A TALE TOLD BY TRAITORS

TALES OF WONDER AND WOE
BOOK 2

R. DUGAN

COPYRIGHT

DEDICATION

For all the people who have ever felt like they were sailing in the wrong direction. It's never too late to change the course of your tale.

May you find your way across the raging seas, to your heart's home and to the truth of what you're made of.

AMERE-DEL
Catrae
Zayir Harbor
Getchmin
Shadewyle Castle
Shadewyle Proper
Mount Shadewyle
Sadir
Sudene
Westyr
Antaross
Monsha
The Everreach
The Spear Teeth
Ravinor
The Barradir Highlands
Tevale
Sennesole Basin
Bashir
Port Krait
The Abbra Foothills
Korsa
Weyval Basin
Drowverge
Port Pyrath
Port Tamsay
Pyrath
Anoram
©2021 JESSICA KHOURY

CHAPTER I
BENEATH THE FIRE

My life's tale ended—and began—with fireworks.

Dazzles of rich, riotous red and blistering, blazing blue caught against the frame of the hastily-done braid that twined from beneath my dark hood. Sparks kissed burning holes in the hem of the bright crimson-and-purple skirts I'd tied at my waist before I'd vaulted this artfully-crafted rooftop; flagrant freckles dusted the long sleeves and exposed peeps of brown skin, leaving small singes in the linen like droplets of dark-chocolate batter.

Though this plot had ruined my finest set of nightclothes, I smiled the broadest I had in some time, crouched on the sculpted edge of one of the minaret towers demarcating the meeting of the districts of Krylan—the southernmost city in the country of Mithra-Sha.

And that grin doubled like rising dough at the whoops and hollers of my fellow immigrants from the neighboring land of Amere-Del, their cheers drumming from the square below.

Though I had laid my roots deep in the Tailbone City—far from this district of jewel-toned clothing and lilting accents like mine, with its kindred love of nightlife and the decadent assault of the fireworks—there was little denying what made us alike in this moment. The same iron lining forged through our hot blood, our veins streaked with a kindred daring that had made this maneuver possible.

When I had come to these people tonight, I had asked for only one thing: a distraction. And they'd given it without hesitation.

They knew little about me but that I was also Ameresh, seller of the finest breads and pastries most had ever sampled—a woman who appeared in the district like a mirage some evenings, vendor cart shimmering into shape here and there in the nightlife quarter. With that and little else, they had agreed to help prime and ignite the detonations that had brought down some of the oldest and ugliest of the district's many minarets.

We had aimed solely for the ones erected by the Mithrans to welcome us…the ones that flew the banner of Amere-Del's ruling regime. That sigil of the mountain capped in a sharp-angled star—a testament to the tale of Del Ahim, our mythic deity descending to give shape to the world—had been an eyesore as long as I'd lived in Krylan.

For the first several months I'd called this city my refuge, that banner had haunted my dreams, suffocating me in its folds, its smothering cocoon dragging me back to places I had sworn never to visit again.

The Mithrans meant well. After all, most of them loved their country's ruler, Sha Lothar, and his generous family. Few were privy to just how deep the contentions in Amere-Del ran…and how the immigrants in particular held no love for Del Graven, the paranoid ruler whose flapping flags they were still forced to walk beneath every day.

So I had aimed for his minarets…a toss of a rude, sharp-fingered gesture in the face of the regime I too had left behind long ago. The leaders of which would have slammed my fingers in a doorjamb for making such an obscene motion.

The aching *cracks* of those collapsing minarets still rattled within my bones, the cheers at their destruction sending a burst of heat swimming in my eyes. All that remained now were the minarets built by immigrants like us, topped in flags of weighted scales: favor and fate perfectly in balance.

Well, only those…and a sky exploding in sizzling garlands of light, cheers still spiraling upward like the tempting waft of aroma from a pan of fresh sourdough cookies.

My gaze tugged irresistibly to the mint-and-currant towers that rose on either side of Krylan's city gates. Satisfaction blazed its own incendiary path through my gut, but in its wake the shimmer settled into sorrow. Missing.

This beauty was not only a diversion. It was a sacrifice.

Success meant loss…it meant the only true friend I had dared make since leaving Amere-Del could escape this city and its cruel, suspicious soldiers who sought to imprison her tonight. And the pair of us would likely never cross paths again.

It had taken such a long time to stop looking over my shoulder and notice the people around me; to be mindful of the half-drowned Mithran migrant who'd stepped into my shop months ago, emanating a desperate need for a kind word as much as for shelter from the rain. Befriending her had been so simple, as carefree as baking a recipe learned by heart. It had been a lovely daydream for us both…and a poignant, painful reminder of other bonds, broken long ago.

Yet Audra Jashowin was different from any friend I'd ever made. She was a Storycrafter, a unique sort of power in Mithra-Sha…a storyteller whose tales had once come alive, creating tangibility from the intangible. The words of Storycrafters could reshape the world, could forge objects and roads and even highly coveted weapons…though I had never witnessed the craft for myself. Audra's tales, like all the rest told by her kind, had been without endings—and therefore, without the power to create—for some time now.

Until tonight.

When I'd found her in her apartment hours ago, later than she had ever been for one of our nights of dice games and dessert tea, she'd told me a new sort of tale.

She'd met a farmhand in the tavern where she tended bar. And in his presence, she'd finished a story for the first time in years.

That was why the soldiers hunted her. That was why she'd fled…before they could make use of her. Make use of *him*.

No one deserves to be treated like a charm, she'd told me.

And how long ago had I spoken such similar words, my voice a blend of terror, desperation, command, and cajole? How long ago—and yet every blink brought the memory of a face the mirror of mine, equal in shape, equal in fear…and then, equal in determination.

I had seen that same determination in Audra tonight. And I knew precisely the path she would walk if I did not offer my aid.

That path ended bloodily, pain and regret its pavestones When I'd peered into Audra's future through the frame of my past, the way had been clear: what her life would become…and what I must do to prevent it.

Laying a hand to my heart now, I measured its thundering beats; it raced, not only from exertion, from the run to the district and the climb to this minaret where I'd set the first fireworks free as a distraction to aid her escape, but from the swell of grief bubbling within it. It roiled hot and thick as burned caramel, bittersweet, tainted with smoke.

"Goodbye, Addie-cat." The nickname rolled over my tongue like syrupy confection, wet and griefstricken. "I hope you find what you are searching for."

A commotion of clamorous sound masked the last of the words as they spilled from my lips; my hand tightened, then tumbled to the edge of the minaret tower. I cocked forward on my knees, peering over the steep plunge to the streets below.

The gleeful shouts of the immigrants devolved swiftly to cries of protest; between the packed handcarts and festive booths, shadows slithered into view.

Mithran soldiers. They were on the hunt.

I begged for the sanity of fear, but it did not come. A simple baker might've plunged into oblivion at the sight of their assault. But all that rose in me was a cool, detestable calm…and then a surge of indignation I fought not to sway to as the soldiers laid hands on the immigrants below, shoving chests against booth tables and minaret walls, tying wrists behind backs.

I would not intervene.

I couldn't.

They had known the risks of this display; and as I lurched from my perch and darted around the edge of the minaret's sculpting, seeking the rooftop I had used as leverage to clamber up to this height, I timed my thoughts to the pound of my racing feet.

There was safety in anonymity. For them, and for me.

Every immigrant in that square was above reproach, so long as they were not entangled with me. After all, setting fireworks was not a crime. How could they have predicted precisely where the wind would carry them…what towers they might strike? And if the soldiers were distracted from a hunt for a certain runaway Storycrafter by such a luminous display, well…that was their own fault.

Fault. The word resounded through my mind as I leaped from the minaret, cutting blade-smooth through the air and tumbling into a crouch on the steepled rooftop below. *Any suffering that comes of this will be your fault.*

Shaking my head sharply to rid it of that chilly echo, I sprinted down the spine of the roof, dodging from one shadow to the next. Wood smashed to splinters in the distance, a furious scream rending the air as the last motes of the final dazzling firework trail tapered to nothing. Guilt hammered in my chest, a twin to my pulse; a stamped-down, neglected flare of protectiveness surged to grate against the backs of my teeth.

These are your *people.*

I shook the notion away.

I had no people. Lionyra Vara straddled two worlds and belonged to neither.

That could not change. I would never belong to anyone again.

Leaning into the swift swell of confidence that arched with that thought, I clambered down from the rooftop to the absolute darkness of the streets below. Behind me, voices stormed, barking questions, doling out demands; wanting to know who had started this. Who had decided to set fireworks off *tonight*, of all nights, in the Ameresh immigrant district that so often kept to itself.

A smirk lit on my lips, dangerous as the depths. I hooked my scarf over my nose and mouth, spinning to the empty street I knew so well—that would take me to my bakery, *The Secret Ingredient*, and the quiet life I had made for myself.

Instead, I whirled into a pair of hands that clapped shackle-tight around my arms.

Panic had no opportunity to take its piece from my flesh, because pain gave it no quarter. Brick stones I could have walked blind ripped against the soles of my feet now as the man's greater weight barreled me backward, hurling me against the side of the home I'd descended from. All the air gasped from my lungs at once, and when I folded over, brutish fingers locked around my chin, wrenching my head up.

Red hair. A bloodied mouth. Half-crazed gray eyes storming with hate. A broad chest heaving from a hard run.

A Mithran soldier. And he was *furious.*

"*There* it is," he snarled in my face, his voice bubbling with agony and triumph. "I knew it. I *knew* it was only a matter of time before you helped her."

My wild, whirling mind had one moment to understand who he meant. And then his savage smile was all I could see, bloody and blasted, filling up my world.

"Lionyra Vara, you are under arrest."

CHAPTER 2
THE RUNAWAY HEIR

For nearly a week, Krylan's jailhouse was my home. I marked the passage of time by the tray of bread, meat, and cheese left inside the bars each day, and by the fresh slag bucket set by the door. Though I never laid eyes on the soldiers who brought these things, I was grateful, at least, that the redheaded fool never returned to sling sideways remarks and taunts.

I did not know what he was waiting for. He'd slammed the door of this small, paltry cell behind me that first night, hung his fingers through the slats, and vowed, "I'll be back for you. Take some time and think about what sort of *mood* you'd like to find me in when I come."

He'd hurled that threat six days ago.

It was almost humorous, that he thought solitary confinement would break me. As if I had never known worse; as if I did not know how to sing songs and play mind games to pass the time. I paced and pirouetted in the narrow cell, keeping my hands and feet busy. I hung my head off the end of the small iron shelf-bed bolted to the wall and recited the finer details of the Mithran orientation I had taken alongside the cluster of fellow refugees with whom I'd crossed the border.

I had never forgotten the laws they'd taught us then—nor forgotten how I'd wept at them, silent and endless, throughout the orientation sessions. The fairness of it all, the justice this army-led city strove for. It had been everything I'd craved and all I'd been denied since girlhood.

It was precisely the opposite of what I was being shown here. *This* treatment reeked of the past. It was bone-achingly familiar.

And I would not stand for it.

I was restless and ready on the sixth day, when I at last saw the face of the soldier who came for me; not the redheaded, gray-eyed fiend who'd accosted me in the street, but a broader, older man with pale locks and soft blue eyes. He had the decency to smile sheepishly when he arrived, keys in hand.

"Lionyra Vara," the Mithran soldier spoke my name in short, clipped syllables, "you've been summoned."

Slowly, I pushed myself upright from where I'd hung over the bed's edge again, tugging my hair over my shoulder. The rank scent of it after a week assaulted my nostrils, and I fought not to wrinkle my nose. "By whom?"

"Officer Fiordona."

I swung my legs from my cold perch and stepped to meet the soldier; he flashed a pair of fetters and raised his brows, and I fixed him with a cold look I'd perfected long ago—one brandished on bread thieves and querulous customers in my shop. The same steely stare that had once sent powerful Ameresh men to their knees. "I see no need for restraints. Those are intended for prisoners, are they not? Men and women being held on charges of which they have been *informed*, and interred through legal processes?"

The soldier tugged his neck and avoided my stare. "It's not…usual, what's happened. But Officer Fiordona said you're not to be released without them."

Blasted depths. I shoved my wrists between the bars. "You might have the courtesy to leave them loose."

To my relief, he did.

We traveled down a lengthy hall strung with cells, each no larger than mine. Some prisoners donned scowls and blistering glares at our passing, unrepentant of whatever crimes had brought them here; others wept or wailed, pleading for justice or mercy. I refused to number how many of those distant shouts carried Ameresh accents. Tried not to wonder if any of them had been arrested on account of the fireworks display and the toppled minarets a week ago.

We descended two levels to the broader ground floor of the jailhouse, a circular affair ringed in strong pillars and arched doorways; then it was down another narrow hall, this one lit with lanterns set in niches along both sides. There were no windows—a familiar precaution—and something sinister beat in the veins of this place as we arrived at a steel door near the corridor's end. The soldier unlocked it with a twist of his wrist, ushering me inside and sealing it swiftly at my back.

He did not follow me in. But I was not alone.

Darkness cloaked the edges of the room—wider than I could see, judging by the clinking echo of my fetters and footsteps when both whispered to a halt. The shadows bent only before a single lantern on a table with two seats, bolted to the floor at the heart of the room. Another Mithran soldier took up one chair in a sprawl, knocking his knuckles out of beat on the cast-metal tabletop.

Beholding the leering Officer Fiordona in the dim lighting rather than the gloom of night, a rogue familiarity prickled in the back of my mind. Bitter dislike dusted my tongue like a waft of inhaled cinnamon; I forced myself to swallow it, stepping toward the table before he could speak—before he could summon me and make this room his place of power.

"Are these truly necessary?" I demanded, flashing my wrists. "I'm no criminal…I have nothing to flee from and nothing to hide."

"We'll see about that." The soldier's smirk was made all the more gruesome by the myriad of bruises peppering his face. It was a comfort to know someone else clearly disliked him as much as I did. "Why don't you—?"

I had already taken the seat across from him, silencing his suggestion with the grind of chair legs on the stone.

He cocked his head, measuring me with blood-simmering arrogance. "You seem nervous."

I settled into the seat, legs folded primly. The demure disarmament…a tactic I knew better than my chosen name. "And you must be dull indeed, to mistake fury for fear."

He clicked his tongue. "Insulting a Mithran soldier comes with its share of consequences, I think you'll find."

"What more could you hope to do to me? You have imprisoned me without charge."

He shrugged. "You attempted to flee."

"And from what was I fleeing, precisely?"

"I think that's something you should tell *me*."

We gazed at one another for a moment, mutual distaste corroding the air.

I balanced my bound hands in my lap, fingertips pressing to my opposite knuckles. "On what charges am I being held?"

"None." His lips curled into a despicable, gloating smile. "Your imprisonment here, you might consider it a…small *favor*."

"To *whom*?"

"That's the question, isn't it?" He inclined, propping his elbows on the table, folding his hands at his mouth; wicked contentment kneaded his lips into a cruel sneer. "I'll give you this…I would have liked to keep you here for anything. For spitting in the street. For breaking some law you weren't even aware of. Luck knows I spent long enough searching for something…so long, in fact, I found *everything*."

From the pocket of his trousers, he withdrew a small, leatherbound journal; flicking it open between his thumb and forefinger, he read aloud with vicious flourish curling around every word.

"Lionyra Vara…immigrant of Amere-Del. Fled to the border when her village was destroyed by Southland raiders." His lip flared a bit at that. "Completed orientation without demerit. Began a small baking venture in the Ameresh district and maintained it for over a year before securing a shopfront on the Mithran side. *The Secret Ingredient*."

Ah, *that* was where I'd seen him. He'd been a frequent, if brusque, customer the last two months, ever since…

A chill dripped down my spine.

Ever since I'd met Addie.

"You didn't do a single thing worth noting…until you befriended our city's latest *Storycrafting* visitor." Pure hate curdled the last words, and Officer Fiordona flicked his eyes to me. "So, I started looking at you a bit more closely."

I dug my fingernails into the meat of my thigh, fighting to anchor myself to the room. A heady, weightless sensation began to crawl up my neck and throat. "It is not a crime to befriend a Storycrafter."

"No. But it is against the laws of Krylan to lie to the military and impersonate someone…or to give a false name upon entering the city."

My breath halted altogether. And his smile grew.

"Lionyra Vara is a model citizen. The perfect immigrant." He quirked his head to one side. "What a pity she doesn't exist."

A whisper of protest flared across my unfeeling lips. "I'm—"

"I know who you are," he interrupted coldly. "Alyona Graven. The Delina, sole inheritor of the ruling regime of Amere-Del."

The name struck like a slap, hurling me flush to the seatback, fingernails springing free of my skin. A chaos of memories all collided at once, hearing those words, those *titles*, spoken for the first time since that night of running, of begging, of choosing my life—and the life of the only person in the world I cared for—over my fear in the span of a heartbeat.

Alyona Graven. Delina. The truth I'd fled for so long. The past I'd cut myself free from, day by day, since I'd escaped from Amere-Del.

"Found you, *Delina*." Victory cut the lines around the soldier's eyes; he cast the journal onto the table between us with a dull, resonate *clap*, reclining with hand to thigh. "Alyona Graven has a *much* more storied history than the baker. We heard you went missing a few years ago…not long before Lionyra Vara made her appearance at the border. Luck flipped its coin in your favor back then, but it looks like it turned the other way this time."

His ogling stare stoked my rage like a hearthfire, the banners of its heat sizzling in my fingertips.

"So, the lost heiress of Amere-Del is found," he mused through a wretched tilt of those overfull lips. "I suppose rumors of the Del's impotence must just be barracks-talk, if he sired the likes of you."

Grief surged beyond my taming. Struggling for breath, I clung to the edge of my seat with fettered hands, gulping down air to soothe my ravaged nerves. And Officer Fiordona watched every flinch, every flicker, the weight of his stare barreling over me; a silent, howling triumph blazed in his smile.

His fangs were at my throat.

"As soon as I put the pieces together," he went on, his gleeful boast faintly muffled by the blood roaring in my ears, "I sent word to our friends at the Ameresh border. You can imagine how eager they were to hear their long-lost Delina was living under an alias in the Tailbone City. Said they would be sending someone to retrieve you forthwith."

Every word pounded at the door of my heart, demanding entrance, heedless of the rage and shame and *hatred* that lurked beyond.

Officer Fiordona inclined against the table's edge again, his burning thatch of hair scorching my view; focus scored the world again, etching every angle of his bruised, grinning face in sharp relief. "I have a feeling you might not want to go back, so I'm willing to make you a deal. You tell me where Audra Jashowin and that farmhand are headed next, and I'll send you out the back way. Tell the Ameresh delegate you escaped…and that will be the end of that."

He dangled the chance at freedom with far, far too much relish—a small man with overlarge wants, who reaped far too great a pleasure from being the player holding all the cards at the betting table.

But he had shown his hand too soon, in a fit of rage in that sidestreet where he had cornered me. His rough-handed rage had revealed precisely how much finding Addie meant to him; no doubt he was the precise sort of soldier she'd been desperate to escape from when she'd begged me for aid. And that knowledge, however slight, placed a kernel of control back into my hands.

Eyes wide open. The old, familiar mantra flickered like a lit candle in my mind. *Take power where you can.*

Fixing a smile to my face—empty and ruthless though it felt—I inclined toward him as well. And for the first time in many years, I let the practiced accent and tone of the Ameresh Northlands fall away, the guise I had used to mask my crossing over the border into this country, the voice that had been another layer of armor against discovery. What emerged instead was *my* voice, the rich accent from the very heart of Amere-Del, the Delina's tone that had rendered trembling imbiciles out of ambitious fools…men no different from this one who had unearthed the long-buried truth of me.

"I would not give you Audra Jashowin if it meant I could disappear like a shadow from this city forever."

Officer Fiordona slowly leaned away, breaths seething audibly through clenched teeth as the shift in my voice, my posture…the strength of my determination. "All right. If that's how you'd like to play the game, you're useless to me. I'll just have to find them myself." Kicking back his chair, he flung a careless hand my way. "She's all yours."

The moment a shadow separated from the corner of the room, I tasted my first wash of true fear in this Mithran prison where I did not belong.

I knew of only one person so capable of companionship with the shadows; only one so utterly deft at the skill, she made her livelihood from it—defending the Del, stomping out dissidence wherever it arose.

Her marks lived on my body. Her lessons were blistered scars scorched into my mind, notions of cruelty I fought daily not to let shape my decisions, my actions, the very definition of who I was.

The Pale Viper was *here.* In Mithra-Sha, my sanctuary, my escape. My *home.*

Every bone and muscle knew her even before the lanternlight grazed across the honed frame of her. And then the glow found the twin blades lashed over her shoulders, and the shorter half-arm daggers belted at each hip. It fingered the twine of silver and crimson that wrapped the grips of every weapon, denoting this woman's place in the Ameresh militar. Not only *in* it—but at the head of it. The one responsible for keeping Shadewyle Castle secure and the country's militar trained and readied for war…and, at one time, to have its Delina prepared for the same.

The Del had sent Lucretzia Nore, his Own Blade, his most trusted warrior, to retrieve me.

CHAPTER 3
THE FIRST TEST

ll at once, various angles of my body began to throb: a somber, screaming, off-kilter tune greeting the dealer of long-ago hurts as she halted in the thin pool of light that puddled around the table's feet. And for the first time in not enough years, I beheld the face of the mentor who had beaten me like untested steel into the woman she believed I ought to be.

Everything about her was made paler against the black of her leather armor, her silver-blonde hair defying even an estimate of age, her skin the hue of sun-bleached flour and her brows nearly the same, all but erasing them from notice.

It made the core dark of her eyes all the more striking when they slit toward Officer Fiordona, brimming with vicious disdain. "You were going to send her out the back way?"

Her voice unleashed a shudder that scurried from the tops of my shoulders to my waist.

Officer Fiordona was silent for a long, long moment. Perhaps Lucretzia was the first woman he had ever esteemed himself lesser than.

"Not really," he grunted at length. "Just trying to get her to talk."

Lucretzia pivoted with a snap of her sable cloak, seizing Fiordona by the throat, hefting him from his seat and hurling him back against the wall; it happened so swiftly, my hand barely leaped to my mouth soon enough to smother my bark of shock at the *crack* of body on brick.

"I do not want to hear that you *ever* interfered in Ameresh business with false promises again." Though Lucretzia's tone was level, the malice breathing behind every word was as unmistakable in this waking horror as it had ever been in my nightmares. "Nor that you dared to even *hint* at freedom for the worst of our criminals."

Criminal. That was how she saw me now.

A well-learned terror frothed in my middle. I had seen countless horrors enacted—and learned my own penchant for cruelty—against those Lucretzia deemed *criminal.*

Her hand flexed out of the folds of Fiordona's neck, and she pivoted back to me.

I had hoped for a lifetime before I ever again beheld that malevolent stare that had so often shrunk me down to my smallest parts. I had prayed myself hoarse that if I ever faced her again, it would be in the cradle of Ahim's arms, defended by the World-Forger himself on the other side of death.

Nowhere else was safe from Lucretzia Nore.

For a long moment, we stared at one another, until shadow and light blurred together and even the Mithran soldier faded away, slouched against the wall, rubbing his neck.

Lucretzia took one step, and I could not help how my body reacted.

I thrust back my seat and lunged for the door.

She was in my path in two strides, my head cracking against the solid bulk of her shoulder when she twisted, slamming her armored bicep straight against my face. The scent of metal filled my nostrils as my nose burst; I stumbled back, pain wracking through my cheekbones and twisting above my eyes.

Officer Fiordona's delighted guffaw was all that winnowed past the thunder of my pulse in my ears when I struck the table's edge.

Lucretzia had laid a test before me in the pause. I had failed.

Her gauntleted hand snatched forward, seizing the chain of my fetters. In one swift, shoulder-aching wrench, she hauled me to her side, then thrust me away from her toward the door—as if she could not bear to breathe the same air as me. "We're leaving, Alyona."

I dug in my heels and bolted my courage to the floor to keep from staggering beneath the force of that shove…and the weight of Lucretzia's loathing stare. "I have things to retrieve. Personal belongings—"

"I don't give a single scrap from the blasted *depths* what you have or what you assume belongs to you." She thrust my chair back into its setting with a harsh screech and an eruptive *bang* that rattled through the marrow of my bones. "If those rags on your back rot and cling to your hide, so be it." She brushed past me, snagging my fetters again and yanking me after her. "Perhaps that will teach you every lesson you have forgotten in your time *away* from us."

Officer Fiordona coughed another satisfied laugh when Lucretzia swung the door open, still dragging me after her like a disruptive child. On the threshold, we both halted and looked back at the smirking Mithran soldier rubbing the welts on his neck.

"Enjoy one another," he croaked.

"I assure you," Lucretzia sneered, "she will enjoy no part of what is to come any more than a woman has ever enjoyed *you.*"

She kicked the door shut on his stunned expression morphing rapidly into rage, hauling my shackles again. The motion tugged me off-balance, setting me staggering wildly after her down the windowless hall.

Fighting to straighten, I tongued strands of limp, filthy hair from my mouth, coating the tip in a thick glaze of blood from my still-pulsing nose. Lucretzia maintained a backhand hold on the chain of my fetters—a precise grip which kept my hands down low at my waist, preventing any attempt I might make to reach for her blades.

I pressed down on my panic like an unruly loaf rising out of form; I pummeled and kneaded it into something malleable, a substance I could make *use* of, as Lucretzia led me back to the columned room and toward the jailhouse doors. Precisely where I deserved to go—outdoors. To freedom.

I had never been less free in all my life. Not even when I had been the Del's captive heir.

And I had no intention of returning to those tortuous confines without a fight.

CHAPTER 4
FOLLOWER NO LONGER

*T*he strong slap of sunlight greeted us when Lucretzia hauled me out of the jailhouse. Midday brilliance bounced off the bright domes and vivid bricking of the sprawling city I called my home—that I had *made* my home. Not by the intimidation and ferocity taught me by the woman who commanded my shackles, but by the kindness that had won me undeserved friends and loyal customers over the years.

It all seemed bleaker when the resplendent colors of Krylan's vaults and narrow streets and archways splashed against the pallor of Lucretzia's frame as she angled for the steps down from the jailhouse.

The change in height was, perhaps, the first nod of encouragement from Ahim since I'd been dragged into this place. A flicker of a plan came to mind, and I batted aside the notion of how I had *learned* to think so swiftly, and to act with as much speed—tutored at the feet of the woman I followed behind.

But I would follow no longer.

Eyes wide open. Take power where you can.

The words I had whispered to myself since girlhood…that I had scarcely needed to lean into for *years*…blew through me like a blistering wind this time.

With a violent thrust, I leaped back up a step; the motion knocked Lucretzia off-balance, towing her halfway toward me, and before she could halt that swivel, I swung my knee with all my might into a scar that crossed her midsection.

A scar I knew still panged now and again. A scar I knew the precise lay and shape of…because *I* had given it to her.

Lucretzia stumbled, snatching for the long hanks of my hair; I met her with a chomp of teeth to her inner wrist, where there was a small, hidden chink her armor. Then I dealt another wild but precise blow to her abdomen.

It would not cripple her. But it loosened her grip just enough that, with the height, I could plant my foot in her clavicle and kick her away. Her fingers unfastened from my shackles, and I did not pause. I did not look back.

I *fled.*

The crowd did not know me, but it parted the same as the frightened masses that had once flocked Shadewyle Castle. Whispers of shock patterned the wind at my back—I was certain I looked a frightening sight, bloodied in the nose, filthy, fettered, and running for my life from the jailhouse.

I dared not even glance over my shoulder. There was no doubt Lucretzia pursued. I had only the fleeting hope that my knowledge of this city would thwart her just as her intimate reckoning of Shadewyle's town had often allowed her to outwit *me* in these same sorts of chases.

I knew the streets of Krylan in all the ways she did not. I knew its arteries and veins; I had surged through them like blood, fleeing my secret fears, fleeing faces I had thought now and again sparkled with recognition in the Ameresh district. If I could simply reach the plaza outside *The Secret Ingredient*, I could slip into a narrow seam between buildings where street rakers kept their tools and slag buckets, and through a hidden door in a smoke shop where illicit trade fumed beneath the Mithran army's noses. I could fold myself into those shadows and disappear until Lucretzia gave up the hunt…or until the White Spice traders moved their stock from the hidden pallets within the shop.

Nearly there. Another two streets, a market district, the bridge across the city's aqueducts, and then—

My fingertips grazed brick, ripping slightly as I angled around the corner into the next side-street…and stumbled to a halt, gasping, swearing in shock, my stomach plummeting to my toes at the sheer wrongness of what lay ahead.

The street simply…ended.

Not an alley wall. Not a bricking-over. But the street itself folded upward at a seamless angle, like a piece of parchment creased neatly. The spires of broken buildings and the shattered street itself jutted into the sky like an elbow bone snapped clean in half.

I could not unstick my feet for a moment. I could only stare, gasping for breath, dizzied by the impossibility of it all.

I had heard rumors of this sort of might, but never seen it for myself. Because it was not meant to be possible…not any longer.

These must be the twists of Storycraft…a powerful pirouetting of tales. A mark left behind by a woman a week gone, and of the man who'd brought her tales to life.

She'd warned me of this sort of power. I'd tried to make sense of it, to give it shape in my mind, but I had never imagined *this*.

"Addie-cat." Her name wisped from my heaving lungs like the peel of a knife.

Her escape had become my downfall.

No sooner had the thought struck me than something else did—a powerful, barreling weight descending from above, a knee slamming into the small of my back. Blinding dapples erupted across my vision, and I hardly registered the ringing impact of my legs with the cobblestone road or how my fingertips tore even further when they plunged down to catch my body…then flattened as that weight crushed me flat to my chest.

A vicious arm hooked me around the waist, swinging me to my feet; despite the pain thundering in my knees and hands, survival instinct took hold. I revived, kicking and writhing, lashing out for that same scar on Lucretzia's middle—but she was prepared for me this time. She snagged a fistful of my hair in her free hand and drove her weight into me, flinging me flush to the wall by my chest.

"Do not," she snarled, "*ever* do that again."

"Oh, *apologies*," I hissed, cheek pressed to the wall, puffs of breath blowing strands of hair from my face. "Are my attempts to save my own life *inconvenient* to you?"

"You are *disgusting* to me." She pressed in, twisting my arm past the point of pain, into a blinding wash of white light. "You are a coward proving her cowardice hasn't changed since she *abandoned* her duties."

My duties. As a Del-forged weapon. As a breeding sow and perpetuator of hurt and heartache.

Howling with rage, I planted my foot against the wall and thrust backward; but Lucretzia was as ready for me as she had ever been, pitching her weight effortlessly with mine. Spinning me with a fistful of my shirt's collar, she rammed me back against the wall again—this time with an arm braced across my clavicles. I swung up my shackled hands to dig my chipped, unpared nails into her arm; she met me with a brutalizing strike to the knuckles, shoving my hands back down against my waist, pinning them with her fingers laced into the links.

We glared at one another, both panting with exertion.

"Look at you." Lucretzia's gaze poured over me like scorched syrup—bitter, blackened, and revolting. "Soft. Plump. *Desperate*. You wasted everything I made of you…in just a few years, you've undone what took more than half a *lifetime* to build."

I bared my teeth in her face, glad for the blood that had seeped over my upper lip and ran into the cracks of my teeth. For an instant, at least, my ferocity was an equal match for hers. "Every day I chose not to run laps or train with blades, every time I returned for second servings or thirds, I thought of you. I *relished* undoing your work."

Lucretzia's smile morphed from scorn to savagery; she wound her free hand into my forelock, wrenching my head back against the alley wall—exposing my throat. "You've only made things more difficult for yourself…and for those you've touched with your selfishness." Even with my head tipped back, it took little effort to meet her gaze; the difference in our heights was striking. I had forgotten how severe her posture was, how much she resembled a blade even in how she carried herself. "You are coming home with me, Delina…and *everything* will be precisely as it was. But the Del is content to let you flounder for a time as punishment…and I find myself agreeable to that."

My pulse stuttered—not at the threat of my own fate, but at the way her voice curled with satisfaction around one sentence in particular:

Everything will be precisely as it was.

"Everything—?"

Lucretzia smothered my mouth with her hand, bearing her weight against me. "*Everything*. Imagine what that means…and not only for you."

Memories slashed free of the prison where I'd kept them for years.

A face so like mine…a mirror image. Fingers entwined, a last embrace, a stolen backward glance as we parted ways for the final time. A bit of my heart fracturing as the only friendship I'd ever allowed myself in Shadewyle Castle came to an agonizing, unknowable end.

"You don't have her." Defiance and fear were a bitter blend of spice on my tongue, the words garbled against her gauntlet.

Lucretzia's forehead wrinkled upward—the only sign her brows had arched. Relishing the terror that bled into my tone, despite my efforts. "Do we not?"

At that, horror doused my resolve, smothering it like a darkening hearth. Three words pounded against the inside of my skull, silencing even my desire to escape, to save my own life: *They have Tristah.*

CHAPTER 5
TESTING PATIENCE, TEMPTING RAGE

Nothing seemed real beyond the confines of that Storycrafted street…as if I had become a figment of one of Audra's tales, not quite tangible, reshaped and turned inside-outward.

I moved in a fog, towed in the footsteps of my captor through the city gates and down the serpentine road that snaked from just south of the Tailbone City to Port Craythin, through a patchwork of drought-stamped farmlands toward the steep-sided cliffs at the seaside.

Most often trod by vendors touting wares from port to city—and occasionally by those seeking a voyage by ship.

There was no doubt in my mind we would be among the latter.

The swiftest way to Shadewyle Castle was by sea, up the Everreach River to the trade haven of Monsha at the beating heart of Amere-Del; and from there, by a smaller vessel along one of the many branching tributaries to the town of Shadewyle in the shadow of the Del's home, Shadewyle Castle, nestled against the mountains.

Which made everything far worse for me. Chances of escape would be far slimmer with nothing around us but the sea.

The crank of cartwheels and the gruff shout of salt-blistered voices greeted us long before the thickening of the alpine trees, where the farmlands had left off lumbering and allowed the natural growth at the foot of Mithra-Sha to flourish. The path wove between their towering trunks for a time, then graded steeply down to Port Craythin.

I had never laid eyes on it before. I'd made my way north on foot through the border wall held by the Mithran army—a precaution against the Graven regime's storied history of paranoia, warmongering, and conquest. But this port suited the descriptions given by sailors who'd wandered into *The Secret Ingredient* for a meal of something other than cheese, dried meat, and hardtack. Every inch of the port was carved out of the sheer-sided rock walls—cleaning stations for catches, places for declaration of wares, and the interspersed inns for sailors who had no desire to venture into bustling Krylan during their brief stay in port.

Those inns stood out only by their wooden awnings; none were named, and altogether they numbered few. Their paltry assortment stood in stark contrast to the sheer volume of stations for preparing fish; I nearly gagged at the robust odor of all their slimy inner parts.

Lucretzia did not flinch. She stormed to the nearest inn, butting the door open with her shoulder.

Her exchange with the innkeeper was brief; in the dim entry chamber, low-roofed and lit by a single roaring hearth, golden, rectangular Ameresh merits traded hands. I rolled my wrists in my shackles and considered testing whether I could raise my hands enough to flash my fetters to the innkeeper. After all, trafficking was forbidden in Krylan.

But Lucretzia held me shackled in far more ways than flesh. Her vicious taunt in the street had not cleared my head yet.

I could not flee until I knew for certain whether the regime held Tristah captive again; the mere thought set my stomach heaving worse than the reek of dead fish.

For Audra, I had set fireworks ablaze. But for Tristah, I had done far more—far *worse*. And Lucretzia knew it.

With key in hand, she marched me from the entry chamber into the chilly twist of a hall boring deep into the cliffs themselves; when we reached the furthest door, she yanked it open, thrust me inside, and shut it at our backs while I took stock of our accommodations.

A single bed, a relief bucket, a washbasin, a lantern strung from a rope at the height of the ceiling. All functional but rudimentary, keeping a rotating list of clientele in mind.

Lucretzia hauled me to the bed and swept my ankles without warning, hurling me down with such force my shoulder clipped the wooden frame. A groan wrenched from my lips.

"Sleep," she ordered. "We leave before dawn."

I rolled onto my back as she strode away, unbelting her weapons but holding them close. She splashed water from the basin onto her face, keeping her back to me—no doubt another test.

Digging my feet into the floor, I pushed myself upright on the bed. "Do you have Tristah."

I did not frame it as a question. Even a tilt of tone with Lucretzia could be a signal of weakness…a chink in one's armor for her to slide a sword into.

She scoffed, rubbing her face on her sleeve. "Do you truly think she would be any more difficult to capture than you?"

I had no answer. For years, I had evaded notice here in Mithra-Sha; for years, I had prayed to Ahim that Tristah managed the same—wherever she'd gone. She had all of the same lessons as me, all of the same trained skills. I had my love of baking and she her love of music, and those were the only secret things we had kept for ourselves…that set us apart.

Which meant that, if they had come for me, they would indeed come for her as well.

I brushed my sweating palms on my knees. "Is she well?"

No answer. Was that an admission of Tristah's freedom, or a taunt?

Bile scorched my throat. "Lucretzia, I beg you—"

She bashed a hand against the side of the basin, the sharp motion and ringing impact doing precisely what they had always done: silencing me. "You do not beg. Nor do you have *permission* any longer to speak my name."

I swallowed back the surge of stomach-curdling tension at her abrupt movements—movements that had often preceded blinding bouts of inescapable pain. The sort that had sent me writhing on the floor from her boot to my gut, her blade pommel to my ribs, her fist to my temple.

Lucretzia let the silence stretch out like overworked dough. Then she yanked the starched towel from the basin's hook and dabbed her face.

"You," she growled into its folds, her voice still carrying loudly in the confined space, "are an absolute disgrace. You fled your country and shirked your duties. For years, Zorast has been holding together Amere-Del *alone*, grieving, without a hope for peace…all because you could not bear to lie down and take what was meant for you."

The way she spoke the Del's name—and spoke of his grief, as if that was all that mattered in the world—struck the dry tinder of my temper alight. Fury took hold before guilt—shame, at the memory of precisely *why* he was alone, why he grieved—could take root. "You mean that I could not bear to be shuttled off as breeding stock to placate the head of the dissenion."

Lucretzia snorted. "Dramatics are unbecoming a Delina."

"An empty insult from a woman forged of Highlands ice."

"Again, the dramatics." Lucretzia belted her weapons back on with slow, meticulous care. I despised the ruffle of an aged fear that scuffed through my veins at the motions—nearly as much as I despised how much this cold-blooded viper *knew* me.

"What you call *shuttling off for breeding,*" Lucretzia added in monotone, "was the greatest hope for quelling an uprising that would tear Amere-Del apart. But you were selfish and narrow-minded, and you sought your own comfort over your sworn obligation to place Amere-Del first."

Frustration burned hearth-hot in my throat, crisping the words I ached to spit in retaliation—words that would fall on deafened ears, as they always had.

I had sworn vows of fealty to our country against my will. The choice had never been mine—not to be chosen and named Delina. Not to be trained in negotiation and intimidation and weaponry. Certainly not in who would claim my hand in a lifelong swearing.

And not only *my* hand, but…

Frustration collapsed into a dry, unseasoned humor. Mirthless laughter prodded my lips; I pressed them thin to hold the untimely chuckle at bay.

Selfish. Narrow-minded. Those words were weapons in Lucretzia's overfull arsenal; they were not the truth of me.

It was the opposite of selfishness that had set me fleeing from Shadewyle Castle after years and years of biting my tongue and enduring the ridicule, the shame, the reshaping of all the things I wished for myself.

I was not selfish; *Lionyra Vara* was not a selfish creature.

Lucretzia would never believe it. Zorast Graven would never believe it, particularly not after what I'd taken from him the night I'd escaped Shadewyle Castle. Long before that vile, fear-soaked night, they had made up their minds about me…the role I would play in the future of Amere-Del.

The man I would be sworn to.

But I knew who I was. Not Alyona Graven, an orphan made heir, plucked from the blind side of Monsha by a childless regime in desperate need of an inheritor…but Lionyra Vara.

The woman self-made. The name and life I had chosen for *myself.*

I was not prepared to let her go without a battle…whatever of it was left in me.

So I planted my hands on the cot frame and thrust myself upright. "If you think me selfish, then you must realize I will fight you. Every step, every mile from this ragged inn to the doors of Shadewyle Castle."

Lucretzia pivoted my way, slow as a curl of smoke and equally sinister…the portent to an inferno that might erupt at any moment. I had spent far too many years—more than half my life—cowering before that unblinking stare. Cowering before threats wielded fiercely and consequences doled out with equal relish.

My years in Mithra-Sha had offered me enough strength, at least, that I could lock my knees and not give ground when I stepped into the churning waters at Lucretzia's iron-plated feet.

"I have spent too long building the life I've wanted," I snarled. "I will not allow you or Zorast to keep taking and taking…I have nothing left that I am willing to give to you. Not the years from my body, not my peace of mind, not my right to choose who I will *love*."

Her expression remained unmoved with every word I spoke; so I summoned the rage that had spurred me to commit my vilest act, the one for which she no doubt despised me most.

I settled my weight and linked my arms at my waist, as best I could with my wrists still shackled together. "I thought I proved well enough I was done serving your whims the night I put a blade in the Della's blasted *belly*."

She was across the room in a blink, a swift and throat-rending sweep of the Del's Own Blade, the Pale Viper uncoiling before I had gathered enough breath to keep shouting. Her hand snaked around the side of my neck, the angled fingerpoints of her gloves brushing my nape, trailing down my spine—not a forceful grip by any means, but the press of her thumb's pad to my windpipe hitched my breathing to a halt.

It was as gentle a touch as a lover's caress. That made it all the more chilling when Lucretzia gazed at that point of contact as if she contemplated precisely how easily she could press inward and crush my throat.

"*If* you test my rage," she said slowly, her tone half-wandering with thoughts I was fortunate not to know, "you will not in any way find it lacking. But my patience…*that* has limits." Her gaze flicked up to mine, glacial as the tips of the Barradir Highlands that jutted like fangs on the eastern maw of Amere-Del. "You have known for *many* years what I am capable of. You do not know how *badly* I want to use every scrap of skill I've learned against *you*. How I have dreamed of it ever since we found Athyna's body in the hall where you and Tristah left her to die while you abandoned your country. Your sworn duty. Everything we ever made the pair of you to be."

Her fingers tightened, hauling me up to her height by the back of my neck until our noses nearly brushed.

"Press me again," her half-murmured words were a gust of hoarfrost and wicked winter wind against my face, "and you will spend the entire voyage home drugged and unconscious."

She shoved me behind her; my ribs clipped the washbasin and burst powdery pain like flour motes across my sternum. I choked it back and staggered around to face her, only to meet the stern fan of flesh between her thumb and forefinger jamming into my windpipe.

Through the billowing haze of panic that accompanied lungs wracked of air, I was dimly mindful that we were here—*again*. That I was a grown woman now, but it was a girl of scarcely sixteen who collapsed to the floor. Just as she had fallen at this same viper's feet again and again in training exercise after training exercise, bested once more. Brutalized. Broken down so that she might be reforged into something that struck to wound and killed without mercy.

Planting my fists on my knees, I struggled back to my feet, wheezing for breath. Again, Lucretzia's forehead creased…this time with chilly amusement and a hint of her signature disdain. "Stay down there where you belong."

I barked a harsh laugh, pressing the throbbing band her strike had left on my windpipe. My voice emerged guttural, but emerge it did: "I belong nowhere. And to no one."

With a scoff, Lucretzia struck again—a foot angled at my hip. This time I thrust my bound hands down to meet her, blocking the jab of her boot.

A new crease forged itself atop all the others.

Swift as a lightning strike, the Pale Viper whirled, trading her weight and spearing her elbow backward into my ribs. This, I was not swift enough to block; the blow erupted like a firework launched against my side, casting me down to the floor again. Lucretzia crowded me with her iron-toed boots, stomping on my fingers and drilling kicks into my legs, shattering pain again and again through my limbs until I pressed myself back against the door; and there she dropped to a knee, seizing a fistful of my hair, shoving my head flush to the wall.

"You sit the night here. Do not move from this corner. And consider very carefully how *much* you care for Tristah. It would require very little effort to make your death seem a tragic accident, and that would leave Tristah shouldering the burden of every role the pair of you once shared."

Air huffed from me in short, staggered bursts. For that, I had no retort—even if my voice had been more than the pain-dulled rasp I'd launched before her strikes.

Lucretzia freed my hair with a yank, keeping several strands for herself and freckling fresh agony across my scalp. "Good. We understand one another."

Understood, yes; I had always understood she was a vile creature, from the first occasion I'd tiptoed into the training room of Shadewyle Castle and introduced myself, and she'd greeted me with a blow to the gut and a knee to the face…testing my never-trained reflexes.

Lucretzia stood, dusting my hair strands from her gauntlets. "Intriguing, is it not, how expendable a woman with a flawless decoy truly is?"

The words jerked my head up like a blade slid beneath my chin; my eyes latched to hers, and she leveled back a silent challenge—daring me to defy.

If they truly had Tristah, then they had everything. They had excuses. They had all but a perfect ruse to mask my death. They had a lie that would fool everyone who did not know me dearly…and in respect to the Del's ferocious determination and the Della's premature death, those who did numbered few.

If I perished, Amere-Del might not miss me. Indeed, they would never know I was gone. But Tristah—my near-twin, my fellow orphan so alike we had once dreamed ourselves secret sisters—would inherit all of the spite and retribution that fumed from the likes of Lucretzia. All of the expectations and horrors once foisted on *me*.

And though I ached to defy, I could not inflict that burden on her.

Not until I knew for certain if she was captive or free.

CHAPTER 6
A SEASIDE LULLABY

After a night robbed of sleep, my haunches and back aching, my thoughts circling from Tristah to Lucretzia to the Del and Della and back again, it was a small mercy to abandon the room at dawn.

Lucretzia rose without a word, slid her blades into hidden sheaths all along her body, and unrolled a far finer cloak than the one she'd worn the day before from the small pack at the back of her waist. This she donned herself, the silver threading and ice-blue accents tucking like scales along her frame; the plainer cloak she cast over my shoulders, binding every clasp down the front—sealing my shackles from view.

Then she shoved me—fettered, sleepless, and sore—ahead of her from the inn and down to the docks.

With every step, pain wrenched in my chest, deeper and more poignant than the ache in my fingers and toes and the tenderness in my abused throat. It was Ahim's endless mercy that dusk's velvet embrace and my leading steps masked my features from Lucretzia's view, the morning fog wiping gently at the salty tracks that still scourged my cheeks.

I did not know when grief had overtaken me; at some point in the night, when the lantern had burned low and Lucretzia's patterned breathing had hinted at slumber, I had curled my knees to my chest, hidden my face, and allowed despair its moment.

I had raged in silence. I had begged Ahim for salvation. I had even considered attempting to smother Lucretzia in her sleep.

But I was no longer any sort of match for her; even in Shadewyle, I had barely been that.

She was right. I had grown soft…a notion that had never bothered me before. I'd *relished* the wasting of muscle once so stiff it chafed my formal gowns in odd places. I'd loved the blunting of my harsh angles, had pinched and grinned at the folds of a stomach once taut with hunger pangs. Every day my exertion came by choice—from lifting sacks of flour and cranking the grain mill in *The Secret Ingredient* rather than by subjecting myself to rigorous hours of training beneath Lucretzia's unrelenting stare—was an absolute gift.

But now—for the first time since I'd enjoyed my welcoming meal unsupervised in Mithra-Sha and wept at the luxury of cleaning my platter unjudged—I ached for the strength that had once bent malevolent men and wicked women to my will.

I needed to bend Lucretzia. And I had only so long to do it.

The rage and despair loosened their hold on me some now that we were moving; but the desperation living beneath my ribs jabbed its blunted tip deeper with every step down the long, gentle grade to the docks. I could hardly focus by the time we reached the crescent of wooden wharfs that ringed the harbor at the base of the cliffs; my hands shook, rattling my fetters, giving a small, tingling voice to the flightiness that fanned like a riot of butterflies in my bone marrow.

I just needed a few moments—just enough to dart out of reach of her blades and leap into the sea—

Lucretzia seized me by the shoulder and thrust me forward, keeping a hand woven into the collar of her cloak draped over my frame as she steered me down the long strain of wooden planks, toward one of the many ships put into port.

At a glance, I knew precisely why she eyed this ship in particular. It was the only one boasting an Ameresh name scripted across its hull.

The Athalion.

Old lessons dusted themselves off in the recesses of my mind: the Athalion was a sword of legend, Ahim's choice weapon after which the title of the Del's Own Blade was fashioned. In the tales of the world's making, the Athalion had been so mighty it pealed like a bell when swung. It was said that by that blade, Ahim had routed the beasts that claimed Amere-Del long ago, driving them up into the Barradir Highlands. His power had cleared a path for the first people to make a home for themselves in the lush folds of the untamed country.

How cruelly fitting, that the Del's Own Blade sought to carry me back to captivity on a vessel bearing such a name.

Much of Port Craythin still slumbered, but an eerie echo pierced the early-morning mist when we drew nearer to the ship: whistling. Long, low, and steady, the song's notes were so haunting that it was a moment before I recognized the Ameresh lullaby shearing through the fog; I had not heard its weaving notes since Tristah had last hummed them to me, two nights before we'd learned of the fate the Del intended for us. Two nights before I had done the only thing I could think of to set us both free.

It was strange to hear the same lullaby sung so bleakly now, more a dirge than a comfort as it reeled us toward the whistler on his perch of an overturned crate, sharpening a boning knife on his pocket whetstone.

He had unmistakable presence, a shadow of Ahim himself from storybooks and fables: equally robust, with dark hair winding down in coils to his waist and his eyes and mouth boasting lines that could only be crafted by swift laughter and broad grins freely given. He wore a deep blue coat and matching pants, both veined in gold, that contrasted starkly with the muddied shades of the fog-shrouded docks.

His broad frame, roped in thick muscle and stamped in ink, might have been built for militar service. But here he was…a shipman of Mithra-Sha, raising kohl-stamped eyes at our arrival; a faint divot creased his brows, as if we were not who he'd expected, but he went on whistling while he tucked away his whetstone.

When he stood, eerie silence enshrouded us all, deeper than the mist.

"Something I can do for you ladies?" His tone was deadpan, but the way he held himself anticipated something…a fight, perhaps. Or a robbery.

"We require passage to Amere-Del." Lucretzia's retort was as blade-sharp as the rest of her.

The man's eyes widened a fraction, his mouth assuming an incredulous tilt. "Is that right? Any particular reason you'd be asking that from a Trade vessel?"

"I care nothing for your trade. It's someone Ameresh I seek."

"Well, you found him. Captain Jularius Cathan." The sailor—the *Captain*—spanned his arms and sketched a sort of mocking curtsey that likened him to a character from one of Addie's tales…but his clever eyes never left our faces. "Still waiting to hear why you're asking that of me and mine."

Scorn drizzled Lucretia's retort like a squeeze of thick amber honey. "I wasn't aware asking a sailor to sail was demanding the impossible."

I couldn't resist the invitation for a waspish retort. "He is not a ferryman. He wears tradesman's clothing…what you ask of him, ferrying flesh aboard a Trade vessel, is illicit activity in Mithran waters."

Lucretzia was silent for a long moment. When she spoke, it was not to me, only to the Captain: "I trust you've sailed the Everreach to Monsha?"

"Done my share of voyages up its blasted back, if that's what you're wondering." Jularius spun his knife into its sheath and perched his hands on his waist, rocking back on his heels. "Not an easy trip, that. We prefer to keep to the coast."

"Nevertheless, you will take it. That will place you *outside* of Mithran waters where such cargo is illicit. And it will be a voyage well-compensated."

His searching gaze slid over us, and the swift shake of his head dismissed whatever he found. "The pair of you don't look as if you could make it worth my while."

"That is where you're wrong." Lucretzia tilted her head. "I would be glad to pay a man of Ameresh heritage for this undertaking…but make no mistake, merits are not the only bargaining piece I bring."

The sailor straightened a bit. "That sounded just enough like a threat. I could boot you off this dock and turn you over to the soldiers for that."

My teeth nicked together, biting back a warning that begged to slither free. This Captain did not know who he was threatening.

"You could," Lucretzia's voice held fast to its even keel, "but you'll not receive a boon like this on any other voyage, and with winter coming, I assume you'd like to keep your crew intact." The pause tolled on, my clamoring heart overworking itself to fill it. The Captain's gaze floated between us, indecision warring across his features; for a moment, his stare focused solely on me. His eyes dropped to the bulge of my bound hands, disguised within Lucretzia's cloak, and my mouth dried.

At last, the sailor blinked. His focus swept back to Lucretzia, and he offered a smile that did not quite awaken all of the dimpled lines etched permanently into his cheeks. "Just so happens we took on a small handful of fresh Ameresh sailors here in port not a week past. Should make sailing the Everreach easier than usual."

Lucretzia offered a smile equally void of mirth. From her hip, she unhooked the same merit pouch from which she'd paid the innkeeper; all the rest of it, she tossed to the sailor. "For your trouble. And your discretion."

"Appreciated." He hefted the pouch in a salute, then stowed it in his trouser pocket. "What can I call you ladies?"

"Cress Matherus," Lucretzia said smoothly. "My husband is the head of the mercantile guild in Monsha, a close friend of Del Graven. This is our servant girl, Lionyra Vara."

For the first time, I despised the sound of the name I had chosen for myself…a creaking, unsteady scaffold to Lucretzia's vicious lies.

The Captain's gaze flicked back to my face, and this time his smile broadened, became truly genuine—something that warmed just an inch of my frozen heart. "Pleasure to make your acquaintance, ladies. Welcome to *The Athalion*." He sidestepped, sweeping an arm toward the lowered gangplank. "Head on up. The crew will see to you."

Beholding the broad span of wood slanting up to the deck, that brief moment of relief perished utterly. Despair flooded into its tomb, stealing all the space for my lungs to expand. My heart shrank like a poorly batch of dough.

Friendly or not, this Captain was like so many others…easily bought.

And he did not know it, but he had just been ransomed for my undoing.

CHAPTER 7
SAILOR SUNSHINE

Lucretzia's silence swore a vow of retribution when she ushered me ahead of her up the gangplank. I dropped my gaze to the water lapping against the support struts of the docks, which plunged deep into the bay on either side.

I could leap over the unwalled edge—I was a proficient swimmer, if by no means a talented one, and if I could free my bound hands of this cloak—

Lucretzia's fingers knotted in the back of the covering, cinching it tight to my bosom and clavicles when she gave a vicious tug, jerking me nearly flush back to her chest. "Do not even *think* of it."

Then she thrust me up the last span of the gangplank, to *The Athalion's* topdeck.

My feet tangled in the cloak's hem when its edge snagged on the gangplank's hinges. My stomach deserted my body as my fettered hands snapped uselessly against the fastenings that contained them.

I had one instant—only one—to dread that *this* was how I would make my arrival on the vessel meant to carry me to Monsha: falling flat on my face before the crew, sporting a twice-bloodied nose, exuding all the grace of a limp cheese loaf.

A scoff from behind me—Lucretzia, laughing perhaps, or the nearest she could manage to it—

And then, smooth and sinuous as an Ameresh dance, a broad hand snagged beneath my armpit, lifting and spinning me back to balance.

The shift in height, when my nose had been a mere hairsbreadth from contact with the deck a heartbeat before, sent the world tilting around me. I wavered, digging in my heels and squinting against the sunlight peeling back the mist like a gauzy veil.

In the brightening glow, I beheld the smirking countenance of one of Captain Jularius's deckhands.

He was tall, strong, built for labor, wearing the trade threads in deep cerulean blue against sun-browned skin; droplets of morning mist floured the fabric like the spangles of a firework. His black hair fell against his brow in strands of licorice, bitter and alluring, a smoky, sensuous challenge to the palate—much like his eyes, a gleaming rosemary-green. Much like his grinning words when he spoke after a moment, hand still fastened beneath my arm.

"Most women who fall for me don't do it *literally*."

Irritation and giddy amusement—a fault, no doubt, of my disoriented senses and near-tumble—braided together like woven dough in my gut, thick and settling. "Most men who save my face from meeting a ship's deck do not boast of their exploits after."

His smile settled into something warmer. "Is that a frequent occurrence for you?"

I couldn't hold back an undignified snort. "Which bit of it? Acquainting my face with the topdeck, or being saved from such a fate?"

His eyes slid over me from head to heels, lingering a moment on my broad hips, and that cheeky smile widened. "Both."

At last, he freed my underarm—and some bit of my heart snapped after that absent touch. Without it, I was keenly aware of how the ship bobbed on the swells beneath us. And how terribly my balance suffered without my hands to catch me.

The sailor jutted out the same callused hand that had rescued me from my stumbling shame. Inkings dotted his knuckles and curved about his wrist, disappearing into the sleeve of his blue tunic. "Bastyan Atreyon."

The name did not suit him. No, I decided, he was a *Bash*, thoroughly and utterly, from the guilelessness of his grin to the powerful brawn of him.

"Lionyra Vara." I dipped my chin. "Thank you for your quick hands, Master Sailor."

"Well, I appreciate that. Most don't bother." His glib retort sundered too quickly, and his spine straightened as his gaze fell past me.

Lucretzia boarded the deck like a blizzard settling over the wastelands of Amere-Del. She joined us in two sharp strides, snagging the back of my cloak. "Forgive my servant's clumsy feet."

"It's hard for anyone to keep their balance when someone shoves them up the gangplank."

I nearly choked. Lucretzia's fingers tightened, strangling the folds between my shoulder blades; her icy smile swore another vow of reckoning. "She stumbled."

"So, why didn't she try to catch herself?"

Before Lucretzia could lie—or more likely, send him toppling overboard—the clap of boots descending on the deck from the rigging arrested the conversation. A second sailor straightened from his landing crouch before us, scratching his dark-bearded jaw, eyes lively as he glanced between us. "What's the word from the Captain? New recruits?"

"Yes." I seized his distraction with a smile that tensed where it hinged to my cheek, relief warming my insides as Lucretzia flicked her gaze away from Bastyan. "Something like that."

"Well, would you look at that!" The man clapped Bastyan on the shoulder. "You've just been promoted, green-gills. Now you'll have company swabbing out the relief buckets!"

Lucretzia's incredulous scoff might have coaxed a laugh from me, if not for the smothering grip she maintained around the back of my cloak.

"Sailed before?" the man added, glancing between us.

We nodded. Ventures to Monsha had been a regular occurrence in my youth, and Lucretzia had sailed often at the Del's behest.

"How's your sea legs?" Bastyan pitched himself back against the mainmast, arms folded and brows raised, eyes pinned on Lucretzia.

"Unreproachable," she replied stiffly.

"Passable," I hedged.

"That, we can work with!" The other sailor propped his elbow on Bastyan's shoulder, observing us with a hearthfire of curiosity burning in his gaze. "What did the Captain promise you, eh?"

"We're to have passage." Lucretzia spared little breath for the clipped syllables. "And privacy."

"Passage?" A sharp-eyed woman with dark, shaggy locks slipped up at Bastyan's other side, her mistrustful gaze landing against us like a blade to the neck. "This isn't a Ferry vessel."

"Today, it is!" Hands clapped down on my shoulder and Lucretzia's from behind; I winced, and Lucretzia stiffened, raking a bone-melting glare toward the

Captain as he arced his chin between our heads. "Syd, find Frixia and tell her we're making a run south."

The dark-haired man whistled, long and low, sliding his elbow from Bastyan's shoulder. "You'll have to explain that one, Captain."

"That's the idea, once the crew's all gathered. Get a move on. Reinera," he added with a touch of softness to the woman—who had not given an inch, but measured us with a glowering intensity I appreciated. "Show these two the hammocks, bring up everyone who's still grinding logs. And if you two ever need a reprieve from the ship's bustle," his fingers tightened over the cap of my shoulder, his chin lifting slightly, "my quarters are open to all."

He shoved back from us and strode around our side, whistling; Reinera measured us with equal parts disbelief and dislike. Then, shaking her head, she beckoned us belowdecks.

With a last warning twist of my cloak in her malevolent fingers, Lucretzia followed. I lingered a moment, though not of my own accord; Bastyan's gaze hung upon me like a millstone, fastening my feet to the deck.

"Lionyra," he mused. "Good name."

"Bastyan," I retorted. "Nearly as good."

He grinned, knocking his head back against the mainmast. "You should hear the other names they call me."

"I'm certain they're unsuitable for mixed company."

He winked. "Depends on the company you keep."

"*Lionyra.*" Lucretzia's warning tone hailed me from the hatch near the Captain's quarters, eviscerating the slim moment of normalcy I'd stolen for myself with the sailor who'd helped me save face—quite literally—before the rest of the crew.

Ducking my chin once more in farewell, I followed Lucretzia and Reinera belowdecks.

The belly of the ship was calmer than the topdeck. The sleeping quarters consumed a broad span of it, strung with the sinew of various woven hammocks. Reinera showed us to an unoccupied pair, one laced above the other; then she rousted her crewmates lazing in their woven cocoons nearby and led them out, still throwing glances over her shoulder.

In the absence of the sailors—all of them—the silence was more than suffocating. A warning knell all its own.

Sweat licked at the creases of my palms.

Lucretzia settled into the lower hammock, boots planted on the floor, wrists hanging from her knees. With the barest tilt of her head, she gestured me to the one across from her. "Sit."

Spoken like an invitation. Leveled like a threat.

Slowly, I lowered myself across from her—then stiffened, feet digging into the floorboards as she snapped a hand forward, seizing me by the collar. I could do nothing to brace or defend myself as she jerked the offhand, corded blade from beneath her own cloak—

And slit the front of mine, exposing my hands to the dim porthole light filtering in from the far wall.

I could barely scrape a breath through the pinhole of panic my throat had become. And though Lucretzia's face registered not a flicker of emotion, I could taste the satisfaction that soaked from her pores, potent as rosemary and tangy as anise, while she jammed the tip of her blade into the lock of my fetters.

With a few deft wrenches, the mechanisms gave.

The moment cool air kissed the bruised skin around my wrists, an iron band of equal tightness eased away from my lungs. I was no longer at the mercy of quickhanded sailors…and no longer unable to defend myself.

I rolled the joints, relishing their free movement, and lifted my gaze to Lucretzia's. She watched me with predatory stillness, knife balanced in hand.

"I do not do this because you deserve freedom." Her voice was a serpent's hiss, rolling from some dark cavern into which no human sight could pierce. "But because I saw how that *Captain* looked at you. And because you cannot escape me here. You do understand that, Alyona? You have *nowhere* to flee. Nowhere to escape. You are not a strong swimmer. You are not a clever woman. You are my prisoner, shackles or none."

Disgust emboldened my tongue. "Have you forgotten I evaded the regime for *years*? It takes a clever woman to do that."

Slowly, Lucretzia bent, hands snaring the hammock's frame on either side of my knees. She tipped us both forward in the same thrust, studying my face. Searching my eyes.

I dared not look away.

After several tenuous moments, Lucretzia hissed, "Zorast failed to find you because the grief of his Della's *murder* clouded his judgement. It blunted his edge. And that was your doing."

Though I had wept and vomited after that hideous act, even days later, I was compelled to meet her blow for blow in this…the way she had trained me. "I *relished* it."

The hilt of her knife swung up, cracking my cheekbone so hard I tumbled from the hammock, slamming to the floor. Fire erupted in my elbow, which took the brunt of my fall, and silver-and-red scorches warred across my vision. A cry surged to my lips, but Lucretzia's hand clamped over my mouth. Fingers digging into the arch of my cheekbone where her pommel had struck, she hauled me up before her. My feet nearly left the floor.

"Let this be a warning to you," she hissed. "What you did to Athyna, I will do to any friends you make aboard this ship. If you tell *any* of them your true name or our purpose in this voyage, I will slit their bellies open and cast their bodies overboard. And I will find ways to inflict pain into every soul you draw close to…beginning with that *charming* deckhand."

Her thumb pressed into the rising welt on my cheekbone with such force, I could not smother the whimper that rose in my throat. Savage pleasure sculpted her smile.

"No friends," she murmured. "No failures. No deaths."

She thrust me into the cocoon of the vacant hammock, so hard it nearly spilled me out the other side. I caught myself with my wounded elbow in the weaving by instinct, then bit my tongue to stifle another yelp as fresh pain beat through my arm.

Lucretzia dropped into her own hammock again, sheathing her blade, as diffident as if she'd never struck me—nor threatened the lives of every innocent soul aboard this vessel. "More than a fortnight to the mouth of the Everreach. But less than a month, if these sailors are worth their salt."

I did not need all of my muddled wits about me to hear what went unspoken: there was little telling how treacherous the Everreach would prove this time of year. It could be longer than a month before we dropped anchor in Monsha.

Longer than a month to keep my secrets. To evade friendships. To avoid anything which might draw attention.

It was a challenge I had failed before.

And through Tristah, the Pale Viper had long ago proven she was unafraid to use allies against me.

CHAPTER 8
PRISONER OF THE WAVES

The first and second days aboard *The Athalion* were long, lonely, and suffocating. I dared not leave my hammock—I could not bear to glance into the communal washbucket and behold the latest damage Lucretzia had wrought to my face. Instead, I feigned sleep while she breathed serpent-silent below, curled on my side in the hammock above her, pain pulsing from my cheekbone and radiating in a grim halo around my eye.

It was not until the second dawn, after all the sailors had fallen asleep or traveled abovedecks, that I gathered the strength to swing my legs over the edge of the hammock and drop to the floor. Even the dull impact of my heels on the wood pounded fresh heat through my cheekbone and eye, but I swallowed a groan when I pivoted to face Lucretzia, seated on the edge of her own hammock.

She regarded me with a sliver of vicious triumph. I arranged my countenance into a cool mask, despite the ache that came with slackening my features. "Good morning."

She stabbed the blade she had been sharpening into the seam of her boot, rising. "And what do you intend to do with it?"

Her tone suggested there was only one proper answer to that question—a test she expected me to fail.

Foregoing it altogether, I swiveled on heel and strode from the room.

"You know better than to walk away from me." Lucretzia's iron-plated heels clipped the floor as she gave chase. "*Lionyra!*"

There was no victory in hearing her speak that name.

Gathering my tattered skirts, I broke into a jog, then into a sprint, wincing as the impact vibrated in my swollen cheekbone with every footfall; but I persisted, down the hall, up the steps, shouldering through the hatch—

Which slammed skin with an audible *clump.*

Someone profaned the depths with such vehemence, I halted on the steps—and wished I could retreat down them when Bastyan circled the hatch, rubbing his shoulder and scowling. "What in Ahim's name was *that*—for...?"

His tone shifted between one word and the next, softening, tilting upward.

The sun beat down relentlessly on the deck, warming my skin. Dimly, I was aware that Lucretzia had reached the base of the steps behind me, but she did not mount them.

Observing. Taking note. The serpent coiled in its cool den, seeking an exposed ankle to strike.

I dropped my skirts to shield mine. "Good day, Bastyan."

"It is, that." His gaze landed on the fresh bruise that swelled along my cheekbone, and his lips twitched mildly. "Quite the shiner you've got there." He touched his smallest finger to the same square of flesh beneath his own eye. "I might've missed it, being knocked stupid when you were falling for me the other day, but was that there when you boarded?"

I flicked up the heel of my hand to mask the bruise. "No, this was—"

Icy awareness prickled at the nape of my neck. *No friends. No failures. No deaths.*

Swallowing, I let my hand fall and kneaded my mouth into a sheepish grin, paired with an offhanded lift of the shoulders. "My own doing, I'm afraid. It's been some years since I've sailed, and when we cast off from the docks, the sea got the better of me."

"Hmm." He stepped a bit nearer, his fingers rising, and for an instant I wondered—feared—that he might palpate the bruise for himself.

But though his hand hovered between us a moment, it finally slid back through his hair, laying it flat to his scalp. He flashed a lopsided smile of his own. "Just so happens, I was on my way to find you. You saved me the extra steps."

Lucretzia's gaze still crawled like branching ice up my back. "And what do you want with me, Master Sailor?"

The swell of his throat bobbed. He retreated a step, restoring the space he'd closed between us. "Captain wants us swabbing the relief buckets."

I blinked.

His mouth turned up at the corner. "What? Did you think Syd was bluffing?"

"No, although I—"

"Captain figures scrubbing out the relief buckets ought to be something a servant girl has some experience with."

A bit of challenge flared beneath my ribs like a prodded coal. "Quite the disappointment, no doubt, that our plight did not entirely free you from such an unpleasant task."

"Unpleasant, ah! Gives me time to think. Besides, it'll go awfully bloody faster with a second pair of hands." He jerked his head, motioning me away from the hatch. "Aboard a Trade vessel, everyone pulls their weight. That means you and your mistress as well." He dropped his tone to a conspiratorial whisper. "Between you and me, what's she good at?"

Intimidation. Cruelty. Gutting with small blades and hacking with large ones. Wielding words with the same daggered proficiency.

I forced a smile. "She is talented in many things. I am certain the Captain can find work for her."

"True of any Captain worth his salt." Bastyan gave another ushering tilt of his head. "Best not waste any time. You think the relief buckets are ripe now, just you wait until they've baked beneath the midday sun on the deck for a bit."

Grimacing, I followed after him; I sensed Lucretzia's ascension abovedecks even without a single spared glance, her gaze tracking after me.

But what could she do? She had pieced together this ruse; I was simply upholding it.

Still, unease needled in the base of my throat as I mounted the steps to the helm and the aft deck where Captain Jularius manned the wheel, deep in conversation with a dark-haired woman of middling age, wearing tasseled blue-and-gold attire similar to his.

And beyond them…the sea.

The sight of open water had always stolen my breath, leaving a certain hollowness where peace curled itself in a pleasant little coil. The beat of the waves on the cliffs beyond Krylan had been a favorite retreat of mine when I'd first immigrated to Mithra-Sha, their ceaseless song silencing the tumult of my thoughts in a way nothing else could.

Now the sea was all I had—miles and miles of it, a vivid, rich blue span which spoke of the trenchless depths below *The Athalion*. Thin, slumbering spines of coast to one side and islands on the other delineated our course, but no deterrents awaited.

Peace. Yet I was its prisoner, captive to those cerulean stretches. I was not a wave-walker like Ahim, whom legend told had sprinted across the face of the sea to hurl bloodthirsty, flesh-eating men from Amere-Del's shores, to the distant islands where they lingered to this day.

No. I was confined to this ship, even unshackled. And I was bound by the piercing stare which jabbed at my back while we ascended to the upper deck.

Lucretzia, watching me with hawkish intensity, until she could see me no more.

CHAPTER 9
NOWHERE ELSE TO GO

The Captain spared me a cursory nod as I trailed Bastyan to the rear of the deck, but the smile that accompanied it carved deep lines into his cheeks. A bit of my spirit warmed at being surrounded by ready grins for the first time since I'd closed *The Secret Ingredient* more than a week ago and gone to freshen up and await Addie's arrival for tea and games.

She had never come. And now I would likely never see her again…nor my shop.

Had it been reclaimed by the bustle of Krylan already, kneaded effortlessly into the ever-rising batch of want for space that grew and doubled with each arrival of fresh immigrants? Had a Mithran baker taken over in the scarce week of my absence, dutifully erasing the first imprint of an Ameresh storefront beyond the immigrant district?

The brief burst of warmth snuffed out, and I trudged across the aft deck to the row of buckets chained to the railing. Already Bastyan had freed and hefted the first, spilling it unceremoniously into the sea.

I followed his example, wrinkling my nose at the odor—not from lack of experience so much as a dearth of exposure. Della Athyna had never thought it beneath Tristah and me to tend the washrooms in Shadewyle Castle when our rare bouts of defiance had stoked one of her frequent migraines.

Thoughts of the Della soaked my hands in a surge of sweat and filled my mouth with bile. Of all the pieces of my past that built such a fractured mosaic of adolescence and womanhood, she was the portion I revisited the least; the piece painted bloodred, the corner fragment that was still sharp enough to slice deeply if I pressed against it the wrong way.

"You're quiet." Bastyan's observation jostled me from thumbing at the edges of that stinging shard. "You're not going to hurl on me, are you?"

Scrunching my nose tighter, I tipped another bucket over the side. "And what's to suggest I'm not always so quiet?"

"You don't seem the type."

I tipped another bucket's contents to the mercy of the sea, then linked it behind the chain and faced Bastyan, scrubbing my filthy hair from my brow with my wrist. "What do you know of *my type*, Master Sailor?"

His smile burned as bright against my face as the sunlight spilling untamed across the deck. "A bit haughty. Too good for your station. No one listens to you as much as you wish they would…so you never stop talking."

"Hmm." I gave him nothing more than that; it was amusing how wrong he was, in so many ways.

And also how right, in other aspects I preferred not to reflect on.

"Except around this mistress of yours," Bastyan added, upending the next bucket into the sea. "What's her story…Cress Matherus?"

"Ask her, if you dare."

"Ah, she doesn't worry me."

"She should."

He dropped his bucket and caught the next just as I lifted it, his hands snaring the base and rim opposite mine. Our eyes met across the bucket. "Does she worry *you*?"

I wrested the bucket from his grasp and took my turn spilling it overboard.

After a long moment, Bastyan swooped up another bucket, deftly changing the subject. "Well, not much has me shaking in my boots, for better or worse. That's why I'm on this ship."

A snort unraveled from me. "Because Captain Jularius Cathan is such a terrifying figure."

"That one? He intimidates me as much as a rat snuffling under my pillow."

"Heard that, you lousy ramblers," the Captain called over his shoulder.

"I meant for you to!" Bastyan pitched back.

"Then why *are* you on this ship, Bastyan Atreyon?" I wheedled as we worked. Safer by far to discuss his past than mine.

"Nowhere else to go." He shrugged. "I'm Ameresh, so I wanted an Ameresh vessel to sail on. This was the only ship taking on new deckhands, and I knew I'd never have another bloody chance to see the world."

"You believe a Trade vessel will take you so far?"

He tilted his bucket back from the edge, gaze trailing over the sea. The errant wind that filled our sails blew strands of thick, dark hair from his brow. "It'll take me far enough."

Curiosity dotted my heart like flakes of butter zested into pastry dough. "Far enough for what, if I may ask?"

He blinked, then flashed one of those sunny smiles my way. "Far enough to stay ahead of all the reasons I left Amere-Del in the first place."

When I set aside the last emptied bucket, mulling that notion, he produced a pair of damp, soapy sponges from a pouch hanging at his opposite hip, tossing one my way.

"All right," he announced, "time for the gritty bits. Still with me?"

"Where else, precisely, would I be?"

Snorting, Bastyan dropped cross-legged onto the deck, rucking his sleeves up to his elbows—revealing tattoos that curled far past his hands, up his elbows, disappearing toward his shoulders. They were a mess of indeterminate shapes and whorls; if they held any significance or told any tales, I could not discern them.

I snapped my gaze away when he settled, hauling a bucket into his lap and plunging his arm into it up to the elbow. "Well, if *I* could be anywhere else, let me tell you…it would be a stretch of beach near the port town of Sudene, down in Amere-Del. I may not have any interest in living there, but the *sands*…"

He rambled on while I sank into the grunge of the task, soothed by the undemanding ease of this chatty sailor's presence. Left to my own devices—even if those devices necessitated holding my face far too near the reek of waste—I could nearly forget where I was. And where I was bound for, against my will. And who might be awaiting me there, already in chains.

We finished our task just past midday; Bastyan stood first, offering his hand and hauling me to my feet with a powerful tug. Together, we stared at the string of cleaned buckets chained before us.

"Such satisfaction," I mused, "for swabbing out slag buckets."

Bastyan guffawed, tossing the sponges into one of them. "Is that what they call them in Mithra-Sha? I bet you could tell some stories about all of that. How long were you and your mistress up there?"

Swallowing a surge of fresh sorrow, I tugged my fingers through my greasy locks, tying them to the nape of my neck to escape the flirting fingers of the wind. "Not long enough."

Bastyan eyed me again; he opened and shut his mouth. Then he tugged off his rich blue tunic, slapping it over his shoulder—baring an abdomen and torso decorated with uncountable markings. Tattoos. Scars. Another tale written in flesh tanned but not quite pocked by the sun.

He gathered a fistful of bucket handles in each hand, straightened, then eyed me full-faced. His gaze lingered on the bruise across my cheek. "If you feel like sharing any of those stories…I'm happy to listen."

Then he was gone—toting the buckets off to their usual places. But I remained, struck silent by his offer…by the kindness among these sailors.

And wishing, with a pang of deep-rooted melancholy, that *this* was my future. And not, perhaps, my last gasp of freedom and friendliness before I was subjected to a life in chains.

It was past darkness when I slipped belowdecks again; I had taken advantage of necessary duties, swabbing the deck at the command of Frixia Armis, *The Athalion's* First Mate. A delicious ache banded my arms from shoulders to wrists—a pain I had chosen—by the time I slipped into the hold where half the crew slept in their hammocks. The other half worked the rigging abovedecks.

No sight of Bastyan among them. And that was some relief, when I saw who had beaten me to the hold.

I had not glimpsed Lucretzia all day—not even from the corners of my eyes. I'd relished her absence until the moment our gazes met across the dim lanternlit room; and then all at once the weight of her presence barreled over me, like a vinegar tang I'd grown unaccustomed to after too much time avoiding it. It scorched my tongue and set my teeth grinding.

Slowly, I approached where she sat on her hammock. If I carried a stench from the harsh soaps and waste I'd spent the day submerging myself in, she did not remark. All she said, keeping her gaze on the knife she turned between her hands, was a quiet, vicious, "What did I tell you of friendships, Lionyra?"

I lifted myself with a swift spring into the upper hammock—nearly out of reach. "It was you who decided we were to be servant and mistress. Servants serve, do they not?"

"Servants do not needlessly chatter."

"He did the chattering. Would you have preferred I froze him out with silence and drummed up contention with our hosts? Suspicion, even?"

She was silent for a time; the haze of hate that fumed perpetually from her adopted an odor of skepticism now—an intensity I could scarcely afford.

"The moment this becomes something more," she warned, "I will know it."

Something more. What *more* could there possibly be, aboard this vessel carrying me to the fate I had feared and fled from?

But I did not indulge her with an answer. I simply rolled to my side and put my back to the room.

The sooner I slept, the sooner I could escape her.

And escape I did…into dreams of white, sandy shores alongside Ameresh port towns. It was the first time since I'd escaped Amere-Del that my dreams of my birth country were pleasant, rather than nightmarish.

And in my dreams, I walked them with a sailor made of sunshine.

CHAPTER 10
BARTERING SKILLS

Life aboard *The Athalion* was, in its own right, a recipe, sprinkled with ingredients both savory and saccharine. And Captain Jularius—or Julas, as the crew called him, which I much preferred—was his own sort of cook, crafting a masterful delicacy out of the talents of his people. Even the newest among us.

I did not mind a shipman's labor; in fact, it quite suited me. Much the same muscles were required for swabbing relief buckets and cleaning the deck as tending *The Secret Ingredient*. To use them was to nourish Lionyra Vara; and I much preferred that over tasting bile when I caught the Pale Viper's gaze lingering a bit too long on whichever sailor I'd deigned to speak to that day.

It had been so long since I'd been trapped anywhere with Lucretzia, I'd forgotten how suffocating it could be. But there she was—awakening the moment I slipped from my hammock each morning. Returning before me to hers, that warning gaze following me when I vaulted into my cocoon and folded it over myself to escape her.

Something—or perhaps *everything*—about Lucretzia tainted the batch of my courage with mold. Every spore of her blackened every bit of me.

Which was the other reason I so enjoyed the tasks Captain Julas assigned me; unpleasant though they were, they certainly befit a servant, keeping Lucretzia and I apart from one another. Often they were done in tandem with the newest sailors—the Ameresh deckhands.

Most often, they were done with Bastyan.

If Lucretzia was a mold, then Bastyan was a fungus…a delightful little mushroom, blackcapped and golden-stemmed, growing perpetually in the cracks wherever I lingered more than a moment. I came to anticipate his morning greetings, often sliding down the rigging from the crow's nest to alight wherever I scrubbed or applied fresh varnish to the deck; or else he would creep up on me while I sponged out buckets, by all means intent on recreating our first meeting with a bright, "*Top* of the morning, Lionyra!" or a bark of wordless sound meant to send me leaping.

He did not know, of course, that my ears were sensitive to his approach—trained to listen for footfalls, and forever attuned while I worked, awaiting a far less pleasant greeting from Lucretzia.

Bastyan's, I enjoyed, inasmuch as his relentless attempts were amusing; and it seemed the crew enjoyed him, as well. I could detect him across the deck by the swell of laughter in any given direction. He and Syd sparred for the position as the most humorous man among the crew—a friendly contest by which all the rest of us benefited. Jokes and banter sugared the air often, interwoven with Mithran shanties and Ameresh sailing tunes flung from rigging rope to rigging rope like a challenge.

Whenever he caught me chuckling at his antics, Bastyan grinned; then he would join me, regardless of his other tasks, and entertain me with tales of his smaller sailing ventures before he'd made his way north and found Julas's crew.

The only stories he would not tell me were of the state of Amere-Del; whether because he did not know, or because it troubled him, he danced around the subject whenever I broached it.

I did not know *why* I broached it; I avoided it fiercely with Lucretzia. But with every mile we sailed down the coast, I became keenly aware that the country of my birth lurked off the portside, waiting to swallow me whole once we turned our course down the Everreach.

As dreams of escape shrank and the days brought us nearer to our destination, rage and resignation slowly crusted over with resolve. If I must return, I would know what I was stepping into, so I might face it with my head high; and so that I might prepare Tristah as well, if indeed she awaited me at the end of this voyage.

So I prodded, and I mused; but Bastyan never gave way. He changed the subject expertly whenever it strayed too near to how Amere-Del was nowadays. Gradually, I relented, reticent of the shadows that lurked within his downcast gaze at the mention of the mainland.

Some people were simply sunshine. I had learned that with Addie-cat. I'd learned it with Tristah, despite the stormclouds she'd sketched across the angles of her life, shielding her glow from those who sought to snuff it.

Bastyan, too, was sunshine. Despite Lucretzia's shrewd warnings, it was a delight to bask in his glow. And I would not smother it for the sake of my own curiosity.

I had grown so used to his greetings that it was disappointment, not delight, that surged in me the day another sailor's whistle pulled me from my task—not Bastyan, but Reinera, approaching where I hemmed a tattered sailcloth on the forecastle. She halted, elbow propped to the railing, watching me; I did not meet her gaze, intent on my work and determined not to prick my fingers with the sharp whalebone needle I wove in and out of the sailcloth.

My fingers were already bruised and pricked enough from the distraction of watching Bastyan and a pair of twin sailors, Nix and Nash, have a knot-tying contest below. He'd beaten them handily three times before they'd each gotten rounds over on him.

A born sailor, indeed.

"You have quite a hand for stitching," Reinera remarked, angular eyes narrowing as she watched me work.

I flashed her a smile—all I was willing to spare before I returned my full attention to my task. "The more I can do for myself, the easier my life becomes."

Which was true of many things; I'd shadowed tradesman after skillwoman in Krylan, dabbling in this and that—learning to make and mend my own clothes, to grow my own produce for the shop, to launder and clean properly, to build and upkeep my vending cart. Over the years, I had lost count of how many occasions I'd bartered skills in exchange for bread—with poorer craftspeople, unhappy immigrants, and destitute sailors who could not afford to pay me for the food they so desperately needed.

The more I knew, the stronger I was; if not in body, then certainly in mind. And my mind was my refuge.

Sliding her hand along the railing, Reinera approached me. "Captain wasn't wrong…you're handy aboard a ship."

"I try to be useful wherever I go." Better than a domineering figurehead paraded as a prize before gawking denizens; better than chattel sold for her title and station, for breeding, for peace.

Reinera halted, shifted her weight, then blurted, "I apologize for my demeanor when you boarded. I was concerned, with Captain Julas bringing so many unfamiliar faces aboard all at once."

I paused in mid-stitch, raising my eyes to hers. "Us, and the Ameresh deckhands?"

Her narrow chin jerked in a curt nod. "Aboard a ship, you never know…the last vessel I sailed with, we were invaded by plainclothes pirates. Only I survived, and that, I owed to Syd…a lonely sailor in his little boat, rowing the wrong direction after a storm." A flicker of a smile teased her mouth, but it settled swiftly into a thin line. "I trust this crew. It's more difficult to trust the new folk Captain brings aboard."

I let the sailcloth fall into my lap, studying her face; I had spotted her often these last several days, watching me across the deck, her hands fisted in the lines as she worked them.

There was no mistaking the harshness of her countenance had slackened somewhat. Vigilance no longer tightened her shoulders.

"Did you come to apologize because I've proven myself?" I strove for a mild tone, though laughter fought to bubble beneath the surface. "Or because we've sailed long enough now that you assume if I planned to strike, I would have done so by now?"

She tapped her knuckles on the railing. "Can it be both?"

The laughter erupted out of me like a firework, and I patted the deck next to me. "I assure you, I am no pirate. Nor am I a good enough performer to pretend otherwise."

That lie branded my tongue a bit. But at least the part I performed would not betray this sailor's fears.

Reinera eased a few steps nearer—then halted. "Actually, I'm here on Captain's orders. He asked me to…well, just come with me."

Unease dabbed sizzling-hot against my nape. Pushing aside the mended sailcloth, I gripped the railing backhand and hauled myself to my feet. "What task does he have for me now?"

Reinera wrinkled her nose so fiercely, lines fanned around her eyes. "Before you do *anything* else, what you need is a bath. And some fresh clothes, flipping *Luck*. Has Bastyan had you *washing* those relief buckets, or soaking in them?"

"Is there a difference?"

"Lionyra, I would like to jest with you, but you have such a truly eyewatering stench, I can't even manage it." Gagging, Reinera pressed her sleeve over her nose and mouth. "Just…come with me."

CHAPTER II
DISSIDENTS AND LOYALISTS

That was how I found myself in the ship's bathing chamber—which I would have preferred to visit long ago, but I had never ducked Lucretzia's eye long enough. And I'd had little doubt she would follow me in, watch as I disrobed…and relish the opportunity to remark on every bit of my body she found flawed. It had been a favored pastime of hers and Athyna's ever since I'd taken my first bath in Shadewyle Castle as a knobby-boned orphan, with parched skin and little fat stuck to my ribs.

While Reinera stood watch, I enjoyed my first soaking since before the jailhouse in Mithra-Sha.

I did not care that the water was chilly, nor the varnished washbarrel cramped, nor that countless sailors had likely used the sponges and soap before me. I basked in every pass of the porous material over my sun-marked skin, relishing removing the tarry residue from my scalp. Scrub after dunk after wash after rinse, I peeled away the layers of abuse that coated my body…a punishment Lucretzia had doled out through withholding. Among her most favored acts of domination.

I emerged from the barrel a new woman, clean and smelling of citrus rather than the stench of bodily grime. To think that the other sailors had been subjected to such a rank odor for the past week was another blade of humiliation laid hilt-first in Lucretzia's hand, so I refused to apologize as I lashed on the simple terrycloth robe slung on a hook at the door—likely another communal piece—and peeled the drab wood open a crack.

It was some relief to find Reinera still lounging against the outer wall, arms folded, boot kicked up against the paneling.

"My clothes?" I prompted; she'd demanded I leave them outside.

"Floating behind us on a current that will hopefully drag them out to sea." Reinera swooped up a heap of fabric from the floor beside her, pushing it through the seam in the door to me. "This should be your size."

And so it was, if a bit tight in the bust. The loose-sleeved linen shirt puffed notes of clove and cinnamon into my nostrils when I shrugged into it, and with hasty fingers, I tied the front laces of the leather vest. I slapped on the belt to hold the layered skirts in place, then hung the robe again and sidestepped to greet my reflection in the stained slab of glass bolted to the opposite wall.

The ensemble was nothing like I had ever worn before; its grays and browns contrasted with the bright tones of classic Ameresh dress, the beaded shawls and fiery hues I had been reluctant to part with even after I'd left my title and the country of my birth far behind. This costume was neither ornate nor drab; it befit a sailor, not a Delina.

And I loved it.

Fierce, functional, and feminine. It was all I craved to be.

Braiding my damp locks swiftly over one shoulder, I stepped to the door and toed it open fully this time. Reinera greeted me with a pivot and a nod. "It suits you."

The glow burned from my chest out to my fingertips, lighting the fuse of my grin as I worked over my hair. "This is possibly the loveliest thing I've ever worn."

Reinera smirked. "Better than those clothes you had before. What were they once—pink?"

"Fuchsia, if you please."

She glanced over me, a gleam of troubled thought shining across her eyes. "Do you mind me asking why you wore them for so long?"

My fingers snagged on a tangle in my hair; I worked over it for a moment, threading out the frayed ends. "When my mistress and I received word to return to Monsha, we had no time to gather our spare things."

Reinera snorted. "It hardly seems wise to go to *Monsha* with just the clothing on your back."

A chill scraped at my belly. "And why is that?"

Slowly, Reinera tilted her shoulder to the wall, then her hip; trouble overtook her gaze in full, washing her burnt-umber eyes with a glassy film.

"I don't know who called you and your mistress home now, or why," she said, "or how long you've been gone. But things in Amere-Del aren't good."

I tugged the end of my braid into a loose knot, then eased the door shut at my back. "What do you mean?"

Reinera glanced shrewdly over her shoulder, then tilted closer to me. "There's talk of closing the Everreach."

Shock rippled bitterly in my throat. "*What?*"

"It has all the captains between the two countries in an absolute whirlwind," Reinera admitted. "The strife between the Del's regime and the dissidents worsens every season…more and more since talk of the Incendiary began."

"What is *that?*"

"Not what. *Who.*" Reinera's tone dropped to a storyteller's cadence—the same tone that had beckoned me to seek out Addie the first night I'd heard her working her craft over a crowd. "The Incendiary is the champion of the dissidents. They've begun to call Algernon Sorai a mere figurehead in the revolt against the Del Graven regime. The Incendiary is the one taking true action."

Sorai's name scathed through me like the flat of a blade laid to my flesh, flaying it from my bones. A violent shiver shook through me; I tipped back against the shut door, pressing my folded hands to my mouth.

"Anyway," Reinera went on, ignorant of the nausea that bubbled in my belly at the mention of the dissident mouthpiece, "the Incendiary is taking Amere-Del by storm. The dissenters have gone from plastering propaganda against the regime on alley walls to ransacking storehouses and disseminating goods among the people. His knowledge extends *far* beyond what the regime's detractors have ever held before…his strikes have been so precise, it's put Del Graven in a panic."

"So he threatens to shut down the Everreach in retaliation." The words floated in a whisper from my half-numb tongue.

Zorast Graven's paranoia wasn't new; it was why there'd ever been want for a decoy at all. But sealing off the Everreach would put to death the trade enterprises across Amere-Del. The blighted, barren Southlands relied on imports from the Northlands to feed their people; the Northlands depended on the ore from the lower Barradir Highlands to forge their defenses against the beasts that roamed the wilds, and the unbreakable stone cut from the Abbra Foothills to construct their homes and cities.

The two halves of Amere-Del, bisected by the Everreach, leaned on one another to survive. For that reason, Del Graven had been willing to do anything to preserve the peace. When dissenters had first begun to grumble about taxes

and trade routes, he'd sent appeals to Sha Lothar for a contingent of
Storycrafters to be sent into Ameresh lands, hoping the power of their stories
could solve our troubles.

When the Sha had declined, the Del had retaliated with marauders—flesh-
thieves sent to capture Storycrafters. I'd sat on needle-tips during that excursion,
shocked they'd made the attempt to capture the Master Storycrafter herself; that
swift bid for absolute control, and the decisive retribution from the Master
Storycrafter's bodyguard and his contingent of soldiers, had ended the Del's
attempts mid-grasp.

I had not remembered that affair for years. Likely because of how all of the
events afterward had pitched Amere-Del into chaos.

Pockets of infighting had broken out. Trade deals had soured between the
Northlands and Southlands. Taxes had multiplied, setting the country on the
sharp edge of turmoil. Soon dissent had cropped up on both sides of the
Everreach, and after years of strife, a leader had shown himself.

Algernon Sorai. Angry, arrogant, and resolute. The voice of the people, he'd
called himself.

And the people had been furious.

His name throbbed within me like spoiled milk, sour in my gut.

The Del and Della had been determined to put an end to the dissonance by
any means. Even if it meant giving Sorai what he craved—or feigning as much.
Providing him a false sense of sway, of power, by offering a prize which made
the power seem to be his.

I slid my palms apart to lay one against my mouth, in case the sweating heat
between my teeth should become something thicker. "Closing off the Everreach
will solve nothing. Dissidents are everywhere, on both sides of the river."

"True." Reinera picked at the loose skin around her nailbeds, scowling.
"Julas doesn't think the act is about solving anything. It's a show of
strength…Graven proving *he's* still the Del. That the Incendiary can raid
storehouses and help people on both sides, but in the end, his reach only goes so
far."

"This Incendiary…would he relent?"

Reinera shrugged. "It's difficult to say. He certainly seems to have interest
in helping the hurting, regardless of whether they come from the Northlands or
Southlands. But he remains a dissident, if the most powerful of them all. Sorai
has publicly decried his actions."

A snort burst from me. "Likely because action on behalf of the people ruins Sorai's chances of seizing power for himself."

Reinera quirked a brow. "I see you have an opinion on things."

I fell silent, studying the tips of my bare toes peeking out from the hem of my borrowed skirts.

A servant should not be allowed opinions; but one who served a mistress from Monsha would no doubt have heard things, even if those things did not directly influence her.

"What I have seen," I offered carefully, "is that the dissidents have good intentions, but they go about them the wrong way. A man like Algernon Sorai in a position of influence, or as Del himself, will only be a voice for the people for so long. He knows nothing of how to lead a country. Sooner or later, self-interest will get the better of him, and both sides will go back to hurting."

"For what it's worth, I agree," Reinera said. "It takes the right sort of person to captain a vessel…to lead a country. Not everyone can be a Jularius Cathan, yeah?" Warmth budded at the corners of her smile. "But Del Graven has a point to make, and he wants to cut off travel and trade across the Everreach to do it."

That explained Lucretzia's haste, her fouler-than-usual mood. She was desperate to return to Shadewyle Castle before things rotted so utterly that they blockaded the river.

And she and Del Graven likely still hoped to swear me off to Sorai. To make peace among the dissidents before this Incendiary lit a spark that raged out of everyone's control.

Would such a swearing even bring peace anymore, with this new figure fighting for those suffering on both sides? What were his intentions, if they set him in opposition to Sorai, voice of the people?

"Anyway," Reinera's sigh cut into the havoc of my thoughts as she shoved herself upright from the wall, "the problem with Monsha is, it's too much in the middle. It's become an absolute breeding ground for chaos…riots, revolts. Militar and dissidents clash there almost daily. The streets aren't safe to walk anymore. Even sailors keep close to the docks and scurry back aboard as soon as they've traded their wares." Her gaze slid sideways to me in the gloom of the ship's narrow corridor, scarcely touched by the lantern swinging high above. "If I was a trademaster with a wife in Mithra-Sha, I'd have told her to stay there until all of this was solved."

I eased out what imitation of a smile I could manage with so much new truth swirling in my head—and so many memories of the trade port that had been the place of my birth and a place of so much death. The city I had called home until my adolescence.

A place whose riots and revolts I knew all too painfully well.

"Thank you for informing me," I managed at last. "My mistress tells me little."

"I gather that." Reinera's smile was as reluctant as mine. "No one should go into Monsha unprepared these days."

And it was a fresh sort of punishment that Lucretzia had intended me to go blindly back into the Del's clutches, unaware of how Amere-Del had sundered near to civil war.

"Thank you for the clothing," I said as we wound our way back toward the steps up to the topdeck. "I wish that I could repay you."

"It was a spare." Reinera shrugged. "Besides, I stole it from Lanah."

Laughter soothed my abraded nerves like honey swallowed down a sore throat. "I suppose I should trust her not to peel these from my back when she sees me in them?"

"Of course not. She prefers to wear corsets rather than vests these days, particularly when Syd is nearby." Reinera wagged her dark, full brows. "Anyway, it's good you're approachable now. We're dropping anchor and going ashore soon."

My bare heels snagged on the rough wooden floor, bringing me to a swift halt. "Ashore? Why?"

Reinera snorted. "All that talk of dissidents made you jumpier than a jackrabbit on hot coals, didn't it?" She gripped my shoulder, nudging me forward. "Sunrise Isle isn't far…another two days off. We always drop anchor there on voyages to and from Amere-Del. It's the best place to replenish our supplies, refill the water barrels, and enjoy a cooked meal of fresh food."

Fresh food.

A true grin, untamed, rose at the corners of my mouth.

When I stepped to her side, Reinera blinked, and a smile cracked her sober countenance as well…as if it could not help itself in the presence of mine.

"Tell me," I said, eagerness spilling all over my tone, "would it be possible to have access to your ship's galley?"

CHAPTER 12
THE SECRET INGREDIENT

It required every ounce of stealth that I had retained over the years—coupled with mercy begged from Ahim himself—to escape my hammock that night without waking Lucretzia.

This was not the first time I had crept off to craft illicit goods. I could scarcely number the times Tristah had slipped into my vacant bed and I had made a mound of blankets shaped like a curled-up form in hers, then stolen off to the kitchens of Shadewyle Castle.

This act of defiance set my heart thundering just as much now as it had then. But excitement and anticipation were familiar, urgent companions nipping at my heels as I stole down the shadowed ship halls in just my long tunic and a pair of muslin undershorts Lanah had given me.

Likely stolen from Syd—or won from him in one of the games of *Poor Man's Dice* I'd watched the crew play, but never joined for fear of Lucretzia's watchful eyes.

The thought of her hounded me to the doorway of the ship's galley…then perished on the threshold as I took in the room.

A chamber full of bolted-down tables and seats; a broad half-counter at the back wall, lined left and right with ration barrels, allowing only a thin seam for a body to slip behind. Those ration barrels were expertly labeled—likely by Henriet, the ship's harried bookkeeper, who'd swiftly proven to be utterly meticulous about how things were inventoried and recorded.

I blessed her in Ahim's name as I snatched an apron from a peg on the counter's nearest support post, wound my braid around itself in a knot at the back of my head, and set to work.

Unpleasant surprise wrinkled my nose as I discovered how much a fortnight without my fingers in dough had altered my intrinsic sense of my beloved craft. I had not gone so long without baking *something* since I'd arrived in Mithra-Sha; now, I struggled to recall the recipe for a simple bread loaf. Measurements molded over in my mind, and it took pitching away two batches with heavy hands and a far heavier heart before it truly struck me what was happening.

This was no mere matter of passing time; it was the Pale Viper's presence aboard the ship strangling the life and levity from my work. This was the loom of Shadewyle Castle casting its sprawling, many-fingered shadows from iron-tipped turrets and jutting towers across the path I had chosen to walk—turning me back to the one chosen for me.

In the silence, I plunged my fingers into the latest batch of dough, puffing flour against my chest. "Leave me be," I rasped. "In Ahim's name, leave me *be*."

I needed only one night. Just one to make these loaves, for my fingers and the joints at my wrists to recall the rhythmic press, shove, and pull, the measuring and mixing that highlighted my life. I had not appreciated this enough the last day I'd closed up *The Secret Ingredient*. I'd been querulous about Farmer Tillion's cheddar in my dough, and how it hadn't mingled well with the rest of my ingredients; I had been irate, unthankful.

I only needed this one night, possibly to bid farewell to baking forever…or at least for so long that my fingers would surely forget, my mind occluded utterly with Lucretzia's hovering presence and Zorast Graven's grief and fury. And with Algernon Sorai's leering intentions.

I would not take this night for granted, however it went.

So I toiled in silence, as I often had in the castle kitchens. For the crew, I made loaf after loaf; for myself, I kneaded and shaped, beat down and smoothed out my fury and hurts and my shame and fear until calm came…not from the stillness of the galley around me, but from a span of quiet in my core.

This was perhaps the deepest mess I'd ever been in, but I was not bereft of options. Though I could not escape Lucretzia now, I knew Shadewyle and its guards, the patterns of its halls and the watches within them.

I had escaped the castle before. And though I had left with blood on my hands, and only with Tristah's help…with her, I could do it again. Our tale would not end where we had left it in Amere-Del, cut off the moment our lives had been offered up as a prize for peace.

No. I was a baker who shaped and molded and battered things to their very best. I would not take my hands out of the batch of my life until it was seasoned and set precisely how I liked it. And if that required great finesse, slipping ingredients where Lucretzia and the Del could not scent or see them…

So be it.

I gave the dough an extra pummel for good measure, a decisive strike laying my intentions by a blow of knuckles into the slick round, the way I had long ago struck Lucretzia's sparring dummies.

"Oi. What did that poor loaf ever do to you?"

The rasp of drowsy humor, delivered in a voice still husky with sleep, unleashed a gale that stirred up the calm waters at my core. Hauling my fist from the dough, I snapped a glance at the galley doorway.

Bastyan leaned his shoulder into the doorless frame, one hand stuffed in the pocket of his trousers, the other scratching beneath his dark hair. The lanterns along the tabletops cast a striking tawny glow along his bare chest, his tattoos rippling as if coming alive in the glass-sheathed firelight.

I only realized I hadn't risen to the bait of his banter when his posture shifted, evoking a fresh dance from the dark ink. His hand threaded out of his hair and clapped to the doorframe above, and he bowed his weight into it, tipping inside the galley. "What are you doing in here, 'ay? It's the dead of dark."

Shoving back from the counter, I brushed a strand of hair from my burning cheek with my wrist. "Kneading dough. What does it look like I'm doing?"

Chuckling, Bastyan shoved fully into the room, his hand sliding from the doorframe above. He leaned across the counter from me, his thumb flicking out—brushing the mending bruise along my cheekbone. Before I could so much as suck in my breath at the unexpected touch, he pulled his thumb back and studied it…dusted with flour.

"Aye, I can see that," he teased, his gaze darting back to mine—then dropping to the loaves in various states of rising and settling, spread across the counter. "But…*why?*"

"Because you need dough to make bread." My lips curved up at the slippery turn of phrase, and he snorted, palming the counter and lurching back from me.

"You also need fire." He sauntered to the gap between the ration barrels and the wall. "And a cooking pot."

"Ah! You know about baking bread, do you?"

"Well, enough to know it doesn't cook itself." Bastyan retrieved a cup from the latched cupboard and tapped one of the casks fitted on the wall behind me, filling the wooden chalice to the brim with stale, oak-tinged water.

"Bake," I couldn't help but correct him. "You *bake* bread. You do not cook it."

"Well, pardon me. Didn't realize bread terms were as particular as sailing ones." Tossing back a deep swallow, he cleaned his mouth on his elbow and offered one of his sunny grins. "So, how do you intend to *bake* it?"

"Reinera claims we're to go ashore soon…I thought perhaps some fresh bread, baked over the fire, would serve as a show of gratitude for this crew's accommodations."

A divot cut between Bastyan's brows. "Your mistress paid for those."

"Yes, but you all have accommodated us in other ways. And the risk you've taken cannot be overlooked."

It deserved to be said—though I could never aptly express my gratitude and sorrow for the burden they unknowingly shouldered, tiptoeing around the Pale Viper slithering across their decks, ready to give a venomous strike if anyone stepped too near.

"Besides," I added, when the silence stretched too long—like dough pulled past its breaking point, every thread and fiber screaming as they slowly came undone, "baking calms me. It is…a sanctuary of sorts."

In Amere-Del, many found sanctuary in shrines built to Del Ahim. Places where violence was forbidden by both dissenters and loyalists to the regime. Even among the feckless criminals who ran illicit drug trade and those who took advantage of the needs of others, few were so brash as to dare disrespect Ahim's name by sullying his sanctuaries. They either feared or revered him too much.

But Lucretzia cared nothing for sanctuary. She had dragged me out of one by my hair once when I'd ducked inside to escape her lessons, warning off the stunned glances of Shadewyle's denizens with a hand to her blade. She had told me that night, with her boot pressed into my back after hours of torturous training, that she did not care for shrines; she cared for legacies. And she was willing to trample over anyone's fealty to Ahim if it meant preserving Del Graven and his regime.

I had never set foot in a shrine after that. Sanctuary had become whichever places I could creep away without catching Lucretzia's eye; and for many years, that had been the kitchens, long after dark.

Slowly, Bastyan lowered his haunches onto the wooden frame that held the ration barrels in place. He leaned his back and shoulders against the casks, tilted his head to meet the iron rims at their tops, but kept his eyes on me. Against the cup laced between the fingers of both hands, his thumbs drummed an inaudible tune. "Why baking?"

I shrugged, turning back to the dough; but even with my side to him, I could not escape the heat of his curious stare. "This was what I did in Mithra-Sha, to earn my living wage. And in…my mistress's house, I would often sneak from my chambers after dark to make the sorts of pastries and breads she wouldn't allow me during meals."

An old, forgotten hunger pang gnawed at my core. Here aboard the ship, Lucretzia did not watch my meals closely; it wasn't as if there was a great deal of variety to be had. But I could not escape the disdain with which she eyed this softer body I'd spent years cultivating. Even tonight, when I'd returned from my shiphand duties in the fresh clothes from Reinera, she had sneered first at my escape from the tattered garments she'd caged me in, and then made a sly remark of how it accentuated my curves, my thickness, the folds of my belly.

How long before she sought to deprive me again, to wrestle me back into the form that she and Del Graven and Algernon found befitting a woman sworn for a peace treaty?

Shaking off that thought with a sharp twist of my head, I shoved the dough a bit flatter than necessary and yanked it back toward myself with more vigor than the action warranted. "I would lose the whole night baking in secret, but it was worth the sleeplessness. Having the opportunity to enjoy those treats to myself, in my bed, while I read the books they foisted on me, I…"

Trailing off, I pulled back my hands, fixing my gaze on the loaf.

If I blinked, the tears would fall.

I had not thought closely of those nights in so long. I had fiercely separated the baker I was in Mithra-Sha from the woman I'd been then, sneaking her craft in here and there.

My chest lifted in a shuddering breath. "I do not know why I am telling you this."

Bastyan said nothing. Fresh heat stained my cheeks at his silence. What must he be thinking?

"Anyway," I added hastily, "it seems a shame to let all of that practice go to waste."

There was no masking the sorrow that touched my voice, nor the scorch of it in my chest like the glistering silver trail of a firework loosed across the face of my heart; it was simple, naked grief at what was lost…what had mattered, perhaps more than anyone would ever truly fathom.

Bastyan's voice cut into my heartache. "Teach me."

Startled, I blinked at last, and trails of heat escaped over my lashes; I stroked them hastily away as I pivoted to face him—sloped forward now, bent over his knees, elbows braced on his thighs, turning the cup between his palms.

"I beg your pardon?"

His mouth tilted up at the shock that webbed my tone; but for a moment I caught the most somber expression I'd ever beheld on his face, the lines deep beside his eyes and the grooves harsh around his downturned lips, as if the chambers of his heart echoed the pain in mine. "Teach me this trade of yours." Setting the cup aside on the counter, he lurched to his feet. "I've got nothing better to do."

My gaze darted to the doorway, half-anticipating the shadow of Lucretzia in it like nightshade pressed between the pages of a poisoner's guidebook.

But it would be little worse if she found me here with Bastyan than alone; and if she appeared, I could always push him down behind the counter.

"All right." Seizing courage in the set of my shoulders, I jerked my chin for him to join me.

Clapping his hands together and rasping the calluses on his palms, he swaggered to my side. "Right, then. What do we do first?"

Laughing, I sidestepped and gestured to the dough. "Pull this in half— good. Now, knead your piece—"

"Right here?"

I struck his bare shoulder. "*Bash!*"

He rubbed the offended spot—a tattoo of a compass cast in sharp relief over a mound of muscle. "Oh, those are the sort of names we're using now, *Lio?*"

I halted altogether as that name washed through me.

Lio. Not Lionyra. Not *Alyona,* Ahim forbid. But *Lio.*

After Officer Fiordona's cruelty in the Mithran jailhouse, a corner of my spirit had feared I would never hear that precise name spoken again.

"I am a woman of nicknames." I kept my tone breezy, though my heart still clamored with glee.

"Well, of all the things I've ever been called, I despise that one the least," Bastyan snorted. "Now, you were saying, about my piece—?"

"Do you know what?" I snatched the loaf away from him. "You haven't earned this."

"Oh, haven't I?" His tone dipped as he swiveled to face me, planting one hand on the counter beside my waist.

This man was not only a sailor, but a scallywag. "No, you have not. You must make your *own* loaf."

"And if I don't know *how*?" His other hand descended on the counter beside my opposite hip; he did not press in against me, but his nearness was oven-warm. The scent of salt and varnish filled my head like a foreign spice at the Krylan markets; I would have shamelessly sucked it down were he not standing so near.

There would be no explaining anything if Lucretzia found us like this. I could not explain it to *myself*—what he intended with his teasing, or why I did not withdraw from it.

For a long moment, we stared at one another.

Then Bastyan receded, smile broadening, pushing himself back from the counter with a thrust from the heels of his palms. "I take it you're going to show me?"

And I did.

We passed the time in a haven of lanternlight and shadows while I taught him which ingredients he needed, and how to measure them. We settled on a cinnamon and sugar loaf—his proclaimed favorite—and banter bled into the familiarity of the work. When he refused to moderate his generous use of the spice blend, I warned him he would ruin it; in retaliation, he flicked five full fingertips of it into my face. Huffing in mock offense, I scooped out the last palmful and mashed it against his mouth, leaving his lips patterned in puffs of cinnamon and granules of sugar like a sunkissed shore.

"Was that supposed to be some sort of punishment?" He swiped the corner of his lips with his tongue. "If so, I should offend you more often."

Scoffing, I covered the loaf with a damp cloth to allow it to rise; Bastyan mournfully tipped the empty spice bowl on its side, setting it spinning on the counter while we waited.

And while we waited, I watched—the tilt of the lanternlight reflecting on his features. The dark circles, offset by the ink of his tattoos, stroked beneath his eyes. A glance at the porthole windows showed it was still a deep, endless night outside the ship—the sort where the horizon and the sea and sky did not know where they ended and met.

Yet, here he was…a sailor of the day's crew, baking and bantering, when only a few short hours from now he would be demanded abovedecks.

"Why are *you* here, Bastyan?"

He halted the bowl before it could drop from its spin, his eyes fixed on it. "Sleep and I aren't always the best bedfellows."

I folded my arms at my waist. "And why is that, if I may ask?"

He turned over the bowl and simply stared at it for a time; emotion flexed soundlessly in the harsh definition of his broad shoulders.

"Sailing is my life," he said at length. "But once, it was…almost the death of me. During the day, I can manage it well enough. Things aren't right now like they were back then. But when I'm sleeping, sometimes it all turns to a bloody, tangled mess in my head. Like all the nets get snared and I'm trapped somewhere in the middle of the fray, drowning."

His eyes flicked to me, rosemary green graying with shame.

"There were some tonics that helped, the last ship I sailed on," he admitted, "but I don't have those here."

Sympathy abraded my throat like a puff of inhaled spice. "Have you struggled with this ever since you sailed on your first ship?"

He blinked, gaze brightening from that somber gray to a brighter green. "Well, what do you know? You actually listened while we swabbed out those buckets."

I was tempted to shrug, but some quiet sense held my body rapt—as if this were not a moment to take lightly. "You said you were only a boy when you left your hometown. Was it aboard that vessel where the sea nearly took your life?"

"Interesting choice of words." He drummed his fingers on the countertop, chin bobbing slightly. "Aye, it was."

There was far more to it—that much was made clear in his brittle tone. But I had learned long ago to tread lightly into conversations where I was not openly invited; so I breached the gap between us with a hand instead, touching his elbow. "When one is given to excessive conversation, others often become deaf to what you're truly trying to say."

His mouth opened—with a quick-witted retort, no doubt—but I spoke my piece over him, before sense could claim the better of me.

"If ever you need someone to hear…truly hear…you have my ear."

He was silent for so long that the rising dough demanded my attention before he spoke again, sinking his haunches against the counter, folding his arms. "You're surprising, for a servant girl." His tone was low, threaded with some emotion I could not name.

"And you…a sailor who has nightmares of the sea."

He chuckled, scratching beneath the line of his hair again. "What a pair we make."

What a pair, indeed. An innocent Ameresh deckhand, long since departed from his country's heart; and me, its Delina, a secret kept by my foes.

What would he think, if he knew all of the ways in which I was surprising?

I did not want to imagine any of it. What did Bastyan Atreyon think of the regime…of the civil divide which separated loyalists and dissenters? Would he fall on the side that revered me as sole heir, or loathed me as the perpetuation of imbalanced power? Would he scorn me, the bride meant for a man he might respect as a lonely voice in places of power? Or would he see me as his salvation, a prize sold off to keep the comfortable life from crumbling beneath him?

Hollowness gnawed at the bits of me that had grown famished, smelling the yeast and flour and all of the spices I'd soaked my hands in these last several hours.

"Oi. Lio." Bastyan's knuckle nudged my chin, and I startled, twisting to face him. The frown made a fresh appearance between his brows. "Where did you go?"

As if I could ever tell him.

Fastening a smile into place, I turned to the array of dishes spread around us. "Here. Help me clean these…this will go much better if we have space to work."

We gathered the dishes and washed them at the corner bucket in silence; I scrubbed, and he dried. My gaze wandered now and again to the tattoos on his knuckles, and not for the first time, I wondered where they had come from…whether he had collected them on his first ship, or more recently.

Given how sore the subject of his earliest voyages seemed, I dared not ask.

When the dishes were neatly stacked, Bastyan slapped the drying cloth over his shoulder and planted his hands on his hipbones, staring down at the cloth covering that hid his cinnamon-sugar loaf. "Shall we?"

I nudged him with a nod, and he lifted the corner to peer inside; then he tugged it away, revealing a perfectly doubled loaf.

"Excellent." I turned the bowl out and divided it in half. "I would like to teach you something."

"What have we been doing all this time, if you're not teaching me?"

"Not baking," I scolded. "Something to do when you have nightmares. A way that this craft helps."

He eyed me askance, but said, "I'm listening."

"Take your *portion of the loaf*," I enunciated carefully, and his grin widened to a broad slice of teeth in the lanternlight.

Striking him with my hip, I shuffled my portion squarely in front of me, settling my stance; then I reared back and pummeled the heels of my hands into it—imagining the loaf held the shape of Lucretzia's face.

"Feel your unwanted thoughts traveling down from your mind, to your shoulders, to your forearms and wrists. Then *shove* them out into the dough." Another thrust of my hands had the thready mound coiling away from me. "In their place, seize the thoughts you want to keep, and bring them back to yourself." I tugged the far edge of the dough toward me, tucking it gracefully into itself. "Then, seal those things with your strength—" I folded the right corner of the dough over "—and your courage—" I folded over the left "—and breathe in."

Rocking back on my heels, I inhaled deeply, resting a hand over my stomach; calm slid along the paths of my bones, chasing out the pain of wondering what this sailor would make out of the truth of me.

Slowly, Bastyan took his half and did as I had done: seizing it, shoving it out, bringing it in and folding. Once, twice, three times, he did it—more forcefully each time. I could only wonder whose face he saw in those threads…who had left such a foul impression on him that it still sent nightmares stalking across his life.

After the third kneading pass, he fell back on his heels as well, imitating my posture: hand to his torso, breathing in through his nose, exhaling through his parted lips.

Some modicum of tension eased from his shoulders when he blew out the air. "Well, what do you know?" His laughter tinged with shock, he swiped the tip of his tongue over his lower lip. "That's something else, Lio."

I grinned. "When I do this enough times, I find my calm. And also find I have more pastries and bread loaves than I know what to do with."

Chuckling, Bastyan went to work on his half of the loaf as I returned to mine; this silence was different, lulled with the calm we'd claimed for ourselves.

It was a companionable understanding I wished I could linger in for the rest of the night—the remainder of the voyage, even.

But, all too soon, the dough was pleading for relief. I stayed Bastyan with a touch to the wrist, and we tucked away the two loaves in deep iron pots alongside the others.

At the counter, we lingered; a thread of reluctance thrummed in the dimness. Little joy awaited either of us in our hammocks tonight. And dawn would claim our tired bodies all too soon.

But I *was* exhausted, and calm enough perhaps even to sleep…and that, I owed to the companionship of the sailor beside me, who followed an invisible stain on the counter with the crescent of his thumb, avoiding my gaze when he said, "We should do this again sometime."

The invitation chiseled at the edges of my heart. I would claim a thousand moments like this, if I did not know how they would ache when I left this ship at my back. "I doubt if any dough would last the rest of the voyage to Monsha."

He deflated a bit. "Right."

Unease encroached on the silence again. To spare us both, I turned to go. "Sleep sweet, Bash."

"'Ay." He caught me under the arm, gently, pivoting me back toward him.

His gaze searched mine, striking as a flood of sunlight cleaving through the depths of dark water. As if I was some sailor sucked below the waves, sinking, drowning in the trenches, and he was the gleam of the surface above—a promise of sweet air and salvation.

"I'm sorry," he said after a beat, tilting his chin toward the counter, "if, before, when I was joking with you, I was—"

"I am my own woman, Bash." For now, at least. "If I had wanted to put distance between us, I would have."

His fingers flexed slightly, his thumb stroking the back of my bicep, crossing to the blade of my shoulder. It was so oddly intimate a place to be touched—somewhere I was not certain even Lucretzia had landed a blow before. Perhaps that was what made my heart leap about it all.

"So," his voice was the rasp of a wave on sea gravel, "what does that mean, exactly?"

What *did* it mean? What could I even *want* it to mean?

Nothing. I could want none of this…because not one moment between here and Shadewyle, where I might find Tristah, could matter. This was a lull, a lurch, that pause of time between when the dough went into the oven and when the bread was finished baking.

Circumstances were baking, rising, crusting over. I could not allow myself to have regrets or melancholy for what befell me aboard *The Athalion*; Tristah was my destination, my greatest goal, my only outcome.

Nothing could dissuade me from reaching her. Not even licorice-dark hair and rosemary-green eyes, and the wonderful relief of my chosen name on lips still freckled with cinnamon and sugar.

Gently, I tugged free of his grip. "It means that tonight was as pleasant a dream as either of us can hope for on this voyage. And nothing more."

And that was true. But it was a dream I would carry with me for quite some time.

Fresh bread. Hours of baking, uninterrupted. Not a trace of Lucretzia's presence all night.

And Bastyan, the secret ingredient I had not expected…but one that had made the night among the sweetest I could recall in all my life.

CHAPTER 13
SUNRISE ISLE

I did not realize how much I had missed the shore until I stood on its sturdy span again, bare toes sinking into the sand. Though it was bitingly cool, I'd pay the price of a few goosebumps to escape the world tossing beneath me, rising and falling on untamable waves.

The only tossing now lurched within my chest.

I had not spoken to Bastyan since we'd parted ways in the galley; he had not been there to greet me when I'd come topside after only an hour of fitful sleep, and it had been Syd who'd directed me to my day's tasks: untangling nets and sorting crab cages with Lanah.

Lucretzia had filled the hole of his absence like a backspill of bile in a sweating mouth. Her gaze hooked into my flesh, inescapable as one of the fishing barbs I'd meticulously unwound that morning.

It was possible she had learned already of my bread-baking excursion; and if she had not yet, then she might well discern it when she saw the offerings toted by the crew up the shore toward the fertile heart of the island.

But she could not know Bastyan had been there with me. Nor would she ever know I had dreamed of little else before dawn had driven me from my hammock again.

Shaking away the notion, I blinked the island reaches into view: a broad crescent of sparkling white sand met the sea where we'd rowed ashore, our boats jammed like splinters into the pale skin of the island's outermost banks. Thin ribbons of seawater shimmered deeper ashore until the land graded upward; there, verdant green grasses pocked the landscape, thickening to a carpet near the jungle treeline, where palm trees hung outstretched and thick ivy twined among the trunks.

From the shelter of leaves and fronds, the chitter of jungle creatures and birds rose in a ceaseless chorus. Their cries wove in harmony with the continuous rush of the waves, giving little breathing room for doubts and worries to raise their shrill, nattering call.

Sunrise Isle was indeed a haven. For a moment, I entertained the notion of stringing up my hammock between two curvaceous palms and making *this* my home. Away from notions of civil unrest and the brink of war. Away from the intentions of Del Graven and Algernon and every person who plotted my life for me.

"Enjoying the view?"

Blinking sharply, I swiveled at the waist to find Reinera behind me, toting a crate on one shoulder. Threads of her dark, disheveled hair had caught in the untreated wood. "You could say as much. What have you got there?"

"Last of the pit fruits and apples." She shrugged her burdened shoulder, jouncing the crate lightly. "Best to steam them while we're ashore, can them, and enjoy them as a treat the rest of the way to Monsha."

"I can't think of a better place for such tasks."

"Neither can the Captain," Reinera snorted, leading me further ashore. "We love it here…no rules or policies, no risk of any regulators boarding to peruse the cargo. Trade sailing can be mind-numbing work, but Julas is good about offering a reprieve anytime we've got enough wind in our sails and time to spare."

Her grin was infectious, even if I did not share her love of the sea or her sense of true reprieve—not when the familiar twinge of vicious attention speared into my back.

From the shallows, Lucretzia watched me, nostrils flaring faintly at the grievance of this unintended diversion…and the costuming it demanded. Today, she wore clothing better befitting a trademaster's wife: thick skirts cut of wool and leather, a well-trimmed blouse with clinging sleeves in the bright, jeweled tones of Amere-Del. They were a stark splash against her natural pallor, an ill-fitting disguise for the Pale Viper to lurk beneath.

Yet even ankles-deep in the shallows, her lurid green skirts floating at the hem around her calves, she reeked of the danger I had known for a good deal of my life. Though she kept her weapons hidden when the crew was near, I had little doubt that blades lurked beneath the seams of her clothing.

Hidden in her skirts. Strapped to her thighs. Tucked into her sturdy boots, which clapped the sand as she strode ashore.

I cast an apologetic glance at Reinera; I would have liked to get to know her better after the kindness she had done me with clothing and information. I would have liked to jest with her in earnest and play cards and learn what she thought of the world, her profession…even Amere-Del.

I would have liked to call her Rei.

But already I risked far too much. And Lucretzia watched me closer still as she halted alongside us, putting her back to Reinera—the indifference befitting both a trademaster's wife and the Del's Own Blade. "Leave these people to their work, Lionyra."

A warning as well as a command. Her tone—and her nearness—left me little choice but to heed, particularly with no ship tasks to occupy my hands. So I followed her as a dutiful servant would, trekking up the slight incline in the dune and across the span of grass to a broad hoop of ancient, deceased kindling. Already, much of the crew set about stacking fresh branches, littering the ground with tinder; but even so, it was clear many fires had burned here.

This was a home for *The Athalion's* crew, away from their ship.

Gratitude and the weight of honor banded around my heart to be shown this place—welcomed into a sacred space, a sanctuary all their own.

Lucretzia's caustic snort plucked me from the depths of my appreciation, and she dropped herself sharply onto a log at the fireside. "It's a wonder these people make a trade with how they lag at every opportunity."

I cast a swift glance around the fireside, ensuring no one had heard her scathing remark—and my gaze landed on Bastyan.

He assembled with a swath of crewmates armed for hunting, snares and traps and spears at hand. Frixia doled out instructions to the new Ameresh recruits, but Bastyan did not appear to be listening.

Instead, he watched me.

For a moment, the island chorus and the conversation among the crew faded away. Warmth spread through my chest and curled itself down my arms, to my fingertips—warmth, like the work of hands in dough. Pride and delight, a sweet aroma that put to death the acrid tang of Lucretzia's dismissive cruelty.

"Sit, Lionyra," she snapped, and ice perforated the warmth in my chest, freezing it like a blizzard's gale.

Before I could lower myself to the log beside her, Captain Julas jogged to join us, hailing with a lift of his hand.

"I hear your servant is handy with baking." He addressed Lucretzia, but his crinkle-eyed gaze settled on me. "We've got more bread loaves than we know what to do with. Mind if we borrow her to help us through them?"

No mention at all that the loaves were my making; I held my features in check, docile and demure, while Lucretzia's narrowed eyes leaped between the Captain and me. Seeking a lie—seeking an excuse to refuse.

"I would have my needs tended," she argued stiffly.

Julas's smile did not waver as he jerked his chin around the fire circle. "I've got Valori pouring the brew, and Nix and Nash doling out rations. I'll make certain they come to you first, and often."

Another moment's hesitation; but the lie Lucretzia had spun herself had thoroughly ensnared her. There was no reason she ought to keep me with her. None but that she despised, down to the hollow chasm where most people kept their hearts, the sliver of freedom the workings of this crew afforded me.

"Very well," she growled at last. "Use her how you will."

For a heartbeat, the smiling crinkles around Julas's eyes deepened. The frame of his face went tight, and in that instant, I had the vaguest glimpse of what it would look like if the ever-smiling captain were to scowl. Were to bare his teeth like a snarling wolf.

Then the expression cleared, and he jerked his head at me. "Lionyra, if you please?"

I certainly did.

We circled around the fire to where the ship's cook laid out the spread for the evening meal. The Captain hooked his thumbs in his belt loops as we walked, sloping one shoulder my way. "Bastyan sends his regards."

My gaze launched back to him like a loosed and furious firework, finding that he still watched me. When our gazes met—when he watched me walk away with the Captain, toward the loaves waiting to be baked—the side of Bastyan's mouth tilted upward, a ray of sun peering around the edge of a stormcloud, dyeing it silver.

Then he turned, and with the rest of the deckhands, he was off to hunt.

For the first time in too many weeks, I baked bread again, filling my nostrils with the aromatic waft of thickening crusts and fragrant dough. Cook told me of his own ventures in baking and sailing—how he had given up the life of a Mithran farmer for the adventure as a ship's galleymaster—and how all of it filled the need to care and nurture he'd found void with his wife's death and his four boys growing into trades of their own.

I told him bits and pieces of my life…nothing embellished, and certainly nothing that would incriminate Lucretzia in her lies. But I told him the truth of my love for baking, and how it had been nurtured in the gentle hands of my mother; how her fingers had worked the dough alongside mine, teaching me the techniques passed down from her mother, and her mother's mother. How we had baked loaves of bread every day when I was a girl, always facing the window that looked out over the sweep of Monsha's sloped back and down the road that would reveal my father, riding his donkey home at the end of a long day of trading.

I told him of my time in the Monshan orphanage; how I had taught this trade to other children to pass the time, to earn a few extra merits we would stash away. All the while I told this, I kept watch on Lucretzia; she was too far to hear me divulge the past that the Del and Della had insisted died with my parents. That I must never speak of again—though I had told it to Tristah, our shared, fretful whispers of our fallen families the only soft-spoken shadows that kept them near.

To my relief, Lucretzia found no excuse to summon me back. Perhaps because, whenever she showed an inkling she might rise, Valori—one of the ship's repairwomen, and a close friend, I gathered, of Reinera and Lanah's— accosted her with another pour of sailor's grog.

The delectable aroma of cinnamon and sugar filled my head when I finished telling Cook all that I could…my life before the foul day when the Del himself had barged through the orphanage door, demanding to ward a girl displaced by the most violent riots Monsha had ever seen.

Sympathy kneaded Cook's weathered brows together, and he scratched a hand through his silvering nutmeg hair as he watched me pull the iron baking pot from over the small fire we'd built. "That's a flipping luckless life you've lived, lass."

I shrugged, careful of the pot's tilt as I set it on a heap of rocks to cool. "It was not entirely unfortunate. I had many good memories with my mother and father, and they loved me…fiercely. They taught me what love *is*." The words stung my throat; I had known enough of love in their arms to be sharply aware how little of it I'd been shown ever since their deaths. "With things as they are in Amere-Del…some have far less."

Like Tristah.

Cook nodded, and for a time, we were quiet; I let my gaze wander across the smaller pockets of flame where Reinera and the others cooked the last few perishable foods, back to where Julas presided over a roaring bonfire fitted with the carcass of some island animal. I had not even seen the hunting parties return, but now they were speckled in among the rest of the crew, raising cups of drink and laughter to welcome the first glints of stars in the darkening dome of the endless blue sky.

Lucretzia was no longer alone with Valori on the log; the ship's fretful bookkeeper, Henriet, fidgeted on the other side of her, shooting uneasy glances at the Pale Viper. Perhaps she could sense the wickedness wafting from Lucretzia's pores, seasoned with the drink Valori kept pouring into her.

The reprieve was not as long-lived as I would have liked; too soon, the bread was finished baking, and I had little more than the scent of it pressed into my clothes to sustain me when Cook and I went to the bonfire, toting the pots.

The anguish of returning to Lucretzia's side was soothed somewhat by the absolute famishment with which the crew fell on the potted bread. The hunting parties in particular jostled and shoved for a portion, tearing off hunks and holding the rest of the loaves out to one another; some swore and others exclaimed aloud, while Syd tumbled back on the nearest log beside Lanah, moaning and chewing like a starved prisoner enjoying his first meal in weeks.

"Lionyra, you *made* this?" he exclaimed around a mouthful.

"I did." And then, my gaze catching on Bastyan, seated beside Captain Julas across the fire, I added, "The baking, that is."

Predictably, the crew turned on Cook to pepper him with praise—and demands for more bread, and here and there some complained that he had been keeping his true talents a secret, and why did he not bake like this for them *every* visit to Sunrise Isle?

Bastyan's eyes flicked to me, and he winked. At that gesture, the spill of writhing nerves in my middle left no room even for bread.

The crew did not savor their meal; they devoured it with a fervor utterly unfit for any sort of fine halls, which made me appreciate them all the more. Laughter and teasing floated among the sparks and embers that drifted on the wind; and the more they bantered, the more the silence swelled from Lucretzia. She visibly fumed by the time darkness unfurled its cloth across the sea, drenching everything beyond the island in shadow. Only the bone-white blots of sand and the kiss of moonlight on the waves lived beyond our firelight.

It was as if all the rest of the world had disappeared. I nearly wished it would.

With much of the food consumed—and the rest stored safely away in the pots, lightly salted to preserve the meat and bread—the crew turned to drinking Valori's grog. Spirits rose and the laughter thickened, until one conversation could hardly be distinguished from another.

Cook was the first to produce a fiddle from the sack he'd lugged ashore. Another sailor near his age—Ribbens, who I had learned was the ship's bosun when we'd patched a hole in the deck together—unearthed one of his own; with a whoop, Syd was on his feet, snatching Lanah's hands. "Let's have ourselves a dance!"

"*Hey!*" Julas cheered, striking out a hand to Reinera. Rolling her eyes, she took it; Frixia lit an Ameresh pipe and reclined, one arm folded over her middle, puffing as she grinned around it.

With the first notes of fiddle bow on strings, all but a handful of the crew leaped to their feet, as if the music was a puppeteer and they the marionettes. Hands clasped and arms locked, the drink-dizzied sailors burst into stomach-splitting laughter as they swept one another off around the campfire.

An ache built beneath my ribs between every breath. The reel the two men played was an Ameresh ceremonial song—the sort that was played at a swearing, when a man and woman vowed themselves to one another. Tristah loved this sort of music; she had played this very tune often while I danced with all my might in our room, as ridiculously as I could, until neither of us could play or dance or breathe for how hard we laughed.

My vision caught on Lucretzia's foot, tapping a bit off-kilter to the beat…a song of the country she loved. One she had likely danced to long ago, at Zorast and Athyna's swearing ceremony.

The ache sharpened to a profound jab, harsh enough to halt my breath.

Would I be expected to dance with such abandon in the arms of Algernon Sorai? Was that the thought that had Lucretzia's mouth crooking off to one side, violent and hungry in a way no food or drink could sate?

A splash of fresh grog into her cup roused me from my thoughts; and while Valori poured, a hand caught around my elbow from behind, drawing me to my feet.

"Don't think," Bastyan breathed against my ear. "Just dance."

He spun me into the array of sailors all jigging and leaping in the firelight, twisting and shouting shanties that blended in among the fiddle notes. My arm snapped from Bastyan's hold as Nix caught me around the waist, wrestling a laugh out of me while he twirled me until the night blurred in a black-and-gold wash.

I lost sight of Lucretzia and of Bastyan and of my own fears and sorrow. There was only the music and the crew around me, singing and swaying, leaping and whirling. Ribbens and Cook guided us through song after song, never pausing; now and again cups dropped into our hands, and I was dimly aware it was oak-soaked water I drank, not grog.

Then back to dancing, back to spinning, back to singing, back to forgetting all the rest of it. I could not recall when I had last laughed so much, held so many different hands, been spun and swung and lifted by so many arms.

One moment popped like a burst of embers from toppling tinder—when I knew the brawny strength that banded around me. When Bastyan spun across my path and swept me against him for an instant, one hand splayed low at the dip of my waist, his other arm outflung to steady us as we swirled. And for that moment, he pressed his brow to mine.

It was only a heartbeat, just long enough for our eyes to meet; then we traded partners, Syd tackling me, Bastyan stealing a dance with Valori.

But it branded me. It burned into my skin like a dusting of cinders on the hem of my skirts. I was still thinking of it nearly an hour later when we all crashed to our seats, sweating, gasping, exhausted and—for my part—faintly ill. In all of the best ways.

Fresh cups in our hands, we settled and panted; I had fallen onto a log, not beside Lucretzia, but between Reinera and Henriet. To my left, I could keep an eye on the Pale Viper—who swayed a bit in her place, the disgust in her expression muddled somewhat.

Before I could consider that more deeply, Syd roared at Julas, "Let's have a story, Captain!"

"Oh, *yes*!" Valori cheered.

"*Story! Story! Story!*" the crew chanted, and fresh melancholy pricked my heart.

How Addie-cat would have loved this tale-thirsty knot of sailors.

"All right, quiet down, you bloodhungry sharks," Julas scoffed. The crew tapered off in their demands as the Captain prodded the fire lower with a piece of kindling, searching our gazes above the banking flames. "Quiet, now, and I'll tell you the tale of the fearsome Captain Blackhand and *The Dread Singer*."

CHAPTER 14
TEMPTING THE SEA

"This is a tale as old as the sea itself," Julas murmured, his bass tone blending with the crackle of the fire and the faraway breathings of the waves. "Just as vast. Just as fathomless. But for as long as there's been ships on the waves and folk willing to brave the back of the wind for treasure and trade…there's been *The Dread Singer.*"

A shiver rippled up my arms. Syd mimed a shudder himself, and Lanah treaded on his boot. Lucretzia scoffed, then tipped forward, blinking drowsily.

"Some say Blackhand was the first pirate ever to pillage and plunder. Some say he's not quite a man…more a myth brought to life by storytelling. Maybe something that crawled out of the depths." Julas prodded the fire again, then rolled the ember-tipped stick between his palms, flaking black char onto his boots. "What's known for certain is this: he's as old as villainy itself, and something keeps the man from dying."

"Greed?" Syd offered.

"Some special herb?" Hasser, the ship's healer, rebutted.

"Feasting on the souls of the ships he sinks?" Henriet fretted, rubbing her shawl-wrapped arms.

"All entirely possible." Julas nodded to each in turn. "A few stories claim it's hate that keeps him breathing and sailing. Hate that his ship's built of. But most believe it's vengeance."

"For what?" Bastyan asked eagerly, bending into the firelight with almost boyish curiosity.

"For a broken heart." Julas swirled the embers, then sketched with the ashen tip of his stick in the sand. "They say when *The Dread Singer* first set sail, Blackhand had a bit of Luck none could match: a musician with a violin so sweet, she could play sea beasts and sirens back to slumber. Her music tempted in fog to shroud the ship and quieted storms in their path. It lulled other vessels until *The Dread Singer* could fall on them like a curse. She'd sit up in the crow's nest and play, and some said you could hear it from halfway across the sea."

A single sweet strain of strings had us all jumping in our seats. Ribbens cast us a gap-toothed grin over his fiddle neck, blending a second, lower, far more sinister note into the first.

Julas's mouth cocked upward, but he kept his storyteller's tone as he went on: "Sailors came to fear that sound…the song that earned the ship its name. They were unstoppable, Blackhand and his lass; so powerful together, their flag bore their marks. A crossed bow and violin for her, and a skull for him—for all the ships he sank."

"He was in love with her," Bastyan said…simple and certain.

My heart stuttered and wrenched.

"That he was." Julas met Bastyan's gaze across the fire when he added, "You see where this tale is going?"

Bastyan's chin bobbed once, sharply. "He betrayed her."

My stomach pinched.

"Aye, but she betrayed him first," Julas murmured. "Sold the secrets of *The Dread Singer* and Captain Blackhand to other pirates for a lifetime's sum of gold. The stories say he sank her with an anchor tied to her ankle for her treachery. But others rumor he stranded her on an island and left her to her fate…and that it's the love they once shared, soured into hate, that's kept them both alive ever since."

Ribbens played a somber, straining tune now, higher-pitched, melancholy and fretting; my heart echoed it in perfect harmony.

"Alive, all this time," Julas went on. "Her song ever-playing across the waves…they say Blackhand can hear it anywhere. That it's driven him mad, like a siren's cry, like an echo from the depths. And that he plunders and sinks ships just for a moment's relief." His eyes trailed over us, from face to face. "Legend tells, only the screams of the dying can sate his madness and buy him a hint of reprieve. He left his heart behind on that island, or sank it in the depths, and now there's no reasoning with him. No bargaining back your life once he's seen fit to take it."

Bastyan and Lanah shivered, sitting back a bit from the flames. I could not move at all; I was far too enraptured by the Captain's tale of such love gone frigid, of such passion spoiled to hate. Of how it could alter the fates of the sea and all who sailed it; how the fears and regrets of one could become the suffering of all.

It was not at all unlike the Del, in many ways.

"That's why every Captain's warned to listen for violin strings on calm, clear nights like this one." Julas sat back as well, gazing through the fire, toward the sea. "They say if no one's playing, but you hear the song, it means Blackhand's close. That he's sharing his madness. And by the time you hear it…there's no escape."

"Can he be laid to rest?" Reinera prodded.

"Might be." Julas offered her a sly grin. "If one could reunite him and his love. If the island she was stranded on wasn't lost to madness and memory. Then, they say, you might be able to free the seas of him, if…"

He fell silent, the stillness enunciated brutally by the pop of the dwindling fire.

"*If?*" Syd prompted.

Julas frowned down into the flames. "Couldn't rightly say. I suppose the tale's still being written."

Along the fireside, the crew traded uneasy glances. Syd scraped the back of his neck, glancing off to the sea as if he expected to see *The Dread Singer* emerging from the blackness. Valori jittered her foot; Henriet jumped and cursed under her breath when Ribbens set aside his fiddle, bow sliding on strings. Even Bastyan rocked his shoulders back, rubbing his forearms, his complexion faintly sallow.

But it was Lucretzia to whom all of us looked.

Lucretzia, who pitched suddenly off the log and fell snoring into the sand.

No one moved. I did not even breathe.

And then Nash said sagely, "Some people can't manage their grog."

The eruption of laughter did not even stir the Pale Viper from her face-first plunge into the ground; but it shattered the fetters of unease by which the Captain's story held us all bound. Rowdy pockets broke off to gamble with dice and cards, or to play Endurance over side-fires.

Reinera flashed me a prized deck of cards, raising her brows. "I won these in a game against men fifteen years my senior on my very first day in Mithra-Sha." Her thumb traced the edge of the deck with loving reverence. "That was the day I started believing in the Mithran lore of fickle Luck. Care to try yours?"

Though my heart sang at the prospect, I declined with a shake of my head. Because, just then, I caught a glimpse of a shadow peeling apart from the rest.

Bastyan, walking away from us all. Headed down toward the solitary slice of the distant shore, still rubbing his arms, his expression remote.

Reinera shrugged and went one way, beckoning Valori and Lanah for a game in my stead; I went the other, snatching up what remained of the last cinnamon-and-sugar loaf.

Perhaps it was the good food in my belly, the captivation of Julas's tale, or the whimsy of the dance; perhaps it was that Lucretzia was thoroughly unconscious, still splayed on the ground, where not a single crewmate had even attempted to move her.

Perhaps it was the scorch of a sun-stamped brow still imprinted against mine.

But for whatever reason only Ahim knew, I followed Bastyan.

The firelight faded and the sounds of revelry dimmed, consumed with the trill of nightbirds and insects and whatever animals called the night their domain on Sunrise Isle. Presently, even those were washed away by the breathings of the sea.

I found Bastyan seated below a deep divot in the shore, so steep I would not have spotted him had I not seen him come this way; he sat with one leg tucked behind the other, his knee cocked to his chest. The surf just barely kissed his bare foot before it pulled away again.

Bracing my heels, I slid down the slope and padded up at his back, offering half the portion of bread over his shoulder. "May I sit?"

"If you dare." His tone was wry, but some emptiness yawned beneath it. "Afraid I'm not the best company tonight."

"I found your company agreeable enough at the dance."

He snorted, but did not reply.

I settled beside him, keeping some distance between us. The salt spray of the sea cooled even the burning track on my brow where his had touched. Where some portion of me wished it still did.

The Bastyan who'd drawn me into the dance and the one I sat beside now were two different men. One had been smiling, full of sunlight; this one was somber, carved of moonbeams. He stared absently at the bread in his hands.

"Are you not fond of pirate tales and superstitions, Master Sailor?" I ventured.

He was silent for a moment longer.

"I've seen things out there, Lio," he said at last. "Things that would gray a lad's beard. They may just be stories to some, but I'm not one to tempt the sea."

Unease dusted my next inhale. "Julas meant nothing ill, I'm certain."

"No, I'm sure he didn't. He's a good man…a good captain."

He offered nothing more. I demanded nothing else. We nibbled our bread in silence, enraptured with the comings and goings of the tide.

"I've seen my share of pirates," Bastyan blurted at last. "Some of them, you'd be better off dead than crossing. When I was a lad, I was…"

He trailed off, cursing colorfully under his breath, streaking a hand back through his dark hair.

"My life wasn't mine to decide," he muttered. "I sailed for a blasted scoundrel who didn't mind using the crop or worse to put boys in their place."

Tension flexed along the muscular planes of his back, pressing against the threads of his shirt; my stomach lurched at the memory of the marks that twined among the tattoos on his body.

"The sea's a merciless place," he added quietly. "Some say Ahim's eye blurs over the waves. That the world-shaper can't see what takes shape out there."

He scooped up a handful of sand, trickling it from his fist while he stared across the waves.

"When you're just a lad," he rasped, "you never think that the worst can happen to you. You never think your grandad, the strongest man you ever knew, the one who taught you how to fish, how to sail, how to be the sort of boy who turned heads in a portside town…you never think that he could drop dead," he snapped his fingers, "just like that. But then he does."

The last of the sand drizzled from his fist; still, the quiet hung in the air before him, like a gavel waiting to fall.

"You never think that your parents could sell you off to the worst blasted drug trader this side of the Everreach," he croaked at last. "Sell you just for a year's ration of their favorite herbs, to be a deckhand on a crew that's notorious for throwing boys into the sea to die. But then they do."

Indignation, pity, *fury* carved pieces from me like a warmed blade through cold butter.

How could any parent even *entertain* such cruelty? Nevermind to inflict it—nevermind against a *boy*, and one like Bastyan, built of carefree smiles and sunshine on sparkling waters.

"You never think," he added, while I wrestled my rage on his behalf in silence, "that someday you'll have to make a choice between staying safe with the pain, or risking something that hurts plenty worse." He shifted slightly, the moonlight reshaping his profile as his head swiveled my way. "You never think someone will have to say to you, *'There's a chance at freedom for all of us. What are you willing to sacrifice to take it?'"*

The second swell of heat in my throat had far less to do with his history than with mine. His face and the surface of the sea rippled in a blackish glaze. Hastily, I blinked it away. "I'm sorry, Bastyan. I am so sorry there was no one to fight for you."

It was his turn to blink, his spine pulling inward a bit as he straightened from his slouch. "Aye. Thank you for that, Lio."

Raucous laughter wafted from the occupied fires behind us—then the thumps of what seemed to be Syd and one of the twins falling into a good-natured wrestling match. We swapped tight-edged smiles, then turned our gazes back to the sea.

"Anyway," Bastyan scrubbed his knuckles in a gentle rasp over his sand-dusted trouser leg, "suppose I'm not much for stories, knowing worse is out there. And that people do nothing about it."

Did Del Graven know of boys being sold for substance in the portside towns of Amere-Del? Did he even care? Or was that of so little consequence to the civil unrest sparking across the country that it was simply a problem for *after*—after the dissenters were appeased? After he had his chokehold firmly around the country again, by use of *my* throat…and Tristah's?

The problem of his tomorrow was the problem of today for boys like Bastyan—and for the men they'd grow into.

"How did you escape the drug runners?" I asked.

"A different captain finally asked me that question…what I'd do for freedom," Bastyan admitted. "When he did, there was no other answer. I'd have given what was left of the skin on my back to make it off that drug ship. Took me a while to clean up, steady off…but here I am."

Here he was. Here *we* were, in the shadows, with his secrets given up to the sea—and to me.

Slowly, I smoothed my skirts down over my bent knees. "Why are you telling me this now?"

The surf's breathings spilled into his silence like a cove, burying hidden gems and wondrous truths beneath its foam.

"I don't really know," he said after a time. "But I figure…maybe our situations aren't so different, aye?" His focus flicked up the beach, then returned to me—swift, but certain enough to send a chill skimming through me. "So I thought maybe you could hear it. Really hear it."

There's a chance at freedom for all of us. What are you willing to sacrifice to take it?

I shivered, turning back to the sea—watching the waves rise and fall, their tides as soothing as they were unpredictable.

Such was life.

And all at once—loosed, perhaps, by the truths I had already shared with Cook today—my honesty manifested itself again in a salt-studded whisper: "You never imagine that your parents will be caught in a riot of dissenters. Struck down on their way home from the market. That one morning you will wake with everything in the world, and when you lay down your head that night, all of it will be gone."

Bastyan cursed under his breath. "Sorry to hear that."

"As was I." A humorless smile kneaded up my lips. "And I am sorry the last words I ever spoke to them were in childish anger…pleading, and then threatening what I would do if they did not bring me a treat from the market."

That day, I had never considered that the sweetest gift of all was one I would never receive: their return, emptyhanded or not.

"How did Cress come into all of that?" Bastyan's question roused me from the barb-tipped grip of my memories. His stare was pointed, his mouth drawn down more somberly than I had ever seen it.

"She found me, years later," I hedged, "and I have served her ever since."

Bastyan shifted his seat a bit, clearing his throat. "Lio…"

"*Lionyra!*"

That cracked, grog-soured shout sent us both leaping in our skins. I scrambled to my feet, and Bastyan rose beside me, taking my elbow to steady me.

"Cress," I groaned.

"Let me help you with her," Bastyan offered.

"No." I laid a hand to his chest, shoving him back a step when he turned for the lip of the shore. Whatever state she was in, the tenor of her bellow suggested her temper was thinly leashed. And that temper was far deadlier than what any sailor aboard *The Athalion* could ever comprehend. "She is my mistress…my duty is to care for her."

Bastyan settled back on his heels, his gaze sweeping me up and down. "Aye. But who cares for *you?*"

Tristah's face flickered across my mind. Then Addie's.

I brushed their memories aside with a smile, unseasoned with even the barest dusting of joy. "I care for myself, Bastyan."

He edged a bit nearer, forcing my upraised palm flat against his chest. "Awful burden to bear alone, that." His thumb brushed my cheek, tracing the faded stamp of the blow Lucretzia had dealt me the day we'd boarded. "Nothing wrong with a bit of help."

No reply came swiftly to my lips. Perhaps it was the grog I'd sampled, or the exhaustion of the fireside dance, but I did not withdraw when he took another step—when my arm folded between us, keeping contact with his chest.

His heart was thudding, thunderous and craving…just like mine.

"Nothing wrong with having something for yourself." His words were a husky breath, spoken as if to himself; but the slide of his hand around my waist was purely *my* pleasure.

Perhaps he was right. No harm could come in this place where the sea drank the sky, where hardly a whisper of a horizon or a tomorrow lay visible in the consuming dark.

Things could happen here—moments could be stolen here—that did not belong to any other person. Even to the serpent hissing my name.

"I suppose that's true," I murmured, and Bastyan's eyes darkened, gray overtaking green. "There's no harm in trying, just to see…"

His head slanted, a whisper of black hair brushing his jaw as he angled his mouth toward mine—

"*Lionyra Vara!*"

My arm stiffened, shot out, shoving Bastyan away—separating us by force. We stumbled apart on the slice of shoreline, his eyes wide, my chest heaving.

That shout had come *far* too close.

He had been far too close.

I knew better. I had *learned* better, so long ago—those lessons were still notched into my very bones.

With Lucretzia, I could not risk this. With Tristah's life in the balance, I could not afford to be distracted.

I could not risk anything *like* this.

"Forgive me, Bastyan." Into those words, I spilled all of the truths I could not freely speak—desire, and regret, and desperation.

His head bobbed faintly, as if my words—and actions—were answers he had already suspected to a question he had not yet asked. "Go. Your mistress is calling."

That made it no easier to gather my skirts and hike up the slope, when all I craved was to stay. To see what might become of this seaside solitude, with a glimmer of truths laid bare between us.

Instead, I found Lucretzia seated on a piece of driftwood not far from the slope, her head cradled in her hands. She did not look up at my approach, and I slowed a bit, disgust twisting in my gut.

I had never seen the Pale Viper so slouched, so shaken…so *weak*.

It was oddly repulsive. And all the more repulsive was what it awakened in me—the notion of how easy she would be to overcome in this state. To bring to her knees with every ruthless, cruel tactic she had taught me.

When I halted before her, Lucretzia raised her head; that black, venomous stare pinned me like a blade through the shoulder to the wall of her fury.

"Get us back to the ship," she snarled. "*Now*."

I was fortunate that a handful of the dawn crew were ready to pack away their rations and retire for the night. I did not endure Lucretzia's attention alone until we stumbled belowdecks nearly an hour later, where she made straight for one of the relief buckets I'd scrubbed out just that morning.

She emptied herself into it three times, shoving me off with an arm when I did a servant's duty of approaching to offer aid. So I retreated to where I preferred myself—at the wall, far from the stench of her illness.

In my mind, I retreated to the seaside…the place I truly wished to be.

At last, Lucretzia gagged and pushed up from her knees, sticking that same arm out blindly my way. "Help me into my hammock."

I obliged, guiding her by as scarce a touch as possible. With a groan, she spilled into the woven netting, rolling from her arm to her back.

Swifter than I could anticipate—or withdraw—she hooked her fingertip through the gold ring fixed in the side of my nose. Pain pierced through my nostril and blinded my eye as she dragged me down in a sharp, contorted angle. The stench of her grog-and-vomit-tinged breath nearly made me heave in turn.

"You have crossed a line tonight," she growled. "I know precisely what you and this crew have done. I know where and with whom you were with when I called you." Her finger curled tighter, threads of skin giving way as the ring bore into my flesh. "You know what comes next."

Tristah's face flashed in the wateriness of my left eye—wounds dealt to every inch of her body that fine dresses concealed.

Wounds dealt because of my defiance. My mistakes.

Horror rose on a surge of bile in my throat. "Lucretzia, *please*—"

"You would have no need to beg if you had obeyed."

She thrust me away so sharply, my feet skidded on the damp planks; I reeled and struck the wall. My knees gave way, and I folded to my seat, staring at Lucretzia as she slumped in her hammock—and fell at once to snoring.

I cupped my hands around my nose and mouth, smothering my quickening breaths—and the hate and horror which spurred me to do the unconscionable. What I had sworn the night we'd escaped Shadewyle Castle that I would never do again.

I could scarcely temper the urge to grip her ratty pillow, or one of her blades, and do to her as I had done to Athyna Graven.

Nothing else would prevent what was coming. Nothing else would save this crew.

Save *Bastyan*.

But I could not will my legs to lift me. I could not peel my hands from my face. I could not force myself to murder the Pale Viper while she slumbered...even knowing what was to come.

CHAPTER 15
SUNK BENEATH THE WAVES

I was out of my hammock when the first bell rang from the quarterdeck the following morning, feet striking the floor soundlessly. I spared only a glance to see that Lucretzia still slept; then I darted out into the hall, wedging past the rousing first-watch crew. I hastened up the steps to the topdeck and emerged into the bleary light of an overcast dawn.

Desperately, I scouted the ship; we floated some distance from Sunrise Isle, its gleaming white shores pulling away as the crew traded spaces, letting out the sails to catch the early breeze. Captain Julas bellowed a greeting from the helm, where he and Frixia and Syd scouted a map to navigate us back into the currents that would carry us along to Amere-Del.

But I paid the Captain no heed. It was not him I searched for; it was the brawny sailor at the railing, hauling up the crab cages and fishing nets we had dropped before we'd gone ashore the previous night.

The sight of him tangled my innards in knots worse than the ones I'd unwound from those same nets. "Bastyan!"

He swiveled to face me, a guarded smile inching along his mouth. "Top of the morning, Lio."

I stepped toward him. "I need to speak to you about—"

"About what, *precisely*, Lionyra?"

That cool voice halted me in my steps, a chill glazing my spine.

Lucretzia had emerged quietly from the hatch, pulling even with me in strides buried beneath the bustle of work as the ship drifted from shore.

There was no trace of the strong spirits she'd consumed left on her to warn me of her approach; there was no scent in the threads of her clothes or the fume of her level breaths. Not a hint of an aching head or a stomach that roiled as mine did when she caught my shoulder, towing me to a halt at the railing beside Bastyan.

Fear lodged like a sideways bone in my throat. Heat stung my eyes.

I wanted her away from him. I did not want them to breathe the same *air*.

Bastyan glanced between us, his expression the most guarded I'd ever seen it; his eyes shadowed nearly full gray as he folded his arms at his waist, pitching his weight against the railing. "Well?"

I had no hope of warning him when Lucretzia's fingers dug into my skin— a warning spasm that flexed free just before a groan escaped me. Gripping the railing, she leaned over the side and mimed a delighted gasp that stung my ears with its false wonder. "Look at this *reef!*"

Bastyan turned his head aside to cast one eye at the barrier reefs drifting beneath the ship's belly. "Aye. Good place for filling the traps."

"Is it?" A note of distaste tinged Lucretzia's tone as she slicked a hand down the railing. "Plenty of crabs, I take it? Fish?"

"Well, it's not full of bloody cows."

"No, of course not."

My pulse hammered so fiercely in my ears, for a moment no sound came to me but the swish of blood hurtling through the paths of my body.

Whatever she was doing—whatever she schemed—I dared not take my eyes off of her.

Her lips moved, framing some question I could not hear over my thundering heart. Bastyan frowned, turning to brace his hands on the railing, peering wherever she pointed—

And Lucretzia stumbled.

She went to a knee, so clumsy and unlike her that for a moment I believed it must be residue of the drink that not even the Pale Viper could pretend away.

"This silly hem!" She tugged and fluffed out the edge of her skirts, false mirth stringing together the words.

I saw what she was prepared to do. But I had no time even to gather a scream.

Lucretzia surged upright at an angle; her shoulder met Bastyan's back first, and then her elbow, hooking into his groin and rising with the full shove of her muscular legs. He stumbled against the railing, and her knee followed the thrust of her arm, catching him between the legs and tilting him over the edge.

Bone cracked against wood as he fell, muffling the shriek that ripped from my mouth. I lunged for the railing, and just when I rammed into it, catching myself on the edge that bit into my belly, Bastyan's shocked, anguished bellow cut short.

He slammed into the water—water which plumed pinkish in the whitecap of his impact.

And he did not reappear.

My gaze flashed to Lucretzia, her hands clapped to her mouth in mock-horror. But the glance she speared my way was glacial, full of vicious satisfaction.

You did this.

And, all in a moment, my racing pulse slowed. And my breaths quickened. Deepened. Swifter and swifter they came, expanding my lungs to their full measure as I gripped the rigging and stepped up on the railing.

Eyes wide open.

Lucretzia blinked. A divot plunged between her brows.

Take power where you can.

And by the time the first of the deckhands reached the railing, shouting in shock and disbelief, by the time Lucretzia realized my intention—and threw out a hand to stop me—I was plummeting into the water.

The cut of the waves closed around me like a cool bath, and I fought not to gasp out all my air as I folded my legs and arms, sinking rapidly beneath the surface.

A gemstone array of reefs unfolded around me. Quicksilver fish flitted among the urchins. A shark wound lazily over a ledge to my right. An octopus performed a long-legged, graceful descent from one coral shelf to the next.

And there, off to the left, a murky trail dusted along the shimmering silver currents—ribbons of red-brown staining the sea.

Unfolding from my sinking posture, I planted my boots on the nearest shelf and dove after it.

Bastyan had not drifted far; I came upon him just over the rise in the reef. He floated in the jeweled bed, blood clouding the water around his head and shoulder; his eyes were open in narrow slits, his face red with strain, cheeks flexing around bitten-back air. His arm looped over a notch of coral, but he did nothing to thrust himself up toward the surface.

Confusion clutched for my held breaths. I shoved it away just as I shoved off from the pinnacle of the reef, stroking toward him.

His eyes caught on me—and widened. His mouth opened in a soundless cry, bubbles rushing from his throat—

And something seized me like a pair of ruthless hands. A snare about my waist, my neck, my ankles.

An undersea current.

It whipped me in a dizzying circle like syrup swirled into batter; then it towed me the same direction it had taken Bastyan, my fingers clawing and ripping at the surface of the reef. Peeling away, again and again.

My scratched, striking palms encountered drenched fabric. Leather. Vibrant blue threads, alive beneath the waves.

Bastyan's free hand swiveled, encircling my wrist; the current tore me to the end of his reach, wrenching my shoulder in its socket. But he held onto me— and I clung to him.

For a moment, the current's relentless reach warred against Bastyan's grip.

In the shadow of *The Athalion*, I met his gaze—shrouded with exhaustion. With disorientation. Blood pluming in the current around him.

Determination seized hold, expanding the capacity of my chest, the strength of my limbs.

He was beneath these waves because of me. I would not let this be his watery tomb.

Sinking my fingers into his boot, I clawed my way up the length of his current-tugged body—anchoring myself to his belt, then his collar. His arm rotated slowly as I hauled myself along the stretch of his body, maintaining his hold on my wrist until we lay chest-to-chest. I wrapped my fingers around his, gripping the coral. And I met his delirious gaze with a sharp nod.

He blinked—once, a drowsy attempt to hold my stare.

Then his head dropped. Bubbles fumed from his nostrils as the air left him…as unconsciousness took hold.

My silent scream freed a few breath bubbles of my own. I tore his arm from around the coral—and let go.

The current snatched us backward, away from *The Athalion*—away from the bulk of its side, the treachery of the waves that threatened to drag us beneath it…away from the dangerous tines of the coral itself. I wrapped my body full around Bastyan's, linking my arms and legs at his neck and waist, sliding one hand into his hair to steady his head.

Then I pressed my mouth over his, breathing life into his lungs as the current shoved us deeper into the sea.

Citrus and salt and blood tarnished my teeth. There was softness to his sun-chapped lips. A faint stirring as his tongue tickled mine.

The coral shelf dropped out from beneath us, making way for the silt seabed…and the trenches of the deep beyond. The current heaved us over a high mound of sand—then plunged all at once, catching us in a rolling twist of the undersea, hurling our bodies downward in a spinning, spiraling vortex.

Direction floundered in the blackening abyss. I crashed my mouth back over Bastyan's, breathing for us both as the current tumbled and swirled us, flinging our bodies deeper into the sea. Pressure pounded at the doors of my lungs, begging them to empty entirely. Shadows lulled the corners of my vision.

Merciful Ahim, please…no, no, no… This could not happen. We could not end here, victims of Lucretzia's cruelty, sunk at the bottom of the sea. *Please—*

My boots met silt. Sand. The sea floor near the isle shores.

With all of my might, I planted my boots, cocked my knees, and *flung* us upward on the backside of the current. Its roiling swirl against the drop in the seafloor was a spiral, thrusting up from below us now; with its aid, I rose, kicking and stroking with one arm, the other banded around Bastyan's chest. The light spilling in watery shafts from the surface clashed violently with the shadows softening the sides of my sight.

Was that light pulling away? Was I sinking?

And then, with my vision fading, dappled and narrow as the gaps in cheesecloth—water broke like shattered glass around our heads.

Gasping, coughing, weeping all at once, I rolled myself to float, holding Bastyan sprawled against my chest, my arms linked around his deadweight.

"Bastyan." My voice abraded with seawater, I shook him slightly. "Bastyan, do you hear me?"

His head lolled. He did not answer.

"Bastyan, *please*…" I choked.

"*Lionyra!*"

Lifting my chin from the water was a feat nearly beyond reckoning. Through hazy, half-lidded eyes, I caught a slim slice of chocolate-brown wood cleaving across the water. A rowboat, manned by Syd and Lanah.

Relief snapped in a violent gust of laughter from my burning throat. "They're here, Bash. They're here for us."

But I wasn't certain we would be any safer aboard. Not after what Lucretzia had done.

CHAPTER 16
CHOOSING BASTYAN

The scrapes on my palms stung only slightly less than my stiff, aching fingers. Every muscle thudded with a dull, mutinous resonance that threatened to sharpen into a debilitating ache when I was least prepared. Likely after a long night of sleep…should I ever bring myself to close my eyes again on this ship.

The pain was all that kept me company in the hall outside the sick bay.

I hadn't moved in hours. I had not spared Lucretzia or the rest of the crew a single glance when we'd boarded again; I'd followed Syd and Jaspyr, another Ameresh deckhand, down into the belly of the ship where they'd borne Bastyan between them.

Hasser had ushered them into the sick bay, then turned to me; I had asked only for a stinging tincture and the spool of bandages that now laced my fingers.

Syd had passed them along on his way out, pausing to muss my hair and drape a thick blanket about my shoulders. I hugged the damp fabric to myself now, leaning my head back against the wall, shutting my eyes to drink in the stillness. The creak of pressure squeezing along the sides of the ship.

We were underway again, as if nothing had transpired. As if Lucretzia had not nearly committed murder aboard *The Athalion*.

As if I had not defied her once more, plunging overboard to drag Bastyan from the deep.

With every breath, guilt gusted into one lung. Fury filled the other. I was nearly breathing fire as hot as my shop's oven by the time the door creaked open at last.

Surging to my feet, I let the blanket fall away. Hasser emerged, drying off his hands. His rich brown skin was dulled somewhat with exhaustion beneath the lanternlight; he brushed his spectacles up the bridge of his long nose and offered a crooked smile. "He's awake."

"Will—" My voice emerged rougher than ever, salted with seawater and strained from hours of silence. "Will he live?"

Hasser's brows tugged together. "He did take in quite a bit of seawater. The blow to his head was heavy, and that coral scrape along his shoulder may take some months to heal. But I am confident, if he avoids infection, he will recover in time." Beneath his breath, he added, "He would do better if he would take the herbs I offered, but he's as stubborn a sailor as I've ever known."

Inching out my breath, I glanced past him at the plain, heavy-set door. "May I look in on him?"

"Of course." Hasser nodded, stepping aside. "He was asking for you."

The sick bay was cool, and quiet—insulated a bit by the walls stuffed full of leather-strapped bottles, the netted rafters dangling with bunches of dried herbs. Several bunks lined one wall, a row of cots the other. Bastyan lay on one, dressed in a fresh, dry tunic, the blanket tucked around his torso. A bandage enshrouded his head, all of his hair flattened beneath it; another swaddle of gauze bulked the angle of his right shoulder. His eyes were shut, his hand resting over his stomach, lifting and settling with his quick, labored breaths.

For a moment, I deliberated the sanity of all of this.

Then I turned for the door.

"'Ay."

The husky croak of his voice halted me with my hand to the knob.

Slowly, I turned back.

Bastyan shifted his head to a more comfortable angle, his chin nearly brushing his shoulder as he peered at me. The lines around his eyes and mouth were soft; no sunshine smile greeted me, but the tenderness in his expression branded my vision with tears.

He offered his hand across his body—the hand that had caught me in the current. That had kept me from being dragged away. "Come here."

I towed Hasser's chair to the bedside. When Bastyan did not withdraw his hand, I settled mine in it—every motion, every moment throbbing with something I could not name.

Gently, Bastyan chafed his thumb over my bandaged knuckles. Confusion knitted his brows together; he did not lift his gaze from our hands. "You dove into the drink for me."

"I could not watch you drown."

His throat bobbed; his eyes flicked up to mine, that heartbreaking confusion still etched across the furrows of his brow.

I did not know what to make of that; nor of the way he held my hand, every rope-abraded callous, every hook-dealt scar muffled by the gauze that cloaked my wounds.

"Hasser says you've refused the herbs for pain," I said—for lack of anything better to say.

"Aye. Well, I told you …after the drug ship, took me a while to steady off." He wagged his head, then winced at the motion. "I don't touch herbs if I can help it."

"You must be in pain."

"I've had worse." His mouth tilted up at the corner. "Besides, I'd rather be in pain than another scrap dangling off the reef."

A shudder whispered along my skin. Did he realize how close he had truly come to that?

The drop of his head. That burst of bubbles as he lost his breath. The sea-swept softness of his mouth as I covered it with mine—

I would always carry with me that moment he could not remember.

"Are *you* all right?" His tone pitched with concern, his thumb still tracing the outlines of my knuckles. "Are these coral scrapes?"

"Whatever they are, I can survive them."

"Don't tell me—you've had worse?"

My skin itched and burned all at once, remembering uncountable blows endured at Lucretzia's hand. Pain seared along my tongue, as if I'd bitten into a scorching pepper. Tearing my hand from his, I shoved back my seat. "I should not be here."

As I should not have been at the shore with him the night before. Or in the galley. Or anywhere that could bring harm to him or this crew.

"Wait—Lio, why?" Bastyan grunted as I rose.

"Because I am *dangerous* to you," I hissed. "This…friendship, this—"

His mouth cocked up. "Friendship?"

"It ends *now*," I barreled on, cladding my heart against the warmth of his smile. "That is the only way to keep you safe."

Curling one hand around his battered shoulder, he hoisted himself up on his opposite elbow. "And what if I'm not interested in *safe*?"

"You do not know what you're saying. My…" I ground my teeth against the title Lucretzia had forced upon me with her ruse—another shackle cuffed around my neck from afar, "…*mistress* does not like me befriending sailors."

Bastyan shrugged. "So, we'll be crafty about it."

"You do not understand, Bastyan—"

"What don't I understand? That you're not allowed to make decisions for yourself? That maybe, your entire life, your friends have been picked for you? By people who chose your clothes, your meals, where you went, what you could say, who you could say it to?"

When I said nothing, he grimaced, hand spasming against his shoulder.

"*No one* chooses my life but me." His voice was gravelly, but his gaze held clear—focused, fixed on me. "And if I choose a bit of danger, that's my choice to make."

A bitter laugh spilled from me. "And this is the sort of danger you desire…that leaves you half-drowned and bedridden?"

"If you're a part of it?" His grin returned in a blink. "You're bloody right I do, sweetheart."

Shaking my head, I banded my arms about myself—warding off the chill that wound into the dampness of my hair and my salt-stiffened clothes. Warding off the weakness that unfurled from within, begging to have a friend. An ally in him.

Perhaps something more.

"Why don't *you* choose, for once, Lio?" Bastyan dared me. Tempted me. "Choose yourself, aye? Choose *me*."

I gazed at him—a bandaged mess, the stain of his blood washed away but the memory of it soiling every stitch of this moment. That dare.

Loosening my arms, I approached the bed. I pressed on his unhurt shoulder until he fell onto his back. Then I allowed myself one moment to sit beside him…to trace the etchings of ink on his forearm. To marvel at the musculature beneath.

To be grateful that he was alive…that my defiance had saved him as surely as it had endangered him.

"You asked what I would be willing to sacrifice for my freedom." I took his hand, lacing my fingers between his. "I am not willing to sacrifice *you*."

Pressing a kiss to his knuckles, I pushed off the bed again and strode from the room, shutting the door behind me.

Eyes closed, I breathed in the silence…and when I breathed out, heat snaked from the corner of my eye, trickling down the side of my nose.

I blinked my eyes open…and there she was.

The Pale Viper, lurking halfway down the hall. Arms folded, she leaned against the wall—the posture of the Del's Own Blade contrasting sharply against the attire of a trademaster's wife.

Every hair on my body stood at attention. Ice cracked in my middle…cold, sharp shards of hate.

"What are you doing here?" I hissed.

In the lanternlight, utter blackness forged her gaze—fixed past me, on the door.

I was all that stood between Bastyan and her hidden blades.

"The crew is muttering about him," she murmured. "A sailor who falls overboard and fails to rescue himself…that isn't the sort of deckhand who inspires confidence. They're beginning to wonder if it was a mistake to bring him aboard."

Heat patterned the back of my neck and dotted across my cheeks. "And I'm certain you had no part in those whispers starting."

Her forehead creased at one side—a pale brow rising, untouched by the rage simmering in my tone. "I warned you what would happen if you did not keep to yourself."

Gritting my teeth, I shoved past her—begging Ahim that she would follow me, angle her weapons at *me*. Not at him.

Her voice floated after me: "You should not have saved his life."

Heels catching on the planks, I whirled on her, my aching hands forming fists at my hips. "Keep away from him. You made your message clear…now leave him *be*."

"You do not command me."

Exhaustion and fury and the profound ache in my chest spilled fresh courage through my veins. I stalked toward her, and she straightened at my approach—as if, perhaps for the first time, I had caught the Pale Viper unawares.

"Not yet," I seethed, halting nearly toe-to-toe with her. "But if your intentions go to plan, then someday, at Sorai's side, as Della…I *will*. He may not realize the swearing would be a sham of the regime—and his ignorance will make him all the more eager to heed my desires." Sipping in a last, strengthening breath, I spat, "At this moment, my greatest desire is to see you hang."

Lucretzia regarded me for a long, tense moment. Then a broad smile, wicked and void of true mirth, peeled her mouth wide. "At *last*. I wondered when you might make use of the things I taught you."

"*No.* Do not pretend as if you planned all of this," I snarled. "You were *thwarted* today. You tried to kill him…you did not succeed. And whatever I am, whatever strength I wield, none of it is owed to you."

"Think what you like." She shrugged up from the wall, striding past me up the hall. "But I hardly believe the soft-bellied *baker* from Mithra-Sha would have been so bold today. Nor managed to survive such a current."

She swaggered away, leaving me alone in the gaping gullet of the hall.

All of the day's events swelled up in me at once, and nausea blazed through my core. Planting a hand to the wall, I bent double, clutching my rebellious middle.

Terror. Determination. The nearness of death. Relief. Heartache. Rage, and rage, and *rage*…

What if this *was* all her ploy to break apart the edges of the woman I had chosen to be—to mold what remained back into the girl who had followed the Del's commands with scarcely any resistance?

I could no longer be certain what was true and what was not…what was Lucretzia's making and what was mine. The clear waters had grown murky—clouded with blood. Clouded with cruelty. Clouded with the seepage of the past spilling over into the present, fogging the future.

I stumbled through lanternlit shadows all the way to the hammock bay, ignoring someone who called my name—Reinera, perhaps, or Valori. Hauling myself into the embrace of the netting, I rolled, putting my back to the room.

And I wept until I could no longer breathe.

CHAPTER 17
AN OFFER OF BLOODSHED

or several days, I kept to my hammock while the fever of the coral scrapes took me, leaving my hands a swollen, itching mess. I stirred only to slather on the tincture Hasser had provided me; then I dove back into the sweet relief of slumber, from which not even Lucretzia roused me.

When the fever abated at last and my hands were of some use again, I returned to the topdeck to perform my duties. I spoke to no one but in moments of absolute necessity—either receiving my assignments or asking how I might fill them. I bowed my head and kept vigorously at my work, ignoring every word tossed my way, every attempt at conversation from the crew. Every scathing glance Lucretzia leveled across the deck, seething with silent triumph.

By retreating so absolutely into myself, I'd made her believe she had won.

And perhaps she had. If her intention had been to petrify me with the notion of wreaking more harm on this crew, then she'd certainly pinned yet another victory to her belt. Merely the latest in a storied history of triumphs that intermixed across our shared past.

Bitterness and helplessness waged war within me while we sailed. I was desperate to claw that victory from her hands…but with the echo of Bastyan's head meeting the side of the deck still resonating viciously in my ears, I could dream of no circumstance where appeasing my own suffering was worth the risk.

I had done enough harm here.

So I worked, and I served, and I refused to ask after Bastyan. I did not see him on the topdeck during our usual rotation; whether he was still bedbound or had requested a different watch, I could not bring myself to pursue.

I prayed he had not been struck from the roster altogether by the whispers that wreathed the air—concern over the state of him. Disbelief at how the sea had nearly taken him.

Ignoring that gossip built on Lucretzia's forked tongue, I retreated into myself. All I carried away were the gifted clothes that I washed every other day, and the memory of a bonfire dance. And the heat of a thumb's brush on my bandaged knuckles that had my hand flexing now and again, long after I'd shed the bandages.

My conduct was above reproach—I made certain of it. So Lucretzia had no reason to complain, nor to argue, the day I was assigned to clean the Captain's quarters.

The request came pertly given by Reinera—against whom I had committed the greatest grievances and ignored the most attempts at conversation since we'd cast off from Sunrise Isle. She thrust it at me alongside a washbucket and feathered duster, her gaze averted from mine.

"Captain's orders," she muttered. "Be sure to empty the relief bucket."

I nearly answered, if only to offer a mumble of gratitude; but Lucretzia's stare pierced me from where she sat primly on a crate across the quarterdeck, taking in the salty sea spray.

So instead I shifted the tools in my grasp, offered a quick nod, and hurried for the cabin, avoiding Lucretzia's slit-eyed look with my own focus trained off the portside railing.

The view had changed some that way in the last two days. No longer a deep sea path of endless blue faintly fringed in rocky coastline, the horizon now swarmed with rich, dark blots like clumps of chocolate in a batch of cookie dough. Frixia, Syd, and the Captain consulted more frequently, often with frowns and quiet mutters I was glad not to hear.

I had no desire to know how swiftly I might trade the pain of being aboard this ship for the pain of returning to Shadewyle.

A poignant ache gnawed in the corner of my belly at the thought; but, like the hunger pangs that had once been my constant companion, I brushed the pain aside and ducked into the chamber.

Quiet, tangible calm enveloped me when I trudged over the threshold, leaving the door slightly ajar. Even with the echoes of the crewmembers at work wafting in my wake, the thick walls offered a sturdy solitude that ushered me deeper into their embrace, one pace at a time.

The bed was strictly made, a mere cot bolted beneath the broad window on the far wall. The washbasin and writing table were warmly functional, emptied and cleared. And along every wall…books. Volumes of every shade, size, and subject, immaculately arranged on shelves grafted to the ship's boards, each one fitted with a short lip to keep the tomes from pitching to the floor as *The Athalion* surged over the waves. The scent of ancient paper and tooled leather brushed my nose, and a lump lodged in my throat.

Addie would have adored this chamber.

Heart scorched with melancholy, I circled the walls, fingertips brushing the spines—storybooks from Mithra-Sha, poetry volumes from Hadrass-Drui, ancient legends and curriculums from Amere-Del. Slowly, I lowered the bucket and raised the duster to the first column of books.

A strained, quiet voice floated from behind me: "You don't have to do that, lass."

If I had not been trained so long to bite back any shout of pain or alarm, I might have screamed. Spinning, hand flattened to my galloping heart, I faced the small sitting area I had not noticed before—a pair of chairs and a low table tucked away where the right wall cornered.

Seated in one of the chairs was Captain Julas, dressed in his usual sailing fare and smiling slightly, though shadows crawled across the surface of his eyes.

"I didn't realize you were here." My voice emerged a croak dulled with days of disuse. "I can return—"

"No, please. Stay."

Shifting my feet, I glanced around at the stuffed shelves. "I see you are quite the connoisseur of the written word."

"Can't help myself. Books make for good cargo, and they can take you a thousand places while you keep your feet on the deck…when you've got the time." Julas shrugged, knocking his knuckles against the low table. "Best way I know of to have adventures while sailing for coin."

"And do you always allow sailors into your private chamber to read?"

He smiled broader at that, the many dimpled lines of his cheeks rippling out. "The ones I can trust not to spill a cup of grog on the pages. Better to let them cool that sea-fire in their bellies with a book than a brawl, you know?" Reclining a bit, he raised his chin at the shelves. "How do you like stories?"

I hooked my hair from around my neck to drape over my opposite shoulder, dodging his stare. "Well enough. In Mithra-Sha, I became acquainted with a girl…I called her Addie-cat. She was so fond of stories, you couldn't help becoming fond of them in her presence. She did all she could to make them come alive…though it cost her."

And it had cost me.

"You sound upset," Julas remarked.

"Addie fell on hard times," I hedged. "I helped her and her friend from Krylan, and…you might say that is part of why I'm aboard your vessel."

Julas's smile was fleeting; it did not touch his eyes as they raked over me, simmering with thought so intent I couldn't bear to hold his gaze. "I figured you being here might be more than just a journey home."

He darted a glance at the door.

With a low creak, it swung shut—revealing Bastyan slouched in the shadow behind it, arms folded, his stare simmering like a rising storm.

Shock—relief—then horror crashed through me, ripping at my resolve with all the force of an undersea current. I jolted backward a step, and Bastyan frowned, shoving up from the wall. "It's all right, Lio."

"What is this?" I demanded.

"Nothing unsafe." The Captain gestured to the seat across from him. "Why don't you join me?"

"I can't…I should not be here with you—"

"Because of Cress?" Bastyan stepped from behind the door, the strong daylight falling through the bay windows in rogue slashes across his face. His head was no longer bandaged, and his hair seemed darker than ever—a fierce contrast with the lingering bruise that blotted his brow and the pale gauze still peeking beneath his shirt collar. "She's occupied. Frixia is seeing to that."

"She will notice I'm gone." The hiss slipped between my gritted teeth. "She *always* notices."

And what would the punishment be this time? Bastyan meeting some untimely demise, impaled on a harpoon? The Captain, his head severed in some strange accident with an anchor?

Julas's gaze flicked to Bastyan; something conferred in that glance sent my heart stumbling. They showed little surprise at my words…and that was not the look a captain shared with a deckhand he hardly trusted.

It was a glimpse traded by allies in some unspoken conflict. Something I had shared countless times with Tristah.

"Lio." The Captain nodded to the opposite seat again. "Give us some trust, will you?"

"Just for a moment," Bastyan pleaded.

It was that heartfelt invitation—extended from him, of all people, still battered and moving stiffly, but upright…and *here*, in the Captain's own quarters—that plumped up my curiosity and battered courage like a well-leavened loaf.

I crossed the chamber slowly, feeling my way along the seatback, sinking carefully onto the edge of its cushion. "Very well. Now, tell me what this is."

The austere tone was the only power I could remand from all of the strange happenings aboard this ship.

Bastyan slipped up to the side, pitching himself against the angle of the wall—so that, should the door open, it would only be me and the Captain visible. That thoughtfulness slowed my racing heart a bit.

"I have a question to ask." The gravity of Julas's stare had me pressing my shoulders and spine to the seatback, fearing the worst. "I'd like a true answer from you, however you can give it…however you feel safe to."

"All right," I answered slowly.

A last glance at Bastyan. Then: "Are you being trafficked against your will?"

Shock broke the floor out of my belly, sending it plummeting to my knees. "I beg your pardon?"

Julas blew out a breath, rubbing his hand over his bearded mouth. "When I agreed to ferry the pair of you…it wasn't for the merits. Something didn't seem right about the way of things back in Port Craythin. Still doesn't feel right now."

"You know I've seen my share of bad dealings out there on the sea," Bastyan added, his gaze graying a bit with the memory of the truths we'd shared on the shores of Sunrise Isle.

"Bastyan's been keeping a close watch on things," Julas added. "My orders. He's pushed at the edges of your mistress, to see what she's capable of…and she's showed us plenty."

"I don't know if I've ever met any trademasters' wives who can lift a sailor clean off his feet." Arms folded, Bastyan frowned down at his boots; then his eyes darted back to me. "*Accident*, my well-shaped backside. I felt the muscle behind that shove…she knew *exactly* what she was doing. And I've never met a woman of her so-called station built that way."

Incredulous, I held his stormy gray-green stare.

He had provoked her—deliberately, deftly—to learn that?

For *my* sake?

Julas sat forward, drawing my attention from Bastyan; his gaze dipped to my sore, mottled hands, then traveled back to my face. That grave expression rearranged itself into something far fiercer—a pained memory. "You see things in this profession, going into the ports we do. Some people choose a Trade vessel over a Ferry because they want less questions. Or, you know…" True malice flickered in the depths of his dark eyes. "Because they see the people they're ferrying *as* cargo."

He shifted, dropping his voice to a secret held in the slim space between us.

"You just say the word," he rumbled, "or say nothing, if it feels unsafe. But if you need her dealt with…my crew and me, we'll handle it discreetly. And we'll take you wherever you need to go."

My breath snared audibly at the impossible offer.

His eyes shot up to search mine, seeking permission in that sound—searching for a silent admission of danger.

I couldn't summon a single word past the disbelief and gratitude raging in my chest.

How many thefts of persons had this Captain quietly managed? How many stolen people had he set free? Perhaps this was why he had become a sailor…because of men like the Del, who saw fit to steal Storycrafters and orphans and whomever else he wished, bartering them for his own ends.

The Del, who treated people as if they were charms dangling at his neck, or weapons in his arsenal primed for use.

The Del, who wanted *me*.

My thoughts stuttered, stumbling over the imaginings of what he might do if he were to learn that I had been nearly in his grasp…and escaped it, felling Lucretzia along the way. How fiercely he would hunt me *then*, until he learned of *The Athalion*—of its crew, and of his Viper, pitched into the sea or otherwise vanished.

Perhaps it would be a seamless escape. Or perhaps he would never stop hunting me, now that he knew for certain I still lived. And Julas and his crew would become casualties on his way to finding the prize he so desperately sought.

Death had been my false guise for many years, my means of escaping the Del's watch and Lucretzia's cruelty. But it would be Julas's truth if the Del learned what he'd done to his Own Blade, and to his carefully-forged Delina.

It would be *Bastyan's* truth, some wound dealt from which I could not save him. From which he would not recover.

All of it a bitter, inevitable end, even *if* they somehow got the better of Lucretzia. And I was not certain they could.

And should I escape, never to be found again—

Tristah.

Alone against Sorai. Alone against the Del. The way we had sworn never to leave one another.

Hopelessness tangled in my chest. I wanted desperately to cry.

These men—these kind, selfless souls—had brought us aboard for *this.* For my safety. For a truth they thought they understood, and never could. That I could never allow them to fully comprehend.

Tying my lips into a faint smile, I shook my head. "I appreciate your concern. Both of you. But I am here of my own will, I assure you."

It was not an absolute lie. Not when Tristah might await at the end of this voyage.

"Cress is a stern woman," I went on, "but a fair mistress. And as for her strength…Monsha is dangerous. She is well-prepared for that."

Julas settled back, his lips pressed thin; Bastyan sank down on the edge of the low table between us. His knees nearly brushed mine as he sat, offering his hands palm-up on his knees.

Betraying him—betraying my own self-preservation and sanity—I laid mine in his, the way I had yearned to since I'd last let go in the sick bay. He trailed a thumb gently along a scar on my wrist that I had hardly notice until now: a thin, white rope of a marking, weeks old, imprinted by the shackle I'd worn my first several days under Lucretzia's control.

"I don't believe that," he said simply.

The words landed like an iron-toed kick to my middle.

"If she's not trafficking you, then she's mistreating you," he forged on. "Mistress or not, she has no right to decide your life."

"You assume, because I rejected your advances—"

"I *know,* because I've seen how you flinch when she touches you." His tone was rough with a fury not angled at me. "How you catch her eye across the deck and crumble. I know what it is to serve beneath someone you respect…and to serve people who show their faces in your nightmares."

He let that hang between us; behind him, Julas's brow furrowed, his gaze drifting from Bastyan's back to my face and returning like the tide.

Bastyan squeezed my hands, inclining until his brow touched mine. "If you look into my eyes and tell me you're safe, we can forget this conversation ever happened. But if you're not safe, sweetheart, help me make you that way."

The ache gathered and grew in my chest, blazing, burning, *begging* to spill out in the truth—

And all at once, the ship gave a violent shudder and a lurch, tossing me out of my seat—straight into Bastyan's lap. He reeled, elbow slamming onto the table, his other arm circling me and bracing me against him as the ship scraped and bucked and bashed against something, heaving sideways.

Julas surged to his feet. "Wicked, blasted *depths*—!"

"What was that?" I cried.

"That," Bastyan gritted out, his breath hot against my ear, "was one of the Spear Teeth."

The name prodded my memory of nautical maps and the most fearsome voyage tales I had heard from sailors my father had bartered with in Monsha.

The Spear Teeth…the juts of murderous stone that foamed at the mouth of the river severing Amere-Del in twain.

We had arrived at the Everreach.

CHAPTER 18
INTO THE EVERREACH

*J*ulas lunged from the room, snatching his Captain's coat from around his chair and snapping it on. By the time he reached the door—barking orders as he went—Bastyan had shoved us both to our feet, his arm still bracing me.

"You're all right?" he demanded. "Steady?"

I nodded, ducking his grasp. We bolted after the Captain, striking out onto a deck already consumed with chaos.

Shouting. Scrambling. There was no first, second, or third watch now; all hands were on deck, launching themselves at pieces of rigging, tying and loosing, performing all manner of sailing feats about which I knew very little.

But danger, I knew well. And it loomed off the side of the ship in jagged stone fangs.

The breath escaped from the very bottom of my lungs as I beheld the sharp, soaring spires—some of which loomed higher than the masts themselves, vanishing into the clouds. They were odd, twisted, misshapen things, utterly menacing; I could not help but shrink in their shadow.

Distantly, but louder in its echo than all the tumult of the crew around us, something plummeted into the water. I leaped in my skin; Bastyan gripped my shoulder, his face grim.

"This stone has been eroding for a long bloody time," he muttered. "Falls apart with the changes in the wind. The danger here's not just beneath us. It's coming on every side."

My gaze flashed to Lucretzia; she was pressed to the mainmast, gripping it backhanded to steady herself. The long, pale column of her throat heaved as she stared up at the monoliths of stone that yawned wide to devour us.

For the first time that I could ever recall, fear flashed in the Pale Viper's eyes, beholding this danger against which her weapons could not defend.

A violent grind of stone on stone roared through the pound of the waves and Julas's commands; then a second echo, dragging its cacophony against my thrumming nerves.

Another clot of stone broke from the nearest of the Spear Teeth, riving the sea just shy of the starboard bow.

A plume of water surged up beneath *The Athalion*, lifting us high and slamming us down again. My feet deserted the decking, and Bastyan gripped my waist, tossing me down and landing over me as shards of stone battered the railing and the varnished wood around us.

"Those blasted Teeth are why a heap of Trade vessels are sleeping at the bottom of the sea!" Julas barked. "Stay lively, sailors!"

Bastyan palmed the deck on either side of me and lurched up, thrusting his hand out to me. "Stay here, under the overhang."

The moment he'd tugged me to my feet, he was gone—dashing across the deck, putting himself to work without pausing for orders. He became a blur with the rest of them, while I pressed myself into the shelter of the thin lip of wood stretching out above the door to Julas's chambers.

Even after weeks of sailing, I did not know the terms and meanings of a ship's language well enough to assess what was befalling us; but desperation seethed in the lurch of *The Athalion's* cumbersome body, in how the helm cranked left and right as we came about to face the Spear Teeth.

The tides of the sea and the rush of the broad-mouthed Everreach foamed where they met, eroding the lethal columns of rock. Vicious rapids and whirlpools swirled at their bases; beyond those treacherous juts of stone, the high walls of the Everreach itself loomed: ancient, black stone capped in alpine tufts, littered with slick footpaths and dangerous narrows.

Sailing to and from Monsha along the Everreach was the most profitable means of trade by water beyond the western coast of Amere-Del. And only the greatest captains and crews had earned the rite of passage against the forces of nature itself.

It was time to learn if we were worthy.

Julas roared another command; high in the rigging, Nix and Nash leaped from a crossbeam like acrobats, swinging on a pair of ropes twin as the sailors themselves. The sails snapped wide, and with a great gust, the wind hammered us toward the slim slice of space between the first two Spear Teeth.

Clinging to the handle of Julas's door, I hissed a prayer to merciful Ahim as we rolled into the treacherous waters.

Sailors vanished and reappeared along the deck, flitting like misplaced spirits among the shrouds and stays. Turbulence dragged at the belly of *The Athalion* as the coming tide of the Everreach shoved against it, and the fingers of the sea's currents lifted and flung it back. We were a child's toy passed from hand to hand in a cruel, vicious game.

My stomach rocked and roiled; unlike the rhythmic churn of the open sea, no reason guided how we sailed now. Desperation manned the wheel, all hard pivots and changing sails as Captain Julas forged a path between the Spear Teeth.

My heart lurched at every errant creak from the ship's body as we sloshed and surged among the tides. I had heard tales of what lurked at the mouth of the Everreach, but to see it for myself—these stone jaws which seethed with sinister intent—I had never been more grateful for the crew we sailed with.

Lucretzia, for all her flaws, had chosen well.

Somewhere ahead of us—above us—stone groaned and crackled. Sailors swore. Lucretzia shoved from the mainmast and retreated several steps, her gaze fixed on the pair of Spear Teeth that lay ahead.

"Steady," Julas called, his voice echoing oddly off the rocks.

"Ahim, please," I breathed—the only prayer I could muster.

We squeezed through the narrow gap, wood groaning against the strain of encroaching stone—

A mighty fracture sounded off the port side.

Screams. Bellowed prayers. Shattering rock, and the deck exploded into fresh chaos as the sailors dove for what little cover could be found. I caught a glimpse of pale hair and ashen skin—Lucretzia lunging belowdecks, yanking the hatch shut over her head.

And then the stone hailed down on us.

Impact after impact thrummed in wicked vibrations along my bones; I lurched back against the door, pressing myself below the overhang, but even that was not enough of a shield. Flying stone clipped my shoulder so fiercely, it knocked my feet out from beneath me. I dropped on the slick wood, my temple thudding against the deck.

Muffled ringing bloomed like yeast in water through my ears. Bleary-eyed, I picked up my head, blinking against the pain that thudded in my skull. A graze of fingers to my hairline unburied no blood—it had been a dull impact only, not a piercing one.

Not all had been so fortunate.

All across the deck, crew had fallen, struck down by the raining stone. Some cried out in anguish; some stanched their bleeding. Some were horrifically silent, unmoving…delirious or dead, I could not tell.

Horror dumped through me, a wicked spice blazing on my tongue, when I recognized Ribbens—the bosun who conveyed orders down from the quarterdeck to the crew. He lay senseless in a sprawl, blood running from his leathery brow, his eyes at half-mast. Fingers that had worked the neck of the fiddle like kneading dough at the bonfire on Sunrise Isle were crushed and splintered by falling stone.

Slowly, I wobbled to my feet. A strident shout caught against the ringing in my ears, allowing trickles of sense to slip through.

Bastyan. That was Bastyan's voice.

Something about the mainsail—something about the rigging, snapped loose by the stonefall—

And then I spotted him; hurtling across the deck, he stepped fearlessly up onto the railing and leaped off of it.

A cry lodged into my throat. My head roared with the echo of him striking the shipside—his body smashing into the water—

But he did not fall. It was as if the wind itself lifted him; his leap had been perfectly timed, and he shot out an arm, catching the slash of a rope I had not even noticed flapping wildly in the wind. In the span of a blink, he was arcing back to the railing and dropping to a crouch on the deck. The tension of his weight against the rope lifted the sail, and it ballooned, driving us forward again. A sharp cheer rose, and Bastyan's head shot up.

Across the deck, his eyes found me. I could not place the war of indecision in his gaze—or how long it held me rooted beneath the overhang.

Then his fingers danced, tying off the rope in a few complicated swivels. He surged to his feet and bellowed orders to the crew—no different from a bosun's command.

"You lot, get over here—tie these off—let the anchor down two spans, we may need to drop it and bank. Get ready to trim the sails on both sides, it'll be a tight squeeze between a few of these teeth—I want eyes on the shrouds, and get someone up there to start patching those holes—!"

On and on, orders poured from him, and no one protested; no one claimed rank or told him to stand down. Frixia and Julas struggled at the helm, Syd with the navigation, guiding us between the Spear Teeth. And far too many of the crew were still bleeding, disposed on the deck.

Desperation twisted my fists to knots.

I could not run the lines of a ship. I could not sail us from these dangerous waters. And I could not leave these people to die.

Bearing down a breath for bravery, I did what no one else seemed keen to do: I disobeyed Bastyan's orders, sliding out into the open even as fresh rock severed from the nearest Spear Teeth, hailing down on the deck. Dodging the smaller clots of stone, I skidded to my knees beside Ribbens, feeling for a pulse beneath his baggy jowls. It met my touch, weak and wavering, and I gasped out a prayer of thanks. Then I hooked my hands beneath the bosun's arms and towed him backward to the hatch belowdecks.

Lucretzia met me there, fierce as a blade, snatching my wrist the moment I reached the base of the steps—still dragging Ribbens with me. "Keep yourself down here."

I held her gaze, seeking any bit of fear to spare for her furious glower. But I had none left; all that remained for her was disgust.

She had retreated. Hidden away. A cowardly serpent cringing in her den.

"Unless you would rather be dead in the water, and *walk* the rest of the way to Shadewyle," I seethed, "this crew needs able hands."

I heaved Ribbens up and thrust him toward her; Lucretzia caught him by sheer instinct, his weight nearly bearing her down in half.

"The Captain suspects you," I added, and her brow furrowed. "I suggest you behave like a trademaster's wife would and *help* these people. Get him to the sick bay."

Leaving him to a fate that would be little worse than if he had remained on the deck, I abandoned Ribbens and Lucretzia, hauling myself back out onto the topdeck.

Chaos still ruled the ship; some sailors were bailing, many working the lines. I slipped through the heart of the upheaval, dropping to my knees beside fallen bodies, feeling for their heartbeats. Those who had them, I hauled to the hatch, slipping and floundering with every toss and heave of the ship. Those who had none, I left, sorrow foaming in my middle.

It seemed more had fallen with every return I made; limbs broken, bodies bleeding, sliced by fallen stone. Dents and gaps littered the deck; terror strangled my throat when I clawed my way abovedecks and spotted the vicious holes rent clean through two sails from broken rock.

But we had not faltered for it; Bastyan paced the yard of the mainmast above like a collared wildcat, peering down across the deck—assessing the turmoil, his jaw firm as he deliberated how to patch the many gaps in the crew and its equipment.

He did not have the look of a deckhand today. There was something fierce, something vibrant and powerful in him. Something so magnificent, it stopped my breath.

Slinging one hand around the nearest line, Bastyan tilted forward so that only the toes of his boots held purchase on the beam; he struck out a hand into the wind, eyes shut, the breeze tugging threads of black hair against his clean-shaven cheeks.

After a breathless moment, his eyes snapped open again; he twined the line around his arm and swung down, landing with practiced ease on the railing before the helm and stepping off to face Julas and Frixia. From below, I caught their voices above the clamor:

"We need to angle the bow to portside."

"*Port?*" Frixia echoed scathingly.

"Have you lost your blasted mind?" Strain cracked Julas's voice as he fought the wheel over the pits and swells of the churning waters. "Every sailor knows that's the weak side of the river mouth! That rock won't hold, and even if it does, the rapids on that half—"

"Trust me, Julas!"

Stillness suffocated the ship; all along the lines, eyes snapped wide and bewildered toward the quarterdeck—toward the rash-mouthed deckhand who addressed Captain Julas as if they were equals.

That quiet held for barely a moment, shattering with the next moan of tearing stone.

Julas cursed. "Take us to portside, Atreyon."

"Aye, Captain."

Boots scuffed wood, and Bastyan dropped beside me in a crouch, then bounded back to his feet. For a heartbeat, his hand flashed up, cupping my cheek, his gaze fastened to mine. A plea roared in the depths of his gaze…for what, I feared I would never know.

"Find something to hang onto," he warned.

Then he tore past me, racing down the deck, crying orders to every sailor he passed. They all broke into a flurry of fresh commotion as we wove through the Spear Teeth, and slowly the ship angled to the left.

Bitten with the sense of narrow time, I scouted the deck for more wounded sailors—and found only one.

Reinera sagged on her seat, pressed against the railing, one hand wrapped around a bleeding gash on her ribs. With the other, she clung fiercely to a loose line.

Cursing, I sprinted across the deck, staggering as the ship bucked and writhed over the waves. Kicking aside clots of stone in my path, I tumbled to my knees beside Reinera, dumping my hair over one shoulder so that I could see her wound clearly.

A gash scoured her side—wide, but not deep. More brutal was the rash that veined her forearm where the rope chafed. Its greedy bite seemed intent on severing that arm completely.

I took the rope above her hand in both of mine. "Let go."

"I do that, and we lose course," she panted between gritted teeth.

"I have it. Let go, Rei."

Her gaze flicked unwillingly up to mine; agony painted a bright glaze across her eyes. "It needs tying off."

"Then tell me how."

A last, breathless, indecisive pause.

"Hold on," she croaked.

I tightened my grip, and her arm slithered from the rope.

The vicious yank of the twine nearly lifted me straight to my feet; I drove my weight down to the deck, grateful all the more that I was not the same lean creature I had once been—and that the muscles I had built through hard labor in my shop were far more accustomed to this sort of counterweight. Still, tears stung my eyes as the rope chafed against the abrasions still healing on my palms.

Reinera slammed back against the railing, barking commands—telling me where to loop the rope around an iron fastening on the deck. How to circle and slip and knot it.

The sail tucked in, and with the rope secured, I shoved forward on my knees, pressing my hand over Reinera's against her bleeding side. "Hasser must see to this."

"No time." Reinera raised her chin. "Look."

Swiveling in my crouch, I followed her gaze.

Bastyan stood on the railing at the portside, hand woven into the rigging. The walls of the Everreach loomed ahead—and at its mouth, the swirling, cascading rapids where sea and river met. Wooden bones pierced from within and around the white-mouthed swirls; for a moment, I thought they must be felled trees, caught in the river's currents and carried out to sea…until I spotted the sinew of a lonely Ameresh standard, hanging limply from the tip of one.

Not a tree. A mast. A graveyard of ships—that one likely recently sunk.

My heart sank as well.

"Tuck in, Lionyra!" Reinera shouted, and I dove against the railing myself, wrapping one arm around its gilled posts. I kept my free hand over her ribs, bracing us both.

Stone and wood ground together from the portside. The ship groaned beneath the strain, and fresh blades of stone punched into the deck and bit through the sails. Julas cursed; I repelled a wince, keeping my eyes on the looming cliffs as they closed in. The roar of those ship-shattering rapids and currents filled my ears.

"Free the helm!" Bastyan's cry carried with the bellow of falling rock.

Julas and Frixia had already snatched their hands back from the wheel, sending it into a wild whirl of spokes, the ship following in an unbound reel toward the right.

"Loose the starboard sails!" Bastyan ordered.

"That's us!" Reinera barked.

Lunging, I yanked at the tail of the knot I'd tied; the cord whipped through my fingers, stinging and ripping flesh as it went. The sail billowed wide, and with a rush of wind in its belly, *The Athalion* pivoted sharply—cutting around behind the foaming rapids at the mouth of the Everreach.

For a moment, the tumultuous waters lifted us up to one side like Ahim himself had gripped the ship in his world-shaping hand. We tilted, a sliver of the ship's belly bared to the overcast sky. A scream lodged behind my teeth as Reinera and I clung to the railing, the world tilting out from beneath us. Someone laughed—wild and wicked, daring the sea and the river both to do their worst.

It sounded like Bastyan.

Then everything toppled, cargo snapping at its fastening, sails guttering, sailors screaming as we smashed back down onto the water, blowing it high, soaking the deck—

—and we sailed around the mouth of the Everreach.

"Anchor!" Bastyan snapped, and someone loosed it, plunging it into the silty riverbed.

"Oars!" Julas ordered, and sailors spilled belowdecks to row the limping ship upstream against the river's current.

With the wind still at our backs, I prayed it would be enough.

Bastyan dropped from the railing, booting rocks from his path as he jogged down the deck. He touched the shoulders of doubled-over sailors, muttering to them, helping them straighten. I towed Reinera to her feet, and we turned to meet him—just as Julas reached us, his dark brows nearly joining at the center of his forehead. The Captain's hand nudged mine away from Reinera's ribs; the other he curled around the side of her neck, steadying her. "All right, there?"

"I'll live," she panted.

Relief sparkled in Julas's crinkled eyes; then they shot to Bastyan. "Quite a head for sailing you've got, Atreyon."

"I've sailed on more than one ship. Been in and out of the Everreach a few times." Bastyan's gaze never strayed from my face; despite the slick cold of the sea settling along my skin, somehow a flush still managed to find patches to burn. "You all right?"

"I'll survive…thanks to you both."

Julas smiled crookedly. "Treacherous waters this time of year."

I hitched Reinera up when she sagged a bit. "We should see Hasser."

"I'll see to that."

I stiffened as Lucretzia picked her way across the deck toward us. Her expression remained icy, remote, but she took Reinera's arm across her shoulders with a gentleness I had not thought her capable of; she pressed a hand carefully over her wound and helped her toward the hatch belowdecks.

For an instant, fear blinded me; an intrusive vision of Lucretzia dragging Reinera behind the steps, digging bare fingers into her gash, ripping it wider and leaving her to bleed to death—

It was some relief when Lanah met them at the hatch, throwing it wide and following them down.

I let out my breath in a gust…then offered the words I knew were expected of me. The reason Lucretzia had approached us at all. "As I told you both, she is stern. But fair."

Julas scowled, rubbing a hand over his mouth; but when Syd called for him across the deck, he went, his coat's sodden hem struggling to lift on the breeze.

Bastyan stayed, sinking his haunches against the railing, rubbing the soaked bandage over his shoulder. "How many did we lose?"

"A half-dozen, by my count." I dared to lay a hand on his arm. "It would have been more if not for you. You have greater sailing prowess than I realized."

A low laugh rumbled in his chest. "Aye, but that makes me a pain in the rear. Hard to keep a man on a ship when he doesn't know how to keep his mouth shut and hold rank."

"I would rather my life be saved by a man breaking rank than be buried alongside one who knew his place."

Bastyan snorted, dropping his fingers from his shoulder. "Tell that to all of the Captains who've booted me off their ships." He jerked his chin after Julas. "Tell that to *him*."

I watched Julas help his crew to their feet—clapping hands on shuddering backs, looking over wounds himself, ordering this and that one belowdecks even when they protested. And I recalled the unity with which these two men had confronted me in the Captain's quarters—equal in their concern. Partners in seeking my wellbeing.

Warmth budded in my chest. "Something tells me I won't need to."

CHAPTER 19
THE CITY BEYOND THE SEAWALL

he Athalion was by no means crippled, but certainly wounded. Night and day as we rowed and sailed up the Everreach, the crew worked in slings to patch and tar the holes driven deep into the hull and decks. The sails were one of my tasks; I mended alongside Reinera, Lanah, and Valori, as well as the Ameresh deckhands. Many of them had sailed the Everreach before; most claimed they had never seen such tactical skill as Julas displayed. And just as many argued that Bastyan ought to be his First Mate.

To his benefit, Bash took their praise humbly, mending with the rest of us and steering the subject to safer waters whenever it arose.

A span at a time, we journeyed upriver…past the treacherous stone walls still shedding clots now and then, to smaller hills made of firmer sediment. Homesteads dotted the clifftops, some wedged into the crags themselves; occasionally, we caught glimpses of people on both sides, children hanging from railings piercing the cliffsides, near enough to wave when we sailed by.

As the landscape altered, so did my mood. Tension tightened my shoulders, pinching in the small of my back until pain stalked my waking hours and poor dreams my sleeping ones. Even with Lucretzia's temper receding—likely for the sake of our ruse—I tossed and turned every night.

For the first time in years, I was inside Ameresh borders. The land to which I had sworn I would never return. The country that desired me…but I had no desire for it.

The ache in me doubled, and doubled again, until at last sleep eluded me entirely. I slipped from my hammock near dawn one day, desperate for a sip of fresh air—not the stifling belowdecks atmosphere that thickened with the perpetual scent of tar.

Up above, the world hung suspended in the last gray hours before sunrise. A small handful of mercantile vessels floated by, their smaller bodies and tighter sails meant for parading the edges of Amere-Del rather than sailing the deeper waters we'd traversed from Mithra-Sha.

I banded myself tightly with a long, flowing purple robe one of the crew, Noveen, had retrieved from the trunks of trading cloth in the hull. Then I made my way to the railing to behold the Everreach.

It was truly a marvel of Amere-Del…and little wonder the largest cities, Monsha and Ravinor, Westyr and Antaross and the like, had established themselves within easy walking distance of it. The broad river, swift-flowing in places and meandering in others, had carved itself down from the Barradir Highlands in the northeast. Along its way, the water spit out shining rocks that paved the riverbed, glowing a bright, iridescent cerulean. The world beneath us sparkled and rippled, casting dancing purple-blue whorls against *The Athalion's* belly as we slid smoothly along its reaches.

The last of the slope-backed hills had petered out to level earth around us, ringed in broad, lovely trees; some were bare from the winter chill. Others burst in the bright maroon foliage of the cold months, their innards fed by warm sap that added richness to dessert teas and coffees. I'd loved to swirl it into my breads when I could afford a small jar.

Stung with melancholy, I folded my robed arms on the railing and laid my chin on them. Dropping my gaze from the vessels that smoothed past us on this glassy span of the Everreach, I watched the glistening stones slip away.

There was such beauty to Amere-Del. I wished I could truly appreciate it…that these did not feel like blinks of beauty in an otherwise grim, cruel land.

Heavy footsteps treaded across the deck behind me, and a hand snagged the rigging above my head. Heat brushed my side as Bastyan stretched out over the water, peering down at the radiant riverbed. "That's always a sight, isn't it?"

I offered a slight smile. "It is that."

Silence tumbled between us as he leaned into his arm, and I rested on mine. We had not held one another's private company since the day we'd sailed into the Everreach. I had been grateful then, but now…

Time felt far too short. And in the melancholy gloom, it occurred to me for the first time that soon, the attentions of Bastyan Atreyon would no longer be my concern. Our paths would diverge forever.

Misery clotted my throat, and I dropped my gaze lest he catch it streaked across my eyes. "What brings you abovedecks at this early hour, Master Sailor?"

"Ahh, I didn't want to miss this." Bastyan bent himself against the railing, mirroring my posture.

Intrigue tattered my melancholy, and I slid a glance his way. "Miss—?"

He pressed his palms together and pointed along the curve of *The Athalion's* bow. "That."

I swiveled to follow his gesture—and the breath raked into my lungs in a soundless sweep.

The river mouth bloomed ahead into a harbor, snaking away in five tributary fingers like a widespread hand. And at the center of that palm, looming on a broad pedestal of slick stone ringed in docks beyond numbering…

Monsha itself. The city of my birth.

I had forgotten the sheer breadth of it. The absolute sprawl of its port, endlessly bustling with trade from the three fingers that branched to the Southlands and the two that fed from the Northlands. The ceaseless chime of labor and revelry rose from its streets, even at this early hour—streets which arced out and built upward from the shore.

Monsha was a city that climbed…first from the red-gabled roofs just beyond the seawall, to the brighter and airier homes and shops on staggered, moss-capped clefts, and finally to the lurching juts of the smaller mountains that braced the city's back. Atop these mountains perched the homesteads of the trademasters responsible for each guild—the Mercantile Guild, the Cloth Guild, the Ferry Guild, and countless more. One of which Lucretzia was meant to be sworn to.

At the notion of her, my wonder took on a sour drizzle. Painful memories winnowed through my heart.

I had once called the middle district my home. I had looked down across the sweeps of this city and loved it fiercely as a girl. I had thought I would never leave; I was determined to marry a fisherman and make my home in Monsha, as my parents had done, and their parents, and theirs. Generations loving and living and growing and perishing in this beautiful Trade City.

That daydream had been consumed by riots…riots that made orphans of little girls. That had altered the trajectory of my life—and Tristah's. That had sent us hurtling toward one another, entirely against our will.

Now, the nearer we sailed toward the distant docks, the swifter I hurtled toward her again. Utterly unstoppable. A journey not of my making…but now my choosing.

Was it resolve or terror that stuck my throat shut?

"'Ay."

Bastyan's quiet summons jerked my gaze back to him; he no longer watched the city, but me, one hand braced to the railing just shy of my arm.

"You really want to be doing this?" he asked quietly.

A last offer to take what had been set before me in the Captain's quarters days ago. The salvation I yearned so desperately for.

Instead, I carved a smile across my cheeks. "This life is all I know. Anything else is only a dream."

And so, because that dream was fading in the gauzy light of dawn crawling slowly across the harbor, I laid my coral-scuffed, needle-notched hand against Bastyan's cheek. I breathed in the scent of tar and varnish and salt from his clothes and committed to memory the precise rasp of the first strands of stubble prodding at my palm.

In all the time I'd known him, I had never seen him anything but clean-shaven. Somehow, that brush against my hand made this parting all the truer.

"*This*," I croaked, "this kindness and care you have shown me during this voyage, the concern you have given me for even a moment…that has also been a lovely dream. And I will miss you, Bastyan Atreyon."

Anguish seared his eyes when they darted up to mine. "You don't have to do this, Lio."

Helplessness reshaped the smile that still hung from my lips. "This is the only way."

For this crew to live. For Tristah and I to have any chance at proper escape…and a life afterward.

It was time to let go.

CHAPTER 20
ONLY CONSTANT, ONLY COMPANION

In our pocket of the sleep bay, I found Lucretzia alone, dressed, and strapping her blades to her body, her armor cinched beneath her flowing trademistress's robes. The jeweled green, yellow, and orange raiment was tied loosely, ready to be cast off the moment we fled sight of *The Athalion.*

The Pale Viper, braced to shed her latest skin.

Her movements slowed at my return, but she did not halt entirely…as if, perhaps, she worried less now if the crew realized she was not all she seemed. Her gaze roved across me with cool consideration; I braced for interrogation, but she only said, "Get your things."

My *things* consisted of only the clothes Reinera and Lanah and Noveen had scrounged together for me. All of it rolled neatly into a bundle I belted on at the small of my back, and there, standing at the side of my hammock, I realized just how little I had in the world to call my own.

No more shop or home in Krylan. All of the clothing and little worthless trinkets I had accumulated simply because they brought me joy…gone. Wherever I escaped to next, I would be starting over from absolutely nothing.

Again.

Pain squeezed beneath my ribs. *Nothing* was not an impossible place to begin from, but it would have been lovely to carry something more with me.

Heavyhearted, I followed Lucretzia abovedecks to rejoin the crew; they loitered a bit, the Ameresh sailors gazing at the sheer span of Monsha with longing and reserve, their Mithran crewmates twittering among themselves.

Lucretzia cast a disdainful gaze over the harbor city, demure and calm as any woman who lived within its walls might be.

"We'll stay in port just long enough to be seen," Captain Julas announced when I slipped through the milling assembly to his side. Lucretzia halted a handsbreadth away. "Do a bit of trade, then make our way back to Mithran waters."

"A *bit of trade* won't be nearly enough to account for this voyage," Henriet fretted, leaning against the railing.

"Only matters if we're audited." Julas winked at her, and she scowled so fiercely, *I* feared her wrath. Then the Captain shot a glance Lucretzia's way; she searched the docks, likely hunting for a worthy vessel among the wharfs that would carry us to Shadewyle proper.

Unease pricked low in my gut like a punctured wineskin; but a sideways embrace from Cook smothered the leakage.

"I'll think of you whenever I eat a loaf of sour bread," he grunted, his breath and body carrying the scent of flour and yeast and sugar…things I would miss for quite some time.

"Or cheat at cards," Reinera grinned, tugging me to her side from the opposite way. "It's been good to meet you, Lionyra. If you're ever in Port Craythin again…"

How I wished I would be.

"If I'm ever there, I'll be sure to find your ship," I lied, wrapping both arms around Reinera and embracing her with all my might.

Julas took my arm and tugged me off to the side while Syd and the twins descended on Lucretzia, loading her with jars of pickled fish and dried fruit. Beneath the shadow of the mainmast, he held my gaze with those lively, sharp eyes. "Last chance to lose your shadow there and sail off into the sunrise."

My throat heated as his jesting tone—at the thread of absolute sincerity spooling beneath it. "You are a good man, Jularius Cathan. You look where others are afraid to see…that is always how I'll remember you."

"And I'll always remember the outrageous stories you tell." Folding a hand around the back of my head, he drew me into his shoulder. "Be well, Lionyra."

"And you, Captain." If my compliance earned me nothing else, I hoped it would ensure that, at least.

We returned to the others, meeting a few eyes misty with farewell, a few smiles strained. I slid dutifully to Lucretzia's side, peering among the assembled crew for one face in particular…a pair of eyes I wished to catch and hold. Just a parting glance I might carry with me away from the ship.

But Bastyan was nowhere to be seen.

Disappointment moldered in my chest as the crew lowered the gangplank. But it was for the better–if he showed his face now, Lucretzia would certainly leave him with something wicked to remember her by.

The moment my heels struck the shore, it was as if I'd stepped from a quiet, muffled side room into a fete that had been underway for some time. At this angle, the vivid daylight pierced through Monsha's heights and slashed across my eyes; I raised a hand to shield my view, but the assault persisted. Sound and sight and scent engulfed me——the bright, striking tones of Ameresh clothing, the bellows of hawkers and fishmongers and mercantilists, the crash of tools at work. Saws chafing wood, hammers beating steel, bone and scale sundering, innards flopping back into the sea.

Monsha had once been a delicacy whose ingredients I knew by heart. My father had known many of the mercantilists by name; he had known which ones to barter our homemade bread with, and which ones would purchase the things he gathered from that bartering.

For a moment, my skin prickled with the memory of precious bangles and jewels he'd acquired from sailors just like Captain Julas. Glittering crystal anklets that sang with my steps and wicked bloodstone necklaces, tiered and lush; a piece of my inheritance. The flash of sizzling sunlight across my eyes might well have been the dance of its rays on the full-length cut glass in my girlhood bedroom, where I'd clapped on every piece my father had ever brought me and worn them all at once.

And now they were all gone. Sold to the orphanage that had taken me in to pay for the stale bread, tasteless meat, and hard cheese that had fed me while I'd waited and waited for something to rouse me from the nightmare of my parents' deaths.

Throat tight, I dropped my hand and squinted to find Lucretzia fording through the crowd. Despite the early morning hour and the bustle of the markets, people made way for her; even if they did not recognize her in her gaudy trademistress's attire, she exuded a lethal grace which others wisely took as a warning.

For a moment, I considered stepping backward, losing myself in the lurch of the Monshan markets. Another city I knew well…another former home into which I might flee. One without Storycraft twisting the streets.

Lucretzia swiveled back, her gaze fastening me in place—the prey caught beneath the viper's eye. She stabbed a finger at the street beside her. *Come.*

A flicker of bravery rose in me—courage reclaimed as I reminded myself why I was enduring this.

For Tristah.

Slowly, I unpeeled my feet from the docks and plodded after her.

We wound some distance along the wharfs, then ducked beneath an open arch in the seawall, where Lucretzia at last shed her disguise. Unthreading her silk belt and casting the garments from her muscled shoulders and sturdy waist, she balled the gauzy material effortlessly with a swirl of her arm and discarded it at the side of the pavestone street climbing up into the heights of Monsha. "We have no time to waste. That scarcely competent captain cost us days sailing up the Everreach, not to mention his worthless stopover at that blasted island. We must find a river-trader who can do better."

The notion made my skin crawl. River-traders were notorious skinflints with a decisive lack of morals; most couldn't balance their scales honestly long enough to create a reputable trade enterprise in Monsha. instead, they sailed up and down the rivers, stealing and swindling, taking advantage of poorer lakeside towns and villages who were overtaxed and undertraded.

I knew all of this because, while those sorts of lessons had left me too heartsick to concentrate while our tutor droned on and on, Tristah had gobbled them up like jam-slathered bread. Indignation had seethed from her every pore as she'd ranted about the entire river-trade profession afterward; how it should be the Del's sworn duty to regulate trade, so that the most desperate people weren't taken advantage of.

But the Del did not care, so long as they paid the exorbitant taxes that came with waterfront living. And any attempt Tristah had made to raise the notion in council sessions had been swiftly and mercilessly silenced.

And no wonder, when the Del's Own Blade unapologetically spoke of hiring those pirates.

Lucretzia spoke to herself as she walked, unslinging her satchel and rooting about in its depths. "With a good river-trader, we can make it up the Sudene River in less than a week. Still within Zorast's timing, no thanks to our *ferrymen.*"

"Must you?" The snarl burst unbidden from my lips. "You despise them. I'm aware. There's no need to air your grievances like a petty child."

Lucretzia halted midstride, wheeling back to face me; her hand caught me beneath the chin, and she stared deep into my eyes. Past them. The blade of her blackened stare pierced into places I fought to keep hidden from her—from most people.

"I must admit, I rather enjoy this streak of defiance you've somehow managed to cobble together over the years, Alyona. Asserting yourself without Tristah at your hip was something I never thought you capable of." Her lip slid back from her teeth—not a smile. A baring of venomous fangs. "It is the *only* improvement I've witnessed so far."

Her hand dropped to my middle, pinching the rolls of my belly with such force I nearly yelped. Every inch of this woman was honed to deliver pain—even the tips of her fingers.

"This will be the first thing to go," she added. "I worry how you'll even keep pace with me up the steps to the castle with all of this extra padding."

Freeing me, she stepped back; but the space to breathe was no escape from her tirade.

"The regimen must be fierce, if you're to hold any appeal at all to Sorai by the time he returns for peace talks. No scrawny, scrap-fed dissident will want a woman who outweighs him." Every word was a throwing knife flung directly into my still-panging middle. "I'll have a watch on your rooms, particularly in the night…and I can assure you the guard has been schooled to detect and mitigate any hint of midnight rebellion."

Her drawl was casual, but the edge of her stare pressed sharp with a stomach-churning malice. For a moment, Della Athyna's name—her fate—hung unspoken between us.

"There are, of course, other measures I've been permitted to take," she went on quietly. "Ones that I assure you I am *exceedingly* eager to make use of. Ways of keeping you where we would like you…particularly in the night."

From within the satchel gripped in her fist, the clank of rattling iron battered my ears. Despair soaked my mouth in a rush of bile.

Not a half-mile from *The Athalion*, and it had already begun.

I was a prisoner without pretense again—a figurehead to be chiseled and carved until presentable. Already my wrists stung with the cold clap of the irons they were bound for; my belly ached with the imminent hunger pangs.

Panic seared my chest.

I could not do this. I could not become this again. I had pushed it away, played it off, treated it like a faraway nightmare while we sailed, distracted by the part we played for the crew.

But there was no fleeing, no hiding, no excusing this. The shackles were in Lucretzia's hands, the satchel dropped to her feet as she stepped nearer to me.

"I know why you've played the part of the battered orphan from Monsha so well these last weeks," she growled. "Why you have kept your head lowered. You assume that with Tristah, some semblance of escape is possible again." Disgust wrinkled the corner of her mouth in a savage upward tilt. "But I assure you, Alyona, I have not been idle in your absence. I have trained, and I have learned, and I have *prepared* for you. You will not find Shadewyle as trusting or trickable a place as you knew."

An iron cuff clapped around my wrist, and I flinched; I had not even seen it approaching, my gaze locked on the void of her pitiless stare.

"Whatever comfort you were given then is gone now," she hissed. "And you will not be permitted to breathe the same air as Tristah. I am your only constant. I am your *only* companion until you are given over to Sorai. I am—"

Something *cracked.*

A burst of sound. Deafening.

Warmth and wetness shattered across my face, and for a moment, the world ceased to be built of sense.

Because Lucretzia had fallen to one knee with a howl of *pain*, letting go of my wrists and clutching her shoulder, blood pumping between her gloved fingers—

And a hand latched under *my* arm, sunbrowned, tattooed. A familiar voice bellowed in my ear, "Lio, weigh anchor and *move your bloody feet!*"

At that moment, I made the coward's choice.

I did not think of Tristah. Or of the fate of my rescuer.

With all my might, I whipped the loose manacle of the chained shackle in a brutal arc, smashing it into the side of Lucretzia's face. Then I ripped the offhand blade from its sheath across her back, put my hand into Bastyan Atreyon's—and I *ran.*

CHAPTER 21
THE ONE WHO LISTENED

Lucretzia's parting howl of rage and retribution echoed in my ears as Bastyan and I shoved and stumbled through the swelling market crowds. It was an animal's snarl, a hunting beast's brutal cry. It would haunt me until the moment she sank her fangs into me again.

But in this moment, all that existed for us was fleeing—leaping over low booths and carts, dodging up shallow side-steps as the city flourished in height around us. Running hand-in-hand.

We were not going back to *The Athalion*. That much I was grateful for.

Lucretzia could return to them if she wished. She could tear the ship apart, search every inch of the hull, and find them all above reproach. But if Julas was as clever as he seemed, I suspected they had never disembarked at all…that they were already sailing out of reach, back toward the river.

I suspected a great many things I'd never dared to consider when Bastyan had not come to say goodbye.

We kept running even as the sun climbed toward its zenith above the city. Though our pace slowed in time, abrupted with aching sides and sore feet, we pressed on—until, all at once, everything gained an edge of heartaching familiarity. I squeezed Bastyan's hand, then veered sharply aside, tugging him after me to a high whitestone wall that followed a curve in the pavestone pathway—just as I remembered it. The foliage on the far side was denser than I recalled, but not enough to inhibit our climb.

"Up and over," Bastyan said when we reached the wall, cupping his hands. With a running leap and a thrust, he had me at the top of the wall; I hauled myself over and dropped to the far side.

He landed beside me, straightening in the gloom of tangled branches. The day changed to dark beneath the thickly-woven boughs; only slim slivers of light winnowed through, falling in chinks at our feet, dappling our skin.

"Where are we, now?" he asked.

"Azayla's orchard." Bracing my arms, I shoved through the undergrowth, the empty shackle beating dully against my thigh. "I used to hide away here when I was in trouble with my mother. If she hasn't changed it—"

And she had not. The seam in the wall was still precisely where I remembered...a split of stone, deep and high and narrow, where I had hidden myself and many of my treasures as a girl.

It was a much tighter fit now, and I struggled to banish Lucretzia's scathing remarks on my softness as I wedged myself into the gap. Bastyan ducked in after me, and we settled on our knees, trembling from our run. Gripping the knees of my skirts in trembling fingers, I bowed my head and fought for breath, my lungs spun tighter than a wet dishcloth.

"'Ay." Bastyan brushed the sweat-soaked hair from my brow, gently tilting my head up. Concern etched lines around his eyes; he stooped forward, his brow brushing mine. His fingers still traced through my hair, a quiet sweep from my brow back to my shoulderblade. "You all right?"

Swallowing burned as if I'd guzzled seawater. "Why did you do that? Why did you come after me?"

He leaned away, his forehead furrowing, erasing every glint of sunshine in his gaze. "Because I saw that look in your eye, at the railing this morning. And I couldn't help but think you're a woman who's used to asking for help and being ignored...so you must've stopped asking." He shrugged. "I figured it was time someone listened."

Gratitude strangled what little air crawled into my lungs. "You shot her."

"Aye." He tapped a finger against a weapon stuffed in his belt. "Pistol. Handier than a Mithran rifle...easier to hide, too."

"Bastyan, you don't know what you've done." Fear and desperation surmounted my surprise—my relief, even—that he had come for me. "She is not who she seems."

"I gathered that, back on the ship. And with those blades on her today..." He whistled lowly, dropping his gaze—and his hand—to the shackle secured around my wrist. "Let's get this thing off of you."

He produced a lockpicking set from his pocket and went to work; I settled on my haunches, measuring my breathing, staring at the top of his head. Dark hair tumbled across his brow and hung in limp strands around his head; he was calming as well, his respirations deepening, his movements smoothing out bit by bit as he worked the tumblers within the keyhole.

A corner of his shirt's collar slid down, baring the vicious, lateral marring from the coral bed. A wound dealt by Lucretzia's treachery.

I swallowed a surge of fresh terror. "Does the crew know?"

"Julas and I parted ways on friendly terms just before Frixia put us to port," Bastyan said. "And that's all that needs saying."

It was. Anything more would make *The Athalion* complicit. As it was, Bastyan Atreyon was simply an Ameresh deckhand who had found his way back to his own shores. What he did now, no longer a crewman of the ship, was no concern of theirs.

"How long have you been planning this?" I murmured.

With an audible *click*, the shackle separated. Bastyan's gaze lifted to mine. "Longer than you'd believe."

He cast the cuff aside, then shifted to sit at an angle from me, our feet tangled in the space between us.

"So," he said, linking his arms loosely around his bent knees, "how did you know this little cleft was here?"

I kneaded my sore ankles, grimacing. "I grew up just the next street over."

His brows arched. "Is that the truth?"

Nodding was some effort. "I would stash animals here that I found in the city…homeless hounds and cats. Infant rabbits. Dormice. I nursed them to health and found homes for them all."

Bastyan's frame vibrated with bitten-back laughter. "Couldn't sneak them into the house?"

"My mother had a terrific sneeze every time I tried. I learned to care for the waifs in hidden ways…and somehow there was always enough food to spare for them. Enough milk in the jar from the local farmer."

Bastyan fell quiet for a moment, an odd line sketched between his brows, diving into the furrows around his eyes. "They must have adored you. Your parents."

The truth—and pain—of those words had lived long in my heart. "They did. My mother is the one who taught me how to dole my frustrations into the dough." A smile edged my lips, but it hurt as well…so near to where that beautiful dream had fallen to pieces. "She was well-loved, and my father was well-known. So he traded our creations at the market, and sold what he traded for. We had a comfortable life."

Bastyan stared out into the overgrown orchard. "Until the riots."

My next breath struggled into my lungs, and it came tinged with the fleeting essence of the smoke that had choked Monsha that night. "They were seeing about a shopfront in the lower district…somewhere she could bake besides our home. They did nothing wrong, they provoked no one. They were simply in the wrong place at the most terrible time. And when fighting broke out between the dissenters and the militar…"

I raked my sleeve against my cheek; a bit of Lucretzia's blood flaked off on my knees.

To my relief, Bastyan did not press further; instead, he shoved up to his feet, offering his hand. "We should move. She'll have the city watch after us soon."

Accepting his hand, I let him draw me to my throbbing feet. "And where are we moving *to*, Master Sailor?"

His lips twitched. "Somewhere safe. We need to get back down toward the waves."

We scrambled over the wall and dropped into the street, its stony span still silent apart from the occasional couple out for a stroll. No marketing or trading took place in this district; the nearest mercantile lay at the bottom of the hill. Here, homes flourished. Families grew together.

Melancholy scrabbled at my heart as Bastyan tightened his hand around mine. "Walk like we're one of them."

So we did—forcing a casual pace while we wound through these places I had known as a girl. Bastyan seemed equally familiar with them; he even went so far as to whistle along the way, offering genial nods to whomever we passed.

Now and again, I tugged Bastyan into side streets and paths that doubled back on themselves, mindful of pursuers. The militar were a profound presence in Monsha, keeping the peace among traders, addressing threats and thefts; it was no doubt Lucretzia had begun to rally them and put them on the hunt. We could trust no one who wore the same red-and-silver cords as she.

It was nearing sunset when the sound of the tide swelled in our ears again; we approached the seawall from above, cast in the shadow of the lower Barradir Highlands that jutted their rounded teeth from the city's aft. At the edge of a perilous, steep hill, Bastyan peered down toward the meeting of the wall and a narrow curl of woodland below—and for the first time since he had found me in the street, he smiled.

"Brilliant." Swiveling, he beckoned me. "It's not far."

We descended the hill, bracing ourselves on the sharp incline. By the time we skidded to safer ground, enough light had faded that the trees retained only their barest definition around us.

Bastyan's hand found mine again. "This way."

He set off as if some clear path lay beneath his feet; I could do little else but trust his sense of direction. I had never been to this side of Monsha; it was the oldest stretch of the seawall, and the most treacherous. My father had told me how it flooded in the rainy season, ponding between these trees, filling old caves and gaps in the wall with a rush of water that could drown even a seasoned swimmer in seconds.

I had lost two childhood playmates to it. I had never dared come this way.

But Bastyan forded fearlessly through the undergrowth as if he knew the precise stirrings and tides of the sea and when to heed them. His courage and determination reminded me sharply of Tristah.

The notion of her stuttered past the ironclad walls of my heart; for the first time since we'd escaped Lucretzia, panic and shame swarmed my chest.

I had abandoned her. I had chosen myself, my own wellbeing, over hers; in a moment of instinct over will, I had shown my true nature. I had not looked back; I had not thought twice. I'd taken Bastyan's hand, and now…

Now we were slowing, and Bastyan tangled his fingers in the thick, hardy ivy growing in untamed swatches along the wall. He whistled as he went, the same shanty from the street, this time even and deliberate. And every few notes, he tugged on an ivy strand. I followed in his shadow, arms wrapped around my middle, warding off the chill that had nothing to do with the late autumn night encroaching on Monsha's outer hills.

With every step, I was making the same choice; the one I had sworn I would never make. That I had vowed to *Tristah* I would not make.

We did not abandon one another. We did not leave one another alone in Lucretzia's hands, at the mercy of the Del's whims.

But every moment, with every step—

Our steps halted.

Bastyan's shanty had come to an end; we were left in windswept, sea-splintered silence, staring up at another tumbling sheaf of ivy the same as all the rest.

But not to Bastyan. With a satisfied hum thrumming deep in his broad chest, he parted the ivy strands and laid his shoulder to the wall, pushing inward and peeling sideways.

A seam opened up as the stone rolled back on itself.

Bastyan stepped clear, dusting off his hands. "You know your streets. I know mine." With a tilt of his head, he beckoned me toward the gap, resting his hand on the overhang of it—the same sway of his lean, muscular body as when he'd leaned into the ship's galley.

I managed only two steps after him before my muscles stiffened. "Bastyan, I…"

No words would come.

He glanced away from the gap. "What?" And then, studying my face, he straightened and turned—paying me his full attention. "What is it, Lio?"

What could I tell him without revealing the truth of who I was? What could I do but ask him to take me back?

Back to Lucretzia, with her scorching remarks and her revulsion at the woman I had made of myself. Lucretzia, with her iron shackles and pinching, perverse fingers. Lucretzia, sporting a hole in her shoulder and a broken face from our escape.

Despair shuddered in my core. I could not draw a full breath past the lump lodged in my throat.

Could I not be of better aid to Tristah if I reached her on my own terms, rather than returning to Shadewyle in chains?

Swallowing the biting tang of selfishness that soaked my tongue, I croaked, "I've never been this way before."

He studied me a moment longer; then he offered one of those blinding grins. "I have. Plenty of times. Trust me, aye? I'll get you through. Nothing comes between us."

Scuffing my jaw with his tattooed knuckles and bumping his forehead to mine, he ducked through the hole in the seawall. With a last glance back the way we had traveled—back toward my faraway captor, who had assured me I would never lay eyes on Tristah again in her charge—I steeled my heart and stepped into the gap behind Bastyan.

CHAPTER 22
SHADOWS COME ALIVE

he darkness did not last.

Only our first few steps were taken in shadow; and then, roused by the brush of our hands on the narrow edges of the hewn tunnel, iridescent silt and glowing worms unfurled among the crags in the rock.

My breath hitched at the sight; Bastyan cast a look over his shoulder, softness touching the lines beside his eyes. "Really something, isn't it?"

"I had nearly forgotten," I confessed, "that such beauty still existed in pockets of Amere-Del."

Bastyan slowed, stretching out the moments that breathed in the lustrous dark; and then he surged forward all at once, tearing aside another clot of hanging ivy, and we slithered from the wall.

At once, we were immersed in the music of the night beyond the confines of Monsha. The jungled foothills of the Barradir Highlands, fed by the salty seawater, encroached on every side. Trilling nightbirds, chattering creatures, and humming insects all raised their voices in a spirited song.

"This way." Bastyan tilted his head.

We moved at a swifter clip now that the city lay behind us. Brushing through thick foliage and clambering over swoop-bodied trees, we pressed deeper into the jungle's decadent embrace. In the absence of Lucretzia's relentless attention laid at the nape of my neck like a blade, courage wound an unbreakable twine around my bones.

I would find a way to free Tristah—my *own* way. Perhaps even with the aid of the sailor who accompanied me, shouldering ahead through the verdant landscape.

"Bastyan." I laid a hand on his shoulder. "there is something I—"

We broke cover all at once, and again my breath tumbled to a halt. My fingers slipped from his back.

Moonlight glowed over a sheer-sided cove below, carved into a basin beneath the nearest foothills. I could not see how one sailed in or out of it, unless by some false wall or invisible seam in the foliage.

But there must be a way; for a ship slumbered in the heart of it, nearly twin to *The Athalion*, its sails run up.

"Whose ship is this?" I demanded.

"A friend's." Bastyan measured the distance with his gaze, then took several steps back from the ledge. "Ever been cliff-jumping?"

"No, I—"

"Well, shouldn't be too bad the first time."

He took a running start—and lunged over the edge.

My startled shout was lost in the impact of Bastyan cleaving into the water, vanishing in a surge of foam. For a moment, my guttering pulse stilled, my ears echoing with the deafening spray of water.

But then he rose again, treading in place, sweeping his hair to lay flat against his head. A pale glint of teeth knifed the shadows below. "Coming?"

"Ahim be *merciful*," I seethed, stripping off my boots.

I dove feet-first; I did not trust the depths of the cove as Bastyan did. But there was a strange peace that came with the surge of water closing over my head; for a moment, I floated within the pause, eyes open. In the crystalline cove, all was defined by vague impressions; glowing rocks far below my feet. A current eddying toward a particular portion of the wall. Gilded fish winnowing past in swift flickers.

Bastyan dipped below the surface, soaked and shining. Shadows clouded the water around him; he jerked his head, and we were off.

It was not a long swim to the ship, but my limbs throbbed with the strain of pulling against my sodden clothes by the time we reached it. There was no ladder; instead, rungs were bolted into the hull. Bastyan mounted them with the confidence of familiarity; I made my ascent much more slowly, wary of my slippery boots and chilled fingers gliding numbly along the iron.

It was a relief to pull myself up at last, spilling onto the deck. Hauling up on my elbows, I gazed about the empty ship; in contrast to the perpetual bustle aboard *The Athalion*, it was all but a boneyard.

Bastyan strode fearlessly into it; he knotted his hair at his nape as he went, whistling that same shanty from the wall.

And when he passed through the midst of the ship, shadows came alive.

They peeled away from the masts and quarterdeck; they rose from the hatch that led below. They crawled like spiders down the rigging and descended on slings in slow, acrobatic spins, not unlike the performing troupes who called Krylan home.

My stomach shriveled. "Bastyan. What *is* this?"

He did not turn my way as the shadows encroached—men and women in threadbare, patchwork raiment. All gaunt in various ways, from lean bodies to hunger-panged eyes. But over his shoulder, Bastyan called, "Best not to call me that aboard this ship."

A man stepped into the slant of the moonlight, nearer than the rest; his skin was dark as pitch, and he reached for me with a three-fingered hand.

I scrambled to my feet, dodging around his hold, hastening after Bastyan as he mounted the steps toward the empty helm. "Tell me what we are *doing here!*"

"Siu," he called to someone behind me, "raise the colors."

"Aye, Captain!" a woman bellowed back—and with a snap, a flag unfurled and ran up the mainmast, echoing the crackling disbelief that railed in my head.

Captain—

A flicker of a symbol halted me halfway up the steps; slack-jawed, I took in the black etchings backdropped against the stained brown flag.

My heart fled my chest.

A skull, splashed against a crossed violin and bow.

My hand slammed down on the railing that curved along the steps; it was all that held me up as I wrenched back around to face the helm.

The helm where Bastyan stood, shedding his blue Trader's tunic…reaching for a coal-black coat strung on a peg behind the wheel.

Words rotted in my mouth, floating like ash over my lips. "Bastyan Atreyon—"

"Does not exist." He flung the coat on over his bare chest—a Captain's coat, sable as the depths of night. "You're aboard *The Dread Singer*, captained by Ryker *Blackhand* Kassian and his Raiders."

Blackhand.

Mad pirate. Plunderer of the depths. Bane of the seas.

No. No, no, no—Ahim, have mercy—

Captain Julas's story could not be coming alive before my eyes—could not be embodied in *him*, the deckhand who had befriended me, the man I had begun to…that I had thought perhaps I might *want* to…

That thought deserted me. Along with every other.

All that remained was a pulsing, flaring coalbed of hurt, of fury, of *betrayal* that throbbed in my core, timed to the erratic tempo of my heart.

"You *liar*," I hissed, pulling myself up the railing hand over hand toward him—toward that smug, smiling countenance. Not sunshine, but flame. A ruthless, consuming wildfire of a grin. "You wicked, blasted *liar*!"

I lunged up the last step, unsheathing Lucretzia's blade, intent on piercing whatever inch of him I could reach; but he pirouetted with vicious ease, catching my wrist and spinning me to rest against the railing. Effortlessly, he turned the knife back to lay against my clavicle. "Already resorting to violence, *Delina*?"

And with that word, he ruined me. Shattered me in ways beyond repairing. He had known. He had *known*, all this time.

I had not befriended a sailor. I had been deceived by a *pirate*.

With a brutal twist of his fingers, he jammed my wrist, freeing the blade. It dropped—straight into his other hand. He sheathed it in his belt as he stepped back, turning me by my wrist and casting me into the hands of the three-fingered sailor who'd crept up the steps behind me.

I did not dodge him this time. I did not fight. My clothes were laden and heavy, my heart heavier still. Shock and grief pounded against me like Lucretzia's fists in a training exercise.

I had not been rescued after all. I had only traded one captor for another.

"Put her in my quarters," Bastyan—*Ryker*—ordered.

I barely mustered the strength to dig my heels in as we descended the steps—to make it some sort of struggle for the man who dragged me along. But that was all the resistance I had left.

The sailor shoved me into the Captain's quarters and drew the twin doors shut at my back. I had only a moment to breathe it in—a warm, polished room, all shimmering wood and deep scarlet and amber tones—

A lock clicked behind me…and the finality of that echo revived my rage.

"*Bastyan*!" I spun away from comfortable cage and lunged to the door; I yanked against its knob, slamming my palms against the wood. "*Blackhand*!"

But no one came.

The sailor I had just begun to trust…the one I had leaped into the sea for, the one I had defied Lucretzia for, the one whose parting smile I had thought might be enough to sustain me all the way to Shadewyle…he was gone.

He had never existed at all. I had been taken in by a *pirate*, of all people.

A pirate who knew precisely who I was.

CHAPTER 23
DEBTS AND MERITS

RYKER

So. That had gone about as well as expected.

The familiar creak of my own ship under my feet was the only sound that made it through the pounding in my skull while I bent over the basin in the sick bay, scrubbing the last of the brick dye out of my hair. Good riddance—the stuff itched something fierce. I'd hated slathering it back on after my tumble into the reef.

Thank the depths none of the Athalion crew had noticed the black sloughing off while they'd toted my sorry, half-conscious hide off to Hasser's little storeroom.

Not to complain about a man who'd shoved the water out of my lungs, pieced my head back together, and somehow kept the pain of a coral scrape in my shoulder to a dull roar...but I hadn't liked his chamber. Sick bay on *The Athalion* had felt like a land-leg's infirmary, and smelled like it, too.

Not here. Not in the realm of Greenfinger—the better healer of the two, if I had to stake my life on it.

He perched on his stitching table behind me, watching me strip my hair back to the color of sand at sunrise. And I kept waiting for him to say what he was thinking—the thing I didn't much care to be thinking about.

Finally, he spoke up in that deep, accented mumble of his. "Kory says the Delina stopped railing about a half-hour after he locked the door."

"Good," I muttered into my dripping palm, slapping another handful of water out of his washbowl and towing it through my hair. I tried to shove out the sound of her screaming my name…the hate in it. The way she'd sounded like I'd just run her through.

"That was the longest con you've ever pulled, brother." He stopped, waiting for me to fill in the gaps. I didn't much feel like it. "Seems like it worked out."

It had, that…better than I'd dreamed. Befriending the long-lost Delina had almost come easy. She hadn't been uptight, suspicious like everyone I'd shook hands with whenever I got close to Del Graven.

She was loose. Easygoing. Sassy and big on opinions, but there was no arguing she'd caught me off guard a few times. She reminded me of the sea like that; and depths if I hadn't just kicked up a maelstrom getting her secured on my ship.

Something nibbled in my gut like a skin-eating fish. I slapped it down and dumped another handful of water over my head, leaning my elbows on the edge of the bowl and watching the last of it drip from the tip of my nose.

Finally clear.

I straightened up, grabbing a towel off the edge of the basin and blotting off my face while I turned to face Gydeon Greenfinger Nassar…the *Singer's* healer and my own brain outside my skull. He slouched on the table's edge, running his fingers through the tangled bush of a beard hanging halfway down his chest.

If I wasn't mistaken, he'd gone a little grayer since I'd hopped aboard *The Athalion*, calling myself Bastyan…a name I'd left behind in the canals down in Korsa when I'd been given the choice to stay a slave or make my way as a pirate.

No looking back. Not on that name. Not on the longest, trickiest con I'd pulled yet…and it wasn't really over. Not with the Delina locked in my quarters.

I wrapped the towel strangling-tight around my fists, leaning back on the washbasin stand. "She seem all right? Did Kory say?"

"Well, she cursed herself hoarse," Gydeon offered, and my mouth tugged off to the side. "But Willy poked his head in when he left the bread and water you asked for. Said she was asleep on the divan."

I let out my breath, slow as a sail. "You mind looking in on her?"

"What for?"

He didn't sound surprised. More like he was searching me out when he already knew what I was sick with.

I shrugged. "They didn't treat her right…before or now. She's got coral-scrapes on her hands and a rash from a shackle. Those could use looking after."

Gydeon's thick brows bunched together. "How do you mean they didn't treat her right?"

I weighed out how much to say. But he was a healer; he did his best work when he knew what he was dealing with. "She was scared, Gyddy. Feisty as a hungry gull when it was just her and me, or her with the crew. But she folded like a cut sail when her *escort* was around."

I couldn't keep my temper quiet when I thought about that black-eyed, fishbelly-pale snake. I'd expected her to shed her skin sometime on the way to the Everreach…I'd tried poking her from every angle, just to see what she'd do.

Hadn't expected her to dump me in the drink.

Hadn't expected Alyona Graven to fish me out, either.

Tonight could've been the best chance for sleep she'd had since we'd left Port Craythin…no hammock strung above a sneering leech, no fork-tongued captor watching her every move. But if I'd learned anything about her, she was dreaming about how to put that knife she'd stolen—the one I'd stolen from her—straight through my eye.

I teased it out of my waistband, striding to the table and setting it next to Gydeon. He swiveled to peer down on it, turning half as green as his namesake.

"That's the Pale Viper's dagger, no doubt," he breathed. "Wilkes would have a fit if he saw this."

"Aye." I pressed my fists into the tabletop on either side of the blade, eyeing it; it looked about as sharp as a viper's fang. Just as lethal, too. "Might have to wait for all of that to blow over before we make our demands to the Del."

"Mmhmm." Gydeon went back to fiddling with his beard.

I shot him a glance. "What, mate?"

"What, nothing. I'm agreeing with you." He kept his tone even—same way he talked to sailors while he pried shrapnel out of their hides.

Usually I didn't much mind it…he talked to everyone that way. But tonight it kicked my hackles up, for no real reason that made sense. "We have to go through with this, Gyddy. She's here. We've got her. There's nothing for it."

"True, that."

I shoved back from the table, pushing the tension out into my knuckles. Felt a bit too much like kneading dough. "Listen. We talked about this…it's the only way. We owe too much to the Old Salts. We don't get enough merits, they'll start collecting…first with the *Singer*, then from our hides." I clamped down on an old swell of panic that tried to seep up my throat at the thought of how those pirate lords played when *collecting* started. "The only way we get all the coin we need at once and slip the tethers together is if we plunder the Del's own coffers."

"I know, brother. We had this talk before you left."

I snatched up and stowed the dagger, scowling. "So why are you on my back about it, ay?"

Gydeon popped a brow up. "I'm not. You're the one in the whitecap."

Blasted chum-for-brains.

I grabbed my coat and threw it back on. "If it's her or every man and woman on this crew, I choose the crew. You've all been to the depths and back with me. Nothing in the last month changes that."

Maybe it changed what I dreamed about. And, sure as salt, it'd made leading the Delina here easier than I'd thought. She'd been so eager to get away from the Del's Own Blade, she'd run without looking back. And she'd trusted me enough to run with *me* wherever I led her.

She wouldn't be making that mistake ever again.

I set my teeth against each other, turning back to Gydeon. "Have Klem put us out on the Bashiri River through Way-In-The-Rock. So long as the Pale Viper doesn't place us, we should be safe bobbing in Sennesole Basin until this all blows over."

Gydeon slid off the table, thick boots thumping on the polished floor. "And then you'll start negotiating with the Del for the release of his heir."

"Aye." Patting off the last of the water from my neck, I bundled up the towel and tossed it into Gydeon's washbasket. "For enough merits, he'll have her back…and we'll finally be free."

The notion had my mouth watering.

Free to do whatever we wanted. Free to sail wherever, without worrying about a faster ship catching us up for trying to outrun what we owed. Free to gather merits for ourselves, not the Old Salts. Free of every blasted debt…the ones we'd stacked up getting out of tight spots, shrugging off past lives, just trying to make it to the next sunrise.

Aye. We'd be *free.*

And all we had to do was toss Lio back in her cage.

That water in my teeth turned sour in a second.

I wasn't a fool…at least, not an entire one. She'd lied through a smile about at least half of what she'd told me on *The Athalion*—who she was, what her escort was to her. But there'd been some truth in it, too.

I knew angry. I knew mistreated. I knew shipped off, choices stolen, prospects skinny and getting skinnier.

That's what Lucretzia—Cress, the Del's Own Blade—had been hauling her back to. It's where I was sending her anyway, a step ahead of the Pale Viper.

Grimacing, I shook off that thought. "Mind if I stay here while she's in my quarters?"

"In the interest of not having to stitch you up when she puts a chair leg through your thick skull?" Gydeon snorted. "You have your pick of the sick cots. I'll let Siu know, so you don't startle her when she comes in off second watch. Can't have *her* putting a chair leg through your skull, either."

"Aye. Thank you for that, Gyddy."

"Whatever and whenever you need it." He thrust out his hand. "Good to have you back aboard, Captain. The ship was going stir-crazy waiting for Blackhand to man the helm again."

I gripped his forearm and tugged him in, clapping him on the back. "It's good to be back, mate."

And that was the truth.

Didn't stop up that hole leaking in my stomach when I laid out on the nearest bed and finally closed my eyes. I'd been awake too blasted long…rolling out of my hammock to see the city with the Delina before sunrise.

I dropped an anchor on those thoughts…sent them floating to the depths.

That was behind me. The first part of the voyage was done. It was time to dodge the Viper's eye; then we would deliver the ransom—and the spoils—to the Del.

The choice had been made before I'd ever laid eyes on Alyona Graven.

Still. Didn't stop me from dreaming.

CHAPTER 24
KINDNESS IN A PLACE OF CRUELTY

espair and rage, sullied together, were like an illness—one which ravaged me for days.

Curled on the divan in my lovely prison, pained with the defeat of doors I could not break and barred windows that refused to shatter despite all I'd ransacked in the room and flung at them, I at last turned to ride the tides of sickness churning in my gut.

For some time, I slept; and when I woke, I wept into the shield of my arm draped over my eyes—wept at my own foolishness and the cruelty of a world that had not yet grown bored of wounding me.

I had so rarely trusted anyone since my parents' passing…and when I had, that trust had been held like a sacred oath. By Tristah. Even by Addie.

But Bastyan—*Ryker*—had trampled on it. Defiled it without care.

That was the way of pirates. I had not ever thought it would be his way with *me*.

Though, truly, I had never known him; and I had never felt more the fool than whenever that thought visited me, kneading my stiff spine and hissing mockery in my ear.

I had told him so much about me…all that I could without risking Lucretzia's wrath raining down on us both. And in turn, he had kept me well-fed on lies. A false name. A false heritage.

Bastyan Atreyon does not exist.

I would never forget those words. They were branded in my mind like the sear of hot oven stones against flesh; just as I wore a scar from such a mishap on my inner wrist, I would always carry the blistering reminder of Ryker Kassian's cruel deception.

And now I had to find a way off his ship…to rescue Tristah entirely on my own.

No sooner did my thoughts stray from my own fury and anguish to that daunting task than, for the first time in my waking hours, a knock came at the cabin door. "Mind if I come in?"

I tore my gaze from the bay windows behind the divan, where I had been staring for hours; these were blackened with pitch, so I had no bearing of where we were. The only light came from the lanterns I lit now and again on the bolted-down desk, shedding light across Blackhand's quarters.

By that light, I'd searched for any weak seams in the bay window; I had found none yet.

"So long as you are not anyone bearing the name Kassian, or Blackhand, or any moniker of his…yes," I snapped.

The door nudged open, and a man entered, carrying a bundle under one arm and a wrapped loaf of bread in the other hand. He was taller, broader than all of the sailors I had met on these terrible voyages…built like a lumberer or even a man of the militar. But there was a gentleness about him, in the creases of his eyes and the perpetual smile that ruffled the edges of his beard.

He reminded me of Julas in a way that panged low in my throat.

Did *The Athalion's* Captain know he had consorted with a pirate?

Before I could tease that thought—and consider the possibility of perhaps another betrayal in my wake—the man toed the door shut and crossed the room. The fragrance of rosemary and goat cheese stroked my nose from the bread in his hand, and water sprinkled between my teeth. I had nibbled at the hard bread and cheese that appeared inside the door each time I woke, but this smelled fresh—warm.

Likely baked in that cove where this pirate vessel had slumbered, awaiting its Captain's return.

"I presume Blackhand told you to ply me with bread?" I eyed the man from my perch on the divan; what a pretty prisoner I must appear, curled against the swooping armrest, hugging my knees to my chest.

Only that huddled posture kept my pieces from cracking apart.

The man smiled without guile as he set the loaf on the Captain's desk. "He might have mentioned your penchant for baked goods, yes."

With some effort, I turned my face back to the window. "I want nothing from him."

"Fair enough. I can see how you'd feel that way. But you're on his ship now, Delina. Everything you touch is his. One way or another, you have something from him."

Sullen, I glanced his way and mumbled, "Do not call me that."

"All right." He leaned against the table's edge, spreading his palms out low at his sides. "What would you like me to call you?"

"Alyona."

He studied me a long moment. "You know, aboard a pirate vessel, everyone has their given name and the name the Captain and crew calls them. You can be Alyona here, but you can be something else, too." Gripping his thighs, he pushed himself up straight, crossing the cabin in only a few strides. "For example…the name's Gydeon Nassar. But the crew calls me Greenfinger."

He offered a broad palm my way; the grooves of it were softened and stained green with herbs.

"You're the ship's healer," I ventured, eyeing that hand.

"I am. So, what can I call you while you're aboard this ship, Alyona?"

I did not lift my gaze from his expectant fingers; a thousand warning cymbals clashed in my head, all of them carrying the echo of Lucretzia's scathing tone. Blackhand's smirking truths.

Bastyan Atreyon does not exist.

But, merciful Ahim…just a bit of kindness. A bit of *decency.* That was all I craved; a makeshift bandage over my broken heart.

"Lio," I whispered, and loosely clasped his hand. "You may call me Lio."

"All right, Lio." His smile gentled, and he reached backward, drawing a chair from the desk and settling into it. "May I have a look at your hands?"

I allowed it; he examined the coral scrapes, which had angered some while climbing the wall in Monsha and swimming the cove. His thumb grazed my sleeve as well, baring the bruise around my wrist where Lucretzia had forced the fetter shut in the streets, pinching skin.

"I can give you tinctures and salves for these," he offered. "If you're willing to accept something from the *Singer's* crew."

I tugged my hands back. "What I would more gladly accept is an explanation. Where are we sailing? What does your *Captain* intend for me?"

"I could tell you that…but I think it's a conversation better had between the two of you."

I scoffed, settling back against the divan. "I would not trust a word from that man's mouth if it came with a thousand merits and an oath to Ahim himself."

"Hmm." Gydeon stroked his beard, folding his other arm across his soft middle. "That creates quite a dilemma, doesn't it? You'd like an explanation, but you won't trust one. What good is it to you, then?"

I opened my mouth, then shut it again.

Another of those thick smiles peeked through his beard. "*I search for clarity in deception's dark waters, where the lines of truth and fiction blur. The ones I once trusted have become strangers, their words a weapon, their promises a curse.*"

A shiver traced along my spine. "And are you the ship's poetmaster as well?"

A quiet chuckle. "No, not by far. I had a friend once who was fond of that sort of thing…that stanza belongs to the infamous Kilgrave."

I'd come across his work now and again in my tutoring—though I had never considered poetry could flash like a firework in the dim depths my life had recently become.

"It's a bit of truth, though, isn't it?" Gydeon added quietly. "It becomes difficult to believe anything when you've faced a betrayal of that depth."

"Yes, it is." All that I would dare give him, with those words still rattling about in my head.

His earnest eyes searched mine. "Would you sooner trust an explanation from *me*?"

Scowling, I tugged my feet onto the divan. "How can I trust anyone who sails beneath the flag of such a liar and a villain?"

"I'm sure I'd say the same, if I was sitting where you are." Gydeon hesitated a moment; then he added, "May I try?"

Confusion softened the harsh edge of my temper. "May you—?"

Lurching up from the chair, he came to the divan, settling himself next to me; I drew as far from him as the seating would allow, and he put distance between us on his side. Hands clasped in his lap, he trailed his eyes around the room; then he leaned his head on the swooped back, gazing up at the dim ceiling.

"Ryker is a liar," he allowed at last—such faultless honesty that it made me sit taller, prodded with shock. "He's a scoundrel, and one of the most notorious pirates in these waters. However…I would suspect you have nothing to lose by making him tell you the truth of why you're here."

The scoff came weakly this time. "And you assume I can believe him? On what grounds?"

"Because he stands to gain nothing by painting a pretty picture of what's to come." Gydeon's brutal honesty speared into my throbbing heart. "You would not believe him if he claimed to be sailing you to some sun-washed island where you might spend the rest of your days in peaceful solitude. You don't trust him enough to expect kindness. So, he has no reason to lie. There is little you can do to turn the rudder on that ship, anyway."

I sank my chin onto my knees. "If not kindness, then…"

Gydeon eyed me sidelong for a moment. Then he said, quietly, "I won't lie and say that you're here for your own good, Lio. But this crew has no cause to mistreat you while you're with us." His gaze dipped to my hands, locked about my ankles tighter than Lucretzia's shackles. "Let me give you something for your wounds. Eat the bread. These might be kindnesses in a place of cruelty, but you aren't punishing *him* by refusing them. You're only harming yourself."

Defiance rippled through my every nerve, but it perished swiftly when my stomach quivered, my next inhale warmed with the scent of rosemary and cheese.

He was right; if I was to escape this ship, a lack of food and drink would not serve me. I would need all of my wits and strength to be rid of this place…and of these pirates.

I had done it from Shadewyle, but I was not the same woman now that I had been then. I required cunning. Power; not just in my mind, but in my body as well.

This task demanded eyes wide open.

Ryker had deceived me to lure me aboard his ship; I had been trained to deceive men far cleverer, to have my way as Delina.

I would take power where I could. Where I *must*.

So, though it felt like handing triumph to the likes of Lucretzia and becoming all she desired of me, I slid my feet down to the floor and twisted to face Gydeon. Once again, I offered him my hands. "You may give me what you wish. And after I eat that bread, I require an audience with your Captain. He will join me for supper, if he ever hopes to lay claim to his rooms in the same order in which he left them."

"There you go." He winked. "I'll have my wife, Siu, come and fetch you. I suspect she can rustle up something for you to wear to this supper."

I marshalled my features to dry mockery. "Is your loyalty to your Captain, or to me, Greenfinger?"

He barked a laugh, rising to retrieve his healer's bundle from the table. "Ryker got himself into this mess. It's not my fault if it's torture for him getting out of it."

I liked this healer.

I did not trust him, nor would I ever. But I liked him well enough that I could build my lies off of that small truth.

And from it, I would undo everything Blackhand had plotted for me.

CHAPTER 25
PIVOT AND PARRY

iu Nassar proved as difficult to dislike as her husband.

She arrived hours after his departure, her arms laden down with silks and muslin and fabrics from likely countless plunders; all of it she tossed onto the foot of the divan, then offered her hand to me.

"Steady Siu. First Mate, mother to these reckless Raiders, and wife of Gydeon," she introduced herself. "If you hurt him in *any* way, I have a pistol on hand at all times, and a lead ball with your name etched into it. Are we clear?"

I measured the absolute sincerity of that threat—in the pinch of her mouth, in the seriousness of the bright blue eyes peering from beneath the fringe of her deep scarlet forelock, in the steadiness of the hand thrust my way.

A truce offered. And a vow demanded on behalf of the ship's healer.

"My contention is not with your husband." I clasped her hand.

"Then I have none with you…yet." Siu gave my fingers a perfunctory squeeze, then stepped back, perching her hands on her broad hips. "I'd apologize for how you've been treated, but you're the only one not sleeping in a hammock or on a cot. Or a mattress on the floor. So, let's get to business, shall we?" She dove into the pile of cloth, tossing various pieces into my lap. "How would you prefer to torture the Captain?"

"What choices are there?"

"I'm delighted you asked." A sharp smile snaked across her lips. "If your intention is to make him regret how he ever wronged you, I suggest purples…a noble color. A reminder that, despite his captaincy, you *far* outrank him."

My heart stumbled at the sight of so much silken purple sliding through her hands—a favorite hue in the Del's household. "Perhaps not."

Her gaze flicked up to me; then she shrugged. "Fair enough. Red, if you're as furious with him as your demeanor suggests."

I glanced down at my fists, pressing into the divan on either side of me. "Is *that* a cause for contention between us?"

She snorted. "Captain makes his own choices. And for what it's worth, I was never fond of this scheme. I won't say I don't see his reasons, but the consequences? The enemies he's making along the way? Those are his battles to fight, not mine." She slid a midriff shirt from the heap, etched in bright green and deep blue threading. "What about this? Traditional Ameresh jewel tones…vitality and femininity. I have a skirt to match."

Bearing down a deep breath, I pushed myself to my feet. "I suppose it will suffice."

In truth, it would more than suffice; I intended to command the galley tonight. I would make known my fury. I would have him trust it…so that he would also trust when I pretended to lose it. So that he would look the other way. And then I would be free of him.

I stepped into the Captain's private washroom to change; it felt like a farewell to a true friend as I removed the clothing Reinera had given me and slipped into the vivid skirt and midriff shirt from the *Singer's* First Mate.

But it was all required of my ruse.

"You have a way with colors," I remarked through the open door, splintering the unnerving silence from the main quarters.

"Well, I was an artist once." Siu offered nothing more.

I stepped from the washroom, bundling my dirty clothes in my arms, the folds stiff with days of sweat and shed tears. Siu eyed me up and down, gave a low whistle, then stuck out her hand.

"I'll wash those after I bring you to the galley."

I cocked a brow. "Must I be escorted everywhere?"

She snorted. "Aye, *Delina*. Captain warned us you're clever. For now, you don't set foot anywhere without an attendant."

Understandable. And the first link in these shackles I would have to break to escape these pirates.

I loathed the recognition—and the brief moment of relief—that came from spotting Blackhand when Siu ushered me through the galley door. But by the time she shut it behind me, the latch clicking softly into place, the relief had already boiled over into fury.

The wicked Captain lounged at a table halfway through the broad galley, its notched surface adorned with twin platters of herb-dusted, lemon-ringed fish; and I was not the only one who had come to this plotted meal with plans to deceive and distress.

He looked like Bastyan again, dressed in a plain linen shirt, trousers stuffed into his boots; except that these were core black, the shade of piracy. They contrasted starkly with his hair…no longer the deep sable hue I had found myself searching for aboard *The Athalion*, but a rich wheat-gold. And against the broad planes of his chest hung a ship's wheel pendant, tarnished silver, blackened as if rubbed a thousand times by his thumb.

Disgust bobbed in the center of my throat. "Captain."

"Delina." His eyes tracked me as I crossed the room, lingering on the soft folds of my stomach peeping through the midriff shirt. "You look lovely."

"And you appear precisely how you truly are…a scoundrel and a pirate, with a mind only for his own desires."

He winced, flashing a sheepish smile. All teeth—a shark's blood-hungry grimace. "I deserved that."

"That is the *least* of what you deserve." I raked out the seat across from him, settling into it with the poise and grace taught me by Athyna Graven.

My palms heated at the thought of her…the reminder that I had worn blood on my hands before. That I might do it again, if this pirate also put himself between me and the path to freedom.

"However," I added sharply when he opened his mouth to speak, "I am feeling gracious this evening. Which is why you are here."

He reclined, the corners of his mouth twisting up—a mere shadow of the sunshine smiles he'd worn aboard *The Athalion*. Another piece of his cruel masquerade. "Now, which of us is Captain?"

"I see no Captain before me. I see only a man who likely won this ship by cheating and bloodshed. You have no more *earned* the title of Captain than I have the title of—"

"Delina?"

A pivot. A parry.

We stared at one another in lanternlight which guttered to the precise tune of a chuckle—as if Ahim himself regarded our exchange with amusement.

"Whatever my origins," I seethed, "I have earned that title a hundred times over."

"So have I." Blackhand's mouth stretched into an arrogant smirk. "So, let's not insult one another, aye? There's only so much hate I can take before it gets me hot under the collar."

The very breath we shared was an insult. Every memory of the sailor I had thought him was an insult. His jesting was an insult.

But I conceded that ground, reaching for my fork. He had not left me a knife.

"Where are we?" I demanded—a safe beginning to test his capacity for truth.

"Sailing up the Bashiri River, to Sennesole Basin." His reply came without hesitation, nor with a trace of dishonesty. But I could not trust myself to sniff out his lies any longer.

"And what will we do there?"

"Float with the docking ships and wait for the Pale Viper to give up hunting us."

A despicable silence encroached, thick with shared memories and knowledge I had no desire to hold in common with him. I did not want to meet Ryker Kassian's eyes across this table and see the grim reflection of what I had once thought I shared with Bastyan Atreyon...what had once united us.

For a moment, I regretted that I had ever leaped overboard to save him from the reef.

But what was done was done; and now we were here, and his recitation of our heading rang true. So I forged ahead: "Something about all of this is a lie. The Blackhand legend is far older than you."

"Sharp as ever." He took up his fork and knife, slicing into his fish. "I'm the *latest* Blackhand. The title's been carried by the Captain of *The Dread Singer* for generations."

"And you are—?"

"The tenth Blackhand, or so the last one told me."

"And what makes you so fearsome…besides your ability to lie with a smile on your face?"

His knife skated shrilly against the plate; we both sucked in our breath. Slowly, his gaze lifted to me.

"Blackhand's reputation is as swarthy as they say." His voice dropped, a bass murmur which matched the creaking of the ship and its slow churn over the water. "I've plundered my share of ships like Julas's. Sunk a few, when the Captains wouldn't give me what I asked. You want to know if I've cheated, murdered, lied? Aye. More than I can count. You weren't the first."

"Tell me why."

He studied me for a long moment. Then he set aside his fork and knife. "Crewing doesn't come for free. When I became Blackhand, I picked up a whole new crew…and all the debts they owed. That made us strong, at first. Now it's made us vulnerable."

"So you plan to sell me, then. Sell me for the merits to pay off your debts."

"I never doubted you were clever, Delina."

And so was he. Reinera had painted a vision of a Del far more desperate than even the one I had known, steeped in paranoia and made cruel by it. Doubtless he would pay a hearty sum to have me returned…Blackhand could all but name his price.

No different from Sorai. I was a prize for yet another man, wielded at his will.

I tossed down my fork and covered it with my napkin. "You use me, then, because you are a poor Captain who cannot choose a worthy crew."

His hand struck the table's edge. "'*Ay*. Insult me all you like…curse my name to Ahim if it makes you feel better. But don't you ever insult *them*. The men and women who crew this ship are cut from a better cloth than all the rest of us. You keep them out of this."

The passion in his tone stilled my tongue. He stood to gain nothing from vulnerability—and the sheen of his eyes spoke of a loyalty to this crew that went deeper than even the camaraderie I had witnessed aboard *The Athalion*.

Deep enough, perhaps, to make capturing and selling off a runaway heir seem conscionable.

Cobbling together the fraying cords of my composure, I perched my hands in my lap and inclined toward him. "And how did you come to find me, Blackhand?"

He matched my posture, though his hands he perched on the table. When he leaned near, a waft of seawater and leather engulfed me—nearly enough to make my mouth sweat again.

"Rumors of you sprouted all over the southern half of the country…how the Delina had been spotted, after she'd been assumed dead all this time. How that would change things for the regime. But the Del's Own Blade didn't go south, she went north. So that's the way I went, too…"

His lips still moved, sketching the outlines of his entire nefarious scheme…but I did not hear them. I heard nothing but the roar of blood swelling in my ears.

Rumors of you sprouted all over the southern half of the country—

And all at once, I was laughing.

Laughing so hard, my sides ached. Laughing until tears budded and ran from the corners of my eyes. Laughing until Blackhand shut his mouth and sat back, staring, one hand squared on the table as if he was prepared to leap away from me. "Delina—?"

"She's all right." I bowed my head into my hands and wept with joy. "She is *safe.*"

Rumors of me in two places could only mean one thing: someone had spotted Tristah. Which meant she was free—somewhere in the Southlands, veiled among the dissenters.

Lucretzia had lied. Tristah was not a prisoner in Shadewyle. She was not Zorast's captive.

Yet.

The notion noosed my runaway joy to a stumbling, gagging halt.

They did not have her *yet.* But now that I was gone, Lucretzia would not hesitate to make good on that first threat she had leveled back in Port Craythin. To hold Tristah as a knife to my back, forcing me to walk the path they set before me.

If they did not pursue us now aboard this ship, they might never try. Instead, they would find *her.*

Because they knew that I had been prepared to go all the way to Shadewyle Castle, the bed of my nightmares and horrors, for her. So that she would not be alone.

Everything will be as it was.

Tristah and I, both slaves to the Del's whims. Tristah and I, returning together to the training grounds where Lucretzia would beat us like unshaped steel. Tristah and I, forced to restrict our eating, forced to wear the same clothes, to style our hair the same way, to learn the same lessons and attend all the same meetings…

Tristah and I, both fodder for the dissident leader the Del found the most influential. Two wives sworn to Algernon Sorai, to maintain the ruse. Two women by which the Del would give the dissidents what they craved…a swipe at leadership in Amere-Del.

A false sense of ruling for a man leashed to the Del by his heir and her decoy.

And Tristah, who beheld romance with caution, against whom intimacy had been wielded as a weapon before she had ever come to us in Shadewyle Castle; Tristah, strong and unyielding, clever and brave, who had wept in my arms at the thought of *belonging* to Sorai, her terror and heartache the very thing that had at long, long last sparked my courage to escape Shadewyle Castle once and for all…

They would force her back into it to lure *me*.

It would not be the Del's schemes. It would be *my* fault.

Blackhand slowly eased forward against the table's edge again. "Delina."

His voice pulsed from far off. I laid a clammy hand to my brow and encountered a sheen of sweat. "He's coming for her."

Eyes wide open.

I measured my breaths, sliding my hand down my face to smother my mouth, staring at the nearest guttering lantern.

Tristah was in the Southlands. Her name in the mouths of dissidents.

I must reach her before Lucretzia does.

Searing determination ripped through me—the same conviction that had emboldened me to rally the immigrants in Krylan. That had sent me over the railing into the sea when Blackhand had fallen. That had set my face against Lucretzia's in the hall outside the sick bay.

Take power where you can.

That furious resolve burned through my blood like hot oil. It shoved my spine straight to the seatback; it likened itself to the sort of heady rage that smoldered in a wildfire.

We would not go back. I would reach her first. No other possibility was worth considering.

And to do it, I needed a swift vessel unhampered by regulation and restrictions. One that would not think twice of undermining the Del's Own Blade.

I did not need a proper crew. I needed piracy.

And in a mere blink, I saw the way before me—a reshaping of what I had considered in the Captain's quarters. How I would use my talents and skills, not for my own sake, but for Tristah's.

Lucretzia, I couldn't match; I had always known it. Tristah had been far more her equal. But this pirate seated across from me, watching me with a balance of unease and suspicion...he was simple. Nefarious, wicked, self-seeking, and built of deception, yes; still, I could outthink him. Outwit him.

I held all of the ingredients in my hands; I had recipe to deceive him as thoroughly as he had deceived me. It required tactics I had not wielded in some time, taught to me by Lucretzia, Athyna, and Zorast. Methods which Lucretzia would never have been beguiled by, would never have trusted.

Blackhand did not *know* not to trust them.

And that would be my greatest weapon.

For Tristah's sake—and for my own—I could play this part.

And then, together, we would cast off the shackles of *all* our captors—the regime and these pirates. We would flee together, far from their manipulations and schemes.

All it required of me was to *act*.

Breathing deeply, I poured in the first ingredient of my deception. "If it's merits you seek, I can double your sum."

Blackhand arched a brow. "Now, this, I *have* to hear."

CHAPTER 26
THE DECOY AND THE DELINA

"In Shadewyle Castle," I began, "I was not alone."

Blackhand did not so much as blink.

"Not long after I was first brought to Shadewyle, there was an attempt on my life." An old, bitter dread curled my insides at the memory—when one of the Del's servants, a dissident in disguise, had cornered me in an empty hall and driven a blade into my side.

I'd still been just a girl; yet there had been no trace of compassion in the woman's face when she'd held me to the wall and smothered my mouth with one hand, piercing my flesh with the knife in the other.

Lucretzia had found us in moments. It was the first time I had witnessed the brutal, murderous efficiency of the Del's Own Blade, severing the servant's head without even a breath.

It took a moment to become aware of my own fingers pressing into my flesh, guarding the scar that remained.

"After," I croaked, "the Del was furious. Frightened." Perhaps the only time he had acted anything like a true father. "So he sent Lucretzia to find someone who could enter dangerous situations in my stead…who could take my place wherever a threat might arise."

I let my eyes fall shut—allowed the memory to manifest in the darkness behind them.

"She found Tristah."

The day we'd first met still burned bright in my mind: when I'd stepped from my chambers and met the girl being hauled toward me by the arm, thrashing and clawing at Lucretzia's gauntlet. We'd frozen when our eyes met…when we'd seen our own faces reflected in one another.

"We looked so alike, it's…it's almost certain we're related." A truth we had held like a special secret, one we'd whispered as girls when it had still mattered whether it was blood or simply love that forged our bond. "Tristah hardly knew her parents…they died of a plague when she was small. And my father had siblings he rarely spoke of, ones he parted ways with on terrible terms. We both hailed from Monsha, even; Lucretzia plucked Tristah from an orphanage not far from the one where the Del found me."

Each of these truths—truths I had never aired to anyone—Blackhand drank down in silence. His eyes never left mine.

"Blood or not, she was the perfect decoy," I went on. "So Lucretzia scarred her precisely where I was wounded, and that day, Tristah was bound to me."

I could still feel the suffocating press of my bed as I'd crumbled face-down into it, hands pressed over my ears, blocking out the shrill screams and spitting threats Tristah had hurled while Lucretzia cut her, deftly and precisely, along her side. I had feared Tristah would despise me for it…that I would wake with her hands around my throat.

Instead, we had become one another's bastion against the horrors of Shadewyle Castle.

"We had all of the same lessons, all of the same schooling," I murmured, fixing my gaze again on the dancing lantern's flame. "We trained step-for-step with Lucretzia. And Tristah…Tristah burned with a fire I did not possess. A passion for Amere-Del that strengthened as mine soured."

Perhaps I was giving away too much; but to convince him to aid in my schemes, I first had to convince him how integral Tristah was to the Del's.

"The night I fled Shadewyle Castle, I begged Tristah to leave with me." I wrenched my gaze to Blackhand's, finding that he still watched me—breathing shallowly, his hands white-knuckled, gripped together on the table. "And she did. I went north, and she fled—"

"South," Blackhand growled. "The rumors about you—"

"Are rumors of her."

Slowly, he sank back, threading a hand through his hair. "How have I *never* heard of this?"

"Because any whisper of it would have defeated the purpose," I scoffed. "No one was aware of Tristah's existence but the Del, his wife, and Lucretzia. The orphanage where she lived burned to cinders the same day they took her."

Another of Lucretzia's cold cruelties. And she would do far worse if she laid hands on Tristah with me still in the wind.

I fisted my trembling hands in the folds of my skirt. "However many merits you would reap ransoming me alone…imagine what you could demand for us both."

Blackhand stiffened. Shock blazed through his eyes, turning the rosemary-gray to a vivid green. "Come again?"

"Tristah is a variable not even Lucretzia has sorted out yet. The Del will be desperate to reclaim her. And you will not find her without my aid."

Blackhand barked an incredulous laugh. "You expect me to believe you're just going to lead me right to your friend…so I can sell you both off?"

I held his gaze, unflinching. "I do not believe you, of all men, have any right to assume what a person would and would not do for those they love. Tristah is *my* crew…she is the only family I have left."

The gleam of his gaze dimmed a bit. "Precisely why I don't expect you want me anywhere near her."

"If it isn't you, it will be Lucretzia," I snapped, and his eyes narrowed. "She will find Tristah to lure me back. She will do *unspeakable* things to my friend, because she has always known we are one another's weakness."

Perhaps, if I had heeded Lucretzia's warnings when she'd first brought Tristah to the castle—when she had told me not to befriend her, to treat her as a shield—we would have both been safer.

But we'd been hopeless from the start…family finding one another in the depths of suffering. Untraceable blood, but sisters in heart.

Blackhand said nothing, but thoughts flickered in his eyes like sprinkles of sugar winking in the sun.

Seizing the advantage of his silence, I plowed on: "You saw how she treated me. For Tristah, it will be far worse…it has always been worse for the decoy than the Delina. You, at least, I can trust to feed us and clothe us. I would rather we find her than the Pale Viper."

Conflict brimmed in his gaze as he studied me. At last, he said, "Betraying her to me…what's in it for you?"

My heart cracked at that word—even if I had no intention at all of truly betraying her. Tristah and I had proven long ago that we could escape the most fortified places in all of Amere-Del as long as we had one another. Escaping this vessel together would be simple compared to that.

But for any of this to go to plan, I had to convince Blackhand of my selfishness. My desperation.

"I gain a friend," I rasped. "Believe me, Blackhand, I care nothing for the merits you gain…but since you only speak the language of plundering and trickery and thieving, yes. I'll happily sell you on the sum. So, suppose we simply agree that we *both* stand to benefit from finding Tristah…and set sail for the Southlands, before everyone meets a worse fate."

He stared me down, his jaw working in a furious, silent grinding of teeth.

"Show me the scar," he said at last.

The demand caught me so utterly off-guard, I could only blink.

"Show me the wound that started all of this," he insisted. "The reason they brought her to stand in for you."

A test. I'd expected one, but there was something utterly intimate about this request; it moored me to the seat, indecision twisting my fingers more tightly into the seams of my skirt.

I had resigned myself to using every method to win his aid. But this…
For Tristah.

Slowly, I rose on unsteady legs and stepped deeper into the lanternlight. And I rolled down my high skirt's cinched waistband to bare the scar to the light.

It was many shades paler than the brown of my skin; as long as my middle finger, the wicked ridge followed the curve of my hip from just beneath my left-side ribs, stretching toward my back.

"The Del forced Tristah to show hers off at a meeting with his council." The words clawed from my tongue before I was even aware they hovered there. "To show the *strength* of the regime was untouched by the dissenters."

Nevermind that two girls, barely of bleeding age, had suffered, wept, and screamed, begged for mercy and cried for their mothers…all to prove the strength of the Graven name.

Blackhand eased his chair backward in a soft grind of wood against wood. He rounded the table's edge, halting before me, staring down at the scar that winked like a cold grin in the lanternlight.

He stretched out his hand; fingers knotted in the waistband of my skirt, I did not retreat.

Slowly, his thumb grazed the line of the scar.

A shudder pulsed through me. I sucked in a breath and held it captive in the depths of my lungs as his hand settled over the bare skin of my hip, fingertips warm and callused against the softest folds of my flesh, his thumb brushing back and forth along the scar.

For a moment, my fingers curled and caved inward, considering a strike—clean and swift. Taught to me by Lucretzia. The sort that would ensure he never touched me again.

And yet, the way his eyes held fast to that old wound, the tug between his brows, the set of his mouth…

It stilled me.

It was precisely how Bastyan had looked at the wound on my wrist from the shackles Lucretzia had forced on me.

After a long moment in which only my thundering heart filled the silence, his eyes lifted to mine. "I hope your friend looked in their faces at that council the way you're looking in mine right now."

He dropped his hand and brushed past me.

"Have Siu bring you to the maproom tomorrow morning," he tossed curtly over his shoulder. "We'll chart a course from there."

The moment the galley door shut, I crumbled down into my seat, pressing the back of my hand to my mouth. It muffled my racing breaths; it did not quiet my hurtling pulse.

I would not be leaving this ship anytime soon, after all…but that was my choice. My doing. My own hand stirring the batch.

I had done it; not made the perfect mix, but something that could be shaped and baked into it.

I had beguiled Blackhand.

And soon, I would find Tristah—before the Pale Viper could add to her scars.

CHAPTER 27
GO DOWN TOGETHER

or the first time since I'd last opened *The Secret Ingredient* for business, I woke in the morning with a blaze of excitement heating the marrow of my bones. It was a complex sort of eagerness, seasoned with determination and defiance—the potency of it would not allow me to lay down a moment longer once my eyes popped open.

I rolled to my feet and hastened to the washroom, my thoughts still hanging where I had fastened them all night: on Tristah. My reunion with my heart-sister awaiting on the horizon…not predicated on the wiles of the Del Graven regime, but on my wits pitted against Lucretzia's.

A harrowing challenge. But for Tristah, I would undertake it a thousand times.

I was already washed and dressed, perched in the chair behind the Captain's desk, when Siu came to fetch me; she greeted me with a raised brow and the slim edge of a smile, leaning cross-armed in the doorway. "You clean up nicely."

"Such is the nature of my upbringing." I pushed myself up from the chair. "Shall we?"

"You do realize this is the First Mate of a pirate vessel you're sassing."

"And I hope your Captain realizes I am the Delina who will have the choice between executing or acquitting him someday."

Siu met the lack of intentionality behind my lie with a hearty squawk of laughter; then she ushered me out onto the topdeck by my elbow.

By night, I had taken little time to survey the make of *The Dread Singer*. At best, it had been a scourge, the trickery of its Captain tarred into every seam. But by daylight, it was the vessel that would carry me to Tristah…and I despised it a little less.

We drifted steadily between the broad shores of the three-fingered Bashiri River…one of the two that flowed into the Southlands from the bay around Monsha. Sturdy trees and steep hills hugged the blue water on either side; it might have been lovely, once.

But that was before the blight.

It was some relief that, over the decades, the wash of powerful waters downstream from the Barradir Highlands and the bay around Monsha had flushed a good deal of the taint from these waters. In my grandmother's time, Southlanders had been wary to drink from even the swiftest-flowing rivers and streams, fearing the sickness that soaked their portion of the country in death.

Though the waters beneath the body of our vessel ran clear now, the rich blue expanse only made the lingering taint sharper on the shores; the evergreens were a mournful, ashen gray, their arms withered and drooping. The sparse foliage between their stiff trunks grew spindly and brittle, a thorny tangle at best.

I wrenched my gaze from the desolate landscape, the twist in my heart pinching into something unbearable. This was one of countless harms in Amere-Del that, even as its Delina, I had been powerless to cure.

So instead, I took measure of the ship and its crew.

They bantered among themselves, singing shanties and work songs as they went about their duties. I glimpsed a handful of faces I had seen the night we'd come aboard, ducking in and out of shadows among the masts and beneath the plain, parchment-brown sails. Those drab colors seemed a disguise for these waters, which all flowed from the Del's hand; on the open seas, doubtless they would run up the standard of the skull and bow again. A ship as built from lies as its Captain.

That notion focused my thoughts as Siu guided me down into the ship's belly, through a handful of slim halls, to a vault of a room strung fore and aft with lanterns. A table took up the bulk of it, bolted by iron fastenings to the floor; only one wall sat bare, two others lined with pigeonholes stuffed full of maps and charts. A map of the named countries in the Wellspoken World sprawled across the third: Mithra-Sha and Amere-Del, Hadrass-Drui and Navar-Bane, Zandrae-Rath, Kayne-Sor, and Torr-Kal—and the islands beyond.

Beneath the bold etchings of our continents, one of its foremost terrors awaited my arrival.

Captain Blackhand stood sturdy at the tableside, one arm crossing his middle and his free palm stroking down his sandy beard and mustache. He wore a pale shirt under his dark coat, that ship's wheel pendant still proudly on display. No glimpse of the Bastyan I'd known remained to disarm me today.

A woman hovered at his side, spinning a brass compass in her hand, then snapping it shut. Her deep sienna skin nearly blended with the wall behind her, but the bright Ameresh sash around her waist spilled like blood across her otherwise plain attire. Her gaze, like the Captain's, was fixed on the map.

When Siu kicked the door shut, Blackhand's attention sprang to us. His hand fell, settling on the tabletop; his arm remained a band around his middle, as if to defend himself from the blows I would've liked to land there.

Not now. I would worry about being rid of him—and perhaps leaving him some pain to remember me by—once Tristah was safe.

"Welcome to the map room." He jerked his chin at the woman. "And say hello to Klement Keen-Eye Drace, ship's navigator. Klem, this is—"

"Our Delina." No respect threaded her rich Ameresh accent; only a tangle of disdain, if I was favored by Ahim. That tone could lend itself just as well to true animosity. And with the numerous knives sheathed among the compasses and spyglasses strung across her hips, I was far from eager to learn if it was indeed the latter.

So different from *The Athalion*, this crew.

Siu dropped my arm, striding to the table. "Well? Let's hear it, Captain. What's the cause for this meeting so secret, I couldn't even whisper it over Gydeon's lips last night?"

"Figured you tossed me out for a reason." He shot her a playful scowl, then bent his knuckles to the tabletop. I joined him there, positioning myself across from Klement; it seemed safest to keep the breadth of the map table between us. "According to Klem, we, roughly, are here." He stabbed a finger at one of the river branches from the Bashiri, then slid it down the wending sketch to a broader pool of water. "Which means we're a day or so from Sennesole Basin, at most."

"Where we'll moor in." Klem gave the compass another spin, watching him through hooded eyes.

"Aye, I did say that." Blackhand tapped the map, keeping his gaze down; then he slashed his finger past it, across a ridge of mountains at the shore of the lake. "But we're sailing through."

Klement's eyes bulged. Siu sucked in a breath, then burst out, "*Through*?"

The Captain's eyes jumped to me. "Do you want to tell them, or should I?"

I cinched my arms at my waist, guarding against both women's incredulous stares as they landed against me. "They're your crew."

"It's your quest."

I gnashed my teeth tightly. "Your merits."

"Your friend."

Ahim have *mercy*.

"We're searching for a member of the Del's household," I muttered, ignoring Blackhand's arched brow. "Someone the Pale Viper will soon be hunting."

Klement's compass whizzed another turn, slicing the thickening silence that filled the cabin like smoke from a gritty hearth. "And why in the depths are we hunting the same prey as the Del's Own Blade? *Again*?"

"Simple. Twice the bodies means twice the ransom." Blackhand jerked his chin my way; I pierced him with a glare so mighty, he wouldn't meet my gaze. *Coward.*

"We already have what we need," Siu argued. "Why risk taking on more danger—more debt—just for the chance to cancel it out again?"

Blackhand quieted for a long moment. "Aye. We have that. But who knows what it'll take to make the Del bend? The more leverage, the better."

"Assuming it doesn't cost us the ship," Klement countered. "Or worse."

"I know what I'm doing."

"Aye. I'm sure you do," Siu said slowly, her gaze drifting between us.

Klement shook her head. "This is a terrible idea. How do we know this person even exists?" She didn't pause for Blackhand—or me—to protest. "We should stick to the plan. Put into port, haggle with the Del—"

"Decision's been made," Blackhand said curtly. "I tell us where to go, you tell us how to get there, Keen-Eye."

She fell into mutinous silence, snapping the compass shut and clenching her fingers around it.

It took effort to drag my eyes from that strangling grip, back to the Captain. "Where do *you* assume she would have gone?"

I was no fool; I knew Tristah, but Blackhand knew deception. He knew ways to and from Monsha I had never heard a whisper of. It would require our combined prowess to find her.

Blackhand dragged his thumb along his lower lip, following the map; then his gaze darted to Siu. "Korsa."

Her swift intake of breath unleashed a shiver of dread in my middle.

"And where, precisely, is Korsa?" I had not heard its name in my studies, nor seen it on any map—not even the one we gazed at now.

"Pirate's haven." Klement's tone was clipped. "Where they put in to trade goods, hide their stolen wares, smuggle their merits…"

"Pick up crews," Ryker added brusquely. "Perfect place for a lass on the run to disappear."

Disbelief scorched my throat. "You believe Tristah would have sailed with *pirates*?"

"If she had any sense? You tell me." Ryker lurched back from the table, fixing me with an unblinking stare. "We're the only ones not keeping names on the books that the Del could audit. If your friend wanted her trail wiped off the face of the country, a pirate vessel would be the only way to do it."

"Plenty of pirating vessels sail in and out of Monsha," Siu croaked, her skin still the pallid color of fresh dough brushed in a sheen of butter. "Wearing false sails…often plundered ones. It takes a sharp eye to spot them, but it can be done."

And doubtless Tristah would have known what to watch for, how to tell apart a pirate vessel and its crew despite their disguises. She had paid closer attention in our lessons than I ever had; if she had been the one to stumble into Ryker Kassian's path, she would not have been taken in.

I swallowed a harsh burn of self-deprecation, fixing my eyes on his detestable face. "If she sailed to this *Korsa*, then so must we."

Blackhand nodded, though reluctance weighed his every motion. "We'll pick up the trail from there."

"*Captain.*" Siu's voice wavered a bit.

"'Ay." Ryker circled the table, gripping her shoulders and giving her the slightest shake. "I won't let anything happen to you in there. To *any* of you…but you and Gyddy especially. Aye?"

Siu's crimson lips pinched into a thin line. She blinked, then rolled her eyes up to stare at the swaying strands of lanterns hanging above.

After a long moment, she twisted out from under Blackhand's grip, facing Klement. "You still remember the way in and out of the port from this side?"

Klement snorted, linking arms with her and tugging her toward the door. "I could sail that bottleneck in my sleep."

"No, you could *navigate* us there, *I* could sail us—"

They slipped out, shutting the door behind them with a ringing echo that reminded me all too harshly of another pair of girls...a Delina and a decoy who had left so many rooms just like this one, masking their fear and disgust beneath banter. Wrapping themselves up in their friendship like a cloak, a defense against the bitter things that hounded their heels.

I leaned back against the table's edge, folding my hands around the sides of my neck. My jolting pulse greeted me, dancing with wicked unease. "What is Siu frightened of?"

Blackhand reclined against the opposite side of the table, staring at the closed door. "You remember those debts I mentioned over dinner last night?" When I nodded, he went on, "We owe them to the Old Salts in Korsa…the pirate lords."

My stomach knotted. "Pirate *lords*?"

"Pirating isn't what it used to be…'least, not in Amere-Del. Taxes are so high and the militar comes down so hard on everyone, you can hardly get your boots off the land without help." He folded his arms tightly over his abdomen. "Trouble is, the Old Salts filled their coffers before things got so bad. So they have ships and merits to spare. Now-days, they don't have to go sailing and plundering for themselves…depths, they don't even have to leave Korsa. They get the new sealegs to do all the hard work for them. And we pay them back for the debts we owe out of the raids we make."

"I take it they are the more fearsome pirates?"

"The ones of legend? Aye." Blackhand grimaced. "The ravagers. The island-sinkers. They aren't afraid to gather debts from stealing pieces of you and selling them off on the skin-trade. And Siu…Siu owes a lot. Gydeon owes a little bit more."

I was almost frightened to ask, but the question forced itself from my stiff lips: "And you? What do *you* owe, Blackhand?"

He skimmed a hand back through his hair. "Let's just say, even if we wring every merit we can out of Del Graven…with only you, the crew gets out of debt, but I'm still in the noose."

Klement's disbelief settled sharply into place now. "Do they know?"

"No. Gydeon's a worrier, and half this crew wouldn't agree to having their debts paid off if I kept mine. They'd rather we all go down a few notches and still owe than leave one of us in the lurch. But I'm their Captain. I can't sail that way."

Surprise jerked my gaze to his face, just as he twisted to peer at me; in the lanternlight, the sharp angles that had shown like blades the night he betrayed me softened a bit. It reminded me too fiercely of a night spent in the galley, baking bread together.

"You can think whatever you want of me," he added, "but this crew is my responsibility. Either they get out of this with the skin on their backs and their debts paid off...or none of us do."

I set my teeth and held his stare. "Then if we go down, we all go down together."

"Now you're sounding like a sailor."

A challenge. A dare, like the one he'd given me in Hasser's sick bay. But this one, I was far more willing to take.

Planting a boot against the table, I shoved myself upright. "Then we have no time to waste."

CHAPTER 28
WASHED OUT TO SEA

On our voyage to Korsa, I did not sit idle. I read to pass the time, peeling through the volumes Captain Blackhand deemed worthy of keeping in his personal quarters: sailing tomes and pieces on Ameresh history, their contents as dry as the wizened pages on which they were writ. I also uncovered a handful of adventure tales stashed beneath his cot, so tarnished with spills and stains they must have been older than all the rest. And far better loved.

Addie would have enjoyed them.

I pushed those thoughts and the books away, and myself with learning all that I could of piracy and seamanship. And what I could not find pressed between the pages, I wrested from those whose company I begrudgingly kept.

Despite her duties as First Mate, Siu became a frequent visitor to the Captain's quarters. Though often stiff and scowling, she brought small tasks for me to do—mending sailcloth and fraying lines, the sorts of things I'd learned under Julas's captaincy. Tasks I would never have put my fingers to, had our heading not been to find Tristah.

To envision our reunion free of the confines of Shadewyle Castle was breathtaking…and nerve-wracking, setting me eagerly to every task which eased us nearer to finding her.

Now and again while we worked, I asked Siu of Korsa; but she remained clam-lipped on the subject, and always left the chamber soon after I broached it.

"You'll have to pardon her," Gydeon said one day, when I raised the matter while he salved a fresh rope burn on my hand. "All of us have Korsa's salt ground into our bootheels, but Siu outlasted worse there than most of us."

I stared at the angry red wheal across my palm until it disappeared beneath a thin layer of gauze. "I never knew that pirates were hosting a small country within Ameresh borders…that people were suffering in such a way."

"Few know. And those who do likely profit from it." Gydeon's smile strained when he flashed it my way. "Piracy is lucrative, and some folk in places of power can't help dipping into coffers that rich." His fingers stilled a moment, the bandage lying limp against them. "The problem with profit is it rattles more coinpurses than consciences. Where there ought to be regulation, there's often backpocketing. And the Old Salts are as talented at making deals as threats."

Nausea simmered low in my throat. How many of the Del's councilors had sat in session with us, knowing and doing nothing for the *children* who were victims of this country's underbelly?

I had thought my fate the worst in Amere-Del…orphaned and dragged to a life in servitude to the regime. I had not known I might have drifted into another fate entirely, washed downstream to Korsa, saddled with unpayable debts.

"I wish I had known," I murmured.

"The trouble isn't knowing the injustice, it's that no one does anything about it…not in there, not out here." Gydeon tied off the bandage and rose, patting my knee. "Perhaps when the regime changes, that also will change."

For the first time, a furrowed knot settled in my gut at the notion of Amere-Del's future.

Without me, who would rise in place of Zorast Graven? He was the first Del to have sired no heirs in all the Graven line, and they had no time to train fresh orphans to their standards.

Perhaps Lucretzia would become Della. Or else Amere-Del would crumble into utter chaos as Northlanders and Southlanders vied for the seat of power in Shadewyle. A war would break out in earnest.

The thought chilled me; lines of succession had rarely been discussed with us. There had never been cause for it. But now…it was no wonder Lucretzia had been so voracious to return me to Shadewyle. And why it was all the more likely she would pursue Tristah now, to tempt me back.

She had captured me with the threat; she would claim me with the truth.

I surged to my feet, fresh fire catching in my bones. "Would you tell me all that you can of Korsa?"

Gydeon gazed at me for a long moment, his mustached upper lip twitching slightly. Then he dipped his head. "I won't say I'd be delighted. But I won't say no, either."

CHAPTER 29
THE INVERSION

My time with Gydeon while he treated my healing hands turned to lessons, of sorts. He told me first of how Korsa had been forged, of ramshackle outer buildings along river channels on the mountainsides that gradually spooled downward. First they had spread into the caverns where the rivers ran through the hearts of the mountains; then into a vast harbor within the mountains themselves, so deep the militar would not travel to it.

The derelict buildings along the riversides now served as sentries and lookouts; if the Del were ever to decide to do something about Korsa, the alarm would be raised. The outer tunnels would collapse in a deluge of fireworks, buying the pirates time to escape through the innermost rivers.

Those rivers were the ones we sailed now, manned by a capable and crafty crew.

I came to know others among them as the days wore on…some by meeting them, others by Gydeon's tales: One Pot Willy, the withered cook, who brought food to my rooms twice a day. Kato, the ship's bosun, the sturdy, silent brother to hook-sharp Klement…and to Kory, the three-fingered man who'd first shoved me into Blackhand's rooms.

Camden, the youngest of the crew, proved difficult to dislike. Straw-headed, freckle-faced, and so sunmarked his skin more closely resembled a tanned hide, he became my most constant companion besides Gydeon and Siu. Scarcely more than a boy, his voice broke and tumbled over every odd word; his sunny disposition reminded me achingly of Blackhand's *Bastyan* façade. He frequented the Captain's quarters during the week of our sailing toward Korsa, dusting the numerous bookcases and shelves while he peppered me with questions about Mithra-Sha…the country, I gathered, of his birth.

"I always wanted to sail," he boasted one day, perched cross-legged on the Captain's desk. I sat in its seat, a sailor's record splayed on my lap—ignored, for now. I had just finished regaling him with tales of *The Secret Ingredient* and why I had opened it…a bit of my heritage shared with a boy too young to make a weapon of that truth.

Smiling hurt today, with the memory of my parents held near to my heart; but I offered him what I could. "And why is that, Cam?"

He grinned at the nickname, as he had since I'd first spoken it the day we'd met. "I mean, who wouldn't? Look at the sea!"

"I would love to, but…" I raised my chin at the tarred window, through which only vague streaks of sunlight winnowed.

"Yeah." Cam balanced his chin glumly on his fist. "Captain did that. Says he doesn't like looking at the waves first thing when he wakes up."

Curiosity prodded me upright in the seat. "Do you have any notion why?"

A crooked shrug. "Cap doesn't tell me much about that. Just says he started out a little like me, and…sometimes the sea reminds him of that."

The prod turned to a press of heat against the small of my back. "And how *did* you start, Cam?"

His hand fell from beneath his jaw, and he gripped his ankles, staring down at the thick, fingerless woolen gloves that covered his hands. "Shipwrecked. Pa's Ferry ship got smashed in a storm, and the only ones who came to help were pirates."

I grimaced. "The *Singer*?"

"No, I mean…" he shuddered. "*Real* pirates. The ones who want to be the next Old Salts, not the ones trying to get out of it like Cap and them."

A frown dragged my mouth down by the sinking of my heart. "You were indebted to them?"

"Sure. I had to eat." Another shrug. "Cap bought me out the second he laid eyes on me. Didn't even *ask* how much of a debt I had. Just, *I'll take him. Get on my ship, lad.*" He swiped his knuckles beneath his nose. "Been here ever since."

Something trembled in my heart, twisting and tightening. "What is your duty aboard this vessel, Master Cam?"

He straightened, his grin making a bright reappearance. "Whatever I'm told! Sometimes I clean, sometimes I mend things, sometimes I keep people company…in sick bay, or, you know, like this." He flagged a hand my way. "But I'm hoping he's training me to be the next Blackhand!"

The door swung open, a stern voice drifting through the frame: "That'll never happen, lad."

For the first time since we'd set our course in the map room, Blackhand and I beheld one another; his gaze dropped to the book open in my lap, then flicked back to my face, brows vaulted in silent question.

I chose not to answer it, clapping the book shut and rising from my seat. "Have you come for a battle of wits? If so, I should warn you I was never taught to show mercy to an unarmed man."

"Oh, I'm sure you weren't." Arms folded, he cocked his weight into the doorframe. "I'm getting fond of this ruthless Delina."

"The feeling, I assure you, could not be further from mutual."

"So you've made clear." All at once, the humor drowned in his gaze. Boosting himself upright again, he tugged his chin. "Cam, you're needed belowdecks."

"On my way, Cap!" He launched down from the table and darted past Blackhand, who gripped the back of his head and gave him a light, friendly shove out onto the topdeck.

In Camden's absence, the Captain lingered, rolling his hand. "You as well."

"Belowdecks?"

"No." He turned from the quarters, but waited for me to reach him before he stepped out. "I don't want the lad to see this. You, on the other hand…"

It was good he trailed off. I would have heard little of what he said after, regardless.

From Gydeon's reports, I'd learned these inner rivers were something most sailors rarely saw. For anyone but the pirates to know of them was a death sentence. It was why I had not been allowed to see us pass into it, or how we found our way along the cavernous rivers that wended into the mountain halls.

But now, it seemed, we were leaving those caverns behind.

Rogue reddish light swathed the bow of *The Dread Singer*, unfurling in vicious, gutting talons backward along its length. The crew worked the lines, bringing us slowly along the current to a port like none I had ever seen.

A port at the heart of a mountain.

It began with a sprinkling of lanternlit hovels, notched deep into the stone along the river mouth; and then, as we peeled free of those shadows—helmed by

Siu, who guided us with ease, true to her steady name—the breadth of Korsa unfolded before us.

The cavernous span at the center of this mountain stood sheer and breathtaking; waterfalls tumbled from furrows in the rock, filling the hollow chamber with a ceaseless, thunderous resonance. Cold wind hummed through the tunnels that led to this place, carrying ships in from outer ports.

The city itself spread out and climbed on crescents of stone, staggered structures slapped together with rock and wood. Most were in some measure of decay—or made to look it—so it was impossible to guess at a glance where the Old Salts made their beds. Though I would have bet my inheritance on the tall, spiraling towers near the city's aft.

Shanties, shouts, and screams peppered the air, muffled by the roar of falling water. Fires burned—some controlled, some eating away at pockets of lumber here and there. Tension bridled the air, as if at any moment another inferno, another brawl, or far worse would crack open and spill across this hidden haven.

Old memories dusted my eyes like flung flour; the gritty smoke of smoldering rubble, curses called down on Del Graven's name, the bite of scattered crumbs against my knees as I hid under our table, praying through tears for my parents to come home.

I swept them from the surface of my mind with a forceful breath out. A deeper breath in.

Eyes wide open.

I would not look away; to look away might mean missing a sign that would lead us to Tristah. So instead I set my knuckles to the railing, kneading nightmares into its salt-stripped surface.

Blackhand clasped his fingers loosely, forearms braced on the railing, his gaze trained on the city toward which we sailed…though occasionally it drifted to my hands. "Some sailors call this place Monsha's Underbelly. Built the same, fills the same purpose…but the Old Salts here make the Del seem like a fair ruler. The trade's in stolen goods…sometimes things. Sometimes people. You can expect plenty of fights, plenty of pickpockets, and plenty of bad memories made if you wander off alone."

And Tristah had come here, we suspected—friendless. Unaccompanied. For the first time, I wondered if we might find her crewing one of the vessels that bobbed along the wharfs, sunk in debt so deep not even a man of lost causes like Blackhand would look her way twice.

Bitter fear coated my tongue. "How do you intend to find word of Tristah in all of this?"

His gaze slid sideways to me. "The only way we're learning anything about your friend's whereabouts is by my lead. I expect you to honor that the way any crewmate would…otherwise we'll land ourselves with more questions than we know how to answer. Savvy?"

"Savvy." The less attention I drew in places like this, the better.

With a grunt, Blackhand pushed himself back from the railing. "In Korsa, the crew sticks together—at least two of us everywhere we go. And believe me, no sailor you lay eyes on out there is going to offer you a better deal than you've got here."

I tore my gaze away from the city, relieved to put my back to it; bracing one arm on the railing, I faced Blackhand instead. "Is that what you fear? That I'll make an escape?"

His eyes tightened at the corners. "That thought's cost me sleep."

There was a hollow grit to his words—a gravelly intensity I had not expected. As if, perhaps, it was more than the notion of losing his ransom that kept him awake at night.

I shook away that troubling idea, fastening a smile in place. "If you trust nothing else about me, Blackhand, you can trust this: I have no intention of doing anything that would compromise our success in finding Tristah."

"Good." He nodded, swift and sharp. "Then let's ready to drop anchor. We have a decoy to find."

CHAPTER 30
A TALE TO TAKE THEM AWAY

We docked among an endless span of vessels at the foot of Korsa, all flying their own flags: stamped in serpents and sea creatures, emblazoned in blades and figures of legend, each one intimidating in its own right. When I emerged from the Captain's quarters, I nearly stumbled over the thick leather satchel Siu dropped outside the door.

"If anyone asks, you're the bosun's assistant." Her tone was clipped, a thin polish of sweat clinging to her brow as she pointed to the satchel. "That's full of tools that need sharpening and replacing. You'll be using that opportunity to poke around and see what you can hear…but mostly, keep your head down and your mouth closed. And for depths' sake, don't accept anything anyone offers you."

I glanced down at the satchel, then back to her strained face. "*You* carry it, then."

Her lips swirled up at the corners. "Any other day, that would have gotten a laugh out of me." Snatching up the leather bag, she thrust it against my chest. "Weigh anchor on those fine boots of yours. And stay close to the group."

Blackhand brought only a small number of us ashore: Gydeon and Siu, Wilkes—the ship's quartermaster—Kato, to whom I would be playing assistant, and me. No one else seemed eager to disembark, and I caught no glimpse of Camden at all before we descended the gangplank into the stench of revelry and wickedness that coated the mountain harbor like a slick film.

Korsa was all the more overwhelming from within. What had blistered hearth-red with firework pulses of ambient color from the height of the *Singer's* deck all but roared when it engulfed us. The scent of brine and sweat and various wares assaulted my nostrils at once—a batter swirled with far too many spices, each one competing for dominance.

Fish. Boiled meat. Fresh leather. Tobacco. Entrancing herbs. Body odor. Bile. Vomit. Cooking oil. My stomach clenched at the nauseating array of aromatics, and I gritted my teeth, tightening the satchel strap across my front.

Eyes wide open. Eyes wide open.

A difficult task, thanks to the haze that clung to the city—its gritty glaze found little escape through the wind vents high above in the mountain's face, or out through the tunnels where the water surged and thundered.

I could manage little better than a squint as I took my first steps into Korsa at the head of the crew; Blackhand moved nearly in step with me, but the others strayed at our heels, eyeing the heaving masses of pirates and destitutes who crowded around the docks. Most of the latter wore thin garments to combat the heat of the fires and the bustle of wadded bodies; threadbare cloth draped over knobby bones and concaved chests, eyes flaring with hunger and craving and worse as they followed our progress along the docks.

Doubtless some tallied our numbers and wondered if we held anything worth stealing—anything that might offset the edge of their debts or keep them fed without accruing more.

The sympathy that had surged in me when I'd discussed this place with Gydeon dimmed somewhat when I caught the glint of too many knives winking at too many waists, all kept just within hand's reach. Heartaching as their plight was, I preferred they not carve their debts out of my flesh.

Blackhand fell into perfect lockstep with me as we wound down the broad crescent of wharfs, the bulk of his sable-coated frame bulwarking between my body and the hungry eyes that littered the landside of the dock. Thumb tucked into the strap of his own satchel—full of what, I dared not speculate—he inclined his head toward mine. "You certainly know how to carry yourself in a crowd."

I spared him a glower; his brows arched.

"I mean it. You move like a prow cutting through the sea."

"The swifter headway we make, the sooner we're rid of this place." And the sooner I would see Tristah—and be rid of *him*.

When he dropped back abruptly, my gut trembled—a quiver of victory, but also of unease—which only mounted when I realized why he had returned to the crew.

To Siu, who had halted some distance behind the rest, eyes shut; her hand was fisted tightly in Gydeon's, who tucked a lock of hair behind her ear, his lips gliding in soothing murmurs I could not hear.

My stomach clenched all the tighter at the grimace that furrowed her brow and twisted her mouth into a corkscrew. At any moment, it seemed tears might escape.

Blackhand strode back to his First Mate, brushing gently between Kato and Wilkes. Shrugging his pack off, he took Siu by both shoulders, his thumbs pressing gently to the hollows of them until she blinked her eyes open.

A single tear escaped, rolling thickly down her cheek; swiftly, Blackhand caught it with his thumb.

"'Ay," he rasped, "you're sure you want to be doing this?"

Siu held his gaze for a moment, then tightened her jaw—and her grip on Gydeon's hand, as if he was the anchor which kept her moored to these moldering docks. "Gyddy needs fresh herbs. I'm not letting my love off into this den of spinestabbers and salt-veins alone."

"That's my girl." The smile Blackhand offered nearly stole my breath: a grin of pure sunshine, bright with pride.

Pain pierced low in my middle. How could a man who betrayed without blinking an eye also carry such love within him? Why could he not be as purely foul as Lucretzia, as detestable as the Del?

Bearing down on the inside of my cheek, I shook away the thought; and I held my place, waiting for the rest of the crew to move up the docks, before I took another step—at Siu's side now, measuring my pace to hers.

"You and Gydeon are favored by Ahim to have found one another." I nodded to their tightly twined hands. "How did you meet?"

Gydeon flashed his wife a smile utterly in conflict with the atmosphere of the city around us; it glowed with adoration, wiping away the clinging taint of Korsa. "Now, that's quite a tale."

Siu hauled in a deep breath and rolled her eyes. "Which version are we telling today, then? The one with you as the dashing hero, or myself in the role of savior?"

"The truth, I suspect." He lifted their hands, pressing a kiss to her knuckles.

"Ha!" Kato's brash bark of laughter whipped all our eyes to him. "*None* of us has heard that version yet."

"And pity the day we do," Wilkes added, a morose smile tightening the sun-squinted creases around his eyes and ruffling his thick, dark beard. "Many of us will have to turn out our pockets for all they're worth."

"Which, in your case, is only a handful of lint." Kato knocked shoulders with him in passing. "Persistent gambler."

"Pocket-pincher," Wilkes fired back, striding after him up the docks. "Oi—Bodey, wait up!"

Kato flipped him a rude gesture at the moniker, which must be his pirate's name…but he did not halt.

"Wait!" Siu called after them. "Don't you want to hear the story?"

"*Not again*!" both men fired back.

Blackhand swiveled his head our way, measuring me with a glance that towed my mind back to the sick bay aboard *The Athalion*, and the dazed sort of look he'd given me then.

"Well, I suppose I'll begin," Gydeon offered. "It was a day here in Korsa like any other…as I'm certain you can imagine. A day when debtors came to collect. A day when a woman with hair of fire and a temper just as hot came to my rescue…"

Gydeon and Siu's unlikely tale—told in snatches of banter and spattered with kisses like flakes of chocolate sprinkled into cookie dough—carried us through the very streets where they'd met in their adolescence. It was a welcome diversion from the sights and sounds that peppered the air…it was hope itself, incarnated with the promise that good endings existed even in this hovel of greed and debauchery.

A possibility I might not have otherwise allowed myself to imagine as we made our way up the switchback roads hewn through the climbing city. Through puddles of questionable origin, past brothels and pits and all manner of dwellings and shops, we trudged until we were sore and tired; until the mountain harbor lay a good distance below, the *Singer* no longer distinguishable by its flag.

At long last, after hours of dodging hawkers and pickpockets—long after even Gydeon and Siu had fallen silent, their story spent, their eyes brimming with suspicion rather than lovestruck memories again—Blackhand called us aside. Together we clustered beneath a dark cloth awning among the many that swooped over one of the market-like districts of Korsa.

The clapboard face of the structure before us seemed unremarkable, at first glance; my gaze hung on the wooden sign above the door, declaring its name: *The Pearl in the Rough.*

"Ryker." Gydeon's gaze followed mine, unease tightening his hand around his own satchel strap. "The *Pearl* belongs to Merry Dred."

"I'm aware." Blackhand stared at the ornate door handles—both iron-rendered clams, mouths agape—as if they were biting serpents poised to strike.

"Then what are we *standing here* for?" Siu hissed.

"Because we want the Old Salts to know we're looking for something." Blackhand offered us a glance over his shoulder. "The more we stir up the waters, the more likely some bottom-lurker who knows something will drift to the surface. Quickest way to do *that* is to start the whispers from the top down."

Wilkes palmed the long twists of black hair from his brow. "I don't like this, Captain."

"However," Kato cut in smoothly, "if it takes us away from this depths-cursed place more quickly…"

"So be it." Siu set her shoulders and stepped forward—the First Mate restored to rank by the task ahead. "Shall we?"

The Pearl in the Rough oozed with deceptive charm. It was far quieter and better lit than the streets, fringed with fireplaces and dotted with tables. A mercantile booth stretched along one wall, a cooking hearth along the opposite side. The smell of freshly baked bread and roasted meat soaked into every inch of me, disarming in its own way.

A cheddar and rosemary scone awaited in one of those hearths. And I craved it desperately.

Blackhand flicked a golden merit to Siu. "Food and board. Make sure there's bread."

With a swift nod, she tugged Gydeon away; the rest of us followed Blackhand to secure one of the tables, our backs to a fireplace and our faces to the room.

The reprieve was short-lived. Within moments of taking our seats, we were assailed by the *crack* of a shattering bottle, the slam of an overturned table—cheaters turning to brawlers, men and women hurling one another against the walls, mouths colliding as disgust boiled over to passion.

Heat climbed the column of my neck, and I set about examining the contents of my satchel: the handful of blunted instruments which required sharpening or replacing.

A notion pricked at my mind; I jerked my gaze up to Wilkes, who gazed around with a quartermaster's keen interest—seeking danger aimed our way.

"Steelheart," I murmured, and his gaze leaped to me, surprise tweaking his brows at the name I'd learned from Gydeon. "You know the weaponsmiths of Korsa, I presume."

"Aye. I know a handful." He cinched his arms over his broad chest, eyes narrowing. "What's your interest?"

"Tristah is a proficient swordswoman. She would have armed herself—if not in Monsha, where her face might've been recognized, then certainly here."

Wilkes tipped his head slowly to the side, firelight dancing on the light brown of his skin. "Right. I'll ask around—"

"I'll accompany you," I said, and his hands bunched into fists in the fold of his brawny arms. "They're hardly likely to remember a woman of Tristah's appearance from some years ago. But if we were to ask them to recall someone who looks precisely like me…"

"That'd jog a few memories." Blackhand nodded. "Clever thinking, Lio."

I ignored him—ignored the burst of warmth at the praise and at the sound of my chosen name carried on his husky tone.

"And what will you give them for this information?" Kato prodded. "They will wring you out like a sail for whatever they believe you'll pay for your friend's whereabouts."

"Let me be concerned with that."

Blackhand frowned; his mouth leaped open to pursue the matter, but Siu and Gydeon spared me with their arrival, setting bowls of stew and a platter of fragrant bread before us. Gydeon slid into the seat beside Blackhand with an apologetic half-smile. "Only a single room, I'm afraid. And only one bed. Who should—?"

Wilkes, Kato, and I all gestured our spoons at him—and at Siu, dropping down beside him, flashing her first true smirk since our disembarking earlier that day. "It's taken enough years, but I'm glad I've finally beaten some respect into you scoundrels."

Blackhand did not join in their banter; his gaze stayed hooked on me, heavy and shrewd, all throughout the quiet meal. I helped myself to as much bread as my heart desired, ignoring him with all my might—but my appetite waned swiftly beneath that pointed stare.

It seemed the torturous meal would never end; when spoons at last scraped empty bowls, Blackhand shoved his half-eaten ration away, his eyes turning to each of the crew in turn. "Go chum the waters, mates."

With swift nods, they were all up, cleaning away their bowls, leaving us facing one another across the table. Blackhand settled his crossed arms on his waist, reclining in his seat.

"How are you settling the scores, Lio?"

"Is it any business of yours?" I retorted.

"It will be if there isn't enough left of you to return to the Del."

Fresh hate shivered along every nerve in my body. "Such gallantry."

"Pirate, sweetheart."

"Even for a pirate, you are detestable, Blackhand."

His lips jerked up humorlessly at the edges. "How are you settling the blasted *scores*?"

"I had intended to accrue a debt. One that will become the Del's."

He shook his head. "Won't work. They're going to need surety of some kind."

"Then what would you suggest?"

His eyes raked me up and down. "We don't ask nicely."

Surprise straightened me in my seat. "You wish to threaten the truth from them?"

He unfolded one arm, balanced his fingers on the tabletop a moment, then flipped his palm up in a shrug. "Quickest way to make people talk in this town."

"And what will that cost us?"

"Be harder to get favors. It'll raise a stink around here, that's for sure. Could land me in hot water if things go on long enough." A shrug of the shoulders this time. "But seeing as I don't intend to be in debt much longer…"

A scoff simmered in my throat; but at its edges there prodded something else. A vulnerable sort of curiosity. "I do not understand," I admitted, "why you would threaten your own kind for the sake of this task."

His brows tugged together slightly. "You think I care more for the turncoats in this harbor than…" A quirk of his mouth at this, "what gets my crew their freedom?"

A fair question. "I think I cannot trust anything you say."

He grimaced. "Aye. Well, let's settle this: if it keeps the crew safe, keeps bread in their bellies and even a chance of freedom on their horizon, it's the truth."

"I wish I could trust *that*." And the painful bit of it all was that I truly did; it had been lovely, those few weeks aboard *The Athalion*, to believe I could put a kernel of faith in the sailor who sat before me.

Or, rather, in the man he'd pretended to be.

Grunting, Blackhand raked his hands back through his long, golden hair, then dropped them on his thighs. He regarded me for a moment. Then, "I want to thank you. For what you did back there, with Gyddy and Siu."

I shrugged. "A friend once taught me the power of stories. How they can take us away from ourselves, to somewhere better."

Blackhand's thumbs scraped the creases of his trousers. "If a story could take you anywhere, where would it be?"

"Back to *The Secret Ingredient*." The answer came without hesitation—from the places in me that ached for a world where Lucretzia had never darkened my path again. "And you, Captain?"

A crooked smile graced his lips. "Nowhere that exists in this life, sweetheart."

Curiosity canted my head. "Into one of the adventures you read about in your storybooks, perhaps?"

He snorted. "Been snooping?"

"I prefer to know the nature of my enemies. It defines my survival."

"And that," he gestured to me with a flick of his hand, "is the answer to your question. I don't have adventures anymore…just good days and bad ones."

He shoved back from the table and started away into the crowd—leaving me with no choice but to follow, or risk being alone in a den of feckless pirates.

CHAPTER 31
FEAR BEGETS FEAR

Our accommodations were what I had expected: a moldering room with rat holes chewed at the bases of the walls, the single bed creaking ominously beneath Gydeon and Siu's combined weight. Sleep did not come easily, despite the exhaustion that towed steadily on my limbs.

After countless hours of tossing and turning, I finally pushed myself up from my sleeping place below the window—the farthest from the ratholes that I could reach. The others drowsed in various states of fitful slumber; Blackhand lay nearest, on his side, face mashed into his pillow. The powerful lines of his back strained against his shirt, flexing as he struggled through a dream I was perhaps fortunate not to know.

I crept across the room, crouching at his side, reaching for his shoulder. "Blackhand."

His arm snapped up, his fingers closing around my wrist like a trapper's snare. In one deft movement, he yanked me over top of him, pinning me against him with one arm curled around the back of my neck and one leg cocked over, trapping both of mine against his.

All of the air squeezed from my lungs at once; I squirmed, but he did not release me. Though it prodded my throat like thorns, I forced a whisper through tingling lips: "*Bastyan.*"

He blinked. Settled. Then frowned.

"Lio?" His gaze panned across the room, settling on each of his crew, one after the other. An agitated breath burst from his rounded lips, and he released me, shoving his body from under mine in one deft thrust of the heels of his hands. Legs bent, arms braced, he stared at me; his chest heaved in knifing breaths, sharing and stealing the gleam of his ship's wheel pendant with the light. "I thought…*depths*, it's the bloody sounds of Korsa. Always makes me think I'm…"

He trailed off again, dragging a hand through his hair. His eyes flicked back up to me, and for a moment the shadows there nearly named themselves *shame*.

"You're all right?" he muttered.

"Startled, but unharmed." I scoured my thumb gently along the inside of my wrist, where his grip had pinched precisely over the markings left by Lucretzia's shackle.

He flexed his fingertips against his scalp. Eyed my wrist like he was searching it for harm himself. "Sorry about that."

Silence engulfed us for a time; were I any braver, I might have asked what he dreamed about. But I had enough of my own nightmares to know how private a matter they could be.

Clearing my throat, I eased nearer to him on my knees. "I came to wake you so that we could begin our search."

"Aye," he mumbled. "Might as well. You kick Wilkes awake. I'll meet the pair of you down in the dining room."

Mercifully, the quartermaster was far easier to rouse; we were downstairs in only a handful of minutes, where a different Blackhand altogether greeted us. He was bright-eyed, a smirk strung gamely on his face, his hair slicked back damply to his scalp.

"All right, you two," he said, "let's get to hunting."

We pushed out through the tavern doors into a city throbbing with precisely the same frenetic chaos as the night before. Korsa did not fully fall to slumber; it might well have been the dead of night beyond the mountain crags for the exhaustion that still draped over me like a foul cloak, but this pirate haven thrived with clamor.

"So," Blackhand said as we walked, his hands thrust into his pockets as if we casually strolled the docks of Monsha—not past brawls every block, illicit activity in the corners, and cruel trade in the shadows. "Tristah is fond of weapons, is she?"

"She would know to defend herself in a place like this. From these sorts of people." A foresight I had unfortunately not shared.

"Aye. Pirates are the worst." Blackhand cast out an arm to slow Wilkes and me as a pair of tussling women spilled from a tavern doorway, beating one another senseless and peppering the path with shards of broken teeth.

We skirted around them, where Wilkes took the lead with a calm, no-nonsense focus I appreciated. I did not want to converse with these Raiders; I did not want to hear their thoughts about this horrible city or wonder what nightmares I had awakened Blackhand from—and which of the shadows gathered at the corners of his eyes belonged to them.

I did not want to care for a single thing except finding Tristah…or finding my way to her.

So I followed dutifully behind Wilkes's guiding to the first blacksmith…and to many, many more after that.

There was no lack of the trade here—nor any lack, it seemed, of weapons and tools in need of service. Wilkes had a small armory hanging from his belts in addition to my bosun's tools. At each blacksmith, he had this or that item sharpened while Blackhand and I peered around, studied the clientele, showed our faces to the smiths, and asked questions.

None flashed a flicker of recognition in turn; this held true for a dozen different forges. And then fifteen.

"Do you truly need *quite* so many blades?" I demanded when we ducked from the cloth overhang of our seventeenth visit that day. We had serviced many of my tools by now, yet Wilkes continued to draw blades from unseen places whenever we required them. "Wouldn't one or two do?"

"Perhaps they would." The quartermaster offered me a crooked grin. "But I was taught otherwise. To always carry more weapons than needed…to arm not only myself, but those around me."

A whisper of forgotten weight grazed my thighs and hips—a memory of when too many knives had once brushed those intimate places like a lover's hands. "I was taught the same."

"I imagine so." Wilkes settled a hand on the hilt of the cutlass lashed at his side while we cut across a marketplace, Blackhand falling back slightly at our heels. "I was militar trained…in the barracks of Shadewyle Castle."

Shock anchored my feet to the path for a moment before Blackhand's palm struck the small of my back, driving me forward. I stumbled after Wilkes again, lengthening my stride to match his, catching the silvering threads in his beard and the slant of his eyes in the lanternlight and bonfire glows that brightened only some of Korsa.

He was not familiar to me. But had I known him once? Had our gazes met, our shoulders brushed in those castle halls?

"When?" I demanded. "And why did you leave?"

"Many years ago. I wasn't fond of their methods." His gaze fell on me for a moment, then fixed ahead again. "Nor did I enjoy the notion of using brute force to beat the last merits from people who could not afford the taxes levied against them."

"So you turned to piracy instead? How is that any better?"

"I chose to sail with *The Dread Singer* for a reason." Wilkes shrugged. "I have no regret stealing from wealthy privateers and trademasters with deeper pockets than consciences. I won't plunder the poor the way Del Graven chooses to."

That would have halted me in my steps again were Blackhand's presence not looming at my back, herding me on.

I did not know what to make of this crew. Pirates with principles. Raiders with limitations on what and where and from whom they stole.

"Nor would I fight in any coming war between Northlanders and Southlanders, or dissidents and loyalists," Wilkes added. "Too many friends and family on both sides."

"And do your friends and family know you turned pirate?" I asked, tucking my shoulders to follow him through a thick throng of squabbling pirates.

Wilkes grasped my elbow, steering me from the mess of tense bodies. "They believe I was butchered on a mission across the Mithran border many years ago, to abduct the Master Storycrafter. Better that way."

He left it at that as we ducked into our next destination: a half-ship's hull mounted at the edge of the latest marketplace, its bulk torn clean down the middle, weapons displayed in barrels and on hooks mounted along the inner wall. A counter ringed the curve of the hull, the forge built along the black stone of the mountain off to the right, where a grizzled, elderly blacksmith beat new steel into shape. He cast us a nod but no glance as Wilkes began to peruse his wares; I leaned against the counter, Blackhand beside me, my head whirling with the revelation of what Wilkes was—and what had brought him here.

"Having trouble swallowing that down?" Blackhand asked after a moment.

"Don't you have anyone on your crew who's a simple *pirate*?" Disbelief— and an unease I could not quite place—sharpened my tone.

Blackhand turned his back to the counter, propping his elbows on it, staring out across the plaza beyond the forge—full of card games, dice games, cursing, bloodletting, rage. "You take a look out there and tell me if you see anything but a whole lot of backstabbers and liars."

"I don't have to look any farther than under this awning for that."

Blackhand grimaced, running a hand over the nape of his neck. "Well, I wasn't much for sailing with the same sort of crew I lived with on my first ship. My grandad always used to say a little kindness makes for a heap of loyalty. A little cruelty makes for fear…and fear goes both ways. You always have to be a little afraid of what's afraid of you." He shrugged. "Figured I could find a crew that wanted to raid and rip their way across the sea…and sooner or later they'd rip me apart, too. Or I could find the sorry sacks like me…the ones who'd do better with a friendly hand than a fist to the face. And I could make something out of them that'd last."

"That hardly seems to fit the legend of Blackhand." Nor did it fit with the image of him I struggled to keep hold of in my mind—the betrayer and liar who used me for ransom.

But then, I was not his crew. He could be however he wished with them…and however he wished with me.

He shrugged. "There's a reason there's been plenty of Blackhands since that legend first got told. Let's just say the story about how he and his lass betrayed each other? True, as far as I can tell. And they weren't the last. Not every Blackhand ended peaceful like the one who signed me on…for most, it was a bloody fate."

Before I could pursue the matter further, steel rammed down on the counter just shy of my fingertips, sending my pulse skittering and pounding, my breath halting in my throat; the blacksmith dipped his tall, lean frame to peer into my eyes—and his stare lit with a surge of recognition and good humor.

"Well, look at you!" he grinned—then spat an impressive wad of chewed leaf into the spittoon on the counter. "It's been a while, hasn't it, lassy?"

I straightened up sharply from the counter, nearly colliding with Blackhand's chest when he twisted to stand behind me. "I beg your pardon?"

"If begging did any good in Korsa, you'd have it, just for not biting my head off the second you strolled under my awning!" The blacksmith chuckled. "Looks like you found what you were looking for out there, after all."

"I think you've got the wrong sailor, mate." Blackhand's tone edged with a faint note of something I could not name…almost defensiveness.

But the certainty in the man's gaze—and the reminiscence of his smile— were not feigned. And all at once, a giddy, proven-right sort of glee bubbled up in my core.

After all this time, I had still known *precisely* what steps Tristah would take.

"You must have sold to my sister." The lie glided near-perfectly from my tongue. "I'm searching for her, as it happens. Can you tell me what you remember of her?"

"Sister?" The man tilted his head, stringy gray hair falling in reckless braids over his shoulder as he tilted in to study me more closely. After a long moment, he nodded, slow and thoughtful. "Aye, now that I look at you nearly, there *was* some difference. She was leaner. *Meaner.* Now, that lass knew how to bargain."

My pulse quickened; my fingers curved, the gritty wooden counter driving a splinter into the nailbed of the middle one. I hardly cared. "*Please.*"

The blacksmith guffawed. "That word's as useful as a shoeshiner or a praying man in these parts, lassy."

Wilkes glanced up from the rack of weapons he examined. "I could easily take my business elsewhere."

The man eyed Wilkes—and the collection of new daggers in his fist, and the axe in his other hand, which he clutched as if he would rather not let them go at all. Then the old man grimaced, rubbing a soot-stained palm over his mouth. "Well, now that you mention it…I remember what a hardy thing she was. Fierce. Full of threats." He grinned almost fondly. "Remember how she came in several times before finding something she liked. Stirred up some squall-worthy arguments with one of my regulars in the meantime. The way they were at each other's throats, they were either going to kill each other or he would've had her up against the wall in a second. Shame I never got to see which."

The skin on my spine tightened like a beaded shawl pulled tight to my flesh. "You sold to her?"

"That I did, once we settled on a price…which included her not running off my best customers, mind. A fine piece—a pair of blades, actually. A cutlass and a dagger."

Wilkes settled the axe and knives on the counter. "What else can you tell us of her?"

The man favored him with a near-reverent smirk. "That she knew her way around weapons, sure enough. Pickier than most. And from here, she said she was heading down to the docks. Asked me what was the cheapest accommodations I knew of, where the most crews gathered."

At least now I knew that Tristah had been armed—and where she had gone next. But that was of little comfort with the next words the blacksmith spoke:

"Aye…from the sound of things, she was planning to charter passage out of Korsa at the tip of that sword. If that regular of mine didn't gut her first."

CHAPTER 32
FRIENDLESS IN THE WORLD

Our time in Korsa after the boon at the blacksmith's shop was not swiftly spent.

The first days following his heading were strung together with a sort of painful hope…a daggered desire to find our answers immediately and be gone. It was a craving held unspoken in every glance we traded across the dining tables in the lower level of the *Pearl* each morning…and it dimmed, day by day, when our excursions into the city proved meaningless. Waiting for an unleavened batch of dough to rise might have gone more quickly. But pirates were built of tricky words and rigamarole, and no threads we tugged unraveled the tapestry of Tristah's disappearance.

From the blacksmith's shop, we gained a tantalizing hope affixed toward the docks, where the old man claimed to have steered her to make good on her need to find passage. But from there, we lost the thread in a tangled knot of countless others.

Some people claimed to have seen a woman of an appearance like mine in Korsa a month or so after our escape from Shadewyle. Yet the places these lookouts pointed us were often darkened roads without an end; and those that did end were in shadowed sidestreets where Blackhand backed us out, shaking his head in a firm, silent command.

Some jaws were loosened only by Blackhand's fearsome reputation. He did not hesitate to fling mouthy pirates up against brick walls, hands fisted in collars, spitting threats that many heeded on trembling legs, pointing us somewhere else to go. Half the directions we gained were only by his force; the way he blew through Korsa like a maelstrom had his crew scowling nervously, but it awakened an odd sort of awe in me.

Disgusted as I was with him, there was still something riveting about seeing a legend living out its truths.

Following directions earned by the bite of his fists on pirates' cheekbones and his fingers twined around heaving throats, we visited taverns where Tristah was said to have been spotted. We shook down crews who claimed she'd approached them. They teased and wheedled at me, drawing broad comparisons between us—and when Blackhand had his hand at their necks, some claimed she'd moved on with a ship. Others warned she'd been sunk at the bottom of the harbor.

A week passed in that pattern, fruitlessness flowering in every crack of our combined resolve.

Wilkes, Siu, and Gydeon returned to the ship; Klement and Kory joined us in their stead, and once again we peeled through the city, searching for leads— and finding none. Kato and I spilled the rest of our tools at every shop we could find, listening with rapt ears while the smiths sharpened them, but hearing no mention of Tristah. Kory and Klement vanished into gambling dens for hours, returning with the sweat of strong drink in their pores and more leads that led to nothing.

Another week of meaningless pursuit. Gydeon and Siu returned to us, and Kato all but chased Kory back aboard the *Singer*. Then Wilkes joined us again with his new axe proudly strapped to his waist…a reminder of that first favored day in Korsa that had given us such worthless hope.

One morning, not long after Wilkes and Gydeon and Siu returned, I woke to the sound of Klement and Blackhand arguing in the corner of the ramshackle room, their voices pitched so low I could scarcely hear them; if I had not trained my ears to catch Tristah's near-inaudible whispers when we were meant to be sleeping, I might have missed it altogether.

And missed that it was me they discussed in harsh undertones.

"Why are we *doing* this, Captain?" Klement seethed; even with my eyes shut, feigning slumber, I could envision the ship's navigator with arms folded, her fearsome scowl pinned to Blackhand like a pistol's muzzle. "We *have* the Delina. We could've had our ransom and dusted her off our hands by now if we'd just kept to the plan."

A rasp of skin on stubble—Blackhand, rubbing his ever-thickening beard. "We need the merits, Klem."

Her silence waxed for a moment.

"I've always respected how you don't share the debt ledger with any of us," she said at length, "but it can't be worth all this, Captain."

"I'll be the one who decides what it's worth."

Their conversation settled heavy on my chest every day that we demanded and hunted and searched to no avail. Whatever steps Tristah had taken after the blacksmith's forge, she'd covered them well...or else threats and merits simply were not enough to tempt these pirates to give up any morsel of real truth. Even one that seemed mundane.

We were running out of time—and not merely to find Tristah, to keep ahead of Lucretzia's wicked intentions for us both. *I* was losing time, and the crew's patience. And if they did indeed mutiny, and took the ransom for themselves...my defenses were few.

Unless I could disappear into Korsa...a possibility I considered deeply one evening when I sat in the *Pearl's* parlor, resting my weary feet after another day of hopeless striving about the city. And this time I'd gone with only Blackhand for company, while the others rested from their own excursions the day before.

I was not merely exhausted; the slope of my back was more than fatigue, the lack of craving in my empty stomach far worse than hunger.

It was hopelessness.

Hopelessness had me mumbling a vague reply when Blackhand left to retrieve mugs of cider from the counter after we'd snatched up a table and set down our plates and bowls in the heaving lurch of patrons coming and going. Despair left a taste of ash in my mouth with every bite of beef flank and mealy beans. Dejection made me yearn almost unduly for my bedroll in the room above.

I was tiring of dark alleyways and dead ends and the lies spun to lead us there. Wearying of the crew's frowns and disbelief, forever angled at me like sword tips. Exhausted from hearing Blackhand threaten and sailors tremble, only for them to spit out more lies. Sick to death of feeling alone and friendless, every lead to Tristah slipping like a fraying cord through my fingers.

Weariness led my mind astray. It made me unaware someone was beckoning me until a finger tapped my arm.

"Oi." A pirate at the next table over grinned when I wrenched around to face him, sitting back in his seat beside a pair of burlier men—twins, by the look of them. His smile showed a broken slide of yellow teeth contrasting sharply with the vanilla-bean-thin mustache perched on his sneering upper lip. "What's a pretty thing like you doing feasting alone at the *Pearl?*"

The parlor came into sharp focus around me—a stark realization that Blackhand had not yet returned with our cider. That these men had freshly retrieved their own platters, still steaming, and that the man's thin mustache struck me as familiar.

They'd been standing at the counter when I'd ordered and retrieved my food. They had watched me—though in Blackhand's presence, I'd paid them no mind.

Warning cast across my mind like a puff of powdered sugar. I folded my arm around my platter, drawing it near. "You think me foolish? I know what becomes of women who dine alone in Korsa. My companion will return soon."

"Well, if he doesn't," one of the twins leered, "we'd be glad to be your companions for the night."

"For as many nights as you'd like," his brother chuckled.

Disgust rattled the fork in my hand. These pirates believed anything they craved was theirs to plunder. Merits, belongings, vessels…people. And the thought of Tristah, alone in this sea of lust and craving, without anyone to share her table or guard her back…

"If I was in need of companionship," I hissed—the only tone that kept the tremble of fury from my voice, "yours would be the last I sought."

The mustached man straightened, laying a hand over his thigh. "That wasn't nice."

"I'm sorry…was I giving the impression I intended nicety? Or shall I rephrase myself to make it absolutely clear: *I want nothing to do with the likes of you.*"

The man's eyes darkened. Narrowed. "I like that mouth better stuffed with food. You were prettier before you talked."

"A pity for *you* I've lost my appetite." Reckless rage had me setting aside my fork. "So, shall we have a conversation?"

His friend bent toward me, lip curling. "Your *companion* should've stayed closer."

"Oi. Who says I didn't?"

I did not expect the relief that flooded through me at Blackhand's arrogant interruption. His strength, his commanding presence were unmistakable as he appeared at the tableside, cider in hand—even to those who might not know the legends of Blackhand.

The swarthy sailors leaned back fully in their seats, and at last I could draw a full breath. There was nothing feigned or forced in the smile that curved my lips when I met Blackhand's gaze; he offered a single long, slow blink in return, striking a path of fire like a flintrock dragged down my spine, straight to my core.

And then he smirked—a crooked, secretive thing, a marriage of sunshine and shadows that undid the last of the tension banded around my spine. He slid in next to me, shoving a cup my way. "Sorry about the delay." He draped an arm around my chair. "Had to beat someone's teeth in for the last two mugs."

"I'm just glad you're here now." Honesty poured itself into my words, and Blackhand straightened a bit, his gaze darting from my face to the pirates leering around us.

Tension settled across his features and set the line of his shoulders. "And I'm not going anywhere."

A promise. A threat.

I pushed my plate toward him and helped myself to my bowl of soup instead—something warm and nourishing to soothe the chill from my bones. Blackhand tucked into his meal without pause, but his eyes never once fell to what he ate. Instead, he watched the pirates at the adjacent table, who'd fallen to muttering between themselves. Memorizing. Measuring.

It wasn't until his arm stiffened against mine that I glanced up as well—and caught a pair of them gesturing our way.

Unease jabbed its paring knife between my ribs. I fixed my eyes on them, unblinking—making it clear I knew the direction of their focus. They held my stare just as levelly, sneering…and the mustached pirate made a vile gesture that turned my stomach on itself, the soup climbing back up my throat.

"I beg your pardon?" I snapped.

Silence descended at the tables around us. Several pirates snickered; the twins lounged in their seats, and the mustached man looked me up and down with shameless leering. "Just wondering if you might give us a *delay*, too. Maybe stay and clean us up, after—"

"'*Ay*."

Blackhand's snarl quaked in the base of my bowl, in the soles of my feet, in the roots of my heart. His ferocious glare pinned the pirate to his seatback, and for an instant, the man's expression brimmed with unease.

"You *do not* speak to her that way." Though Blackhand's voice held level, we all might have been less breathtaken if he'd bellowed. "Not to her. Not in front of me. Not with your sorry crew behind closed doors. Is that bloody *clear*?"

And though he only said it as a pirate guarding a catch…something fissured in my core at his ferocity. Chills capered down my arms, and my hair stood on end. And gratitude, sweet, hot, and choking, filled my throat.

The men said nothing, only fixed him with mutinous smirks.

"*Ay!*" The bark of Blackhand's voice and the scrape of his chair as he kicked back from the table set the twins flinching. "If you so much as breathe her name in your sleep, I'll hear about it. And we'll have a *talk* about that. Understood?"

Pure glee gleamed like the trail of a lit firework in my throat when the mustached man bobbed his head. "Aye. *Understood.*"

"Good." Blackhand swiped up his plate, then my bowl, and stood. "Let's finish this upstairs."

I had never been so grateful to desert the *Pearl's* parlor; to leave the watchful eyes of those pirates behind. And it struck like a well-aimed blow, the unfairness of the need I held for *this* pirate.

Swallowing felt as if I'd drunk a bowl full of thorns. The steps blurred before my eyes as I mounted them behind Blackhand to the upper landing. "What you did back there—you—"

He stumbled over the top step, slamming to one knee in the wooden hall, the bowl and platter dropping from his hands. A strangled yelp burst from me, and I caught his arm, hauling at his weight.

"Black—Ryker—?" Had he always weighed so much?

"Blasted…*depths*…" His hand struck the wall, then slid off. "The food. Something in the bloody *food*…"

The needling pain in my throat scraped itself across my tongue; I sucked in a breath and fought to scream—for the crew down the hall, for Gydeon, for *someone*—but all that emerged was a pitiful whimper.

Hands closed around my shoulders from behind, wrenching me away from Blackhand. A burst of harsh breath escaped him as he struggled around on his knees—only to meet a fist to the jaw, blunting him sideways.

The mustached pirate loomed above him, snagging Blackhand by a fistful of hair, wrenching his head back.

But he did not pierce a knife through his throat. He did not fire a pistol into his face. Words were his weapon—a deft cut wielded at both our hearts.

"Should have played nice, *mates.*" He hauled Blackhand up by the head, shoving him into the hands of the second twin—the one who was not holding me. "Merry Dred wants a word with you two."

CHAPTER 33
THE DEBT OF TRUTH

The power of speech had returned to me by the time we reached our destination: a narrow box of a structure fitted on stilts, clapped between an abandoned pair of shops somewhere in the winding curve of Korsa, more than a mile from the *Pearl*.

But though my tongue served me again, I knew better than to scream for help. No one would come, just as no one had intervened on my behalf before Blackhand had returned to me in the parlor. He was all I'd had then; he was all the help I had now as the pirates shoved us up a rickety flight of steps and into the stilted room, where they thrust us to our knees.

The box was an odd, amalgam imitation of the sort of studies the Del and Della had worked from in Shadewyle Castle. The trappings were much the same: bookcases stuffed with ledgers, a broad desk and wingbacked chair taking up the far wall. But here the floorboards were scraped and swollen, marred by drippings from the cavern recesses high above the unroofed room; there were only swaths of cloth draped this way and that above our heads, chinks of city light tumbling through their haphazard web.

That light splashed across the room's single occupant, seated in the chair: a man who appeared carved from the same pale slab of wood as the desk. He lounged behind it in a brocade vest and linen sleeves tucked beneath a black coat, his hair tamed from his creased, suntanned brow by a scarlet sash. Dark kohl stamped his eyes, highlighting the age that notched his flesh—and the cunning it had failed to dim.

An Old Salt. Merry Dred, these pirates had named him. The *Pearl's* owner—a pirate the Raiders feared.

Terror bladed into my middle.

"Captain Blackhand." Dred spoke with the same sort of deep churning that had whispered from the sea currents when I'd flung myself overboard to save Bastyan from the reef. "You have been causing quite a stir in this city these past several days."

Blackhand grunted, shoving off the hands of the pirate who held him down; the man receded only at a nod from the Old Salt, and the grip binding my arms behind my waist released in tandem. Blackhand hauled me up beneath my arm, and he did not let go until the pirates at our backs vanished through the door, their heavy boots creaking on every step back down to the streets of Korsa.

In their absence, Merry Dred regarded us with a hooded stare. "I see you've accrued new debts in your time at sea."

"Doesn't have anything to do with the debts between *us*," Blackhand growled. "Tell me what you're after so we can go our separate ways."

"I think you know I'd like you to stop manhandling other crews." Dred propped one boot on the edge of the desk, flashing a hint of metal beaten into the toes. "It's becoming a source of contention between myself and other Salts, having my most renowned Captain at *their* Captains' throats."

"Sounds like we have ourselves at an impasse." Blackhand folded his arms. "Or an accord."

Dred's chuckle rolled through the room, dark and thick as molasses. "And what sort of accord might that be?"

I spoke before Blackhand could, following the thread of his reasoning. "If you've heard what we've done, then you've heard what knowledge we seek." A smirk slipped onto my lips when Blackhand nodded. "A woman who passed through this way, years ago. Her face would have looked like mine."

The Old Salt's gaze pierced flesh and bore down to the bone. It lifted the hairs on my neck, the imminence of danger sliding over my skin, smothering my moment of confidence.

It keenly reminded me of the time I'd stuck my hand inside the gap in Azalya's orchard wall to greet the orphaned rabbits I'd hidden there…only to encounter the serpent who'd eaten them for its morning meal instead.

"Aye. I remember her. The spitting image of you." At last, he reclined at his desk, fingers tapping an off-kilter tune across its notched surface. "Imagine that. They say everyone in the world has a lookalike, but yours…if I didn't know better, I'd say you were twin sisters. Though she possessed something you lack…had a heat to her. You're a cold little coal, aren't you?"

"'Ay," Blackhand cut in sharply, "stay on the subject. Where did the girl get off to?"

Dred's eyes shifted to him; freed from the clutches of his stare, my lungs expanded at last to gather a full breath. "Now, Blackhand. You of all folk know that sort of information doesn't come for free."

Tension unfurled through the room like a loosed sailcloth; dread sprinkled down my bones. "What cost?"

Those lethal eyes flashed back to me. "It takes something memorable to jog a memory as ancient as mine, lass. Particularly when it's been so crowded with reports of *your Captain's* conduct these last few weeks."

"And how do we know your *memory* will prove worth the price?"

An upward dart of one hoop-lined brow. Then he said, with slow, caustic enunciation, "*Levanthya.*"

My heart lunged.

Tristah had scarcely ever whispered her family name in Shadewyle Castle, holding that last scrap of her life before the orphanage like a sacred oath, never to be relinquished. It had taken more than a full year of friendship before she'd dared breathe it to me.

If she had spoken it here, then she had been desperate, indeed.

Fear shivered through my hands. "What do you know of her?"

"From what I recall, she was seeking passage to the farthest reaches of the Southlands. Shaking down whichever captains would look her way twice, not unlike Blackhand here." His head slanted. "There *was* something else. Afraid I can't recall what it was."

"All right, enough of the games." Blackhand brushed forward, rubbing his coral-scraped shoulder, where perhaps the burly pirate had shoved him too hard. "Name the price, Dred. Let's get this over with."

Shock seared through me. I snagged his elbow, yanking him back a step. "*Blackhand.*"

"'Ay. You wanted to find her? This is how you barter in Korsa. It was always going to come down to this, one way or another." He shrugged me off, turning back to Merry Dred. "So, what's the price?"

I seized him beneath the arm again, wrenching him around to face me. "Tristah is *my* friend. Let the debt also be mine!"

His hand slammed against the swollen wooden wall beside my head, a resonance that rang like a clarion call demanding to be heeded. He towered before me, and for a fleeting instant, vulnerability blistered along the angles of his face…the openness I had thought I'd known in Bastyan.

Worry. Desperation. A fear that went deeper than I could name—and a determination entwined with it. The same determination that had stared down the fury of the Spear Teeth…and sailed us through.

"You don't know what you're asking for, sweetheart," he growled. "Trust me on this, aye?"

I did. The words blistered on my tongue. *I did trust you, with more than I have trusted anyone in so long…and see where that led us?*

His gaze searched mine—and shuttered, as if he'd fished out the thoughts swimming in my mind.

Skin rasped wood as his hand slid off to grip my upper arm. And then his brow settled against mine.

For a moment, we shared the same breath. All the world shrank to the narrow seam between our bodies—a distance some traitorous part of my battered heart ached to close.

"Lio, I'm begging you." His voice was a husky rasp. "Let me take this."

I could not fathom what he stood to gain from the offer, what angle this tempestuous pirate scourge sought to play. That I would be indebted to him? That he would hold this knowledge Dred dangled before us—and perhaps keep it from me?

All I knew for certain was that I had been taking blows for so much of my life—blows from Lucretzia. Blows meant for Tristah. The blows of a country teetering on the brink of civil war. A marriage not my choosing. A life I had never wished for. All strikes rained down on me.

And for once—for one selfish, awful moment—it was wonderful to feel the weight lift from my back. As it slid onto Blackhand's.

My brow to his, I barely edged out a nod.

Blackhand squeezed my arm once; then he withdrew, striding toward Merry Dred, who regarded us with the sort of wicked pleasure I had beheld and reviled so often in Lucretzia's gleaming gaze.

"All right," Blackhand drawled, "let's get this over with. You give me the name of the crew the girl sailed away with, you can add one hundred merits to my ledger."

Dred flashed a palm, halting him across the desk. "'Fraid I'm going to need more than your word this time, Blackhand."

He halted. I pushed up from the wall, a chill seeping through my blood.

"What more do you want?" Blackhand snapped.

Dred reclined, folding his hands over his leather-clad middle, thumbs tapping idly at his coat's polished brass buttons. "Just so happens another Old Salt is in a bind. He's gotten frisky with his debtors…started sending bits of their friends off to them, a piece at a time. Only thing is, he's run out of fingers to cut loose—and the skin market's been drier than a shore the sea don't love, lately."

A harsh, grinding rasp filled the room; it was a moment before I recognized the sound as my own breaths, doubling and tripling, staggering all over themselves.

"I give Dulledge Cleaver a finger," Dred went on, as casually as if they discussed bartering for flour rather than flesh, "he's indebted to me. And you know best how high a price skin and bone accrues."

"I know what it's worth." Blackhand's voice did not tremble, but the pitch was wrong; it grated against my ears. "To you, and to me. So, if I give you that…I want to hear the crew, the ship, *and* the harbor they sailed for."

Dred tilted his head. And I had never so desperately wished before—wished against my *own* ends—that someone would reject an offer.

"Done," he said at last. "Hand on the desk, boy."

"*Blackhand!*" His name ripped from me, shriller than I had intended—wilder than I had believed myself to be.

Blackhand tossed out a palm—halting me when I lurched a step across the small, confined space. His gaze was trained on Merry Dred, who had yet to stop smiling at the spectacle we made.

"Crew first," he said. "I'll take the ship name and port once you have your prize."

Dred clicked his tongue. "Almost seems fair, doesn't it? And we pirates don't play fair."

"*Almost,*" Blackhand hurled back. A challenge.

Dred was quiet for a moment. Then his callused, craggy fingers whipped a silver-shafted cleaver from a sheath at his waist. "The Dredgers."

Blackhand dipped his chin. His hand slammed down on the desk, and his knees hit the dilapidated wooden floor.

"*Wait—*"

My plea was lost to the first hack of steel on flesh.

A scream erupted from my throat; Blackhand's head yanked back, his face thrust skyward, the muscles in his neck and shoulders convulsing as he fought to swallow an agonized bellow. The rich, mineral scent of blood burst across the air, soiling my next strangled breath; Dred lurched to his feet and took a second swing.

Metal crunched through bone. A staggered moan tore from Blackhand's lurching throat.

My feet unstuck from the floor with the third swing; I reached them just as the metal whisked down and finished its task.

I caught Blackhand as he crumbled back from the desk, his slumped weight barreling against my chest. Snaking an arm beneath both of his, I snatched his bloodied hand and wrapped it swiftly in my skirts; I dared not look at it. Dared not take my eyes from the ruthless Old Salt who so casually picked up Blackhand's severed finger, wrapping it in a blemished, filthy kerchief from his own soiled pocket.

"Give us the *blasted* name!" I snarled.

Dred's eyes skipped to me, his brows tilting just slightly upward. "Ah, *now* you're truly her double." His grin was a broken slide of yellowing teeth. "She sailed away with the Dredgers, aboard *The Haverknot*. Bound for Bashir, it was, through Port Krait and up the way…and then for Port Tamsay across the basin, to Anoram."

For once, I blessed the Della's ceaseless insistence on the lessons Tristah and I had shared; I could map these places perfectly in my mind. The route which Tristah had undertaken opened like one of Addie's tales before me…a storybook of a years-ago past I would soon be sailing into.

But, first…before anything else…

I planted my heels and bore my strength into the breadth of my thighs, heaving Blackhand back to his feet. There he wavered, unsteady and pallid as thin batter. His remaining fingers tangled tightly in the folds of my skirt, keeping pressure on the severed stub.

Bile blistered my throat.

"You're something the silt-feeders wouldn't sip on, Dred," he panted.

"Aye." The Old Salt didn't pay us a glance, his gaze riveted on the finger he tucked away in a leather pouch strung at his side. "And you never were much good at insults. I'd watch my step, if I were you…Bashir is where that blasted Incendiary does his work. And he has a habit of chumming the waters when it comes to piracy."

Reinera's whispered tale of revolution in the Southlands collided against the choking need to escape this room.

I would ponder the rest later.

I tugged Blackhand away from the desk, toward the door; I couldn't abide a moment longer in Dred's presence. He would have been better than a match for Lucretzia…he might have even given her pause with his brutality.

Dred's parting words halted us just over the threshold: "Oh, and Bastyan?"

That name struck me like a three-fold cord, dashing heat and shock through my core. Blackhand stiffened as well, but he did not look back.

"If you ever darken the docks of this city with threats and demands rather than merits again, I'll take more than a finger," Dred warned. "And I'll take the same from all of that crew whose debts you decided to scrape in before you paid me back for *yours*."

The door slammed shut at our backs, kicked by a steel-toed boot. The draft of its closing jolted me toward the steep stairwell and the pulsing streets of Korsa beyond—and with the revival of motion, my thoughts staggered into step as well.

Bastyan.

Dred knew the name. Spoke it as if it were *true*.

"Blackhand…?" The question sizzled on the tip of my tongue.

"Get me to Gydeon," he croaked, slumping against me a bit. "And if anyone grabs for us…you drop me and run back to the *Pearl*. Bring him to wherever you left me."

Gritting my teeth, I slung his free arm across my shoulders and anchored his wrist; the other hand I wrapped around his waist. "Just keep pressure on that wound."

And as we descended back into the havoc that was Korsa, I breathed life into the fire Dred had seen in me—the same fire he claimed Tristah had stoked to barter passage with the Dredgers, aboard *The Haverknot*, to sail to Bashir.

And with that fire kindled, I turned its blistering rage against anyone who so much as looked twice at me…and the pirate who leaned against me. And I did not let go of him, all the way back to the *Pearl*, even when stalking steps pursued. Even when shouts and taunts and far, far worse hounded our heels.

I held on to him. And he to me.

CHAPTER 34
LOST NAMES

I could not watch Gydeon clean and bandage the stump of Blackhand's missing finger.

He did his work in a room that was not ours by merits; instead, Siu picked the lock of an empty hovel down the hall, full of far fewer rats, where Gydeon artfully spread out his tools on the only table and went to work. The others all gathered with us, unshy of the blood—though their rage on their Captain's behalf choked the borrowed quarters in a palpable fume. I leaned beside the door, my gaze fixed on my feet, memories of Hasser's sick bay wreaking havoc on my heart.

"I knew something like this would happen," Siu muttered. "Staying in Dred's own den was a *mistake*."

"No, it was the whole bloody plan," Blackhand shot back—then cursed, wincing audibly at something Gydeon did. I winced in turn, though I still dared not look. "You lot know nothing gets done quick in this city without an Old Salt stirring the pot. It was just a matter of time before Dred noticed us."

"Quick?" Klement snorted. "It's been *three weeks*."

"And losing a finger was not part of the plan," Gydeon retorted, his tone unreasonably mild for the subject at hand. "You can't convince me otherwise."

A beat. "Aye, well," Blackhand mumbled, "pity whatever sorry sod takes the Blackhand name after me. It'll cost him a finger to keep the tale alive."

My stomach churned at the nonchalant remark…as if it meant nothing that he had lost a piece of himself in this search for Tristah.

A piece that would otherwise have come from me.

Nausea spilled up the shaft of my throat; I cleared it sharply, but no one turned my way.

"Did you at least get what you wanted out of him?" Wilkes demanded.

"Some of it," Blackhand grunted. "Anyone ever hear a whisper of some so-called *Incendiary*?"

Siu and Klement exchanged a long, heated glance.

"In Monsha, first," Siu admitted. "While we were waiting in the cove for you, Captain. Talk of raided storehouses and strikes against the militar when they go to collect on unpaid taxes. 'Specially in the Southlands."

"But there's rumors in the gambling dens here in Korsa, too," Klement added. "They say there are fewer and fewer waifs climbing aboard vessels. They've been…disappearing instead."

My breath caught, my head shooting up. Blackhand shoved himself upright on the bed, cradling his bandaged hand carefully in his lap. "Disappearing *how*?"

"Not stolen, by the sound of it. They don't seem to be leaving against their will." My breath inched out at Klement's assurance, memories of the orphanage in Monsha evaporating beneath the heat of relief. "More like they're finding better prospects."

"With whom?" Gydeon tipped forward from his seat beside Blackhand on the edge of the cot, intrigue lifting his brows. "This Incendiary?"

"Dred did say he chummed the waters with pirates." I met Blackhand's gaze for a heartbeat—all that I could manage before the heat in my neck burned too hot to endure. "What better way to do it than by removing the chance for new debtors?"

Silence overwhelmed the room—a hefty, stricken thing. In every pair of eyes, the same wistful disbelief reflected: the notion of how their own lives might have been different, had such prospects existed in their youth.

Pain pricked my heart. What might the same offer at the orphanage door have changed for *me*?

I shook the thought away. "If the Incendiary is indeed often in Bashir, as Dred implied, and if his name was known *here*, then it stands to reason Tristah might have some dealings with him. She was passionate about the plights of orphans and the underprivileged…their interests aligned."

"Might be he helped *her* disappear," Blackhand mused. "Doesn't sound like we'll get a better lead than Bashir."

"That city is crawling with dissidents," Siu warned. "Besides Ravinor, it's the biggest hotpot of anti-regime propaganda south of the Everreach. Sure you want *her* going there, Captain?"

Blackhand said nothing, his gaze fixed on me; it was a moment before I realized he was awaiting my retort.

I straightened, wetting my dry mouth with a harsh swallow. "It's possible I'll be recognized…more possible there than here. But if it's also possible this Incendiary knew of Tristah, or aided in her escape…I agree, we'll find no better place to uncover that truth."

"You heard her," Blackhand said. "Let's clear out the room. I want us all breathing clean air by this time tomorrow."

There was no mistaking the relief that unfurled among the crew at the notion of leaving this vile city. They all hurried out to do as he ordered; in moments, only Blackhand and I remained. He took a swig of the brandy Gydeon had used to douse his wound, left on the floor beside the low cot; then he set it aside and capped it with a slam of his palm.

"Why are you still here?" he grunted.

Because I was weary from all that the day had wrought. Because I had not yet caught my breath from our futile search today, and the encounter with the sinister pirates in the parlor, and our horrific meeting with Dred.

Because his agony was imprinted behind every blink of my eyes, and despite Gydeon's ministrations, I was not yet convinced he was all right. And for this blow he had taken on *my* behalf, to spare me that fate—

It mattered. More than I could ever allow the crew to witness.

Least of all him.

So I settled instead for the burning question—the one that had nipped my heels all the way from Dred's refuge, back to the *Pearl*.

"You told me that Bastyan Atreyon does not exist." I leaned back against the wall, trapping my hands behind me, flush to the splintering wood. "Explain to me why Dred called you that."

"Why bother?" he scoffed. "Whatever I say, you'll just call it a lie."

I despised the truth of that nearly as much as I despised the part of me that wished for something to believe in. For something about *him* to be true.

"You can lie about plenty," I said, "but you did not force Dred to lie for you. He is clearly no ally of yours." The muscles of his shoulders bunched, and I barreled on, "He spoke that name to wound you…degrade you." Just as Lucretzia had called me *Alyona*, tarnishing the name my parents had given me with her cold mockery. "Who is *Bastyan* to *him*?"

A muscle in his jaw feathered. His abdomen swelled inward with the force of his breath.

"Bastyan is the name my *parents* gave me, all right?" He spat the title with such contempt, it set me back against the wall. "It's who I was when I fell into debt with Dred." His hands knotted tightly in his lap…then sprang apart, a low hiss escaping his gritted teeth. He flexed out his fingers, gaze fixed to the bandaged stump. "That lad didn't have it in him to make pirate. He was a fine enough sailor with his grandad, or pitched onto a drug runner's vessel…but Korsa would've minced him for chum." His eyes lifted at last to mine. "So I put him down. And that's where Ryker Kassian was born."

Ryker Kassian, who had sailed with the latest in a long heritage of Blackhands—and then *become* Blackhand when the time was right.

Bastyan was as lost to him as *Alyona* was to me. And yet, some piece of Bastyan must still live in him…just as the pieces of Alyona breathed with my lungs and beat in my heart.

My careful knowledge of baking. My love of needy and desperate things. My sharp mind for maps and places.

His sunshine smiles. His devastating concern for the people he called his own. His rough-edged gallantry.

What a pair we were. Not entirely self-made; not entirely the sum of what we'd been.

He was a scoundrel. A captor. A pirate.

And today, he had lost a finger for me.

A debt I had been willing to pay—one he had not been required to take on for himself. Yet he had. An act I would have expected of the man aboard *The Athalion*. Something Bash would've done.

I shifted my feet. "Was it Bastyan or Ryker who nearly perished at sea— who has nightmares and tonics he takes for them?"

The corner of his mouth tilted upward. "That was with the drug runners. Still Bastyan."

"And what nightmares does Ryker Kassian have?"

Slowly, he struggled to his feet, a bit of pallor still lightening his sunmarked skin. "Tonight, it's going to be your hand taking that cleaver instead of mine."

My stomach lifted on the crest of a tidal wave; I opened my mouth to give it some escape, to give voice to what blazed in my chest—

A scream crashed thinly along the walls of the outer hall.

Blackhand jerked toward the door, his breaths halting all at once; by his wide eyes and the dread that pooled in them, I knew I had not misheard.

Siu.

CHAPTER 35
A BLADE BETWEEN

I did not want to feel fear for this crew. I did not want to feel anything at all…Not after so many betrayals. Not with all the things that set us apart.

And yet, it *was* fear souring my throat; fear clamoring in my heart as Blackhand and I tore from the room and thundered down the *Pearl's* tilted staircase, hastening toward Siu's relentless, wrathful shrieks.

"Get your hands off of him—get your hands *off of him*! *Let go of me*—Gyddy! No, *no, no, no!*"

I leaped down from the last step, staggering when my heels struck against the uneven floorboards. Blackhand slung an arm around my waist, halting my wild stumble, towing me back against his chest. His heart hammered between my shoulders; the imprint of his pendant practically blazed against my back.

The *Pearl's* lower room was dredged in havoc—chairs tossed aside, tables tipped, tankards overturned, steaming plates of food scattered. The door flailed on its hinges, as if the last few patrons had only recently escaped. For the first time in our long weeks here, the food and mercantile counters were unmanned.

All that remained were the Raiders—and a band of pirates I did not know.

They outnumbered Blackhand's crew by painful odds—more than a dozen against four. And nearly half of them were occupied with Siu, the rest with blades and pistols on Klement and Wilkes; wisely, both had abated from what seemed a brutal fistfight. Bruises and blood marred their noses and cheekbones, and Klement gripped her ribs, sagging over them as if they'd cracked.

But Siu…Siu was primal. She thrashed with ferocity made flesh, bucking and biting at the hands that pinned her against the serving counter as she struggled for her freedom…to get to Gydeon, held against the opposite wall by a man dressed in a black Captain's coat.

Gydeon did not fight. And I could only imagine what threats this captain had breathed against Siu to keep him from snapping loose and ripping those men off of her.

"Hold her," the Captain spat to his mates. "I said, *hold her!*"

And they did—three to each arm now, pinning them outstretched to the counter, another sliding over the worn top to band his thick arm around Siu's throat from behind. Still, she struggled with such violence it heated the air around her like an oven. It coaxed up a bloodthirst in me I had not known since my days dueling with Lucretzia, fed by Tristah's rage and hate.

But all of the fighting ceased when the Captain whipped out a notched, rust-handled dagger, laying its blade to the leaping pulse at the side of Gydeon's neck. Even Siu's vicious writhing stilled.

"I don't see a coinpurse on you, Greenfinger." The pirate's croaky chuckle danced like the fingertips of an iron-clawed gauntlet down my spine. "You know what that means?"

He tipped up Gydeon's chin with the flat of the blade, stroking the tip slowly, tauntingly, to the other side of his neck. Siu sobbed with killing desperation.

"It means it's *almost* my time."

A sizzling flash of light burst across my vision—the memory of Blackhand facing the same sort of cruelty only hours ago. The same heartless violence.

And I thought of Tristah, meritless, without a friend at her side, navigating these treacherous waters.

And Gydeon, right here before me…the gentlest, most compassionate of the Raiders, with a thin sliver of blood trickling down his neck.

Even Siu in all her fury could not escape the cage of a dozen hands. Wilkes and Klement could not bat away bullets with blades.

But only Blackhand held me back.

And this time, that was not enough to keep me captive.

I shoved down his arm with one hand, and with the other, I plucked Lucretzia's stolen blade from its sheath at his side.

And I leaped.

It had been years since I had sparred; years since I had drawn a single one of Lucretzia's methods from the dusty corner of my mind where I'd stashed them away. But that did not erase more than a decade of training pounded into my blood and bones, day by day.

These were pirates, brawlers, full of stabbing brawn and treachery. They had not been trained by the delegator of the Graven regime's militar.

I slithered between two of them, throwing kicks and punches at the soft spots that would wound the worst; they toppled side and side before their crewmates even noticed they'd been struck…and by then, I'd swiveled beneath the Captain's knife hand. I jerked my shoulder upward into his wrist, a maneuver I had practiced countless times—freeing Tristah from Lucretzia's unsheathed daggers in much the same way. In the same moment, I spiraled, my blade shrieking in an overhead arch along his…lifting it away from Gydeon's neck, ensuring not a fleck of steel skimmed skin.

My pivot finished with a boot to the pirate's gut, landing him solidly on his haunches. I braced myself between him and Gydeon, the knife laid backhand to my wrist…twice as stable, twice as deadly as a blade held out from the body. And twice as difficult to steal.

The Captain stared at me, stunned.

The Raiders stared at me. Equally stunned.

Athyna's stunned face, blood bubbling at her lips, struggled into my mind's eye; I blinked it forcefully away.

I did not have to draw blood. I needed only to convince them that I could. And that I *would*.

"He leaves this hovel unharmed," I snarled, flicking my eyes from pirate to pirate, "or *none of you* do."

"He killed my brother," the Captain seethed.

Though that did not seem like anything Gydeon could do, I hardly cared whose blood he'd once spilled. Not when these pirates threatened to spill his— *all* of ours. "And would you like me to make your mother *childless?*"

The cords around Lucretzia's blade winked in the low tavern light; the crew did not all swarm me at once. They were wolves measuring their prey; ready to kill, but wary to lose blood in the battle.

A pistol clicked, silencing every breath in the room.

"See, now, that's the sort of sound I like to hear." Blackhand slouched a bit, the thumb of his bandaged hand hooked casually in his belt; in the other, he held his pistol, aimed at the Captain slumped on the floor before me. "All right, there, sweetheart?"

I shot him a glare; he hefted a brow.

Behind me, Gydeon scoffed. "Bit shaken, but I'll live."

The maddening urge to laugh bubbled caramel-thick in my throat.

"Now that we're all in a position to have a *civilized* conversation." Blackhand stepped over the instigator, doubling the layer between him and Gydeon—and, mercifully, ensuring that *I* would not be forced to draw blood. "What is it you think you're going to have this time, Sharkteeth?"

The man bared his mouth in a scowl, and revulsion rippled through me; his teeth were rived to fine points, the gums around them blackened and blistered. Whether it was some illness or a modification meant to make him more fearsome, the effect was the same; I had little desire even to look him in the face.

"You know the deal with Wash Rackham," he spat. "Nassar doesn't pay the life debt, I get my way with him."

"Aye. Didn't think old Rackham gave an acquittal." Blackhand's head slanted. "Didn't realize he used the Leeches to gather his debts on the streets same as the seas, either."

"*Unpaid* debts," Sharkteeth enunciated bitterly.

"We were just on our way to make a payment, as a matter of fact," Blackhand drawled. "You Leeches are welcome to join us, if it cools your fins."

He holstered the pistol and mustered the Raiders with a jerk of his chin; slowly, uneasily, the Leeches relinquished their hold on them.

Siu shot forward, ramming past Sharkteeth just as he gained his feet and sending him tumbling back to the floor. She ducked around me with a flick of a glance, clapping a hand to the side of Gydeon's neck; his fingers wound deftly into her hair.

"All right, Blackhand," Sharkteeth sneered, regaining his feet much less gracefully now—favoring his left hip. "Let's pay the Old Salt a visit."

At the bark of his voice, his crew enclosed us, shuffling us from the tavern and out into the city streets.

CHAPTER 36
BELOW THE SOUND THE WORLD MAKES

My nerves frayed at the notion of meeting another Old Salt—two of them in a single day. And, judging by how our last encounter had gone…

I dropped my gaze to the blood-freckled bandage still hanging low at Blackhand's waist.

He kept perfect stride with me, but his gaze bounced about the crew; from Wilkes and Klement, taking the lead, to Gydeon and Siu just ahead of us, arms wrapped around one another's waists as if they would never be parted again.

I inclined toward Blackhand. "Why didn't you draw that pistol to begin with?"

He leaned back, so near his lips grazed the top of my head. "Because the Leeches know me. They know the whole crew. They've been watching us a long time, because that sucking little loach wants the half of the debt he can't have…blood for blood." His fingers flexed on his pistol grip. "You saw how they had Siu and Klem and Wil. I saw them watching me, too. What they didn't have eyes on was *you*. So, I figured…you were the best chance we had of getting to Gyddy before something happened none of us could come back from."

Faith.

He'd put *faith* in me…had entrusted the life of his ship's healer into my hands. Hands he had no reason to believe were capable of saving that life.

"And now what?" I rasped, before I could show a glint of gratitude I might later regret.

"Well, unless you have any particular interest in meeting a man so old, he looks like he was carved for a ship's head, and smells just as briney?" Blackhand drew back far enough to level his gaze with mine.

Readiness tightened through me. I shook my head.

"Guessed as much."

Without another word, Blackhand slammed on his heels, whipped the pistol from below his cloak, and pivoted back, leading with his arm outstretched—firing straight through Sharkteeth's shoulder.

Pandemonium erupted on the current of the pirate's piercing bellow; Wilkes and Klem turned on the Leeches as if they'd been waiting for this moment, slinging punches and hammering kicks like seasoned brawlers. Siu and Gydeon ducked and swiveled, hurling great casks of rum into the street from outside the taverns on both edges of it. With deft shoves, they sent them rolling down the angled way ahead of us, Wilkes and Klement handspringing over them to land back beside us.

"There's our trail!" Blackhand stuffed his pistol away, snatched my hand…and we flew.

The barrels set a tremendous, thundering procession before us. Their weighty descent removed pirates left and right from our path—some forcibly, others with shocked yelps as they dove for safety at the roadside. Behind us, the Leeches gave chase; but in the wake of the tumbling barrels, the sea of pirates closed back in, forging a wall at our backs.

All of us were gasping and heaving from the run by the time we reached the harbor docks; Blackhand flagged in particular, thicker stains of fresh blood marring his bandage.

Behind us, a bellow split the cacophony of the harbor. *"Stop the Raiders! Rackham wants them!"*

We swerved down the curve of the harbor, and Blackhand stumbled, weaving on his feet. With the flex of his hand around mine, he nearly dragged me down to the docks with him. Cursing, I ducked beneath his arm and wrenched him forward, calling ahead in a voice so breathlessly raspy, I hardly recognized it as my own: "Wilkes, we need a distraction!"

The quartermaster pulled ahead of us, adding speed to his sprint that I wasn't certain I could've managed; drawing the faithful cutlass at his side, he spun and slashed, again and again—not striking bodies, but bollards.

Mooring twine snapped beneath the slick cut of the sharpest blade I had ever beheld. With great, guttural creaks, ships began to shift, tilting precariously in the falls-fed water.

Crews hollered, aboard and at the portside. They rushed to save the lines; in seconds, the docks were swarming with bodies, few of them paying any mind to Sharkteeth's command.

But those that did were a barreling tide at our backs; their footsteps shook the docks as we reached the shadow of *The Dread Singer*, where I shoved Blackhand over against Klement and Wilkes and whirled on Siu.

"Get the ship moving. Do not wait for me," I commanded.

With a jerk of the chin, she was up the gangplank, Gydeon pressed on her heels. Klement and Wilkes jerked Blackhand after them, but he dragged his feet, slinging an arm back my way. "Lio!"

I caught his hand, grazed my thumb gently over the soiled, bloody stump— then shoved his arm away. "Get on board!"

From Wilkes' waist, I snatched the axe he'd bartered at the blacksmith's half-hull. And then I sprinted back down the docks.

With every step, it was the past—not the warped, wooden wharfs—which rose to meet me. Lessons Tristah had taught me. Not Lucretzia.

The trick to crossing ice is to listen, she'd breathed in clouded plumes while we strapped on ice skates and prepared to conquer the frozen lake behind Shadewyle Castle. *Listen with your whole heart, Aly. Get quiet inside you, and you can hear below the sounds the world makes.*

I dragged breath in through rounded lips and pushed it back out again, blowing away fear like loose flour from the kneading block.

Listen, Aly.

Besides my parents, only she had ever called me that.

Listen.

There it was—the creak in the rotting planks, in the precise place where Blackhand had stumbled.

Weakness. Something to be exploited.

That, I *had* learned from Lucretzia.

Eyes wide open.

Skidding to a halt, I raised my gaze to the cluster of pirates hurtling down the docks…the ones who had heard the name of an Old Salt and leapt to task. Who perhaps thought that by dragging us to Wash Rackham, they would lessen their own debts.

Unfortunately for them, I was thoroughly finished paying dues to this place. *Take power where you can.*

Planting my feet, I hefted the axe over my shoulder; and with a cry to bear that power down into every bone, I swung it overhead with all my might—and slammed it into the weakened portion of the docks.

A mighty groan snaked through the belly of the wood; prying the axehead loose, I hefted and swung again. And again. And again.

My muscles gloried in it—in a motion not unlike lifting and throwing sacks of flour and grain from the wagons which had delivered them weekly to *The Secret Ingredient.*

This strength belonged to Lionyra Vara. This power made *sense.*

I barely heard the sixth swing over the pounding of boots converging down the docks. The seventh suffocated beneath the snap of sailcloth and the grind of an anchor being weighed.

Another heft. Another strike.

Wood crunched. Splintered.

Powder blasted.

The pistolshot screamed past my face, so near its heat skimmed my cheek. Shock—and horror—stole the bottom from my stomach. My next lift and slam of the axe was weaker, wobbling with disbelief at how near death had sketched the lines of my life.

Another shot—then another, and another. But these came from behind me, aimed at the pirates who rounded the curve of the wharfs, sprinting my way.

They came from the *Raiders*, lining the railing, pistols in hand and rifles shouldered. And from Blackhand, his unhurt arm raised, pistol aimed, sighted—

Another powder eruption.

The pirate nearest to me dropped, two others stumbling over him.

"*Lio, move!*" Blackhand bellowed, casting his pistol aside; his hands slapped the railing, preparing to leap from the ship to my side. But Gydeon and Kory were on his arms in an instant, heaving him back before he could hurl himself down to the gangplank. He tore and wrenched at their hold, his eyes still fixed on me. "Get your backside on this ship! Forget the blasted—"

But I paid him no heed; I settled my weight, dug into the very depths of myself, and looked down into the splintered mess I'd made of the docks.

I envisioned Lucretzia's face as I heaved back and *hurled* down.

With a tremendous, spine-shuddering *crack*, the docks sundered.

Wood planks caved, wrenching apart; moldering struts crumbled into the black waters below. Pirates tipped and crashed over the edge, buried under a fresh onslaught as more and more boards broke loose and gave way beneath their piled weight.

The planks beneath my own feet bucked. And slanted.

A cry burst from my throat as I slipped, dragged by the axe's weight, tipping forward—

Fingers snared in the back of my vest. With a vicious shout, Siu wrenched me away from the edge, whipping the axe from my hand and shoving me toward the end of the docks. "*Run!*"

And we did—the First Mate hefting the axe over her shoulder as if it weighed nothing. Already the *Singer* was pulling away from the docks, picking up speed as the crew rowed belowdecks, long oars striking the water in a monotonous drumbeat. We hurtled alongside it as it withdrew, the gangplank lifted but the rungs still in reach.

On deck, Blackhand kept perfect pace with us, his black cloak snapping behind him as he sprinted down the railing line. "Come on, *come on!*"

Ducking pistolfire, we reached the edge of the dock—and with no other choice, we jumped.

My outstretched hands snagged the lowest rung, iron chafes erupting across my palms. All the breath punched from my lungs when my chest struck the unyielding hull; Siu landed below me, nothing to grasp onto but the shaft of the axe with its head buried in the wood.

But she did not hesitate; nimble as a cat, she flipped herself up to stand on the axe's handle, then lunged for the rungs above me—just as the axe broke free, tumbling into the water.

With all our strength, we started to climb.

The ascent dizzied me; numbness sparked in pockets along my arms and shoulders, spiraling like smoke curls down my back. A warning that, after months without practice, my muscles were no longer so fit for the tasks I had put them to today, no matter how I'd relished them.

There would be pain. There would be *time* for pain, once we reached the deck.

Siu made it first, slipping above, her barked orders peppering the air. I struggled up after her, eyes fixed on the next rung, and the next—

Another bark of pistolfire; pain slashed along my upper arm, and my fingers erupted with blistering pain—then fell numb. Loosed from the rung, I swung wildly to the side, facing back toward the docks…toward Sharkteeth, who had conquered the gap and reached the end of the long wharf.

His pistol was raised, those cruel teeth bared in a hateful snarl.

Blood erupted. A deadshot.

Sharkteeth crumbled, bleeding profusely from the head; and over the crackling echo that had come from the deck—from Wilkes's own rifle, still shouldered, angled above the railing—a voice spoke my name.

"Lionyra. Look at me."

Blinking the sparkling swarm of damp heat from my vision, I met Blackhand's gaze.

Flat on his stomach, he reached his unhurt arm down to me. Concern etched every sun-loved line around his piercing green eyes. "Sweetheart, I can't pull you up if you don't give me your hand."

Setting my teeth, I slung my laden arm up to him, pain crying out from the lead track in my bicep.

Blackhand caught my fingers, squeezed them once, then hauled against my weight; and with his added strength, I conquered the last half-dozen rungs, spilling onto the topdeck of *The Dread Singer*, half in its Captain's lap.

For a moment, neither of us moved; cast against the tangle of his legs, I searched out his gaze. The concern there had not dimmed—only darkened when his thumb swiped the burn on my cheek; when his hand encountered my sleeve, stained with blood.

"Get to my chambers," he growled. "Gyddy's on his way."

And I went; not because I craved confinement. Not because it was an order worth obeying.

But because I knew myself. I knew what was to come.

I barely reached Blackhand's private washroom in time to snatch the relief bucket from the corner.

Then I vomited until I had nothing left in me.

CHAPTER 37
THE REFINING FIRE

By Ahim's mercy, Gydeon did not visit me until the sickness passed.

I lay curled on the divan when the door opened at long last, huddled beneath a woven blanket that smelled of salt and damp. Even with that reprieve, the click of the latch spilled a heavy pour of sour adrenaline into my veins, my whirling thoughts mistaking it as the precedent to thunderous pistolshot. I thrust up to one hand, only for my elbow to collapse like a poorly done souffle; a groan punched against my teeth as my burned cheek chafed against the pillow.

"Only me," Gydeon said; when I failed to answer, unable to trawl breath back into my lungs, he slipped inside, bag in tow. I pushed myself gingerly this time, gathering my hair over my shoulder…away from the wound I had bandaged with a worn kerchief from Blackhand's desk drawer. Gydeon, to my relief, was bandaged as well, his neck padded with soft gauze.

He drew his usual chair beside the divan, set his healer's bag on the floor, and rustled about within it. Then he drew a tincture free, pressing it into my hand. "For the nausea."

Wincing, I uncorked it, taking all of the mixture at once. It stung, cloying and cold, but the tang of ginger soothed my sickness almost at once. "How did you know?"

"I saw that look on your face when the Captain sent you off." Apology edged his tone as he began laying out things from his bag—suture thread and needles, and several corked bottles. "I'm sorry I didn't come to you sooner. I intended to, but Siu…"

"She wanted you to see to yourself first," I hazarded. "As she should. You had a blade to your neck only hours ago, Gydeon."

"It was not the first time. Doubtful it will be the last. But my wife worries." With his thumb and forefinger, he parted the tear in my sleeve, shaking his head a bit. "Let me clean this. Then we'll move to stitching."

It had been so long since I'd had wounds that needed to be sutured…since I'd done anything so dangerous as to necessitate it. I steadied myself with both feet swung onto the floor, gripping the sculpted edges of the divan beside my knees while Gydeon dabbed a stinging tonic on the torn lips of my skin. To distract myself from the burn, I indulged in the question that had plagued me since the *Pearl.* "What happened with Sharkteeth's brother?"

Gydeon's hands stilled a moment; and then, for the first time since they'd treated my coral scrapes, a tremor shifted through them.

"Before Sharkteeth took the helm, his brother, Silver-Eyes, captained *The Depth Treachery,*" he said, so quietly I had to brace forward to catch his words, "and led the Leeches. It was the first vessel that agreed to take Siu on. The *Treachery* is a ship indebted to Wash Rackham, one of the oldest and wealthiest of the Old Salts. His crews are proud. Too proud. They think too highly of themselves, and initiation is…bitter. Painful. *Brutal.*"

His fingers lifted away from my skin, flexing slightly; when they steadied again, he returned to his work.

"Siu was only a girl when she joined them, but that…I think it spurred them to greater cruelty. She and I turned friends while she was serving aboard their ship, after I landed myself in Korsa…and I watched as she returned from plunders and voyages with fresh scars and burns. As she told tales of all the dangerous tasks she'd undertaken…the suffering she endured to keep her place on the only crew that would have her."

His eyes took on a distant quality, lost in pain-stricken memory…a look I knew all too well from mirrors I'd gazed into for years and years.

"Korsa thought her weak, easy prey. Because she is an artist at heart…because she would have rather decorated the walls of a pirate city with paint than with blood." His voice roughened; he shook his head, setting aside the stained dabbing cloth and rinsing his hands in a wash of antiseptic. He dried them, then patted his face dry, his next words muffled by the towel: "No one else would take her aboard. So she stayed, and she experienced unspeakable hurts…and then one night she returned to Korsa nearly dead. Her back a bloodied slab."

Nausea peppered my throat again—not for things *I* had suffered this time, but for the agony of the woman who'd come back for me at the docks. "The Leeches?"

"Silver-Eyes himself," Gydeon growled. "He punished her for showing compassion during a raid on a Trade vessel to a girl half her age. Whipped her bloody and gave her nothing for her wounds while they sailed back."

He took up the needle and thread, but his hands trembled so violently now he could not guide the sutures through.

I gripped his wrists, bringing his hands down to settle in his lap. He stared at them while I held them in place, my thumbs brushing the backs of his knuckles—all the comfort I could offer to a man whose past held such pain for a woman he loved so fiercely.

"By the time they returned to Korsa, the infection ran deep, and the pain far deeper," he croaked. "Enough that delirium had taken her when they dropped anchor. Her only clear thought was to reach me. The debt I accrued acquiring items for her healing was…" He stole in a shuddering breath, freeing one hand to wipe his eyes. "I still do not know the extent of it. Someday, I'm certain it will come to collect. But at the time, I could think of nothing but what I needed to save her."

"And you did," I reminded him quietly. "She lives because of your faithful labor. Your love."

His eyes lifted to mine, rimmed in gleaming silver and blushed pink; his smile wobbled as fiercely as his hands. "I'm afraid there was more than love in me, those days. There was vengeance."

His fingers steadying at last, he turned me gently beneath the arm, rinsed my wound, and spoke as he worked—a tale that silenced the pain.

"While Siu healed, I hunted. I found *The Depth Treachery* and Silver-Eyes, and I made absolutely certain he could harm no other waifs, no other women, as he had harmed her."

A chill scampered down my spine, absent entirely from the draft that leaked beneath the door. It was only faintly alarming, to hear such words from the man who tended my wounds.

"It was a clean death, but not a painless one," Gydeon went on. "And the methods were precise, but I was clumsy…made careless by my rage. Sharkteeth found the trail back to me, and he dragged me before Rackham—hoping, I'm certain, to receive a ransom for finding the killer of one of Rackham's indebted captains, as well avenging his brother."

A swift shake of his head; the needle dipped in and out of my skin, pricking and burning as it tugged flesh shut.

"But the Old Salt recognized more in me than murderous hands…he saw a finesse to it." Gydeon's lip curled, mustache rustling at the scathing compliment. "He asked if I'd been trained by Hadrassi poisoners. I told him I had not."

"And was that the truth?"

His skilled hands paused, his eyes leveling into me.

The infinite silence took on a warning resonance.

"Rackham saw more use in me alive than dead," he said at last, his focus returning to his work. "He saw purposes my skills might serve. So he cut a new debt for us…a lifetime's worth of merits, or half that and my services at his beck and call." He shrugged crookedly, though the stilted gesture held no nonchalance whatsoever. "Or else Sharkteeth would have his way with me."

He snipped the thread, tempered a bandage around the wound, then knuckled my jaw gently, turning my head so he could apply a salve to the pistolshot scrape on my cheek.

"Afterward, Sharkteeth gained the *Treachery*, and when I told Siu what I'd done…she hauled herself from her cot for the first time in nearly a week. And she said that we would waste no time repaying that debt." A new light sparkled in his gaze—the same love that bubbled beneath every word. "She marched us down to the docks with a fire in her I had never seen before. She was no longer asking, or pleading…she was *demanding* to be taken aboard. And when we collided with the newest ship's Captain sailing into port…it was a match made in the depths. He asked her on as his First Mate between one breath and the next."

An unbidden smile tugged at my mouth. "Blackhand."

It was no wonder the truth of this tale had never been shared among the crew; it was soaked in far more sorrow and anguish and cruelty than the bantering tale they'd told on the way to the *Pearl*. And yet the sketchings of it remained there…a man and a woman, their talents twisted by the desperation born in the pirate haven, finding and clinging to one another. Saving one another in their own ways…finding their strengths through the refining fire as they traversed it hand in hand.

And in that tale, there was another sort of hero…one guised at first in shadow. A stranger who had seen the potential in them both.

I shut my eyes as Gydeon streaked salve along my cheekbone. "Ahim favored you both, to find such a love."

"Aye." Gydeon chuckled quietly. "We wouldn't have known it was love, at first. But that's how it goes, isn't it? The longer you're in something, the more it changes…all the different ways you see it."

"And sometimes a leech is just a leech." A new voice joined our conversation, heavy and gruff. "Aye, Gyddy?"

I blinked my eyes open—which took more effort than I had anticipated, my lashes clinging with exhaustion.

The Captain slouched in the doorway of his own quarters, one hand gripping the upper frame, the other with its missing finger tucked securely beneath the pit of his opposite shoulder. Heaviness hung around the contours of his face, dragging the corners of his mouth into a scowl.

Gydeon brushed his thumb once more along my cheekbone, tapped my jaw, then got to his feet and gathered his things. "I'll have a look at those bandages soon, ensure the stitches are holding well. For now, I suggest sleep for you both."

"Wait." Desperation had me catching his wrist again, despite the miserable heat of vulnerability that climbed my cheeks in the Captain's presence. "Do you have a tonic for that?"

I could only begin to imagine what would haunt my dreams tonight, when my waking hours had sickened me to the point of emptying my insides.

Gydeon opened his mouth, but before he could speak, Blackhand shrugged up from the doorframe. "I've got her, Gyddy. Go curl up with your wife…depths know she's waiting for you."

Gydeon's forehead reddened; he blew out a curse under his breath, clapped Blackhand on the shoulder, and ducked out. The door whispered shut behind him, and silence infused itself into our presence…the same charged quiet that had hung between us in the borrowed room at the *Pearl*.

The quiet creak of boots on floorboards shattered it as he crossed to his bed, dropping to root beneath the iron-fastened legs. In a moment he straightened, an amber bottle caught by the neck between his fingers.

"This ought to do the trick." He lobbed it to me with his good hand; I caught it deftly, but pain tugged through the strained muscles of my shoulders. At my hiss, Blackhand's brows drew together. "You all right?"

"I will be." Popping the cork, I inhaled the scent of a valerian tincture; it stirred memories of a tale he had told me, washed in lanternlight and the smell of yeast and dough. Comforts I still craved, even now.

I helped myself to a swallow of the tincture, wincing at the syrupy thickness. Blackhand chuckled quietly, settling into the seat Gydeon had vacated before me. "You get used to it."

"I'd rather if it was just for the night." I offered the bottle out to him; he took it, rolling it against his palm. Shadows darkened the green of his eyes to deep gray.

"So would I." Sighing, he tossed back a swallow of his own, then cleaned his lips on his sleeve.

I settled deeper into the divan, applying slight pressure to the hot wound on my upper arm; it alleviated a bit of the sting, as if touching it dispersed the pain into my muscles. "Where are we now?"

"In the tunnels." Blackhand reclined as well, his unhurt hand braced on his thigh, the bottle still dangling between his fingers. "Should come out of a spillway into the Abbra Foothills in a few days. Port Krait's not far from there…then it's about a day on foot to Bashir."

Excitement thrummed low in my belly, muted beneath the tincture and the weight of exhaustion settling over me like a damp shawl. "And then, with any favor from Ahim…we find word of Tristah."

Blackhand nodded, his gaze dancing over me; an odd sheen coated his eyes, coaxing out rumors of green amidst the gray. "Back there, at the docks…that was the most blasted foolhardy thing I've ever seen."

A low snort spun itself from my throat, my eyes rolling shut. "Yes, well—"

"And the bravest."

His voice hitched slightly on those three soft, husky words, and shock unstuck my lashes far more swiftly this time; the Captain gazed at me with a sort of raw reverence that no words could properly name.

"Ever since I started taking this crew aboard…feels like it's been me against everyone else, everything in this blasted country and the seas beyond that's trying to tear us apart. Take them away from me." His thumb grazed the tight furrows of his brow, his gaze averting from mine. "Don't even know how to thank you for taking that risk. For Gyddy, back in the tavern. And with the axe."

His gratitude rendered me speechless; I could detect no lie in it, no matter how fine a sieve I sifted it through. How could there be, when I had seen how much he loved his crew—how they adored him? The man who'd taken a wounded woman and a kindhearted poisoner aboard, named them First Mate and healer…entrusted so much of himself to them that he slept in their quarters and risked life and limb to protect them from those who sought their deaths.

Today, he had entrusted them to me, as well. And I had not thought twice of defending them, all of them. Just as Siu had not hesitated to come back for me; just as the Captain had not hesitated to reach for me when I'd dangled above the doom of the depths.

A lump forged in my throat. I swallowed it away, sat forward—then slumped as a dizzying wave of sleepiness surged through my head. My jaws cracked in an ear-splitting yawn, so deafening I nearly missed Blackhand's chuckle. "You and me both, sweetheart."

His hands caught my shoulders—gentle with the right—and he guided me down to lie on the divan. Warmth snapped over me, puffing out scents of leather and smoke and sea salt; a blanket tucked under my chin.

The hair drifted away from my cheek, guided by rope-rough fingers to drape behind my ear.

"Thank you." A brush of raspy words breathed against my temple. Tonic-softened lips followed.

I pried my eyes open to find him already at the door—leaving it partially ajar as he slipped out into the night.

Confusion prodded up my head. "Ryker?"

He paused astride the deck, glancing at me over his shoulder. Anguish stroked the angles of his face. "The door is open," he said simply. "And you'll find the galley is stocked with plenty of flour."

Then he was gone. And I toppled back onto the divan, certain I would wake to find that exchange—and the brand of his lips on my skin—had all been part of some confused, tonic-touched dream.

CHAPTER 38
NO SIMPLE RANSOM

The door remained open. I knew that to be true the moment I woke to Camden's weight landing on my ankles.

"Oi!" His boyish shout startled me awake like a splash of cold water to the face; I struggled up, dazed and bleary, to find him grinning at me from his post on my feet, cross-legged and grinning. "That was some work you did on the docks, Seasplitter!"

"Sea—I beg your pardon?" The vestiges of a dream—one of floating and sinking in the most pleasant, bathwater-warm sea—slowly dripped away, and the slash of lanternlight from the deck paved across my face through the open door.

Still open. The bustle of the crew beyond seemed to be the dream now.

"Yeah!" Camden crowed, one hand planted on the swoopbacked divan, the other on its edge as he tilted to snare my gaze. "The crew's been jabbering about it all day…what you did to the docks back in port, with the axe! Depths, I wish I'd seen it, but Kory hasn't let me topside in *weeks*. Did you really use the axe to take off some pirate's head?"

"Cam—"

"No, I know…too *violent* for me." He flapped a hand. "But if you *could* tell me anything…was there a lot of blood?"

"*Camden!*" We both jolted at that rough feminine shout floating through the open door; the firelight rippled around the frame of Siu's body, hands planted on her hips. We did not need to see her eyes in the dimness to feel the fire of her stare.

"Oops. Blast it," Camden muttered, scrambling off the divan.

"Hey!" Siu stalked into the room, scruffing him and hoisting him to his tiptoes. "What did Gydeon say about waking her?"

"Aw, I wasn't doing any harm!" Cam protested, dangling from her grip with a disarming grin. "Just wanted a story is all."

"Well, when you find a Storycrafter, you can have one." Siu pushed him toward the open door, popping him on the haunches with her foot. "Go take your lessons from Kato. He's waiting."

"Sure he is," Camden sulked; but around Siu's back, he winked at me, pointed two fingers at my chest, then jabbed his thumbs into his own. *We'll talk*, he mouthed.

"Plucky runt," Siu muttered as he darted off. Her gaze trailed over me, and she scratched beneath the kerchief that tamed her red locks tight to her scalp. "How are you?"

"Wide awake now," I laughed breathlessly, towing myself up with a hand on the seatback. A dim throb pulsed in my injured arm and scoured cheek, but they were far less painful than many injuries I'd suffered before. "Gydeon?"

"Still sleeping, thank Ahim. He needed it." Siu shifted her weight, her hands falling limp at her sides now. After a moment, she cinched them behind her waist. "I…wanted to thank you. For what you did for him yesterday."

Embarrassment warmed beneath my skin. "It was—"

"Don't say it was nothing," Siu cut across me sharply. "Don't ever say that to someone when you saved the person they love most in the world."

Heat stamped my throat. "Well," I offered, "then it was my pleasure."

She winked. "Better."

"Thank *you*," I added, struggling to my feet; sleep still clung to my curves like an ill-fitting cloak. "For coming back for me."

"I'd do it again." There was no hint of regret or doubt in her steady tone. "From now on, you need anything aboard this vessel, you come to me or Gyddy. We'll make sure you're taken care of."

The firmness of that vow set my already-dizzied head spinning. I leaned one hand into the curved arm of the divan, setting my teeth against a grimace. "Just like that? A prisoner becomes a friend, for the sake of a saved life?"

Perhaps to anyone else, the question would have been insulting; but Siu's gaze brimmed with respect as it searched mine.

"Piracy is a cutthroat trade," she said. "From what Gydeon told you, you understand see it was that way for me more than most. I don't take it lightly that folk who aren't Raiders wouldn't have looked twice at what was happening in that tavern. And you had less reason to intervene than any of them, because of…what we are to one another." She scraped a hand up her arm, bunching her loose-fitting, billowy linen shirt up at the elbow. "But you did it anyway. Says plenty about the sort of woman you are, titles and ransoms be sunk."

"Well, I do appreciate it," I admitted. "And, the things you suffered among the Leeches...our tales may not be the same, but I suspect there is more written into the lines of our stories that is alike than different. So, if you would ever like someone you can discuss it with..."

"I just might." Siu flicked a smile my way; then she offered the hook of her elbow to me. "But, for now...let's get you cleaned up, aye? And, I don't know if you've spent much time with One-Pot Willy, but he gets a bit lonely down in the galley."

My fingers all but itched for the feel of dough beneath them—something to erase the impression left by the hilt of a dagger and the grip of an axe. "I'd love to."

The voyage away from Korsa proved so much more pleasant than the one that had brought us to its docks, I could nearly believe I sailed aboard another vessel altogether.

Though the crew was not entirely friendly—indeed, frosty silence still punctuated my occasional encounters with Klement in particular—grudging respect spread as rapidly as Camden's tales of my feat at the docks. I suspected Gydeon and Siu had as much to do with that as the boy; and Wilkes, though bemoaning the loss of his axe, was adamant it had perished for a good cause.

A certain notoriety among pirates was not something I had ever envisioned myself in possession of; but I hardly minded. Particularly when that reputation began to shift from my daring with the axe to the bread I made.

The moment we sailed clear of the spillway and into the Abbra Foothills, Siu and Ryker tucked us away into a cove to replenish supplies and cook perishables. I chose to remain aboard the vessel, forcing my impatience at our necessary delay into several new batches of dough and then sending them ashore to be baked.

That night, when we cast out from the cove, the mood among the crew was markedly different; a levity I had never seen among them saturated every corner of the galley where they assembled to eat, passing fragrant loaves of bread and cinnamon pastries around the narrow cluster of tables.

"Drop me in the *depths*," Kato roared, slamming his hand on the tabletop and gesturing to me—at the counter, still kneading out my frustrations. "I would kill a man for this bread, Seasplitter."

"I would kill *you* for it," Kory volleyed off, ripping the bread loaf from his brother's hands. "I don't know *what* they make the loaves out of in Korsa, but it must not be flour if this is what bread's meant to be."

"It isn't, and I've warned you about that a thousand times!" One-Pot Willy growled from behind me, tossing the freshly skinned meat they'd trapped that day into a salting brine.

Camden draped himself over the back of his seat, shoveling another handful of cinnamon pastry into his mouth. "I'm going to die. I am going to *die* from this, and it's going to be all *Lio's* fault."

"Worse ways to go, mate," the Captain teased, ruffling a hand through the boy's hair and firing a wink my way.

It was odd beyond measure, to find such camaraderie from a crew of pirates...my captors, no less.

And yet...the door to my quarters remained unlocked.

At night, I walked the deck, a plum cloak banded around myself courtesy of Siu's plunder chest, watching the river float past. The blight-scarred shores stretched away in uneven clumps like overworked dough, but the waters, at least, were beautiful. And I could watch them whenever they beckoned me, whenever sleep eluded and questions took power.

What was I now? Still a captive—a ransom?

Yet we sailed to a port of *my* choosing; I had not seen Lucretzia's face in over a month, had not worn her shackles since I had chosen to flee. I'd baked bread. I traversed the deck unbound. I now knew this crew by name...and held their grudging respect, though I'd never intended to obtain it.

I had learned long ago that survival necessitated I accept things as they were...not as I wished them to be.

That I would not have a family again, after my parents' passing. That Tristah and I would never find love in the arms of Algernon Sorai. That, for our own safety, our farewell had been necessary. That Lucretzia had hunted me. That Ryker Kassian had lied to me...at least in part.

And I could not deny this truth any more than the rest of them: this was not a simple ransom for merits. Not anymore.

CHAPTER 39
A TRENCH FULL OF SECRETS

The confusion of where I stood with the crew had not abated by the time we sailed into Port Krait a week after our departure from Korsa. The distraction of next steps proved to be a relief; in the hunt for Tristah, at least, I knew my footing precisely.

I perched on the foredeck when we made port; Camden crouched beside me, silent for once. The intensity of his stare nearly branded my fingers as I demonstrated one of the many skills I had traded for in Krylan: how to repair one of the handcarts we would use to ferry cargo from Bashir back to the ship, under the guise of fair trade rather than piracy. We'd been delegated this task by Wyst, the *Singer's* quiet, reclusive carpenter, who was overseeing the tarring of the false name for common port and patching the small wound on the ship's side dealt by Siu burying the axehead in it.

All at once, a shadow fell across us, blotting out the light; we were passing beneath an arch of the sturdy, sparkling stone for which the Southlands were known.

With a traded glance, Camden and I bounded to our feet, rushing to the railing to watch the slim canopy of stone pass overhead. Its far side revealed a small port, more a town than a city, with several ships bobbing in its waters. A single, lofty tower and a waterwheel dominated much of the landscape, the rest framed with the blighted lofts of the Abbra Foothills.

As unlike Korsa as possible. And I could not help the sigh I heaved at the sight of it, solace casting all the breath from my lungs.

"Not much for looks, is it?" Klement's strident drawl had us both straightening against the railing; the Second Mate cast herself on Camden's other side, arms folded, body sloped to the wood. A jerk of her chin indicated the gradients behind the port. "Bashir lies that way, about a day's walk. We'll do some trade with the plunder in the hull while you lot sniff around for your friend."

Excitement tingled in my fingertips; only a day from learning more of Tristah's whereabouts.

"I want to go," Camden whined, spinning with his back to the railing and clutching Klement by the arm. "Please don't make me stay on this ship *again*, Klem."

"Aye, Captain says you can come ashore." Her troubled gaze raked over him. "Finish with that cart, and you can help Bodey load up the wares."

"On it!" Camden grinned. "I'll take it from here, thanks, Lio!"

He darted back to the tools and wood we'd left scattered across the deck; Klement watched him go, dark brows furrowed, and I watched her—rolling out a pang of unease in my middle until it became curiosity instead.

"You'd prefer he didn't come," I ventured cautiously.

"Bashir's not a safe city." Klement cinched her arms at her waist. "Never has been. My brothers and I, we scraped for everything there. The dissidents may have their hearts in the right place…doesn't mean they always do things the right *way*. I'd hate for Cam to see the wicked side of things in there. He's seen enough."

"Yes, he has." Something we could agree on. "But we will protect him."

Klement's sideways stare raked over me. "I don't understand your angle, Delina."

"Interesting words, from a pirate. Must everyone have an *angle*?"

She snorted. "I like pirates. They're predictable because you can't ever trust them. But rulers, city officials…they're too coy and clever. They say one thing and do another. Difficult to navigate seas of that sort."

I held her gaze without shying from the challenge in its gleaming depths. "Your brothers…you would do anything for them, yes?"

A keen edge sharpened her eyes—proof of her namesake. "Anything. I've slit throats for them."

Somehow, that did not surprise me. "The woman we search for…Tristah. She is like a sister to me. *That* is my angle. Nothing more or less."

And that was true; it accounted for all I had done and all I planned to do. Including vanishing from this ship with Tristah at my side, never to be found by the Raiders or Lucretzia or anyone else who wished us ill again.

"Lio, look!" Camden's proud shout floated across the deck, half-muffled by the grind of the anchor being dropped. "I did it! Wait 'til I show Wyst…bet he couldn't do it any better himself!"

As he flipped the cart over, testing its mended wheel and knocking on the fresh slats of wood we'd fixed to its one rotting side, something pinched low in my heart.

I would miss little about Amere-Del. But that boy's eagerness made up some of it.

"Would you slit *our* throats for her?"

Klement's question startled my gaze from Camden, straight back to her. She stared at me. I stared back.

A wolfish smile overtook her full lips. "*That's* the angle. Every sailor thinks they'll keep their salt when merits are on the line. But once they've got the prize gleaming in their faces…that's when you learn who's cutthroat. Who's pirate."

Heat flared at her insinuation—and the truth behind it, as if she could see clearly how I planned to desert this ship the moment Tristah and I were reunited. "And you?" I retorted. "Would you slit *my* throat for this crew, Keen-Eye?"

"Oh, in a heartbeat. But that's the difference between us, Delina. If I'm a friend, you'll know why. Same if I'm a foe." Her head tilted, her gaze climbing slowly over me. "You, on the other hand…you're a trench full of secrets, aren't you? And the trouble is, no one knows what's lurking under that surface…least of all the Captain."

Unease blistered in my middle. "What do you mean?"

Klement's brows arched. "You seem clever. Why don't you sort it out?"

Siu's whistle cut toward us from the helm, interrupting the conversation just as it began to slide into treacherous waters. With a tilt of her fingers, Klement swaggered off to answer the summons—leaving me staring at the modest dappling of homes and shops that comprised Port Krait, my joy cooling like an oven left open.

We were a voyage nearer to discovering the truth about Tristah. But what would Bashir demand of me, to find the next whisper of her whereabouts?

What price would I be willing to pay, to catch those murmurs before the wind carried them away?

CHAPTER 40
MARK OF FIRE

A long, well-trodden road carved into the Foothills from the aft of Port Krait, paving the way to Bashir. With our wares declared—and a false name given for our ship, spewed with such confidence from Ryker's mouth I assumed it had been a vessel signature stolen many Blackhands before—we were on our way.

The landscape offered little in the way of distraction, the hills rugged and rich brown, dotted with long-dead trees; but with the bulk of the crew all traveling together, even One-Pot Willy—the slowest of us, with a staggered gait and puffing lungs that required frequent stops—there was at least no dearth of humor.

None of the same reserve breathed through the ranks as when we'd docked in Korsa; everyone was full of jest and good humor, and Camden whizzed about the edges of our group like a hummingbird full of sugar water, pointing out whatever caught his interest.

Everything delighted him…particularly the cart he pushed, topped with plunder, which he boasted more than once he'd repaired himself. Even as the day darkened toward the early sunsets of mid-winter and we all turned up our collars against the chill that edged on freezing, spirits soared.

I kept stride with Willy at the rear, stoking enthusiasm to keep me warm as we conversed about our favorite dishes to make and breads to bake. The embers of my resolve had cooled after my conversation with Klement; it took some effort to rejuvenate my determination.

The first flare that rose, not of my own making, came when darkness set in; when the hills ahead glinted, not with the cool glow of dusk, but with rich, reddish warmth. A distant reel of fiddle music and the whistle of a well-played flute beckoned us onward, keeping us on Camden's heels as he took the lead. We jogged past caravans of traders and traveling mercantilists and rounded a bend in the road, beholding at last the city of Bashir.

I had never visited before—Lucretzia deemed it too dangerous for any Northlanders to set foot inside, most of all members of the regime. It towered over us, magnificent and monolithic, full of piercing minarets, dome-capped rotundas, and sloped, gabled roofs; its broad span was dished in a bowl of the foothills so steep, the ridges caught shadows and dumped them in long, smoky spirals down the cragged cliffsides.

To enter, we had to pass beneath vaulting watchtowers arched over the road, the gates manned by the militar—not unlike Krylan. Beyond their watch, the city pulsed in lanternlight and fire-glow, its shimmering brownstone walls gleaming like a daydream. At the sight of it, the embers in my gut erupted into flame; determination seized my bones like a weaponmaker's vise, and I shouldered forward to join Ryker near the fore, just behind Camden.

"I can't be seen at the gate," I whispered. "There's little telling which militar might recognize their long-lost Delina."

"Aye," he said, keeping his gaze forward. "Ideas?"

I glanced around at the crew—at the various burdens they carried, shouldered, or pushed. "Plunder."

His mouth curled up at one corner. "Kory?"

The ship's Third Mate slipped to our side, shooting me the same hesitant smile he did whenever our paths crossed; it seemed he had not forgiven himself yet for tossing me into the Captain's quarters my first night aboard the *Singer.* "Aye, Captain?"

"Have your brother drop back to the rear with his handcart."

And that was how I found myself entering Bashir; not beholding its majesty up close, but lying face-down in a heap of trading furs, sweltering under my cloak, Ryker's false crimson cloak, and a heap of baubles for good measure.

A bosun's handcart playing a Delina's carriage. Tristah would have cackled to see it.

A stifling, half-suffocating way to venture in—but it certainly had its merits. When the militar poked and prodded within Kato's cart, likely searching for stashed barrels and hidden goods, my body melted in among the stiff furs; I ceased to breathe.

At long last, muffled voices floated above, and then the wheels trundled beneath me again. The motion was utterly smooth, Kato's musculature giving no hint at all as to his true burden; not a heap of furs, but a well-endowed woman.

Moments later, the handcart veered sharply; the crushing heat lifted, and blessedly chilly air snaked down over my cheeks. Then a kinder warmth brushed over the back of my neck and found my chin, prying my downturned face from among the furs.

"Still breathing, there, sweetheart?"

I rolled over in my oven-hot shelter, tossing off pelts and coats, pinning Ryker with a wry look. "Death by suffocation among the coats. What would your ransom become then, I wonder?"

Scoffing, he jutted out his hand. "Let's get searching, shall we?"

Leftover heat bubbled up from my core, swarming my throat; with a grin of glee uncontained, I took his hand.

Bashir, I swiftly learned as we wound through its streets, did not host taverns and inns, but rather compounds—small, walled accommodations within larger, walled complexes. Finial-tipped and three times as tall as Wilkes—who was the tallest among us, soaring nearly six-and-a-half feet in height—they cast shadows with more than their impressive loft.

Propaganda leaflets tarred each and every wall we passed; some newly-pasted, others leaking from the corners of their bindings, curling at the edges. All scrawled in dissident notes.

Reform the Regime, some declared, with a slash scoured through the dewdrop-diamond and mountain crest of the Del Graven household.

Northlands, Southlands, One Land, read another.

Others boasted fouler language: *Death to Del Graven. Choke the Everreach, Choke Us All. Crush the Viper.*

I glanced at Klement; her eyes were already turned my way, her mouth wound tightly to one side.

I strayed further along the complex walls, pulling away from the crew to read; to drink in the proof of everything Klement and Reinera had warned me about.

The dissidents were passionate; they were powerful. These were the sorts of messages we had discussed years ago in council meetings at Shadewyle Castle, the Del and Della and Lucretzia's fury mounting with every report of these notes spattered across the cities.

Except, back then, they had been fewer. They had been hidden in alleyways and handed out from the shadows, not tarred in public view; and it had been a chief task of the militar to tear them down.

Now, there were too many to count, too many to rip away; and buried among them, littered on parchment half-tucked behind propaganda…

A single flame's etching, speckled with castaway embers like leaves. Like new growth. Like *hope.*

The Incendiary.

My fingers skimmed over his mark, my throat tightening.

There was no message that accompanied his symbol, yet it carried a power different from the furious voices slapped to these soaring structures.

Action. Work being done on behalf of the suffering. A true challenge to Del Graven…one that could not be silenced by selling off women against their will to appease ambitious, vocal mouthpieces.

A man whose cause would have drawn Tristah. A woman he would certainly have helped.

"'Ay, sweetheart." Fingers brushed lightly against the curve of my shoulder. "You still with us?"

I blinked, swiveling to face Ryker; the others had halted some distance off, peering at me with a mix of curiosity and scorn. "Is…is this where we'll stay?"

His eyes darted to the bulletin of flame plastered on the wall. "Aye."

While he ducked inside the compound's guardhouse to make arrangements, Klement and her brothers slipped off another way; curiosity nibbled at my belly, and I dropped back beside Gydeon and Siu. "Where are they off to?"

"Scouting around," Siu said. "The three of them used to be swindlers and cardsharps here in the city, back before they landed aboard the *Singer.* All together, they can run a con like you wouldn't believe."

"Most of the crew are years and merits in debt to them," Gydeon chuckled fondly. "The only wise way to play against the Drace siblings is to never get into the game at all."

"They'll find our first whispers of your friend here, no doubt," Siu added. "Whatever those whispers may be."

Dread cooled the edges of my excitement again, but there was little time to dwell on it; Ryker had already returned, jerking his head toward the gatehouse and the dark corridor that lay beyond. "We've got ourselves a courtyard. Let's get settled."

CHAPTER 41
WHAT THE SEA KEEPS

A scattering of old, hand-carved braziers warmed the private compound's variegated cobblestones, their fiery glister dotted among potted trees imported from the Northlands. Even in these cold winter months, the boughs hung heavy, warmed by the firelight and water moats dug around their bases. Half a dozen canvas tents sprawled about the yard, their roofs decked in rich blue silks and their sides unlaced to allow glimpses of pillowed and blanketed floors within.

"All right." Ryker clapped his hands—wincing a bit—and the crew circled up around him, myself included. "Park the carts and divvy up the tents...leave one aside for the Draces. I want most of you trading and peddling starting tomorrow. Wilkes, you keep the rest of the crew moving. Gyddy, Siu, you're with the Draces, Lio, and me. We'll sniff around for our mark."

Anticipation tingled in my fingertips, the heat of that ember in my gut pulsing into every nerve.

Rapidly, the crew splintered off to their tents: Siu pulling Gydeon into one and lacing it firmly and finally behind them; Wilkes setting one aside for himself and the Draces and sealing it just as sharply. One-Pot Willy ambled off to his own refuge in the smallest tent, with no one hastening to join him. A handful of crewmates I had come to know over the weeks—Wyst, along with the ship's cooper, Brant, its master gunner, Nella, and the musicians, Rhea, Maryon, and Rynshaw—all ducked into a single tent together, decks of cards and dice already flashing in their hands. Other deckhands I had not yet associated by name scurried into the rest of the tents, not a single one flashing a glance or an invitation my way.

In moments, there were only three of us left: myself, Camden, and Ryker.

Camden beamed at me. "Good times! You're stuck with us."

"Unless you prefer Willy for a tentmate." Ryker hooked his thumbs in his belt, tilting his head conspiratorially. "But I'll warn you, sweetheart, the man *snores*."

"Like a *hacksaw*." Camden shuddered. "I don't think I slept a *wink* the last time we shared quarters."

Ryker chuckled, striding toward the last remaining tent. "There's a reason he keeps his hammock strung in the galley, half a ship away from everyone else."

Despite the touch of reservation grazing the small of my back, I gathered my satchel of meager belongings and followed after them.

Our tent tallied among the smaller ones, but no less cozy; the braided burlap trapped the heat of a smaller brazier within, its smoke escaping through the narrow hatch at the height of the roof. The cushioned floor was the softest thing I had set my feet on since the sands of Sunrise Isle; I kicked off my boots and buried my toes in the fabric, sighing with contentment.

"Tell me about it!" Camden flung his own pack to the side and dropped on his back, stretching out beside the tent's central post and swimming his sprawled limbs through the quilts and cushions. "Oh, a man could get used to this."

"Oi. You're a few seasons short of a *man* yet, mate." Ryker dropped his own pack straight onto Camden's chest, puffing a high-pitched yelp from him. "'Til I can do that without getting a crack out of you, you're still a lad."

"Do you have to insult me in front of the *Seasplitter*?"

Their banter eased a bit of the tension that seethed beneath my skin at the notion of sharing a tent with Ryker. Thank merciful Ahim we were not alone, at least.

We took our places around the tent post and brazier; I lay on one side, Camden on the other, Ryker stretching out along the back wall. In minutes, the boy was snoring, spent from a full day's walk and our hard labor over the cart since sunrise. The soothing scent of incense in the warm, humid air lulled me toward sleep after him, the first vestiges of thoughts trailing over into dreams of high-sketched fire—

"Lio."

I jolted, hiking myself up on my elbows, heart thundering. "What?"

Ryker propped himself on an elbow as well, his face half-shrouded in shadows as the brazier dimmed. "Sorry. Didn't mean to startle you."

I swiped a strand of stray hair from my brow. "What *is* it?"

"Hand me my pack, would you?" His voice barely reached a whisper. "Forgot to take my tonic."

I rooted about, half-blind with drowsiness, until I caught the strap of his pack near Camden's feet. Feeling through the sparse innards, I caught the tonic bottle and passed it to him.

"First night on land's always the hardest," Ryker muttered, popping the cork. "Don't want the lad to see or hear anything."

Heat seared through my wrist—the memory of how he'd startled awake in Korsa that first morning when I'd shaken him. The regret in his eyes when he'd realized what he'd done.

My heart bobbed into my throat. "Does nothing else help?"

"Nothing I've tried." Taking a deep swig, he corked the bottle and set it aside. "Well. Except what they gave me on the drug ship, after I almost sank."

Compassion wrapped its hand around my throat. "You've never told me what happened."

Ryker settled back among the blankets, head balanced on his hand, his elbow folded upright beside his head. He stayed quiet for so long, I suspected he would not tell me at all; and I would never force him to dredge up that pain from his past.

Then his husky voice rose among the dimming embers, toward the vent in the tent's woven roof. "I wasn't the only skin that got sold onto that ship when we sailed out of Zayir Harbor. There was a lass…Antigony. Never let us call her anything else, even when the Captain tried calling her *Ann* just to cut her down."

A faint smile threaded his words…then swiftly faded.

"She was two years older than me, and her aunt sold her off to pay some debts for drugs she shouldn't have touched in the first place. Antigony tried to take care of the rest of us, keep us fed. I thought the bloody sun rose out of that golden head of hers…I'd have walked off the plank with her if she asked me to."

An ache built in the chasms of my chest; because he was here, and she was not…this girl he spoke so fondly of, with a child's never-forgotten adoration.

This tale would not have a pleasant ending.

"Storm came up while we were on our way to some island." Ryker's voice barely peaked above a rough whisper now. "Bad as it was, they still had all the runts on the topdeck, doing the work of seasoned sailors. Antigony was a great deckhand for a lass of ten, but…the sea was just bloody better."

The wheel around his neck chafed on its chain, sliding slowly one way and the other.

"She was watching out for me, but neither of us saw this wave coming. It washed me right over the railing, and she didn't stop to breathe. Just jumped in after me."

The flash of sunlight on a reef pierced my mind. The slam of his body against wood and water echoed over my shuddering pulse.

"We grabbed each other out there in the swells, swam back to the ship, and held on hard…grabbed the rungs on the side and tried to ride it out." His head wagged slowly against the cradle of his hand, his gaze still fixed on the canvas roof and the smoke making its escape. "Not one of those blasted sailors even threw us a rope. And somewhere in the toss…Antigony's arms gave out. I had her by the collar, I tried as hard as I blasted could to pull her up, but the sea yanked her right out of my hands."

Both those hands rose now, smothering his face, muffling his next words.

"All I had left was her bloody ship's wheel necklace and the sound of her mouth filling up with water when the sea sucked her down. I couldn't hold onto her…barely held onto the rungs myself until they remembered to look for me the next morning."

Rage bubbled in my throat—for a younger Ryker, desperate to save his friend. For a boy growing into a man, shouldering a guilt and grief he should have been spared. That he *could* have been spared, had his life not been stamped by the cruelty of parents and strangers alike.

His hands fell from his face, slack over his stomach. Roughness took his voice when he went on—a sound that did not belong to exhaustion or to the tonic's work. "She was the only thing that made that ship bearable. With her gone, we were all at each other's throats. Closest thing I'd had to a home since my grandad passed was that lass, and sometimes…I have dreams where I held on a little longer. Where someone cared enough to toss us a lifeline." After a quiet moment, he added, "Sometimes feels like I started looking for what *home* was, ever since she slipped through my hands."

His words thundered through me, awakening a desperate yearning I had danced with all throughout my days…ever since my parents' deaths. In Krylan, among the Ameresh immigrants I refused to embrace as *my* people; in *The Secret Ingredient,* where satisfied days had bled into lonely nights; with Addie, the first friend I had dared make after Tristah.

"Did you ever find it?" I murmured. "Your home?"

"Not sure that's an option for someone like me anymore."

"Not even aboard the *Singer*?"

He lifted one shoulder in a crooked shrug. "It's my ship, but not really. Not until I pay off Dred."

I had no comfort to offer but simple, honest words: "I'm sorry for how you've suffered."

And I was. Even if did not excuse so many of his choices…I could hold both. The pain for myself and the pain on his behalf.

After a long moment, he spoke again, drowsy and hoarse. "After the worst happens, you never think piracy could be better…until the choice is between Captain Blackhand and *The Dread Singer*, or Captain Varsi and *The Silver Spice*. And you realize maybe turning pirate is better than sailing with a bastard who didn't bother looking twice for the girl he let drown."

"How old were you, in all of this?"

"Six when they sold me. Ten when Blackhand found me. Eight when Antigony drowned."

Speaking through my tight throat proved painful, nearly impossible; yet the words tugged themselves free, desperate to be spoken. "After your parents perish, you don't think anything could be worse. And you truly never imagine that after months of begging Ahim for rescue from being forgotten in an overfull orphanage, the person who would step in to rescue you would be Zorast Del Graven. Or that his first act as your warden would be to slap you so hard for questioning where he's sailing you, it knocks the last of your milk teeth straight down your throat."

Ryker stiffened, rolling to his side, rosemary gaze burned tawny by the ember glow. "That blasted son of sea-snake—"

"It was equally terrible for Tristah." I turned onto my stomach, propping my chin on my folded arms. "Lucretzia dragged her into the castle like trapped prey, bound and gagged."

Rage flickered in the depths of his eyes. "Why the pair of you? Out of all the orphans these cities churn out—"

"Because of how my parents perished. Del Graven chose me because he believed my hate would make me his finest weapon…that I would be ruthless against his dissidents. That I would do anything to punish the people who took my parents from me."

People like those in this city; people who plastered propaganda on high walls, crying for reformation at any cost…a cost their orphan children paid in their stead.

People who also gave board to travelers. People who bought and bartered. People who were not terrible…only desperate.

Ryker let the silence breathe a bit. Then he asked the question I was certain had driven Zorast and Athyna to the precipice of madness during the two decades I had been their ward. "Why didn't you?"

Somehow, after all this time, it finally felt right to speak it—to him, of all people. "The dissidents lashed out from a place of hurt…not of greed, not of desire to control. They hurt because they were hurting. And if I hurt them because of *my* hurt, what would I be doing but perpetuating the cycle?" I blinked tears from my eyes. "I would create more orphaned girls, and someday they would come for whatever semblance of a life I had built, and my descendants would be left to avenge me…and what then?"

"Death on top of death," Ryker agreed quietly. "Like the Leeches, with Gyddy. Aye. I can see that."

For a time, we held that quiet between us, facing the magnitude of a world seasoned with vengeance and emptiness and death that stole too soon. A bitter mouthful, impossible to swallow.

"Tristah always said plights should be heard, not silenced," I admitted after a time. "Only the selfish and frightened and weak-willed would gag their opponents rather than weighing opposing views. I see that in Del Graven now, with what he intends with the Everreach."

"And this Incendiary? You think he's any different? Seems he's a man of action, same as the Del."

My mind trailed back to the mark of fire on the walls—a call to arms. A clarion cry sending out rumors of a shuttered Everreach. Of more suffering on both sides. "I'm afraid his actions will lead to more riots…and more orphans. But I also heard what you heard, in Korsa. Of the Incendiary's reputation there."

Sinking my chin back onto my folded arms, I let my eyes fall shut.

"I think that nothing about this is simple," I murmured, "except that I want no part in any of it. I only want to find Tristah."

I could not afford to care any more than that. I could not fear for the fate of Amere-Del. And it could not need me.

I had never been the Delina who could save it. And nothing would change that now.

CHAPTER 42
PLAYING THE STAKES

aylight found the whole crew gathered, yawning and bleary-eyed, at the largest of the braziers in the courtyard; the Drace siblings alone were wide awake, though according to Wilkes, they had not returned all night. He'd bragged about his ample leg room to Rhea over breakfast—then changed the subject as deftly as he traded blades when she dryly inquired whether he was offering to share with those less fortunate.

Even the groggiest among us thrummed with a fresh life I'd not yet seen in these sailors—the Draces in particular as if they'd drunk a pot of the most strongly brewed coffee ever roasted in the Southlands. They fidgeted and flustered, bundled side-by-side in the furs from Kato's cart, a dark-skinned blur of tapping fingers, folded arms, and weight trading from foot to foot.

Whatever Klement claimed of the city's nature, they clearly knew its beating heart; scraping and conning their way through it brought about a vim that not even sailing awakened in their bones.

"No sign of *The Haverknot* in Port Krait, though records have its false name on the books coming and going less than a week ago," Klement reported when we had all mustered—even Camden, yawning and leaning into Gydeon's side, the healer's arm wrapped around the boy's narrow shoulders.

"But there's word of a man who sails with them in and out...some claim he's a skin trader," Kory flung in, hands propped on his hips, beating a tune against the thick sash that belted his tapered waist. "Ember, they call him."

"Interesting." Ryker's eyes darted to me.

"Embers and incendiaries," I murmured, turning to Klem. "Is there a connection?"

"I'd bet merits on it," she said.

The notion set my gut churning. A skin-trader, aboard the same vessel that had brought Tristah here… "What connection does he seem to have?"

Kato shrugged. "Difficult to say. Could be an associate. Could be someone the Incendiary is fighting off."

"All we gathered is that their names are tied up together when you ask around the city," Kory offered.

"That's what we have to learn," Klement added. "Seems if your friend did sail in aboard *The Haverknot*, she may have crossed paths with Ember. Might be he pointed her toward the Incendiary."

"Then that's our heading," Ryker confirmed. "Ask around, see what you can learn about this so-called Ember, the Incendiary, whatever ties them together."

A simple task—but one that sparked like a flint struck against my bones.

Find the Ember. Find the Incendiary.

And force him to lead us to Tristah by any means necessary.

Unlike Korsa, we discovered no lack of whispers bearing the names *Ember* or *Incendiary* in Bashir.

From Reinera's account of this revolutionary, I had expected a man fully guised in shadow, his name only breathed in secretive circles. Instead, the people of the city discussed the Incendiary and Ember as if they were local legends. Klement reported several gambling dens had open pots where visitors bet on the identities of these men, whether they were allies or enemies, and what their eventual aims might be.

Even with the prevalence of gossip, the Drace siblings could glean no further truth about either man. Many of the gamblers were not eager to play against them…which was unfortunate, given they were the best cardsharps and dice-throwers among us.

Or, at the very least, the best they *knew* of.

"Could raise an issue," Ryker remarked when Klement brought the report of another day's dealings at the gambling dens. "Merits loosen lips. The more merits on the table, the more tongues start wagging." Every few words he spoke were punctuated with the throw of a dagger, nailing into the body of one of the potted trees scattered throughout the courtyard. The impact resonated in my breastbone where I sat behind Ryker at one of the courtyard's many benched tables, several feet from his target. "But if they won't play you…"

"It doesn't matter how loose their tongues might get." Kato stalked across the yard to loosen the knives, returned to his seat at Ryker's side, and took his turn throwing them—one after another.

"We found one promising den," Kory muttered, rubbing the stumps of his three-fingered hand. "There's plenty of talk of the Ember and Incendiary there. It might be enough to—"

"You're dreaming," Klement scoffed, plucking a knife from Kato's hand and giving it a hurl; it dug in precisely blade-to-blade with the last one he'd thrown. "You saw the gambling pots there…all about the Ember's dealings. *She* obviously knows a thing or two about him." The stress on the words breathed of a long-buried contention. "She's not going to give it up without good pay."

"Or a better threat." Kato hurled the last knife, ending a perfect line of blades embedded down the trunk.

"Which we can't afford." Toppling back on the seat beside her brother, Klement settled her chin glumly in her palms. "Not if we plan to be here any length of time."

Ryker retrieved the blades, laying them out on the table. Curiosity—and a deep, nagging compulsion—drew my fingers to their hilts, wondering if their weights remained the same as I recalled from years ago.

They did—an absolute balance my muscles corded to greet. The anticipation of throwing.

"I could do it," I offered, and the conversation ebbed to a halt around me. Wide eyes all swung my way, but it was Ryker's gaze I met—him who needed convincing, because only by his orders would such a ruse be possible. "Send the Drace siblings with me, to draw the attention of the crowd…but I will make the gamble for the truths we need."

"You'll lose," Klement scoffed.

I shot her a glance. "You have not seen me play."

"Isn't much *to* lose," Ryker pointed out, bending one foot on the bench beside me. "They're already keeping their mouths shut."

"Oh, I intend to take a few merits as well," I smiled, and Ryker's eyes narrowed. "First, the coin to make their mouths open. Then the game, so I can hear what pours out."

"We don't have much to spare," Kory warned.

"Unless we're really doubling our ransom demand here in Bashir, *Captain*." Klement laid a harsh-edged look at Ryker, striking like a blade to the jugular.

He did not look away from me. "You think you can outplay port town gamblers, sweetheart?"

"I think," I replied, "I can outplay anyone, if the stakes are finding Tristah."

Sliding from the bench, I snatched up one of the knives, flipped it from hilt to tip, and flung it in a smooth, blinding arc—straight into the knot at the tree's heart.

The Drace siblings sucked in their breaths all at once; Ryker smirked, shaking back his hair, pinning me with a look of such knowing, it sent heat puddling low in my belly.

Bolstered by that full-body flush—and by the thrill of muscle memory—I added, "Because I cannot afford to lose."

CHAPTER 43
PORT TOWN GAMBLERS

A day later, I set foot into my first Bashiri gambling house—an act that would have turned Lucretzia red-faced with rage.

I entered *The Coin Toss* dressed to mingle with its patrons: my sleeves flowing, a pair of loose trousers tucked into my boots, my hair braided over one shoulder and a coinpurse rattling loudly on my hip beneath my plum velvet cloak. The scent of incense and pipesmoke made itself known at once in my nostrils; beneath it, the rich roll of brandy and the floral notes of wine softened the palate.

Curious stares and lustful whispers found us from every corner of the misty room, precisely built of such sharp angles that, from the proper vantage point, one could see all of its two-dozen tables at once. Just such a point happened to teeter atop the spiraled fountain at the room's center, from which a constant deluge of water splashed into a lanternlit pool; and at the apex of the fountain, on a broad slab of marble, the den's mistress did her dealings, her lissome figure visible through the railing slats.

"That's Selyna Anterys." Klement landed an elbow on my shoulder as we halted just over the threshold. "Most famous gossip and most popular gambling mistress in all of Bashir." Her face twisted in a scowl. "We used to run games for her, back when this was our home."

I kept my eyes on the splash of shadow atop the marble, whose hawkish eyes spanned the room in search of threats. "And she remembers, I take it."

"We may have a lifetime ban on gambling here," Kory muttered from my other side, scrubbing a hand over his braids.

"Not that the Captain needs to hear those particulars," Kato warned.

Fighting a smile, I ducked a glance toward the gambling pots lined up just to the right of the door: a series of bronze dishes, familiar throughout the city, full of bets on things yet to be revealed about the mysterious Incendiary and his associate, Ember.

I could see now why this den had drawn the Draces' interest; besides their inherent familiarity with its inner workings, these pots were for far different bets than any of the gambling dens I'd peered into with Siu, Gydeon, and Wilkes. These placards invited guesses of where Ember made his dwelling place—three pots each for three vastly different locations: one in the Barradir Highlands, another near Sennesole Basin, and a third across the Weyval Basin, where Krait was one of several ports and Bashir one of its many cities.

Another boasted a two-pot guess: was the Ember an ally or enemy of the Incendiary? And further down the row—bets on when Ember or the Incendiary might next be seen in the city.

My gaze lingered longest on that crooked inscription; with every blink, fresh vigor bore deep into my marrow.

"Lio?" Klement slid her elbow from my shoulder, then spoke to her brothers: "What in the depths is *that* look?"

"I don't know, but it reminds me of the Captain when he's scheming something foul." Kory stepped back from me. "I *hate* that look."

I strode away from them, to the serving counter that wrapped around the fountain's basin. The tall man behind it, his skin the warm shade of strong, fresh-brewed tea, paused swabbing out a glass and raised his eyes at my arrival— at the heavy *thunk* of my coinpurse on the counter.

"Tell me how I must play to earn a round with the den mistress."

He cocked a brow, pierced through with several gold hoops—and eyed the cluster of bodies that swarmed behind me. "She's with you three?"

"We lost a bet," Klement muttered. "Now we're her protection for the week."

"Pity you. She'll be dead inside it, flashing coin that way." The tender folded his broad arms on the counter, bending at my level. "To play Anterys, you must play—and win—every other table."

"Fair enough." I raked the bag back to myself. "Point me to the first."

I'd been honest with Ryker and the Draces, back at the compound: I could not afford to squander this chance. But the truth—a truth I had told no one, not even Addie when we'd played *Poor Man's Dice* in my home after long days in Krylan—was that I was not a particularly affluent card player or dice thrower.

However, thanks to the many methods Tristah had taught me, I happened to be quite the expert *cheater.*

I wasn't the only cheater here, either. The method such gambling required was the same I had used at my supper with Ryker aboard *The Dread Singer*. I must lie better than the best liar among them.

This strategy had served me well in council meetings and dangerous scrapes. It had won me food when I might have otherwise gone hungry during my first few months in Krylan. And once again, it played to my benefit as we took the tables in *The Coin Toss*; the blinks and head tilts and glances of the Drace siblings helped to isolate the greatest cheaters at any given table, and from there, the game was on.

I simply ignored the rest of the players. I played against those who were playing the same game as me—played them as if they were Tristah, seated across from me on my bed in Shadewyle Castle.

I played Tristah in my mind. And I beat her, over and over again.

Twenty-four times.

Uncountable hours passed, the sun nearly lost through the grit-filmed windows; my sloped shoulderblades throbbed as if a knife had been driven between them. But when the last table folded, the last of the dice thrown in my favor, I scraped together my sizeable pot of merits—one I had raised table after table, enticing and unraveling the focus of my opponents—and swiveled in my seat to look up the height of the fountain.

There I found Selyna Anterys regarding me with unabashed contempt.

Her gnarled fingers curled over the railing encircling the fountain's upper setting; her hair, a bright chestnut shade ombred with a thick sheen of silver at the roots, hung loose about her shoulders as if tossed by a storm that could not be seen or felt…one that roiled within the sheath of her amber skin.

When our gazes met, her scowl deepened, slicing her full lips down at the corners. With a jerk of her head, she beckoned me to her.

Merits in fist, I went.

Up the winding staircase, with the Drace siblings on my heels; there was a small commotion between them and the tender at the counter, but something Kato muttered made the man sidestep at once, hands kept to himself. And then they followed doggedly after me, up to the pinnacle of the fountain, where a single table dominated the broad marble square.

"You flaunt boldly, for a woman of your stature," Selyna said by way of greeting—not a compliment by any means.

I tossed the merits onto the table. "I have a bargain to make with you."

She eyed the satchel, then slid herself into the chair she had vacated at some point to watch the proceedings below. "My ears are perked."

"Play me a game of *Poor Man's Dice*." I settled into the seat across from her, brushing the satchel aside so I might face her squarely; she followed its passing with ravenous eyes. "If you win, you may keep all of the merits I've earned today."

"And in the unlikely event *you* should win?"

"I will take the *truth* you know about Ember and the Incendiary."

Her gaze flashed back to me; when I did not blink, her scowl turned to a snarl. "I don't like your sort in my den."

"Of course you don't. Because the truth would dry up your most lucrative ventures." I tipped my head toward the guessing pots below. "But I can assure you, this is for personal business, not public knowledge."

"What good is the word of a cheat?"

"Why don't you play me and find out?"

She licked her lips and shot a glance at the Draces. "Did you tell this one about me?"

Klement folded her arms, dropping her weight back into the railing. "Just told her where was the best den for gambling in Bashir."

Hate sparked in Selyna's gaze. "I should have drowned you all in the Weyval before I let you crawl out of this place."

Rage tightened my fingertips around the table's edge; before I could snap a retort, Kato drawled, "Your mistake. Now, are you going to play her, or are you too much a coward?"

"We have bets on that, too." Kory flashed a smile that lacked any of its usual sincerity; it was all teeth, much more like his elder sister's.

Selyna hesitated a moment longer; then she grunted, "The buy-in to play the gambling mistress is fifteen merits."

I surrendered them without contest, ignoring Klement's quiet, reproachful grunt. I wasn't certain it was aimed at me this time. "Fifteen merits, and we play to two hundred marks. The first to reach is the winner."

Playing against Selyna was nothing like the other tables; *Poor Man's Dice* was a game with better odds the more players were present. The pot filled much quicker that way, so the stakes were far greater. But here, there was a single pot, laden with a satchel and secrets; and for us both, the stakes could be no higher.

Sweat soaked the small of my back with every roll of the dice. They were clearly weighted—the precise lay of the corners rubbed stark as a callous against the scarred flesh of my hands. It took several rounds before I determined the axis where that weight leaned and tilted—rounds that put Selyna many marks ahead.

Kato, Kory, and Klement kept the score, their tones rough with unease when I rolled low numbers round after round; but trepidation turned to dull hope, then to mounting anticipation when my numbers angled higher and higher.

Selyna's smug grin shifted to a scowl and then to a smirk again, the course of the game an endless tide changing the shape of her shores. Neither of us spoke a word; my throat ached as if this she-wolf pinned me to my chair, her teeth pressed against my thudding pulse.

Her daggered grin only grew when Kory named the count once again, and then added, softly, "Last toss."

Across the table, Selyna and I speared one another with narrowed eyes.

We were each within a roll of two hundred marks, dependent on the dice; and I was far nearer to two hundred, which made the odds of crossing the threshold and spoiling the count—thus forfeiting the game—far likelier.

Selyna watched me weigh the dice between my fingers, her smile crooked and cocky and absolutely, cruelly certain.

She had played her game well. Even the highest score she rolled would not cause her to spoil.

No one breathed as I squared the dice between my fingers—and shut my eyes.

A glimpse of the compound's courtyard. Sunlight on knives. The flicker of Ryker's smirk when I took up the blade—rolled my wrist—breathed—

And threw.

The same precise toss—the same muscle memory that had sung through my body then—sent the dice clattering across the table, whirling on their weighted corners…and falling again.

A precise, exact two hundred.

The Drace siblings went *mad.*

They all exploded, whooping and cheering—Kato clapping his hands on his thighs, Klement shoving up and spinning a full circle with fingers tangled in her hair, Kory shaking me by the back of the chair and then bending to wrap both his arms around my shoulders and twist me back and forth in my seat.

Though grinning, I never took my eyes from Selyna, who fell back in her seat with a violent curse, swiping a hand down her face. "Girl—who taught you to *throw*?"

"I believe the winner's question belongs to me," I retorted, and at once Kory released me, straightening at my back. Kato closed in on one side, Klement on the other, as I shoved the dice toward Selyna. "You have your fifteen merits, and I have the score. Now, tell us who Ember truly is."

Selyna glared me down, an impressive one-sided snarl to accompany it; there was a bested ferocity in her glower that might have made me fearful for my life were the Draces not fanned at my flanks, a veritable wall of muscle and intent as powerful as a storm spotted across the sea.

"He associates with the Incendiary," she said at long last. "Moves skin for him."

"What sort of *skin*?" Klement demanded.

"The sort that doesn't want to be watched." Selyna folded her arms beneath the heft of her bust; when none of us so much as twitched, her mouth jerked to the side, baring the other half of her teeth in a truly wolfish leer. "I've got no opinion, one way or the other. I just hear things."

"As do we." Kory's tone was calm, nearly placating; but his three-fingered grip on the back of my chair set the wood creaking.

Selyna hesitated a moment longer; then, eyeing the bosun's tools strapped to Kato's belt, she relented. "Folk who are on the outs with the regime. The ones who can't pay their taxes, or they lose their homes and shops paying them. My sister's husband's relatives, they were some of the ones Ember—" she snapped her fingers "—made disappear."

Unease gnawed at the edge of my belly.

It sounded like Lucretzia's methods. Like something the militar would do to debtors, stealing them away to prisons…or worse, to work camps in the Highlands to pay out their service by forced labor.

And yet…

I knocked my knuckles on the table. "Where can this *Ember* be found?"

She scoffed. "You don't find him. He finds you, if he wants to be seen."

"Humor us." Klement's voice held a flash of her own teeth—not a smile. "You should remember we are *quite* good at finding things."

"The only reason you still draw breath in my presence, *Klement*." Selyna rolled her eyes; then she bent toward me, her hands in dangerous reach of the coinpurse. "Gossip around the taverns is, he's gone again. Folk caught a glimpse of his cloak disappearing around corners, snapping up a few for the vanishing…and now he's blown off like cookfire smoke."

"For how long?" I demanded.

"Hard to say. Usually rumors about him taper off for six weeks at a time; sometimes eight. Then they pick up again…sightings all around the city."

Her querulous tone was all too familiar—not unlike a latchbox clattering shut. I had learned the precise tenor of imminent mutiny in Tristah's voice whenever she and Lucretzia sparred with words.

Shoving back my chair, I shook out another ten merits in addition to the fifteen, and shoved them to her across the table. "For what you've said." I cut a smile across my mouth, sharp as a dagger. "And for what you will *not* repeat."

Her eyes flicked from the merits up to me. Her jaw shifted as if she might say more; and then deciding, perhaps, that I was not worth whatever warning or threat settled on her tongue, she merely nodded, scraping the merits nearer.

I left the gambling den as swiftly as I could, halting on the curb outside to gulp down lungfuls of air. The rich, clean wind sweeping down from the hillsides cleansed me of the persona I'd clad around myself in that place…and chased out the eagerness for another round of dice. Another chance to play and seize fate for myself.

"What are you thinking?" Klement demanded, stepping out beside me, her hands perched on her hips. "I can see that scheming mind of yours kneading something out."

"Aye, now we know the look," Kato teased, falling in next to his sister.

"These people who are being taken, they are certainly not disappearing into servitude to the regime," I murmured. "I wonder if the Incendiary is…hiding them."

"Hiding them *from* servitude?" Kory scraped both palms down his cheeks.

"Just like the orphans in Korsa." Kato scratched a hand over his cropped, curly hair. "Moving skin—but not for harm."

"Ember must travel with *The Haverknot* to and from port in Korsa," I went on, the sketchings of their system taking shape in my mind, "gathering up waifs from the pirate city and Bashir and moving them to safety."

"But where in the depths are they going?" Klement muttered.

"Where he's gone right now, I imagine," Kory said.

"Six *or* eight weeks—not *between* six and eight. A staggered pattern." I started down the street, the Drace siblings falling into step around and behind me. "But it's long enough, regardless. Long enough to take a sizeable number of people somewhere far away…somewhere the militar cannot track them."

"Somewhere up in the Foothills," Klement ventured. "Maybe even as far as the Barradir Highlands."

My guts writhed with triumph at this mosaic we pieced together—but dread knotted up victory into a noose. "It seems likely they helped Tristah disappear the same way."

For a moment, we were all quiet, soaking in the implications of that.

If my theory held water, these revolutionaries had helped her vanish years ago. She could be anywhere now.

I shoved aside the thick, suffocating weight of despair that crept about my shoulders at the notion. Ryker had mentioned rumors of my face appearing in the Southlands *recently*. If those rumors indeed mapped Tristah's trail, then she had not fled entirely beyond my reach.

Someone knew where she was. And where she had been.

Drawing my shoulders back, I raised my heavy head. "In six or eight weeks, we will have our answer." I jerked my chin. "Come. Let's tell the others."

CHAPTER 44
WHAT DRIVES A DISSIDENT TO FLEE

A month and a half, or two months." Ryker's tone tilted with quiet thought as he soaked in our report, sitting at one of the ramshackle tables beneath one of the imported trees in the courtyard. Siu sat on one side of him; I'd taken the other after Klement and Kory plopped themselves beside Gydeon, across from us. The game of cards on the tabletop sat forgotten—or, mostly forgotten.

Klement flicked a gaze over the mingling of old, tattered cards and dice, then shot me a raised brow. I rolled my eyes in retort, and she stifled a snort.

Ryker blinked, glancing between us; then he started to gather the cards. "Steady Siu?"

"Too long to keep the ship in port." She drummed her fingers on the tabletop. "Folk like us know better than to linger too long in one place."

"Krait's not the only port here in the Weyval Basin," Klement offered. "Port Tamsay is across the breadth of it, right on the outskirts of Anoram."

I glanced at Ryker. He looked at me.

"Merry Dred mentioned Anoram," I reminded him. "Another destination of *The Haverknot* when Tristah left port."

Silence consumed the table; Gydeon's eyes weighed heavily on Ryker's swaddled hand, his missing finger.

"What are you thinking, Klem?" A faint growl edged Ryker's words—an unspoken *I'm all right* aimed at Gydeon, just as his gaze was.

It was Siu who answered, with a glance at the Second Mate for her nod of assent. "We could sail the ship across the Basin in a fortnight or so, maybe three weeks. Put in at Tamsay, leave a few rowboats behind."

"Send the crew in batches across, once they've had their fill of this place," Klement added. "We can poke our noses in, see if we hear anything about our friend Tristah in Anoram. And if it takes the full eight weeks, we'll make our way to some of the other ports around the Basin…Pyrath Harbor, maybe."

Gratitude swelled in my chest, though none of this was particularly for my sake. "That would certainly give us other avenues to pursue, if the Incendiary and Ember manage to evade us."

"They won't," Ryker said with the sort of brash confidence that had made it so simple to defy Lucretzia in his presence aboard *The Athalion*. "Spread the word, Klem. You'll take the first batch aboard the ship for Tamsay. I'll send you more with supplies in tow."

"My pleasure, Captain." Klement rose, nudging Kory up with her; but on her feet, she hesitated, gazing down at me. "You know, I've never seen anyone play *Poor Man's Dice* the way you did today."

"Tristah taught me," I admitted. "She used to swindle the older children in her orphanage for rations and clothing."

"Hm." Klement slanted her head, knocking her fist on the table. "I'll have to have her teach me, when we find her. Or I suppose *you* could."

I pounced on that offer of truce like a priceless sachet of saffron. "I'd be delighted to."

Her one-sided smirk nearly crinkled her left eye shut. "You'll only be saying that until I'm the one swindling *you* for information."

A threat. A challenge. A promise.

She and her brother swaggered away, and Siu rose with a yawn and a stretch. "I'll muster up the crew and gather volunteers for the first sail across the Basin with Klem. Anyone in particular you want to send?"

"Kory," Ryker replied without hesitation. "Klem's got old connections in Anoram she can shake down. And Three-Finger will have her back if they start trying to shake her in turn."

"Smart," Gydeon said, leaning up into the kiss Siu planted on his temple. She hurried toward the scattering of tents, barking the sailors to attention, while Gydeon lingered with us. "Now, what's that look for, brother?"

I turned my attention back to Ryker; he drummed his hand on the tabletop, the tune slightly uneven with his missing finger.

"*Haverknot* sailed out of port in Korsa ahead of us, but she's already gone again," he mused. "If Ember was on that ship, it means he barely dug his heels in here before he shoved back off the deck."

"A swift departure." Nerves tangled in my core.

"Could be nothing," Gydeon cautioned. "He may have had a flock of orphans to get to safety, if we're riding the right current as to his dealings."

"Aye." Ryker's drumming increased, his gaze sliding out of focus as he stared across the courtyard. "But then, why make an appearance in the city at all? Could've just touched down in Port Krait and headed out straight from there."

"He intended to stay in Bashir," I murmured. "Something sent him away."

"That's what I'm thinking."

"But what," Gydeon dragged his fingertips through his beard, "would drive such a bold dissident to flee?"

"Question of the day, Gyddy." Ryker planted a hand on my shoulder, boosting himself easily to his feet. "Let's keep our eyes open and our steps light, aye? Something's breathing in this city, and I don't want to step on it until I know what it is."

CHAPTER 45
THE CHANGE THAT TIPS THE BALANCE

t was Ahim's mercy that I had so rarely visited the Southlands as Delina; our tours of the Northlands, quashing dissidence with Lucretzia's ferocity and mustering support for higher taxes, would have made it too dangerous for me to roam if we were searching for Tristah on the other side of the Everreach.

But, odd as it was, the Southlands—rifer with propaganda against the regime, far more vocal about its disgust with high taxes and a lack of voice in the ruling of the country—was the safer place by far for a runaway Delina.

So much safer, in fact, that within a handful of days, I had acquired employment in Bashir.

The Love of the Loaf was a modest bakery tucked away among the staggered stacks of eateries and mercantilists not far from the plaza, where traveling traders plied people with their wares. But—as I reminded Ryker firmly when I returned from my wanderings one day, coated in flour and no better able to wipe the foolish smile from my face—it was the perfect place to continue gathering information. I had learned swiftly in owning *The Secret Ingredient* that good food loosened tongues.

"Two months," I reminded Ryker when he frowned, pitched against one of the courtyard trees, watching Siu and Klement grapple for a pair of blades; the weapons traded hands so swiftly, they nearly blurred. "We came to Bashir under guise as immigrants seeking honest labor. I can think of no better way to uphold that ruse."

To say nothing of how it served my own ruse, with the earnings that hung heavy in the pouch belted around my upper thigh. Those would be mine and Tristah's sustenance when we cast away from the crew, embarking on a quest of our own.

"And if you're recognized?" Ryker challenged, swiveling troubled eyes to me—more gray than green today.

I snorted lightly, blowing a flour stain from the tip of my nose. "The owner is half-blind and arthritic. It's why she's so desperately in need of an assistant. Even if she wasn't, she wouldn't believe me if I told her outright who I am…and she kept me all day today in the back, kneading dough." I folded my arms, bracing my weight against the table's edge behind me. "No one will be the wiser."

Grunting, Ryker scratched beneath his hair. Then he dropped his arm and hooked his thumb in his belt. "Up to you, sweetheart."

"The bakery it is, then." And in that moment, my glee was so absolute, I could not stop myself: I planted a kiss on the Captain's cheek before I hurried away.

I couldn't hide my brighter mood in the days that followed; they slid by swiftly, each one crammed full of doing what I loved best. In the shop, with Dorcas for company, I tried my hand at new recipes handed down through her family line. We chatted about her roots sunk deep into the crust of Bashir…how her ancestors had been present at its laying. How it had changed since. What had changed just in her lifetime.

"This is hardly the same city I knew as a girl," she croaked one day, perching on a stool and shaving chocolate for the pastry dough I worked at the counter. "So much unrest. So many speeches. And that Incendiary…"

My fingers caught a bit in the dough. This was the first she'd made mention of him in the fortnight I'd been working for her.

"What do you know of him?" I ventured…then added hastily, "Where I come from, it's such a small village in the foothills. I'd never heard even a whisper of any *Incendiary* before I set foot in Bashir."

Lucretzia would have smiled at my easy lie. I chased away the notion of her face with the next fold of pastry dough.

Dorcas sighed, shoving loose silver curls behind her ear with the back of her wrist—and still managing to lay a stripe of chocolate on her brow, melted by the heat of her stiff hands. "He has made things different in this city. Some say he's stoking the tension, and I suppose that's true…but there is also less violence."

I frowned at her over the kneading block. "In what way?"

She shrugged. "Before, militar and dissidents would squabble every now and again. Sometimes, it dissolved into arguments. Sometimes, it was worse." A pained memory streaked across her countenance in a twist of brows and lips—an agony that echoed across the hollow place in my heart where my parents had lived. "But that happens less now, with the Incendiary. I know the dissidents are torn between him and Sorai, but I tend to think they both do some good."

I fought not to scoff; it was difficult to imagine Algernon Sorai doing good for anyone but himself.

I must have accidentally made a sound regardless—or else she read the weight of what went unsaid in my silence. Dorcas shot me an amused half-smile. "You young people are so precise in how you think. But the way I see it, Sorai gives the elderly folk something to do…a sense of being heard. And this Incendiary, he gives the young and angry somewhere useful to pour out their rage. It's why the dissidents love them both, I think."

"I'm one for action over speeches, myself." Particularly when Sorai gave those speeches only to ingratiate himself to the Del…to remain close to the title and power he hoped to someday inherit. "A man unwilling to inconvenience himself to bring about change *now* will not be bothered to do it in the future."

"That is fair," Dorcas allowed, "and why the Incendiary may be right, after all. It's the elder folk who like Sorai's talking, because talking is all *we* have ever done. But this Incendiary…well. He certainly is not afraid to be inconvenienced, with how the Del seeks his head." She shook hers at the thought, returning to the slow, steady grate of chocolate. "And that may be the change that tips the balance, after all."

CHAPTER 46
THE BLADE LAID TO REST

The clatter of weapons roused me from sleep days later, rattling my skull in tune with Dorcas's lingering words while I dressed in the tent I shared with Ryker and Camden. Both had been perfect gentlemen since our arrival; they always made themselves scarce before I had even risen each day, granting me the luxury of changing in peace.

But today was different; when I stepped out, tying the laces of my bodice, I saw they'd deserted the tent for a new pursuit.

My stomach dropped at the bark of sparring shouts echoing from the heart of the courtyard where the crew circled up—trading merits, hollering encouragement and derision, laughing among themselves. The spectacle clashed uncomfortably against memories of dueling with Lucretzia and Tristah until I was too wearied and wounded to get to my feet for the hundredth time.

But it was not Lucretzia's scowling face I found when I elbowed through the crew to Camden, who greeted me with a tilted chin and a broad grin.

It was Ryker and Wilkes, a whirling dervish of striking blades.

I forgot the bakery that called me and the imminent danger of tardiness, my innards cringing as I recognized the dance of militar training in motion.

I needed no more than a few seconds of watching to find the familiarity in their form. They slithered around each other and lashed out like cobras, their wicked steel fangs seething in brilliant, firework-bright arcs; both were shirtless, their skin dappled in the shade cast by stone and tree blocking the early morning sun that inched above the courtyard's inner wall.

I had never seen Ryker wield a blade before, only a pistol; though he hefted a longsword in one hand and Lucretzia's stolen dagger in the other, both seemed the same weight in his hands. Some old, sore rage bellowed from every thrust of the dagger and swing of the sword, liquid and leonine; and though the sight moored me in place with fascination and even a spark of fear, the crew had clearly seen this spectacle before.

Gydeon and Siu sat atop the nearest table, shoulders pressed together, grinning as they flipped merits back and forth. The Draces sipped coffee and teased both men as they danced around one another. Rhea and Maryon took up two sides of the nearest potted tree, dueling in fiddle reels that kept tempo with the sparring sailors; Rhea shouted encouragement to Wilkes, Maryon to the Captain.

Side by side with Camden, I could not tear my gaze for longer than a heartbeat from Ryker.

He was…magnificent. I was not too proud to admit it, if only ever to myself. Every inch the pirate legend of Julas's fable—though I knew now that there were Old Salts more fearsome and ruthless than he. Ryker spared no expense in muscle or might, and every other movement had his dagger at Wilkes's throat, his kidney, his rigid abdomen. The quartermaster would pull back and spin to strike, lissome on his feet—and yet Ryker was already there to block with one blade, backhanding the other to a vulnerable spot.

It was as if the world whispered to him, warning him of Wilkes's movements before he ever made them; or as if Ryker held an innate sense of whatever lay ahead, his foresight a hairsbreadth ahead of us all. Whatever he translated from his quartermaster's inhalings, his barest shiftings, he turned back on him in the span of a heartbeat.

With every powerful thrust—every sharp pivot on heel and ball of foot, forward and back again, parrying, catching, blocking, swinging and spinning…with every slam of blade toward an inch of flesh that would have ended Wilkes if not for Ryker's well-honed restraint—it struck me that this man might, after all, be a match for Lucretzia.

And I was so relieved by that notion, it punched the breath from my lungs.

The absurdity of my own joy struck a gasping laugh from me, and I wrapped my arm around Camden's shoulders. He hugged my waist in turn, and we raised a cheer as Ryker tossed both sword and dagger high in the air, trading them effortlessly between hands while he backstepped from a slash Wilkes aimed at his middle.

And that was when I saw it.

The faintest dip in his right hand when he caught the longsword in it—the one relieved of a finger by Merry Dred. The slightest tremble in that same forearm as he compensated for the weakening of a four-fingered grip around a far heavier blade.

Eyes narrowing, Wilkes whirled around Ryker, abrupting his line of vision; and when Ryker spun to strike, Wilkes feinted, dodged back, and swung a full strike at Ryker's right leg. Ryker thrust the sword down to parry; but when metal shrieked on metal, it bent his fingers backward. With a shout, he let go—let the blade drop to the cobblestones with a resounding *bang*. And Wilkes's sword swept his ankles.

Down Ryker went, nearly slamming to his knees; but Wilkes lunged, caught him beneath the arm before his legs fully folded, and spun deftly behind him, drawing him back to his feet. He steadied him with his free arm draped around the back of Ryker's neck, clapping him soundly on the chest—just above his wheel pendant—and muttering something in his ear; even with the profound silence that insinuated itself among the crew, that whisper was too low for anyone else to hear.

Ryker heaved for breath, flexing his wounded hand, his eyes fixed on me. That look was impossible to discern; I wanted no part in trying to define it.

Gydeon clapped loudly, startling us all from our reverie. "All right, show's over, you lot! Don't you all have places to be?"

"Gambling houses to go spend that coin in that you just traded?" Siu added sharply, springing down from the table. "And don't try to shuffle off, Willy…you *do* owe me two merits."

Camden glanced up at me, his bright gaze seeded with doubt. "Cap lost. What's that mean?"

I squeezed him sideways. "That he is still healing. We all heal at our own pace, Cam. Even the strongest among us."

Thoughtfulness eased the tense line between his brows. "You don't think Cap's weak?"

"Everyone is weak in certain ways." I unwound my arm from around his shoulders. "But do I think another captain might swoop in and steal this crew from him? Doubtful. And even if one should try, Ryker has himself surrounded with people he trusts. People who would never allow such a mutiny."

Camden brightened fully at that. "Yeah, I doubt it, too. Thanks, Lio." He bumped his fist against my limp knuckles, then tore off after the Drace siblings—already begging them to take him to a gambling house before they'd even set foot in their tent.

I shook my head, a smile curling my lips; that boy was equal parts treasure and trouble. Ahim help this crew raising him amongst themselves.

"Enjoy the show?"

Heat poured down my back like a pot of honey tipped in the sun. Stubble brushed along my temple, teasing and tugging a few loose strands of hair as Ryker circled around me, his shoulder grazing mine. He donned his shirt as he passed, towing on the stained, tan linen and fluffing the hem out over his tattooed hipbones, walking backward while he faced me.

"Wilkes's idea," he offered when I didn't speak. "The duel. Training the grip back into my hand."

My gaze dropped to his missing finger—and my heart with it.

"Appreciate you having a word with Cam," Ryker added. "The lad carries more worry for this crew than a boy his age ought to carry for everything in his whole life. He needs mothering, and you have the talent for that."

"Well, I had an excellent example." For the first half of my life, at least.

Ryker's brows knitted, and for a moment, he looked as if he would say something else; but before he could, Wilkes's strident voice rang across the courtyard.

"Oi, Seasplitter!" With a jolt, I remembered that meant *me*. "Care for a duel?"

Dryness swept through my mouth; in its wake, sourness budded so boldly I nearly gagged. "I beg your pardon?"

"The way you wielded my axe back in Korsa, I'd wager you're handy with a sword." Wilkes spread his arms, blade dangling loose and easy in his grip. "How about a show, then?"

The heat doused. A cold chill of fear scraped along my bones—bones that remembered the thrust of a knife into the sheath of stomach-flesh, bones that remembered themselves fracturing and aching beneath the torture of repetitive motions, blades against blades, over and over and *over* again—

"*No.*" The word slashed from me with more force than I'd intended; yet even when Wilkes fell back on his heels, frowning, the swelling of fear and resentment left no pocket for sympathy to squeeze into. "Do not ask me again."

And I turned, hurrying out of the courtyard, free from the wide-eyed crew who'd halted to see if I would accept the challenge.

Blindly, I pushed out into the streets, the nearness of the past snapping viciously at my heels. My fingers grew clammy, soaked in sweat that congealed like blood.

I ached to bury them in flour, in dough—in the present.

Footsteps struck stone. "Lio!"

Ryker.

I did not pause for him; I shouldered between the marketers crowding Bashir's streets, shrinking into their midst. Every brush of a body against mine, every pop of color and light in my periphery, seared like a sunburn.

If I could only reach Dorcas's shop, lose myself in the rich scents of hot butter and yeast, then...

"Wait. Wait." Ryker's hand snared gently beneath my arm. "'Ay. Where are you running off to, sweetheart?"

Tugging from his grip, I scrubbed away the gooseflesh that still freckled my arms. "Work."

"Aye. All right." He fell into step with me, and his broad-shouldered presence broke the tide of passersby, affording me a bit more room to breathe. "But what's with that face?"

"Nothing. This is simply my face." I plastered a well-trained scowl across it for good measure. "If you do not *appreciate* it, I can find someone who will."

"Oh, I appreciate it plenty," he said—which threw me off my balance altogether until he added, "Wilkes didn't mean anything by it. He's not trying to rile you up...he's concerned, same as the rest of us."

"Concerned about *what?*" I rounded on him, feet planted. Sense warned he did not deserve my panic-frothed fury...but in some ways, he deserved it more than anyone. Him, and this crew who did not know me, but pushed me, and pushed me, and *pushed me*— "Concerned that I won't lift a sword? Shouldn't you *want* me weak and helpless...a damsel who cannot free herself?"

The crowd broke around us with mutters of annoyance, and after a moment, Ryker seized my shoulder and backed me off the street, tucking me into a niche between two looming, brick-sided buildings. The space was so narrow, our chests contacted with every breath; he braced his forearm against the wall above my head, the muscles in his bare bicep and shoulder flexing until the ink etched across them nearly danced. "What we're up against, with the beehive we kicked in Korsa, not to mention the Del's Own Blade at our backs...everyone needs to be in top form. Everyone needs to be able to stand for themselves. He wants you there, too."

Lucretzia's voice trickled into my mind, condescending and conniving. *Everyone in the Del's household must be prepared for the worst. Or would you prefer the feeling of another blade slipping into your side, Delina?*

An itch throbbed above my hipbone. "And who is to say I'm not in *top form*, Master Sailor?"

His brows did not so much as inch upward. "Why won't you pick up a sword?"

Swallowing a snappish retort, I ducked beneath his arm, slipping back into the street. He followed, keeping stride beneath the awning-laced avenues…as I'd hoped he would, but could not untangle my tongue enough to ask.

While we walked, I gazed at my hands…empty and clean. Yet in my eyes, they carried the perpetual shade of blood.

"You must know that Del Graven is a widower," I murmured. "That he has been for some years."

"Aye, word floated down the rivers that—"

"It was my doing."

Absolute quiet engulfed us for nearly a half-mile after that.

I had never told another soul this story. I had sworn I never would.

But now it eased from me, word over word, kneaded out by my tingling tongue. "It was the night Tristah and I escaped Shadewyle Castle. I had studied the watch changes for months by then. Tristah had gathered the supplies. Our scheme was flawless…but we did not expect Athyna."

Even with eyes wide open, I could envision the night all too clearly; the tacky humidity that made breathing so difficult. The precise pattern of the shadows on the walls. The summer lightning erupting like the fete fireworks that had ended hours before.

"We chose that evening for the drunken revelry that celebrated our betrothal…a supposition of looming peace—"

"Wait. Wait a *bloody minute*." Ryker snared my shoulder again, twisting me toward him. "You're *betrothed*? To who in the *depths*—?"

"To the spokesman of the dissidents. Algernon Sorai." I shrugged him off, his touch burning in the mess of this conversation—my confession. "Del Graven called it a betrothal. Truly, we were chattel sold to quiet his most outspoken denigrators."

Ryker's mouth roped to the side, straining as his jaw feathered and a muscle along the side of his neck bunched. "That bloody, blackhearted, blasted son of a—"

"This tale is not about him," I interrupted firmly; if I did not continue now, I never would. So I kept talking as we made our path through the thinning crowd. "In the inebriated aftermath of that celebration, only Tristah and I remained sober. So we made our escape through the castle halls, precisely as planned…but the Della intercepted us."

My next blink recalled the state of her—a spirit poised in our way, dipped in silken silver robes, her frame cut in the lightning which flashed over the mountainside.

"She threatened us," I murmured. "We had truly believed there was no worse they could do, but the punishments she promised if we did not return to our room were far beyond what we'd imagined in the worst outcomes of our attempted escape."

Until that night, I had thought Athyna the least of our imprisoners in Shadewyle; far less intimidating than her paranoid, cruel husband. Far less terrifying than ruthless, immoral Lucretzia.

But when she had found us creeping through the halls, the Della had flung insults and threats that had made my skin crawl and my ears burn. That had frozen Tristah in place, her mind dragged back to wounds she had suffered long ago…and spent so many years binding and healing, until they'd scarred at last.

Until Athyna tore them open again with unbridled savagery.

"We could hardly move." Every word was a dry croak clawing from my throat. "And she advanced on us. And when she tried to seize me, I acted without thinking. I trusted the training Lucretzia had beaten into us, and I…"

My fingers flexed, curling over the precise measure of the dagger I'd held that night. That I'd left behind in its new sheath when we'd fled…a mortal one made of flesh.

I jolted when calluses and sunmarks brushed away the phantom trace of blood and blade; Ryker's steady hand covered the tremble in my palm. His fingers pushed mine out from their crooked cage, every finger laid perfectly together except his missing one.

"You don't have to tell me," he offered.

That was true; I did not *have* to. And the choice to tell him was what made me say it: "I drew my knife and buried it to the hilt in her stomach."

Ryker's fingers flexed slightly; then they pivoted, sliding into the spaces between mine.

When sanity returned, perhaps, I would regret what I did then; that, rather than wrenching away as I ought to, I laced my fingers between his. That I held his hand while we walked the streets, as I might've held Bastyan's aboard *The Athalion*…a stolen touch sampled between Lucretzia's piercing looks.

I had yearned for an anchor then. I craved one again in this telling.

"My hands were soaked in blood in moments," I whispered, fixing my gaze across the staggered buildings ahead. "I might never have run if Tristah had not grabbed hold of me. We fled, and we left her in that hall to die…slowly and painfully. And we let her suffering bolster our escape."

I'd always suspected that they had found her dying before they'd found us missing. That the time spent failing to save the Della had cost them the precious moments that would have caught them up to us. That her death had been the steppingstone to our survival.

"After that night, I vowed to never wield another blade against a person," I rasped. "Not unless I can trust why I use it."

We had nearly reached Dorcas's shop; the streets were emptying, the crowds flowing past us to the nearby marketer's plaza. It would be some hours yet before they wandered away from the baubles and trinkets, desperate for sustenance…hours I would spend baking and frosting things, kneading dough and pushing my troubles out into the batch.

But for now, I stopped; and Ryker halted with me, his hand slipping from mine, his face angled slightly away, up the deserted avenue.

"I'll tell Wilkes to lay off," he said. "Whatever it is you need to feel ready for what's coming… you let one of us know."

Gratitude heated the base of my throat. "I will."

Scrubbing the back of his neck, he slanted his gaze my way. "I don't want you helpless. That's never been—"

"I know." But I didn't. It was too complicated, too unsure, this strange thing we had become.

Unwilling partners, united on the hunt for Tristah. A hunt I wanted to go one way, for our sakes. A hunt he wanted to go the other, for his crew.

Ryker pivoted to face me fully, his expression hollowed with the same exhaustion that had hounded me since I'd realized we would be waiting weeks in this city for a man who might not even be able to lead us to the Incendiary. "You're already more than a match for what's out there, most ways. You don't need a blade in your hand to be the best of yourself." A shrug tilted his shoulders. "And you can have a weapon in your hand and still be the weakest person in the room, if you're drawing it for the wrong reasons."

"Lucretzia would disagree."

"Lucretzia's not here." Finally, he arched that brow. "Maybe that ought to tell you both something, aye?"

"She only isn't here because a pirate lord outwitted her."

He shrugged. "That pirate was only alive to do it because a baker was brave enough to jump into the drink and fish him out."

Warmth saturated my insides. "There's simply no arguing with you, is there, Captain?"

"Eh." He scratched beneath his hair again. "Wilkes beat me today. Got to earn my wins somewhere."

The vision of them dueling floated to my mind again, and all at once a flustered sort of energy stole through my hands. I gripped my skirt at the thighs, pivoting away. "I should go. Dorcas needs my help."

"Aye, I'll see you back at the compound tonight. And…Lio, I'm sorry," he called after me as I hurried toward *The Love of the Loaf.* "For what the Del sold you to."

Halting on the threshold, my hand braced to the door, I looked back at him over my shoulder. "Little different from a ransom of merits for paid off debts, isn't it?"

His jaw slipped. Shock, then comprehension, then horror unleashed in his gaze.

I ducked inside, shutting the door on all three.

CHAPTER 47
A SHADOW OF THE PAST

omething shifted between Ryker and I the day of the duel…something that could not be put back as it once was.

Now and again, he accompanied me to Dorcas's shop in the mornings; and most evenings, he was there to walk me back to the compound, our arms laden with sacks of leftover bread the elderly shopowner insisted I take.

It was a strange escort, at first…one I could not make sense of until it struck me one evening—watching him canvass the streets for trouble, a sharp gaze overlaying a gamely grin—that he was the blade at my side. The dagger I refused to draw.

A man protecting his prized ransom, perhaps; but his presence comforted me nonetheless. Particularly when the first batch of crew, led by Klement, sailed the *Singer* across the Weyval Basin to Port Tamsay.

And particularly when, not long after their departure, a sense of anticipation spilled through the city like spoiled milk tipped from a cracked pitcher.

It leaked into everything; the essence of Bashir itself curdled from demure to dreadful. Shopkeepers scowled and frowned; marketers were hurried and harried, their reckonings with us swift and curt—nearly rude. The walls of the complex were plastered in fresh propaganda each morning when I departed and each evening when Ryker and I returned.

Tensioned seethed beneath every footfall I took down the city streets. It was not entirely an unfamiliar sensation, but a fully unwelcome one.

It reminded me far too strongly of the last days in Monsha before my safe, sugar-sweet childhood had erupted into lurid firework-flames.

"The city seems…unsettled," I remarked to Dorcas one day, watching another patron scurry from the shop, clutching a loaf of bread like a shield over his chest.

"It's a city near a port, Lionyra," Dorcas snorted. "It is always unsettled."

"Fair." A smile tugged at my mouth. "But…more than usual."

"True, it does seem that." She angled a weather-beaten frown at the sliced loaves she was carefully bagging in brown paper sacks. "I've heard murmurs from rumor-mongers that this has to do with the dissidents."

The dread that had beaten like a pulse against the soles of my feet for days spiked higher, lancing my stomach. "What of them?"

"You've seen the fresh propaganda, I take it?"

"Every day." I carved through another loaf and slid the uniform pieces down the counter to her.

"Well, to hear the loosest tongues and most speculative minds tell it, they're expecting something."

"Expecting—?"

The bell above the door sang its sweet silver chime, and a familiar fair-haired figure swaggered in, thumbs hooked in his belt.

Dorcas glanced from Ryker to me, her gray brows arching. "Something noteworthy to come through the door, I suppose."

"'Ay, now," Ryker drawled, leaning his folded arms on the counter; his tattoos popped starkly against the fine dusting of flour where we'd worked all day. "You know we can't flirt in front of her, Dory. She's a jealous one."

A disbelieving snort burst from me. "Please! You may flirt with whomever you wish…whoever is unfortunate enough to catch your fancy."

"Flirting with someone and fancying them aren't the same thing."

I chuckled under my breath, raising my brows but keeping my gaze on the bread, sparing my fingers from a nicking by the only sort of blade I cared to wield. "Yes, that much, I suppose, you've made quite clear."

"Not clear enough, by the way you won't look me in the eye."

His husky tone made a liar of him—it *did* draw my gaze to his. A pang wrenched through my heart at the untrustworthy earnestness there…at the way my heart stretched out, hungry for it. Aching for it.

Dorcas's laughter shattered the stare which held us both captive. "Leave the heating of the shop to the ovens, will you? Lionyra, you're free to go."

I pushed back from the counter, turning to face her—freeing myself from the Captain's captivating attention. "So early?"

She sobered a bit, peering through the street-facing windows of the shopfront. Shadows scurried beyond, moving with haste all in one direction…as if no one could arrive at their destinations swiftly enough. "All jest aside, I see what you see. Feel it, too. I'd prefer none of us be out later than necessary."

Ryker shifted back from the counter, knocking his fist on it. "Sure you're not a born sailor?"

She huffed a laugh dryer than the bread-filled sacks before her. "If I was, I'd be soaking these old bones in a saltwater surf somewhere, not warming them by flirting hopelessly with the likes of you."

"Ah, but I do warm those bones, don't I?"

Yanking loose the hand-cleaning cloth that hung at her waist, Dorcas snapped it playfully at his bicep. "Get out!"

Laughing, we stole out into the streets, each with a loaf tucked under one arm…and I carried a bag of cinnamon rolls just for Camden. Watching him wager—and lose—his pastries in round after round of cards with the Drace siblings had become a favorite pastime in the evenings; it was what I would miss the most now that Kory and Klement had sailed off aboard the *Singer*. At least there was Kato still, though he let Camden win far fewer rounds than his soft-souled brother did.

"Hear any good rumors today?" Ryker asked as we passed through shadow after shadow, the spring sunset deepening early thanks to the steep hills and high vaults of Bashir. It was a practiced question—one he asked every day.

"No mention of anyone like Ember returning to the city," I replied…as I did every day. "Nor of the Incendiary."

"They'll come." Nothing cracked the confident swagger in his tone. "They've been dancing around the Basin for years, by the sound of it. No sense they'd disappear as soon as we start sniffing around for them."

"Unless they've caught wind we're sniffing."

"Give me some credit, sweetheart." Ryker smirked. "Raiders know how to sniff in ways that don't get them caught."

That much, I could trust…if for no other reason than the intrigue the gamblers in *The Coin Toss* had showed when the Drace siblings breezed inside. It struck such an odd discord in me; how the Raiders could be so feared among the common folk, yet suffer so much at the hands of their own kind in Korsa.

And yet…was that any different from the carvings of my own past? The untouchable Delina, cold as a Highlands hoarfrost, sweeping down to blanket council sessions in rime-ice threats and frigid, unblinking stares; a woman whispered about and feared by city rulers and councilors of the Del himself, respected for her bladed tongue and the spine-shuddering, knee-bending force by which she delivered her opinions.

The Delina who had laid awake more nights than she could number in Shadewyle Castle, fear seizing its fist around her heart, terrified that every step creaking outside her door must belong to the Pale Viper.

Perhaps we were all no more than charlatans playing at strength, broken up with the weaknesses we hid from the world. Each of us feigning power in the light and trembling in the dark.

Or perhaps the strength and the weakness were both the truth of us, each of us taking back power where we could.

My stride hitched, shifting to match Ryker's. "Well, there are certainly worse cities to wait in."

"Aye?" Ryker hefted the bread beneath his arm. "All about this, isn't it?"

"You've found me out," I laughed. "I have joy anywhere I can bake bread."

"That simple a life, is it?"

"Well, when you have a past so complicated—"

The words perished in my mouth, a last wisp of vapor floating off my tongue as we stepped into one of the many plazas that pockmarked the path back to the compound—and a phantom of the past grazed across my vision, sweeping all sense from my head.

My feet stuck to the cobblestones. My chest shriveled to a husk.

He crossed my way without looking twice…a tall man, broad-shouldered and barrel-chested, his dark hair tied in a knot that swept down the thick drape of his jewel-toned green cloak. A scar twisted up from the curve of his jaw, curling across his cheekbone, halfway to his left eye. He strode with purpose, chin high, and people parted to make way for him to the crier's pedestal erected in the plaza center.

He did not see me. But I saw him—here, and splashed against the garish hearthlight of Shadewyle Castle in my memory, a booming, blustering presence that swept through like a gale. A man who had seen me only fleetingly, though I'd spied on him with Tristah in every council session he'd held in private with Del Graven.

The world blurred. Tilted. Heaved and bucked beneath me like a ship on the waves. My lungs had yet to expand, and everything began to darken, graying on the edges and flickering with silver sugar-sprinkles that grew to yeast blooms in my vision—

And then…heat.

Heat erupted from around my clavicles, shooting down my breastbone, my ribs, digging into my pelvis in a single long, violent, body-quaking shiver that forced breath back into my lungs.

A hot palm seized my shoulder, and all at once I returned to my trembling body. To Bastyan—to *Ryker*—his arm slung around my collarbones from behind, his hand with the missing finger anchored to my opposite shoulder.

"Breathe, sweetheart," he murmured against the shell of my ear, producing another shiver that forced air through my strangled lungs. "What're you seeing that I'm not?"

I twisted in his grip, chest-to-chest with him, his arm casing my shoulders now, his pendant scraping against my throat; that faint twinge of pain dredged my voice up from the depths where the sight of that detestable face had sent it cowering.

"*Sorai*," I choked. "That man was Algernon Sorai."

CHAPTER 48
THE MOUTHPIECE

The moment that hated name left my lips, Ryker hauled me aside, loaves of bread dropped, shoving me into a seam between two of the buildings that made up the plaza's edge. The cinnamon rolls, I somehow kept in my fist; my fingers had spasmed so tightly, it would have required a chisel to pry them apart.

Ryker set me against the bricks, then laid his back against them as well, bending to peer out of the alley. Collaring myself with one hand, I shut my eyes and fought for calm.

I had seen him. He had not seen me, and even if he did, we had only crossed paths once—and I had looked a different woman altogether then, done up in cosmetics and a many-stranded braid and an orchid-pink dress. Little of that refined Delina remained in my flour-stained frame, my muted attire and plum cloak.

Still, he'd spent enough time with Tristah that there wasn't an inconsiderable risk of being recognized.

My fingers flew to my braid, undoing it rapidly, severing that similarity in my appearance; and that motion gave me a moment to gather my wits.

"Well, I think we know why Ember disappeared so quickly," I muttered.

"Aye. Didn't want to start a fight with the mouthpiece of the people." Raw hatred seethed in Ryker's voice—an unearned disgust.

Sorai's presence explained other things, too; the outbreak of dissent. The rise in propaganda. The restlessness that had overtaken the city.

His coming had been known, at least to some. Which likely meant the Del had sent him…a test of his loyalty. Perhaps to prove that, after all this time, Sorai could still be reasoned with. Could still be *bought*, for the proper price.

I knocked my head back against the stones, struggling to bear down my next inhale; my fingers unleashed all at once, and the bag of sweets dropped with a dull *thump* at my feet.

Ryker swiveled in the alleyway, his broad frame blocking my view of the plaza. "'Ay. How do you want to get out of this?"

Blinking away tears, I turned my cheek flush to the warm stones, meeting his gaze; tempestuous emotion grayed his eyes, but he held his ground. He did not usher me down the alley or force me back into the plaza.

The choice was firmly in my hands. How did *I* want to get out of this?

Did I want to get out of it?

All at once, indecision—not shock, not dread—stuck my feet in place instead.

Sorai was more than a mouthpiece of the people; he was a glimpse into the Del's schemes. Through him, I could ascertain what Del Graven was plotting. For the country as a whole…and for the Incendiary.

If I possessed that knowledge, it would almost certainly ingratiate me to him…perhaps even provide bargaining power for Tristah's whereabouts.

Setting my jaw, I pressed each fingertip to the stone wall at my back until the whorls memorized the brush of stone. Then I pushed myself lightly away from it, stooping to snatch up the bag. "I would hear what this mouthpiece is yammering about."

The corner of Ryker's mouth tugged up—a fleeting glimpse of a sunshine grin. "Atta girl. How are you about climbing walls?"

"Just go, will you?"

With a grunt of laughter, he fitted his sturdy boots to the bricks and started to climb—slow, faltering a bit with his four-fingered hand, but determined in the ascent. Seizing the seam of the sweets bag in my teeth, I followed after him.

Climbing this way reminisced of the minaret towers I'd scaled in Krylan the night I'd fallen captive to Officer Fiordona. My hatred for the soldier who'd set this mess in motion became the strength in my fingers, the sturdiness of my feet. It coaxed me to greater heights, rising like a well-made souffle until I spilled over onto the rooftop, gasping for breath; Ryker caught me beneath the arm, and we scurried to the edge of the rooftop on hands and knees.

Lying on our bellies, we peered down into the plaza: it was packed nearly to the seams with Bashiri residents of all ages, all sorts. A palpable energy hummed in their midst like one torch lighting another, and another, and another, until smoke and fire rose from the hearth of bodies.

A righteous anger veined the cracks in the cobblestones, lighting the eyes of the assembled. Simmering coals impatiently waiting to be stoked into flame.

They carried no pamphlets. No tar marred their fingertips. But I knew in the marrow of my bones that this crowd contained a double-helping of dissenters…and that somewhere nearby, the militar must be taking note of who assembled.

I shot a glance at Ryker; his grim countenance, the deep grooves framing his mouth, spoke of the same certainty.

My hatred doubled when I laid eyes on Sorai; he'd taken to the crier's pedestal, emanating the same power as a hawker or a mercantilist who was certain of the wares he sold and wished to share them with the world.

Or he simply knew the power of good salesmanship. I had seen far too many people who sold only what they knew could earn them profit, regardless if they believed in the product itself.

Today, Algernon Sorai had come to sell discord.

"For years now, I've kept my ears toward Bashir." He had already made his introductions and plunged knee-deep into speech-making…and already, he held the people captive with the curve of his inflections, with the power he pushed behind this word and that. "I've heard your plights. You can trust that I have brought them before Del Graven himself!" He waited for the uproar of gratitude at that—then calmed it with a brush of his hand, pivoting to round the pedestal. "But the regime has concerns. *I* have concerns."

Halting in the center of the upraised platform, he spread his hands—an inviting gesture. A deadly embrace.

"Where is the Incendiary whose name travels from this city in every direction? I would speak with him now!"

No one stepped forward.

"Blowhard," Ryker muttered. "What's he doing—spoiling for a fight?"

"All he has are words," I breathed back. "And who knows if the Incendiary is proficient at speeches? If Sorai can outspeak him, he may yet win the favor of some of the dissenters who haven't chosen rebellion over reticence."

"Keep them docile, you mean."

Sorai dropped his arms, arresting my focus and halting my retort. "I thought not." A grim smile, a patronizing wag of his head. "You know, as difficult as matters have been between the dissenters and the regime, I have never once shied away from the calling. I have been present; I have shown my face. I have made public appearances and stood before the Del himself, despite the risk to my own person. But what do you do, *Incendiary*?" He raised the challenge to an invisible opponent—or, at the very least, an unknowable one. "You call the shadows your home. You won't show your face in the Del's presence. You cower and cringe and swing from the darkness!"

A few murmurs rose among the crowd, chasing a chill down my spine.

"You say you are for the people, *Incendiary*!" Sorai's strident words possessed the whole plaza, hushing the gathering at once; his robes glinted like emeralds freshly mined from the Highlands as he paced the pedestal, his hands framing his words in cuts and slashes.

I couldn't deny he had presence. There was a reason, after all, he had named himself the voice of the people.

And he had intended to steal *mine*.

"You say you are *for the people*." In this repetition, his tone dipped with scorn, his tongue unfurling a bit to paint his lower lip—as if he was cleansing a lie from the chapped flesh. "Yet you lead them into acts of rebellion that will foment war!"

A few voices struck out in fervent agreement. Others grumbled among themselves so lowly, their opinions might have gone either way.

"Raiding storehouses will solve nothing!" A half-dozen cries spiked at that, and Algernon paced more swiftly, goaded by the support of the crowd. "Disrupting the *militar* will solve *nothing*! Withholding due taxes will solve nothing!"

There were fewer tones of support at that; I cast a glance at Ryker, and he smirked, rolling his eyes.

"You are not changing laws by your actions. You make nothing *better* for this country. Your defiance *will* cost you," Algernon went on, muting the square once more with a sweep of his outstretched arm. "It will cost us all. There is a way to have what we want…a true voice in the leadership of our beloved country. Yet you *spit* on talks of peace if they do not include you. You defy Del Graven to his face, rather than seeking compromise."

He flicked his cloak back from his hips and planted his hands on his waist, glaring across the crowd, arms akimbo—as if any one of them might be the Incendiary, target of his wrath.

"If your intentions were pure, you would do as *I* have done…you would show yourself. You would negotiate for the good of all. Instead, you hide behind a false title and drive us nearer and nearer to a place from which we will never return." He shook his head, lips curling with sour disgust. "If you are listening,

Incendiary, I hope you're not too stuffed full of pride to hear these words: *stand down*. I am so blasted *near* to sealing a compromise that will forever grant the people a true voice in the regime…not in cruel acts carried out from the shadows."

Ryker's head snapped my way, and my heart pounded against my ribs like a dancing drum.

A compromise.

He meant my *hand* forced into his. So he knew I had been found in Mithra-Sha…that Lucretzia and Del Graven hunted me still.

"You *have* quelled the riots…I'll give you that," Algernon's grudging concession whipped my head up as if he'd seized me by the chin. "You've given unreasonable malcontents a place to spend their energy. But I fear that will only make things worse in the end."

Disgruntled mutters curled up in smoky tendrils from below. Ryker's hand crawled across the space between us, gripping my shoulder. "Steady, Lio."

The whisper of my chosen name eased my trembling rage; I blinked a sheen of furious tears from my vision, bringing Sorai's shivering form back into view.

"…have any love for this country you claim to fight for, you *will* stand down." His tone had shifted in the moments that rage thudded in my ears.

I had never thought Algernon Sorai fearsome, only blustering at best. But his narrowed eyes and stinging smile flashed with the fanatical determination of a man who was within reach of what he craved most in the world—who would fight for it by any means. Even bloody ones.

"Stand *out of my way*," he warned, "or when I broker peace for the Northlands and Southlands both, you will find you have an enemy in myself as well as the Del. And that is a union you do not wish to *light a fire* against."

Union.

The word roared through me, marrying with the havoc of cheers, shouts, and questions that vaulted from the crowd below. The chaos of frenzied defiance winnowed into my ears like the tip of a blade, scraping the walls of my skull. Pain pulsed in my temples in tune to their stomps and shouts, their cheers.

Were these the death-sounds that had ushered my parents to their graves— the last things they'd ever heard before the riots had consumed them? How would they have reacted when those cries were raised again at the mention of their daughter sold off, a prize to the highest bidder?

The little girl in me begged for a kitchen table to hide under; instead, I let Ryker's hand anchor me in the rising tide of dissidence.

My fingers crooked into fists; I tucked them tightly beneath my folded arms, staring Algernon Sorai down as if he could feel the heat of my glare.

Eyes wide open. Take power where you can.

He would not have me. He would not have Tristah. Not while there was still breath in my lungs.

"He will *not* have me," I hissed aloud.

Ryker's hand tightened on my shoulder, his eyes gleaming a bright, ash-edged green. "You're bloody right he won't."

While the crowd stormed and questioned and raved below us, we crawled as one back from the rooftop's edge, clambering down into the alley. The moment our boots struck stone, a mirrored urgency tightened our spines; we pivoted to face one another in the narrow split of stone.

"Every street'll be packed while this lot breaks up and heads for home." Ryker jerked his chin at the alley mouth. "Wait it out, or use the cover?"

"Cover." I strangled the bag in my fist. "There's no telling how long Sorai will linger. Perhaps he'll hope for a meeting with the Incendiary."

"Fair enough." Ryker rolled his shoulders, then offered his hand. "Ready to run with me one more time?"

Something chafed in my core at those words; but I said nothing, only laid my hand in his.

We stepped from the alley as if our intentions there had been anything but to hide; and all at once, the muttering, agitated mob swelled around us, swallowing us like hot, swollen flesh around a splinter.

Thoughts of my parents crowded nearer than the press of bodies on every side; the air corroded against my face, throttled with friction, with discord against the Incendiary and jeers against Sorai. Arguments splintered in pockets all around us.

Ryker's grip flexed. "Don't stop, whatever you do. And don't let go of my hand."

I had no intentions otherwise.

CHAPTER 49
NOTHING BUT YOURS

We forded through the dangerous waters of dissent, the brand of militar gazes landing on us from side avenues; and worse, the heat of Algernon's stare, raking the crowd. Searching for the Incendiary among us…seeking an opponent who knew better than to challenge him to his face.

A shoving pair of bodies, shouting and cursing, jostled against my side, throwing my feet into a stumbling swerve; Ryker's hand seized, his grip scrabbling with its stolen finger, then separating from mine.

The sea of bodies tore him away from me; and when I thrust through the flow of the crowd in the direction it had carried him, he was no longer there.

His name leaped to my tongue—then perished.

Ryker Kassian didn't exist in this city. Not a single one of us had called him by name outside the compound walls since we'd set foot in Port Krait. He could not be that famed pirate, could not be Blackhand in such a place; and I could not be heard calling a name bound to theft and high-seas plundering.

Cursing, I raised my voice. "Bastyan!"

No reply.

Deadweight struck cobblestones nearby; someone screamed, and bone snapped as boots crushed bodies. Panic scoured my throat like a hot poker, and I choked on it, my next scream of Ryker's name emerging as a horrified wheeze.

Riots.

A body lost in a rampage, a body crushed, a man or woman—a father or mother—never coming home.

With my next blink, my mind taunted me with the imaginings of *Ryker* stampeded beneath the feet of this heaving crowd. Ryker, never returning to his crew, his life snuffed in a fire, unrest and anger stamped across the last memories of him that I would ever hold.

Something violent seized me, a cruel need that swallowed all clear thought and reason. Screaming, I threw elbows and kicked wildly, shoving the crowd out of my path, hurling myself in the direction their rogue swells had carried him. "Bastyan! Bastyan, where are you? *Bastyan!*"

"Lio!" Faintly, his voice floated among the chaos of shouts that choked the plaza; the tide of bodies had dragged him back toward the crier's stand. They were so thick there, shouting at Algernon's feet, demanding answers and attention, weeping over taxes and suppression and need—

Only one need howled through me as fresh bursts of squabbling broke out among the onlookers:

Bastyan.

Bastyan.

Bastyan.

I chased his voice, ducking the assembly's bickering and brawling, holding my breath to keep the smell of smoke at bay. Treading waves of memory crashing over and over against my mind. A successful escape from everything, I thought—until I risked a glance up at the crier's platform.

Until my eyes met Algernon Sorai's.

They widened, confused. Then…

"You!" He stabbed a finger my way. "Come up here!"

Choking back the brutal profanity that coated my tongue, braided with the grimy taste of smoke, I tore my gaze away and hunted wildly for Ryker's face among the crowd. But there was no one familiar, nothing but panicked memories encroaching on every side.

With no other choice left, I flung myself away from the platform and sprinted as best I could through the crowd; still, the *thud* of Algernon leaping down from the stand rang in my ears like a physical blow. "Wait a moment!"

Heart seizing, I quickened my pace, shoving between the battling bodies and knocking shoulders with simple Bashiri residents and hidden dissidents alike. I did not look back when Sorai hollered after me to halt again. And again.

"Someone *seize that woman!*"

Terror whipped through me, and I wrenched backward as a pair of men— his loyalists, little doubt, by how swiftly they moved at his command—rounded in my path. Their gazes landed on me at once, given away by my telltale back-step; then they forded through the stream of the crowd, moving against its current, determination setting their ruddy countenances.

Pastry bag in fist, I whirled—and slammed into rope-scarred hands, one missing a finger.

Sweat streaked Ryker's face, and a bruise bloomed along his jaw; someone was cursing off to the left, voice muffled with blood. As if he'd thrown fists to reach me.

Relief buckled my knees; I dipped, gripping his forearms—the only strength that kept me standing.

"You were gone," I rambled, hardly knowing the weak, thready pitch of my own voice. "You were *gone*, the crowd took you, I couldn't find you—"

His hands flexed around my elbows, and he heaved for breath, unspeaking. But his eyes, blown wide and brimming with urgency, and his touch, tender but steady, spoke tales I needed no Storycrafter's penchant like Addie's to understand.

Let me handle this.

Then his hands dipped to squeeze my fingers; his brow and mine met, sweat and dirt and a bit of blood streaking my forehead. And once again, I nearly broke down where I stood; I squeezed my eyes shut, burying my forehead against his, leaning into the comfort his presence whispered.

I'm here.

He pivoted to face Sorai as the mouthpiece jostled through the crowd toward us, keeping one arm braced before me and his shoulder angled in my path—blocking the way to me. "Any particular reason you're yelling at my wife, out of everyone at your little assembly?"

Sorai jogged to a halt, confusion tracing the sharp lines of his high cheekbones and sunken eyes. "This woman is your wife?"

"I'd say so, considering I vowed my worthless hide to her six years ago." Ryker slanted his head. "So unless she has a decoy somewhere out there…"

It took effort not to drill my boot into his shin.

Frowning, Sorai bent, fighting to peer around Ryker's bulk at me. "I could've sworn—"

"*'Ay!*" Ryker snapped—the same vicious tone that had undercut his voice at the tavern in Korsa, before Dred's men had taken us. He angled his body with the tilt of Sorai's, matching him motion for motion. "I'm right here, *friend*. If she wants to talk to you, she will."

And I wanted nothing less.

"Your…*wife* bears a resemblance to someone I once knew," Sorai said.

"That so? Well, you keep harassing her, and that sort of thing's all your little supporters will be able to say about *you* after tonight."

Sorai leaned back, arms folded. "Do you have any idea who I am?"

"I know exactly who you are." Ryker eased forward a step. "And if you had the same luxury, you'd be pissing yourself and running the other way. So let's leave it at this: she's with me. You don't know her. And she's not going anywhere with you or your little trouser-sniffers here."

The jerk of his head was a warning; I spun, placing my back to his, and the two men who'd moved to seize me at Sorai's word froze—a step from laying hold of me from behind.

Heart thundering so wildly it sent spirals of pain jouncing through my breastbone and into my throat, I pressed every inch of myself to Ryker's back…the only place of safety in this eruptive square.

"Now," Ryker said, "let us pass."

Sorai grimaced; then, after a long moment, he cut his gaze to the side.

The two men receded at once, trailing off with mutinous frowns flung our way. Ryker reached aside, his hand snaring mine, and I did not look back at Sorai again as Ryker pivoted on heel and shoved us both into the crowd.

My heart refused to calm—a lingering fear I blamed at first on the crush of the crowd and the clots of conflict still breaking out. The odd peace or pause the Incendiary had evoked in Bashir was faltering moment by moment with the touch of Algernon's influence.

But even after we slipped into the darker streets, leaving the crowd behind, the tension did not ease. I could not draw a full breath, nor escape the prickling at the nape of my neck.

It was too much like Korsa.

"He's pursuing us," I hissed.

"Aye." Ryker kept his gaze firmly ahead. "Those two lackeys of his are on our flanks."

My mind stumbled, tearing ahead; we had far to go to the compound, and I had no interest in leading Sorai somewhere he could watch us. Nor would I become a prisoner within the stone walls of our courtyard, fearing that his friends lurked outside.

He did not believe Ryker's lie—did not believe what we were.

Very well. I would give him something to believe in.

Another hundred paces along, our surroundings took on a familiar sheen. I hauled Ryker off the darkened avenue, down a sidestreet, into a polished courtyard ringed in soaring columns. Tables and chairs littered its face, and numerous eateries and taverns faced into it—a perfect place for dining, drinking, and playing music. Rhea had brought me wandering by it while we'd sought whispers of Ember and the Incendiary, the same day I'd found Dorcas's shop; Rhea's grin had glowed brighter than her rich auburn hair at the hum of chatter that arrested its broad flagstone span, her voice sweet as music and crafty as a con when she'd noted how perfect a place this would be to earn merits with sweet fiddle tunes.

Now it hung quiet but for the distant pulse of riotous shouts from the plaza, only the breeze of our passing stirring the boxed ivy that dangled down from atop the ornate columns as I hauled Ryker by the hand into the midst of the courtyard.

"What are you *doing?*" he panted, feet scuffing the flagstones as he kept pace with me. "What is this, a shortcut? Sweetheart—"

I freed his hand only to swivel and grip his shoulders, boosting myself up to perch on the edge of the nearest table. Ryker's hands caught my hips by instinct, it seemed; his eyes widened when I twined my legs around his waist, binding him close, my fingers flexing in the folds of his vest…giving myself one moment to question whether this was the road I wished to take.

Eyes wide open.

I would not give myself more than that breathless heartbeat to doubt how desperately I wanted this—how believing I'd lost him in the burgeoning riots tonight had cut the tethers of every restraint that had held me captive since we'd first boarded *The Dread Singer* together.

Take power where you can.

I gripped Ryker's cheek, wrenching his head toward mine when he swiveled to glance back at the shadow-drenched street we'd left, where the echo of footfalls pounded now in tune with my racing heart. "Kiss me."

His jaw unhinged. The blood drained from his face so rapidly, his skin turned clammy beneath my fingers. "What—?"

"Kiss me! Do you want to sell the tale you told him? Then kiss me like a husband would!"

"You *can't* be—"

Sliding my hand from his cheek, around the back of his neck, I tugged him so near I could smell the sea salt living in the pores of his skin. He fisted a hand in my tangled hair, holding me at bay when our brows touched, when my nose brushed his; I met his disbelieving stare and poured every inch of the fear and relief of losing and finding him again into my hiss: "I will not give them reason to believe I am anything but *yours*."

His eyes fixed on me with a last, held-breath warning…a final opportunity to flee from something I ought to have been running from all this time.

When I did not retreat, his fist wrapped up sharply in my hair, and he wrenched my mouth to his.

The collision of our lips was nothing soft, nothing sacred; it was furious and bruising, and the grip of his other hand around my waist, anchoring me against the tabletop, had a nearly painful bite. But despite that, Ryker Kassian knew his way around a kiss…a practiced experience that danced beneath the layers of desire and hurt where our lips and tongues and bodies met.

He made it seem *real*—real enough that when his weight landed over me, sinking me to my back on the table, both my hands twined of their own volition in the wheat-gold locks of his hair and guided him down against me. His knuckles defended my skull from the stone, his fingers flexing, burying themselves against my scalp, stroking deeply and setting chills flaring down my neck and shoulders.

Distantly, over the thudding of my wild, rebellious heart, I came aware of boots striking the courtyard stones—then silencing altogether.

Ryker's hand released my waist, sliding up to my knee, hitching my leg more tightly around him and then finding its way back to my hip. His touch was a branding fire, catching my gasp for air, burning it up to vapors. His lips possessed mine, his mouth gentling slightly as he stole my breath, taking every part of me into every part of him—

The steps resumed, hurrying on past the courtyard.

Ryker broke away at once, tearing himself free and slamming his palms against the tabletop on either side of my head; my spine unbowed and I pressed a hand to my stomach, holding captive a body that craved to return for more.

We stared at one another, panting, him looming above me and me slack beneath him, and something bittersweet unfurled in my middle…a sense of the forbidden taking hold. The notion that I had just done something which could never be undone.

"If that didn't bloody convince him," Ryker croaked, "nothing will."

I should not have wished Sorai unconvinced, just for the chance to kiss this Captain again. I should not have wished for another excuse to taste the citrus and salt in the mouth of the man who would hold me ransom.

The man who'd given up a finger to spare me the same pain. Who'd shouted for me with broken tones from the ship's deck while his crew held him back from leaping to my aid. Who was in this city and these straits to find Tristah with me.

I should not have yearned for the name *Bastyan* on my tongue again—or for the way he'd shouted back to me when he'd heard it cried above the crowd tonight. As if the sailor aboard the ship that had carried us to Monsha was fighting his way back to me.

My eyes swarmed with heat. "We should return to the compound…as indirectly as possible."

Slowly, his hands trailed from the tabletop, passing my thighs, my bent legs that had fallen from around his waist. His arms tumbled limp at his sides, and I sat up, my stare never leaving his. "Aye. Shouldn't be too hard to find our way."

That was true, but still it was a slow journey, a darkened one, and we spoke not one word as we made it; and I was both grateful and full of nerves, every step we took, refusing to look at him even once.

Because if I peered into his eyes and saw a sunshine smile, saw any hint of Bastyan Atreyon looking back at me from that face tonight…

I would come utterly undone.

CHAPTER 50
THE RISING TIDE

RYKER

It was the kind of absolute bloody mess that dared the depths to spit up something worse—then laughed straight in their trenches when they couldn't manage it.

I'd kissed Lionyra Vara.

Not just kissed her…I'd about blasted lost myself in her. Forgot who I was and why I was doing any of this. Why I'd lied and cheated and played deckhand just to get her aboard my ship. Why we were in this city her depths-sunk *betrothed* strolled in and out of in one night, leaving some riot fires burning on his heels.

Fires I helped put out before dawn just so Lio wouldn't wake up and smell them burning.

It was half a day later, with soot smeared all over my face and lungs itching from the smoke, before I finally woke up enough to stare myself down in the bucket I was washing the stains off in and get serious about it all.

To forget for a second how badly I wanted to go back to that courtyard and find out what would happen if neither of us had to stop to breathe. To forget what I'd been doing all day, and who I was doing it for, and why. To forget that I was dreaming wide awake, and just look myself in the eye.

This was supposed to be a *job*. The kind of piracy the last Blackhand had dumped into all the parts of me Varsi had scraped out. The kind of run that looked only at the merits in the coffers, not the faces you handed over—or worse—to get them.

I wasn't supposed to look twice at that face. Wasn't supposed to have some craving for the smiling mouth on it that always had a dab of chocolate at the corner…or spend a whole day walking around like some lovestruck runt, dreaming about another taste.

"You stupid son of a sea urchin." I grabbed both sides of the bucket, groaning down at my own face. "What did you *do*?"

Then I dunked my head into the water and didn't come up for a long time.

The next chance I had to breathe, next time I felt like myself—like I even knew who that was or what in the depths he was *doing*—didn't come for weeks after. And it came on a day that stuck in me like a harpoon, jagged end shoved all the way through.

When I walked Kato, Nella, Wyst, and most of the deckhands out to edge of the city to say goodbye.

From the jump, I figured sending the first batch of crew off across the Basin was the hardest thing I'd ever done—worse than looking into men's eyes when I'd slit their throats. Because I'd always had Korsa's sanction on every ship I'd sunk, every crew I sent down to the depths. Had Merry Dred breathing down my back that if it wasn't some ferry crew or trade ship without a name who went to meet Ahim in the deep, it'd be *my* crew, *my* ship…and that wasn't about to happen. I'd sullied my hands more times than I could count, keeping the promise of a better life I'd made to every soul who crewed the *Singer*.

This was worse than killing to keep my Raiders alive. I hated sending them off without me, not knowing if I'd ever see them again. If some Old Salt's bootlickers caught up to them in Tamsay or another port, they'd drag them back to Korsa hogtied like a spit roast. They'd tow the *Singer* back inside those mountains with hooks sunk in her sides. And then they'd wait for me, Dred with his boots up on a desk already stained with my blood…that blasted, wrinkled sack of greed and old debts just slobbering at the chance to finish what he'd started with my finger.

But I didn't have much choice; that's what I told myself the first time. The second time, when I watched Kato saunter off with the other half of the crew in tow, ready to catch up with the *Singer* and get them ready to move from Tamsay to Pyrath…excuses were getting harder.

I just kept Siu and Gyddy, Cam, Rhea, and Wilkes back this time—and now we were a tighter bunch. Restless. Flightier. We'd never stayed in one place this long…at least, not a city. The crew had scattered and come back together a few times before they'd come to meet me in Monsha.

Moving was what kept us steady. It kept us alive.

The only one who didn't seem too bothered by the long stay was Lio. And depths if it didn't quiet the storm in my belly, being around her. I soaked in her calm like a sea sponge.

So that was where I went, after I saw Kato and the rest of them off to the rowboats his sister had stashed in a cove near the Foothills; straight to that bakery without stopping for anything. Even though it was a few hours too early to walk her back, I sat on the stoop with my head in my hands and just *listened* to the city.

Really listened. I hadn't had time to do that in a while.

Things had finally settled since Sorai's visit. The riots had stayed small, contained to that plaza where he gave his grandiose speech…and settled out with a few arrests that had the militar grinning like the gull that got the crab.

The crew had spooked about that, at first. They'd kept close to the compound, especially Cam. Even if we did most of our raids out on the high seas where no one ever saw our faces, a pirate's a pirate…the second they made us, there'd be no chance for swindling.

Playing the part of good citizens and keeping a step ahead of the militar was part of the life. Didn't mean it was our favorite part.

Now that things had settled, though, they'd maybe even gotten better. The crew was stretching their wings; Gydeon had a few folk he was helping around the city with their health. Siu'd scrounged up some art supplies thanks to Klem's bets and started selling off a few portraits to the deep pockets in the city. I'd caught Cam doing every sort of odd job, from running to messaging to sweeping stoops and raking streets.

Everyone did their share to scrape in some merits. Not enough to settle debts, but enough that we weren't about to be living on the streets and eating out of trash bins—enough that we didn't have to think about stealing, either.

I knew why they were doing it. Knew whose example they were following.

It had been a depths-blasted long time since we'd had anyone with an honest trade aboard our ship…if ever. Everything we needed, we took where we could find, and tried not to think of whoever else would end up in the hole for it. But Lio wasn't like that; and the good work she did every day, it leaked over the crew in a swelling tide.

That tide lifted my heart like an unmoored ship when the shop door creaked open and she finally came down the steps, bread loaves under her arms…same as every day. She caught a look at me when I shoved to my feet, and her eyes flashed—some tricky way the light caught them that I never could sort out.

And I tried to. More than I could justify.

"Bastyan," she greeted—just a little reticent, saying the name. The same as every day since Algernon had showed his smug face and I'd had to drop anchors on my fists to keep from finding out how hard that bastard's pearly teeth cut on ink-covered knuckles.

Repeatedly.

"Lio." I raised a brow, disarming the tension with a smirk.

She was waiting for one of us to mention it—what'd happened in that courtyard. But I wasn't going to be the one to break the silence…that was up to her. Not my choice to make.

I'd already stolen enough choices from her.

That reminder sucked out the tide from my chest and ran my heart aground on the reefs underneath. Scraping the back of my neck with my uneven hand, I shoved the line of my jaw toward the street. "Best we get moving. Crew's starving tonight."

"They've been busy." Lio's laugh bubbled with relief—another day, another talk we didn't have to have.

No use wondering why that put a spring in her step.

"Aye." Pocketing my hands, I looked both ways before I stepped off the curb to join her. Algernon's goons hadn't showed their faces since they'd tried to grab her that night, weeks ago—when her screaming my old name over that crowd had turned me wild. When her hush afterward had bashed the breath from me like a boom swung by a storm. When I'd started hitting everyone who stepped an inch in my way, fighting to get back to her.

When I'd had my first nightmare wide awake, her face a mirage wavering over every trampled body, every poor sod left to choke on their own blood or riot-fire smoke. Might've found her faster if I hadn't stopped to look twice at each before the crowd closed up around them.

Still. Couldn't hurt to be careful. And I wasn't much less than eager to teach them the lesson I'd had to let go of that night so I could play the part of her husband.

Another thing we just weren't going to discuss.

I shook that thought off and focused on the street in front of me, and her expectant face waiting for more than a grunt.

"Saw most of them off this morning to the next horizon," I added—letting her figure out the rest. "But Rhea's picked up a job with a performing troupe, and Wilkes has some arrangement with a local forge now."

"I'm glad. It seems good for them," Lio offered. "They aren't looking over their shoulders quite so much."

Aye. And we owe that to you.

"Funny how staying in one place long enough teaches you about people," I shot back instead.

"That it does." Lio looked me up and down—and didn't say anything else.

This blasted woman was going to be the death of me long before Merry Dred got his hooks in my ship.

CHAPTER 51
SHOT TO THE HEART

RYKER

The rest of the walk, we took in silence, soaking in the city. It was quiet, mostly; calmer than I was used to, like someone had rocked it back to sleep. I couldn't help feeling like my back was exposed with Kory, Klement, and Kato all off on the ship now…would've liked keeping their ears in their old gambling dens, just for some extra security.

But Kato had mentioned folk were starting to clam up. Acting suspicious around him. The safer thing for the Draces was a shorter stopover in Bashir…and they'd already overstayed their welcome.

So I just had to listen to the wind and mind the hairs tingling on the back of my neck by the time we reached the compound—and almost crashed into Cam outside it.

"Evening, Lio! Ca—Ry—Bastyan," he stumbled over a few names before he got to the right one, tugging down the ratty knit cap slouched on his head.

I laughed to let him off the hook, tugging the cap back up. "What's this, then?"

"Oh, lay off," he mumbled, swiping my arm away. "A girl—I mean, a client—a girl I was running for today, she paid me with it on top of the merits. Said my ears were turning red from cold."

Not that Bashir wasn't chilly still this time of spring, being in the bowl of the mountains. Still, I couldn't fight the smirk that unfurled on my face. "Aye? Is *that* why she thought they were turning red?" Clicking my tongue, I mussed the cap over his hair. "Must not know what a blush looks like on you."

"Don't be cruel," Lio chided, but she was smiling too when she looped an arm around Cam's shoulders, steering him toward the compound. "And what did you run for this girl?"

He perked up like she'd landed on his favorite subject—which tended to change week to week. "She works in her pa's clockwork shop! I've never seen anything like it, Lio…"

He cannoned off into the tale, and I trailed after them, catching Lio's smile over her shoulder.

This time, the tide left its mark with a deposit of writhing sea-eels setting up shop in my gut.

We ate with the paltry crew that we'd kept back, tearing into Lio's bread and the meat Wilkes had bought on his way back from the forge. After Cam finished telling us all about his day, he trickled out a pocketful of orange sweets he'd gotten to keep after a delivery went sour; whether that had been an accident or that mischievous streak in him, he wouldn't say. Just told us all to shut our yaks and enjoy the candy.

I shot Lio a shrug, and she rolled her eyes; you could *maybe* convince a pirate to work for an honest living, but in the depths of him, he was still a pirate.

Rhea pulled out her fiddle and struck up a tune once the food settled a bit, her new strings sounding a whole lot stronger than the frayed ones she'd been making do with for the last handful of months. Gyddy didn't miss a beat; he pulled Siu up off the bench seat and took her dancing, dropping a kiss on a streak of paint that stuck out like a welt on her cheekbone.

After an awkward few seconds, Cam tugged the cap down on his brow again and swiveled on the bench toward Lio. "Would you…um…?"

She squeezed his shoulder. "I would be delighted to dance."

Good thing he had on that cap, because I could feel the heat of him blushing from across the table. "I don't really know how."

Lio didn't miss a beat, smooth on his slippery shyness as Gyddy was on spinning his wife around the courtyard. "Then I'd be delighted to *teach* you."

She carted him off to the middle of the circle and started putting him through his paces…placements and steps some clockworker's daughter would most likely learn for herself in a day or two.

Wilkes started in on a bottle of brandy I had a feeling the forgemaster didn't know was missing, slouching with his elbows back on the tabletop; when he passed the amber bottle my way, I took it without thinking twice.

Herbs, I didn't do well with; but a little brandy took the edge off the stupid in me that wouldn't quit…the part that remembered the daydream of Sunrise Isle and how, for a firelit second, *I'd* been the one dancing with Lionyra Vara.

The part of me that wished I still could.

"City's stirring," Wilkes said all of a sudden, jerking my focus off of Lio and Cam stumbling through the first steps of the dance. "Can you feel it?"

An anchor dropped through my gut. "Aye. Seemed off today."

I didn't put full stock by what *I* thought was off-kilter. I'd been proven wrong too many times. But Wilkes had been militar before he'd been one of us…he was the only reason I'd known enough about the Pale Viper to get the jump on her in Monsha's streets.

So, if he was picking up something on the breeze…it sure as salt explained why the hairs on my neck still wouldn't lay flat.

I coaxed them down with another swig of brandy. "Any idea what it is?"

"Nothing yet." Wilkes took the bottle back when I passed it. "I've plied a few of the city militar, and they're keeping their lips stitched tight."

"So, have Gyddy teach you how to rip out the threads."

"Comedian doesn't suit you, Captain." Another deft swallow, then he wiped his mouth on his arm and added, "I'll keep my eyes and ears open. But consider keeping Camden closer to the compound…and if you'd like, I could escort Rhea to the performing hall." His gaze flicked to her, the edge of his mouth curling up like pipesmoke while he watched her play. "It would set me back on the labor, but it's worth the coins to keep her safe in these streets."

"Aye. But what about after? You're at the forge later than the troupe plays."

Wilkes frowned. "There is that."

Cursing, I rubbed those offending hairs again. "Wish I'd kept on more of the crew."

"You kept the ones who were willing to stay. Everyone else was itching for a change of scenery."

That was true. I couldn't have put up with another day of One-Pot Willy complaining about how his blanket itched and how much he missed the sound of a creaking ship. A sailor kept against his will was more likely to be a problem than a help.

Still. Having one more person to keep an eye out, set the balance, walk Cam and Rhea back from their duties…

Unless *I* did it.

But given the timing, I'd have to let Lio walk herself back.

I weighed it out in my head; Cam, who trusted too easy, and Rhea, who couldn't bring herself to break her fiddle over someone's head if it meant busting her family's heirloom instrument…or Lio, who'd faced down charging pirates with an axe in hand.

Lio, who'd gone so pale I could've counted every freckle on her face when she laid eyes on her depths-blasted *betrothed.*

I flexed my hand, letting my knuckles air out the craving for a bite of smug dissident teeth on the bone. "I'll sort it out."

But not tonight; tonight was for dancing.

Rhea's fiddle upped its tempo, turning from raw music to a cheeky challenge, and with a laugh, Gyddy swept Siu along faster. Lio and Cam tripped through things a bit before they hit their stride; then they traded partners, Gydeon dragging Cam in, Siu and Lio whirling off together, cackling madly like they'd been friends all their blasted lives.

I swiped the bottle back from Wilkes and took a long drink, wetting the dryness that stole over my throat like a depths-blasted thief.

But not even brandy's burn could settle me when Lio spun out of Siu's grip, staggering a bit when she halted before me. Locks of hair tumbled loose from the braid she always wore at the *Loaf,* and she stuck her hand out with a look that hung somewhere between a challenge and a plea.

"Don't think," she panted, "just dance."

I slammed the brandy bottle down and grabbed her hand; guffawing, Wilkes surged up and sauntered over to Rhea, breaking into a proper sailor's jig in front of her until she burst into laughter. Rhea countered him like a knife fight, twisting and sashaying on the balls of her feet, shimmying with her back to his.

And then we were all making a mess of it, spinning together around the courtyard.

I forgot everything outside the compound walls. Forgot about changing winds and a scattered crew and Merry blasted Dred. I just kept my eyes on Lio, on that sneaky smile, on the way she danced. On the way her body fit into my arms and her hips filled my hands and how badly I never wanted to let her go.

To the depths with Shadewyle Castle. To the depths with the bloody *ransom.*

I didn't want to let her go for all the merits in all the countries in the Wellspoken World.

Heat crowded in my face. My vision turned blurry. And when I blinked, when I got my focus back…

That smile on her face clobbered me like a rogue wave, and I plunged back under, towed by the currents, drowning in a way that didn't hurt. That didn't give me a warning to find the surface and clear my head.

Depths sink me…

I was in love with her.

Loved the way she sassed me and set me straight. Loved the way my name sounded in her mouth. Loved the way that mouth felt all over mine. Loved every curve of her, how she melted into my hands like my blasted fingers had been reaching, grabbing for her for longer than I'd even noticed.

I wasn't just in love with Lionyra Vara, I was bloody *sunk*. To the depths for her…and sunk in my own skin.

No one was getting out of this without a pistolshot through the heart. Not when the choice was her or my crew.

I didn't even realize I'd let go until she stopped dancing, too. The others were still going, but we just stood stock, staring at one another.

Rhea's fiddle caught a bit, and that discordant note finally woke me up. But it didn't stop the dragged-down bits of me from bleeding when I stepped back, ripping her hooks from my hull.

"Need a drink," I muttered.

I went to our tent, brandy in hand, but I didn't touch a drop of it. I just sat there, staring at the canvas walls, hating every blasted piece of myself. Hating what this had come to. And hating that I wished I'd never stepped into it in the first place.

If I'd just said *no* to this mad scheme for her friend Tristah, maybe I could've spared us both the trouble. She could've gone on hating me like she had after I'd tossed Bastyan back overboard, his mutiny put to a swift end at the tip of Blackhand's blade pressed against the Delina's throat.

But that was the trouble. Even back then, I hadn't wanted her to hate me.

Klem was right; I wasn't here for the merits, wasn't here for enough ransom to cancel my debt. I was here because she wanted her bloody friend back, and…

Maybe it was penance. Maybe it was the last bit of me that was Bastyan, that gold-hearted fool of a lad who'd trusted his strung-out parents all the way up the gangplank of a drug runner's ship. Maybe it was the fool Lio kept fishing back out of the depths I tried to sink him in.

But I wanted her to be happy. Wanted her smiling like she had during our dance tonight, *every* night.

Depths. I wanted her smiling that way at *me*. Even though I didn't deserve it after everything I'd done.

Shoving the bottle aside, I crashed on my back and flung an arm over my eyes, covering out the fiddle notes and laughter from the courtyard.

I was so blasted sunk, there wasn't any hope left for me.

I was going to drown. And maybe that would be better than the shot to the heart, in the end.

CHAPTER 52
THE EMBER IN THE SHADOWS

Fiddle notes strained in my head—a desperately romantic tune I smothered with all my might in the push and pull of kneading dough, nearly a full day after the instrument had fallen silent.

I wished that Rhea's fiddling the night before had not reminded me desperately of how Tristah used to play. I had been so lost in the moment, caught up in the memories of a friend's music and in the relief of another day without seeing Sorai, and then—

Then I had asked Ryker to dance.

Utter foolishness.

I should not have done that. Not with all of the things unspoken between us. And not when, the last time I'd pulled him so close, it had been to catch the taste of his tongue. A necessity at the time, but…

I heaved the dough toward me and pounded it so harshly, a pocket of air gasped and died with a sad, small puff.

In truth, I had revisited that courtyard many times since, both waking and sleeping.

I had thought perhaps satisfying the curiosity I had held near to my heart ever since Lucretzia's cruelty had disrupted our solitary moment on Sunrise Isle would be the end of it. Instead, curiosity had sharpened into craving. One that wouldn't settle unless I stole another taste.

He was my captor. My ally. And…

And if I was to derive anything from the way he had looked at me when he'd stepped back from our dance last night, gaping like a man torn through the middle—like someone left with a knife stuck in their belly, bleeding in the dark—the desire to sample that taste of passion was not entirely mutual.

After all, he had not mentioned it once since.

Pull. Pound. Fold.

The fiddle notes still warbled in my ears.

"Best head for home early today, Lio." Dorcas's strained voice floated over the counter that separated us; today she leaned on things more than she stood, and now, without a customer to help, she bent and kneaded her painful knees. "Bad spring rain's coming. I can feel it."

I worked out a smile so she would not think my dour mood was her doing. "I thought such feelings were superstition."

"Well, Ahim be merciful, you'll live as long as I have and experience the *joys* of such aches and pains for yourself." Dorcas flashed me an equally forced grin, settling herself on her faithful stool. "You go on."

"Let me finish this batch," I begged. "Otherwise, I'll have to knead the dough again come morning."

She puffed out a breath, blowing corkscrew curls from her veined brow. "I've never had an assistant who didn't bolt for the door when the words *head for home* left my lips…even if I planned to say *late, so you can help me close up shop.*"

"You've had some poor assistants in the past, then."

"Or I have one now who's running *from* something."

The heels of my palms wrenched into the dough, halting.

We stared at one another for a moment.

"Lio," Dorcas added slowly, still working the sore joints of her knee, "whatever things you bury in your work will still be there when you go home. Best you find a way to face them, not bake them."

My next exhale trembled. "There are some things that are impossible to face. That you cannot make sense of."

"There is always sense to be made. I find it's rather often a matter of whether we like the way sense looks, or if we would rather pretend what we see is the unsensible thing."

I could not argue that. Not when violin notes echoed the very beat of my heart.

Sweeping the dough off into the baking pot, I flashed her another smile. To this one, I could coax no warmth at all, only exhaustion. "I'll be finished with this soon."

But not soon enough, it seemed; the rain Dorcas had predicted unleashed itself violently against the windowpanes by the time I slid the dough into the dry cask-chest, ready for Dorcas to bake before I arrived in the morning. She enfolded me in a rare embrace as I gathered my coat, her powdered-sugar scent so painfully familiar that it was as if my own mother held me again.

"Face it," she whispered in my ear. "Face what you fear. It is the only way to have mastery over yourself."

The very notion made my bones quiver with dread; but for her sake, I said that I would try. Then I stepped into the deluge, drawing up my hood, my eyes going by habit to the curb beside the shop's stoop, where—

Where no one waited.

My gaze tripped along the storm-blackened avenue, pulse stumbling/

Ryker was not there.

A deserted stoop. An empty street.

He had not come.

Pain erupted in a low flare across my belly, like a dim firework fizzing before it could light up the dark.

It should not have troubled me. Not after the previous night. Not when things were so entangled between us.

And yet…my heart did not know that it shouldn't ache. My spirit did not resist a stab of rejection at his absence, or avoid the fleeting recollection of how abruptly he had released me the night before, the flash of immutable emotion in his eyes cutting across my chest in turn.

He had abandoned us all for a bottle of amber spirits and the solitude of the tent, where Cam and I had found him already asleep hours later, drowsing with his back to us, the bottle neck in his fist.

We had not spoken since. And he was not here.

Stuffing my hands into my pockets, I descended the stoop, head ducked against the rain. And for the first time since I'd told him of Athyna's fate, I made the walk back toward the compound alone.

The solitude was not entirely meritless—and it was by no means silent, filled with the drum of rain on shop awnings and stone streets, the wiser folk already tucked away from the brunt of the storm.

A dull thought flickered to life in the back of my mind: that if I fled now, I could be halfway to Port Krait by sunrise. I could join an honest mercantile vessel and vanish before the crew began to search for me in earnest.

Yet my feet did not even tilt that way.

I was bruised with exhaustion, bound up in this search for Tristah, and…I was so tired of running.

Ever since that night of fireworks in Mithra-Sha, I had been fleeing. Sometimes of my own volition; sometimes at the behest of others. And now, when the choice was fully mine, when nothing but rain-wrapped streets lay between me and the next flight toward the horizon…

I stayed.

What that said about me, I did not dare wonder.

I was so *tired.*

That exhaustion—and the rain—dimmed everything. They dimmed the heartache that thrummed in my chest. Dulled the sounds all around me. Robed my senses in the scent of petrichor, the echo of the driving deluge around me, so that I did not know I was no longer alone until it was already too late.

Until a hand shot from a shadowed alley cove as I passed by, clapping over the lower half of my face, hauling me back against a heaving, armor-plated chest.

Militar.

Dissident.

Sorai.

No matter which proved true, they would not have me.

I threw an elbow on instinct, and pain hammered through my whole arm, numbing the stricken limb like a dip in a bucket of ice water when the nerves encountered pure steel layered beneath leather.

I lunged against the hand, but it muzzled me utterly; it twisted my neck, pinning me back against the brawn of a man starkly taller than me. One who seemed perfectly at ease trapping smaller women in his clutches.

"Bastyan!"

The scream burst from me like a breath knocked from my lungs, perishing against the glove that covered my mouth.

My heels skidded on slick cobblestone as a strong arm banded my waist, wrenching me backward—hauling me away from the rain-blurred city lights. Into the gutted sidestreets, warded off to prevent rioters from returning to the state of their mess.

I thrashed and fought and bucked all the way, but his body was an infuriating twist of shadow; every blow slid off or dealt me more pain than I traded to him. It was only when I managed to land a single sharp strike— beneath the armpit, a surprisingly painful place Tristah had taught me to hit in our sessions with Lucretzia—that he reacted at all.

But then, it was only to halt in the thicker shadows of a butcher's shop, the iron tang of spilled blood coagulating at our feet as he folded me nearer against his broad chest. "Stop! It's me, it's *me*…it's *Ember!*"

And I *did* freeze—not reassured at the bass thrum of his voice, but struck still by that name.

Ember.

He whipped me about to face him, backing me against the side of the butcher's shop, and in the slice of poled lanternlight from the street to our left, I caught a vague definition of his face: black hair that dripped like sugarless, melted chocolate in rain-soaked hanks around his prominent cheekbones. A thick, ashen cloak that shrouded wide shoulders and chiseled muscles that strained against his charcoal attire. When he hauled down his woven cowl, it revealed a stern mouth enshrouded by a thick mustache and a well-trimmed, dark beard that met worry lines carved backward into his cheeks.

Unfamiliar in the uttermost. And yet he gazed at me as if I was the lodestone around which his world found its center.

"Hey." The hands that rose to frame my face, sheathed in leather gloves, were shockingly gentle. "Talk to me. What are you doing out in the streets without your mask, Tristah?"

Another name that knocked my wits flat as unleavened pastry.

He knows Tristah.

The thought pierced like lightning, and my body answered—a boom of thunder rocking through every muscle and bone.

I snapped his grip from me with the same deft hold-break I'd used to escape Lucretzia in Krylan. Shock had scarcely registered on that rugged face before I sidestepped his empty hands, swiveled around behind him, and launched an elbow into his temple—another precise blow taught to me by the Pale Viper. The only place I could strike for a guaranteed, if short-lived, respite.

The man crumbled in a senseless heap at my feet; I dropped as well, straddling him, and pinched the bundle of nerves at the top of his shoulder—an area I rarely managed to reach, my height being as it was.

But he did not fight. In moments, he went limp.

I thrust to my feet, staggering back from him, utterly dizzied by what had transpired…what I had done.

When I slammed into another warm body emerging at my back, I did not hesitate again; I drove my heel into the groin and hooked my elbow deftly into the ribcage of the second person who dared creep up on me tonight.

A familiar profane grunt gusted across the side of my face. Then an arm encircled my clavicles, towing me back into a heaving chest—and this time, I let him take me.

Because I knew *him*. Knew the dig of his pendant between my shoulders, the heat of his breath against my head. And for a moment, terror still spiking through my head and deadening the feeling in my fingertips, I needed a sailor's strength to lean on.

I dug my fingers into Ryker's forearm, sagging into his grip.

"Easy. Easy, love." His pained panting sent a shiver whirling in my core. "Are you hurt? *'Ay!*" His tone sharpened when I gave no answer, and his fingers tightened around my bicep, whipping me around to face him. His gaze slashed over me, searching for wounds, his hands trailing from my shoulders down my arms, to my hips and back again. "Bloody *answer me*, Lio, *did he*—?"

"No," I choked out, my voice bereft of strength. "No, he only frightened me a little."

The steel-stiff tension melted from Ryker like gelatin powder in water; he whistled lowly, draping his arm around my shoulders now. "He's no small lad, either. Atta girl, Seasplitter."

Still, he hauled me close to his side as he stepped us both forward, peering down into the man's slack face.

"Who is he?" A bit more venom leaked into Ryker's tone; his fingers curled, forming a fist against my arm. "One of Sorai's goons?"

"This is Ember." I tasted and tested the marvel of that truth on my tongue.

Ryker's arm loosened. Then he whirled me to face him a second time, his hands landing on my shoulders. "You sure about that?"

"He told me himself. And…" I rubbed a bit of the sodden chill from my deadweight arms. "He called me Tristah."

Ryker stared at me for a moment, his face a conflict of countless emotions. Then he bent, snaring Ember's arm, hauling the hefty man up to his feet. "I know a place we can take him. You lead, I'll tell you where to step."

CHAPTER 53
GAME OF WAITING, GAME OF BREAKING

For two months, we had waited. For two months, we had watched, and learned, and gleaned. And now, by Ahim's mercy—or some capricious humor I had not been aware the world-shaper possessed—Ember was in our possession.

And he knew Tristah's name. Had seen her face in mine.

Excitement and trepidation warred in my chest as I reclined against the door in the small, shabby room where Ryker had dragged the unconscious Ember. It was a den meant for piracy, of that I had little doubt; moldered sheets half-guised the rusted-out chests that had been plundered long ago. The room itself was barely a seam folded between two abandoned shops, its single window masked in grit, allowing only the narrowest puddle of poled lanternlight through.

By that light, Ryker tested the bonds with which I'd secured Ember in the chair where Ryker had dumped him…a complicated series of rope turns and small nooses I had learned from Lucretzia. I had missed countless meals bound to chairs this way, my freedom—and my supper—only promised by what I could manage with my own hands.

Ryker's presence warmed me far more than it should. I would have recovered my wits and hauled Ember off myself, with Tristah's fate in the balance, but I was glad not to be huddling in solitude in this fetid hole, listening to the storm beat the world to death outside.

But it was not enough to silence the nagging rejection that chattered beneath my breastbone.

"Why did you not come today?" I murmured.

Ryker did up a few extra sailor's knots in the ropes, then made his way to the room's only doorway. Bracing both hands to the frame, he leaned out, peering down the deserted corridor.

With a faint stab of alarm—and illness—I realized how much this room reminded me of Merry Dred's roofless den in Korsa. It even leaked the same.

Satisfied at last that we had not been followed—or perhaps he'd simply given himself enough time to think—Ryker pivoted to face me, the shadows and lanternlight taking turns teasing his eyes. "I was walking Cam and Rhea back to the compound. Ran halfway across the city to get to the bakery, but you were gone by the time I got there."

His words soothed my heart like salve on a stovetop burn. "Then how did you find me?"

"I was walking the route we usually take. Heard something that sounded like my name…then I saw him hauling you off at the opposite side of the next street." He was quiet for a moment, his fingers finding their way through the rain-soaked mess of his hair; his expression was vacant of emotion, a rare thing for him. "Tried to chase you down, but he's quick. Makes sense, if he's Ember."

"I can hardly believe it." I searched the man's features for a twitch of wakefulness. "He knows Tristah. He knows her by *name*."

"Aye." Ryker's voice was as void as his expression, bereft of its usual swagger. "You almost have your answers."

He did not sound as thrilled as a man who believed he was near to claiming not one, but two outrageous ransoms ought to.

A chill blurred with the raindrops that still rolled down my arms, dripping from the ends of my sodden hair. "How long do you suppose before he wakes?"

Ryker shrugged. "Can't say. You struck him in the right place." His eyes flitted up to mine, then jerked away—the same as they had after our dance the night before. "I take it the Viper taught you that."

I edged out a stilted nod.

We went back to staring at our captive for a moment; disbelief still battled with my anticipation. As if after these months of searching and sailing, I might wake to find this a dream.

"I'm going to see Tristah." I tested the words aloud, a hushed whisper gathered among the cobwebs and rain-flattened dust; anything more substantial felt irreverent, threatening to shatter the wondrous and deadly impossibility that I was so near to finding my friend.

Ryker said nothing this time—not to confirm or to argue.

And then, at long last, he spoke, just as quietly as I had: "So. How are you planning to do it, once we find her?"

"How am I—?"

"Planning your escape."

I froze.

Across the doorway, our gazes locked—and this time, he did not look away.

"I'm not blind," Ryker added softly. "There's no chance you were ever going back to that castle without a fight…depths, I wouldn't go if I were you. And there's no chance either you struck this bargain to find your friend unless you had a plan to give us the slip."

I sought for words, but none would come when the notion of my escape was met not with taunts, or threats…

But with a smile. One lit with sunbright sadness.

"You're using me, same as I used you." He shrugged. "And I can't blame you for it. Part of me wishes you'd just get it over with."

"As if you would let me leave so easily." The words emerged with far less bladed disdain than I'd intended. They were very nearly a plea.

His smile stayed fixed, but pain flashed through his eyes—pain I could never trust. He folded his arms, dropping one shoulder against the doorframe, his body slanted across the moldered opening. "That's the thing, sweetheart. If it was just you and me, without the crew in the spin…I'd settle my debts my own way, and let you walk out of my life like I never knew you."

That offer, shaped like truth and far too tantalizing, was an opponent I had never been taught to face. A customer I did not know how to haggle with, a tricky bit of sticky, stretchy dough I couldn't shape how I wanted.

Because I did not know *how* I wanted it to be. I did not know what I wanted from Blackhand, from Ryker…from Bastyan. I only knew that in the impossible, knotted mess of our lives, I could certainly not have *everything* I craved.

So I settled for the only thing I knew for certain…the truth that had torn my heart in two: "You lie."

Ryker winced, buckling a bit against the doorframe. He pinched the bridge of his nose and heaved a breath; then he looked at me again, jaw tight. "Sometimes. Doesn't change the fact that if I had the choice between my debt alone, and your freedom, I'd choose your freedom every time."

He let that hang in the air between us…let it consume me with a violent, unkind sort of hope.

"But I'm the Captain," he added at last. "I don't get to choose anything, because choosing *them* always comes first." An empty smile carved across his mouth. "Either they win, or you win. And either way, I lose."

If those words were indeed a lie, then I had never met an actor so proficient as him…not even Tristah, who'd played the part of *me* for years. The agony in his voice knocked the breath from my chest.

"And you want to know what the worst part is?" His eyes searched mine, hunting for something I did not know if I could ever give. "Since I made that choice, you'll never believe I could be anything but a bastard spinning lies to keep you in line."

I did not deny it. He did not seem to expect me to.

But beneath the calm veneer I had perfected in council meetings when I had plastered on a demure smile while inwardly I screamed for relief—

I *shattered*.

I couldn't stop remembering *all* of it…every moment we had shared aboard *The Athalion*. The dance on Sunrise Isle. The dance in the compound the night before. The veiled truths he had shared about himself…about Bastyan Atreyon.

His missing finger. His bleeding hand drawing me to safety aboard the *Singer's* deck.

The open cabin door. Every walk from the bakery to the compound. Every genuine laugh, every smile, every scrap of understanding that had twined me nearer to him over our months together.

The way he'd touched my hip in the galley when we'd dined aboard his ship, the flare of rage in his eyes at the lingering scar of a life nearly taken…a life nothing like I'd ever wanted for myself.

The way he had fought through the beginnings of a riot to reach me—and how he'd slipped from the tent the morning after, putting out riot fires, returning with soot on his face and red-rimmed eyes. Asking before I could catch a breath at the state of him how *I* was faring.

The way he had kissed me in that courtyard. The way he had made himself the blade I did not have to draw, braced at Algernon's throat. Slicing to my rescue tonight. His panic when he'd thought me wounded by Ember, even if I would have been a salvageable ransom still.

Perhaps these were all deceptions to make me feel precisely how I did…as if my rage and hate were burning shards of glass I could no longer grasp hold of.

Or perhaps Ryker was no worse than any desperate man, after all. A captain who loved his patchwork crew and truly saw no other means of saving them.

Perhaps I had been an answer to prayers flung to Ahim for so long, he had truly lost all hope they would be answered. Perhaps he was willing to sell all but the very last good parts of himself to save the crew from missing fingers and far, far worse.

And perhaps those last good parts truly did regret this. Truly did wish that he could find some other way.

"The way I see it," he muttered at last, when I did not speak, "I've got to do my best for my people. But if you outwit *me* the way you outwitted the depths-blasted Pale Viper and the Del himself…that's always a risk, isn't it?"

The notion stopped my breath altogether.

Because, in the wake of them, I saw him as he truly was.

Ryker Kassian was as trapped in piracy as I had been in Shadewyle Castle. Both of us had committed unspeakable acts we regretted. Both of us had tried to build different names and different lives…and still found ourselves on the same path back to our shadows.

He would not forgive himself if he did not fight for his crew. And he would not forgive himself if he let me go.

But if I escaped of my own volition…

An ending we both could endure. A farewell that would break as few hearts as possible.

But there were still debts to be paid. The crew would be hunted for the weighty things they had chosen for themselves…and things they had chosen for my sake. The trouble we'd stirred in Korsa. The enemy Ryker had likely made of Algernon Sorai.

Could I run with Tristah and never look back—never wonder if Dred or Rackham had caught the crew up, if they had exacted more flesh from them? Could I not wonder if Camden was being cared for? If Siu and Gydeon were forced apart? If Kory's quiet, shy charm was forever shadowed, if Wilkes's strength was stolen, if Klement's cool sass was spent, if Kato's booming presence was burned to a wick?

What if Rhea and Maryon never played again, their fiddles smashed, their fingers broken for punishment? If One-Pot Willy was left without a pot to bake in? If Wyst was broken to splinters? If all of them were sold away to other crews, to unimaginable horrors, to settle the merits the Old Salts craved?

If I walked away—*when* I walked away—would I be able to forget them, as I had struggled to forget Zorast and Lucretzia and nearly succeeded? Just another band of captors better left in my past?

A wash of tears gathered in my eyes.

I had known captivity for so much of my life. Perhaps that made me blind, weak…convincible. But I could not recall when I had last thought of *The Dread Singer's* crew as my enemies. Nor, truly, as my captors. They were not like *The Athalion's* sailors, easy allies all about; they were rough-hewn, salty, and suspicious. And yet…

The angry, defiant pieces of me, the jagged fragments that ached to throw off my shackles, that both yearned and feared to defy…they belonged here. They fit. So perhaps these people had uncovered a bit of pirate in me, too.

A dull groan sliced into my thoughts, abrupting the hopeless spiral of wondering.

I looked to Ember just in time to catch the flicker of enviably-long lashes, a slow hitch of his head up from where it had slumped against his shoulder. He blinked several times, bringing the definition of the room into focus.

Then he throttled forward all at once, slamming to the ends of his ropes so sharply, the chair would have upended and flattened him had I not dove as well, catching the warped backing and thrusting its feet to the floor again.

"Tell me what you know of Tristah," I hissed.

His eyes swooped up to meet mine; revulsion cut through their bruise-blue depths, as if he had bitten into a sweet bun and found spoil in its center.

"You're not her." He lashed against his bonds, lips peeling back in a snarl. "What is this? *Where is she?*"

"Wouldn't know, mate." Ryker's tone was lively, but the knife he drew and dangled between his fingers was anything but. "That's what we need *you* for."

"Tell us how you know her," I snapped, "and where I can find her."

He craned forward, taut muscles straining at his bonds. "*I would rather die.*"

I raked a glance toward Ryker; he did not move, or speak, or blink. Leaving this interrogation entirely in my hands.

Steadying myself with a deep breath, I crouched, keeping one hand to the seatback. "*Please.* It is…desperately important that I find Tristah. She knows me…she will *want* to see me."

He dipped his head nearly to my level, slanting it just a bit—so that his murmured answer, pitched mockingly to the same tone as mine, wafted across my face. "I don't believe you."

Anger shoved me back to my feet and forced me away from the chair. "Then you do not know Tristah."

"I know that she's never mentioned a woman who could be her twin," he snarled. "And she tells me everything."

The impossibility of that forced a mirthless laugh from my lips. "Tristah trusts no one."

He snorted in turn. "And *you* claim to know her."

Frustration singed my fingertips like a hot cooking pot. "You are not leaving that chair until I know where Tristah is."

"Then I hope you're prepared to wait a good while." He flopped against the seatback, emanating as much calm and infuriating superiority as any man in his position possibly could. "She knows I will die before I give her up."

And yet a thin sheen of sweat blotted his brow as he strained against his ropes—an unconscious reaction, perhaps. But one we could make use of.

It seemed this was to be a game of waiting…and a game of breaking.

But he did not know of my time in Shadewyle Castle. He did not know how to play a game as long as I did.

I flashed him a sultry smile, and he stiffened, rocking forward an inch. "Well," I said—sweet as turned sugar, delicious before it cloyed on the tongue, "we will decide *that* in time."

I caught a glimpse of my face in the stained window beyond him—and my blood ran cold.

I was wearing the smirk Lucretzia had given me.

CHAPTER 54
BENEATH THE FALLING RAIN

For two months, we had waited.

And for days after, we waited some more.

Ember gave us nothing. Not when we plied him with food and drink; not when we withheld them, either. Not when Ryker threatened him with a blade; not when I coerced and cajoled. Crumbs of my own training—my own suffering—flaked from my mouth like bitter chocolate shavings every now and again…methods we might try in order to make him crumble.

Withholding sleep. Startling him awake from it. Ryker even stole back to the compound and filched Rhea's fiddle, playing off-tune, aching notes that had me stuffing my ears to keep a headache at bay.

Nothing. Nothing. Nothing.

The only rare seams in Ember's death-cold exterior came on the verge of sleeping and waking, when often he would jerk sharply upright in the chair where we kept him bound. It always took a moment before his breaths rearranged themselves into the slow, even pattern befitting a man of such enigmatic nature.

If Ryker noticed it as well, he said nothing.

Nor did I.

We were not like the captors we'd once been subjugated to. And I was not yet so desperate to find Tristah as to willfully take advantage of the terrors jolting this stalwart man from slumber, his eyes darting feverishly until he oriented himself to this festering hole in the corner of Bashir…which somehow seemed more comforting to him than whatever places he visited in his dreams.

I could not have done that even to Lucretzia. And certainly not to a man who'd held my face so tenderly when he'd called me *Tristah*.

On another stormy night several days later, no sleep found me or Ryker, even while Ember dozed in his fastenings. Ryker had adjusted them, giving relief to various points in the man's broad, burly frame; unfortunately, that kindness had won us no favors. He had not even graced us with a reply in days.

"Something's got to give," Ryker muttered, joining me in the doorway where I slouched and sipped hot dessert tea. He'd returned Rhea's fiddle earlier that day and brought cups of drink for us both—and one for Ember.

Who had not even blinked when I'd offered him a sip.

"I hardly know what else to try." The confession burned hotter than the first scorching sip of tea stripping the buds on my tongue. "It's clear he's been trained to withstand duress."

"Aye." Ryker leaned against the opposite side of the doorframe, a foot cocked back on the supple wood, arms folded across his chest—one hand tweaking the wheel that hung there. "No wonder the Incendiary trusts him."

For a moment, we both were silent, watching Ember sleep fitfully in his bonds. The roof above him leaked where we'd moved his chair today, a steady stream of water pelting the top of his head—but even that did not rouse him.

That was little surprise. He had kept himself stubbornly awake more than a full day this time…or perhaps that had been Ryker's atrocious fiddle-playing.

Fabric chafed beneath callouses as Ryker rubbed his thumbs on his elbows. He did not look at me when he said, "I could break him. Maybe. But you wouldn't like it."

Dread puddled low in my belly. "Ryker…"

"You learn things," he spoke over me, his tone vague, as if he had not heard me…as if his thoughts were elsewhere. "You don't want to keep them like cargo stuffed in the hull of your head, but you can't help picking them up as a lad. With the *Spice*. In Korsa. Aboard a ship like the *Singer*. And I crew it differently than most, but…"

But he knew how other captains kept their people in check. He had learned at the feet of the last Blackhand. At the table of Merry Dred.

Sickness rolled up my throat, souring the tea. I set it hastily aside, trapping my trembling hands in my opposite sleeves. "You want to hurt him."

"Depths, I don't *want* to," Ryker cursed, his eyes flashing to me. "But threats aren't working. Making good on them might."

His hand flexed when he spoke—the hand missing its finger.

Lucretzia would have done it; she would have begun there. And if she found this man herself, she still might.

Was Ember simply collateral in the race to find Tristah? Was his fate sealed regardless, a path ending in bloodshed no matter who walked it?

I balled my fists inside my sleeves, shaking away the thought. "It's clear he cares for Tristah. Why should he sell the truth of her to those who would use such methods?"

Ryker stayed quiet for a moment. Then, "Pain doesn't always make the choice easy, sweetheart. If something hurts badly enough, you might give up anything to make it stop. Even things you'd never give up otherwise."

A chill scampered down my spine; the way his gaze landed on me, the depth of anguish in his voice—

All at once, I did not think it was Ember and his secrets we spoke of.

"Lucretzia's forcing your hand," he added after a long moment. "Might be we have to force his."

I opened my mouth and waited—waited for a clever retort, for a solution, for an argument to brand itself across my still-numb tongue—

Wood scraped wood. Ember started awake all at once…but not how he had before. He gasped back to consciousness with the desperation of a drowning man, with a wild grunt that blistered over into a bellow; then he rocked and thrashed, fighting at his restraints, twisting and writhing like a cat on a leash.

Ryker and I shoved up from the doorway at the same moment, but I struck the back of my hand to Ryker's chest, halting him in place. Confusion moored my feet to the rotting floorboards as I watched Ember buck and heave; watched him fight for breath, spitting off the rainwater that tumbled in a deluge over his face. Watched him *shake* as if we had buried him in the ice cap of the Barradir Highlands and left him to suffocate.

Senseless words huffed off his tongue—a tongue that *bled* as he bit through it, struggling and straining at his ropes, desperate to be rid of them. "*Please, please, please, please…*"

He was not speaking to us. The feral flash of his eyes suggested he did not even see us at all…that, this time, he couldn't blink himself back to awareness.

He was lost in something. Fighting something. Seeing something to which we were not privy.

Ryker caught my wrist; his hand flexed around the bone, a silent question that jolted my gaze to him. And despite the fearsomeness of his suggestion mere moments ago, the agony in his face spoke true of the man he was beneath the Captain's coat. A man who drank tonics to sleep away his nightmares of drowning.

I ripped my hand away, and Ryker surged across the room, gripping the back of Ember's seat and slinging him from beneath the pouring rainfall. The man doubled up over his own knees, spitting, gasping, panting as if we'd beaten him raw.

Shame lurched in my chest, but a shock of possibility snatched it and flung it back into the shadows. And then *I* lurched forward, ducking through the spray of tumbling rain, halting before Ember's chair.

I swept the hair from his brow with both hands, holding it back to his temples, and a violent shudder racked through him. But the stare that pierced me now was different than the one I'd come to know over the days…furious and unbending, yes, but also pained and confused.

This time, I wielded my likeness to Tristah like a balm, not a weapon.

"I can see how much you care for Tristah." I stroked my thumbs from the hinges of his jaw back to his temples again. "You've endured so much for her sake…so much I wish had not been necessary. I just want to know *where she is*."

He offered me no response this time; he only seethed in air and wrestled with his ropes.

But perhaps that meant he was truly listening. Perhaps this bout of panic had stripped his defenses.

"Something is coming for her…*Lucretzia* is coming." I tightened my hold on him, refusing to let him tear his gaze from my face. From *her* face. "I do not know when, or where…but she *will* come. She will come to steal Tristah for herself. To return her to Shadewyle, a slave to the Del's whims."

His jaw tightened, the sides of his neck pulsing with tension. Emotion shimmered across the surface of his eyes.

"Depths," Ryker cursed behind me. "He's in love with her."

I did not ask how he had reached that outlandish assumption; I merely trusted it, pouring it into the mix, letting it fuel the desperation we held in common.

Sliding the heels of my hands beneath Ember's square jaw, I cleaned the water from his face with my sleeve. "She is in too much danger to face alone. I think you know it…I think you *have* known it. That's why you were so worried when you snatched me…why you asked why I was unmasked. You know it is only a matter of time before her past catches up to her…and I can assure you, I would not be here if it was not close at hand."

"*Stop.*" The first word he had spoken in two days that was not a curse or a panicked plea; the shivers that accompanied it were so violent, the chair rattled against the floor.

"Help me find her," I begged, sinking to my knees before him. "Please. Before Lucretzia does. *Please.*"

His gleaming eyes fluttered shut. The strain along the lines of his muscles redoubled, tension honing every contour of his body.

Fresh dampness escaped the corner of his eye, joining the rain-slickness of his face.

"You can't have her," he snarled, his head falling heavy into my hands; but whether he spoke to me, or to his own secret fears, or to the shadow of Lucretzia cast over all our lives, I did not know.

And it did not matter.

"Ember, *please.*" I softened my voice even as I steeled my grip on the frame of his face, forcing his head up again until his eyes met mine. "Help me——"

The next boom of thunder did not merely shake the room—it brought destruction in its wake.

Fire erupted.

Glass shattered.

The world exploded in fireworks.

CHAPTER 55
THROUGH THE FLAMES

The room ignited in a spray of fire hues and fractals and *pain*, tearing into my flesh, shredding the clothes Siu had given me. Blood coated my tongue, the first thing I tasted when I roused from my stupor a moment later; I lay against the base of the room's far wall, my nose tingling with the smell of smoke and burning cobwebs.

Groaning, I shoved my hands into the warped wooden floorboards, lifting a body that felt as if it had been weighed down beneath sacks of flour. "Ryker?" My own voice sounded tinny, muffled, living in the folded space between my ears; everything else muddled into a blackened roar of indistinct noise.

No answer found its way through.

I broke down on one elbow, hefting my head to survey the room.

The window behind Ember had blown inward, the larger, more lethal shards of glass cut in a mosaic across the floor. Ember's chair had tipped, his head and shoulder laid to the floor. And Ryker…

Ryker was gone. Buried in what remained of a corner of the room that had collapsed, sending a fresh deluge of rainwater pouring through the broken roof.

Panic brought the world howling back into focus all at once. Digging my toes into the floor, I shoved myself staggering to my feet. "*Ryker—!*"

A streak of soot flipped into the windowsill—and my heart stopped altogether.

Horror consumed my fear. My need to reach Ryker.

It swallowed *everything*.

I knew the precision of Lucretzia's movements like I knew every angle of my own nightmares. The way she lunged into the room with a deft flip. The way she palmed two knives as she straightened, stalking toward me. I knew the grace of her movements, the bend of her muscular frame. The lethality in the way she flipped the knives backhand to her wrists, then broke all at once from a predatory prowl to a leap, her blade aimed at my bloodied neck, my ash-and-dust-stained face—

I could not make myself move, not even to scream, as her knives crossed and cut for my throat.

I knew the flash of her gaze. What those soulless, pitted depths looked like, painted in firelight and cruelty. Glimmering amber eyes, incensed, hardly seeing me above the cowl that robed her nose and mouth—

But I did not find those eyes in the shadow of that hood.

Impossible, true recognition gave me back my voice, a heartbeat before those knives aimed to take it forever: "*Tristah!*"

Blade nicked flesh.

She froze.

Everything, all at once, *froze.*

With her knives at my throat and her weight shoving me back into the glass-studded wood, Tristah and I beheld one another for the first time since our parting on the banks of the Sudene River.

I could see nothing but her eyes, and her stocky frame—so like mine, even after all this time, but fitted with cords of muscle in all the places I was soft, shaped in sturdy armor—and even so, I knew it was her. I knew that incredulous stare like my own.

And she proved it when she hooked a finger into her cowl, yanking it down, baring that face so like mine it had marked us long-forgotten kin. Delina and decoy. Mirrored images of one another.

"*Aly?*" Her voice pitched upward with more than shock—accusation lived there, too. *Fury* I had not felt directed my way from her since her first days in Shadewyle. "What in the blasted—what in *Ahim's name*—?"

"I can explain—"

"*Ugh!*" She tore the knives back and ripped away from me. "Stay here!"

Then she spun and darted to Ember's chair. I blinked after her, dazed, as she fell to her knees beside his chair and sawed against the bonds. At the sight of her thinly-veiled desperation, sense screamed through me.

Ryker.

Shoving up from the wall, I stumbled across the smoke-choked room until I reached the rubble heap of the fallen roof; my scarred, bloodstained hands blurred in and out of focus as I clawed through the debris, screaming for him without pausing to heed any answer. My pulse thundered painfully against my chest; nothing lived in my head but terror and need and his name, crying out like the riot in the streets all over again.

Too many painstaking moments that felt like hours grated against my tender nerves before I finally uncovered a scrap of cloth—the edge of his coat.

Gasping with relief, I moved to his head; there I found him barely conscious, stirring just a bit, a rotting beam fallen across his shoulder at just the right angle that he could not unpin either of his arms. Blood trickled from his temple; his eyes were murky and unfocused when they found mine.

"Lie still." Relief turned my voice wetter than the waterfall pouring in through the gap-torn roof. "I'm getting you out, just lie still…"

My shaking hands took longer to accomplish the task than I could stand; I trembled through and through by the time I shoved aside the last beam, freeing Ryker to roll onto his back. Groaning, he planted his hands and slid himself the rest of the way from the rubble—only to sag against my chest the moment his legs slipped free. I wrapped my arms around him from behind, dizzied by heady relief as I buried my face in his smoke-stained hair. His hand curled around my elbow. "You…you all right?"

"Wounded, but not…" I lost whatever words came after that, my eyes darting across the confines to our companions: Ember, on his feet now, hauling Tristah up by the hand. "That's Tristah."

Ryker said nothing; when I shook him, whispered his name, he did not respond. He had fallen unconscious, slumped in the crook of my arm.

"Tristah!" I shouted…then stilled.

There in the velvet grip of smoke from the fire she had sent ahead of her, Tristah embraced Ember with all her might; her arms tied around his neck, her fingers buried in his hair, her face pressed into the thudding pulse above his collarbone.

"It's all right. You're all right," she said, with a quiet ferocity that as if by her words alone, she could make it true. "This is not the island. Do you hear me? You are not back in that cave. Breathe. Breathe with me. Where's your depths-blasted *bracelet*?"

"Took it off," he mumbled sheepishly, folding his broad arms around her shoulders, holding her with a sort of gentle intimacy I had never seen her allow from any man. "I didn't think I would need it."

"You always need it, you mad oaf."

"I'm sorry." Emotion robbed his muted tones of even a slim corner of strength. Panic had wrung him to a wick, it seemed…or perhaps that was the relief of seeing her, no less potent than what throbbed in every place where Ryker's body laid against mine. "I'm sorry. I almost—"

"Enough!" Tristah cut him off with a fervor so familiar, it stained my eyes with tears. "I care about precisely *none of it*, do you hear me?"

His hands fastened to her biceps, unwinding her arms from around his neck, pushing them back to her sides so that he could grip her shoulders instead. A note of intensity sharpened his voice. "Why are you *here?*"

She fell back sharply on her heels. "Oh, you know, just going for a stroll. Figured I might as well stop and save your sorry skin while I was out."

"Tristah—"

"Don't *Tristah* me. Why do you *think* I'm here? They had you."

"For the love of—"

She sighed heavily. "Don't start."

"Don't *you* start!" All at once, he was a man transformed—soothed into a rhythm of argument with her that had once sustained me the same. "We have a code. An understanding. We—"

"*Enough.*" The word came differently this time—cracking in the midst of it, anguish seeping into the seam. "They had you."

"That doesn't—"

"*They. Had. You.*" Every syllable was its own stepping stone, leading to some shared conclusion that left them both silent for a heartbeat. Then Tristah added softly, "Do you really believe, after *all* this time, I wouldn't come for *you,* Killian?"

His true name flashed through me; far more sundering than the quiet intimacy of how she spoke it was the way it stripped the fight from him. His eyes tumbled shut, and he gathered her hands in the space between their chests, pressing his temple against hers.

An unspeakable anguish tightened my throat—and tightened my arms around Ryker's inert form, my chin settling on his head.

At long last, Tristah pivoted out of Ember—Killian's—grip. She faced me, hands on her hips, her scowl unchanged through the years. "I have somewhere we can go. Somewhere safe, where the militar won't find us."

And it was at that moment—beholding the cool confidence of her, and the way her strength had not faltered, but grown in our time apart…and that she was *here*, and how she had entered, how she had come for Ember—that the truth occurred to me at last.

Belatedly.

That never used to happen with Tristah.

"You're the Incendiary," I whispered.

For the first time, a twitch of a smile curled the corner of her mouth. Then she jerked her head. "Move, Aly. I'll help your friend."

And because everything else brought too many questions—and too much pain to fathom—I did as she ordered.

CHAPTER 56
MADE WITHOUT MERCY

To my untamable relief, Ryker woke once we arrived at our destination—lobbing several choice words at Killian when the man towered over him beside a sturdy iron cot and, without so much as a grunt of warning, dumped a packet of some stinging, peppery-smelling herbal powder on his head wound.

"You'll live," Killian informed him curtly.

"Which is more than I can say for you if you don't keep your bloody hands to yourself," Ryker groaned.

I forced a smile at their barbed exchange, though the heady gladness to have him awake—absurdly, to not be alone with Tristah and Killian—curled my fists closed over the edge of my tabletop perch.

I could not have found my way to this place alone through the raging storm…nor did I know precisely where it was. Only that it was some gutted stone edifice overlaid with wood, made up of sharp angles and broad, adjacent rooms, which we had entered through a long corridor of stone after more than an hour of walking. Its windows were veiled, but the crisp air suggested it was wedged into the crags of the Abbra Foothills.

Tristah had thought of everything.

That odd sensation of unbelonging reared in my chest again; I silenced it with the next curl of my fingers, which found a glass shard I'd failed to pare out. Hissing under my breath, I went to work on it.

"'Ay," Ryker called across the room, perching himself on an elbow atop the cot. "You all right over there, sweetheart?"

"Perfectly," I muttered, trapping the tip of my tongue between my teeth as I worried at the glass splinter. Tears pricked my eyes from the needling pain, separating my view of the single shard into several.

Iron creaked. Boots struck wood, a lopsided gait. Killian cursed. "Fine! Bleed to death. It's your funeral."

Ryker's callused hands enclosed mine. Shockingly deft, his salt-roughened fingernails encircled the shard and slid it free; then his fingers twisted, pressing against the small, bleeding puncture.

"You pick up a few things," he said, "having Gyddy as a best mate."

My eyes darted up to his; he gazed at me, unblinking, brows faintly raised. A question.

Did I truly want to be here? To do this with Tristah still, knowing she was the Incendiary?

I despised how my heart pulled two ways. That it was not a simple, affirmative answer.

Before I could muster a retort, Tristah ducked into the room from where she'd vanished a moment ago; in one hand, she carried a satchel. In the other, something small she tossed underhand to Killian. "Put this on, will you?"

He looped it over his wrist—a bracelet which made a sound like falling rain as the beads strung across its face all knocked together. He leaned on the wall, snapping them against his skin, sliding his thumb over the painted, whorled surface. In the dim light Tristah coaxed to life within the tabletop lantern, I spotted the melding of darker and paler beads…places where his fingertips had smoothed the texture and paint down to nothing.

Ryker watched him as well, his own fingers wandering to the pendant wheel he never went without.

"Move," Tristah ordered Ryker, thrusting the bag against his chest when he didn't oblige at once. Then her arms enveloped me in a waft of smoke and leather, and for the first time in so long, I felt truly safe.

"You are an idiot," she breathed against my hair. "You are an *idiot*, Alyona Vassera."

My family's name—my full, true name, stomped out by the Del long ago— slashed through me, its brutal edge softened by the only voice that had spoken it at all since my parents' deaths. I wrapped my arms around her strong, sturdy waist, burying my face in her shoulder. "An idiot who is so desperately glad to see you, I could weep."

"Don't. It will ruin my image as the Incendiary." Tristah leaned back in my embrace, taking my face in her hands. Surprise—and perhaps even disdain—scrunched her nose. "Speaking of *ruining one's image*, what is *this?*" She tweaked the gold hoop that pierced my nostril.

Swatting her hand away, I rubbed my knuckles against my upper lip. "Just a bit of ornamentation."

"You fight with a *metal hook* in your face? Do you even realize how dangerous that is?"

"I don't *fight* at all."

That muting silence descended over us again. Tristah peeled back a bit further; we stared at one another.

When her gaze dipped to my hands, the knowing that crawled between us nearly stifled me.

Ryker shook the bag loudly. "All right, so, what's in the sack? And more importantly, how's it going to help the absolute fishmonger's mother of a headache I've got thanks to the pair of you?"

"Thanks to *us?*" Tristah spun from me to face him. "You were interrogating my spymaster!"

I slid to my feet, resting a hand on Tristah's shoulder. "I'm sorry. *We* are sorry, I—"

"You did what you thought necessary to protect Tristah." Killian folded his arms, shrugging his gray cloak forward to enshroud his arms; he stared at Tristah with both understanding and faint accusation. "I can't fault you for that."

"I don't *need* protection," Tristah laughed, beckoning Ryker back to the cot. He went when I nodded him along, and when he sat, she dug into the satchel, pulling out bandages and fastenings and a smattering of spirits in a small glass bottle. "Though I appreciate you're still the same Aly as always."

Was I? Had that Alyona held the courage to defy Lucretzia so many times? To flee her? To square up to pirates and also make her peace among them? To search for what she held most precious, even with Lucretzia's hounding breaths on her heels?

I was not entirely certain that Alyona Vassera *or* Alyona Graven had ever possessed such tenacity. But Lionyra Vara…

"How did you find me?" Tristah's tone remained lively, but a thin metal edge undercut the words.

Sending a warning glance Ryker's way, I spoke for us both: "We traced the whispers of the Incendiary. Particularly here in Bashir."

Her gaze cut to me over her shoulder, even while she dribbled the spirits on the side of Ryker's head, flushing the wound at his temple. "And you somehow gathered it was me?"

Killian stiffened, a thunderous rolling of tension that he shrugged down from his shoulders to his shifting feet.

"No," I confessed, "not until you came for Em—for Killian." I pushed away from the table's edge to lean against the cot's wrought-iron headboard instead. "But I know you, Tristah. Everything I heard of the Incendiary seemed the precise sort of person you would have aligned yourself with."

"Well, you aren't wrong," she preened a bit, slapping a bandage against Ryker's head and scoffing when he groaned. "Oh, swallow it, you giant oaf. I'm sure you've had worse."

"Rumor holds that the Incendiary is a man," I added, "and that he has been doing this for quite some time."

Tristah cast a wink Killian's way. "I'd say all your hard work is paying off, then, Killi."

He affected the most infinitesimal of bows, his ashen cloak hardly ruffling more than the shadows that broke around him, his eyes still fixed on us.

"To most of Amere-Del, the Incendiary is precisely what we've made it— made *him*," Tristah added, binding the bandage gently to Ryker's wound. "Few know the truth."

"How few?"

She paused, rocking her knuckles against his bandage. "The four of us."

There was something oddly gratifying in being privy still to some of Tristah's deepest secrets…even if she had never intended to share them with me.

"To most, the Incendiary is a faraway figure," she went on. "And to those who have seen my face as a dissenter, I'm known as a mouthpiece of his."

"Well, they're not the only ones who have seen your face around these parts," Ryker grunted, fingering the bandage. "And believe me, that's about to become *everyone's* problem."

Tristah's eyes dodged between us. "What is *that* supposed to mean?"

"You've been spotted, lass. Everyone knows the Delina is back…and there are rumors bubbling over from these parts up to the border that she's been spotted down in the south."

Tristah was quiet for a long moment, a silent battle waging in her eyes. At last, she shrugged. "If we spooked at every rumor, we'd never stop running. There are always a few flying. Killian is excellent at quashing them."

"There's no quashing these ones," I warned. "They've reached too far. Lucretzia is hunting us."

Killian's teeth flickered to sight in a snarl, and Tristah settled back on her heels, breath swelling her chest.

"She and Zorast will do whatever necessary to reclaim their prized Delina," I added. "They're determined to put an end to the dissidence through us."

At that, Tristah snorted, folding her arms across her middle. "Nothing's changed, then."

Killian shot her a glance, then bowed against the wall, one foot propped back on the curved stone. "What do the Del's plans have to do with *you*?"

I opened my mouth to reply, but Tristah cut across me sharply. "Aly was in Shadewyle with me. All of the same things I told you about…they were going to happen to her." She shot a warning look my way before she added, softly, "We were all each other had, and I thought…I thought I would never see her again."

My inability to discern whether relief or rebuke lined the hooding of her eyes struck a fresh sort of pain in my chest.

"I had to warn you," I croaked. "I could never leave you undefended while Lucretzia roamed the country. I feared she would find you, use you to—"

Tristah scoffed, silencing me. "She's tried. For years. She's hunted me, and she's hunted the Incendiary, and she's never come close." A savage smile accosted her mouth. "Everything she ever taught me, I've turned against her."

Admiration and dread poured into my gut—a collision of oil and water.

"That won't stop her looking," Ryker warned. "Not when Lio's already slipped through her fingers."

Tristah's brow snapped down. "Lio?"

Embarrassment spread across the nape of my neck in a crimson flush. "I adopted a different name when I traveled north."

Tristah nodded, slow and sagely. But I could not name the gleam that lit across her eyes; and it had been so long since Tristah's thoughts had been beyond my reckoning.

"She had you?" Her question was calm, but the next flare in her features— the tightening of her mouth, the slant of her stare, the way her tongue ticked the words off—all festered with familiar fury.

I nodded. "For a time."

"How did you escape?"

A glance at Ryker. "It is…quite a tale."

"Clearly," Killian grunted.

Tristah turned to me, coaxing me back to the table. When I perched on its edge again, she laid out her tools—pickers for the stubborn glass shards, as well as tincture blends I had grown familiar with under Gydeon's care.

I stared at my coral-scraped, glass-cut hands, wondering dully just how long it would be before I could knead dough without pain again.

"Ask your questions, then," Tristah sighed as she set to work over my hands—a familiar practice from countless times tending one another's wounds in Shadewyle.

"How long have you been the Incendiary?"

"Since I came here from Korsa." She cast a shrewd glance up from my hands. "That's—"

"A pirate city in the mountain caverns. I know. I've been there."

A snort escaped her. "You've been busy, *Lio*."

"Not as busy as you. What are you thinking, stirring up an active revolt against the Del?"

"That I couldn't flee and leave this country how I found it…how I *truly* found it while we lived in Shadewyle." Silence settled for a moment, a bit of guilt twining about my heart while she plucked out glass bits and dropped them onto the tabletop. "I almost fled, I really did. But the longer I spent in Korsa, and here in Bashir…I realized how desperately Amere-Del needed someone to help the people. Someone who lacked all that strutting pomp and useless hot air in Sorai." Derision sharpened her tone. "They needed a fighting chance."

"And you created the Incendiary to meet that need."

She shot a crooked smile over one shoulder. "With Killian's help."

"Tristah, if the Del learns the truth of what you've done…what you *are*…"

He would never allow her back. Me, they would capture; they would hold me in chains, ransom me off to Sorai with a gag in my mouth. But Tristah…

There would be no mercy for this. And her unaffected stare suggested she knew as much.

She had not *become* without mercy. She had made herself this way.

"I've given him an ultimatum," she said simply. "Destroy me as Tristah, or destroy me as the Incendiary. Either way, I will never belong to him again."

CHAPTER 57
THE PIRATE'S LIFE

illian made some sound in the base of his throat, as if he'd been run through by an unseen blade. Had I not been struck breathless by the notion of Tristah's demise—and how fearlessly she spoke of it—I might have done the same.

"Is that why you've done *all* of this?" I demanded. "To ensure if he ever found you, he would put an *end* to you?"

She snorted. "Of course not. This is for our people. For the orphans, for the exploited children, for…" The words broke, and Tristah's eyes flashed with tears. "For you and me, Aly."

For a time, we were all silent, the men watching as Tristah dug the last of the glass from my arms and slowly wrapped me from wrist to elbow with bandages.

"But for all I've done, Sorai is right about one thing," Tristah muttered at last. "I am not changing the laws this way. The work of the Incendiary brings relief to those who would otherwise crumble before a true solution can be found. But it's not *the* solution."

"What is?"

She cast me a crooked smile. "That's what I'm buying time to find out."

I winced as she tightened and tied off the bandage on my left arm. "I suppose little can help if you aren't the Del."

She bowed her head over her work, hiding from my mirrored gaze. "The thought has crossed my mind."

Her cool diffidence sent chills skittering down my arms and legs. "You would take his place?"

"If there was a way to do it and become his inheritor, rather than his murderer?" She blinked up at me. "In a heartbeat, Aly."

No cruelty in her tone; merely common sense.

Zorast was a dangerous man and a cruel ruler. He expanded his cruelty by the hand of the Del's Own Blade. I couldn't deny much of the country would breathe easier without the fear of Zorast's will, held at their necks by way of Lucretzia's blade. "Then why haven't you done it?"

A sharp laugh splintered from her. "Because I can't bring myself to set foot near Shadewyle Castle. I've tried, but whenever I draw near, I just…I lose my sense. The memories, the sights and smells of the town…they consume me. I'm not keen enough when I'm close enough to do the deed."

"And Zorast never leaves the castle," I murmured.

Tristah nodded. "Too paranoid after what you did to Athyna."

In the pause that followed that shared memory, both Ryker and Killian shifted in place.

At last, Tristah went on, "You were the reason I did any of this, Aly. Every mission, every raid, every person I've stolen off to safety and stashed away in places where the militar can't hurt them, I've thought of you. You've been with me all this time."

Now it was my turn to blink away years. "And it's a good thing you've done for all of them. Better, I suppose, than forsaking Amere-Del altogether." I had never regretted that decision until now, beholding what she had made of herself. I had never once imagined staying in Amere-Del after we'd escaped the castle; I had not *wanted* to stay, even if I might have done some good. I still had no desire for that. But the guilt that she had remained, and fought, and I had not…

I had broken our vow. I had forsaken her long ago, without even realizing.

Tristah straightened, taking my shoulders, peering into my eyes. "I never blamed you for leaving Amere-Del."

My throat squeezed impossibly tight. "Perhaps you should."

"But I *don't*. Some people heal by helping others. Some have to heal themselves first. One isn't better than the other, and there's no shame in either." She shrugged. "You just couldn't stay. I could."

And the people were better for it. Better with the decoy who remained than the Delina who fled.

"I'm sorry about this," Tristah added softly, tying down the edge of the bandage around my forearm. "I didn't know it was you. If I'd had any idea you were in that room, I never would've come through the window that way."

A shudder grazed my limbs at the memory of precisely how she had appeared. "When you came through the window…I saw Lucretzia. Your movements, your methods…they are precisely like hers, even after all this time."

Tristah gathered her things silently, and I stirred one foot through the air, meeting Ryker's gaze over her shoulder. This exchange had been, perhaps, the longest he'd ever held his tongue in a conversation; his gaze defied interpretation.

"There was nothing terrible in what they taught us," Tristah said at last. "Only the methods with which they taught it."

"I prefer to make use of the talents I've cultivated for myself."

"Well, that's *your* choice. But I worked and bled to the bone for these skills. *I* choose to wield them to help people who are suffering as we did." Returning all of her things to her satchel, she added, "And you can sound as superior as you like, but don't tell me your *cultivated skills* are what gave you the upper hand over my spymaster."

"A slim upper hand," Killian muttered.

Discomfort knotted in the base of my throat at the faint scorn in Tristah's tone; to evade it, I pivoted the subject back to her. "I still find it strange you *have* a spymaster."

"Not just any spymaster. The best in Amere-Del." Fondness tugged at the corners of those words; she ignored how Killian rolled his eyes. "He listens and lurks. He spreads the lies we need stoked about the Incendiary. He finds targets, and I strike them. And he helps move the people who need it most…he gives them places of refuge all throughout the mountains."

My stomach pinched. "How did you meet him?"

"That is a *very* long story." Tristah pitched the satchel to Killian, and he swiveled into a side room with it. "Too long for tonight. For now, we should all rest…I promise, no one is going to find us here. We have food and water stored, and the rest we'll sort out in the morning."

I gaped after her as she hurried to a chest in the corner, pulling out blankets and down-stuffed pillows; my head whirled so viciously, I feared I would pitch from my perch on the tabletop.

I had envisioned this moment for so long…the opportunity to lay everything before Tristah. To beg her to run away with me. To find safety and a home together.

I had not imagined her with her feet so firmly planted. With a cause to fight for. With a man whose embrace she welcomed…who she had been ready to kill for without question. Who read her silent looks and gestures as easily as I once had…and no longer could.

All along, I had imagined myself running toward a Tristah who was adrift, unaware, unwilling to lift a blade to defend herself—a woman shielded by loneliness, seeking an unassuming life while danger stalked at the fringes.

I…

I had envisioned rescuing *myself*.

But Tristah did not need rescuing. Not the sort I wished that someone— anyone—had offered when Lucretzia had slithered back into my life.

If you're not safe, sweetheart, help me make you that way.

My stomach tumbled over itself. "Thank you for your kindness."

"What else would I do?" Tristah snorted. "Though perhaps I shouldn't offer you any pillows, at least…just so Killian feels avenged."

"To be fair, we weren't sure if he was a friend of yours or not," Ryker spoke for the first time in countless minutes, catching the blankets and pillows Tristah flung into his arms.

"I would say you should keep the torture to a bare minimum before you know someone…but then, what should I expect from Blackhand, captain of *The Dread Singer*?"

Ryker's smile was all teeth. "Ah, so you've heard of me."

"None of it good." Tristah glanced between us. "I'd love to hear how you convinced *Alyona Vassera* to sail with you."

A bristle of indignation raced up my spine.

Ryker flicked a hand. "All her idea, coming here after you. I'm just her ferryman."

Tristah laughed. "Save it for the morning, Captain." She nodded to Killian as he stepped back in. "For now, there's some dry clothes in that bundle of blankets as well. And I can give you both some herbs for the pain, to help—"

"No herbs," we chorused in harmony.

Tristah hesitated, looking my way. I swallowed a curse and moved to the cot, perching beside Ryker, offering what I prayed to Ahim was a disarming smile. "We'll be all right."

Tristah held her place a moment longer; then she turned and strode back to the side room, clapping Killian on the chest in passing. He shrugged up from the wall, pinning us both with curious, distrusting eyes; after a long moment potent with unspoken threat, he slipped out after her.

Ryker sagged, carding his hands back through his hair. "How much of this am I imagining after that blow to the head?"

"That depends. Are there small gingerbread folk dancing about the room?"

He swept his hands down the sides of his neck, then dropped them, pinning me with a wide-eyed look. "You can see them, too?"

A laugh scraped from my throat, and I pitched forward, burying my face in my swaddled palms. "None of this went how I planned."

"Aye. That's a pirate's life, I'm afraid." Ryker's heavy hand settled on my back, fanning warmth through my rain-soaked body. When I didn't duck away, he slowly slid his fingers up to my shoulderblades and down to the small of my back. "You'll have to talk her onto the ship if you want her to leave this town. Leave *him*."

"I know." The Tristah I'd walked away from had held no one and nothing in the world but me. In my mind, she had been easy to convince…as desperate to see me as I had been to see her.

This Tristah…this woman was all but a stranger. How was I to convince a *stranger* to give up her life's cause for me?

The question was too overwhelming for one night; I allowed it to slip out the same way Tristah and Killian had gone, leaving my mind floating in a warm in-between…a space occupied only by Ryker and me.

That space proved little safer; behind the darkness of my cradled hands, I saw fire. I saw wood and blood. I saw the same detached confusion in his face that had greeted me when I'd come for him in the reef…when we'd spoken in *The Athalion's* sick bay afterward.

Tension furrowed my shoulders, fighting to shrug off the memory of that brief, blinding terror tonight, between when I'd seen the rubble and when I'd unburied him from beneath it.

Ryker's fingers hesitated on my back; then his palm splayed wider, unleashing fresh heat through me. "'Ay. What's the matter?"

"I'm…" The truth chafed my throat. Perhaps I was no better acquainted with speaking it than him. "I am so relieved you're all right."

"That makes two of us." His hand resumed its careful journey along my bent spine—and with a dull shiver, I arched into the warmth of it. "When that blast went off…I tried to get to you. Get in front of you." His free hand crossed our bodies, brushing over my bandaged arms. "Sorry I wasn't fast enough."

"*I'm* the one who's sorry. Now you've lost a finger *and* had your head dented in on my account."

"No one'll be able to tell if I'm a little loopier than I used to be."

Tying my fingers together, I propped my elbows on my thighs and laid my cheek to my knuckles. When I met his eyes, they brimmed with sincerity—and exhaustion.

"You're impossible," I muttered.

His mouth tipped at the corner. "Been called a lot worse than that."

Even by me. Heart pricked by a fatigued sort of grief, I gripped his shoulder, pushing to my feet. "You ought to rest. I—"

"Trim your sails right there." He hooked me around the waist, towing me back down on the bedside. "I've got a concussion I know better than to sleep through. *You* take a rest."

"Here?"

"I don't see another bed, and I'll be sunk if I let you sleep on the floor one more night. You've been sharing your breathing space with spiders for too long already."

On a saner day, I might have protested; but I had spent more nights than I preferred catching glimpses of slumber stretched out on the floor of the leaking pirate trap where we'd held Killian. The desire for restful sleep frothed over into the desperate *craving* for it the moment he made the offer.

I plucked his arm from around me, only to retrieve the toss of blankets and extract a muslin sleep gown from within. At my pointed look, Ryker pivoted on his seat to face the wall; still, I stripped from my singed, soaked clothes and slipped into the dry gown more swiftly than I ever had in my life, my body flushed with a heat that chased out all of the chill left to my skin by the time I cast myself back on the edge of the bed.

"Your turn." I nudged him.

I kept my eyes on the wall while he tossed off his sodden clothes with heavy *splats.* He fumbled over something, groused and cursed; then he said my name, quietly. Tense.

My bleary gaze found him with the shirt strung in his fists, his bare torso visible in the light—exposing an impressive span of bruises already blooming where the wood beams had struck him.

"I could use a little help, if you're willing," he muttered gruffly.

Feeling a bit as if I were dreaming—and made dangerous by how few consequences lived in the choices made during such fantasies—I crossed the room to him. Slowly, he held out the unbuttoned linen shirt…likely Killian's, a bit too long and broad in the chest for him.

He turned his back to me, exposing scars and inkings that danced together with the harsh contusions across the planes of his back—a tale of many hurts all melding in the guttering lanternlight.

A tale I knew far too well.

Wary of his new wounds and old ones, I eased the shirt onto his arms, sliding it carefully over the muscular contours of his shoulders. He stiffened now and again, small, pained increments of breath clawing at the back of his throat and escaping his nostrils; but he relaxed some when he gingerly shrugged the shirt over the tops of his arms. My fingers followed the roll of his muscles, guiding the open halves of the shirt to rest over his tattooed chest.

"Turn," I whispered, and he slowly pivoted—his head first, his eyes finding mine over his shoulder before he faced me in full.

I held his gaze while I did up the lower buttons—masking many of the bruises. Wishing I could erase them all.

His throat hitched when my fingers brushed against his ribs; seizing my hand, he let out his breath in a long, low sweep, a groan veiled behind the sound. All that time, his eyes fastened to mine; his thumb slowly brushed my knuckles.

"Whatever happens here," he rasped, "between you and her…I've got your back, Vassera."

The way he spoke my family's name bolted through me like a lightning strike on the open sea—brilliant and dazzling and doing no harm. A silent vow that he would never speak it again; that it was safe in his mind and memory.

"Thank you." All I could offer for what had brought us this far. All that we had done, and shared…and all the things we perhaps never would.

Swiveling my hand in his, I led him back to the bed; he helped me step up onto it, then swung his knee tentatively over the edge, pushing himself back to rest with legs outstretched, his back to the wall.

"Wake me if your head worsens," I warned, settling myself cross-legged beside him.

"Not going to lie down?"

Resting my head back against the cool stone, I let my eyes tumble shut. The blessed relief of the smothering shadows overwhelmed me at once, loosening every inch of tension from my body. I could barely force a mumble through my weighted lips: "I want to be ready if you need me."

"Aye." Ryker stayed quiet for so long, I drifted to the edge of slumber before his breath brushed the side of my face—as if he'd laid his cheek to the wall, studying me in the gloom. "That's the trouble, sweetheart. Starting to think I'm always going to need you."

I ran from the piercing strike of those words, from the brush of his breath against my face, from the graze of the tip of his nose against mine; the same way I'd fled from Amere-Del, delving into the shadows of Mithra-Sha, I now took shelter in sleep.

But not before the sensation of falling. Of warmth scraping my cheek.

Not before my head tumbled down on Ryker's shoulder, finding a comfortable home in the crook of his neck…a lullaby in the tender, steady beat of his heart.

CHAPTER 58
WHAT LIES BETWEEN

For four days, we took refuge in Tristah's shelter. And every dawn, I assured myself now would be the time I told her the truth…about the ransoms and the schemes that swirled around our names. How I'd come to sail with Ryker…and how I planned to flee.

Every day, I woke next to Ryker on the cot, one of us propped to the wall and the other stretched out, our feet inevitably tangled together among the blankets. And every day I woke before he did, studying the gentleness that found its way into his slack countenance. Tracing the contours of *Bastyan*, so visible now beneath the sternness of the pirate captain. Aching to run my fingers over the angles of that face…and feeling all of the same panic and terror and *heartache* that had seized me as I'd dug him out of the rubble heap. The same craving that had not abated since I'd helped him slip into his fresh shirt.

Every day, I felt him waiting and watching; waiting for me to leave. Watching for me to break beneath the burden of the truth that sizzled on my tongue. Every day, he whispered the same question whenever we were alone: "When are you going to bloody *tell her*?"

And every day, I hissed the same response: "When she's prepared to *listen*."

That time never came.

The fourth morning, I sat on the tabletop with Tristah, both of us cross-legged, spooning bites of porridge while we chatted about her work as the Incendiary—about the good she had done already for Amere-Del.

In some regards, the dreams and visions she had stirred up in Shadewyle Castle, brought to bear now in her work as the Incendiary, overwhelmed me. These were not the fantasies of a woman caged; the work of her hands proved the truth of passions more than a decade nurtured.

"Some dissidents are just full of hot air," she allowed, speaking with rounded lips around a mouthful of steaming porridge, "but most—in the Northlands *and* Southlands—are just tired. They're so *tired*, Aly. They want change, and they'll claim it any way they can."

"And the Incendiary gives them a means to do that."

"Well, she does try." Tristah winked; then, abruptly, her expression hollowed. "If all it ever does is keep the riots to a minimum, then I consider it worth the risk."

Gratitude warmed my chest better than any bite of hot porridge—but in its wake burned a cold path of dread.

The last four days had taught me how dedicated Tristah truly was to her cause. It seemed impossible she would be coaxed away from it, and I had yet to settle on any angle of suggestion which might make the notion of leaving Amere-Del behind as appealing to her as it was to me.

"So," Tristah added when I didn't speak—perhaps hoping to pull my focus away from the unhealing bruise of dissident riots, "do you think Blackhand and Killian have murdered one another yet?"

It was a distinct possibility. Tristah had dispatched them to the market for supplies…and to listen for whispers of unrest. But I suspected she'd actually wanted time alone with me, and for that, I was more grateful than I could say.

"I wonder who would win if it came to blows between them," I mused, stirring my porridge to release pockets of steam from within. "Ryker is well-trained. I've seen him duel."

"Yes, but Killian is…" A shadow grazed Tristah's eyes, and something like regret bent her lips. "His path has been…different. From anyone else's I've ever met. He's been many places and seen many things. There's a good reason he makes for such an invaluable spymaster."

Her faith in him made me doubt if we would have ever succeeded in finding him at all, had he not been drawn in by the lure of my likeness to Tristah. "He cares very much for you."

She straightened, brushing a hand down the length of herself "He ought to. Have you *met* me? I'm fabulous."

A snort tickled the back of my nose. "What you are is *ridiculous*, Tristah Levanthya."

"Well, I'm not the only one." She settled her weight back on her hands, tossing her chin against her shoulder to peer at me sidelong. "You've been coy, but you *still* haven't explained how you came to sail with Blackhand."

Groaning, I spooned in a mouthful of porridge, buying myself a moment to think. I had not yet devised a lie that would slip by her sharp guard; nor did I wish to tell her the truth. Not without the assurance she wouldn't destroy Ryker…or refuse to flee with me aboard his ship, only to flee *again* at the first opportunity.

Perhaps Ember would come in handy for that.

Though the notion of the two resorting to violence had been amusing mere moments ago…for whatever reason, shifting the setting from a Bashiri market to *The Dread Singer* soured my stomach.

There was no crew in the market. No steady-spirited first mate with a passion for art, who wore *vermillion* or *peach* instead of red or pink; nor her beloved, doting husband, his fingers stained from dealing life and death in comparable measure. No Draces throwing knives in perfect rows or shamelessly fleecing a kindhearted boy's pastries from him night after night. No graceful quartermaster dancing a klutzy jig around a beaming violinist, who dueled with bow and string rather than blade and pistol.

"I've told you all the parts that matter," I hedged. "Lucretzia came for me in Mithra-Sha. Ryker intercepted her and aided my escape. And I bargained with him to help me find you."

"Mm*hm*." Tristah rolled her eyes, rocking her head around to peer toward the gritty window across the room. "Well, no surprise he went for it. The man is utterly smitten with you."

Shock blistered my fingertips, and I dropped my spoon into the porridge. "*Tristah!*"

"What?" she snapped back, defensiveness rocking her tone. "You think Killian cares for *me*? That pirate hardly takes his eyes off of you!"

"Because I'm—" *A ransom.* The words did not find their home on my lips.

And that was the trouble I kept finding myself in now; I had never been particularly talented at lying to Tristah, of all people.

"What lies between us is…complicated," I amended at last.

"Define *complicated*, Aly."

"You first," I volleyed back.

Tristah frowned at me; I arched a brow, meeting her incredulous stare without falter. Her lips twitched at the familiar, silent sparring match—the sort that had kept us sane during long meals with the Del and Della and Lucretzia years ago.

"Killian is my…friend, as well as my spymaster," she said. "Although he wasn't at first. Not when we met back in Korsa—in fact, I've still got a scar from—"

"You met in *Korsa?*"

She dismissed me with a wave, as if the pirate city I'd hardly escaped with my life was beneath her notice. "It's not important. What *is* important is that we've been together ever since, and…I understand him. He understands me." Her tone gentled with memories to which I was not privy. "He's the only reason I can do any of this confidently…that I *have* done so much in so little time. I trust him with my life. He knows everything about my past, my origins…my time in Shadewyle."

"Yet you did not trust him with the truth about me."

She smiled faintly. "I trust *no one* with you."

Warmth swirled in my chest. "What *did* you tell him, then?"

"That *I'm* the Delina."

The breath gushed from me all at once. "That will be difficult to correct."

She winced. "Indeed."

"Why didn't you tell him the *truth?* Would that have been so terrible?"

Her lips strained upward at the corners. "There are some things about the past few years I can't make you understand."

"Perhaps the same can be said for—"

"Stop," Tristah interrupted sharply, and heat flushed up my neck. Defensiveness surged on my tongue, ready to deny whatever ridiculous conclusions she was lunging toward—

But instead, she hopped from the table and went to the window, resting her palm against the gritty glass, a wisp of her breath clearing a small port to peer through.

Tension soaked my bones. Shoving my bowl aside, I lowered myself to the floor as well. "Tristah?"

"Someone is here." The announcement rang hollow off the walls.

"Ryker and Killian?"

"No, Killi knows how to announce himself." Tristah stepped back from the window, sliding a pair of knives free of the many sheaths strung from her belt. "They're scaling the hillside…climbing the walls. It's the blasted militar."

CHAPTER 59
NO LOOKING BACK

Shock, then horror, doused whatever ease had crept over me while we'd bantered. I sprang to Tristah's side; together we pressed our backs to the wall beside the window, our faces toward the door—a familiar, defensive posture, as natural as it was loathsome.

"They're crawling all over this place," she cursed, knocking her head against the wall, her gaze tracking invisible enemies ascending over her refuge. "How did they find us here?"

"Perhaps they're not here for us," I whispered. "A training exercise in the Foothills?"

"Not in those numbers. Not armed that way."

A brush of sound in the outer corridor had us both stiffening; the moment the door eased open, Tristah hurled one of the knives, a keen silver arc cleaving through the musty air.

Steel embedded in the door an inch from the side of Ryker's head as Killian gripped his collar, yanking him out of its path.

The spymaster's eyes rounded out, his head slanting in silent reproach. Tristah bobbed a shrug.

"We've got company," Ryker announced.

"Militar. We know." Tristah beckoned them into the room. "Positions?"

"Coordinated." Killian shoved Ryker inside and stepped after him. "Closing in quickly."

"Blasted depths," Tristah swore. "So we lose this place."

Something like anguish tightened her frame; a shared pain darted through the depths of Killian's night-blue eyes.

"Aye, well, better that than our skins," Ryker said. "Word all over the markets was that the militar had a target on the Incendiary. We came back as soon as we heard."

Cursing again, Tristah shoved up from the wall, wrenching her dagger from the door in passing. "Let's move."

Ryker jerked his chin at me. "You stay right behind me, sweetheart."

I had little intention otherwise.

Closing the distance to Tristah as we reached the doorway, I unhooked a pair of sturdy weapons from her belt—the sort of incendiaries with which she'd blown her way into our pirate den to rescue Killian. The sort, I assumed, from which she'd built her name and reputation.

She had fought desperately for those things. They would not end today.

We slipped out into the blackened halls which ate deep into the face of the Foothills, their innocuous entrances cut between gaps in the outer rock. They were framed in old tapestries and cloth shrouds that muffled footsteps…yet even those were not sturdy enough to quiet the echo of *so many* feet creeping ahead of us, whisper-soft and reeking of malice.

Ryker and I hugged one wall, Killian and Tristah the other; across the way, Ryker caught their eyes and flashed six fingers.

Killian nodded. Tristah laid her blades back, preparing for battle. Ryker pulled a pistol and settled his weight on his heels.

He moved first—firing down the corridor, lighting up the shadows with a spark of pistolshot that tore between the half-dozen militar creeping down the corridor. Then he whirled back, snared me by the shoulder, and butted open one of the doors along the hall, thrusting me into the room beyond.

Metal met flesh in our wake; the militar screamed as they fell beneath Tristah and Killian's assault. Ryker pulled another pistol and threw the empty one to me, bending around the doorframe to fire as he barked: "Reload!"

My fingers flew through one of the many tasks I'd learned aboard the *Singer* on our way to Bashir, drawing lead and powder from the pouches strapped at Ryker's hips, filling and priming and shoving the pistol into his hands just as he drew back around the doorframe. He tossed the second spent pistol my way, caught the loaded one, then drew another from beneath his cloak and stepped full-flush into the hall, shouting abuse as he took aim and fired. Once. Twice.

My hands shook nearly beyond use as I loaded the powder and lead, then ducked out of the room to shove the loaded pistol into its holster across Ryker's chest. I caught the two he'd already spent when he flipped them muzzles-first over his shoulders, and squared my back to his, reloading, priming, returning them to their holsters at his hips.

The fight had moved beyond us, a clash of blades down the hall; but Ryker's aim was precise, and the confidence of his stance and the shouts trading between Tristah and Killian fortified my courage. All shaking had ceased when Ryker whirled, snagging me around the waist and hurling me down the hall. "Let's move!"

We tore into the shadows, lunging over the fallen militar, catching up to Tristah and Killian just as the echo of smashing wood splintered the air behind us. We all whirled back at once—toward the heart of their refuge and the dark bodies swarming over the sills and window ledges, corrupting its comforting confines like a taint of mold through a warm loaf.

Rage drove into my temples; I ripped an incendiary from my belt, tore out its stopper with my teeth, and hurled it back up the hall. Then it was my turn to grip Ryker and Tristah by their collars, shout at Killian to *run*—and do the same.

We made it only a few paces before the blast knocked all of us to our knees. Stone and wood erupted in a violent cacophony, and fire bent to my will just as Tristah had bent it to hers: it collapsed the hall in a torrent of hurtling stone and falling beams, a chaos of heart-bending memory that had me grasping and squeezing Ryker's hand while the deluge sealed us away from the militar.

For now. But they had caught the scent of our retreat—escaping them altogether would be another trial entirely.

Heart in throat, I scrabbled for a tapestry and hauled myself up against it. "We can't stop."

Tristah sprang nimbly to her feet, wrathful heat pulsing from her body. "Apparently not."

She took the lead in a breakneck dash through the halls, hardly slowing even where the wood paneling of the floor gave way to slick stone. My feet skidded, but Ryker caught me beneath the arm, hauling me back up; I could not see his face in the gloom, but the roughness of his breath suggested fury and focus equal to mine.

We burst into the open several miles later—into another pelting, driving rainstorm threatening to sweep us down from the Foothills. Tristah and Killian had not waited for us; they were like spiders scuttling and lunging from stone crop to stone crop, moving down the hills by the light of fire above…a fire that had utterly consumed their sanctuary.

I halted a moment, swiping my rain-drenched hair from my face, my heart clambering into my throat.

If the militar were wiser than they were desperate to capture the Incendiary, they might have slipped back out through the windows they'd broken in through; if so, we were likely to encounter some on the path down to Bashir.

I did not know which was worse…that my toss of the incendiary might have killed them all, or that they might yet have to die for us to escape.

"'Ay. It's a lost cause, love." Ryker tugged against my arm. "No looking back."

He was right. Even if that truth tore at something deep in my heart.

I shook his hand off my arm only to seize it in mine. To find the balance that kept my feet beneath me while we fled—and Tristah and Killian's refuge went up in flames behind us.

CHAPTER 60
BY BLOOD AND CAUSE

It was deep in the night when we dared pause again for a breath, far down the twisting streets of Bashir. Dread encroached like the shadows that swarmed on our heels. The avenues were vacant, windows and doors shuttered—likely a curfew in place. One we had missed from our hideaway.

The militar had cleared their path to hunt us. And though we had encountered only the pursuing shouts of a few survivors on our way down from the Foothills, an occasional shot fired after us from a distance …the reprieve would not last long.

Skidding into a seam between buildings, we halted to catch our breath; Ryker and I tumbled back against one wall, Tristah and Killian against the other. For several moments, only our knifing gasps and the drumming rain filled the silence—but it bristled with rage and grew fangs with every passing moment.

It was Tristah who broke it, lurching up straight, gripping a stitch in her side. "What just *happened?*"

"Might be they followed us from the market," Ryker grunted.

Killian shook his head in a single sharp, deft jerk. "They were ahead of us as well as behind. They were already searching…they've *been* searching."

"But not for the Incendiary. Not this time." Tristah's face hosted a conflict between the smoky light and the shadows that dipped the other half of her countenance—a furious look she had never before turned my way. "How do *you* think they would have known where we were, Alyona?"

I squeezed my eyes shut, forcing my thoughts past the lash of pain dealt by that name—even from her mouth, this time. In a moment, despair took the place of anguish, a cut marring straight across the small of my back.

"Sorai." My eyes sprang open, leaping to Ryker. "Perhaps he truly recognized me after all, and—"

"Reported you to the militar here in the city." Ryker palmed his bearded mouth, muttering, "Blasted *depths*."

"You're out of practice," Tristah spat. "You stopped looking over your shoulder. This wasn't coincidence, them finding me right after you did…this happened *because* of you!"

Horror thudded in the base of my throat. "Tristah, that isn't—"

"I told you, I've evaded the Del for years—for *years*! Do you truly think it's *happenstance* that the militar found me just *days* after you did?" She flung out her arms, animated in her anger. "You led them right *to me*, Alyona!"

"'Ay!" Ryker shrugged forward off the bricks. "That's enough—"

"No." I cut his tirade short. "She…it's true. This *is* my doing."

Because no one else—not even Lucretzia—knew Tristah as I did. No one else would have strummed the precise threads I had in Korsa, and again in Bashir. And for no one else would Ember have revealed himself so recklessly…except that he had believed I was her.

All of the pieces had fallen perfectly into place because, in my desperation to reach her, to save her…I had not considered I might become her downfall.

Tristah cursed, striking her knuckles back against Killian's chest. "Let's get out of the city, before things get any worse."

"Oi!" Ryker snapped. "I'm not leaving without my crew!"

"He's right." The haste of my agreement surprised even me. "If the militar finds them, it will be absolute havoc."

Tristah and Killian conferred with only a look passed between them, and something dark and hideous churned in the pits of me.

There had been a time when Tristah and I had communicated so effortlessly. Now I could not read the intention behind the slope of her head, the tilt of her brows…whether these things spoke in favor of the Raiders or against them. And I wasn't certain what I would do if she decided they were worthy fodder for *our* escape.

At last, Tristah said, "We'll draw the militar's attention. You get your friends and get out your own way."

She shoved off the wall, and desperation seized my limbs; I thrust out a hand, snaring her under the arm.

It was now, or never.

"Come with us, Tristah," I pleaded. "We can escape together—escape all of this. We can finally be free."

"Free—where? Aboard a pirate vessel?" She jerked her chin at Ryker. "I know Captain Blackhand, Aly. He's as cutthroat as they come. He's certainly not helping you out of the goodness of his heart…so what is this, really?"

My mouth opened and shut; I cut a glance at Ryker, who rasped a hand along the nape of his neck—and said nothing in defense of himself.

"We…struck an accord. He took me for a ransom against the Del, yes, but I—*Tristah!*" Anger pulsed in my chest as she cursed aloud, snatching herself out of my grip; compulsion had me stepping after her, caring nothing that my plan spilled from my lips—even in front of Ryker. "We can escape *together*, once we've left Lucretzia and the Del behind—"

Incredulous laughter burst through the seam of her wretched, mirthless grin. "Why would I want that? Why would I *ever* want to flee with your *captor*? What selfish *madness* made you think I would risk sailing with you back toward Shadewyle, even if you had some grandiose plan to escape along the way?"

My teeth cut against my tongue, indignation rising from the core of me; but before I could speak in my own defense, Tristah spun to face me in full, jabbing a finger toward my heart

"I am not running. Not from them, not from anyone. And I don't need *rescuing*," she snarled. "I *am* the rescuer. I have a purpose here…I am serving and saving this country, the way *you* never cared to!"

The accusation rammed to the hilt in my chest—such a sharp pivot from her kind and knowing words the night we'd reunited. The truth of a rage she could no longer hide…the same abandonment that had flared in my chest when she and Killian spoke without a single uttered syllable.

Words were pretty things, crafted to reassure and placate. But fury…fury was honest. Fury did not powder itself with sugar and sweet reassurance.

This was the truth of Tristah's simmering resentment, this disdain offered in sideways glances and curt retorts these last several days. So I gave her the truth of mine, a surge of outrage that flowed hot and red as blood. "You said that you *understood.* You know what this country did to me—what it took from me."

"It takes from *everyone!*" Tears built behind Tristah's voice—not grief, but damp, smoldering wrath. "I'm not built to stand down and let it happen. Perhaps *you* can run while Amere-Del burns to ashes, but this is my *home*, Alyona. There are *my* people. If I don't fight for them, who will?"

Her home.

Her people.

We had been that for each other, once. But now…

Tristah had bound herself by blood and cause to the very heart of Amere-Del…and left no place in any of it for me. Not in her schemes. Not in her life. Not in this country or in the future she sought for it.

I had saved her from nothing. Instead, I'd endangered her plans. Brought the militar to her door.

"Tristah…" My voice was as shallow as my uneven breaths.

"You should never have come back." She flung the words at my feet like a curse. "You should never have found me. You broke your word, Alyona…now you may have broken *everything*."

She pivoted away from me, beckoning to Killian—the silent watcher.

"Muster the dissidents," she told him. "We shake the militar at the ports and move somewhere we can lay low and still do some good, until they've given up our scent."

"Don't walk away from me!" I surged after her. "*Tristah!*"

"You need to leave," she snarled over her shoulder, "before they find you. And so do I."

"Tris—"

"Go *home*, Alyona!" she barked, spinning back to face me; fury and heartbreak warred across the twist of her features. "And if you don't have one, find where that is. We're *finished*. Get out of my city before you do any more damage!"

With that, she hooked her cowl over her nose and mouth, turned again, and sprinted toward the faraway sounds of shouting and searching, Killian a shadow on her heels.

Neither of them looked back.

CHAPTER 61
THE GREATEST ADVENTURE

As the streets blurred past my feet, awash in the driving rain, all I knew was the heat of Ryker's hand wrapped around mine.

It was all that grounded me. All that was true and tangible in this world where Tristah had cast me out. Abandoned me. Accused me. And been horrifically *right* about it all.

Dimly, I wondered if perhaps I looked a bit like Addie had when she'd first stumbled into my shop…friendless. Deserted. Soaked through with more exhaustion than rain.

Yet as we fled toward the compound, Ryker's hold never wavered. His stride was sure, his focus set for his crew—those he would never forsake or abandon. And somehow, that undying loyalty which had made enemies of us when I'd learned the truth of his name and his intentions for me…it anchored me now. I clung to that lifeline as all the rest of the world I'd known slipped my reach, peeling away one piece at a time.

Tristah had thrown me aside.

Ryker did not let go.

And so I fled with him, each of us taking turns dragging the other down alleyways and sidestreets that had become familiar during our months in Bashir—in Tristah's city. Sometimes Ryker marked the militar presence ahead or aside; sometimes I did. And an unspoken trust built like the heat between our palms as we followed each other through one detour after another. Until, at long last, the militar presence began to thin on the street that snaked around the rear of the compound; their pistolshots and shouts to mark our maneuvers lessened, dimmed, dulled beneath the pouring rain.

That much, at least, Tristah had given me: a chance to run, as I always did. As I had run from Shadewyle. From the immigrants being arrested in Krylan. From Bastyan. From Lucretzia. From Ryker. From so many things, even Dorcas had seen that truth in me.

"Almost there," Ryker panted, giving my hand a sharp squeeze. "You get Cam and stick close to Siu, all right? I'll cover Gyddy and Rhea. Wilkes should have all our backs."

"Where will we go?" I wheezed, every breath shearing against my ribs like a planer on hard cheese. "Surely they're watching the roads from the city."

His smile burned like a brand in the night. "Pirate, sweetheart. Thought you'd figured it out by now…I don't use doors."

He whistled a few breathless notes of a familiar shanty, and absurdly, a smile kneaded the tense corners of my mouth.

"'Ay." Ryker fitted his fingers more tightly between mine, slowing as we jogged toward the compound. "Chin up, love. I've still got your back."

I opened my mouth to answer—then winced as lightning cut across the sky, paving the last few yards to the compound's outermost wall.

Not lightning.

The next bark of pistolshot half-deafened me. Ryker's stride hitched at the rain-dimmed echo, and mine followed fashion; but his hand dropped mine, then seized the back of my neck instead and thrust me along, his voice rougher than his grip beneath my hair. *Don't you bloody stop.*

My ears pulsed with a strange, tinny resonance, my boots slipping on the damp cobblestones, and still Ryker shoved me along—until all at once his hand slid from my neck.

"Keep moving!" he barked. "Get inside. *Go!* I'll catch up."

Disbelief snatched me around on heel. "Why in Ahim's name would I—?"

"*Lio.*"

He had never said my name that way before. A command. A plea.

He was the vision of the pirate captain at my back, arrayed against a faint haze of smoke, another cut of lightning. And yet he sagged against the compound's outer wall, shoulder dipped, one hand tucked beneath his coat.

"Sweetheart, you *do this*. For me," he croaked. "Run and don't look back."

His shoulder slipped, and he plunged to his knees.

"*Ryker!*"

The threads of my skirt shredded on the cobblestone as I tumbled down before him, splaying my hand to his back—and finding it tacky, his coat soaked with blood.

Horror choked me—horror doubled, foul and suffocating, when I gripped his collar and tilted him back on his knees only to expose a twin hole in his side, dripping crimson onto the cobblestones.

A shot blown straight through him, from back to front.

"*No!*" The sob wrenched from me, useless, tearing my voice. I had nothing else to give.

Ryker panted, one hand finding the wound at his front, the other fastening over the folds of my hip. "Lio—*go*—"

Wavering in my grip, he broke down against me, his forehead lolling in the crook of my neck, and the *weight* of him drove the terror from me in a shouted plea. "Ryker, no—*please*—"

"Run." His breaths were stilted and staggered and so full of agony, it stole what remained of my courage. Yet he kept pushing at me—pushing me *away*. "Run, Lio, you don't have time—"

"I'm not leaving you!" Panic bolted through my voice as his blood surged against my hand.

"Sweetheart, you *have* to."

"Not without you!" I freed his middle to grip his collar, hauling against the deadweight of him. "Get up—get on your feet—*Ryker, get on your feet!*"

I would never forget that he tried.

For me, he tried.

A drunken stirring of boots against cobblestones. A tenuous rattle of those powerful legs that had carried him across numerous ship decks, in utter command, devoid of fear…always, somehow, angling in my direction. And always, somehow, that was the direction I had hoped he would come.

His fingers wrapped my elbows. He supported himself against me, wobbled up to a half-bend…

And then he crumbled again. He slipped through my fingers and slammed into the street, rolling onto his back, agonized puffs of breath emerging in a stuttering, forceful "*Ha, ha, ha,*" over and over as he fought not to weep. Fought not to scream.

I crashed back down before him, blinded by terror, by the rain sopping my hair to my neck, by the tears that blurred across my eyes as I thrust my hands into the gritty hole torn into him.

Pistolshot. But who had *fired*? Why had they not descended on us by now?

"Ryker, get up, *please*…we're so close—don't you see?" My head spun as I whipped it toward the compound, dizzied by the smoke-scent on my clothes, the blood on my hands, his head on the cobblestones…dissident screams, far-off fires that blistered high, threatening to consume what was most precious in my world. "Lift your head, I need you to *look*…look how close we are! Gyddy will help you—*Gydeon!*"

I screamed for him, even knowing he couldn't hear me. That we *were* so close, and yet so far—*too* far.

"'Ay. 'Ay." Ryker's hand fumbled up my arm to my neck, finding and cradling my cheek. Pain blackened the depths of his stare, all but eclipsing the green and gray. "You know you're the greatest adventure I've ever had?"

A sob built and broke from me swifter than I could swallow it. I clutched his bloodstained hand to my cheek, gripping the folds of his shirt with the other. "Don't—Ryker, please, *don't—*"

"Touching. Truly."

That cold, venomous voice, issuing from an alley at my back.

The reek of pistol powder beaten down into the streets by the driving rain.

The precise shot through Ryker's back and side.

All of it, all at once, I understood. And I spun on my knees, just for a gauntleted slap to strike me full-palmed across the face, knocking me back against Ryker. My elbow drilled into his gut, and he arched and bellowed as agony at last broke free—and his arm flung up, fighting to wrap around me, to shield me, to draw me back against him as Lucretzia towered above us.

Our months apart had unraveled her. The stern knot of her silver-blond hair hung in ragged hanks, and the fury she had once tamed so well seethed from every pore as she beheld us—at her feet, where she had always liked me best.

"Stay *down*," she snarled. "Where you *belong*."

Ryker's arm flexed around me—a weak surge of tightening muscle. As if he pushed all the strength out of his body and into mine.

I planted my hand on his bent knee and shoved myself upright, so swiftly Lucretzia bowed back a single step. She gave an inch of ground to whatever she saw in my face—the wrath and ruination that pulsed from her handprint on my cheek, from Ryker's blood on my fingers.

She had shot Ryker.

She had shot *Ryker*.

"I am," I rasped, "*precisely* where I belong. Between you and him."

The barest, scoffing lilt of her lips. And then the Pale Viper struck again.

I did not see her hand lift, but I flinched at the *crack* of the firing pistol.

And the second shot struck Ryker, punching him backward into the street.

He did not even cry out.

He did not move again.

Shrieking with terror, with horror, with fury, I whipped toward him, falling to my knees, fumbling for his shirt collar, for the side of his neck, his name pouring from me in a ceaseless tide—and Lucretzia lashed out once more.

Her fingers hooked like fangs into my hair, nails ripping bloody gouges into my scalp. She lifted and spun me away as if I weighed nothing, my fingers tangling hopelessly in chained links and ripping the wheel pendant from around Ryker's neck.

And though I thrashed, beat on her body, whipped the chain of Ryker's pendant like a garrot at her face, she remained an adamant wall. She hauled me away like a rip current from that slump of black clothing in the street, blood pooling beneath him.

"*No!*" I screamed, clawing to free myself from the cage of her arms. "Ryker! Ryker, *please*, look at me, open your eyes—*no!* Let me go back to him! *Let me save him!*"

"As you allowed Athyna to be saved?" Lucretzia's retort was flat, but beneath it, sizzling satisfaction soaked every syllable.

And though I knew it was useless, hopeless, I screamed and screamed and *screamed* his name—a tether to tie me back to him. A hysterical hope that it was more than just my precarious sanity that made it seem as if his hand flexed and crawled across the cobblestones toward me.

As if he reached, even in unconsciousness—even in death—when Lucretzia dragged me away.

CHAPTER 62
A SHADOW OF NIGHT AND FURY

My sobs transformed to snarling somewhere between one street and the next. I was no longer a woman, no longer the runaway Delina. I was a storm wrapped in flesh, I was destruction made woman, a Seasplitter, a savage thing. I bit and kicked and hit until finally, *finally*, one of my blows landed true—on that familiar wound in Lucretzia's side.

She buckled, casting me away from her with a snarl. I slammed chest-first into the brick side of a building with such force all the breath burst from me— and it took the form of Ryker's name.

I spun and darted for the narrow alley mouth; but Lucretzia recovered in a heartbeat, catching me with a hand around the throat and thrusting me against the wall again.

"You will *never* learn, will you?" she scoffed.

"Why didn't you just *take me*?" I screamed in her face, spittle flecking from my lips. "You could have stolen me without anyone being the wiser!"

"Yes. But I had the pirate to repay for this." She shrugged forward one shoulder—the shoulder Ryker had blown through in Monsha—and a chill skimmed down my spine.

"How do you know what he—?"

"Korsa." She enunciated the word like a threat, and my spine arched of its own will back into the wall—cringing away from her. "I have set my feet to every path you've taken, Alyona. Or did you truly think yourself so cunning that you'd *evaded* me all this time? That you could have *ever* escaped, even that first day in Monsha, if I did not *let* you leave with *Captain Blackhand*?"

Her grip did not shift—yet it felt as if she pinched my windpipe shut altogether.

"Do you truly believe I taught you *all* of my tricks?" she sneered. "Every rope pattern, every knot?"

I fell back further in her grip, fixing her with a glare. "Not knowing your mind in its entirety has always been one of my greatest prides."

"And that is why you failed where Tristah succeeded." Lucretzia shifted her weight forward, her talon-tipped gloves scraping the brick on either side of my neck. "And why I am almost finished with you, now that you've shown me where she dwells."

Cold dread pulsed in my throat beneath the heel of her hand.

"Finished with me?" My voice was paper-thin, corroded from screaming. "You *have* me. What do you need with Tristah?"

Lucretzia settled back on her heels—and then, when I lifted up from the wall, she slammed me back again, those talons curling about to slice into the nape of my neck. I sealed my lips tight against a shriek as pain pierced and light sparkled across my eyes.

"Did you truly think," Lucretzia hissed, "that after what you did—after you *murdered* Athyna in cold blood—that I would ever allow *you* to sit in a seat of power over Amere-Del? I would not have abided that even if Zorast had ordered me on pain of death." Fingers tightening, she inclined until her nose nearly brushed mine. "This was always about Tristah. Her anger is her weakness and her strength, and she is your *perfect* decoy. You could never be strong enough to be malleated into something useful. Her, I was prepared to work with…to beat into the steel needed to hold this country together. But she was infinitely more clever about hiding herself, so I retrieved the one weapon that she could never defend against."

Horror doused my hate all at once.

The Del's Own Blade had never dulled. After all this time, she knew Tristah and I better than we knew ourselves. The way she'd watched us duel as girls, the secret codes we'd developed that she'd no doubt cracked, the hidden conversations and stolen dreams and wild wishes whispered into the snowfall tumbling over Shadewyle Castle, when we'd begged Ahim to set us free…

She had heard it all. Marked it. Tucked every secret away like arrows in her quiver, ready to be notched and fired at such a time as this.

Tristah had always been the more defiant between us. She had driven Lucretzia to rage far more times than I had ever dared. Lucretzia had not been able to hunt Tristah down …so instead, she'd made *me* her weapon, the same as she herself was Del Graven's.

The only person Tristah would have revealed herself to. The only one she thought Tristah would come for.

I had never been meant to take power from the Del. To return, to be sworn to Sorai, to ascend to the role of Della.

It was all Tristah. Tristah she wanted, Tristah meant for these places, these roles, these sufferings. My end was death, retribution for Athyna's murder. But Tristah's…

Tristah's, in Lucretzia's mind, was to become *me*.

It was cruel. It was horrific. It was utterly *brilliant*.

And I would never allow it to happen.

"You are wrong," I hissed, and Lucretzia blinked, tilting her head. "She and I are not what we once were. She will never reveal herself to you."

"Won't she?" Lucretzia's mouth unfurled into a heinous smirk. "I don't suppose she has *ever* heard you scream as you did when I dragged you away from Blackhand, has she?"

My breath caught.

"I am certain the whole *city* heard you." The Pale Viper withdrew her fingertips at last from my flesh. "It is only a matter of time until—"

Heat.

Fire.

An *eruption*.

This time, the explosion did not pepper me with glass or cast the world from its axis; it rained down fire and smoke from above, and when Lucretzia flinched, I seized my only chance; I tore forward, gasping as her gauntlet constricted, shearing against the angle of my neck and shoulder. But I persisted, ramming my shoulder into her sternum, twisting and ducking beneath her arm.

And when she pivoted with me, a thrown dagger pierced into her bicep, flinging her back against the alley wall.

I retreated two more steps, and a shadow of night and fury descended between us, shoving back her hood. Her stance was square, her feet planted— not a trace of the horror that had bent me at my first reunion with Lucretzia.

Tristah did not bow. She merely drew a second blade, watching with her back heaving as Lucretzia bared her teeth and wrenched the first knife free, wiping her own blood from its blade. "It's been quite some time, Tristah."

"Not long enough," Tristah spat. "Ten lifetimes would not be long enough rid of you, Viper."

Glee sparked along the slide of Lucretzia's smile. "I see you've made a manifestation of that fire in you."

"My fire is not something for you to remark on." Tristah's tone softened, but the metal edge honed sharper. "Or to control."

"Isn't it?"

"Tristah," I rasped, "it's you she wants, not—"

"I know. I heard." Hate splintered through those short, clipped words. "I'm sorry you were caught in the middle of this, Aly. It's time to get yourself out of the game."

My pulse thundered in my ears. "You can't do this alone."

"But you can't do it at all." Tristah shifted her weight, drawing another blade. "I like my chances better than you might think. And I have been waiting *years* for this."

"Likewise." Lucretzia pushed up from the wall.

"Go, Aly!" Laying her blades back against her arms, Tristah squared up to Lucretzia—utterly fearless. A revolutionary built of vengeance. "She is *mine*."

"Tris—"

"Get to your friends. Ember is with them." She spared me one swift glance over her shoulder. "I'll be right behind you."

I did not want to run again.

I did not want to leave two friends in a single night.

But I knew this battleground, this dance they'd sunk into…I had maneuvered its steps until my feet bled, and I was no longer fit for that ballroom. To Tristah, I would be a liability. To Lucretzia, a target. I was unarmed. And somewhere in these rain-drenched city streets, bleeding, dying, if not already dead…

Ryker.

"You come back to me," I whispered—the same command Tristah and I had always breathed when one or the other was dragged off to training alone, or to endless council sessions.

The barest smile grazed her mouth. "*Go.*"

Then she lunged to meet Lucretzia, while I tore from the sidestreet—my ears ringing with the slam of blades shrieking along their edges, of panted, howling battle-cries as the friend I loved with so much of me and the woman I despised with all the rest went to a war of their mutual craving.

My breaths slashed up from my chest, panic tearing me two ways with every stride—on the road I took, and the one back to Tristah. If Killian indeed waited at the compound with the Raiders, then I would find him…I would send him back to help her. I had scarcely seen them in combat together, yet what little I had witnessed left no doubt: together, they would be a match for the Pale Viper. Two against one was not always enough for Lucretzia—Tristah and I were living proof of that—but if anyone could best her, it was them.

So I ran. For Tristah, and for…

"*Ryker!*" I cried out his name when I slid back into the street where I'd left him, where Lucretzia had dragged me away—

And I slammed to a halt.

There was no crumbled Captain's form huddled on the stones.

The blood remained. So much blood, I nearly choked at the sight of it. Nearly spilled the contents of my heaving, havocked insides to join it.

But he was not there.

"No," I panted, spinning a full circle; my scarlet-stained fingers knotted into the fabric of my torn, sodden skirts, and my body bent of its own accord, my spine curling into the sob of his name. "*Bash!*"

Again and again, I screamed for him; but if he had dragged himself away somewhere for shelter, to tend those horrific wounds, then he did not hear me. He did not call back to me, even when his name broke and spilled over my rain-numb lips like a prayer to Ahim. A plea for mercy to the torrential sky.

When my voice failed me…that was when I moved. Shoving my feet into a jog, I splashed through his blood and tore for the compound, winging around its far side, fumbling out the key I had worn around my neck since the day we arrived in Bashir. While I worked the door, I was already screaming for Gydeon. Already begging him to help me, telling him I needed him, I needed him, *please.*

My hands shook and slipped and fumbled a half-dozen times before I managed to enter the compound, and then I stumbled toward our own sealed, private courtyard, sliding the key into its lock—

And before I even twisted my wrist, the door gave way, jolting inward on broken hinges.

My arm swung limp at my side. I could not scream, or shout, or do anything but stare at the fresh horror that awaited beyond.

Our sanctuary lay in ruin. Every tent was toppled, every tree gouged with blademarks and punched through with lead holes. Siu's fine clothes and paints were dumped everywhere like sails shredded from the masts. Rhea's prized fiddle lay smashed into splinters, the bow warped and bent. Wilkes's weapons, Gydeon's tinctures and salves, Cam's candies—

"*No!*" Howling in desperate fury, I bolted for the center of the courtyard. "Gyddy! Siu? *Camden!*"

No replies. Not a whisper of voices.

"Please, please, please…" I choked breathless prayers to Ahim as I kicked and dragged aside the canvas tents, searching for some sign, *any* sign of them.

And when the answer to those prayers came, it was in the toss of the tent that Rhea and Wilkes had shared after the rest of the crew left us, batch by batch. They came in the form of a pale, freckled arm, outcast, bloodstained. Fiddle-friendly fingers bent, broken, crushed.

I stumbled backward from Rhea's corpse while it was still half-buried, breaking down to my knees in the center of the ransacked courtyard where we had danced to her music—those sweet, haunting, romantic notes I would never hear played again. Because she lay dead in the tangle of burlap and ties, blood branching out into the courtyard cracks all around her.

And in the center of her chest stuck out the dagger we had stolen from Lucretzia. That I had used to defend Gydeon in Korsa.

It was nailed into her heart like a warning. Like a testament. Like a threat and a challenge.

Though I was weeping so hard I could see no more than a lick of light along the blade, I hauled myself to Rhea's side on hands and knees and wrenched the weapon free, gasping apologies to the sweet musician who had not deserved any of this. Who had only yearned for sacred halls and columned courtyards to play her family's heirloom instrument in.

And then I shoved myself backward until my shoulders and spine struck the wall; I huddled against it, soaked in rain, my eyes fixed on Rhea. Shock numbed everything…every pain, every fear, every thought.

All but one.

They were gone. They were all gone.

Gydeon and Siu. Wilkes and Camden. Rhea. Even Killian.

Ryker.

Ryker.

Ryker.

With Gydeon vanished…it was impossible he had survived those wounds. I was not even certain he had survived the second pistolshot at all.

Because of me. Because of Tristah.

Because of *me.*

I waited all that night, sitting amongst the ruins of the compound, Ryker's pendant draped between my shaking fingers, the militar dagger clutched in my fist—readier than I had ever been to drive it into Lucretzia's heart if she dared show her face again.

But she did not come for me.

And neither did Tristah.

CHAPTER 63
ON THE RUN

The cold, cruel light of dawn found me on the road to Port Krait.

I could linger no longer—not with the militar still on the hunt. So I gathered what few supplies were left to me and abandoned the courtyard at last, dodging the eyes of the city watch and the murmuring marketers, my ears catching flakes of gossip like spoiled coconut melting against my tongue—each bit rancid and nauseating.

They spoke of pirates seen throughout the city the night before.

Of the militar hunting ruthlessly for dissenters.

Of Ember and the Incendiary, caught up in it all.

Of pistolshots and screams that had people locking their doors and windows, praying to Ahim for salvation. Some still refused to emerge today.

In the gray of dawn, I crept out of the city by rooftop vaults and a seam I found in the outer wall, walking and humming a shanty as familiar as the Monshan countryside and the ivy-tressed stone where Ryker and I had slipped away in the dark together. I wept as I hummed it, staggering the notes; but I still found the way out to the song I'd heard all those months ago. That he'd whistled to me last night.

And then I was running for Port Krait—and when I reached it, turning aside for the crags where Kory had told me the rowboats were stashed. I found them after a half-day of searching, moored in a cleft within the rock; and there I curled up in the belly of the boat to sleep.

I had not closed my eyes in two days. And that was the only reason I was able to drift off at all, even into a fitful in-between of nightmares where Lucretzia lurked and Ryker and Tristah died over and over, while pirates leered and laughed and carved the Raiders into pieces.

Waking had never been such a relief, though I came back to the empty world with tearstained cheeks and hands that trembled while they fumbled up to grip Ryker's wheel pendant—hanging warm and reassuring as a kiss pressed between my collarbones.

I could not pause. I could not think. I could only act.

With what little strength had returned, I cut the rowboat loose and aimed its prow across Weyval Basin. And I rowed for Anoram.

Singular purpose sustained me through the days of traveling across the Basin. When the rations of hardtack and dried beef I dug up from below the rowboat seat and even the bread I'd rummaged from the courtyard tasted of ash on my tongue, I reminded myself I had a cause. A task. A last good thing I could do, that I *must* do.

I had to reach Klem and her brothers, and Nella and Maryon, and Wyst and Brant. All the rest of the crew. I had to warn them of the blade I'd found in Rhea's chest and what it meant.

We had to do something.

And Klem had to know that, until we found Siu—presuming she still lived—Klem herself was Captain.

I rowed until the bandages on my forearms unraveled to nothing, revealing the reddish marring from glass shards beneath. Until the muscles in my back and shoulders spent themselves to their limits and began to fray. Until pain, not grief, kept me awake, slumped over against the oars as I fought the current that threatened to carry me far from my heading.

I did not even know the heading well; I only knew the Della's lessons and Klem's maps and the sparse navigation she had taught me—almost as if it were a dare that I fail it—in exchange for the dice-throwing I'd shown her in Bashir.

It was by the larger ships that I found my way at last—when, after nearly a week of rowing, I spotted their looming bodies and three masts churning across the Basin. Many of them dotted the horizon, all bound in a single direction.

So I aimed my course to theirs, and rowed with all my might.

And at long last, I reached Port Tamsay…and beyond it, the imperious heights of Anoram.

CHAPTER 64
WAR ON THE DOCKS

Port Tamsay was not as far from the Anoram as Port Krait was from Bashir; I was already cast in the shadows of the city's many minaret towers when I ran aground at the Weyval's edge, lashing my rowboat to a bollard and scouting down the lengthy sweep of docks with itching, stinging eyes.

I caught no glimpse of *The Dread Singer's* familiar body, hidden in its guise…nor had I ever thought I would ache so desperately for a hint of the ship that had once been my prison. But I refused to give sway to fear as I hastened down the docks, dodging countless sailors marching to their own ships or merchants unloading their wares. It was a large port, after all; they might be docked further along. Klem might have hidden the ship in some inland cove.

I wouldn't panic. I needed a clear head to tell my story when I found them.

First, I scoured the docks; finding no flicker of familiar faces in the crowds or among the ships themselves, I turned with the tide of merchants down the short path between the port's edge and the breadth of Anoram.

Grief sickened my heart as I slipped into the city full of high, arched footpaths and broad steps leading up to greater and greater spans of buildings above. Like Monsha, this city's layers were richly frosted with mercantiles and hawkers and vendors. Every street corner burst with color and light—streamers, garlands, bright attire, and papered handcarts. Music echoed around the twists in the road, and often I had to halt while folk danced by, arms linked, laughing.

Their joy hardly grazed by the tips of my boots. I could only think how Tristah must have loved the music that beat in the blood of this city; how Rhea would have gloried in it just as much, joining her fiddle to the countless quartets playing on the street corners. How Siu would have relished the colors, the artful murals dripping on brick and stone…and how Gydeon would've been thrilled simply to see his wife so full of joy. How Camden would've sickened himself on the candies and dances. How Wilkes would have watched over it all with a grin, keeping close to Rhea's side.

How Ryker had vowed to bring me here, once, when we'd strolled back from *The Love of the Loaf*. How he'd sworn I would love it, this image he'd sketched with words of a city I had never visited…and how I'd believed him. That he would one day take me to the most infamous bakery in the Southlands, founded here in Anoram, and buy me whatever pastries I wished.

My feet ached to go to there, to seek solace and refuge in the smells of dough and sugar…in the echoes of an unkept promise. Not the first he had broken; yet somehow, now, it was the only lie that mattered anymore. The only oath he had not severed of his own choice.

So I kept my half of it for us both.

The tightness in the base of my throat unknotted for the first time in a week when I slipped into the pearlescent confines of the infamous *Sugared Starlight* bakery. My hands, blistered and splinter-riddled from working the oars, pulsed with need rather than dull anguish this time—the desire to bury themselves in dough. To knead my problems away.

But my fears and my heartache and my *grief* could not be solved by working even the finest pastry mix. Not this time.

I followed my rumbling stomach's wild cravings to the counter and ordered a pair of pastries and a hot dessert tea from the middle-aged baker there; then I shrank back into the amalgamation of customers loitering at the tables and awaiting their own delicacies and drinks. And I did as I had done in Shadewyle, and Krylan, and aboard both *The Athalion* and *The Dread Singer*.

I listened.

In the Del's regime, I had been bidden always to make my voice known—in council sessions and among the Del's supporters and detractors alike. Only in the privacy of our own wing of the castle had my voice been suppressed, silenced with threats—and the truth—of pain. I had become a barreling mouthpiece of the regime, little different from Algernon Sorai…that covetous betrayer on whose head all of my griefs now hung.

Curling my fists around the thought of him, I brought his name close and shoved it out from me again. And I focused on the conversations swirling all around me.

The Secret Ingredient had been more a hive for gossip than any public house or tavern; it had always amused me how I'd often had more scintillating stories to tell from my shop than Addie did from *The Tiller's Tankard*. And *The Sugared Starlight* was no different.

When I pressed my back to the counter and shut my eyes, an absolute havoc of sound assailed my ears. Fretting about waning jobs; concerns over whether the Everreach would shut; the lack of fresh produce being sailed downriver from the Northlands and whether that indicated the regime's tightening fist, or that the Northlands mercantilists themselves were growing wary of their southerly neighbors who were often given to dissidence.

Infedelious spouses. Squabbling sisters. Men who'd challenged one another to duels of blade or pistol. All the gossip hummed around me, raising a sickening lump in my throat.

How long ago had I smiled at these conversations as they'd floated to me from the eager customers awaiting my wares? How could my hands have become so empty now, and my heart—

It gave a painful, unsteady thump against the pendant hanging between my breasts, sharpening all of my senses at once.

And that was when I heard it.

"Bashir is a—"

The name of that city caught my attention like a loose apron thread snagging on a splinter. My eyes popped wide, and I fixed my stare on the floor as I angled my body toward the conversers: a man and a woman dressed in sailing attire, sharing a scone further down the counter.

Whatever the woman had said of Bashir, the sudden racing of my heart had smothered it; when I soothed that aching rhythm and bent back into listening, the man was shaking his head.

"No worse than what we had here," he scoffed. "Did you hear that ruckus near the docks a few days ago? Thought the Del had sent his militar to war out the dissidents for good, the fight that broke out…"

Dread folded around every joint, curling my body in on itself. Clutching the counter tightly behind me, I strained to listen.

"I heard about it," the woman conceded. "Though I was across the city at the time. What was it, anyhow? Some sort of riot at the docks—a fight between a couple of crews?"

"That's the word. Though if you believe the rumors, one of them was flying a pirate flag."

I no longer felt the heat of the other patrons pressing in around me. My hunger perished. Horror filled every bit of me that had ever known a craving, a want, a need of any kind.

Ahim, have mercy—not this, not this—

I had suspected our enemies were in Bashir…the dagger in my belt, cleaned of Rhea's blood, was proof of that. But the crew that had been *here*, in Port Tamsay, in Anoram…

They should have been *safe*.

"A pirate attack? *Here?*" the woman yelped—then quieted to a hoarse whisper when the man shushed her. "Why hasn't the city council said anything?"

"Think they're hoping it's all blown by." He sipped his tea. "They raided just one ship in port, then tore off for the river mouth up near Pyrath with their chains in it like their sails were on fire. No one's seen 'em since."

"Were there any losses? Casualties?"

"A few, by the sound of it. Heard whoever survived was taken to the infirmary, but the damage at the docks has the whole west side under repairs."

"Thank Ahim we docked on the east—"

Heart in my throat, I abandoned eavesdropping to snag the baker's sleeve as she set my pastries and tea before me; she froze, glancing from my hand to my face. At whatever she saw there, she paled, setting aside my things to squeeze my hand instead. "Are you all right, love?"

"Please," I choked. "Where can I find the city's infirmary?"

CHAPTER 65
TAKE THEM BACK

he Della had insisted we visit Shadewyle's infirmaries now and again—a charlatan show of support for the people. I doubted her vacant smile had fooled any of the ill and injured we'd tried to cheer up. She had refused to hold sickened hands, had grimaced at bloodstains peeking through bandages. The wards for the children she had avoided altogether, her face twisting into an indescribable rictus of emotion whenever she heard an infant's wail echoing through the stone halls.

The infirmaries always cleaved my skin to my bones, unease and overwhelm gumming up my body. I had desperately counted down the minutes I was forced to spend in them, the onslaught of heartbreak and suffering leaving me clammy and sweating. So many hurts and needs I'd ached to soothe…and been powerless to help.

Knowing the Del only sent us to visit those who had suffered from dissident riots and pockets of uprising made it worse. All of it had been a reminder of my parents, of Monsha, of what I had lost and what all of Amere-Del stood to lose. What he had hoped I would crush with my own cruelty.

But Tristah had thrived in those places.

Some gentleness had emerged from the scowling visage she often wore in the Della's presence. We had never gone together, only she as my decoy when my attempts at feigning my own sickness had spared me the visits. But I had heard the Della lecture her afterward of how much time she wasted holding arthritic, fragile hands, stroking sweaty hair from ashen brows, murmuring words of peace and comfort, praying and joking and soothing wherever she could.

Tristah had made love her armor inside halls of sickness and suffering and death. So I did the same; sustained on the memory of my friend, I entered

Anoram's public infirmary and begged the attending healer to show me anyone who had been brought in from the skirmish at the docks.

"It was not a pretty encounter," the man warned, thrusting his spectacles up the severe slope of his nose and fixing me with an uneasy look over the broad wooden counter at the entrance. "Are you certain you——?"

"I'm certain," I croaked. "Show me."

Even then, I was not prepared for how another corner of my heart fractured when the man escorted me to a remote corner of the infirmary——dingy and dark, lit only by a single lantern alongside a bed, hidden behind a veil. I was too late to stop the sob that rolled up my throat, and only scarcely smothered it with my hand when the physician towed the curtain aside to reveal One-Pot Willy twitching and groaning feverishly on that lonely bed.

Both of his legs were gone below the knee, his hands severed at the wrists.

"I'm so sorry," the physician murmured, his broad fingers covering my shoulder. "It will be soon. He came to us this way, and the loss of blood was…" He tapered off at the shudder that rocked through me, entirely beyond my control. "Is he family?"

The sob found its way out between my fingers in a shattering croak: "*Yes.*"

Then I went to Willy, shrugging off the healer's grip, my feet bonding to the cold infirmary stones and separating painfully with every step. I wept in earnest before I even reached the bedside, at war within myself against fear, against revulsion, against hate and sorrow and that bottomless well of grief first torn through the middle of me when Ryker had fallen to the street.

I was despicably glad it was not him on this bed. I was heartbroken it was not, because we had not said goodbye. *I* had not said any of the things I should have offered so much sooner. To him. To the whole crew.

I lowered myself onto the edge of the bed, shoving away my own sickened cowardice in favor of cradling the swaddled stump of Willy's left forearm in both hands. "Willy?"

He groaned and shuddered, tears leaking from the corners of his eyes, disappearing into the many soft, wrinkled folds around them. "Let me die, please, *please*, I beg you, just let me *die*——"

And there, in the break of that soft voice that had praised my efforts in the *Singer's* galley, that had marveled at my work and also taught me techniques I had never known before of kneading and mixing and storing and inspiring my craft…in that crack through his strength, I found the first wisp of mine.

Encircling his arm more firmly, I shifted until the bend of my leg braced gently to the ruined stumps of his. "Willy, it's Lio. I came to find you."

At the sound of my name, his rapid, jerking breaths eased a bit. His lashes flickered, and his eyes peeled open, finding me down the length of himself. His chest hurtled upward and sank again—halfway to a chuckle. Or a sob. "Lio, girl. By my…what—how—?"

"Shh." I cradled his weatherworn cheek in one hand, whiskers tickling my palm. "I'm here, that's all that matters."

"No. No, it—the crew, the crew's—"

"Taken. By the Leeches," I choked, and he answered with a swift blink. "I know. They came to Bashir first."

His neck flexed, his throat working harshly. "Captain—?"

He could not frame the question. He already knew that, had Ryker escaped—had he *lived*—he would be here in my place. He would have perhaps even gathered the old sailor into his arms and rocked him like the sea, to the threshold of this life and beyond it.

How I wished I could've begged Ryker to hold *me* now. To be a fortress, a strength, a bastion while I broke.

But I had been breaking alone for a week now. Clutching his pendant and clinging to that last surge of strength that I'd felt in his arm around me, before Lucretzia's second shot had landed true.

"They're all gone." My tremulous whimper would have sent Lucretzia into fits. I no longer cared.

My friends. The *Singer's* crew. Tristah and Killian. *Ryker*.

They were *gone*.

"I'm so glad I found you." I shifted nearer to Willy—the only friend who remained in this world torn to tatters by Lucretzia's treachery, by my own mistakes and failings. "I do not know what I would do if—"

"Find them."

In a blink, startled disbelief cleared the haze from my eyes. I stared at the old man, whose breathing grew more labored by the moment—whose gaze had sharpened to the daggered intensity I had come to expect from every Raider. "Willy, I…I'm only…"

A woman alone. A Delina turned baker. A piece in the game Lucretzia had played against *Tristah*, without either of us knowing, all this time.

"Shh, girl." His forearm flexed weakly in my grip. "What you are is good. And…it's strong. It's what this world needs now. What…what the Captain's needed, long as I've known him."

Fresh tears leaked down the sides of my nose. "Ryker is gone, Willy."

"Aye. He…he's been gone since he…brought you aboard." A barest twitch of his snow-white lips. "You're a world-shaper, Lio, girl. You're…better than the—the best of them." He broke off, struggled for a breath, a swallow, his eyes fighting every blink to remain open. "You take the left path where the…the Sennesole branches. Get through…the mountains. You show them what a baker with steel in her…in her mix is…is made of."

The last three words were nearly a whisper; I had to bend nearer to hear them, my fingertips catching his tears as they slid down his cheeks.

"You make them *pay*."

His breath gusted against my cheek.

He did not draw another.

Horror seared in my throat; I wrenched back, slipping from the edge of the cot, staggering backward through the curtain. Only with the press of both hands did I smother my sobs—and even then, one emerged when I cried for the healer.

I did not wait to hear the pronouncement. I did not wait for another word of death to join the many stuck to the surface of my heart.

When the healer came, I fled.

I only made it down the infirmary's steps before I broke. Before my legs refused to carry me; before the sensation of Willy's last breath on my cheek swept my feet from under me.

My shoulder scraped against the building's sun-warmed bricks, and I buckled into the outer tower, pressing my back against it.

And I gave over to the grief I had kept at bay since the compound.

I wept for Willy. I sobbed aloud for Ryker. I cried for the crew that had counted me among their own, despite all the complicated things between us.

I wept for Tristah, taken by a fate worse than death…back to the place I had sworn I would never allow either of us to go.

I wept at how vast and impossible it all seemed, and how utterly alone I was…alone with Willy's dying words taking root in my heart.

And I wept—in rage, in self-deprecation—over how some selfish piece of me still pleaded to run.

For the first time since the night my life in Mithra-Sha had gone up in fireworks, no one pursued me. Not Lucretzia, not pirate crews, not anyone at all. I could slip away, be forgotten, begin anew.

And yet…

That new life no longer held the appeal it once had. It was a hollow road, reeking of heartache. A new life in a new land offered nothing if I had no one to start it with. To *share* it with.

Someone like Tristah. Like Addie.

Like Ryker.

I had been running for years. Running away from something. Away from everything.

I wanted—I *needed*—something to run *toward*.

Not a new life, but the pieces of one I had already begun to build…without ever fully intending to. A perfect, powerful mix I had stumbled upon through serendipity, a new creation born of a misread recipe.

And it was out there. Beckoning me, like a call across seas and borders.

To run toward Korsa.

To run toward Shadewyle.

Toward Tristah. Toward Siu and Gydeon and Camden. Toward Wilkes and the Drace siblings. Toward whoever was left.

Toward the truth of who *I* was.

Baker. Schemer. Caretaker. Survivor. Rescuer of hurt and forgotten and broken things. Like this patchwork crew I had come to care for, and the Captain I'd begged Lucretzia to let me save—a mercy she had denied me, because she knew. She *knew*.

Because she had heard me scream for him like I had never screamed for anyone in my life.

I had run from him, from this warm, wishful thing growing within me, until it was too late. And it might still be too late.

But for him…for Bastyan Atreyon, for Ryker Kassian, who had sold every last bit of himself to save the crew he loved, and even still struggled with that choice, because he had come to care for *me*, as well…

I could change course. I could run a different race. I could finally run *toward* something instead.

For his sake. For theirs. For mine.

Alyona Graven had fled from everything. But Lionyra Vara had faced cruelty and hate and set it alight with fireworks. Sent it all up in flame.

I had burned the world for Audra Jashowin…the first friend I had made since Tristah. And I was depths-blasted ready to do it again, for the unlikely friends I had found in the months since.

Eyes wide open.

I forced my stinging eyes wide. I blinked and blinked until the film of tears cleared…

And in its place settled a haze of red.

Take power where you can.

I was not coming to take power.

Power was already *in* me. Power…rage…love…they curled my fists against the infirmary's bricks. Set me back on my feet, steadfast beneath me.

For the first time in too many months, I stood firm on my own chosen path. And the harms of the world broke around me like the tides that had carried me this far.

I was not coming to take power.

Lucretzia and these blasted pirates had taken what was mine. My crew. My friends.

My people.

I was coming to take it *all*.

CHAPTER 66
LONELY ROADS AND WORDLESS PRAYERS

There were roads through Amere-Del only known to the ruling regime…and to those formerly part of it.

The water would have provided a more direct route…but also a more crowded one. With the Leeches' warning belted to my waist, I had no desire to find myself aboard another shrouded pirate vessel. I had no intention of returning to Korsa on anyone's terms but mine.

So I went by horseback instead, astride a mount I commandeered from Port Tamsay, flying from its furthest reaches in the dead of dark before the stallion could be missed from the stockyards. And though it had been years since I'd ridden, I found my seat as sure in the saddle as the horse found his footing through the craggy passes carved out by the paranoia of the Graven regime, long before Zorast's particular breed of fear had rotted the country.

These were lonely, isolated paths, winding through the higher parts of the Abbra Foothills and the lower passes of the Barradir Highlands, hewn out for the Graven family to escape beyond the western border to the country of Zandrae-Rath, should revolt ever come about in earnest. I only ate what I could gather and trap; it did not fill me, but that was just as well. Grief and rage left little room for appetite.

And all that time, traversing through narrow, dug-out creases that unraveled mile by mile through the grueling mountains, crossing streams and galloping across level meadows where I could at last give the horse his head, I spoke only to him…and to Ahim.

I prayed for mercy for the crew. Prayed that they would survive, somehow, until I could reach them.

I prayed for Tristah, likely to arrive at Shadewyle any day; that she would evade the Del's wrath for her deeds as the Incendiary, and cling to her life and her strength until I came for her.

I prayed for Ryker, his pendant clutched in my fist; and these prayers had no words, only a desperate, pleading hope, a wish that somehow, *somehow*, he lived. And that, if he did not, some portion of his reckless, wild spirit lingered with me, and would remain when I infiltrated the pirate haven to save those he cared for most.

I prayed so long most days that I lost my voice before the last light faded. And even then, I kept hoping. Wishing. Clinging to that ship's wheel to keep my head above grief's thrashing waves.

And then at long last—after nearly a month of traveling alone, having seen not another face in all that time—I reached the harbor of my intentions.

I emerged from a lonely path arching through a splinter of the Highlands, my body days unbathed, my belly filled with a hunger nothing could slake, my scarred fingers woven into the reins so tightly they had all but forgotten the softness of kneading dough; and yet they still recalled the precise slickness of Ryker's blood imprinted on every callous, the heat of Willy's ruined flesh, the brand of the wheel that hung against my throat.

And finally, through stinging eyes, I gazed down again into the city of my birth.

I had returned to Monsha.

CHAPTER 67
IN THE HEART OF MONSHA

No one knew the former Delina had made her return to the greatest trade city in Amere-Del. And I did not intend that to change; so I exchanged the stallion for a small craft and rowed across the bay's splendid waters, seeking a cove both familiar and strange.

I found it after nearly a full day's searching, entering it at sunset to find it as empty as the hollow center of my chest. I knew its etchings best as they had looked in the shadows of night, framed in silver, cleverly cloaking the pirate Captain who'd beckoned me to leap with him.

And, guided by the memory of the Bastyan I had known then, I dragged myself up the cliff from which we'd dove to meet the *Singer*.

I looked back for only a moment at the quiet cove; and that was all it took to build tears in my eyes.

I entered Monsha through the seam in the outer wall, humming a tune that freed those tears; when I walked in the glistering dark, I let them fall. Let them soothe like rainfall, though they healed nothing. Mended nothing.

When I emerged on the far side of the sliver in the stone, I dried them, facing up the hill toward the sprawl of Monsha high above.

And then the truth of my work began.

Monsha was not how we had left it.

That much became evident within a handful of days; simmering tensions had bubbled over in a frothing vat of rage. Streets I had known since childhood were cordoned off, forcing my feet to learn new paths; few doors were unbarred and even fewer windows unshuttered in the residential areas. Suspicious eyes gathered imaginary enemies across avenues as neighbors envisioned dissidence or misplaced loyalty among those with whom they'd once cheerily shared gossip and food and all the things of life.

Talk floated like flour dust flung into the wind—that the Everreach would soon be collapsed. That the Del would then start shutting other ports, trapping dissidents wherever he found them, crushing them utterly. The rumors I had heard aboard *The Athalion* and in whispers in Anoram now dripped in tones of fear or fury from nearly every mouth in Monsha. And I knew precisely why these speculations and threats against the dissidents had become such a public affair.

The Del was punishing Tristah.

He knew by now the truth of who she was; and it seemed, if he would not put her to death for her defiance, then he would ensure there was no defiance left for her, or for those who called upon the Incendiary's name.

For days—and then a week—and then longer—I scoured the city on the heels of those rumors, making my bed in a squalid home for penniless sailors; I certainly looked the part, and no one glanced twice at me…not with the dagger I wore, which marked me a conqueror of some high-ranking militar official. And not with the good I did for them, either.

Using the talents I had gathered in Krylan and aboard *The Athalion* and the *Singer*, I mended bits and pieces of the boarding house. I sewed and darned, I chiseled and hammered and varnished. And I listened…to talk from the other sailors who shared the five small rooms with their numerous cots. To gossip floating in through the cracked shutters, rambled out at the fishmongers with whom we shared this stretch of street…and to whom we owed the perpetual reek of fish that clung to the walls, the linens, and the skin and clothing of everyone who stayed in the house.

No whispers reeked of hidden piracy. Nor did my scouting along the docks reveal a single ship that had the *Singer's* look from port—a craft in disguise.

The pirates seemed to be avoiding Monsha altogether. Was that because of the threat to the Everreach? The talk of the Del's mounting paranoia and eagerness to quell any uprising? Or were they perhaps otherwise occupied—

distracted by a captured crew to whom some wicked imitation of justice was being dealt, day by day?

Despair spoiled, sour and thick, in my stomach as a fortnight in Monsha approached without a sprinkle of promise. Every day I wasted seeking to secure passage was another day nearer to finding all of the Raiders dead—if they were not already. And every day was another promise broken to Tristah…another sunrise and sunset she was forced to endure alone in Shadewyle Castle.

The beginning of my second week in the city dawned bleak, and my outlook even bleaker; the ceaseless storm of conversation near the docks was more stifling than it had ever been, and another fruitless hunt revealed nothing of promise…no ship that might be eager to sail forbidden paths for whatever false promise of merits I could muster.

Seated on the end of a crumbling wharf far from those where ships still docked, I buried my sunburned face in one hand; with the other, I dragged Ryker's pendant along its chain.

If I could not find a ship, I would simply have to row in the boat still tied off at the cove. But the way was mercilessly long, and the only path I knew was a vague imprint of Willy's dying breaths…not a clear map, but the faintest impression of one.

"Perhaps I should travel to Shadewyle first," I muttered. "Free Tristah, and then…"

The notion shriveled on my tongue.

Creeping out of the castle the first time had been a feat balanced between skill and fortune. Creeping *in*, when Zorast's distrust had only grown, with Tristah in his grasp and Lucretzia once again at his side…

It would be impossible. I needed more bodies…distractions. Trusted friends at my back.

A whisper of a cruel memory teased against the shell of my ear as the wind blew against my hair, brushing it back from my brow like a four-fingered hand.

Chin up, love. I've still got your back.

A furious sob bobbed at the base of my throat. Lifting my head and fixing my gaze across the swaying tides of Monsha's harbor, I clutched the wheel pendant until its spokes sank into my palm. "Merciful Ahim, if you can hear the prayers of a runaway Delina…I need you now," I whispered into the caress of the wind. "I know what I must do. But *how* to do it…"

No more words would come; nor did any answer breathe back on the settling breeze.

The lump doubled in my throat, and I released the pendant to push myself to my feet.

Back to the markets it was, then. Back to rumors and gossip and the hope that somewhere, the news might turn in my favor.

Dense crowds closed around me as I reentered Monsha, my body folding into the gaps between all the sailors and marketers. Wherever I stepped, fresh conversation assailed my ears—hawking, haggling, arguments, threats, fears, prayers—

"Flipping *Luck*! Lio, is that *you*?"

I slammed to a halt at that Mithran curse, heedless all at once of the bodies that crashed into me and the Ameresh insults they flung my way. All the sound left my ears but that voice.

That *voice*—

A voice of hammock beds and the gift of clothing, card and dice games and a ship that had felt like both prison and refuge. A voice of laughter and dances and an offer of friendship when I had thought my chances of it had fled forever.

I spun toward the echo of that cry, hardly able to breathe. "*Reinera?*"

And all at once the crowd broke between a shove of muscle-banded arms, and there she was—her shaggy, pepper-dark hair grown out to the base of her shoulders, her face gaunter than I remembered, her skin marked with healing scars that sketched down from her cheek to her neck and shoulder, disappearing into the collar of her shirt.

But she was *here*. Somehow, impossibly, in the last place I had seen her, that I had ever thought I *would* see her…

Reinera had found me.

Ahim had heard me, after all.

With a whooping cry, she threw her arms around me, crushing me to her chest. And all at once, for the first time since Willy's last breath had cooled against my cheek—

I was not alone in the world.

CHAPTER 68
SAILORS ADRIFT

My shock did not abate after Reinera found me.

Instead, it grew when she unwound her arms from around me, only to guide me by the arm to a boarding house adjacent to the city infirmary. There she towed me inside, shouting people up from the tables scattered about the lower parlor…a room so like the *Pearl* with its mercantile booth and serving counter, the familiarity knocked the breath from me.

I had no chance to reclaim it before Syd, Lanah, Hasser, Noveen, and a handful of the crew all rushed to greet us; stunned, delighted cries heralded their backslapping arrival, and then I was engulfed in embrace after embrace, each one squeezing tears nearer and nearer to the surface of my eyes.

"I just—I can hardly believe—" was all I managed to gasp out; peering about the room, I spotted a handful of other crewmembers still seated…far more somber than during our voyage together. Their greetings were halfhearted; a flip of the hand, a crooked, off-kilter smile.

The parlor lacked a certain presence. A boisterousness chiseling at the edge of my focus.

"Why are all of you *here*?" I demanded. "Where is Julas?"

And that was when it happened.

The drop of their shoulders, the aversion of their gazes—it all told a horrific, tragic tale. Reinera stiffened, and Syd—who had draped an arm around my shoulders and not let go even while Noveen embraced me—dragged his free hand back through his hair. The others withdrew, all at once, as if I'd struck out at them.

Tears began to track down my cheeks at last. "*No.*" A plea. A desperate wish for this to be one of the brawny Captain's crinkle-eyed pranks.

I could not endure one more grief. One more loss. Already my hand sought the weight of Ryker's pendant around my throat, mooring me to something—*anything*—as the anguish lashed across the crew's faces. Across the surface of my tattered, pain-weary heart.

"We sailed somewhere we…." Syd broke off, rasping a hand over his bearded mouth, his eyes filling as well. "Captain didn't make it."

My knees buckled; Syd's arm tightened around me, holding me to my feet even as agony played through his own crumpled features.

"It's a long…story." Reinera's voice twisted on the last word, her gaze darting first to Syd, then to Lanah.

"Better we tell it in private," Syd decided.

The others broke away at that, with a respect for his word that had not been…*absent*, precisely, but certainly not so swift when I'd parted from them in this city months ago.

Curiosity unfastened my feet from the floor; I followed them through a door at the side of the parlor and into a long wing of plain doors set across from tall windows. Once, those might have allowed a truly breathtaking view of the Monshan streets. Now they were boarded, keeping out trouble—or the fear of it.

Reinera led us to the farthest door and opened it to a modest room; cots bearing discarded satchels of effects lined the walls, with a single washbasin at the end. The pair of windows was also boarded.

At the first cot, Reinera collapsed, burying her head in her hands. I sank down beside her; Syd and Lanah took another cot across from us, sitting nearer than I had ever seen them. And when Lanah shivered, bending over her knees, Syd laced his fingers with hers and pressed a kiss to her temple.

Quite a bit had changed, then.

"We sailed some friends out of Fallshyre Bay," Reinera began softly, her words aimed at the floor. "One of them, I think you might know."

"She introduced herself as Addie," Syd explained.

Shock rammed through my chest, followed by a joy in such conflict with the grief I had carried ever since Bashir, I could not breathe past it. Gripping my throat with one shaking hand—begging my lungs to remember their function—I gaped at Syd.

"Yes, *that* Addie," Lanah said. "Your Addie-cat."

My heart wedged into my throat, and I smothered my yelp of delight with both hands.

I had wondered so often where her story had taken her…whether the fireworks had sent her life bursting into better paths, or worse ones. And now, at long last, I *knew*.

"We sailed her and her companion—Julas's friend, Jaik—out to an island called the Illusionarium," Reinera went on, her gaze still fixed on her boots. "There was something they intended to do with Storycraft there, and…"

"It succeeded," Lanah rasped. "But while they were gone, we were at the mercy of the currents."

"There are bad things out in those waters." Syd's tone tensed, his grip around Lanah's hand tightening until she winced; he loosened his hold at once, but the color paled from his cheeks. "Things I've never seen before…and I hope we never see them again."

"One, we faced with the help of Addie's Storycraft." Reinera's voice brittled slightly. "Most of the crew survived…but we lost Valori and the twins. Henriet, as well."

Grief, grief, grief. I had thought myself familiar with its blows by now, but each one skimmed past my guard, riving holes into my aching middle.

Quiet Henriet, who had balanced Julas's wild whims. Valori, who had seen to it Lucretzia was occupied so I might have one night free of her ashore Sunrise Isle. Nix and Nash, faithful hunters and beloved brothers.

Gone without so much as a final farewell.

"The second time…well, by then, we were adrift," Syd picked up the tale when Reinera gave a wordless shake of her head, covering her mouth. "Got boarded by some Mithran soldiers, and…"

"They murdered the Captain." Lanah's tone was fierce with a hate that found no target…that craved an undealt vengeance. It blistered against my flesh, raising the hairs on my arms. "Slit his throat and threw his body aside to rot."

"Then they took Jaik and Addie. Don't worry," Syd added hastily when horror shoved me to the edge of the cot, halfway to rising. "They got free…they sent help back for us. Soldiers who helped tow the ship here to Amere-Del, back to the people who crafted it…for repairs. Sha's orders. Yes, *the* Sha," he scoffed when my eyes blew wide. "Seems your friend has quite some pull."

"But by the time they found us, we had already faced a second attack from some abomination haunting those waters." Reinera dropped her hand, her jaw firming in a rigid slash that set the scars all down her neck twitching. "It took Frixia and Cook. And a handful of others."

I buckled forward, the strength leaving me in a single gust, and I, too, hid my face in my hands.

How could I rejoice that Addie had endured—that she had made it so far in her search for answers—when it had cost *The Athalion* so *much*?

Perhaps the world had not only darkened in these last weeks because of what had befallen us in Bashir; perhaps it had also darkened because Jularius Cathan was no longer a part of it. Nor Valori, or Nix and Nash, or Henriet or Frixia or Cook.

So many sailors I had yearned to call friends, and now…now I would never have the chance.

Not with *them*. But with those who survived…

Towing up my head, I turned my gaze to each of my companions in turn. "I am so sorry for your losses. And I am also so glad you all survived…my friends."

Reinera's mouth tugged up at the corner. "And you. I can't believe I spotted you in that market—were you running an errand for Cress?"

Before I could choke out a disbelieving laugh, Lanah added, "And did Bastyan ever find you after you disembarked? I'll be honest, you being here without him on your heels is costing me some coin."

And now I *did* laugh—a terrible, painful, humorless sound that had them all sitting back on their haunches, brows sketched in various levels of uncertainty…even concern.

"Oh, depths," I croaked, strangling Ryker's pendant once more in my grip. "No. No, she…*Lucretzia* was not my mistress. Oh, I have so much to tell you all. The truth, this time."

So I told them everything.

CHAPTER 69
COMPASS, SAILS, AND WHEEL

At long last, I explained who I was. What I had once been. Who *Lucretzia* was, and Bastyan. And the more I spoke that name—the only name they had ever known him by—the truer that piece of him felt. A piece irrevocably ingrained in the complicated whole.

And I had seen it far too late…how much the kindness and care of Bastyan had been the truth of swaggering, armored Ryker. How the men had blended and complemented one another. How I had come to care for—to admire, even—both sides.

How much I *yearned* for one more moment with him, now that he was gone.

Tears flowed ceaselessly when I told them of Bashir. And somewhere in the telling, Reinera took my hand and clasped it in both of hers. She held me as I had held Willy in his dying moments…her strength a harbor for my pain until, at long last, the tale had spent itself, the harshness of its currents receding.

For a time, all was silent.

Then Syd whistled, long and low. "So…Bastyan was *Blackhand*. From the Captain's story."

"And his crew named you *Seasplitter*?" Reinera tilted her head, her gaze raking me up and down. "Quite the title."

"I knew there was something strange about him." Lanah tucked her hands into her opposite sleeves, an uncharacteristic scowl still marring her features. "He never took orders like a deckhand. He gave them like a captain."

"A *pirate* captain." Slowly, Reinera shook her head. "If Julas had known…"

"He suspected something." My mind flashed over the memory like silver sunlight on waves…of my parting with Julas. Of his confidence that I would be cared for. "They had an understanding, of sorts."

A soft snort. "Of course they did."

Silence, again. Then Lanah ventured, so quietly I hardly heard her, "And now the pirate lords have his crew."

Dread curdled once more in my gut. "Yes. And I'm going to retrieve them…and then Tristah."

"Right. There is *that* part." Syd cocked his head, searching me with a curious gaze, not quite convinced. "You're really the *Delina*?"

"I was. That title is no longer any part of me."

"I can understand that." Lanah's smile gentled at last into something far more familiar. "I'm grateful you told us."

"And we can certainly understand why you didn't before," Reinera added. "From what you say of the Del's Own Blade…we would not have allowed her aboard our ship if we had known."

"But I was glad to have met all of you regardless. I *am* glad." I squeezed her hand. "And I'm sorry you've endured so much."

"And you." Syd cracked his knuckles. "I'll have to have a word with *Bastyan* when we see him again."

The words struck a deep chord within me, resonating like a summons to battle. Particularly that faith-filled, uncompromising *when*, and… "We?"

Reinera glanced at Syd and Lanah, then swiveled toward me. "You need to reach this *Korsa*, and if you could have done it alone, our paths would never have crossed here."

"So, you're waiting for something." Lanah searched me with penetrating focus. "What is it?"

Hunger gleamed in all their gazes, trained on me…a need for purpose. A craving for some gust of breeze to fill their sails and carry them to new horizons. The same hunger that had filled me when I had waited that long night in Bashir, alone…and Tristah had never come.

"A vessel," I confessed. "I cannot make the voyage alone."

"Well, what do you know—you're *not* alone now, are you?" Syd flashed me a lopsided grin.

"We may not have a captain anymore," Reinera's voice tightened with restrained emotion, "but we can still sail."

"We don't have a ship," Lanah reminded them. "*The Athalion* is still being repaired…and will be for some time."

"Right." Syd scrubbed a hand back through his hair. "There's that."

A bit of daring—a bit of wicked excitement—bubbled in my core. "But *The Athalion* is not the only choice."

There was one path I had not yet considered, because it was far too much for one woman to attempt. But with many…with a *crew*…

Reinera's hand tightened sharply, then released mine. "What are you scheming, Lio?"

I gazed at the boarded-shut window, envisioning the port that encircled Monsha, my heart racing at the thought. "We may not have a water-worthy vessel now…but we could certainly steal one."

The silence deafened; Lanah, surprisingly, was the first to break it. "You mean turn *pirate*." None of the anxious disbelief I'd come to expect when we'd sailed to Monsha lived in her voice now. Her tone was level and cool…as if little surprised her anymore.

I lifted my shoulders a bit. "That was always my intention. To find a pirate vessel, or else commandeer some river-worthy craft."

"But you can getter a bigger, better craft with our help." Syd chafed his palms together, glancing from Reinera to Lanah and back again. "The three of us…even though I was Second Mate, captaining never really suited me. We've been sharing the role ever since Frixia went into the sea."

"Compass." Lanah pointed to Syd, who flashed her a smile so soft, it nearly hurt to behold. "Sails." She jerked a thumb into her own chest. "Wheel." She nodded to Reinera, who nodded curtly back.

"If we tell the crew to go, they'll go," Reinera agreed. "We've just been waiting for the wind and waves to point our way from Monsha."

"And Luck just kicked up a breeze." Syd grinned my way.

Disbelief of a different sort battled the anguish that had seethed in my middle for so many weeks. "All of you have endured so much. You hardly knew Bastyan, and you knew me even less. Why—?"

"It's clear this pirate crew means something to you," Reinera interrupted gently. "There is a fire in you that I *rarely* saw when you sailed with us, Lio. And I've seen too many fires in too many friends put out lately."

"No more dead friends," Syd added fiercely. "Not for any of us."

"Besides," Reinera went on, "Bastyan *was* our friend. Our crewmate, even if he didn't tell us the truth of who he was. We would've *all* sunk in the Spear

Teeth if not for him. And I for one am not content to let his people rot just for the lies he told."

"Nor am I," I croaked.

"So. You know how to sail to this pirate haven, *Seasplitter*?" Syd prodded.

"Not precisely. I have a bit of a direction, but—"

"I can point us that way."

Wide-eyed, we all looked at Lanah. She met our gazes levelly, her cheeks blotting red.

"It was before either of you joined," she mumbled to Reinera and Syd. "I was part of a pirate crew sent to board *The Athalion* during one of its trade voyages. It was just after Julas became Captain, and he…well, he knew the black coat for what it was." A rueful smile curled her lips. "But he was Ameresh, too. He'd heard the whispers of Korsa, of what it was like there. He asked me if I needed help, and…"

Syd blinked at last, and it reminded me to do the same. "He got you out?"

"He paid off my debt. He said that having someone who knew pirates would make it safer for all of us to sail."

"And we always *have* been safer than most," Reinera breathed. "I've often wondered how we avoided pirates so well."

Lanah flashed her a reluctant half-grin.

"Then you can show us the way to Korsa?" I demanded.

Bearing down a deep breath, Lanah nodded. "I can. And I can help find us a proper vessel to sail there."

"So, we're really doing this?" Reinera glanced between all of us. "We're turning pirate?"

Syd dragged a hand back through his hair. "What've we got to lose? We're captainless. *The Athalion* might not be salvageable. And after what we've seen, what those Mithran soldiers did to the crew—"

"I'd rather be a pirate again than a trader of Mithra-Sha," Lanah threw in fiercely, folding her arms.

Reinera edged out a slow nod. "All right. Let's spread the word to the crew…anyone who'd rather not be a part of this can cut their lines from us now. But at dawn, we're scouting for ships."

Lanah rose with a sharp nod. Syd stood as well, still gawking at her. "All this time, I've been in love with a *pirate*?"

She winced, hooking her hair behind her ear. "Does that—is that—?"

"Let me stop you right there." He pressed a finger to her lips, his grin unfurling like a sail. "It's perfect, is what it is. You have to teach me everything…how to do the swagger, how to curse like a pirate, how—"

Laughing, she captured his hand, bringing his finger down from her mouth. "Let's begin with how to navigate to the pirate haven."

They ducked from the room, leaving Reinera and I alone, gazing after them. A shared, poignant melancholy stormed the air between us.

"Did you know?" I murmured at last.

Slowly, she shook her head. "Julas never mentioned it."

I studied her face for a moment…the heavy angles of her brow and mouth. The profound ache in her voice when it curled around his name. "I take it there were many things he did not mention that he should have."

She tossed me a wistful smile. "It's quite likely."

Silence, for a time.

Then I asked the question that had haunted me since Anoram—that I had not yet found a way to fit my hands around, so I had broken it down to coals that fueled my determination. "How do you endure the regret of that?"

It was her turn to mount a halfhearted shrug. "I grieve. I look after the rest of them the way he would have done. I save what I can…the ship, if possible. The people who sailed on it. And I choose to be fiercely thankful for every moment we shared, even if it was all borrowed time…and much of it not spent the way I wished it had been."

I stared down into the cradle of my scarred palms. Then I swept in a breath, curling my fingers into fists, lifting my gaze to hers. "We save what we can."

Squeezing my wrist, she murmured, "Thank you. For giving them…for giving *us* something good to do. We've been adrift, ever since Julas…and we needed this. Despite the risk, it helps ease the pain of what we couldn't save."

Willy's slack face flashed through my mind again.

Ryker's body, slumped on the cobblestones.

My last glimpse of Julas, smiling with confidence that I would be cared for…knowing Bastyan was poised to leap to my aid.

I swallowed the lump in my throat. "Then let's find a ship, shall we?"

Reinera's smile broadened into a grin—something feral. Something that would have endeared her to the Raiders in a heartbeat. "Lead the way, *Seasplitter.*"

CHAPTER 70
THE PIRATE AND THE PANTHER

RYKER

The only thing worse than being caged in Korsa was having to share that cage with the Incendiary's bloody spymaster.

Sailing aboard the *Spice*, we'd been paid once by some islander with a black panther for an equal weight of his favorite drug. I'd kept that wildcat company all the way from the banks to port, hiding out in the hull with it, sharing the scraps they fed me.

It'd been the closest thing to a friend I'd had on that ship after Antigony drowned…and it'd still tried to gnaw my arm off.

Ember wasn't much different.

"Would you give it a rest?" A groan slipped through my teeth when I finally found a place to rest my head on the frigid stone wall that didn't hurt as much as the rest. "Unless you're scheming to walk a rut so deep you fall through, pacing's not getting you out of this cage."

That much was obvious. Korsa didn't play loose with its prisoners.

I'd never actually set foot in the prison here before. Heard enough screams floating down from this dank, high-walled building to steer as clear of it as I could, all these years. But in the last few weeks since the Leeches had dragged us and the *Singer* back into this mountain pit, I'd gotten too well acquainted with how those screams sounded up close.

And how it reeked. Depths, that *stench*. Body odor and waste and blood and sick. Cam's had joined the rest when the Leeches had barreled him through the door of his cage, and ever since, the lad was quiet—so blasted quiet it gave me the chills.

Most of them were, all down the row they'd shut us in. I at least had Gyddy in here with me, keeping an eye on the hole in my middle and the scrape carved along the side of my head. That one, he'd had to shave with his razor to keep clean…but it should've been a deadshot. It had slammed my head against the street hard enough I'd blacked out until Ember shook me awake so he could drag me back into the compound.

Ahim loved me, Gyddy kept saying. The Pale Viper was barely beatable with a sword, but her pistolwork was on the shoddier side. I liked to think that was thanks to the hole I'd put through her shoulder.

Boots twisted on rock, dragging through my head like trawling hooks. Groaning, I pushed up from the wall and found that panther of a spymaster still prowling by the cage bars, giving them a few rattles, testing them out. As if he hadn't scouted this cell a dozen bloody times already. "Oi. You're not going to *find* anything, mate. Or you'd've found it by now."

"Unlike *you*, I'm not content to sit and wait to see what these *pirates* have in store for us." He spat out that title the same way most of the crew had spat out bile before we'd all adjusted to the stink of this place. "Tristah is out there. Alone. In a city the Pale Viper was slithering through." He aimed another kick at the base of the bars. "I have to get back to her."

Anger rocked through me like a rogue swell tipping a ship. I shoved up to my feet against the wall, grabbing my middle when it gave off a warning pang. "You hear me singing shanties and making myself a cozy bed? Mate, I'm trying to keep us all alive so we can actually *do* something."

Ember scoffed. "I shouldn't have left her side that night. I shouldn't have wasted my time saving *you*."

We both clammed up at a scuffle and a snort from across the cell—the sound of Gydeon, wrapped up in Ember's gray cloak, fighting through a nightmare I didn't want to know anything about. Not after what he'd been through, worse than the rest of us.

At least me and Ember had that in common: we both knew better than to disturb Gyddy.

We waited for him to go quiet before I finally lobbed back the only retort I had: "Aye. You shouldn't have."

But he had. I didn't remember much from that night—not after that second pistolshot blew past me, anyway—but I remembered *him*. Those fingers wrapped up in my collar; him dragging me into the compound. Gyddy getting to me and starting to patch me up, right before the Leeches got to all of us.

Which was the only reason I hadn't tried clobbering him senseless to stop all that bloody *pacing*.

It wasn't like there was much else to do in these cages. And I hated it more every day that the Old Salts hadn't made their move yet. *Weeks* we'd been here, festering in the dark. Weeks they'd let me stay with Gyddy, so obviously they wanted me alive. But what were they bloody *waiting for?*

"Content or not, I don't see you doing much," Ember shot back. "I'd expect a captain to do more to fight for his crew…for the people who depend on him."

One of those hooks stuck in my craw and *yanked*—yanked me straight back to that slick street and the pain that'd pulled me down like a tide, and the only thing keeping my head above water—

Lio, screaming my name like the whole world was cracking under her feet.

Lio, begging me to get up.

Lio, spitting right back in the Viper's face, holding her own between the two of us, when everything in me had been yelling at her to *just bloody run.*

Lio, and that damned panicked shriek splitting me apart from bow to stern, the last thing I'd heard before that shot had smacked my head against the street and dropped me like a sack of gull fodder.

Lightning bolted along my fingertips like sailing straight into the belly of a storm. I took a step toward Ember—ignoring how that made my middle ache like I'd taken a punch straight below the ribs. "Listen, chum-for-brains, you're not the only one with someone left behind, all right?" The snarl tore up my throat, and that felt good—felt better than how most of us had been whispering since they'd thrown us in here. "Yours at least had more than a few blades on her. Mine…"

Blasted heat scorched over my eyes. That scream just kept ringing and ringing in my head, like a cannon had gone off right next to me, blurring out everything else.

"She already had Lio." That hook dragged her name up like something dead in the depths. "And Lio's the one she wanted. So, chances are, your *Incendiary* is just out there plotting how to get you back."

Stupid slow, my feet finally shuffled me over to meet him beside the bars; he didn't move, thank Ahim. I didn't feel much like chasing more panthers around their cages.

"This isn't your world, friend," I reminded him, bracing my arm up against the bars above us, leaning my weight into it. "These aren't your *kind*. I know how they think, how they walk and talk, how they act. And this?" I knocked on the iron for good measure. "I know how they build their bloody cages. So, aye, I'm not *doing much*…because I know there isn't much to *do*. Yet. So as long as we're in here, we might as well rally, keep up our strength, and try not to go absolutely blasted mad. Aye?"

Ember folded his arms, dropping his shoulder into the bars, measuring me with those midnight eyes. Maybe it should've rattled me, being trapped with a spymaster who'd managed to stay a step ahead of the whole bloody regime for years, but I liked my chances. Mostly because he'd already showed his hand, dragging me back to the compound when he could've left me in the street to rot.

Finally, he said something that didn't have barbs in it—first time since they'd thrown us all in the brig aboard *The Depth Treachery*, when he'd yelled himself hoarse trying to break *those* bars, too. "I don't enjoy confinement."

I couldn't bite down a smirk. "First thing I figured out about you, mate."

His mouth curled in a way that was almost smiling back. "Got a plan?"

"It's being made."

Siu's snort carried from the next cell. "Best lie you've ever told, Captain."

I shot her a glare; she sat against the back wall of the cage they'd thrown her into, Cam sprawled out with his head in her lap. Still sleeping, thank Ahim…he'd slept most of these days away, too rattled to face what was happening. What had *already* happened.

Siu had whispered to me that he'd propped his eyes open the first full day and night here while *I* slept off the rest of that pistolshot, making sure my half-dead carcass didn't flip belly-up; that he'd only keeled over himself when Gyddy gave the all-clear on me.

Pain sparked down the shaved side of my head, and I knuckled it off, leaning my weight more heavily into the bars. "That's the thing with pirates. It's hard to plan anything around them…wily bottom-feeders to the last." I offered the spymaster a wink. "But we're pirates too, mate. We'll think of something."

CHAPTER 71
COUNCILMEET

RYKER

*S*omething didn't make itself clear in two more days. And that was when they came for us.

It should've been a relief, waking up against the wall with Gydeon throwing fresh bandages over my middle and spotting pirates on the *other* side of the cage, for once. But instead, it just felt like someone dropped a barrel full of powder straight through my chest…and I was waiting for something to set it off.

I pushed myself up straight, swatting Gydeon off. "What do they want?"

"They're taking us." All he said—and the most he'd said in weeks.

The Old Salts had given him enough stock to keep me alive. They hadn't left more for him to take care of his own hurts…his beaten-in face, the things that made him limp and had him sleeping deep and long ever since we'd landed in this cage, trying to heal what he could the best way he knew how.

The worst part aboard the *Treachery*—the part that ran thick in my nightmares—was how the newest Captain and his thugs had made a mess out of Gyddy every day. Usually in the brig…usually right in front of us.

Beating him bloody. Making him scream. Making *Siu* scream and threaten and *beg* them off of him while they were still pinning him down and breaking ribs and toes and pulling fingernails off for sport.

Cam had gotten sick then, too; Wilkes and Kato had bent the bars trying to get to Gyddy, and still hadn't gotten out.

I'd never heard Siu sob like that. Gyddy, either. And all I'd been able to do, halfway-dead myself, was reach through the bars and grab his hand and hold on for all I was worth once they finally left him there on the floor, heaving and weeping, too hurt to move.

I hated this bloody life. I hated the flag we sailed under. I hated that they'd dragged us back under it.

I hated that this was all my depths-blasted *fault*.

I tried to show Gyddy as much with just a look, grabbing onto his arm when he tucked the bandage into place. He shot me what could have been a smile—hard to tell with his busted-up cheekbone and crooked jaw. But we got up together, and Ember dropped back beside us, swinging his cloak back on and bunching the folds in his fist like he'd whip it up and carve these silt-sippers in half with the corner.

Almost wished he could.

"Merry Dred wants a word," sneered the pirate who opened our gate— same one who'd crowded up on Lio in the *Pearl*. He trained the muzzle of the pistol, not on any one of us, but out in the hall—straight on the back of Camden's ducked, shivering head.

We went without a fight.

The news had spread during the weeks we'd been rotting in the dark; pirates from just about every crew I'd ever had the misfortune of crossing paths with lined up both sides of the twisting road out of the compound, peppering the air with a whole lot of jeering. A whole lot of bawdy talk I'd tried to keep Cam from ever hearing. They lobbed rotten food at us, whistled and made lewd remarks after Siu and Klem and Maryon and the other ladies…the sort of things they wouldn't have dared if we weren't all being marched at muzzlepoint toward the tallest building in Korsa.

I'd never been inside it; never seen anyone else there, either, in all the years I'd been sailing. The Councilmeet, the last Blackhand had called it; it only got any use when something came up an Old Salt couldn't figure out on their own. So they all pulled their heads together to dream up the worst ways to make someone bleed.

That was where they led us—straight toward that spired building at the top of Korsa's stacked-up streets. My crew were all staggering and soaked with flung rot and their own filth by the time we reached the doors at the base of the tower, and a pair of pirates pulled ahead. They grabbed the greening bronze fish-body handles and dragged the doors open, shoving us inside…then ducking in after us, shutting the doors.

There wasn't much to the tower; just a wide-open, round floor, the tip of the tower blown out and letting in a view of the cavern roof high up. Ropes braided the air above us, most hanging a flag or two—different emblems from different ships. Sunk ones, conquered ones, retired ones.

And in their shadows, in seats scattered around a wheel-shaped table, were all the Old Salts.

My spine prickled; the hairs on my arms jumped up like riding the bow of the *Singer* in bad weather. I'd never seen this many of the pirate lords in one place before…didn't even recognize all of them. Too many craggy, mottled bodies, full up on herbs and drinks and the fat of the land…the things their debt-crews scrounged up for them.

I shoved to the front of mine, spreading my stance even when my gut twinged, clasping my hands low in front of me…drawing all those sharp eyes like pistols aimed straight at my heart.

"So," I drawled, keeping my voice as casual as I could manage when Cam was sobbing quiet-like behind me, "you sent your dogs to hunt us. Let them drag us back. Stuffed us in *cages* and made us wait." I bobbed my shoulders. "And for what?"

"If I stood where you stand, Blackhand," Merry Dred's voice echoed hollow through the Councilmeet, "having done what you've done…I would not be so flippant."

My tongue stuck to the roof of my mouth. Someone—sounded like Klem—shifted behind me.

Notched and pallid and not even smirking, Merry Dred pushed up from the table to stare me down, keeping his hand on the wood like he wanted to throw himself over it and strangle me himself.

Staring him right back, it felt like the whole room shifted. Like I was seeing him—seeing this whole life—real and clear for the first time.

I'd been ready to sell off the best thing that ever came my way, just to line his gold-trimmed pockets with more merits he didn't need. So he could buy off more strays and runts without a wink of hope. So they could bring him merits to buy more.

I was such a part of the bloody problem.

Hating the Old Salts wasn't enough…not while I was still doing their dirty work. Saving my crew meant selling other people just like them to something worse, most likely; because once we were gone, there wouldn't be someone who gave enough of a care to save lads like Camden. To pull in people like Gyddy and Siu without working them to the bone. To look twice at women like Lio and stop thinking like pirates long enough to see her for what she was: a *treasure*, not a bloody ransom.

These pirates weren't any different from the Del or the Pale Viper or even Captain *depths-blasted* Varsi.

I wasn't much different, as long as I kept choosing to play their game.

"All right, Dred, I'll bite." I stepped forward, keeping his eyes on me—off my crew. "Where exactly is it I'm standing?"

The way that top lip curled, it meant he wanted me to ask that question. Which meant I wasn't going to like the answer.

"You stand accused by your fellow captains of destruction, theft, and badgering. None of which we have much concern for, here in Korsa." He pushed himself back lightly from the table. "But those were *my* docks you broke. *My* ship you stole. And Rackham's Leeches you badgered…one of his Captains you killed." He shot a glance at the fidgety, scowling Old Salt to his left, who stared at me with eyes layered in so many bags, most likely he was hiding a whiskey flask under every one. "It's taken a bloody long time to pick a punishment worth all that."

The stump of my finger gave a twinge. I tucked it behind my other hand. "Well, don't leave me hanging, Dred. Let's hear it…which part of me are you selling off first?"

Dred's eyes narrowed.

Right then, I knew. But I wasn't thinking straight—and even if I had been, the scrape in Bashir had already proved I wasn't faster than a pistolshot.

The only thing that made it out of me was a half-step to stop him, a shout of "*No!*"

Then his pistol barked.

Smoke stained the air.

A body dropped behind me.

CHAPTER 72
SOLD OFF FOR DEBTS

RYKER

yst!" Camden yelled, jerking toward our carpenter's corpse folding over at the edge of the cluster of us. He went down to the depths as quiet as he'd lived—a hole blown clean through his head, blood spraying out the back.

Shock heaved my chest up and let it drop again while I stared at him, reached for him, my fist stuck out in the air like I could've grabbed the lead that pierced his skull.

It was a warning. Cannonfire straight across the bow.

The Pale Viper wasn't a crackshot; but every Old Salt in this room was.

"Perhaps that clarifies the seriousness of the conversation." The chafe of powder and lead while Dred reloaded hit my ears off-tune; I spun back on him, my throat so tight I could barely scrape air out, let alone shape it into words.

"What do you *bloody want with us*?" I finally snarled.

"That fear, for starters." Dred settled back in his seat, pistol braced on the table's edge—angled our way. "And now, we come to the exciting part."

I spread my arms, ushering the crew back from the mouth of that pistol. I couldn't look at Wyst, or I'd lose whatever steel was keeping my spine straight.

"The debts your crew has racked up are…unattainable, Blackhand," Dred purred. "It might be admirable, the silt you've sunk yourself in…if it wasn't our pockets you're thieving from, waiting to repay."

The pistol tapped the tabletop.

"So I've sold them all off."

I stared him down. Couldn't make sense of that.

Sold off—what? The *debts*?

"Plenty of crews need new faces all the time," Dred went on. "Accidents happen. So I've decided the best way to put a stop to the leak in my coffers from the *Singer* is to make sure its crew is no longer my problem."

He nodded over to another Old Salt—Chesney Covington, a blond-bearded, braided-haired bastard who leered at us like he'd just won the greatest pot in the greatest card game ever played.

"*The Dread Singer* now sails under Convington's care, for a hefty sum of merits," Dred announced, "and its crew has been bought off by several other ships."

No.

The word sparked in me like a flint on rock.

"Say that again," I growled.

Dred arched both brows. "I've sold them all off for the sum of their debts. They will be sailing with new ships out of this city, and you, Blackhand…you're to be stripped of your title, flogged, and chained to this city's walls. You'll serve me personally in any way I choose, until your debts are paid…which I don't imagine will be while there's still life in your body."

"You're *splitting up our crew*?" Klem snarled, barging forward at my side.

"Oi, Keen-Eye, let me handle this!" I snapped—even though I didn't know how in the *depths* I would.

Dred had us. And he'd made up his bloody mind, most likely as soon as I'd left his little hovel missing a finger.

"There's nothing to handle," Dred sneered. "They're all to be taken to their new vessels forthwith. The lad and your navigator have already been sold off to skin-ships. There's a market for flesh of every kind, of every age, in every port."

My hearing went out—almost all the way. I wished it had, because I didn't want to know what came next.

"And your First Mate…the Leeches were quick to barter for her."

"*Over my rotting bones!*" Gydeon roared, and he jumped toward the table—the same second Kory grabbed Klem, throwing her behind him—

And a second shot blasted through the Councilmeet.

"*Kory!*" Klem shrieked, catching her younger brother when he staggered back, blood spraying across his front.

Panic fired through me like another pistol; belting out every profanity I ever knew, I hurtled toward them, and Ember grabbed Gyddy, slinging him back toward the crew.

My knees barked with pain when I hit the stone floor beside Kory, shoving both hands into his jerking chest, blood spewing out between my fingers. "No, no, *no*," I panted. "Look at me, mate, stay with us…"

"Kory, please, *please*," Klem sobbed—depths, I'd never even seen her cry, and now she was hacking on every breath, clutching her brother against her, kissing the top of his head. "Hold on, baby boy, *hold on*—"

Kory's hand fumbled up to seize mine. Desperation, pleading, agony, *terror* in that stare—

Then his chest jumped up into my hands one more time…and went slack.

Klem let out an animal wail, rocking her brother's body against her. Kato's bellow split the air, and he went hurtling toward the table, too.

Everything was spinning out of my hands faster than I could whip the wheel and steer us out of the storm. The whole crew was yelling, fighting, a couple of Dred's pirates grabbing Kato and shoving him down on his knees, Ember flattening Gydeon down, Siu with both her arms wrapped around Camden but staring between her husband and Dred, dead-eyed like her spirit had left her body—

"Pity for my pockets, there were no bids for a carpenter," Dred said lazily, stuffing more powder into his pistol, angling a nod at Wyst's body, "or a log keeper. Nor, as it happens…" he leveled the muzzle at us again, "for a healer."

Slipping in Kory's blood, I launched to my feet. "*Dred*—!"

"I'd heard pirate councils were a mess," a drawling voice floated down from above, stopping us all in our tracks, "but this is defying even *my* expectations."

Dred stiffened, his gaze shooting up to ropes that hemmed us in.

To the figure swinging down those thick lines, vault to vault, then planting her feet and skimming down the thickest braid to catch herself against one of the tower's support columns. She winged around it, still a good half a mast's height above us, her dark hair tumbling over her shoulder as she bent to peer down at the carnage we'd all made.

Dressed in armored black leathers under a cloak purple as a bruise. Knives singing from her belt. Lively eyes fixed on Dred.

"Who in the bloody depths is *that*?" Rackham barked.

"Tristah," Ember breathed, taking his knee out of Gydeon's back.

Aye, that was her—sure as the sun sparkling on the sea.

"Sorry to drop in unannounced," she drawled, "but word on the street says this is where all of the fun would be today."

Dred's eyes narrowed. "Do I know you?"

Her eyes narrowed right back. "You thought you did."

My hands twisted to fists at my sides. *Wait a bloody second—*

Her gaze dropped on me, and something changed.

Just for a second, her lips pressed tight together. Just for a blink, her brows scrunched and swapped angles, and something darted through that face—something that made me think of island sunsets and a fireside dance. A courtyard and a hand latched into my hair. Fingers tied to mine under the waves.

My knees almost gave out again. If not for my crew, I'd have let them go.

That wasn't the Incendiary.

That was Lionyra Vara, stepping onto the ropes again, easing her way out over the room full of Old Salts like she belonged there. Like she *owned* it…dressed to defy, smirking again, ignoring the blood painted on the floor and the pistol in Dred's hand.

She was fierce. She was as beautiful as a storm raging across the sea. She was a *pirate*, perched up there in the ropes—swaggering and sultry.

She was just like Tristah, right then…and it cracked something in half in me, seeing her like that.

Because it was just a ruse. But depths if she didn't play it well.

"I'm sure you're all sore from patting yourselves on the back about splitting up such a troublesome crew," she said. "But I've come with a better offer…something I'm willing to give in exchange for their freedom."

"And what could that possibly be?" Convington guffawed.

"Me." She dropped down on the table and straightened back up, spreading her arms wide.

"You," Dred echoed flatly.

"You might recall when we last met." Lio curled a finger between them. "I was searching for Tristah Levanthya. You took Blackhand's finger for the information."

His kohl-stamped eyes blew wide. "Well, well—the double."

"As a matter of fact, she was my *decoy*." Lio perched her hands akimbo on her waist. "Rackham might know a bit more…his Leeches were just tangled up in all of this."

Dred blinked, his gaze shooting across the table to Rackham. "Tangled in *what*, precisely?"

"Didn't he tell you?" Lio cocked her head. "No sharing among pirates, I suppose."

Rackham scoffed. "I don't know what this wench is rattling off about—"

"Then you don't know how handsomely your Leeches were paid by the Del's Own Blade to sail her to Bashir, so that she could retrieve *me*?" Lio perched a lacquered finger on her lips, tapping slowly. "Or perhaps the *Treachery's* Captain only informed you that retrieving the *Singer* was the prize. You might check his coffers, then."

"What reason would the Pale Viper have to retrieve the likes of *you*?" another of the Old Salts scoffed.

Horror dripped down my throat. *Lio, don't you bloody do it—*

"The same reason Blackhand ever had me at all: I'm what the Del wants more than anything in the country." Lio shrugged. "I'm the lost Delina."

For a moment, no one spoke. Or breathed.

Dred shoved back his seat, bolting upright. "That can't be bloody true."

"I can show you the scars, if you wish." Lio stepped down off the table. "I can lay the secrets of the Graven regime at your feet. Or we can haggle properly…for every piece of truth I give, you set one of the Raiders free."

"Why in the depths would the *Delina* make such a wager?" Rackham demanded—a little higher pitched than before. Like finding Lio out in a lie might save his hide.

Judging by the way the other Old Salts were staring him down, that wasn't happening either way.

"Because these people are my friends." She said it so easy, so simple, like it was the most obvious thing in the seas.

I almost choked on my own air. *Depths, I missed you.*

"And so you give yourself up as…what? A ransom?" Dred sneered, rounding the table toward her; but I knew that pasty cuttlefish well enough to see he was wavering. She'd just offered up the same thing that had tempted all my darker parts—the ransom of a lifetime.

If it had swayed me, it would sure as salt sway him.

Snorting, Lio stepped nearer to him. "Oh, Dred, Dred, Dred…" She patted his chest, a strike for every word, circling him with that lazy swagger that was all trained—all Tristah. "Still only seeing things through the *small* end of the spyglass, aren't you?" She halted behind him, one arm draped around the back of his neck, keeping that wary Old Salt stiff in her hold. "I'm not the ransom."

She rested her chin on his shoulder, her gaze stuck on something past me.

"I'm the diversion."

She reared back and shoved him with all the strength she had in those brawny baker's arms—

Straight into Ember. Who pulled a blade from *depths-knew-where* and threw it straight through Dred's shoulder, nailing him back on the tabletop.

I didn't wait for him to scream. And I didn't wait for the rest of the Old Salts to jump up, to draw their pistols and take aim.

I threw myself at Cam and Siu, grabbed them both, and hit the deck—right when the first explosion rocked Korsa to its roots.

And then, it was all the way I liked it.

Pure, bloody *chaos*.

CHAPTER 73
BLUE LIKE FLAME

Once again, my life was going up in fireworks.

Calamity descended over the building Lanah had called the *Councilmeet*. It wrecked and ravaged its way through the smoke-choked interior as pistols fired wildly on every side. In the havoc, something—*someone*—struck me, a knife ripping a flaming line down my jaw and shoving tears from my eyes.

I staggered away from the table, whirling to place my back to the wall; half of the Old Salts were rushing for the doors, barreling between the Raiders. But the other half were lunging for me, intent on snatching up the unignorable prize of my life, just as I had hoped they would. And feared.

Bodies cut through the smoke. Screaming profanities, Klem threw herself at Merry Dred, dodging the knife he tore from his shoulder and sent sailing at her chest. Kato caught it from its end-over-end whirl by the hilt, and spun, hurling it back—nailing Dred straight through the throat. Klem gripped the handle and tore, severing his head from his shoulders.

Stomach churning ferociously at the deluge of blood, I sidestepped the grasping hands of another Old Salt, ducking beneath him and tripping him with a slide of my boot. I shoved him straight into Killian—who'd drawn more knives and whirled among the pirates, riving chests and severing fingers.

"Everyone, *get to the docks!*" I shouted to the Raiders—then choked as a hand smothered my mouth from behind, a blade pressing into my kidney.

"You're going nowhere, *Delina*," an Old Salt hissed, spittle flecking my ear.

I chomped down on her palm, speared an elbow upward into her eye socket, and kicked her away. But a second pair of hands met me, then a third;

then a fourth pounded into the weeping cut on my jaw, throwing a sheen of sugar-silver across my vision.

Through the glittering haze, I caught a glimpse of black and gold. A powerful figure wading through the throng, snatching up his crew, shoving them toward the door, pairing them off to help one another stagger from the mess as another explosion bucked through the very walls of the Councilmeet.

I could not help the sob that tore from me at the sight of him—standing. Healed. *Alive.*

"*Bash!*" I cried.

His eyes cut straight to me—and ignited with enough fury to burn the world to its roots.

Ryker aimed and unleashed before two of the four pirates even realized who I'd summoned; then he barreled into the woman who'd first seized me, shoving her into the man whose grip pinched my upper arms now. We all struck the table at once, and when Ryker's hand reared my way, I seized it. He hauled me across the table, out from under them; then he plucked two knives from my belt and, with a shout, tossed them to Killian. In a deft pirouette, the spymaster caught them, whirled, and impaled both Old Salts backward through their chests.

Ryker and I tumbled down behind the table as the next blast shook the tower. His hands, bloodslick and shaking, covered my shoulders. "*What in the bloody depths did you do?*"

I could not make any sense of the question; I could make sense of *nothing* but that he was here, *living,* beyond every hope I'd held, beyond every wish I'd flung to the stars, every prayer I'd breathed to Ahim.

"You're all right. You're *all right.*" My hands rose to frame his face, one palm sliding back to meet the furrow carved into his skull and the shorn hair around it. "Oh, look at you—look at your *hair*—"

"Oi! How hard did they hit you?" His eyes flashed, his thumb dropping to brush the edges of my cut; then he held his sleeve against it. "Lio, how in the depths did you find us? How did you get away?"

"Lucretzia didn't want me, she…" I bit back the tumble of words pressing against my teeth. "I'll explain later. For now—"

"You could have run." Ryker's hands encircled the sides of my neck. "Why did you come back for us?"

As if they were not worth it. As if they did not deserve to be saved.

I held his gaze, desperate, anguished, and the same pain bubbled up in me. "I chose you."

It was all I could say…because then I was kissing him, not a second more wasted.

I kissed him as if we were back beneath the waves, breathing life into him. And taking it for myself, when the sure and steady pressure of his mouth proved what I had not dared to allow myself to truly believe, ever since Bashir.

He was alive. Alive. *Alive.*

When we broke apart, gasping for breath, I leaned my forehead against his for a moment. Soaked in the warmth of him…nearer and more real than any dream I'd had in these lonely weeks we'd spent apart.

"We have to run," I managed at last. "Help is waiting at the docks."

"Help?" he echoed, pulling back fully. "What bloody *help* did you find that could sail to *Korsa*?"

"You'll see." I snatched his hand, pulled us both to our feet—and froze.

Most of the crew had fled—but Wilkes and Kato, Nella, and Killian had been taken at pistolpoint, held to the walls. The Leeches had them captive…snarling figures who had not been in this room when I'd descended among the ropes from above. And only one Old Salt remained: Rackham, prowling toward us, eyes alight with base lust.

"We're going on a voyage, you and I…*Delina.*" He jerked a pistol from his waistband and trained it toward us; Ryker angled himself before me, one arm spread, his other hand hovering over his own holstered weapon. "I for one am eager to know why the Pale Viper let you slip through her fingers when we laid the way for her in Bashir…and what price she might pay for your *second* capture."

I tensed, braced to run, or to dodge him—whatever way this went.

And then something concussive, something earth-shattering and inescapable, blasted through the room. Its invisible force tore across my body, stealing the breath from my lungs and spinning my head in a shrouded gray veil.

Not an explosion. Not fireworks or smoke. It made no more of an impact than a foul and wicked wind, and yet…

Whatever it was, it sent the whole world tilting off-kilter.

Everything buckled and bowed—the walls, the table, the chairs, the very bones of the world all bulged out of joint. Reshaped. Rearranged. Unbearable pressure crowded against our bodies, forcing itself along every angle of my skin, shoving, shifting, changing things. I could not breathe; it felt as if a great bubble expanded in our midst, thrusting everything out-of-sorts, odd-angled, rearranging the world in a deft, violent sweep—

And then I blinked, and it was over.

Everything righted itself. My innards. The tower. The pirates within it, many of them blinking, the swift trade of their glances the only sign they had felt that silent cataclysm, too.

And then, from against the wall…a wild, disbelieving, whooping bark of a laugh. A sound I had never heard before.

Coming from *Killian*, who was all at once weeping, grinning, cackling, with a pistol in his face and tears carving down his cheeks.

Because something utterly absurd was happening—something which defied all reason.

From the pinnacle of his broad shoulders, where his ashen cloak was forever draped…*color* spilled forth.

A rich, noble blue, the precise shade of the depthless seas beneath the midday sky, ran like spilled water down every seam and stitch, igniting the cloth like the heart of a blazing flame.

Such an impossibility, and yet…there it was, drawing every eye, bringing curses and gasps from the Leeches and Raiders alike.

Killian's eyes snapped to mine, of everyone in the room—sharing a moment of wonder and disbelief with the nearest face to someone he cared for.

"*Finally*," he gasped, choked—*exulted.*

Then he grabbed the pistol aimed at his face, jerked it skyward, and slammed a punch into the pirate's throat, flinging her away from him. And he cast the pistol aside, hurling a cry toward the depths of the tower.

"*Let me tell you a story!*"

CHAPTER 74
A FOREVER ECHO

We escaped from Korsa on a tide of power I had only heard tales of in Amere-Del, in Krylan…but never borne witness to myself.

The power which could only be described as *Storycraft*.

Killian unleashed a tale of a city besieged, and he spoke it with such vigor, such passion, such surety, it was as if he had been there himself. Had witnessed a destruction like it. At first, nothing came of his words; but the further we ran, guided by Ryker with his arm around my shoulders, a web of power began to weave itself around us.

By the time we reached the lower city, Killian's story was *alive*.

His words flattened avenues and struck down towers at our heels while we fled, blocking the paths of the pirates who pursued us. By the trappings of a tale, he carved our way toward the docks, where countless pirate vessels had gone up in smoke, others with sails singed and tattered from the fireworks *The Athalion's* crew had launched off the edge of the stone harbor.

They waited for us, our stolen mercantile vessel already cut loose; and though I had prepared to swim, there was no need. Killian's tale crafted a bridge of glass that spanned out over the water; and by his word, it shattered just behind Nella's heels, bringing up the rear. We crossed the blackened depths of the mountain harbor and tumbled aboard the topdeck, fetching up against the masts and siding; gripping the slick wood, I dragged myself up to peer over the railing at the city behind us.

Korsa sparkled in flame, embers catching alight where they'd tumbled on wood-topped roofs and awnings. Bellows and curses rose among the ashes and smoke, Old Salts crying for their crews to pursue us.

I cast a swift glance at Syd, and he shot me a grin in passing; all the evidence I needed that no ship would be fit to follow us, thanks to the deft work of *The Athalion's* crew.

Waiting days for the assembly at the Councilmeet to draw most of the pirates deeper into Korsa had been agony. Agony, to only listen to the rumors and not to try and reach the crew where they were imprisoned; agony, to work quietly during that time, disabling the ships around us whenever their crews changed watch.

But now we were here, together, the deck a hive of hectic energy. The crew was already at work, a melding of pirates and traders-turned-pirate; Syd and Siu barking orders, Reinera and Rynshaw running lines side by side. Gydeon and Hasser saw to the injured together; Klem and Lanah worked the sails as if they had always been shipmates, one aiding where the other fumbled.

Camden huddled against the mainmast, arms wrapped around his legs, face buried in his knees. Concern spurred me toward him, and when I slipped an arm around his shoulders, he flinched, jerking up his head. "L-Lio?"

My heart wrenched at the paths of tears trailing down his freckled cheeks, both new and long-dried. I brushed them away with my knuckles. "That is *the Seasplitter* to you, Master Sailor."

His chin trembled; he turned toward me, arms wrapped around my middle, and buried his face in my shoulder. I held him to me as the others dragged themselves up from our tumble to the deck.

Killian alone did not rise; he splayed on his seat, legs cocked, fistfuls of his cloak gathered in his fingers. He stared at the fabric as if at any moment, it might once more dip to ashen gray.

"What happened?" I demanded.

His eyes rose slowly to find mine again. "I have no idea," he admitted. "I thought…I thought the color was gone for good. That stories had no power anymore. No endings."

His smile was wide, joyous; I could not coax one to meet it.

Ryker limped across the deck, taking a line from Klem, murmuring something in her ear; he squeezed her shoulder, and she turned away from him just as her face crumbled. Striding to the railing, she slammed the heels of her hands against it, then curled her fingers around the wood and braced her weight against her outlocked arms. Her head fell; her shoulders heaved as if she would vomit over the side of the ship.

Kato dropped his tasks and went to her; he wrapped his broad arms around her, and she turned to bury herself in his chest. Witnessing her seldom-seen grief turned my own sorrow stale and heavy, choking me.

For many of them, we had come in time. But the pistolshot I'd heard before I'd slipped in among the flags, and Klem's screams that had followed—that had frozen me for a moment among the ropes, my mind lashing back to Bashir, to the street, to Lucretzia, to my own sobs tearing from my chest—would be a forever echo in my head and heart.

A reminder that, for some—for sweet, noble Kory, for steady, quiet Wyst—we had come too late.

Bowing beneath the weight of shame and sorrow, I kissed Camden's hair, clutching him tight to me. Wishing with all my might I could bring his pain into myself as well, and lighten the burden that fell across his too-young shoulders.

"Oi, I'm surprised to see your sorry hides here!" Ryker's shout to Syd lifted my head just in time to catch him swatting the sailor's haunches in passing.

"Long story, *Bastyan!*" Syd flung back, his voice echoing oddly as we barreled into one of the many dark tunnels winding away from Korsa.

"Right, right." Ryker waved him off. "Where's Julas? Expected to see him captaining this little gravy boat, with all of you aboard."

The Athalion's crew slowed; some even halted. Heartache twisted its talons all the more viciously in my throat as Reinera dug her bloodstained fingertips into her scalp, glancing first at Syd—stiffened at the mainmast—and Lanah, who'd frozen with a line wrapped around her arm.

"It was…it was a storm," Reinera murmured, confusion lining her brow. "Wasn't it?"

"Right." Mourning softened Syd's voice. "First storm after we sailed out of Fallshyre Bay in the spring. *The Athalion* was wrecked, and…"

"The Captain died saving as many of us as he could from the waves." Lanah's voice thickened with tears.

And I wept with her—wept at the relief of our escape from Korsa. The agony of those who had not fled with us. The sheer joy at having the crew back with me. Having *Ryker* back with me.

And I also wept for a grief I could not name. A grief that felt as if it traveled far deeper than for Wyst and Kory, for Julas and the fallen crew of *The Athalion*, even.

As if I mourned some chasm torn within me that had no hope of ever being mended.

CHAPTER 75
GROWING IN THE DARK

None of us took a full, deep breath until the nightlike shadows of the mountain halls swallowed us up; and then, by glow of lanterns alone, Klem and Syd and Lanah took to navigating us through the dark. Ryker manned the ship's helm and growled the same warning to anyone who approached: "Get yourself seen to by Gyddy and Hasser before you come snarling at me."

I lingered by the mainmast, my arms around Camden until his weight grew heavy against me with sleep; then I met Wilkes's eyes across the ship as he emerged from the Captain's cabin, where Gydeon was seeing to the last of the injured among the crew. With a sharp nod, he came to us, scooping Camden up behind the knees and neck, hoisting him off the deck.

"Come, lad," he murmured. "Let's get you off to a proper rest."

I accompanied them belowdecks, to the small bay where I and *The Athalion's* crew had slept on our voyage from Monsha. Camden hardly stirred when Wilkes lowered him into the first hammock—only a slight shudder, only a soft moan.

"Thank you." I touched Wilkes's arm when he withdrew; his answering smile was void of joy, stamped with mourning weeks old…a pain that echoed the sort I'd seen in Reinera's face ever since she'd told me of Julas, of…

A shipwreck. Such a strange, impossible end for such a talented, fearless Captain.

Shaking away that plaguing notion, I dove into the pocket of my bloodstained plum cloak, withdrawing one of the few things I'd kept with me since I'd left the compound…that I had kept for *him*.

"I wish I had saved more," I whispered, offering the token to him: a shard of rosined wood. All I had salvaged from Rhea's smashed fiddle.

Wilkes opened a quaking palm to me, and I dropped the fingerling shard among the weapon-calluses patching his rich brown skin. Slowly, he rolled the piece across his hand; a deep sniff bowed his chest inward. "She broke it herself. Over a Leech's head, when he grabbed Siu."

"She loved her fiddle." Gently, I closed his fingers over the shard. "She loved her crew far more."

His eyes flicked to me; a strained smile graced his lips, and those he brushed against my head fleetingly as he strode past me; without another word, he vanished.

My eyes warm, my throat aching, I sat with Cam in the silence—holding his hand and stroking the dirty hair from his brow until the ship's rocking lulled him into deeper slumber. And still I did not move, until Noveen slipped belowdecks and settled next to me.

"I'll look after him." Her smile hung rich with pain as she took over stroking Camden's hair. "He's hardly younger than my daughter back in Krylan. I'm sure I can mother him proper…you go have your hurts seen to."

With a murmur of thanks, I returned abovedecks to find many of the crew sleeping there—free of confinement, casting blankets along the deck and huddling near one another. Siu held the wheel now, her face set, jaw tight; but she edged out a halfhearted smile when our gazes met and stabbed a finger down toward the floor of the helm. To the Captain's cabin below.

With a nod of thanks, I made my way to the cabin door; it opened just as I arrived, and Gydeon limped out, cleaning his splinted fingers on a damp cloth. We halted, gazing at one another, my heart plummeting at my first true glimpse of his utterly marred face: his nose and jaw bent out of shape, both eye sockets blackened, the angles of his cheeks misshapen. I had seen kinder wounds left on dissenters Lucretzia had beaten senseless.

I stepped nearer, lost for words; Gydeon broke the silence first. "Thank you for intervening when you did." He slapped the cloth over his shoulder, glancing up toward the helm. "That's twice you've saved my life, and both times…both times made it clearer than ever I'm not ready to say goodbye."

"Nor are we to you." I offered my open arms; Gydeon smiled, his eyes crinkling.

"Gently, if you please."

So it was gently that I held him, shy of ribs and spine and any bones that might ache, judging by how he held himself; and though he embraced me lightly, the press of his cheek to my hair felt like a sort of homecoming I'd longed for since my parents were taken from me.

"Thank you, for coming back for us," he murmured against my head.

"Thank *you*," I croaked into his collar. "For saving his life."

Gydeon's fingers grazed my spine. "It was—"

I craned back, cupping my hand over his mouth for a moment. "Don't say that it was nothing."

He gazed down at me as my hand fell away, understanding warming the depths of his eyes. Then he pressed a kiss to my cheek. "It was my pleasure."

We stepped away from one another, though I kept my hands balanced beneath his elbows—ensuring myself that he, too, was still here, sturdy and breathing despite the new shadows gathered among the contusions and lacerations that scarred his face. "Will you be all right?"

He did not answer at once; heaviness bore down on his back, as if my words carried a weight he had shrugged off until now.

"I hope to be, in time." The raw honesty when his voice emerged again at last made me wish desperately I had reached the crew sooner—that I might have followed them straight from Bashir and freed them weeks ago. "For now, I am going to have my first hearty meal since that compound, and I am going to sleep next to my wife. And I owe those comforts to you."

"Nothing is owed. We'll carry no debts between us, Gydeon Nassar. I'm glad to have helped…and I'm glad that you have those things."

"Fair." He grazed his knuckles against the gash on my jaw, which throbbed but no longer bled. "Would you like me to see to this?"

It was what I had come to do; but now, knowing what awaited me beyond the cabin door, my hurts were all but forgotten. "In the morning."

Understanding sprinkled his gaze like powdered sugar. "Go see him. He was asking where you'd gone."

Squeezing his arm one last time, I let myself into the cabin.

Ryker sat astride the room's only table, his contours framed in a rich amber glow shed by the lonely lantern that swayed among the woven nets webbing the ceiling. Fresh bandages covered his middle, guarded beneath the splay of his palm; salve glinted tackily against the wound along his scalp.

I allowed myself a moment to watch him while he stared at the floor. Though hurt, he was alive—despite Lucretzia's best efforts. And that was more wonderful and complicated than if our final parting had been in that street.

I shut the door, and his eyes leaped to me; they were steely at first, shrouded with restraint—as if, after these many weeks apart, he had come to expect any aberrant sound to signify enemies prowling at the door.

And then, all at once, his features loosened; the harsh tilt of his spine eased, and he sat up straighter.

"'Ay." His eyes softened, and he stretched out a hand. "Come here."

I slipped between his knees, and he folded his arms around my waist; I wrapped mine around his neck, lacing my fingers behind his head, settling my brow to his. For a time, we lingered that way, the ship rocking us gently.

He broke the pause first, sliding his hand up to encircle the nape of my neck, his face angling slightly until his nose brushed the hinge of my shoulder. "You all right, sweetheart?"

"Better than I have been since Bashir."

His frame tightened, a cringe that bored into the depths of him. "I wouldn't have left you alone with that bloody serpent if the choice had been mine."

"Nor would I have left you in that street if she hadn't dragged me away." I tousled the tips of his hair, dripping and frigid, and wondered if Gydeon had insisted he bathe before he would see to him. "Your wounds?"

"It was close." His blunt admission scraped against my throat like a bone swallowed sideways. "But no one's as good as Gyddy. He got the lead out and patched me up before we left Bashir…at least, that's what Siu says. I wasn't awake for much of it."

My fingers wandered to the puckered line along his scalp, a shudder wracking through me when swollen, still-healing flesh met my fingertips. "Lucretzia intended you for death."

"Aye, well. Ahim's not finished with me yet."

"Nor am I."

I let that hang unexplained between us—let my actions in the shelter of the table in the Councilmeet and the way I'd screamed his name in the streets of Bashir tell all the rest.

"You have no idea how bloody relieved I was to see you up in those ropes." His breath grazed my neck, unleashing a deluge of shivers down my spine. "Spent the last…I don't know how many weeks it's been, wondering how in the depths I was going to get you out of Shadewyle, dreaming about rescuing you…turns out, I was the damsel needing to be saved."

A laugh dragged from my throat. "Well, I hope you dreamed up some truly spectacular schemes. We still have need of them."

He tugged away to look me in the eyes. "What—?"

"Later." I laid my fingers to his lips. "When we've rested. For now, I have something for you."

Drawing back further still, I slid the chain of his wheel pendant from around my neck. My skin bore a chill in its absence; I had grown so used to the weight of it, consoled by the chafe of the chain running against my skin like the errant touches of the Captain for whom my soul yearned.

I had no small difficulty offering it out to him, the skin-warmed metal tucked in my fist, the wheel itself catching the dim lanternlight from above.

"I know what this means to you." My hand, and my voice, trembled a bit. "It was never my intention to take it."

"Ah, keep it. It suits you." His throat bobbed with emotion.

"Are…are you certain?" I hadn't seen him without it since the night he'd traded coats aboard the *Singer*.

He gazed at the pendant for a moment; then he tugged it from my grasp. When I let it coil in his palm instead, it was only for him to span the chain between his sunkissed fingers and slip it over my head again.

"That's twice you've gone into the drink for me." He settled the pendant between my collarbones. "Not sure I deserved it either time. But seeing this on you, it reminds me what matters. Not saving ships from storms. Saving *people* from theirs."

His eyes hunted for mine, clouded with exhaustion and the horrors he had witnessed in Korsa—and likely aboard *The Depth Treachery*. And still, sincerity pierced through…the truth of Bastyan I had come to know beneath the tattered guise of Ryker and the darker shroud of Blackhand.

"You know I would've come for you, aye?" he murmured. "If they hadn't thrown me in the brig…I would've set every city on fire from here to Shadewyle until I got you out."

"I know." And I did. I *had* known—for far longer than I'd allowed even myself to believe—that whenever danger found me, this man was swift on its heels. Swift to step between me and any threat…and swift to guard my flanks when I chose to face the threats myself.

"I'm sorry for every rotten thing I did that made you doubt that." His hands twisted over mine, holding them to his shoulders. "Sorry I ever planned to make you a ransom. Sorry I acted like an Old Salt."

"It's forgiven." Truly, I had forgiven it long ago. "I know you wouldn't trade me now."

"Not a bloody chance in the depths," he muttered under his breath.

And even though I had known that to be true for some time—for weeks, now—still, it fanned warmth out from my core, hearing him speak the words his actions had long ago made clear.

"I know I don't deserve you," he added hoarsely, his gaze searching mine. "But I'm ready to spend the rest of my sorry life working to change that."

I brushed my thumb over the scarred cleft of his chin, dampness building in my eyes. "It's mine to decide what I deserve…and what I desire. And you, for every brilliant and rotten part, are both of those things." I pressed my lips to his brow. "I have not always been above reproach, either. My hands are no cleaner than yours."

His eyes rolled shut, and the arch of his throat bobbed. "What a pair we make, 'ay?"

He'd said as much before, when we'd baked bread together and freed the first steam-soft wisps of our secrets. But now, it was all laid bare…his truths and mine. His false name and mine. All of the ingredients of us, the stuff that made up who we were. Who we wished to be. And there, in the fragrant mix of it all, was the honesty we could not flee from. Not now…perhaps never again.

I had seized the fire within me and turned pirate for his crew. For *him*.

He had lost his ship and his legacy, even some of his friends, on this mad venture to find Tristah. For *me*.

"What a pair, indeed, Captain," I sighed.

He reared back slightly at that, bringing my hands down from his shoulders, finding them a resting place over his chest. "Oi. Say my name."

Another shiver tumbled through me. "Ryker—"

"Not that one."

I withdrew a bit. Blinked at him. "Bastyan?"

"Try again."

A laugh rose in my throat, and I brushed my nose against his. "*Bash.*"

His eyes fluttered shut. A sunshine grin curled up the side of his mouth, and his hand snared in the hair that straggled loose at the back of my neck. "I love the sound of that coming from your mouth."

With a snorting laugh, I let him lead me into a kiss; an unhurried one, as full of pain as it was full of pleasure…him, releasing his agony and sorrow into the press of our lips. Me, welcoming it and claiming it—my battle to fight alongside him. Those uncertain waters mine to tread with him until he found calm again.

I would fight no more battles that I did not choose. But I chose his.

He drew back several moments later, tilting his gaze up to mine, his hands still snared in my hair and along the breadth of my hip—these anchors, these places where he had drawn me so near to him, the table's edge beneath him bit into my skin.

"Do me a favor?" he muttered. "Stay the night. None of that bloody tonic on this boat, and…"

The rest went unspoken, a tale told by the harsh glint in his eyes.

The crew had suffered much. So much healing lay ahead.

And our task was not yet done.

So I stepped back and took his hands; I tugged him from the table and across the cabin to the bed. I pushed him down into it, and when he stretched out carefully, shifting and rocking to adjust to the bandages along his middle, I settled with him.

We lay facing one another, his head resting on the curl of his arm, mine propped up on my hand.

"I'll keep awake until you're sleeping peacefully," I offered.

Emotion shone in his eyes; his thumb grazed my lower lip. "Depths, I really bloody missed you, Lio."

I nipped at his thumb, drawing another sunshine smile from that mouth otherwise carved in lines of weariness. "And I you."

And I showed him again, with another kiss to quiet his fears. And again, with my leg curled over his hips and my arms tied about his neck. He held me, his hand splayed wide in the small of my back, his face buried in the crook of my neck. His warm breaths found paths over my shoulder, spilling along my spine— and presently, tears followed.

I held him while he wept. And I held him long after he eased into sleep, his face still hidden against my skin, his fingers still tangled in my shirt. I kissed his brow, and his hair, and ran my fingers along the mark on his scalp…the most detestable wound Lucretzia had ever dealt. A blow meant to shatter us both.

It had done the opposite. It had bound me to Bastyan Atreyon, to Ryker Kassian, to Captain Blackhand by the same blood and cause that made Tristah fight so fiercely for this country.

I had fought my way back to him. And now…

There was another fight to be had. One we would wage together.

But for tonight, I simply held him…soothed him when he stirred. Shielded him with my body from the terrors that lurked in the shadows. And in that tender darkness, some new power bloomed in me. Something undeniable; something impassioned and strong and determined beyond words.

Love took root in the dark.

And when it grew in me, petals unfurling to reveal the truth at its center, I knew—why I had come so far for him. Why his betrayals had hurt so terribly, and his kindness meant so much. Why the thought of his death in that street had nearly been my undoing.

I wrapped my arms tight around Ryker's shoulders, and wept—for once— with joy.

After so many months ripped away from Krylan, from my shop, from the life and choices I had built for myself…

At long last, I had found a home.

CHAPTER 76
RECKLESS, RELENTLESS LOVE

When the soft rap of knuckles on wood pierced the gauzy shawl of slumber, for a moment I thought that I was dreaming.

That belief did not fade at first; not when I opened my eyes to the near-gloom of the Captain's cabin and became aware of Ryker's arm draped around my waist, his breaths brushing the side of my neck.

I clamped my eyes shut again, burrowing deeper into these things—certain that if I roused fully, they would float away. Just as they had every time I had dreamed them since Bashir.

But when the knock came again, the weight of Ryker's arm shifted, changed; he drew me nearer to him, tucking me against his side. And no dream could replicate that comfort.

Squinting through the dim, I spied a shadow dripping beneath the cabin door from the deck...someone waiting for one of us.

Carefully, I eased my body from beneath Ryker's arm; I held my place alongside him when he stirred, gripping his hand until he settled again. Then I slipped from the cot, found his discarded Captain's coat by touch, and drew it on over my shoulders as I slipped from the room.

Killian stepped back on the deck to give me space when I emerged, his brows furrowing as he beheld my attire; I laced the coat over my chest, waiting for his gaze to find mine. "You knocked?"

He jerked his chin at the railing. "Let's talk."

Even through the lingering haze of bleary slumber, I was surprised he hadn't sought me sooner.

We went to the ship's side, leaning ourselves into the railing, watching the lanternlight paint flagrant steaks across the tunnel's stone walls. I wondered if the fire made him think of Tristah…if *everything* did.

He held his silence for a long, bracing moment—preparing himself to ask the question that had no doubt ravaged him since the Councilmeet. And preparing to hear the answer he likely already expected.

"Where is she?" When the words emerged at last, they stood strong—until the very end. Until the soft crack in his voice buckled on the last word. Until the way his fists tightened as he crossed his arms over his broad chest.

Heat blistered in my nose and scoured the backs of my eyes. "Lucretzia took her."

A single bob of his head was the only warning he gave.

Then he swiveled, smashing his fist into the rigging post that jutted from the railing. I could only wince at the crack of bone on wood, the rip of giving flesh; I could not save him from it. Nor from the rage that drew his breaths in and shoved them out again, a brutal, vicious kneading of lungs desperate to pull in air. To stave off panic.

"*Damn it!*" he howled. "*Damn it, damn it, damn it!*" Every foreign profanity he punctuated with another blow…until his knuckles were thatched with cuts and whoever had taken watch up in the crow's nest barked for him to be quiet.

"Killian." I caught him beneath the arm when he reared back for another strike. "You cannot punish yourself into protecting her. It's done. She chose to face Lucretzia."

"She chose *you*." The accusation lived only in the words, not in the grief-cracked rasp of his voice.

"She *chose*," I repeated. "And that was what mattered most to her. Now we *choose* how to get her back."

He shrugged me off only to shake out his fist, to swipe blood from his knuckles. "What are they doing to her?"

"I don't know." One of the countless truths I'd fled from since that eternal night spent in the empty compound courtyard, waiting for a sister who never came. "Their aims for her have changed. Lucretzia cannot afford her damaged, but the Del will not wish her to live."

"It wasn't enough," he growled. "It wasn't *enough*, every risk she took, making herself his enemy. They took her *anyway*."

"Better they took her than executed her. We can cheat at this game Lucretzia plays. We cannot cheat death."

"Maybe." Killian's gaze dropped with his fist, winding into the folds of his deep blue cloak. "Maybe not."

"Killian. We *will* retrieve her. I have absolute faith in this crew, and Tristah's faith in *you* was absolute." I hesitated before I gave him the next words—an assurance I could only speak because I knew Tristah as intimately as my own heart. "She would not have faced the risk of falling to Lucretzia if she did not believe you would come for her."

As she had come for him, when we'd had him in our clutches; despite their *code*, their *understanding*, she had come. I did not know him as she did; but I knew enough to be certain because of these things that when I returned to face Shadewyle, I would not do it alone.

His gaze darted to me, glassy, nearly unfocused. "She never wanted to go to that place again."

Following some impulse, my hand darted out, catching a tear before it escaped the corner of his eye. "We will not let her stay there."

With a gruff curse, he twisted his face to the crook of his elbow, dashing more tears before they escaped. The blue of his cloak fluttered in the darkness— a reminder of the power that had blazed forth from him like an inferno in the Councilmeet. A power like none I had ever witnessed before.

"Your Storycraft…that was a sight to behold," I offered—a merciful distraction for us both.

He snorted quietly. "Tristah would've lost her mind."

"She always wanted to see it, I'm sure."

"With the things I told her about what it could do? She knew it could've changed everything for Amere-Del. For the dissenters." He paused, his mouth twisting to the side. "Maybe it still can."

My bones ached at his reverent tone; they had not quite forgotten the shudder, the bow, the bend of the world as unseen power had blown through the Councilmeet. As it had bled color into his cloak. "What happened today in that tower?"

"Storycraft came back." The words were simple, but the feverbrightness of his eyes roared brighter than any hearth. "It's been gone…the endings, all of it, for years. But I've been telling little stories to myself ever since we set sail, and I'm ending them. Every one."

The relief in his tone was not quite fully realized—as if he could celebrate nothing without Tristah here to share it. But at least he was no longer striking the rigging, bloodying himself. So for his sake—and for Tristah's, who would never want to see him harmed—I pursued the matter.

"Whatever became of Storycraft?" I felt as if I had been told the finer points back in Krylan, but that knowledge had been carved out of me. Perhaps by time. Perhaps by all the perils I had faced since leaving Mithra-Sha.

For a long moment, Killian was quiet. Then, "I don't really know," he confessed at length—a truth twisted brutally from his chest, as if the Incendiary's spymaster was not used to being caught unawares. "No one does."

"No one at all?"

"At least no one I've found…that's why I was in Korsa when I met Tristah. I was searching for a vessel to sail me to a place where all the tales of the world are chronicled. I just got…distracted."

By meeting Tristah. By a cause more tangible than the answers to an unsolvable problem. And how could anyone lay blame on him? In a world of broken stories and impossible things, Tristah had been absolute. Real.

"I graduated from Fablehaven Academy more than a decade ago with a cloak this color," Killian added softly. "All Storycrafters have a colored cloak that darkens as they train their craft…different colors for the different kinds of telling they're best at. I fought for years for this, for the blue. Tales of adventures. Epics. Quests. The stories my mother used to tell me, that my brother and I would act out with our toy swords and shields." Emotion roughened his voice again; he cleared it away. "I left Fablehaven and came straight to Amere-Del to start a new life, helping people where I could, dodging the Del's eyes looking everywhere for Storycraft. And then one day, a few years ago, this cloak just…" A helpless bob of his shoulders. "It turned gray. And I couldn't end a single story anymore. All the power was gone."

A flit of ashen color traced my mind—his cloak as I had first seen it, that night in the alley in Bashir. The cloaks of Storycrafters I had spotted now and again in Krylan, though they had never stayed in the city long. "You never learned why it lost its color?"

He shook his head. "And I don't know what brought it back now. But it's good I have it, because we're going to need this power to rewrite the ending these people have in mind for Tristah. It can reshape the world. Create something from nothing. Change your fate." Chafing a corner of the cloth between his fingers, he scoffed quietly. "It can change *everything*."

"Then it can help us save her."

His gaze darted to mine, a sheen of emotion stark across his night-blue eyes. "It had *better.*"

It might have frightened me, once, that tone in his voice—that warning hurled against a world-shaping power like Ahim's, daring and challenging creation incarnate to bow to his whims. As if he would go to war, might against might, if it did not serve him.

It frightened me no longer. I ran with pirates now. I had seen power in so many shapes and forms—not merely what people like Zorast and Athyna and Lucretzia wielded. But the power of determination. The power of undying inner fire. The power of reckless, relentless love.

And I wanted nothing less than Killian at his most brutal at my side when it came to rescuing Tristah.

"We will find her," I vowed. "And we will write the end of our stories our own way, Storycrafter."

A spirit of a smile flitted on his lips. "You sound just like her."

"Naturally." I affected Tristah's confident drawl for his sake. "You thought I *was* her, in the Councilmeet, did you not?"

I'd hoped to soothe him; instead, pain flickered in the depths of his eyes. He turned them back to the lanterns sparkling on the prow of the ship, resting his folded arms on the railing. "I was seeing what I wanted to see."

Grief burned like spatters of hot oil on the surface of my heart. I leaned against the railing as well, posture mirroring his. "Ryker was right about you, wasn't he? You love her."

Killian stiffened, his focus cutting my way; I kept mine ahead, giving him a wide berth to make his own way to whatever answer he would give.

After a moment, he grunted, "Love is not the right word for it."

No. Love was not fierce enough. It did not capture every dimension of it.

It was fealty. Adoration. Dedication. The spark that lit the ember aflame.

"Whatever it is, keep it burning." I pushed back from the railing. "It will help us keep her—and each other—alive."

That parting notion invited a chill that clung to my skin, seeping deep like filthy water into a cleaning sponge, when I slipped back into the cabin. Shivers twisted my muscles into damp dishrag knots at the thought of Tristah spending this night in the prison of our shared nightmares; and at the thought of what price that prison might demand of both Killian and I, in the end, to set her free.

The cold only eased when I neared the bedside, and Ryker rolled to an elbow. He peered blearily at me, frown lines etched deep into his sunweathered brow. "How's he holding water?" A rare and unexpected concern textured his tone. He must have woken when I left.

"I suspect you would say his hull is full of holes." I dredged a small smile for him—what little I could manage in the face of what lay ahead. And what I had left behind on me on the deck…the suffering and fear Killian grappled with. And most of it alone.

"Not surprised," Ryker grunted. "We'll keep him busy aboard…help him spend all that energy somewhere useful."

I paused to coax one of the lanterns to life, just enough to chase away the shadows. "Are you certain you wouldn't prefer him to simmer?"

"Not this time." Slowly, Ryker rolled himself over to face me. "If I was standing where he's standing, with everything he's got to lose right now…I'd sail this fish barrel of a boat so hard and fast, every board would come apart and it would just be a few scraps floating into the harbor. And I'd paddle those planks with my bare hands until I got wherever you were."

Gratitude finally eased my chills; I padded to the bedside, and he pushed himself gingerly upright, gripping the halves of my borrowed coat and drawing me near.

"This is a good look on you," he offered—a bit sleep-muddled, and his smile made all the sunnier by it.

Snorting a breath, I tumbled—not reluctantly in the least—into his lap. Tying my arms around his neck and my legs around his waist, I buried my face in his shoulder; his missing-fingered hand tangled in my hair, his other arm tucking around my back, banding me so near to him that my shivers rattled him, too.

"We'll find her, sweetheart. We'll steal her back, aye? No one better for the job than pirates." The words rumbled through him, into me. Making themselves a home. Making themselves believed, if only for a moment. A promise these shadows could not steal.

With a powerful thrust of his legs, he rolled us onto the bed, me atop him, without a falter in his grip. His hand left my back only to toss the starched blankets over us both; then he held me again, fingers finding sea-forged paths like maps and starlines along my spine, to my nape, and back to my waist.

I wasn't certain when the chill left me entirely. I only knew, on the cusp of sleep, that it made sense. That fear could not survive in this place. In his arms.

This time, it was me who slept, and him who took watch.

I had not slept so well since Bashir.

CHAPTER 77
FLAG AND COUNTRY

e sailed for days in utter darkness, broken only by the thin, distant sheen of mineral ore and the lanterns we burned low along the ship, preserving the fat that lit them. In the passing of time, the motley crew found its rhythm in shifts that allowed for those who most needed to rest—to heal—to make the time for it. The rest worked the lines and watched the current, guiding our voyage through tunnels I would not have had a prayer to Ahim of navigating were it not for our keen and talented Second Mates.

The work seemed to do Klem a great deal of good; she did not beat against the ship or rage in word and gaze when she worked the helm with Ryker or Siu. And she did not quite snarl when I approached her the third day of our journey through the mountains—though her curled lip nearly sent me away.

Steadfast nonetheless, I stuck my feet to the deck at her side and spoke the words that had been building in me ever since we'd fled Korsa: "I am more sorry about Kory than I can say. He was one of the kindest souls I've ever known."

Her lip unfurling, she peered ahead into the blackness, and for a moment I wondered if she wished I would vanish into it; but when I held my place, she muttered at last, "He was the youngest. Our baby brother. Kato and I raised him, you know? Our mother...she broke when he was born. Just went out gambling in Bashir and never came home."

"Was...was it she who taught you to gamble?"

A long pause; then Klem nodded. "We used to play cards to pass the time, waiting for Da to sail back into Port Krait. When she was pregnant with Kory, a storm came up, and..." Klem slanted one shoulder. "She was unraveling the whole time she was pregnant with him. Five days after he was born—as soon as she could get out of bed—she was gone. Never came back."

I hesitated a moment before cautiously setting my hand on her shoulder. She shuddered, but she did not pull away.

"I did not know you then," I murmured, "but from the moment I met this crew, it was clear you and Kato loved Kory enough to make up for all the love he never knew from her."

With a deep, shaking inhale, Klement wiped her fingers beneath her nose. "It was our responsibility to protect him. He shouldn't have put himself in the way for me."

"He loved you." All I could offer in the face of her pain. "My love for Tristah might not be a blood sister's, but it's the nearest I know. And for her, I would have done the same. Even staring down Dred's pistol."

Klem glanced my way. "So, where is she? Cap says you found her back in Bashir."

"I did." The truth stuck in my throat. "The Pale Viper has her."

Her breath dragged in, then rattled out. "So, what are you planning to do about it, Seasplitter?"

A challenge lived in her voice—but also, perhaps, a plea.

Like *The Athalion's* crew, the Raiders were adrift now, in need of purpose…somewhere to aim their blows. Something to sail toward; a cause to make them come alive again.

"I'm planning a siege," I confessed. "One that requires all hands on deck."

She studied me a long moment; then she called without turning, "Oi! Syd, take the prow. Lanah, hold the helm." Without awaiting their reply from up at the wheel, Klem caught me under the arm and towed me down the deck. "We're going to have a talk with the Captain."

For the first time since the compound, we had an assembly of sorts—several warm bodies stuffed in the Captain's cabin. But it was different now; the gathering was both painful and intriguing in its own merits.

Ryker, Siu, Gydeon, Wilkes, Kato, and Klem made up the seasoned Raiders among us, sprawled on the small variety of cots and seats and chests all bolted to the floor. Camden had joined us as well—uninvited, but undiscouraged. He sat cross-legged on the floor next to Killian, whose shimmering cloak spilled like sea waves across his lap.

Reinera, Noveen, Hasser, and Osred—the gunner of *The Athalion* and the oldest of us by some years—made up the representatives of their crew. They dotted among the Raiders, sharing seats and floor space, Noveen with one arm tucked around Camden's blanket-shrouded shoulders from the other side. Their carpenter, Annet, we had also invited; but she had declined, consumed with learning the particulars of how Wyst had run his duties among the crew.

And then there was me, seated on the rim of the small desk against which Ryker leaned with folded arms. My heart thudded in my throat as I took in all of their faces, marked with trials and tribulations endured, together and apart, in the months that lay behind us.

And I had more to ask of them yet.

Ryker finally broke the pause once Killian had shut the door and sat against it; the spymaster's eyes were on me, drying up the words in my throat with the scorch of their intensity.

"So. You're a Storycrafter," Ryker lobbed at Killian—a blast across the bow.

"So. You're an idiot," he shot back without skipping a breath.

"As long as we're stating the obvious," Gydeon added, jerking a thumb at Siu, "that's my wife, the light of my life."

"We *noticed*," Reinera, Noveen, and Hasser all groaned, and Osred guffawed.

"Apparently, half the people on this ship are love-struck fools," Reinera added with a cheeky smirk my way. "What makes you so special?"

"Nothing. Scribbles here is the special one." Ryker nodded to Killian, "Which might just help us survive what's coming next."

Wilkes sat forward on his perch, hands braced on his knees; the low lanternlight caught against the wooden shard dangling by a leather cord against his chest. "Which is—?"

"Getting Tristah back." Killian was serious all at once—deathly so.

I nodded. "Rescuing this crew was only one half of my plan. The rest is a siege on Shadewyle Castle."

Siu scoffed. "A *siege* on the paranoid Del's home? Are you mad?"

"Yes, I am. Furious, to be specific," I retorted. "And I know that all of you are as well. The Del's Own Blade facilitated your capture. She is the reason everything fell apart in Bashir. It's time to pay her back her dues."

No one argued that. *The Athalion's* crew watched me with intrigue as keen as the Raiders'.

I beat my heel gently against the side of the desk, giving my thoughts a moment to form before I spoke them. "Tristah and I swore long ago that we would never leave one another in the Del's clutches…and that we would never go back to Shadewyle Castle. Tristah has done everything in her power to ensure the latter, but Lucretzia has other schemes."

"What schemes, *precisely*?" Killian growled.

"Schemes to make Tristah the Della. She believes she can manipulate Tristah…that she can shape her into whatever she wishes."

He snorted. "She would have better odds bending a blade with her hands."

"I know…and that is precisely what I fear. Lucretzia has no mercy, no compassion, no lines she will not cross to achieve her ends. And her ends are to see Amere-Del made peaceful by deception. A puppet Del—Algernon Sorai—controlled by marriage to a puppet Della."

Killian blanched—so utterly, the stark blue of the veins in his eyelids and beneath his jaw paired intricately to the shade of his cloak.

"If that happens, Tristah suffers unimaginably." I could coax little breath to the words. "Because, to force her into that, Lucretzia *must* shatter her. In every conceivable way." Splinters from the desk dug beneath my fingernails. "And, if it does not happen, it means that Tristah is dead."

Silence enfolded the room, heavy with the rank stench of death—too many deaths in too short a time.

Rhea. Wyst. Kory. Willy. Julas. Frixia. Cook. Henriet. Nix and Nash. And others, crewmates lost in the skirmish in Anoram, and in a storm—a *storm*, of all things—just beyond Fallshyre Bay.

We had all faced death enough of late.

"It is not a matter of whether a siege is going to happen," I added when the silence did not break. "I am going to Shadewyle. So is Killian. It's only a matter of whether we do it as two, or as many."

Glances traded all around the room—the crews looking among themselves. Asking the silent, heavy questions.

I swallowed, battling the unease that coated my throat like flour poured on the kneading block. "It has been so long since I stood for anything but myself. I chose long ago to have no people…but you have all changed that. Tristah changed that when we were only girls. *You* are my people. *You* are my flag and country. And so is she." I slid from the desk, landing at Ryker's side. "Will you help me?"

"We will," Reinera said, and all around her the crew of *The Athalion* nodded. "Del Graven is nothing but a pain to traders and sailors and his own flipping country. And no one deserves to suffer through the sort of things you and Tristah have."

I turned to Ryker, but he did not look my way; instead, he conferred with Siu in a long, silent stare. Then he said, quietly, "Would you lot give the Raiders the room?"

I had anticipated their hesitation. They were only days free of Korsa's cruel hold; now I asked a new, dangerous task of them. Still, my heart twisted and my stomach curled in on itself as Reinera led her crew from the room, and Killian stalked out after them.

"You, too, sweetheart." Ryker's tone was steady, but his gaze pleaded for faith. And though I had once sworn I would never do so again…I put my trust in him.

I shut the door behind me as I stepped out onto the darkened topdeck; Killian waited at the mainmast, pitched against it with folded arms and a foot cast back on the wood. I leaned against the opposite side, shutting my eyes, breathing in the same damp air that had coated my lungs ever since we'd set sail for Korsa.

I was almost beginning to like it.

"It will be enough," Killian said after a moment; fabric chafed between calluses, and then he murmured, "with my power, it will be enough. Even if it's only us and Reinera's crew."

"I know." The heat in my throat stifled the words to wisps. "But I would feel much more settled if the Raiders joined us."

Particularly with the strategy I had concocted on the long, empty journey through the mountain passes by horseback, reflecting on the generational paranoia that had first carved those paths into the world. The same paranoia I would have to circumvent in order to ever be truly free.

That strategy was best executed with the Raiders in our ranks. Otherwise, I was far less certain I would survive what was to come.

CHAPTER 78
NO RANSOM, NO MERITS

RYKER

The quiet in the cabin after Lio shut the door was like the quiet deep under the sea—the kind that made your ears pop, the pushed in on every side. Like it was trying to drown you…like it wanted to make itself a home under your skin.

For a while, no one opened their mouths. No one let the water in. They just sat there, thinking; Gydeon tucked Siu up under his arm, and she held onto his waist, leaning her head into the side of him. Kato pitched himself against the wall and slid down beside Cam, and Klem stood over them like a wolf keeping watch, hackles up. Wilkes bent forward on the empty chest he'd made into his seat, rubbing his face with both hands.

It was probably the most thinking we'd all ever done together. I had to roll the kinks out of my neck and crack my fingers under the fold of my arms, one by one, to keep myself from being the one who shoved us off the next edge.

"A siege on the Del's own castle." Wilkes whistled quietly, finally—and I could've kissed him for breaking up the silence. "It hasn't been tried in a hundred years."

"Not even the Old Salts would make the attempt," Gydeon agreed.

"Could you help us through the cracks?" I prodded Wilkes.

He sat back on the chest, running his fingers through his beard. "Sure the patterns have changed since I turned pirate, but…the castle is the same as when I served under the Pale Viper."

"Between what Wilkes knows about the militar and what Lio knows of creeping in and out, a siege does stand a better chance for us than for most," Kato allowed.

A *better* chance still didn't mean a surefire one. It didn't mean we wouldn't leave with more holes blown in our hull…more dead friends and brothers.

My tongue knotted up like a mooring line. What would've come out like an order before—like telling them we were staying in the *Pearl* in Korsa or setting course to Bashir or stealing the Delina for ransom, no questions asked—couldn't sail out with that snag in its ropes.

There were too many gaps in our crew because of the bloody orders I gave. The ones that belonged to Blackhand…that made me a pirate. That made me a bastard like Varsi, like Merry Dred.

I was done with that life. Done owning the choices for this crew. It was no use saving them for their debts if I drowned them on the way out.

"I'm not telling you all to take this on," I said. "After what we just went through, no one has the right to order you—"

"*Ask us*, then," Siu groaned, picking her head up off of Gyddy. "Just bloody ask us, you fool!"

I looked between all of them—my ragged, scowling, beaten-to-the-bone crew. "We do this, there's no ransom. No merits. We just blew our way out of Korsa for the second time…whoever's left after that, they'll never stop hunting us. So we've got it worse than we ever did, and no way to pay off the debts."

"Just *more* debts," Kato muttered, "if we fail."

"If we give the Del a reason to hunt us, too, you mean," Siu scoffed.

"There's no chance of a ransom that can buy us out of that," I agreed.

Gyddy busted up laughing—and hearing that sound for the first time in weeks made his next words sting a lot less: "We knew the ransom was sunk a long time ago, brother."

Siu's snort had me flushing redder than a boiled lobster. "A *long time*, Gyddy? You owe me fifty merits."

"My merits *are* your merits, love."

"That's not what you said when you made the bet!"

"He made a bet with *you*?" Camden whined, pushing himself up tall against the door with both feet. "He made a bet with *me!*"

"How many times have I told you, you're too young to gamble," Kato grumbled.

"Should have taken your own advice, mate," Wilkes scoffed. "This might be the first time you owe *me*."

"I'll carve it out of your debt to me, then."

My teeth skinned themselves on each other when I looked around at all their smug, sourpuss faces. "How long?"

Wilkes swapped a look with Klem; she cracked her first real smile since Korsa, a tiny little thing that spelled out *hope* like writing in the sand. "I don't know, maybe when you *ignored* your Second Mate's good sense and started this mad hunt for the decoy in the first place?"

"How 'bout when you dropped me like a hot biscuit at the compound and *ran* to get her from the bakery that one night?" Camden sulked.

"When we had to tackle you to stop you jumping off the *Singer* back the first time we escaped Korsa, going after her?" Wilkes chimed in.

"When Scribbles hauled your bleeding, half-dead hide into the compound the night the Leeches took us, and all you rambled on about was *getting her*?" Kato scoffed.

"The absolute *second* you brought her onto the *Singer* that first night," Siu tossed in, brows peaking. "I saw the way you walked beside her, the way you leaned your whole self her way, and I knew right then we wouldn't be sending any sort of letter of ransom to the Del."

"At least not one that had anything but a long list of places he could go and things he could do to himself on the way there," Gydeon snickered.

"If you didn't get to him first." Wilkes folded his arms and flicked me a look that dared me to argue.

I really wasn't enjoying this mutiny.

"All right," I bit out, "so I'm sunk for her and none of you blasted pirates are surprised. Joy. The question stands: what are we gonna do about it?"

"The Del is a crab's armored ass." Klem flicked his name off like chum from her fingernails. "And Lio's right, his little snake is the reason the Salts got their hands on us. At least this way, we know the pain we're getting into, and we can pay it back. I'm in."

"I can't think of another crew I'd rather be on the run with for the rest of my days." Kato smirked, propping an elbow on Cam's shoulder.

"Debt's not worth paying off if you have to turn into someone like the Leeches to pay it, anyway." Cam scowled up at me. "I'll never be like them. Especially if it means leaving behind someone who matters to *Lio*."

"Aye, that's my thinking," I moved to crouch on his level. I owed him that. "But you've tasted the worst side of this life now, lad. It could be worse again."

Cam's eyes tightened at the corners, but he set his jaw like steel. "We'll be all right. Sometimes it takes strong people a while to heal, too…and we're the strongest there is. So we'll find our way through this, all of us, together. With Lio's friend. Right?"

Grimacing, I rested a hand on his sandy hair. "Aye, mate. All right. We'll find a way through."

"I always hated that ransom idea, anyway," Gydeon added, and the rest of the crew raised their voices in agreement—some sheepish, most relieved.

A knot twisted in my guts. Depths, this all would've been easier if I'd asked them in the first bloody place.

But maybe they hadn't felt like they could tell me how they felt about the ransom—how they felt about *Lio*. Because I'd never given the truth to them, either…how much debt I had to pay off for myself. Or how I'd come back from sneaking onto *The Athalion* already hating the ransom plan, because somewhere sailing from Port Craythin to Monsha, Bastyan Atreyon woke up again, hearing his name from Lio's mouth.

And that lad had never turned pirate. He'd stuck his feet in shallower waters…he knew how to open himself so wide, he drank the deep. And he'd found something to hold onto, down in those depths.

He'd grabbed hold of the woman who jumped into the drink to pull him out…and he'd never let go. Even when Ryker Kassian tried to.

It took Lio sanding down my edges before the crew could see me straight…see the Bastyan in me. Someone who was a lot more like them—waifs and debtors and dreamers—than any sorry sod playing Blackhand could ever hope to be.

I'd had a crew before. Now I had a family, something I'd stopped wishing for ever since my grandad died and my parents threw me onto *The Silver Spice*, ever since the sea had ripped Antigony away…some recipe that had been missing its secret ingredient, right until Lio stepped onto the ship that first night.

"We made a deal a long time ago…none of us gets left behind. When we pay off our debts, when we sink in the deep—we go down together," Siu reminded us, her eyes firebright. "Lio is one of us now. Her friends are, too. And the Raiders never leave their own."

"That's right." Gydeon's mouth crinkled up at the corner. "Call her and that Storycrafter back in, Captain. Let's go get their girl."

CHAPTER 79
THE DELINA IT DESERVES

The relief of both crews' agreement to my suicidal scheme devolved swiftly into tension over the particulars…which had many of us gathered in the Captain's cabin long into the night, arguments flying like flung sparking powder.

Certain things seemed obvious; where we would sail, where we would dock, what flags we would fly. Who would stage a raid on the town of Shadewyle to draw militar attention. But as for who would take the path of truest danger…that remained in contestation long after we all should have slept off our tempers.

Ryker pitched himself against the wall, his cropped hair tossed casually over to hide the wound on his head, his arms folded to guard his middle. Once more a Captain; once more a man in command. "The fewer we take inside the castle, the better chance we have of doing this right."

"And you think the *right* way is just you, Steelheart," Siu jerked her chin at Wilkes, "and the Storycrafter?"

"For facing the Viper? Aye." Ryker shoved his hair back when it strayed across his brow. "Any more than that, and I'll just have to worry about how to cover them."

"Why should the numbers matter, when a Storycrafter is one of them?" Reinera demanded, folding her arms on the edge of the desk and easing her back into the bend of it. "I've seen what his kind are capable of, and since it seems stories have their endings back now—"

"It matters because I won't be the one facing the Del's Own Blade." One arm banded across his chest, his free hand tucked against his mouth and muffling the flat words, Killian studied the crude sketch of Shadewyle Castle we had drawn up and spread out on the desk. "My Storycraft will be a diversion."

Ryker snapped his fingers and pointed to Killian. "Spot on."

"The Pale Viper commands legions," Wilkes agreed. "And likely she has them prepared for almost any sort of siege. Only something unexpected like Storycraft will be enough to lure them from their posts…and, that being the case, we want them lured away from *her*."

"The Viper stranded, and two against one…" Ryker shrugged. "I like those odds well enough."

I did not; not when their last confrontation had ended with a hole blasted through his middle. My hands shuddered at the memory, and I tucked them into the pockets of my skirt, leaning into the edge of the desk when exhaustion threatened to sweep my feet from beneath me.

We had been having this same argument for *hours*.

"The truth," I broke into the argument still being waged between Ryker and Siu, "is that we will need at least two diversions to make a rescue attempt possible. Maybe even three."

"Why that many?" Klem demanded.

"Because the militar guard every way into Shadewyle Castle…and since Tristah and I escaped through them, they likely guard the tunnels below as well." I tapped the sketch Siu had drawn up from mine and Wilkes's memories, staggered and stacked from the lower halls Tristah and I had fled down, up to the heights of the towers the Graven family occupied. "After the first diversion, they will become suspicious. After the second, they will move to guard the Del. We will need a third to draw them back from him."

"So we can depose him." Killian's eyes flared with vicious light. "Kill him."

The gravity of that—the notion of murdering the ruler of Amere-Del—stole the air from the room.

Even if it was necessary. Even if was the only way to prevent the Everreach from being destroyed, and war between the Northlands and Southlands, and taxation so grievous only the regime and the pirate lords in Korsa would hold a scrap of merits after this…

It was death premeditated.

It was something Lucretzia would have done.

"There is that." Ryker flattened his mustache with a thumb and forefinger. "Getting to the Viper's one thing…she ought to be spoiling for a fight."

"The best way to have that fight is for *you* to challenge her," Wilkes said. "She presumes you dead. I can hold off any militar she brings along, but your face will knock her off balance."

My guts snarled in a knot. I met Ryker's gaze—and, predictably, found nothing there but eagerness salted with a bit of vengeance. No fear, to face the woman who had tried to murder him—and nearly succeeded—to punish *me*.

"So if Scribs and Steelheart and me are on diversion and Del's Own Blade duty," Ryker tipped his thumb and smallest finger between himself and Killian, "who's taking the Del?"

"Tristah has the talent," Killian said, "but I don't…" He smoothed his hand over his mouth again, and left it settled there when he surrendered the brutal truth we had both dodged thus far like artful dancers, "I don't know what state I'll find her in. Whether she'll be fit to fight."

"I'm happy to do it," Klem growled. "For Kory."

"Not a chance," Ryker shot back. "You and Siu are handling the city, and I'll be sunk to the depths before I let you take on a fight like that before your head's clear."

"What about *your* crew?" Gydeon asked of Reinera. "Do you have any bodies capable of this?"

The pallor of Reinera's complexion—showing off a soft spattering of sienna freckles that had never been visible before—drew the clearest line in the sands I had ever seen between these crews. "We can fight for our ship…we've fought for it before. But, no. No one I know of could manage…this. Not even Lanah, with her history among pirates."

I leaned my hands into the map, staring down at the rough sketch of a castle I knew like my own shadow. A castle I could surely slip back into, now that I'd escaped it once.

Nausea unspooled in my belly. Denial singed the tip of every nerve. But when I ached to withdraw from the table, I bowed my weight into it instead, feeling every crease and crinkle of the dry paper against my palms.

Eyes wide open.

No one else could do this the way I could. No one else could free Tristah forever by ending the threat of Del Graven. No one else could truly set *me* free, except the one who had been able to all along…who had chosen her own name, who had *made* her freedom among pirate captors and schemes for a future that belonged only to her.

Take power where you can.

"Enough," I said; though my voice was quiet, it halted the arguing around me. "I will do this."

Ryker pushed up sharply from the wall. Killian's hand dropped from his mouth, swinging loose at his side. Wide-eyed, Siu straightened, staring at me as if she had never seen me before.

Because they did not know *this* Lio quite so well.

This Lio, who was also Alyona. Who had found the places they met, in the long and empty journey from Bashir to Monsha.

"Lucretzia has long coveted Tristah…but I know Zorast. He wanted *me*, and he will have only grown to want me more if he has learned the truth of who Tristah is." I cast a glance at Killian, whose jaw tightened. "That is a weakness in their shared mind which I can exploit. I am the only one who can appear before the Del without being struck down on sight…and I am the only one he will not expect a double-cross from."

Siu snorted. "Then he's a fool."

Gratitude nudged out my smile. "He does not know me as I am now…only as I was. And that woman did not often fight for herself."

Ryker's eyes narrowed, and he averted his gaze—glanced away from the truth he, too, had once exploited.

I forced my smile wider and warmer for his sake, a reminder of another truth equally as powerful: he had also helped strengthen the woman who *would* take that fight. Who would do whatever she must to save Tristah.

And by saving her, perhaps I would save Amere-Del. Perhaps it was the only way I ever could—by giving the country the Delina it deserved.

"Lucretzia intends to shape Tristah into the absolute vision of the Delina in every way. As if she *is*, and always was, Alyona Graven," I said. "I intend for that as well, and more. Tristah will become me…and I will become her."

The crew swapped looks full of uncertainty. Disbelief. Confusion.

All except Ryker, whose scowl deepened with every throbbing heartbeat; and Killian, who settled back on his heels, eyes wide with realization.

"She wasn't the Delina," he breathed. "That was *you*. She was *your* decoy."

I bobbed a nod his way. Tristah had truly chosen her spymaster well. "But you can see why she told you otherwise, can you not? Those who knew Alyona Graven are far more likely to believe in the image *Tristah* presents now…the fearless one. The warrior. The woman who stands with blade in hand, who commands the room with a single breath."

My next blink unleashed a shimmer across my vision; in its dancing freckles, I beheld the memory of Tristah as she'd come through the blown-apart window to rescue Killian.

Shaking the notion away, I swept a hand down the length of my body…this version of myself I had fought so hard to build, and to heal, and to love.

"Not this," I added. "This, they would far more expect of a decoy…the softness. The love of baking. A gentle woman with a taste for sweets, with a ring in her nose and hands used to sewing and building and day labor." All things I had made and claimed for myself. "Tristah is everything the people dreamed of, and everything they need. And so we must give them precisely that…and let the decoy take the blame."

Killian tilted his head. "It's…precise spywork, actually. The decoy lives and dies in a single day."

"Oi!" Ryker's arms fell from their cross, his gaze flashing between us. "Who said anything about anyone *dying*?"

"We *will* have to see it through to the end." I shared a nod with Killian. "There will never be a sense of safety among the people once they learn their Delina has a mirrored face…not unless they hear Alyona Graven condemn me, and see me fall."

"Herbs," Gydeon put in suddenly, his own arms folded, a thoughtful tilt to his brows. "There are herbs that can do the trick. That can imitate death."

Hope bloomed in my chest, and I nodded his way. *This* was precisely why I'd coveted the Raiders' aid in this siege on Shadewyle Castle.

"Stop. *Stop*." Ryker flashed his palms at both of us. "Slow down and think this through for a bloody minute—"

"I've been thinking it ever since I left Anoram." I stepped forward, snaring his hand, bringing it to rest over my heart—letting him feel its steady, unhurried beat. Letting my confidence soak into him. "For the first time in all my life, I do not fear them. For the *first* time, I know how to make good on every day they held me prisoner. On everything they ever did to me."

His fingers contracted slightly; then they shifted, sliding up my clavicle, winding gently around the column of my neck. "Sweetheart…you don't have to do this." His eyes shone with anguish on my behalf—the pain of knowing what this would cost me. And I trusted that pain; it gave me strength.

"For all that they know, I won't." Gently, I tied my fingers between Ryker's—and brought his hand down from my neck. "It will be Tristah who does this deed…and that is why it must be me."

"For the ruse to hold, they must believe Tristah is the one fully responsible for the Del's demise," Killian agreed.

"She can do this, Captain," Gydeon said; his faith warmed me through.

"I know she can *do* it." Ryker's eyes held mine. "I don't like that she doesn't have a choice."

But I *did* have a choice. I could walk away and leave Tristah in Lucretzia's clutches. I could allow her to ascend, to become the Della on another man's terms—by the Del's sordid dealings. At the side of Algernon Sorai, forsaking that heated spark between her and Killian; forsaking *her* choice in any matters at all. I could flee, the target removed from my chest, Lucretzia's nefarious schemes all coming to fruition and my part in them undone. Or...

I could stay. I could run *back* to her, to the place we'd fled from together. I could keep the vow that had first empowered me to walk into the chaos of Lucretzia's cruel schemes and the Del's morbid determination to claim us at any cost. And in so doing, I could clear the way for Tristah to become the ruler that Amere-Del so desperately needed.

A fair Della. One who fought for the destitutes and orphans. One who cared for its infirm and brokenhearted. One who had tasted poverty and power both, and held the balance of favor in her outstretched hands.

Amere-Del did not need Lionyra Vara as its leader. But, just this once, it needed me as its savior; and I would become that, even if it bloodied my name...for Tristah. For the child I had once been. For the people who prayed to merciful Ahim every day for salvation and sanctuary.

I squeezed Ryker's hand, soaking in his stone-solid courage. And then I unwound my fingers from between his. "I hesitated before...with Lucretzia, aboard *The Athalion*. If I had done what needed doing then, we would not be in these straits. I will not hesitate again."

I glanced at Gydeon, watching me with his arm wrapped around Siu's waist; pain flickered deep in his gaze, but also respect—the sort that nearly knocked the breath from me.

"If I am to do this," I said, "it's your help I need."

He dipped his head. "*Whatever* you need, you have it."

"Good." I dragged in a deep breath; and then I spoke the words that had once ached within me, begging to be freed—before I had known the weight of death held in my fingers:

"The Del is *mine*."

CHAPTER 80
FAVOR, DEATH, SALVATION

No amount of scheming and strategizing during the weeks of sailing from the Sennesole Basin up through the Sudene River could truly prepare me. There was no armoring myself against the dread that stole the feeling from my limbs when Ryker shook me awake one night from a restless slumber in the Captain's cabin.

Somehow, I knew—before he even spoke a word. The truth lived in the frame of his profile as he crouched at the side of the bed we'd shared throughout the voyage, an odd tenderness in his gaze…and tension strung through that finger-robbed hand clasping my arm.

"Come have a look, love," he murmured.

I had never woken so fully, so swiftly. Snatching up my plum cloak, I stepped out onto the deck behind Ryker—and I caught my breath at what we sailed through.

The town of Shadewyle Proper slumbered in the dark like a figment from a children's book of tales—cautionary fables of cannibals masquerading as sweet elders. Warning stories of misbehaving boys and girls cooked in kilns or trapped in traveling circuses for all eternity. Brutal myths meant to frighten little ears into respectable behavior…just as this town had long frightened me.

The shadow of the mountain range looming behind it bruised the streets…and shaped the harsh angles of Shadewyle Castle itself, perched among the crags of Mount Shadewyle, the highest and most imposing peak. Moonlight spilled between the castle's many turrets, forging long-fingered strands of night that twisted down the cobblestones and basted the homes in uneasy gloom. The rich red glow of lanterns shone from countless windows, sinister as the watchful eyes of ravenous beasts; and though our modest trade vessel was not the only one cutting through Shadewyle Channel tonight, bound for the town harbor, it felt as if those eyes watched only for us.

Shuddering, I cinched my cloak and turned up its hood, following Ryker up the steps to the helm. Siu manned the wheel, offering me a nod and freeing the spokes to squeeze my hand—a silent show of support from a woman who knew all too well the anguish of returning to the place of her suffering.

I squeezed back, then bound both hands into the folds of my soft linen sleep pants to halt their shaking.

With a whisper of churning threads and shadow-soft bootsteps against the stairs, Killian joined us on the deck. The depths of night muted the rich tones of his Storycrafter's cloak, harkening back to the gray he had worn when we'd first met. His somber countenance set his broad jaw like adamant; he leaned a shoulder to the flagmast before the helm, his eyes hooked on the city with the ruthless intensity of one beholding a legend.

Likely it was, from the morbid tales Tristah had told him—the same memories that sucked the strength from my bones when I leaned my shoulder into the flagmast across from him.

"She's in there." Killian's voice was void of even a trace of uncertainty—as if whatever bond he and Tristah shared gave him a sense of her, stretching along those darkened paths, crawling up the heights of stone clefts to the towers of the castle itself.

"She is." That spoken truth allowed only the thinnest seam of courage to seep back into my marrow—but a bit of courage was all the fire in me needed for kindling. Freeing my fingers from the folds of my trousers, I flexed them out and breathed deeply. "And soon, we will be with her."

"Captain," Siu announced, "I have eyes on the docks."

Weightlessness seized my belly. *It's time.*

"Put us into port." Ryker pivoted on heel. "Seasplitter, with me."

"Hold," said Gydeon. When I turned, he strode to us, a smile peeking through his thick beard. But even the shadows of night could not hide the worry lines digging deep trenches into his sunbeaten brow.

My heart stuttered as I beheld the glass vials he pinched between his fingertips: one filled to the brim with life-giving green, one clear as crystal, and the last packed with a substance resembling sugar-dust.

The only weapons *I* would be carrying into this fight.

I took them gingerly from him, forcing my fingers not to rattle as I closed my fist. "Will this be enough?"

"More than." He laid a green-tinted palm to my cheek, not a glint of unbelieving in his eyes when they moored to mine. "Happy hunting, Seasplitter."

Gratitude burned in my throat like I'd swallowed a spoonful of strong spice. I slid the vials into my pocket. "Thank you, Greenfinger."

Hand in hand, Ryker and I descended belowdecks—not to the crew's quarters, where Killian moved ahead of us to rouse the others. We slipped into the shadowed hull instead, where we lit the row of lanterns strung from the ceiling. Ryker flipped open one of the trade chests, and from within he drew the materials we had cobbled together for this siege.

First, he held up the costume Siu and I had chosen; he pitched it my way with a scoff. When the weight of the bulky, lurid green-and-blue dress landed in my grip, it felt as if a millstone had descended on me instead. I spilled the length of it through the spread of my arms, watching as Ryker freed his own accoutrements: numerous pistols he spun into straps across his body, a blade belted at his waist, the stolen militar dagger slipped into an offhand sheath at the small of his back.

He would be going armed—and yet I still feared for him as much as myself.

Heart in my throat, I bundled the dress into the watertight pack Ryker also tossed to me. Slinging the straps over my shoulders, I blew loose a long, slow breath, praying to Ahim the weight would calm me.

It did not.

Ryker's gaze jumped to my face, his brow pinching. "You're scared out of your skull."

"I do not want to go back to this place." A truth I would surrender only to him…to the man whose wheel hung above my heart. Who knew as well as I did what it felt like to drown on dry land.

Ryker uncocked and holstered the last pistol, crossing the hull toward me. I retreated until my back met the wall beside the door and I could surrender to the weakness that knocked my knees together.

His palm settled against the rosined wood above my shoulder; then his free hand curled around the nape of my neck, and he pulled me against him. Into the thunderous rush of his pulse. Into the heat that emanated from him, riled and ready to meet the danger ahead.

"The second I'm finished with the Viper," he muttered, his chin grazing my temple, "I'll come find you. If I have to tear that whole blasted castle down to its depths…I'll be there, sweetheart."

"The ruse—"

"I know, I know, the bloody ruse." His fingers slid along the line of my jaw, to my chin; he tilted my head back until my gaze found the irresistible anchor of his. "You need me there. So I'll be there."

The way he saw to the furthest, unspoken depths of me, as he had aboard *The Athalion* the day we'd reached Monsha, gave my fear somewhere to go— somewhere to find rest.

I wrapped my arms around his neck, and he hauled me to him with an embrace like a safe harbor, lifting my feet from the dank floor.

"Give me strength," I whispered into the strands of wheat-gold hair that tumbled over his shoulder.

His arms tightened around me. "Everything I've got is yours."

And somehow, those words—throbbing with sincerity, rich with a feeling and a *choice* I had seized hold of ever since we abandoned Korsa—was the last of the armoring my spine needed to hold me steady.

When we abandoned the hull, we walked hand-in-hand once more; and when I faced Shadewyle Castle again from the deck, I met it with the defiance of an unblinking stare.

I had cowered before this place for so much of my life. But tonight, I could not afford to show it my weakness; those bits of me would remain tucked in the shadows of the hull, safe in the memory of Ryker's embrace, until I could gather them to myself and nurture and heal them.

Tonight required my power. My fire. The talents of Lionyra Vara.

At the helm, Ryker turned us both to face the united crews; he pitched his voice to the tune of the churning waters and the shadows leaking past as we drew near to the docks. "All right. No need to discuss the details…we've all known our part in this for weeks." His gaze flashed to Siu. "No one else sunk."

"No more dead friends," Syd agreed, cracking his knuckles.

"Get in, get busy, and get out," Klem reminded us.

"Light 'em up," Ryker shot back, and she replied with a sinister, sharktoothed smile.

Together, Ryker, Wilkes, Killian, and I scrambled to the stern of the ship; I stepped up onto the railing at the far aft deck, gazing down at the whitecapped waters in our wake.

"'Ay." Ryker squeezed my fingers, and I gripped the rigging to swivel on heel, glancing back at him. The smile he flashed me was a swift, bright burst of sunshine in the dark. "See you on the other side, sweetheart."

I clung to that promise, even as I finally let go of his hand.

As I stepped from the railing.

The fall into the harbor ended with the icy bite of snowmelt water, the shock of bitter cold chasing away my errant thoughts; purpose drove me in a kicking lunge back to the surface, and I broke it just as Ryker, Wilkes, and Killian took their own steps overboard, diving into the depths with me.

Dark stains in the blackness of the night, they struck out for the underbelly of the docks; I set my teeth against chattering and swam opposite them, bound for the roots of Mount Shadewyle where stone plunged into water.

It was a fast swim, if frigid; but when I hauled myself ashore in the mouth of an underwater tunnel, the shallow grade feeding out beneath a rocky ledge into the harbor, the heat of determination began to thaw my limbs at once.

With trembling fingers, I pried myself from my wet clothes and struggled into the gown. Tugging its loose, hammocked sleeves over my shoulders felt no different from wearing shackles—except that these were a part of the costume. They were the beautiful petals by which a poisonous flower lured its prey.

I would not enter the household of my former captors and decades-long adversaries in armor. I would do it in disguise—crafting the face the Del desired.

Still, my skin itched at the drape of silken fabric, and sweat pooled in the small of my back when I strung a leather belt around my waist and rolled my sodden clothes into the waterproof satchel. I warmed myself a moment in the dry garments, huddled against the stones.

Then, with a last prayer whispered on plumes of chilly breath, I pushed myself up, faced the dark—and stepped into it of my own will.

And so it was that I returned to Shadewyle precisely as I had left it: a Delina in a fine, dripping dress, creeping through the shadows toward the lower tunnels which snaked up into the belly of the castle, through miles of rock.

But I would not enter it the same woman who had fled.

I was a baker now with three vials in her pocket—one for favor, one for death, one for salvation. I was a woman who had forged *herself*. I had not come as a captive on the end of Lucretzia's chain, but as a pirate holding the power to rescue her most beloved friend.

I was entering with eyes wide open, the scales of life and death weighed in my hands. And mine would be the last face the Del beheld before he perished.

CHAPTER 81
AGAINST TIME

Between Ryker and Wilkes's work and whatever in Ahim's merciful name Killian was doing out there among the halls, I found the grates at the lower castle sparsely manned upon my arrival—only a single guard on watch.

With the nimble fingers and the quick-footed grace I had learned in Lucretzia's shadow, I uncorked the proper vial from my pocket, shoved the grate up with my shoulder, pirouetted into the man's path, and blew its contents like powdered sugar across his face. And, just as Gydeon had vowed, the guard was unconscious before he had a heartbeat to draw his sword.

Winding up through the tunnels from there, I made my way not at once to the Del's wing; instead, I went to the kitchens.

The low-roofed, arched chambers with their flues bored deep into the mountainsides were dark, deserted…as I had so often found them. For a moment, I stood within the familiar confines, breathing in the scent of the herb sachets strung from the cross-beamed ceiling, the tang of spices in jars on shelves, the faint fragrance of cooked meat and dough.

Then I unstuck myself from the past and set to work.

Much of what I needed was precisely where it had been stored when I had still called Shadewyle Castle my home…as if no time at all had passed. Yet there was a confidence in my craft I had not known then, a certainty that steadied my hands—even knowing what was to come.

While I mixed the batter, I brought Ryker's face to me in the shadows; I sank into the memories of making bread aboard *The Athalion*. I gathered my reservations and fears and heartache and blended them into the batch; and while

I inhaled the aroma of vanilla and chocolate shavings and sugar, I breathed in courage to stoke the fire that had burned in me since Anoram.

Eyes wide open.

I uncorked the second vial—the colorless one—and added it to the batter with a trembling hand.

Take power where you can.

Tonight, I would not merely take power—I would hand it to Tristah, where it belonged. Where it would never rest if Lucretzia and Zorast still drew breath.

Fortified by the thought, I drizzled the batter onto a cooking skillet.

Several long, prayer-filled minutes later—armed without a single weapon, only one vial left in my pocket, and a fragrant platter of cookies in my hands—I went to confront Zorast Graven.

I avoided the castle halls, taking the servant corridors instead; every other step was punctuated with rattling, banging, and concussive blasts that knocked my shoulders into the narrow walls. Likely Killian's work, if not the crews mopping up matters in the town and making their way to the castle.

Through the narrow windows framing the serving hall up to the Graven quarters, I caught glimpses of fireworks rocketing into the sky; silver showers flung against a backdrop of night like new stars. Fiery red embers, a mirror to the heat blazing in my core. Gold flares like the first streaks of a new dawn stealing the night. Sizzling streaks of blue, like Storycraft made manifest.

Gathering strength from their flagrant echoes, I hastened up the steps and emerged in the hallway that housed Zorast and Athyna's private chambers, dining hall, personal studies, and recreational parlors. They could have survived a siege here in great comfort for many, many weeks; yet there was something oddly derelict in these rooms. An absence…an emptiness to it all.

Perhaps because of the lack of militar on watch.

That was not intentional; no, they *had* been coming to defend the Del. But something had stopped them. Judging by the vague pounding that throbbed through the tower walls, I suspected that *something* was a piece of Killian's power—an impenetrable, story-built shield flung my way.

I offered a prayer for him in return; and then I made my way to the door at the very end of the hall, testing it silently.

Locked. But I had expected that. It was why I had spent countless hours with Cam aboard our stolen trade vessel, practicing picking every locked chest in the ship's hull.

With those curated talents put to use, I gained entrance to the Del's private quarters in moments.

I had entered Zorast's bedchamber very few times; it was sparsely adorned, scarcely furnished, functional in the uttermost. Tonight, the curtains were drawn against firework flickers and the sight of the mountain slopes that reflected them. The hearth was dim. There was scarcely any light by which to see Zorast himself—or for him to see me.

And yet, we both froze when I crossed the threshold.

My arms—suddenly heavier than they had ever been, even after full days of hauling flour sacks and kneading dough until my fingers ached—begged to drop the platter and wrap around myself instead.

Zorast held a blade across his knees, his grip so white-knuckled on its hewn handle that every bloodpath strained bruise-blue against his freckled skin; he huddled on the edge of his bed, rich black hair streaked with gray from the temples, tossed haphazardly across his brow.

The years had more than aged him...they had weathered him.

New lines framed his eyes. Haggardness punched in the hollows of his cheeks. He was grizzled, unshaven, sleepless and stiff on his perch. At my arrival, he straightened—wrenched back his shoulders and tautened his spine, as if he had expected anyone else to come through the door.

And then he merely gaped, as I did. For long, uncountable moments.

"*You.*" Only his voice remained as I remembered—the harsh baritone that had resonated after his slap to my face when I had asked where we were going when we left the Monshan orphanage.

The memory of that blow tingled in the heat that grazed my cheekbones. Goaded by the dim echo of pain—the same sort he dealt unblinking to all of Amere-Del, to *Tristah*—I crossed the room to his seating place before the fire, setting the tray on the low table between the pair of seats.

"Do you even know which one I am?" I asked, not looking his way.

He was silent for a long moment; then, cautiously, curtly, "Alyona?"

My eyes stuck shut on a blink, and I fought a repulsed shudder at that name from his mouth. He always spoke it the same way—with a hint of disgust and a hint of greed, as if he despised the girl from the orphanage as much as he coveted the woman he hoped to shape her into.

He would never stop shaping. Not until both Tristah and I were utterly broken to his whim.

Tempering my revulsion, I straightened, pivoting to face him. "Do you know why I am here?"

His grip, if possible, tightened further around the blade. "That depends entirely on how foolish the years have made you."

I eyed the blade; judging by the faint slur of his words and the stubble framing his jaws and neck, he had not faced this night—nor possibly many before it—sober. The siege on the castle might have cleared his head a bit, but not entirely.

I weighed my chances of dodging that knife should he choose to use it; and then, throwing my trust on my training, I beckoned him with a tilt of my head. "I've come to bargain for something you have."

"Is that right." He pushed himself to his feet. "And what might that be?"

"Something you do not want. And something I want very much."

His eyes narrowed with a spite I had seen unleashed in so many council sessions, against so many dissidents and loyalists alike. "The *Incendiary*."

Rage rippled along my hackles at the way he spoke Tristah's chosen title. "I would like to discuss the terms of a trade…my place for hers."

Zorast hesitated for a long, uneasy moment; then he took the first of the many slow, hesitant strides that would bring him to the seating before the hearth. "Lucretzia would not approve."

"Surely so much has not changed in my absence that she is now deciding the Del's steps?"

His lip curled back, baring his teeth. "Ruling this country has become more difficult than you could possibly *imagine* with Athyna gone. The havoc you and that gutter orphan wrought has nearly broken the spine of this country."

As if none of it was his doing. As if he would not have done far worse, had Athyna's cruelty—buried beneath glittering rhinestones and false pleasantries— still whispered in his ear.

"I have seen that difficulty. I've seen the suffering." I settled myself into one of the seats, spanning an arm to invite him to the other. "It's Tristah's suffering that concerns me now."

Zorast moved behind the chair across from me, balancing his folded arms on the sculpted wooden back and pinning me with one of his infamous glares. Tristah had always said this man's eyes were made of melted ore; staring into the near-silver blue at their depths, I was tempted to agree.

"What's happening out there…" he jerked his chin at the windows, "this is from you?"

I folded my legs at the knee, measuring my breaths—and my words—carefully. "Lucretzia would never have allowed me through the tunnel grates, much less the front doors. So, yes, a diversion was required…so that I could find you. Speak with you, Del and Delina, without any distractions between us."

He gazed at me a moment longer, jaw working, eyes still narrowed. Then he flipped the blade against his arm and back again, dropping his stare to it. "That woman has grown…opinionated."

My heart surged at the contention in his tone. "I had noticed that."

"I told her to bring *you* back to me," he scoffed, "and instead she brings me the spare. And not only that, but the most gutless of all these worthless dissidents. And she expected that somehow, we could craft that wretched Incendiary into my Delina? My *heir*?"

"Lucretzia does not command the country. It has always been the Graven regime that chooses its inheritor…as you chose me. I am offering you the opportunity to choose me again."

I reached for the plate, took up one of the thin cookies, and bit into it.

Sweet notes of chocolate drizzle, cinnamon, and sugar burst across my tongue—and that was all. Just as Gydeon had assured me.

My pulse quickened as I forced myself to chew and swallow, despite my mind's rebellion against what my mouth did not detect.

Time worked against me now.

CHAPTER 82
THE CAPTAIN WHO WOULDN'T DIE

RYKER

had never much liked Del Graven—and ever since meeting Lio, I'd have really enjoyed sticking my knife through his eye and watching him twitch.

Couldn't care less about his militar, either…especially the ones we carved out on our way into the castle. The ones Wilkes took down, the ones I shot through, the ones Scribs stuck full of holes before he pounced off to whichever tower he was going to use to raise a distraction…I wouldn't remember their faces in the morning. Perks of being a pirate.

I didn't care much for anything that had a stamp of the regime on it. But I had to admit…the view from their dining hall was bloody *fantastic.*

My heart was still running off like a whipped-free line; my nerves were dancing on a dagger's edge from fighting our way through the lower castle, all the way up to this mid-level, walled-in balcony where the Del and his kind ate. Where Lio had probably taken plenty of meals…when they actually let her bloody *eat.* And thinking about that made me feel a lot less core-rotten about swiping a bowl of grapes off the middle of the long table and dumping myself in the Del's chair to have a snack while I waited.

And waited.

And *waited.*

Heels kicked up on the table, bowl in my lap, I watched the sky light up with fireworks down by the harbor—and pride lit up inside me just as bright.

That was my crew down there, raising a ruckus that had thinned the ranks for us. And somewhere in another wing of the castle, stone bones were knocking out of joint…Scribs, doing whatever it was Storycrafters did that changed the world. Which left me counting down the minutes, tossing grapes to myself and catching them, and watching the show out the window.

And bloody *waiting*.

Finally—*finally*—something moved out in the hall. A lot of footsteps all running in one direction. Sounded like formation to me, but what in the depths did I know? So I shot a look at Wilkes—standing behind the dining hall door, dagger in one hand, cutlass in the other. Head cocked, he was on the sound like a hound on a scent…and after a second, he jerked a nod my way.

Brilliant. Scribs had moved the castle around so the militar only had one way to run: right past us.

Time to up the ruckus.

"Go have yourself some sport." I waved at Wilkes. "Be right behind you."

He rolled his eyes. "Steady, Captain."

"Who's not steady? I'm not bloody shaking." I held out a flat hand just to show him. "Get moving, will you?"

He held his ground until two packs of militar rushed past—then he was out like a mirage on the water, speeding off after them.

I gave him a minute and kept listening for what was moving behind the militar…that formation Wilkes knew like his own heartbeat. The one he and the other militar had drilled through in case of a siege.

And then I finally heard it—the footsteps I'd been straining for.

Pulse kicking, I hefted myself up, polished off the bowl, and stepped out of the room, pulling out my last pistol on the way.

The hallway was littered with militar bodies…some old, some fresh. Some Wilkes had cut down at the rear on his way out. They lined the place like more ornaments tucked into the grottos and grooves up and down the hall. They bled the same red as the carpet that masked the footsteps moving past them—one stride sure and sharp like stabbing blades, the other dragging against fetters locked around her ankles and fists bound behind her back.

They were already past me, down the hall, hustling the same direction Wilkes had gone. That structure was smart, I'd give them that; not that I was a militar man myself, but if I was moving a prisoner this important, I'd have sent at least two lines ahead of me to cut down whatever was in my way, too.

Pity them they didn't check the side rooms that should've been locked.

Betting all my merits on what *wasn't* on either of those people halfway down the hall, I aimed my pistol at their backs and whistled after them.

With how fast the Pale Viper turned—and how quick she had her blade at Tristah's throat, shoved up underneath the filthy hair tangled around her shoulders—she'd been expecting something. But the way those black eyes went wide, she hadn't been expecting *me*.

Tristah didn't look much surprised. Underneath the forelock that curled into her face, past the bruises that swelled up on her cheeks and chin, her stare knifed me like a blade to the liver in a back alley.

Because, for just a *second*, I could see Lio in her. Could see my Seasplitter being the one in the Viper's maw again.

Blasted depths, I was ready to make someone *bleed*.

"Let her go before I count to three," I thumbed the pistol, cocking it, "or this lead's going in your head."

Lucretzia planted her feet and tightened the knife under Tristah's chin, curving herself to the side. "Do you think you're such a remarkable shot, *Captain*? Then do it."

"Just shoot her!" Tristah barked—then winced when the knife nibbled at her skin. Blood dribbled down her neck, but she just clenched her teeth and stared me down. "End this, Blackhand. *End it!*"

"Can't do that." I centered my stance again, following the Viper's little ducking maneuver. "You don't know how bloody important you are."

"Oh, she knows." Lucretzia's free hand snaked around Tristah's chin, those talon nails biting into her skin. "We've discussed it at *length* these last few weeks."

The hand holding my pistol finally did me wrong.

It shook.

I could hit her, no question…if I shot through them both.

But then we all lost. Because Lio wouldn't be able to walk away from all of this without Tristah to take over. And she'd never look at me again if I took out Tristah while trying to bring down the Pale Viper.

Sweat rolled down my temple and found a cut on my jaw from the skirmish against the militar. It stung like a taunt—reminding me that nothing we'd gotten through so far mattered if I didn't get past *her*.

"It takes you this long to count to three?" the Viper sneered, skimming the knife a little along Tristah's neck.

My teeth snapped together when she drew blood. She had the power in this hall, and she bloody *knew* it.

"Blackhand, you're a *pirate*," Tristah snarled. "Act like it—*shoot!*"

Easy for her to say. She didn't know the plan.

"Yes, shoot. If you dare," the Viper taunted. "Shoot us *both*. Show us what you're made of…the Captain who wouldn't die."

The Captain who wouldn't die.

Who in the blasted depths *was* that, even? Who was making this shot?

I wasn't Bastyan Atreyon anymore, that dreamy runt who'd padded meek-faced after his parents, still dull enough to love them right up until they sold him off to a slave ship for a year's supply of their favorite spices.

But I wasn't just Ryker Kassian, either, a scoundrel with a coin purse bigger than his heart, conning and coasting through the world. Someone who'd arrive at the end of it with nothing, because nothing was going to save him and his crew.

And I wasn't Blackhand. Even when I'd inherited the title, the coat had never really fit. Blackhands were ruthless. They were piracy in the flesh. Pillagers and plunderers looking after their own wants. Home was just *The Dread Singer*, and that was the only thing they made space for in their hearts.

But I'd left that ship behind me, let it sink in Korsa with the rest. I'd ended the Blackhands. And even before that, I'd sullied the name. With Gydeon, with Siu, with Kory and Klem and Kato. With Cam and Wilkes and all the rest of them.

With *Lio*.

I wasn't any of those men anymore. I was someone made out of the meeting in the middle where they all shook hands.

So, who was going to take this shot?

The man I was growing into. The one I wanted to be.

Bash.

That name ignited through me, and it brought the whole hallway into focus…and everything outside of it. The firework blasts lighting up the drapes. The taint of blood on the air. The corpses all around us.

The shadow peeling off from the rest behind Tristah and the Viper— slipping out of a hole in the wall that hadn't been there when Wilkes and I had cut our way down this hallway before.

The plan finally shaped up in my head. Better late than never.

I squared up and looked Tristah in the eyes—looked for everything in her face that reminded me of Lio.

The rattle in my hand stopped. I finally breathed *deep*.

"Oi. Firebrand." Her gaze sharpened on my face. "Think of something blue."

Then I pulled the trigger.

Tristah was already moving before the shot went off—yanking back, throwing both her and the Viper out of the path. And hauling them straight into the knife Scribs sent flying from the dark along the wall.

The blade buried itself right to the hilt in the Viper's shoulder. Her arm went dead, dropped in its socket, and Tristah bucked away from it. Scribs shot out of the shadows, shoving the Viper aside, putting his back to her so he caught the blade she whipped around and slashed backward with—straight across his shoulders.

His bark of pain cut through the room like another pistolshot, and he went down, burying Tristah under his weight. I blocked out her screaming—blocked out everything—and yanked my cutlass loose.

Time to see what the Pale Viper was made of.

All my pistols used up, I went after her, blade to blade.

I'd dueled Wilkes plenty—sometimes daily, when we were on long voyages and I needed to let out the steam somehow. Her moves were like a spirit of his, but a whole lot bloody sharper. She moved quick—she moved *dangerous*, even with one arm dead at her side. The other was as close to nicking an artery every other strike as two hands on your average sailor.

She moved like the whole world better bend out of her way. Like she'd cut the wind if it got between her and me.

The fight took us down the hall, stepping over bodies, and every time her blade slammed into mine, it bellowed like a threat that I was about to join them.

I couldn't go on the offensive. Couldn't rear back enough to make *her* defend against *me*. Inside two minutes, sweat was dripping into my eyes and my side was screaming, *Oi, you remember what she did to you last time?*

Those dark eyes of hers were crazed. Killing-ready. Whatever plans she'd been cooking up here, she wasn't about to let them go.

Come on, Steelheart, come on!

Her blade caught mine and swiveled it—yanking against the side where her pistolshot had blown through me, firing pain up into my armpit. My arm jerked up and back, and my fingers went watery; her next hit sent my cutlass clattered off down the hall. Right out of reach.

"You're a fool," the Viper hissed, backing me down the hall at the tip of her blade. "You should have never boarded *The Athalion*. You bet for the wrong prize, *Captain*."

"Aye, well," I panted, working to keep her eyes on my face, "never said I was a good gambler."

A boot met steel behind her—kicking my cutlass spinning back to me. By the time I dove for it, Wilkes had closed the distance to the Pale Viper and drawn her focus. Her snarl when she glimpsed his face was the best music I'd heard since Bashir.

With that chip of Rhea's violin around his neck, I liked to think it was her giving us one last song to dance to—a tune for a battle to the death.

Then it was two against one; and like we'd hoped, it was just about enough.

Wilkes and I were both flagging; he was bleeding from places I couldn't see, sprinkling drops all over the floor. But between us, we kept the Viper's attention. Whatever was happening down the hall, between Tristah and Scribs…it could wait until we wore this snake down to the scales.

Fireworks lit the path. Blood thumped in my ears. If I hadn't known the way Wilkes moved like I knew my own body, I'd have spent more time back in that Bashiri street in my head, waiting for her to draw mortal blood. Because even with just one arm, she kept us both blocked; even on the defensive, she was better than a match for us.

But there was one thing she couldn't match. A fire she'd started she couldn't control.

It was an incendiary, lighting up the dark. It was Tristah bloody Levanthya, with her spymaster bleeding all over the floor.

When I heard her shout my name, I didn't think twice. Depths, knowing her, I didn't even have time to think *once*.

I grabbed Wilkes and hauled him sideways, toward the wall…and he was still barely fast enough to miss the knife Tristah sent flying down the hall.

It slid straight into the seam Wilkes and I had left—too fast for the Viper to see. To block. To dodge.

The dagger slammed into her belly so hard, it took her off her feet, shoving her to her seat on the floor. And Tristah—hands and feet unbound, rope burns flaring like blisters on her wrists—tore down the same path her throwing knife had sailed.

The Viper struggled up to meet her, but not fast enough. Tristah yanked the knife free in a gush of blood—and then those ladies went to *war*.

Wilkes and I couldn't have jumped in even if we'd wanted to. I'd never seen a fight like it…all sparking steel screaming on its edges, all hatred cursed up at the vaulted ceiling above us.

Maybe one against one wasn't enough when it was Wilkes or me against the Viper. But with Tristah, it was.

She played with her prey—wore that bleeding, one-armed serpent down to a gasping, staggering mess. Then she caught her with a knee to the chin that sent her tripping back over the bodies of her militar, sliding on the blood-soaked carpet, and Tristah didn't even stop for a breather. She shoved off the sodden floor, slamming her knee into the stab wound on Viper's belly, hurling her down on her back. They slid into the wall, and Tristah pinned her—first with a hand around her throat, then with the knife shoved into her other shoulder, killing both arms.

"You wanted a perfect heir?" she snarled down into the Viper's bone-white face. "You wanted to make me a decoy, then a Delina? You don't decide that for me! You don't choose what I am!"

The Viper coughed up a laugh, freckling blood on Tristah's face. "And what…are you, *Incendiary?*"

Tristah's mouth warped into one downright terrifying grin. "Something strong enough to kill *you.*"

Then she pulled that blade out, whipped it around in one hand, and tore it straight across her throat.

The Viper went limp…not even twitching. Not one more bloody sound.

Tristah wrenched the knife out, the beads on the bracelet around her wrist whispering like ocean fathoms swallowing something down into the depths.

That bracelet—

Scribs.

I jerked around to find him slumped on his elbow, the back of his cloak turning purple where blood met blue threads.

Cursing, I shoved up from the wall; I got to him right when Tristah did. She threw the knife down and fell to her knees in the mess of cords he'd cut off of her. Probably his wounds were why he'd taken so long to do it.

"You *idiot,*" Tristah rasped, shoving her hands against his back and wincing when he arched and groaned. "Killi—"

"I know. I know," he mumbled, going slack. His eyes blinked quick, fighting to stay open. "I'm *your* idiot."

"Don't you *dare* die on me, Brax."

His lips twitched. "Wasn't planning to."

I pulled his cloak back to get a look at that gash across his shoulders; it looped all the way over, but hadn't gone deep enough to sever something important. He'd still lift a blade, most likely. But he needed Gydeon to see him.

"Can you save the cloak?" he panted when I let it fall.

"Bloody Storycrafters." I glanced at Wilkes. "You all right?"

He held a hand under his ribs, blood trickling over his fingers. "I'll live."

Tristah turned on me, grabbing my wrist. "What are you *doing* here, Blackhand? Have you seen Aly—did she get back to you?"

Aly.

Lio.

I blinked, came back to myself, heat building in my blood again.

I had a promise to keep.

Rocking to my feet, I turned to Wilkes. "You got them?"

"I got 'em." His voice was brittle, but I trusted the nod he tossed my way.

"Fill her in on the plan." I stepped away from them, moving up the hall. "I'm going for Lio."

Tristah's head shot up, her eyes clapping on mine. "She's here—you brought her back *here?*"

"She brought herself back!" I barked. "And it's my job to make sure she gets out again—you call off the militar, *Delina*, you might just be top rank in this castle by now!"

I left Wilkes to explain that to her. I'd done my part—Tristah was safe. Probably this was the safest place in the country for her.

Next thing I knew, I was running for something that mattered more than my own life.

Lio's.

CHAPTER 83
A SEA OF SILVER STARS

I waited until the last of the pan cookie had dissolved on my tongue; then, with a deft swallow that fully set the sands in the hourglass turning against me, I nodded to the chair across the table. "Shall we discuss terms?"

Slowly, Zorast eased around the edge of the seat, lowering himself onto the arm of it. He did not release the dagger. "I find it curious you expect some level of trust from me when you have brought this siege to my doors. How am I to know this is not an assassination attempt?"

"Because I am here, and I come alone." I spread my arms a bit. "Search me, if you wish. You will find no weapon."

He did not move nearer; he only stared at me.

Moments trickled by—moments I did not have to spare.

"Which of you killed her?" he asked suddenly.

So, then, Lucretzia had surmised the culprit of Athyna's demise…but he had not. Perhaps he had not *wanted* to put the blame on either of us, to make one less forgivable than the other for the sake of his schemes.

And it was that desperation—coupled with his doubt of my capabilities— on which this scheme hinged.

Heat flushed in my core. Was that anticipation and dread splashing like hot oil from a sizzling pan? Or something far worse taking root within me?

I swallowed the burning surge, forcing myself to hold Zorast's gaze. "Which do you think?"

He glanced down at my hands, then back to my face. "You always lacked the stomach for death, despite all the training we wasted on you. Tristah has proven she relishes it with this Incendiary business."

I bit into the tip of my tongue, then offered a consolation that had never been any sort of truth. "I tried to stop it from happening. I never wanted anyone to be hurt…I only wanted a taste of freedom."

"At the price of my wife's life," Zorast spat. "And now you expect that I should believe you'd come crawling back, after you bought that *freedom* with shed blood?"

"You have seen me crawl for Tristah before." I did not have to craft the metal that clad my retort. "You have heard me beg and grovel for her. What else did you expect I would do, knowing Lucretzia dragged her back here?"

Zorast scoffed, but his gaze floated down to the plate of cookies between us. A peace offering that sheathed a sword. "I see you have continued your banal pursuits in your absence."

"I suspect these are the last cookies I will ever bake, if you have your way." I took another; and, holding his stare unblinking, I bit into it.

This time, my stomach revolted—not at the sweetness, nor with fear of him, but at the terrible thing writhing deep in my belly…a sure sign that my time was trickling away.

"I couldn't miss the opportunity," I added, offering the bitten cookie out to him. "Now, are you ready to discuss terms?"

He stared at the cookie for a long moment; then, slowly, he took it from me, turning it around between his fingers.

"Name them," he muttered.

A bit of silver sparkled on the edges of my vision. I blinked it hastily away.

"Tristah," I began, steadying my voice with a sharp pinch of teeth against my cheek, "goes free."

"*Never.* Not after what she's done."

"She lives in the dungeon, then," I amended hastily. "Where I can visit her whenever I wish."

His eyes narrowed again. "With a guard at all times."

"So long as Lucretzia is forbidden to visit her."

Zorast hesitated a moment. Then, "What else?"

"We negotiate the terms of *my* marriage to Sorai. Tristah has no part in it."

"Done," he snorted. "Dissidents marrying dissidents would only weaken Amere-Del."

I curbed my hate behind a tongue that tingled strangely, a fine, ashen taste coating its surface. "I would like some say on your council. In exchange, I will report on all that I overhear from Sorai. Any notion of rising dissidence will be brought to your ears at once."

"You will submit to lessons from Lucretzia again."

I swallowed; the burnished metal tang did not abate from my mouth. "Within reason."

"The only *reason* you will require is my command."

A test of my mettle. A test of my sincerity.

Fixing Tristah's face in my mind and my fingers to the armrests, I nodded. "So long as she remains away from Tristah."

"Agreed." Zorast sloped his head. "All of this…for your decoy?"

"I know it is the only way to spare her, after what she has done. And *you* know that I love her. That she has always been more a sister to me than a spare."

"An unfortunate weakness we could never quite stomp out of you. But perhaps that weakness can serve the regime, after all." Zorast studied the cookie in his hand; and then, grunting, he shoved it fully into his mouth.

A heady rush of relief poured from shoulders down to my tailbone. Tears freckled my vision, and did not disappear even when I blinked furiously. The heat built and blistered, a downward tumble and an upward surge meeting in the midst of me.

Sweat broke across my scalp. Illness curdled in my throat. My stomach swiveled, and I shifted sharply on my seat—but Zorast did not seem aware. He took another cookie, aiming it at me with the same brutality as the blade on the cushion beside him. "I always knew you would return to us someday."

I anchored my fingers more tightly to the arms of the seat; blinking did nothing to scatter the colorless sparks that danced across my vision now, setting the room alight like fireworks. "And why is that?"

"Because you have never changed," Zorast snorted. "You have always been a desperate little girl wanting to go home. Crying for a *family*."

My next blink sent a vision of faces dancing across my mind.

Reinera, offering a change of clothes out to me aboard *The Athalion*, freely giving her knowledge of Amere-Del's fate.

Jularius Cathan, his warm parting embrace beside Monsha's docks, the concern in his eyes when he'd offered to deal with Lucretzia for my sake.

Siu, coming back for me on the failing wharfs in Korsa, and Gydeon tending my wounds after, his smile full of gratitude and kinship I had not known how to embrace at the time.

Rhea, walking me through columned courtyards full of light and music, linked arm-in-arm like old friends. Klem and Kory and Kato, guarding my back in the Bashiri gambling den, treating my victories as theirs. Camden, dancing with me to spirited fiddle reels until our feet ached. Syd and Lanah, their faces alight with glee and determination as they prepared to send Korsa and its ships ablaze at my word. Wilkes, his smile full of mischief and mirth when he watched me weigh his new axe in the pirate market, and the brush of his kiss to my head when I'd given him that shard of Rhea's fiddle.

A flicker of something warm and wavering—dessert tea and dice games. A smell of rain and a taste of power on the back of my tongue.

Tristah, grinning at me over her bowl of porridge in the safehouse. Killian, his Storycraft erupting from him, setting us free and bringing us back to the ship.

Ryker. His arms around my back. Our brows pressed together. His heart beating beneath my ear, setting a tune for mine as it stuttered, stumbled, and revived again in this room, where Zorast's face floated in a sea of stars.

"And you…what are you without us?" His voice reached me from a distance. "Without the things we *made* of you, Alyona?"

All at once, power snapped back into me; I shoved up from the seat, towering above Zorast Graven, who silenced at once.

"I am Lionyra Vara," I snarled. "I am a baker. And a sailor. I am a depths-blasted *pirate*…and whatever else I choose to be." I stepped back from his reach, putting my chair between us. "The only thing I will never be is *yours*."

His mouth jerked taut at the corners, and he surged up after me—then doubled over, loosing the sort of scream that had been building in me for minutes now. "*What in Ahim's merciful—?*"

Before his piercing, agonized shriek had fully formed words, I plunged my hand into my satchel; I retreated from him again, fumbling at the cork of the final vial—the antidote to the Hadrassi poison, tasteless and mortal, that I'd baked into the cookies. Death disguised in a peace offering.

Footsteps pounded in the outer hall; the bark of orders raked my ears, filling me to the depths with dread.

A militar command.

Vial in one hand, I stumbled to the suite door and kicked it shut; then I flung my shoulder against the chest-of-drawers beside it and hurled it down, barring the way to the room.

My knees gave way, spilling me down to the floor; the whole world hid behind a haze of gray and white, all of it muted, hollow, echoing. I fumbled at the lip of the vial, tearing up the cork as my lungs began to tighten, as—

As a heavy weight slammed into me, flinging me from my knees.

Pain burst through my ribs when they contacted the chest-of-drawers, and the agonized gasp that followed filled my lungs with breath, clearing the fog like a gust of ocean wind.

One hand encircling his own throat, Zorast crawled toward the vial, knocked from my fist at the impact of his staggering weight.

"*No!*" I choked, diving after him, snaring his ankle and wrenching with all my might. He flopped to his chest at my frantic yank, and I scrambled over him, clumsy and panicked, grabbing for the vial. But his longer arm shot out beneath me, sending the antidote rolling toward the hearth.

Gasping, my vision veiled in a pattern of smoke and cobwebs again, I hauled myself arm over arm after the vial; but Zorast gripped a fistful of my skirts, towing me to a halt. Screaming in a vain effort to carry breath back into my squeezing, shrinking lungs, I kicked desperately at his face.

Something gave with a horrific crunch; he howled, a garbled, choking sound, his nails clawing ribbons into my bare leg. He dragged me toward him, slapping with floundering, weakening blows, his hot breath retching over my face as I fought beneath his heavier weight.

Not here, not in this place, not like this.

Pistolshots rang in the hall. The door slammed against the chest. Again. Again. Again.

Zorast cringed at the sound; I seized the advantage, kicking blindly for his groin, pushing myself from beneath him, rolling to my chest to find the vial with my gaze—

And his deadweight slammed over my back.

Deadweight.

I thrashed, wheezed, clawed for that vial just beyond arm's reach…but my body lacked the strength to shrug off the corpse of Zorast Graven, strangled by poison, draped over me like a cloak.

"No," I croaked, tears salting my lips. "No, no, no…"

And then I could not speak.

I was not breathing.

CHAPTER 84
LOST NO LONGER

loating.

Adrift in the sea. Adrift in a world without color.

I was lost. Orphaned. Alone.

Lio. Lio! I'm here. I'm right here. I'm here, sweetheart, 'ay—open your eyes!

Death's cords bound my hands and feet, my eyes and ears, my blood and bones. My heart and lungs. They no longer responded to my commands.

Reach. Take. Drink. Look. Listen.

Take this. Take it. Take it.

Please.

Love, please…

A pinprick of warmth at the nape of my neck. At the tip of my tongue. Like a name longing to be spoken.

Don't you leave me. Don't you depths-blasted leave me, Lionyra—

Lionyra.

A name of softness. A name of warm dough and rainy afternoons. A powdered-sugar name. A bread-and-cookies name. A kneading, teasing, taunting, truth-telling name.

A name of warm sunrise sands. Of sick bays and desolate rooms, city streets and ship hulls. Of anger and adventure and a shipwrecking, world-changing love found where it should never have grown at all.

A name that brought a brush of warmth sliding along the side of my face.

You think after this whole mad voyage, I'm letting you go that easy?

A bloom of heat between my brows.

Nah. Not a chance.

A warm wind grazing my lips.

You come back to me, Alyona Vassera. Do you hear me?

Come back, sweetheart.

Breath rushed into my lungs. Ash dusted across my tongue.

Heat. Need. Desire.

Life.

Life flooded through me. Life poured into every empty crevice of me. Life thundered into my heart, filled my lungs, roared through my veins.

I gasped, arched, cried out—gasped again.

And Ryker Kassian swept me up tight against him, sprawled across his outstretched legs, one hand shoving against my cheek, pushing my hair aside. "'Ay, there she is! There you are—I've got you, love, I've got you. Breathe, Lio, breathe for me—"

Something struck the floor. Tinny glass, cracking where it landed.

The vial.

And all at once, I was sobbing—sobbing with terror. Sobbing with relief. Sobbing as he rocked me, clutching my head to his chest.

"It's over," I wept. "I killed...I killed—"

"Aye. You did it, Seasplitter."

Fisting my hands in his collar, I arched upward of my own accord this time, tucking my head beneath his chin. Every breath that staggered down my throat was an effort...and each one a gift. Salvation rendered at the hands of a pirate.

The man I loved.

"You came," I choked, sinking back to meet his gaze.

"Made you a promise, didn't I?" He touched his forehead to mine—then jerked back at the drumming of steps in the hall. "Blasted depths! Not *again*."

Sense winnowed through the shadows that near-death had rendered of my mind. With what little strength remained, I shoved away from him. "Go," I croaked. "You must leave, Bash, if they find you here—"

"You expect me to leave you in this bloody condition?"

"*Yes.*" Panting, I gripped his wrist, holding his hand to my face a moment longer. "Remember—*Tristah* did this."

His gaze shuttered; he shifted his fingers to twine between mine. "Last chance to run."

"With you? Always." I tugged both our hands down, pressing my dry lips to his knuckles. "And soon. But for now..."

A shout echoed through the open door—barely a crack widened. Just enough for Ryker to have shoved his way through. But I caught a glimpse of the bodies he'd felled in the hall beyond…a misstep from the plan that I could not find fault in.

Not when he had saved me from choking to death on Hadrassi poison.

"For now…go." I jerked my chin at the window.

Cursing, Ryker slid from beneath me and leaned me against the wall where he'd propped us both; then he bent for a moment, one hand on my shoulder, pressing his lips swift and fierce to the top of my head. "*Soon* isn't soon enough."

He kicked Zorast's body in passing with a brief but truly filthy string of insults, crossing to the window and pulling the panes inward. Then he stepped up onto the sill and glanced back at me; one hand guarding my pounding heart, I met his strained gaze.

"I love you," he said.

My heart faltered and skipped beneath my palm. A strange, silly grin worked itself across my tingling face. "*Go*, will you?"

With a roll of his eyes, he sidestepped the sill—and I was alone.

Alone, with Zorast's body.

Alone, in a world without the Graven regime overtaking it.

Alone, and alive…a life debt owed to a pirate.

And then I was laughing, my tears turning to cackles of disbelief, and glee, and imminent hysteria.

Fitting, somehow, that the militar found me that way: laughing and laughing, alone in a room with a dead man.

CHAPTER 85
A RULER'S RESPECT

RYKER

My second time walking into Shadewyle Castle wasn't much like the first.

A lot fewer pistols and swords this time; not even a lick of hacking and shooting our way through the Del's militar. Plenty more eyes wide as a full moon over the sea, enough whispers to prove that folks knew something about who us pirates were. Or at least, whose side we were on.

It helped that we had an escort from the new Della's Own Blade.

For a man who could make a life out of stories, Scribs sure didn't have much to say on the way through the halls—halls full of servants sweeping up broken glass and putting things back together after our little siege. Every overseer looked like they hadn't slept a wink in the few days since the Del's so-called assassination…and they could get in bloody line.

I'd about lost my bearings and drunk my bodyweight in brandy, hopping from tavern to tavern, trying to catch *some* piece of gossip about what in the depths was happening in the castle. When that hadn't turned up much, I'd decided to show my face and let that be the Della's problem.

Then I'd walked through the door, and Scribs had been there, waiting. Like he'd been expecting me.

"You look good," I'd greeted him.

He shot me a look and just said, "Follow me."

That was *all* he said while he took me up through those long halls, shaped different in the daylight. They were brighter than I'd imagined…mostly from tapestries and the kind of plunder you'd expect aboard a pirate vessel. Which said a lot about where all those merits they taxed out of the country's backside were going.

And, judging by the layers of dust floating in the air and the way the long drapes over those floor-to-ceiling windows were tied off with every kind of twine you could find, didn't seem like they'd been opened in a long while. Didn't seem like this place had seen a lot of life since Lio and Tristah had run out on it.

Plenty was changing. And most of it seemed like a river flowing from one source: the office Scribs led me into, where the Della sat bent over a desk— doing her best, it looked like, to win a record for how many pieces of parchment she could read at once.

I got that same gut-knotted feeling when I saw her as every time we'd locked eyes since Bashir. Still Lio's perfect double, but it felt off, somehow. Like catching a glimpse in a mirror and thinking the face was wrong, but you couldn't put your finger on *why*.

Scribs shifted, and the Della looked up—giving me a good view of that bruised cheekbone and the scrapes on her neck. And the layers of shadows clumped under her eyes.

Probably a better man would've asked how she was doing, but when I opened up my mouth, the first words out were, "Tell me she's all right."

Tristah sat back, tapping her quill on the side of the desk. "She's as good as she can be. Still sleeping off the effects of whatever drug that healer of yours gave her. But she should make a full recovery."

"Just in time to poison her *again*," Scribs muttered, sacking his weight against the door.

"Oi." I threw up a hand his way. "Didn't ask you."

"You never do."

I angled the next question at Tristah: "When."

"Three days from now." She brushed over her forehead with the quill feather. "Enough time to gather your crew and make preparations…and enough time for word to spread."

The sunlight falling through the window behind her caught on a piece of the desk that she'd hidden behind her elbow…maybe on purpose. A thin little headpiece, mostly chains and diamonds; something that would look ridiculous on anyone's head but a ruler's.

The Della's Diadem. I'd heard stories about that piece all over Korsa…it was worth a fool's ransom in merits, enough that it would have covered half of mine *and* my crew's debts if we'd had a blasted prayer of getting into the castle ourselves. Almost wished I could steal it anyway, just for one last good pillage.

But with Scribs burning holes in my back with his eyes, there was no chance I'd get away with it.

I plucked my stare off of it and looked at Tristah instead. "For word to spread about the new Della, I'm guessing?"

Her lips tugged off to the side—the kind of smirk I'd only seen Lio wear in Korsa when she was playing pirate. "The official report from the regime is that I've been a captive all this time…and that Lucretzia rescued me." She flipped a rude gesture at Scribs when he snorted, chafing his hand over his chin. "She returned me to Shadewyle Castle, but before they could make my return public, our captors tried again…those being my decoy, and her trusted band of pirates."

"Aye?" I hitched my thumbs in my belt, leaning back across the doorframe from Scribs. "Guessing we're not *those* pirates, considering I walked in here without irons clapped on me."

Tristah's eyes widened innocently. "Of course not. *You* were the pirates who aided Lucretzia in my retrieval."

All right, that was good, given the bargain she'd struck with the Leeches in Korsa. "So, who came up with *that* story?"

Scribs rolled his eyes. "Who do you *think*?"

"Wasn't talking to you. Still getting used to you being good for much more than popping around corners and scaring the pants off old ladies."

"Spywork involves much more than stealth."

"Aye? And we captured your arse."

"Boys, boys!" Tristah flicked her quill between us. "That's enough. Captain, I have a commendation for you…but I also need you to get out of my city."

My brows cocked up at that. "Scribs never mentioned you were such a sweet-talker."

"Enough with the *name*," he groaned, pinching the bridge of his nose like I was the reason for every headache he'd ever suffered.

And gladly.

"The fact is, this tale of ours is holding well for now," Tristah allowed, "mostly because the people are shaken, and they're terrified. They want something to believe in…and they believed in Alyona Graven for longer than she was gone." A furrow tugged between her brows. "But all it's going to take is the first suspicious councilman raising questions, and then we're likely to end up with more of them than we know how to answer."

"So you want us to make ourselves scarce." I knew that game. Played it plenty enough before and after raids.

"Not because I'm not grateful," Tristah said, "but because I've got a country to run, and, frankly, having a pirate crew in the city is bad for my reputation…supposed allies and rescue-helpers or not."

"Aye. Well, I've been called worse." I thumbed my nose. "We'll be out of your hair as soon as we've got Lio…but we'll lay lower until then." I was about fed up with the local taverns, anyway. And staying in a city where everything was changing so quickly had everyone—even *The Athalion's* crew—getting restless.

Change would flow a lot slower downstream…somewhere like Monsha. Somewhere like Bashir. We could catch our breath out there.

"Guess this is goodbye, then." I shifted my feet, trying to figure out what to say. Gyddy was always better at speeches than me, kept himself handy to woo his wife with a touch of Hadrassi poetry that had no business taking up space in a pirate's craw…but I was the Captain. And I owed these people a lot, even if I hardly knew them.

I cleared the stupid out of my throat in a couple quick coughs, then said, "Listen. I'm not much for authority—"

"Really?" Tristah's lips quirked. "The piracy was not at all a tell of that."

"Oi. Just let me finish." I stuffed my hands in my pockets. "I prefer being a Captain under no one's command. And that's not about to change. But if it was anyone, Della…it could be you."

Her head slanted. "Well, that's as much of a compliment as I suppose I'll get from you. So let me pay you one in kind." She settled forward against the desk, arms folded on her parchments. "Lio trusts you. That's rare. She might even love you…and believe me, that's even rarer. But even if you didn't somehow win her heart, you've won my respect, Captain."

"How's that?"

"Because you looked me in the eyes when Lucretzia had a knife to my throat," she said, "and you shot anyway."

Scribs cleared his throat, tightened his arms across his chest—then winced at whatever it did to his shoulders. But for once, Tristah didn't search him out when he made a sound. She didn't look away from me.

Right then, I realized there was a part of Tristah I'd always understand better than I could ever understand Lio. It took a lot of guts to sheathe your sword forever. It took a different kind to take aim and fire, knowing someone's life was on the line.

Her and I, we were the same…we took the shot. We kept our swords sharp. And the truth was, it changed us…loving someone who chose to leave hers in the sheath. And we wouldn't have it any other bloody way.

I tipped her a salute, turning through the door. "Be seeing you, Della."

"Blackhand."

I ground to stop in the doorway, shifting back to face her.

"I think the Graven regime owes you a debt…for the selfless, safe return of its long-lost Delina." That stone-solid smirk didn't so much as tilt while the lies poured out of her mouth; she would've made a bloody good pirate, if the Old Salts had played their hand right with her. "Take from the treasury what you think is fair. But keep in mind I have an overtaxed, overworked population to make amends with."

Glee lit through me and started my fingers drumming on the doorframe. "Enough to cover some debts should—"

"Forget the debts. I plan to deal with the Old Salts myself." Tristah waved me off like that would be the easiest thing in the seas…like starting a war with pirates wouldn't be the greatest show any of us had ever seen.

I planned to be halfway across the world before she kicked it off.

"Focus on what's ahead of you," she added, pinning me with that stare that hit just below the belt…too much like Lio and not enough like her for my taste. "And invest in *that*."

I flashed her a grin. "I'm liking this new regime already."

"The feeling is not mutual," Scribs grunted, stalking toward me.

I gave him ground, backing out the door, rounding my lips in a genial, windblown kiss. "Still time for you to warm up to me, Scribs."

He slammed the door shut in my face.

Eh. Fair enough.

Siu and Gyddy met me at the end of the hall, falling into stride. My head already bounced ahead of us, thinking through what needed done—every step between now and when we could put this depths-blasted castle behind us. I was sick of wiping my stern with silk.

"Let's hear it," I said to Siu.

"Our vessel is already patched," she announced. "Rations acquired…enough to sail us to Monsha, anyway."

"Good. We'll chart a course from there." I glanced at Gydeon. "Got everything in place, mate?"

"All the herbs, measured out to the proper dose…four times measured," he added before I could ask. "Calm, Captain. I've got her. And I left the herbs in Killian's quarters just now."

I wished that was enough to settle me. Not a chance, though—I wasn't about to feel anything but wound up like the last line in a storm, holding all the rigging together while it frayed apart.

Not until Lio was on the other side of her so-called *execution*.

At the doors of the castle, shouldering out between the militar on watch, Klem and Kato waited for us. They still looked unbalanced, two Drace siblings instead of three; but on the other side of that first wave of grief, like a rip current spilling out to sea, satisfaction capped their smiles.

"What's the gossip?" I demanded, clapping one hand on Kato's shoulder, the other on Klem's.

"Exactly what we want it to be." She shot her brother a smirk. "We dropped the story in the biggest gambling houses and taverns a few days ago, and it's already spread like wildfire."

"Grown a few new details of its own, even." Kato rubbed the back of his neck. "Seems most of the city already believes it…that Tristah is Alyona, and Lio is Tristah. Now they're saying Lio offed the Del *and* the Pale Viper, and she tried to off Alyona, too."

"Any doubters?" Siu asked.

Klem shrugged. "Not enough to be concerned about. And anyone who moves beyond that, I'm sure Scribs will handle it."

I cracked a grin. If I was leaving anything for this city to remember me by, it was that blight of a pirate's name plastered all over Ember's tarnished backside. And I wouldn't have it any other way.

"All right, we've got more work to do," I announced. "This castle's about to host an execution…and that means a perfect time for some plundering."

Klem raised a brow. "Plundering?"

"Permitted," I grunted. "But they don't *all* need to know that, aye?"

Kato scoffed. "Consider it done, Captain."

And while they were stealing the merits and treasures, the rest of us would be stealing back something even more valuable.

That depths-blasted execution couldn't happen soon enough.

CHAPTER 86
SONGS IN THE SHADOWS

The soft strum of six humming strings sang me back to awareness, deep beneath Shadewyle Castle.

I knew where I was even with my eyes closed—by the pungency of wet stone and damp iron, by the incense Della Athyna had long ago ordered burned to cover over the stench of waste from the relief buckets kept in each cell. My body recognized the stiffness of the cot beneath it, the scratchiness of the pillow against my cheek, the roughness of the hand-woven blanket cast over my shoulders.

I had slept on these same cots before—a punishment from Lucretzia for some long-forgotten defiance. She had banished Tristah and me to these cold confines, and though I did not recall for what, I had never forgotten that night.

It had been among the few I'd loved in Shadewyle Castle; because, at long last, Tristah and I had not feared our conversations being overhead, our laughter silenced, our stories cut short by guards—or worse, but Lucretzia herself. We had not slept at all that night; we'd spoken loudly and freely and laughed until our sides hurt.

How strange that in a castle of such glamor, the dungeon held the best memories of all.

Stranger still, that I was not frightened here; even as I flexed my wrists against the loose shackles that bound them and shifted my feet in the sheath of the blanket, relieved to find that all of my limbs functioned as they ought despite the near-disaster with the antidote in the Del's room, no fear took bloom.

Music sat with me in the dark.

For a time, I lay quietly, the pillow snugged to my head—and I listened. To the familiar cadence of those strings. To the hands that played them with expert skill, and the soft curses drizzled throughout when a string plucked askew, when a note emerged wrong. Then the tightening and turning of knobs took precedence before the song began again.

I could've been content to lay there, feigning sleep until it became truth for me again. My body still ached from the poison, a dull throb in every muscle and joint; it would be some time before I fully recovered, and there were more herbs yet on my horizon.

But that was what jolted me fully awake…the realization that, for this moment to be possible, the time must be soon.

I had slept away the days until my own death. And someone did not wish me to wake alone in the dark…a darkness we both knew so intimately, it had taken root in our deepest parts.

My eyes snapped open, a harsh breath abrading my throat, and there I found her: Tristah, on the other side of the dungeon bars I had laid the map of in my mind. She sat perched on the guardstool, one leg cocked over the other, her six-string instrument balanced in her lap. Her loose hair spilled over her shoulder, her head tucked as she paid all her attention to the instrument…or pretended to.

The sight of her this way—dressed in a fine, jewel-toned shirt over trousers, bangles on her wrists and rings sparkling on her fingers—wedged a lump in my throat. When I had last laid eyes on her, she had been armored and viperous, standing between me and Lucretzia in a Bashiri alleyway. And now…

Now she was the vision of a woman in power. A Della in title as well as practice, arrayed in our country's dazzling colors.

"Thank Ahim we reached you in time," I croaked.

Her fingers skipped a string, bringing forth a truly ear-grating, discordant note; I winced, but she did not, her eyes flashing to me. Relief broke through her gaze, her thumb jolting the same string over and over in a single repetitive strum as she held my stare.

"You scared the *life* out of me, do you know that?" she demanded. "You looked half-dead when the guards dragged you down here. When I visited you the first time after, I thought you *were* dead."

"Things did not go entirely according to plan," I confessed.

"Understatement." Slowly, she shook her head. "Killian told me this absolutely mad rescue scheme was all your idea. That you insisted on dealing with Zorast yourself, so that I could…"

When she tapered off, I nodded; I had no words to add.

A second string joined the first in the humming repetition. "Aly. I don't know what to say."

"When have we ever needed words?"

"No. This is different." She shook her head. "I wasn't kind to you in Bashir. I blamed you for everything, even after I said I understood your reasons. And then you went and did *this*, gave me *this*…" Her hand skimmed over her hair, as if feeling for a diadem she had grown used to wearing and only recently removed…a diadem I had never coveted for myself.

"Because *you* are what Amere-Del needs." I slid from the cot and trudged to sit nearer to the bars; even that left me winded, panting when I lowered myself cross-legged before her. "I may hold no love for this country, but I will always hold love for you, Tristah…and for what you aspire to do. Just because I want no part in it does not mean I don't wish you to have *all* of it."

She blew out a sharp breath. "And now, somehow, I'm Della. The council wasted no time once word spread of Zorast's death. Most of them didn't even know I was back in the castle yet…I never thought I'd have them fawning at my feet again."

"How does that feel?"

"Like an impossible dream." A third string joined the chorus. "I wanted the title and this chance for so long, but I didn't see how I would manage it. Now I know that's because I only had half the picture…the other half was always you."

Gratitude swelled in my leaden chest. "And now you have it, free of the strings of Zorast and Lucretzia at your back…free of Algernon Sorai's hand."

A hint of color darkened her cheeks. Her jaw shifted; then she said, quietly, "Lucretzia is dead."

Relief set me back harshly on my haunches, and I rested my palm to my brow—feeling the clammy sweat that bloomed there, then faded as a wish of half my life settled into a certain truth. "Who?"

"Me. But it wouldn't have happened if not for Blackhand and his friends."

Thankfulness branched out from my chest like warm buttermilk spreading through dry dough, bringing it new life. My eyes snapped up to find Tristah's. "He's all right? And Wilkes?"

She nodded. "Both a bit scuffed up—Killi, too. Which, what else do you expect from people who go blade-to-blade against the Pale Viper? But they're all going to be fine. And he's been asking after you…around the town and to my face. He's a real character, that one."

I wiped my knuckles beneath my eyes, then forced the question I was both eager and reluctant to ask. "How badly did she hurt you?"

Tristah's lips bunched off to the side, her gaze dropping to her instrument as she summoned all of the strings to begin the next song. "It's not something I want to discuss with anyone yet."

Dread blistered my throat. "I'm so sorry I didn't come for you sooner."

"From what I hear, you had your hands full with other rescue missions…and, let's be frank, you wouldn't have gotten into this castle without help. Lucretzia had it tied down too tightly this time." Tristah's smile held no animosity, only the exhaustion that came with sharing the Pale Viper's company for too long. "I'm going to find a Hadrassi scholar to speak with about all of it…someone who can help with clearing the mind and accepting things, so you can function beyond them. The people deserve that. *I* deserve to be all right."

"Yes, you do." As did I. And in a world free at last of the Del's paranoid power-gathering, the threat of civil war, and Lucretzia's cruelty…we could pursue it, unshackled, unbound.

"What about you?" Tristah ventured after a moment full of string-songs and nothing else. "I saw the Del…and that lovestruck healer, Siu's husband, he explained it. How are you?"

"His name is Gydeon."

One of her brows rose. "Would he protest the title?"

I pondered that. "He honestly may prefer it."

"I guessed as much. Just as I can guess you're dodging me, which you know very well won't work. How *are* you, really?"

I settled for a moment, whispering that question to the depths of myself…searching the portion of me blackened with the stain of the Del and Della's blood that I'd never wanted to shed. The piece that reflected the shadows Lucretzia had breathed into me for years.

"It…it isn't the same as Athyna," I decided at last. "It weighs differently. Not guilt, it isn't that…but all life taken carries substance. I'm sure you've felt that, as the Incendiary."

She nodded slowly. "I have. So, what are you going to do about it?"

"Find someone to speak with about it." I smiled slightly. "And remind myself that I did not take life from an innocent man…he was a tyrant, and a wounder of young women, and he enabled far worse than that by Lucretzia's hand. I could not allow those woundings to continue. And I will always remember that it was my choice, to free myself of that torment…to free *you*, and the people of Amere-Del."

Each word blunted the edges of the weight; they chiseled and chipped at it and made it far easier to balance in my hands. To carry it as I would carry Zorast's death, and Athyna's, for the rest of my days.

"And for now," I added, "I am going to listen to your music, because it has been one of my greatest comforts, always."

Tristah laughed, shaking her head. "I'm afraid I'm badly out of practice."

"You know I am far too uncultured to notice." Folding my legs beneath me, I rolled my wrists in their bonds and leaned into the strength of the music that crossed the cage bars with no restraint. "It's been so long since I've heard you play."

Her fingers worked the strings in a relentless, soothing melody, even as her gaze lifted to mine. "It's been a long time since I've wanted to."

For a bit, neither of us spoke. She played, and I listened—a habit many years made, when Tristah's music was all that could calm me to slumber on the worst nights in our shared room, here in this same castle. And it had the same effect now; when I leaned my head to the bars and closed my eyes, the music took me away from this place I had never desired to see again.

"Everything is ready," Tristah added at last, her voice blending in harmony with the music her deft fingers made. "*Gydeon* has the herbs measured out. Siu's contraption is tested and true. It will be just like going to sleep for you, and then…"

"And then I will be gone."

Her fingers missed a note, twinging another string wrong.

My eyes popped open as her hands halted altogether. We stared at one another.

I would be gone. And this time, Tristah would remain—her choice. Her own volition.

"Will you be all right?" I whispered.

She bore down a deep breath. "Someday. This castle…I hate it. I hate the memories hiding around every corner of it." A faint smile twitched her lips. "But

I have Killian…and I have my contacts as the Incendiary. And I can finally, *finally* do the kind of good I always wanted to."

"I'm glad." And that was true, even as a deep pinch twisted my insides.

She had a place here, now. A true future in Shadewyle Castle. She had Killian, and her people.

She did not need me.

Tristah draped her arm over the swooped body of her instrument, resting her chin on the crook of her elbow. "You'll be all right, too, Aly. I know it. You can finally stop looking over your shoulder. You have somewhere you belong, and people who are waiting for you." She chuckled lightly. "People who have been badgering me nonstop for *days*, making sure all the affairs are in order."

My laughter bubbled up to join hers, infected with the same eagerness as the crew who'd harassed her on my behalf. "I can't wait to see them."

Tristah hesitated a moment, tapping her thumb and smallest finger in alternation on the instrument's body. "Will *you* be all right? With them?"

"Yes." That truth was steady earth beneath my feet. It was the path I would walk from this place, to my sham execution…knowing what lay beyond. "You've found what freedom holds for you, Tristah. So have I."

A sheen slid across her eyes, and she reached across her instrument, toward the bars. "I'm never going to stop wishing there was a way freedom could keep us together."

Heat snaked down the side of my nose as I bound my fingers with hers. "Some things aren't meant to last a lifetime. That doesn't make them any less precious."

Tristah nodded, but the groove that carved between her brows and the flattening of her lips spoke of imminent weeping—an expression as familiar to me as my own face reflected in glass. "You were the best part of my life for so long, Aly. You were the reason I held on." With a deep, trembling breath, she seized my other hand as well. "I just want you to know that no matter where you go, and no matter what this title demands of me…some part of me will always be staying alive for you. Just like I promised."

"And I for you." I squeezed her hands with all my might, as if that would tie us to one another forever. "The parts of me that were built from you are the parts of myself I love the most, Tristah. Thank you for teaching me to be brave, and to take power wherever I can."

"And thank *you*, for teaching me to face the world with eyes wide open." Her laughter was hoarse with tears. "Those are lessons that will carry us both through what's ahead, I think."

"You will make the best Della this country has ever seen."

"And you…you'll be a fantastic pirate." Her face twisted, and she freed one hand, wiping away the dampness that scoured her cheeks. "Merciful Ahim, is that a good or a very, very *bad* thing?"

"We're going to find out," I laughed. "And that is the joy, isn't it? We're finally free to do what we want, without fearing the shadows."

Her chin trembled, and her smile came slowly; but when it did, it came strong and sure, coaxing up mine in turn. "Finally free."

She sat back then and played a song of what freedom sounded like to her—the resonance of deep, thrumming strings and lighter, airy notes. A tune that carried us both away from this place, to chart the horizon that lay ahead…on the other side of a death pretended. On the other side of letting go, and of saying goodbye—perhaps, truly, forever this time.

She played, and we wept, our gazes meeting now and again through the bars—a thousand apologies, a thousand memories, a thousand regrets and joys all bound up in those shared looks which no words dared encroach upon.

I'd nearly fallen asleep again, slumped against the bars, when Tristah's fingers tired—or perhaps the sacred song of new duty called her from elsewhere. A clarion cry I had never heard for myself, nor desired to; nor ever would.

Stirring when the strings tapered, I raised my head; and Tristah's hand curled in my hair, the way my mother's had whenever I'd told a joke or spoken some childhood profundity that brought her joy. And she pressed a kiss to my brow, a touch of a wind turning my life to a different course.

"Goodbye, Lio," she whispered. "Love you forever, my sweet sister."

And with that, Tristah and her songs left my life for the last time.

Slumped to the bars, cold in her absence, I curled my fist around the wheel pendant hanging hidden in the folds of my collar.

There in the dark, alone…a new tune began to play in my head.

A shanty. A fireside fiddle reel. A song of the sea.

It was a clarion call of a different sort. And it was calling me home.

CHAPTER 87
THE TALE OF LIONYRA VARA

RYKER

n Amere-Del, they say the tale of Tristah Levanthya lived and died in just one day.

It's the sort of story that takes on a different face, depending who tells it. The details get scattered. The things she did change and grow.

Sometimes, they say the decoy was a trickster wearing a fancy mask. That she deceived her way into the regime, always planning to kill the Del. That she was some Ahim-crafted test for the Gravens…and they found out too late. The tale usually spins that she and some band of pirates stole the Delina and held her captive for a few years, and once Alyona Graven escaped, the decoy made her move—tried to wipe out the whole regime in one go.

They don't usually say the truth: that Tristah Levanthya was an orphan with the whole world to lose. That she loved the Delina so much, she turned to a life of rebellion, all staked in her memory.

Some things, though, the stories always get right.

They hung the woman who killed Athyna and Zorast Graven. Hung her with the gold hoop still in her nose and the daylight squaring off every one of her features, from those striking eyes to the folds of her belly to her steady stance, so there was no doubting she looked exactly like the newly-named Della…the one who gave the order for her to hang.

When Tristah Levanthya died, Alyona Graven lived again.

And so did Lionyra Vara.

You'd need a Storycrafter to capture all the details…the heat baking the cobblestones in the middle of the town of Shadewyle. The way the people shouted for her death. The way all of them just wanted something to feel right after losing the Del and the Pale Viper.

Me, I'm no Storycrafter. All I can tell are the moments that mattered to me.

The way her eyes found mine across that courtyard, while the executioner—a bear of a man with bandaged shoulders and a cloak blue as the sea—laid the noose.

The way there wasn't any fear on her face…and no surprise at how much hate they threw her way. It was going to take a depths-blasted *long* time for this country to heal. And we didn't have time for it.

That was Alyona's problem.

I can tell the worst part of the tale…when the executioner pulled the lever, and the world went out from under her.

Even knowing what I knew, it took *everything* in me not to tear across that courtyard and cut her down. I couldn't watch her writhe and buck against the way they'd tied her up. I couldn't just watch and do *nothing*.

So, one last time in my miserable life, I let myself look away from what was hurting her—swearing to Ahim I'd never, ever do that again. Then I prayed like a pious oaf in a sanctuary until it was done; until the relief barreled over the whole courtyard, and everyone started chanting for her body to get hauled off.

That was the worst part of it all.

I can tell the best part of it, too.

When I made it down to the tunnels she'd come in through, the night we handed power over Amere-Del to someone who could do right by it. And down there I found most of the crew waiting—and Gyddy, working his own special craft. Bringing Lio back from the herbs that made them think she was gone.

I can tell how the stone felt when my knees smacked it. How my fingers went straight to the rope burns on her neck and learned for themselves how those marks weren't half as raised and ugly as the ones around her waist—where Scribs had rigged the harness Siu made, some rope contraption that spread the noose's weight down through a hook into the rest of her body.

I can tell how her hand felt, cool but not stiff—not like Kory's in the Councilmeet. And how I still held onto it, hard as I could, while Gydeon worked her over.

I can tell, and not even feel like a fool, how I just stared him down and just kept saying, "Bring her back, Gyddy, bring her back, bring her back to me."

Fear makes fools of us all…rambling, stupid fools. And I'd been a fool for her for a long bloody time.

I can tell—and this is my favorite part—when the herbs finally did their spicy little trick. When she whooped in a good, deep breath, and started coming around. When the whole crew started yelling and cheering and circling up around us, squeezing her hand, stroking her hair, shaking her by the shoulders— and how she elbowed all of them aside to reach for me.

"'Ay, well done, Seasplitter," I choked out, wrapping my arms around her, hauling her across the spread of my lap. "You got out of Shadewyle twice."

"Let's not make it three times." That croaky joke broke every part of me the rest of this mad quest hadn't. And it healed a whole lot more.

"Faking your death, sweetheart?" The laugh that came out of me was shaky. I didn't bloody care. "Now you're a real pirate."

She flashed me the widest grin I'd ever seen, and then she grabbed my face between those perfect hands and dragged me right back down where I wanted to be: kissing her breathless.

And that's when the tale *really* began.

EPILOGUE
GOING UP IN FIREWORKS

ithout the threat of civil war hanging above its streets any longer, Monsha sang again.

I couldn't help pausing on every familiar street corner, drinking deeply of the portside air, refreshing myself on somber strings and bright fiddle reels. I could not help dancing and tossing merits to street performers, since we had plenty left to spare. Nor could I help the thrill that no one looked twice my way, all taken in by the disguise I had worn during more than a month in harbor.

The city of my birth—the city of my *rebirth*—seemed as full of gladness as I was. It sparkled and shone. Delegates had been hard at work this last month, soothing tensions between Northland and Southland visitors, quelling suspicions between inhabitant neighbors.

What had seemed a city on the brink of riot during my last stay was one reaching out its hands toward peace again. Compromise. By no means fully healed—nothing was, not yet—but there were cheerful shouts rather than aggressive accusations from hawkers along the streets. More smiles than scowls. Hands raised in greeting rather than rude gestures; some even called out helloes as I made my way to the docks, a sack of supplies flung over my shoulder, glorying in the feeling of the wind in my hair and lungs that ached less today.

A small victory, perhaps, when Gydeon said I had so much healing left ahead of me from the poisons I had ingested. So much time before I would be able to run and dance and stand at the baking counter all day without growing winded. But victories were victories, no matter how small. These days, I was pirating flickers of hope like coins and treasures for my hoard.

A larger victory awaited around the bend in the docks: the sight of a ship half familiar and half foreign. One that had spent months in carpentry and resining and patching, and at long last—scarcely a week past—had finally come due for its payment.

Ryker had fronted not a small amount of merits for the cost of *The Athalion's* repairs. And now she bobbed seaworthy in the harbor, where we had all chosen our hammocks, spent a good deal of time introducing Gydeon to the sick bay he and Hasser would oversee, and letting Syd and Klem spar for the navigating instruments. I had made my way through the galley that was my own small country to rule, and let the tears flow for Cook and Willy and all those who would never see this ship of two crews. Those who had died, and those whose destinies had simply led them down a different path, away from the sea.

Even now, I dashed off another tear on my knuckles and let a smile ease my grief as I wound through the crowds, making my way to *The Athalion*. The gangplank was dropped, as it had been for days; and the mingled crews moved in tandem, loading supplies to carry us to our next voyage. Though we had not decided yet what that would be.

I nodded to Wilkes and blew a kiss to Cam where they sparred on the forecastle; I waved to Noveen and Brant, Osred and Nella and Annet and Rynshaw. Every face brimmed with smiles, every body relaxed to the uttermost as I mounted the steps to the helm.

It was empty, yet I felt the shadow of Jularius Cathan cast against the decking as I stood where he once had. I felt his brilliant grin in the sun that warmed my back and heard the echo of his laughter in the wind that tugged my dye-tinted, reddish locks over my shoulders.

Capturing the strands behind my ear, I palmed the spokes and breathed deep of the contentment that seemed to seep from the city streets onto the ship.

Monsha was healing. Amere-Del was healing, with Tristah at its helm. And here, today, standing at *this* helm...so was I.

"Oi! That's the Captain's spot, sweetheart."

I grinned, but kept my hand to the wheel, a play of defiance as I cast my head back to glimpse the dark-coated figure sliding down from the rigging with a rope bound around his arm. "Why don't you remove me, then, Captain?"

With a bend of twine, he swept in behind me like a figment of the wind, cuffing one arm around my waist and spinning me to kiss him, my back pressed against the wheel.

"Report?" Ryker grinned against my lips.

I tossed the satchel full of baking supplies beside the helm and buried my fingers in his hair. "The Northlands and Southlands have chosen representatives already. They'll make the pilgrimage to Shadewyle Castle to meet with the new Della and the mouthpiece of the dissidents…and word has it the Incendiary will send a representative of *his* own."

Leaning back from me, Ryker arched a brow. "Is that so?"

I tapped my fingers on the wheel. "Perhaps *I* could—"

"Not a bloody chance." He hooked me tighter around the waist when I burst out laughing, hauling me against him and turning me to face Siu and Reinera as they mounted the steps—bantering, shoving one another, arguing about nothing consequential. Behind them, Syd trailed, hand-in-hand with Lanah; Klem was fast on their heels, one arm slung around Camden's sweat-streaked shoulders. He shrugged her off and came to join Ryker and me at the helm, looping his lanky arms between the spokes and slouching his weight into them. In our month in port, in all the trials we had faced since Bashir, I could have vowed he'd grown an inch and a half.

"So," he said, "we've got ourselves a ship. What now?"

"Now we pitch this lot overboard," Klem hiked a thumb at Syd, Lanah, and Reinera, "and commandeer it for ourselves."

"That was the *old* Raiders," Siu reminded her. "We're reformed."

"Mostly." Ryker smirked; I pinched beneath his arm, and he jerked in place, cursing so profanely Cam shot him a look of pure reproach.

"Well, word in the gambling dens today is that Mithra-Sha just named its new ruler," Klem offered, far more seriously this time. "Sha Arias Lothar just took power from his abdicant father."

"Two countries trading rulers in the same space." Reinera whistled. "That ought to go over well."

"Traders coming up the Everreach say the Sha's cobbling together a fleet to manage some Misspoken manifestations of Storycraft that are spilling out of an island called the Illusionarium. Starting with the beasties in the sea." Syd shot a grin at Klem. "The Sha and his inner circle, they've got a plan to rid the trade routes of what haunts 'em. To put an end to those things for good."

"Must be nice," Siu drawled. "Must *pay* well, a dangerous job like that."

Ryker raised his hands, chuckling. "Let's not mutiny over this. We can have a civil discussion."

"What's there to discuss?" Klem scoffed, leaning with folded arms against the railing. "We can't go back to Korsa."

"Nor would we, even if the choice was there," Siu added fervently.

"We've got no trade, no commission, no hope, no prospects…" Syd ticked each item off on his fingers.

"No *tact*," Lanah added crossly, nudging him with her hip.

"But what we do have is a captain." Reinera's declaration jolted through me; I met her gaze, brimming with a sorrow that would perhaps never fully scar, for what the seas had stolen—but also with contentment for where those same seas had carried us now. "And a crew we're proud to sail with."

"We're all looking for the next thing," Siu said. "So, what'll it be?"

Klem balanced her forearms backward on the railing beside Siu, eyeing Ryker shrewdly. "Give us a heading, Captain."

He glanced around at all of them; then, meeting all stalwart and resolute faces, he shrugged. "Let's toss our names in the pot and see what this new Sha is paying."

With scattered whoops and eager cheers, the crew hastened off to their duties—all but Syd and Reinera.

"We were thinking," Syd began carefully once the others had gone, "since you're Captain, this'll be your ship, obviously—"

"'Ay. She's all ours now," Ryker protested. "And she belonged to you lot first. This pirate doesn't take that lightly."

"Right. That's sort of what we were hoping you'd say." Syd smiled sheepishly. "Because the hull did get shredded in the storm. It took off the name…so we thought we might could give her a new one, Captain." He thumbed his nose, glancing sidelong at Reinera.

She let out a slow and steady breath, blinking against the luster of tears that glossed her eyes. "*The Cathan*."

Ryker and I traded a glance; the rush of warmth in the base of my throat perfectly mirrored the harsh swallow of his.

"Aye," he said huskily, "a new name for a new era."

"It suits this ship well," I agreed. "And the legacy under which it sails."

Ryker nodded. "Give Kato the word."

"On our way, Cap." With twin salutes, Syd and Reinera dashed down to meet the bosun on the deck. Soon the deckhands would be in their harness slings, swinging over the side of the ship, paving over the refurbished hull with its fresh name.

Like myself—like the Captain and the mingled crew—it would carry a new title across the horizon.

Contentment welled within me, freeing a fresh tear from my eye. Ryker caught it before it could fall, frowning. "What's that all about? You all right?"

"I am happier in this moment than I thought perhaps I would ever be." I leaned back into his chest. "I never want to forget what this feels like."

"You won't have to." One arm wrapped around my middle, he draped the wheel with the other. "We'll make a whole lifetime of moments like these, what do you say?"

A lifetime with this crew. With the seas and my galley and all the baking I could ever want to do. A lifetime of freedom.

A life with *him*.

"I say," I laughed, snaking one arm up behind his neck, "that such vows ought to be sealed with a token."

A chuckle rumbled through his chest. "You've already got one of those, sweetheart." His hand dipped to splay between my collarbones, his thumb brushing the tarnished pendant I was never without…a reminder that wherever we sailed now, the winds guided us the same. Wherever we ran now, we would run together. And we would keep one another from drowning, whatever depths we crossed.

After a moment, Ryker's hand drifted upward…fingers coasting along the sides of my neck, his palm sliding up to cup my chin, guiding my head to lean back against the crook of his shoulder. My face uplifted as his bent toward mine.

"How about a kiss instead?" he offered in that husky, rolling tone of seaside bonfires and cavern shadows where I'd come back to life. Over and over again.

Always coming back to *him*.

"Aye, Captain," I grinned.

And when I tangled my hand back in his hair—when he dipped his head to follow the curve of my temple, the line of my jaw and my ear, with liquid light shimmering and shattering in his rosemary-green eyes—when he teased me a moment, noses brushing, breaths mingling, and at long last his mouth crashed over mine—

Fireworks.

CHARACTER GUIDE

Lionyra Vara (lee-oh-NYE-ruh VAR-uh)/Alyona Graven (al-ee-OWN-uh gray-ven): A runaway heiress who has built a new life as a baker

Galan Fiordona (gay-len fee-or-DOAN-uh): A soldier in the city of Krylan

Audra Jashowin (aw-druh JASH-oh-win): A disgraced Storycrafter; Lio's first friend in Mithra-Sha

Lucretzia Nore (lou-CRET-zee-uh noor): Leader of the Del's fighting forces and his right-hand warrior

Tristah Levanthya (triss-tuh leh-ven-THIGH-uh): Lio's former decoy, stand-in as Alyona Graven

Del Zorast Graven (zore-ahst gray-ven): Ruler of Amere-Del, ward to Lio and Tristah since adolescence.

Della Athyna Graven (ah-THIN-uh gray-ven): Wife of Zorast, second ruler over Amere-Del.

Algernon Sorai (al-jer-non SORE-eye): Mouthpiece of the dissidents

Killian Brax (kill-ee-en): Right-hand to the Incendiary.

Dorcas (door-cahs): Owner of *The Love of the Loaf*

SHIP CREWS

The Athalion
Jularius Cathan: Captain
Frixia Armes: First Mate
Syd: Second Mate/Navigator
Lanah: Deckhand
Reinera (ray-NARE-uh): Deckhand
Henriet: Bookkeeper
Nix: Deckhand
Nash: Deckhand
Valori (val-OR-ee): Deckhand
Hasser: Healer
Cook: Ship's Cook
Ribbens: Bosun
Noveen: Cooper
Osred: Gunner
Annet: Carpenter

The Dread Singer:
Ryker "Blackhand" Kassian: Captain
"Steady" Siu Nassar (soo nuh-SAR): First Mate
Klement "Keen-Eye" Drace: Navigator/Second Mate
Kory "Three-Finger" Drace: Third Mate/Log Keeper
Gydeon "Greenfinger" Nassar: Healer
"One-Pot" Willy: Ship's Cook
Kato "Bodey" Drace: Bosun
Camden: Jack-of-all-trades
Wilkes "Steelheart" Krait: Quartermaster/weapon's keeper
Brant: Cooper
Wyst: Carpenter
Nella: Master Gunner
Rhea: Musician
Maryon: Musician
Rynshaw: Deckhand

LOCATION GUIDE

Amere-Del (AH-meer dehl): Country to the south of Mithra-Sha. Ruled by the Del and Della.

Antaross (an-TARE-ose): Seaside Ameresh town.

Abbra Foothills (ahb-rah): The smaller peaks in the Southlands of Amere-Del

Anoram (ah-NORE-ahm): One of the trade cities surrounding the Wayval Basin

Bashir (buh-SHEER): The largest of the trade cities surrounding the Weyval Basin; a breeding ground for dissent

The Barradir Highlands (bar-uh-deer): The high mountain peaks that frame the east of Amere-Del; a shared border with Navar-Bane and Hadrass-Drui

Catrae (cat-ray): An important Northlands city; the last city before the northern border

Drowverge: An important Southlands city

The Everreach: The river bisecting Amere-Del, dividing the Northlands and Southlands

Getchmin: An important Northlands city

Korsa: A pirate city hidden deep in the Abbra Foothills

Krylan (cry-lan): The southernmost city in Mithra-Sha; Lio's home

Monsha: The greatest trade city in Amere-Del; Lio's city of birth

Mount Shadewyle (shade-while): The large mountain where the Del's castle is perched.

The Northlands: The expanse of Amere-Del from the Everreach up to the northern border.

Port Krait: The small port that receives goods and wares for Bashir

Port Pyrath: The small port that receives goods and wares for Pyrath

Port Tamsay: The small port that receives goods and wares for Anoram

Pyrath: One of the trade cities surrounding the Weyval Basin

Ravinor: An important trade city along the Everreach; also a well-known place of dissent against the regime

Sadir (suh-DEER): An important city nestled in the Barradir Highlands.

Sennesole Basin (sen-ah-soul): One of the basins connected by rivers to important trade locations across the Southlands.

Shadewyle Castle: Home of the Del and his family

Shadewyle Proper: The castle town of Amere-Del

The Southlands: The expanse of Amere-Del from the Everreach down to the southern border.

Sudene (soo-DEEN): An important Northlands city; controls some of the river trade.

Sunrise Isle: A favorite stopping place for *The Athalion* during southern voyages.

Westyr: An important Northlands city.

Weyval Basin (way-vahl): The greatest hub for trade in the Southlands; home to a number of important trade ports and their cities.

Zayir Harbor (zie-EAR): Port Town in northern Amere-Del; Ryker's city of birth

ACKNOWLEDGMENTS

Every story is a journey.

A Tale Told by Traitors was one that really challenged me—from getting 70,000 words into the wrong story, to starting over, to pushing through. Each step of this book was made possible by the support that guided me along the way.

To the World-Shaper who helped me shape this book…thank You for the reminders that sometimes we get it all wrong on the way to getting it right. Thank You for never giving up on this Storycrafter whenever I fumble and fret and doubt. Thank You for always shaping new worlds in me. It's an honor to share them…even the hardest ones.

To Cassidy, for not letting me give up even when I was so sure I couldn't put one more line on the page. Thank you for your essays on Killian Brax and Ryker Kassian and for daydreaming with me what spies and sailors do beyond the edge of the world.

To Danny and JD, for all the ways you sacrificed (even when you didn't know you did) to help bring this story to life. Thank you both for being the greatest adventure I've ever had. <3

A special thanks to my mother-in-law for first inspiring the love of baking in me as a 14-year-old that made Lio's character come alive in my mind. She lived in me because you loved me first, long before I was part of the family.

To Lina and Kristin, who continue to support, encourage, and inspire me in bringing this series to life. Thank you both for believing in me and in these Tales. Every word I write, I hold you both in my heart.

To every reader who took a chance on the *Tales of Wonder and Woe*—and found something to love in its pages. May we all face the world with eyes wide open, taking power where we can…and writing our life's tale in ways that help guide us to shore.

ABOUT THE AUTHOR

Renee Dugan is an Indiana-based author who grew up reading fantasy books, chasing stray cats, and writing stories full of dashing heroes and evil masterminds. Now with over a decade of professional editing, administrative work, and writing every spare second under her belt, she has authored several fantasy standalones and series. Living with her husband, son, and not-so-stray cats in the magical Midwest, she continues to explore new worlds and spends her time in this one encouraging and helping other writers on their journey to fulfilling their dreams.

ALSO BY R. DUGAN

You can find other R. Dugan books, including…

The Chaos Circus (YA Portal Fantasy)

The Starchaser Saga (NA Epic Fantasy Series)

The Curse of the Blessed (Adult Fantasy Trilogy)

and

The Tales of Wonder and Woe (NA Fantasy)

at online retailers Amazon, Barnes & Noble, and more,
and at **reneeduganwriting.com/shop**

Find Renee Dugan online at: **Reneeduganwriting.com**
And on social media: **@reneeduganwriting**